STRANGE HARVEST

STRANGE HARVEST

Ashley Carter

W.H. ALLEN · LONDON
1986

Copyright © Harry Whittington 1985

Printed and bound in Great Britain by
Biddles Ltd, Guildford and King's Lynn
for the Publishers, W.H. Allen & Co. PLC
44 Hill Street, London W1X 8LB

ISBN 0 491 03751 1

Part One:

THE FATHER

'And much as Wine has played the Infidel
And robbed me of my Robe of Honour — well,
I often wonder what the Vintners buy
One half so precious as the Goods they sell.'

Omar Khayyám

I

The old man limped on swollen feet across the bare yard and climbed with a grimace of reluctance up into the wagon beside the pregnant girl. At this show of impatience, the girl's mouth twisted petulantly and she fanned herself rapidly with a religious-illustrated reed fan. 'You came only at last,' she said. She stared straight ahead. 'You took your time.'

'One has much to do.' Manuel spoke in raspy acrimony, letting his wife see his displeasure at being torn in the middle of the morning from his work which was their livelihood. She did not bother to look at him. She remained remote, languid, unaware of his scowl. She seldom looked at him and was never moved to emotion, no matter what she read in his whiskered, leathery and age-yellowed face. Julia did not care what Manuel thought as long as he responded to her demands and her whims.

'I am anxious to go. I am in a hurry to be at the house of my sister, old one. You know this. I told you.'

He smiled and touched her protruberant belly. 'Did I refuse? Do I deny anything to the mother of my son?'

Julia thrust his hand away. 'Don't start that pawing at me. Let us go. I am in a great hurry.'

He shook his head in wonder at her, smiling despite his frustration. 'You are lovely, mia Julia. Muy bellisima. . . . The Mother of God must have had breasts such as yours.'

'Never mind my breasts, old one. Move this horse.'

He nodded and took up the reins, still hesitant, troubled. Sighing, he glanced once more towards the bee house where he'd been in the midst of extracting honey from its combs when Julia interrrupted him. The little extraction shed was strung tightly with cheese-cloth against the onslaught of bees at extracting time. He had robbed the superimposed boxes from half a dozen hives and carried the heavy combs of ripe

6

honey into the shed. His extracting machine was small, holding only a single frame at a time. The crank which propelled its centrifugal action had to be turned by hand. It was back-breaking labour, but this was the moment of harvest and his joy and pleasure was ever in the honey, joy deeper than the mere knowledge of any profit derived from its sale. He saw in all this the rewards of his labour, the product of his small factory with its numberless employees, the thrift of the hives, the evidence of God's provision for His children, the richness of his land.

Manuel's ancient buggy once had been painted an imitation oak. Coats of dust, time and numerous owners, each more negligent than his predecessor, had reduced that oaken colour to a dung-heap yellow. These weather beaten, sand-scarred sideboards blended the buggy into the sere landscape. Tall rear wheels converged at the ground and diverged at their top; the forward wheels, somewhat lower, wobbled loosely as they turned on the hard-packed brown road.

The big, clumsy sorrel gelding wearily drawing this buggy was higher at the withers than at the hips; so long of neck that he had a giraffe-like aspect. His ribs were visible, yet he was pot-bellied. A white blaze decorated the abnormally long face with its large ears. His off eye was blind, his feet too big, his joints swollen. Plodding along the road, he hitched first to one side of the buggy and then the other. Sal had been named for Salvator, in honour of the turf's great hero and in the hope that Sal would emulate the purebred.

Sal was not old in years, and he envinced his skittish youth occasionally by shying mildly at a brush or rock or other equally harmless roadside object. The harness, on a more spirited horse than Sal, would have been less than dependable. It was patched with wire and rope in several places and, even where whole, it was unwholesomely dry and cracked. In the whip-rack of the dashboard reposed a long, gnarled olive branch with dead leaves pendant like a tuft, a fitting earnest of the driver's attitude towards his beast of draught.

Between the rear wheels, under the bed of the buggy, a bitch loped laguidly. Forty-five pounds of slab-sided, loose-hipped boniness, she glowed blackly except for lemon yellow eyes and a patch of white on her brisket. Her flat coat was just long enough to feather slightly on her legs, tail, and high-set, pendulous ears. Her master referred to Rosa as his hunting dog, but what she hunted remained a mystery.

At the roadside, crestfallen, sauntered the black bitch's half-grown son. Only in his yellow eyes did he bear the faintest resemblence to his dam. His short, bristly coat was white, flea-riddled, with liver ticking; his small, velvety ears buttoned forward; his tail curled upright over his long back. This journey was too long for his tender months. Frequently he would sink down in the shade of a bush to rest, keeping his yellow eyes fixed upon the dusty buggy under which his dam moved mechanically. Timing his reponse by the distance traversed by the buggy, he would rise reluctantly and gallop break-neck to overtake the vehicle, and so his progress was a succession of relaxations and violent spurts from shade to shade.

On the spindle-enclosed platform behind the seat of the buggy reposed a wooden box into which fitted snugly two tins somewhat less than a foot square and approximately eighteen inches high. These tins contained the honey Manuel had been able to extract for marketing.

Manuel held the reins loosely. Sixty-three years had heightened his cheek-bones, intensified the aquilinity of his nose, furrowed bold crow's-feet from the corners of his eyes, tanned to a single tone the smallpox-pitted leather skin of his seared face, brought his thin, short amorphous beard from black to burnished grey, deepened the red furrows in the red hide of his dewlapped neck, and made more apparent the incredible play of his Adam's apple. But the years had not robbed the small brown eyes of their inner glitter nor his protuberant lips of their ruddiness.

A flat-brimmed felt sombrero, banded with metallic braid and conventionally dented in the crown, shaded his face. This head covering was out of all proportion to the size of the little man. His small, neat feet and fragile hands, withered by years and sun, made him seem smaller than ever.

The blaze of sun, enveloping dust, fatigue of the journey, and lingering rancor at being disturbed at his work with his precious bees, wilted Senor O'Brien's usual jauntiness. The heavy handkerchief of yellow silk draped around his neck and caught in front with a ten-dollar gold-piece mounting, was fouled with sweat and dust.

Julia O'Brien rode silently at her husband's side, her hands folded idly in the lap of her loose white frock with its ruffled yoke and flared skirt. Not yet seventeen, married to old Manuel, approaching the ordeal of parturition, Julia betrayed nothing of her inner thoughts. For a long time hers had been the apathy of a dead calm and stagnant pond, so still that not even a stone skipped across its green-scummed surface aroused a visible ripple. Julia was not happy but she was resigned. And too, that Madonna-like, liquid quietude which comes over the faces of women with child filled the almond-shaped, olive-black eyes. The corners of her full mouth drooped with a hint of nausea. Her slender figure was tautly swollen across the middle. She sat, listless and complacent.

There was no doubt that Manuel's Mexican ancestry was as real as his young wife's. His manner of existence, his dress, his prejudices were all thoroughly California-Spanish, but an Irish sailor had given Manuel's family its surname and Manuel insisted that the bood of that remote Irish grandparent determined his race. He pretended to disdain the local patois which passed for Spanish, but found it the only true medium of communication. However, he frequently exercised his English, on the specious pretext that it was easier to express himself. He even insisted upon conversing thus with his Spanish-speaking acquaintances, to whom only the most common English words were intelligible at all. Had he been aware there existed a Gaelic language, he would have tried to learn it in the belief that such knowledge would denote and affirm his Hibernian lineage.

'A journey on such a hot day is too wearisome for you, my Julia.' Manuel broke the brittle taciturnity of many miles.

'I wish to go.' Julia shrugged. 'I wish to arrive at the house of my sister. I shall endure the journey.'

Manuel sighed and glanced back across his shoulder. 'Some of the hives are crowded. I shall lose some swarms in going away.' He wanted to emphasize the sacrifice and reluctance with which he made this journey to Los Angeles, although he knew, as Julia did not, that the infrequent swarms of bees at this time of the year were hardly worth the hiving. He exhaled deeply. 'But it is to be as you wish, my dear young wife. . . In my old age you shall bear me a son who shall be for the Church. Our son, I shall raise him up to serve the good Jehovah, and he shall say prayers to the blessed Mother for the soul of me when I am dead.'

His wife made no answer.

'You wish it so, do you not, that our son should be for the Church?' Manuel peered at her, seeking confirmation of the purpose on which he was intent.

The passive girl shrugged again. 'But if our child should not be a son?' Julia did not share her spouse's religious ardour. It seemed God has done little enough for her that she should give Him her son.

'Ah, then we should have another, a boy who shall become a priest. And the girl, she shall enter the order of the holy sisters. It is as I would have it.'

'It remains to be known.' Julia sighed wearily. To be done with the subject, she added, 'I am impatient to come to the house of my sister.'

Manuel slapped the reins and reached towards the olive-wood whip. As a sort of promise of haste, Sal took one long stride and resumed the lazy tempo of his pace.

A haze veiled and enhanced the beauties of the earth. The brown hills rimming the San Gabriel Valley blended through grey to purple in the distant approaches to the mountains. A crouching foothill wore a single twisted juniper like a jaunty feather in its brim. Circular patches of shade where live oaks raised leaf-shields against the sun were oases where cattle gathered. Dried stalks of wild mustard grated and rattled in the infrequent gusts of breeze. Downy milkweed floated over the fields in search of sites for new colonies. Regiments of blackbirds foraged, soaring in bands like jet jewels of intricate design. Sal's hoofs disturbed the dust of the lazy road. Clouds of gnats rose like heat waves to glitter in the sun.

2

Manuel O'Brien's espousal of Julia Martinez was not his first experience of matrimony. After a bibulous and lecherous youth, Manuel, with the acquiesence of the Holy Church to which he was devoted all his life, settled down to conjugality with Anna Verdugo, a woman of the race of the conquista-dores who had followed the Franciscan Monks along the shores of the Pacific Ocean. Anna was a faithful wife and bore Manuel numerous offspring. Of the seven who survivied infancy, all succumbed to a smallpox epidemic which also claimed Anna's life. Manuel, too, had fallen victim to the same malady. It left his skin pitted, pocked and coarse, a constant reminder of his tragedy.

The poor man was desolated at the loss of his family. After many Masses and prayers for the souls of his dead, and after some two years of lonely celibacy, Manuel again entered the holy estate, this time without clerical benefit or church blessing. He met Anna Smith in a boarding house in Los Angeles where he stayed on his frequent visits to the town. He was aware that Anna Smith's past had not been impeccable, but he was lonely and her red mouth dripped promise. He believed that the four years she lived with him had been devoted to him alone until, returning one night late unexpectedly from a journey to Los Angeles to buy supplies for his bee-hives, he found his women in dalliance with a rugged blond man, a man Manuel had never seen before. Irate, O'Brien attacked the interloper with the heavy hunting knife which he always carried. The man disregarded the thrust after thrust that Manuel aimed at his chest and throat. He grabbed Manuel at the neck as if he were a mastiff and with his overwhelming size and strength, quickly pinioned the little man against the wall and unhurriedly pounded his face with huge fists until the aggrieved husband sprawled prostrate and insensible on the floor.

Manuel had faint recollection of the affray when, hours later, consciousness returned to him. He remembered Anna's shrill screams with which the whole combat had been punctuated, but in his mind those cries echoed like the maddened wails in some boxing arena. He remembered his futile efforts to stab the intruder. Spots of blood not his own over the bed and floor evidenced that he had not been without a degree of success, but most of all he remembered the initial terrible impact of the stranger's fist on his cheek. Manuel writhed in his own blood, sore and feverish and thirsty. Anna and the blond man were gone, with the woman's few personal belongings and all the cash from Manuel's pockets — whither, Manuel never ascertained. He never heard of either of them again. Anna Smith's issue by Manuel O'Brien had been two still-born daughters.

With occasional deep-bellied sighs, Manuel reviewed his life as he drove through the dusty September landscape with Julia silent, passive and withdrawn at his side. None of the incidents was vivid to him. All his personal history was softened and veiled by a kind of self-willed haze of disremembering, the same kind of haze that softened and veiled the outlines of the mountains and made supportable the heat of the afternoon. His was not a conscious effort to recall his past. He had long refused to look backward to pain, and even to the memory of pain. He preferred not to relive the unbroken span of disappointments and disillusions, the longings unfulfilled, the assaults of conscience, the futilities and errors and virulent fortune that comprised his existence. It was only that suddenly Manuel was no longer afraid of the past. Sitting beside his young and beauteous bride who was about to bear him the child for which he'd longed, a child who could comfort his age and should, in its dedication to the Church, make up for all his own sins and omissions, Manuel could permit to trickle hazily into his consciousness events which had previously caused him nausea and terror when he chanced, through some lapse of memory's guard, to face them.

3

The reason for Julia's having allowed herself to be married to old Manuel caused conjecture among her acquaintances. Some of them even hinted that her dalliance with Pedro Grandos Luiz, the husband of her sister, had brought embarrassment and that a husband of Julia's own must be taken as a bulwark for her good name against the ooze of gossip. Only that Clara Luiz did not confirm these suspicions seemed to the fair-minded ample warrant that the slander was without foundation. In the first place, Clara Luiz was insanely jealous of her man and stood firm that Pedro should confine his amorous attentions to her own plump charms, else, Clara declared, she would kill him with a knife as he slept. So the scandal, never more than the buzz of persistent rumour, finally abated.

The union of Pedro and Clara had been blessed with four children, two of whom had died of some alimentary infection before reaching their first year. The surviving two, however, Pedrillo, seven, and Concha, three, were as vigorous and robust as might be expected from their parentage. Pedro wasted precious little time with his first-born and namesake. Pedrillo was mature enough to rely upon his own resources and the resources of other neglected urchins of similar age for his entertainment. Pedrillo came in from the street only to sleep and to appease his craving for food. But to Conchita the father was, if not devoted, at least tolerant of her antics and amused by her pranks. Her femininity perhaps excited in Pedro an interest he did not feel toward his son. Clara was again with child. To Pedro this was but one more amorphous mouth for which sooner or later he would have to earn extra food by the sweat of his brow. He looked forward without anticipation.

Manuel O'Brien had known Julia Martinez almost from the day of her birth. Without particular interest, he had watched her grow through romping childhood into demure adolescence and, when maturity ripened her contours, he began to watch her with secret concupiscent glances. Julia's mother had died in Julia's babyhood and Clara had served her young sister in a mother's stead. Their father too had died shortly after Clara's marriage to Pedro Luiz. Julia found herself at home with Clara and Clara's man.

Julia was young and pleasant to look on, beautiful with a warm, sleepy kind of beauty, still not full grown, short of maturity in contours and feminine wisdom. Pedro was still under twenty-five, lithe of muscle, amorous of nature. He had a way of stretching himself like a great, well-nigh six-foot cat. He did this so frequently that to stretch like a stalking feline was a habit with him. Still, despite this seeming languid drowsiness, Pedro was capable of sudden flashes of rapier-like activity. His burnished black eyes, wide apart and liquid under thick brows that met over the bridge of his chiseled nose, followed his sister-in-law wherever she moved in his presence.

Julia was admired for her beauty and an apathetic passivity which many men interpret as elusive and mysterious. Sought by many lovers, Julia in her shy bashfulness, its urgency increased by her secret inner fantasies, repulsed the youths who wooed her.

Within the circle of Pedro's family, however, Julia displayed no such reserve. Her mouth was a machine-gun of Spanish words. She bantered and joked with Pedro, plainly found him godlike. She caressed and spanked and fed Pedrillo and Concha, gossiped unceasingly with Clara, bright and bold and vulnerable. In this family O'Brien was a frequent and welcomed guest. Before so old and accustomed a friend, Julia pretended none of the maidenly reserve with which she unintentionally repulsed advances of young males. In her immaturity, she did not even sense the ardour of Manuel's covetous gaze and she failed to draw any modest curtain of defense against it.

Pedro taunted the girl over her inability to attract suitors. 'No novio yet, little bird?' he would ask, keeping her blood astir with self-consciousness. 'Whenever shall we celebrate a feast of marriage?'

And when Julia blushed and tears welled in her black eyes, Pedro flung his arms about her to tickle and fondle and embrace her. When she struggled to escape he held her tighter and smothered her mouth with kisses. Though this play occurred many times a day and often in front of Clara, she seemed not to resent it. She appeared hardly to notice and she smiled complacently; this was Pedro's way with children and to Clara, Julia was still a child.

One Sunday afternoon when the wine jug had warmed the veins of the party and Pedro was more vexatious than usual, holding Julia fiercely upon his lap, tickling her roughly while he insisted she settle for a bridegroom, Manuel, in earnest jest, proposed himself for Julia's husband. He had for months awaited the opportune time; it had arrived and the glasses of wine gave him the courage to seize it.

'Why not old Manuel as husband for the chica?' He heard himself saying the words, his face flushed, his eyes glittering and sweat marbling across his forehead.

Julia blushed red. She broke free from Pedro's arms and braced herself against the wall, half-smiling, half-frightened. Watching her, Manuel felt encouraged. He got up and went to her. 'Manuel is not too old to love a pretty young wife.'

When Julia only went on staring at him, Manuel slipped his arm tentatively about her waist. She drew away from him, in instinctive repulsion of youth for age. Pedro stretched in embarrassment as he looked into Clara's complacent face and found there an unanticipated satisfaction. She offered no protest.

'Come, Julia. Consent to be Manuel's wife,' the old man urged.

14

'There.' Clara nodded and folded her arms across her swollen stomach. 'The little sister wants a husband. Who better then our amigo bueno, Senor O'Brien?'

Pedro's eyes chilled, his face flattened, almost pallid under the swarthy tan. He shook his head. 'There is time. There is time. She is yet a young girl. Tomorrow a lover will come.'

Clara merely gazed at him in her passive, immovable way. 'But who better than the Senor O'Brien for the little sister? The Senor O'Brien is a fitting husband for any girl. The senor owns his rancho and orchard and his own house in the country. He owes no debts and has money in the big bank on Spring Street. The young sister should look with great favour to marry such a one.'

Julia held her breath, crouched against the wall, watching them as the words flew like bats about her head. Nobody consulted her. She turned her frightened eyes to Pedro in mute appeal for succour, an appeal that Pedro failed to sense or lacked the courage to heed, given the state of Clara's mind.

Pedro sat forward on his chair, tasting the burn of hot wine rising up into his throat. Another man sought to deprive him of one of his women. The alcohol moiling in his stomach aggravated his feelings of jelousy and anger. But plainly Clara approved the arrangement. He knew better than to balk her in this matter. Senor O'Brien continued with some fever to urge consent. Senor O'Brien, an old friend. Friends must be obliged, even if the loss nauseated and distressed one. With Pedro there was a further consideration: Julia's marriage to Manuel O'Brien meant alliance of Pedro's house with a man of property and of ready money, a man who would be unable to refuse a small loan to a brother-in-law when, now and again, having squandered his means upon wine, the fickle cards and adorable women, that brother-in-law needed money for the meagre sustenance of his family. One could almost sacrifice the little sister in such a situation.

Pedro stood up, red face, slightly unsteady, but serious and unsmiling. He nodded his head. 'The gracious senor does our little sister much honour. She will hardly refuse his generous offer of marriage.' Pedro's acquiescence as head of his house was tantamount to acceptance, but he nodded towards the girl, taut and pale against the wall. 'Come, Julia. Speak, Julia. Thank the good senor. Say that you consent to be his wife.'

Julia seemed unable for some moments to breathe at all.

15

Her eyes moved across their faces. Her hands remained slack at her sides. At last, she spoke in a halting way. 'Yes. Yes, I thank Senor O'Brien and I accept the honour he offers me.' She nodded, looking as if she might vomit, but smiling in an anguished way. 'I shall become the bride of him.'

A stunned silence enveloped the room. Manuel O'Brien was unable yet to comprehend his great good fortune. Pedro slumped back into his chair. Clara sat rocking, with her arms folded, watching the little sister.

Through the Luiz's window the drizzling rain could be seen falling in the streets that Sunday afternoon in late March. Julia rocked back and forth against the wall. Through her consciousness flashed visions of the inviting leer of the worthless Jose Gonzales whose advances her maidenly shyness had repulsed but treasured and would know no more; visions too of other unworthy but ardent youths, with supple backs and amorous eyes and lips that dripped with passion, youths to whose embraces she might have yielded her warm body with fearful ecstasy. Through her mind coursed fiery visions too of Pedro as he stretched his muscles prior to orgies of romping merriment when Clara was out of the house. She considered all that she was giving up for the security of life with a man of property, an old man who would be kind to her on his ranch out in the distant San Gabriel Valley. It was a place that had never seemed so far away. She would have preferred starvation and cruelty and misery with Jose, would have preferred to be beaten by him as she had seen Pedro beat Clara, would even have preferred final abandonment by Jose rather than constancy from old Manuel. She looked at Clara, saw the way she beamed. She held her breath for a long time. A woman must accept what is offered.

The wine jug circulated and the laughter swelled to fever pitch while the spring rain fell beyond the window.

4

The following Sunday their banns were published. Manuel was open-handed and generous. He bought Julia a trousseau of vivid hues and presents of turquoise jewelry. On the wedding morning, he hired a barouche with driver to bear the bridal couple to the little Church of the Queen of the Angels on the Plaza. Here, a small rotund priest with swinish eyes and bulbous, sensual lips administered in a rapid sing-song the sacrament that made Manuel and Julia man and wife.

Returned to Pedro's home, the festive party squandered the day with meat and wine and ribald jokes. As the sun lowered Manuel became itchily impatient to be gone with his new wife to their home. At the kerb, Sal was harnessed to the oaken buggy. Farewells were shouted amid the riotous revelry. Julia kissed Pedrillo and Concha. Kneeling and hugging the children to whom she had served as a second mother, she wept abruptly. She clung to them, weeping. This was the worst parting of all, so final and so unbearable. This leave-taking was the end of so happy an epoch. Julia doubted that the era about to unfold would prove happy. Clara's laughter was mixed with tears and her embrace was smothering. Pedro stood and looking up, Julia was shocked to find his black eyes brimmed with tears. He crushed her to him and his kisses were passionate on her lips. Julia felt herself near to fainting in surrender to his ardour in her sudden and fearfully aroused desires. She trembled visibly when she pushed him from her and turned away without looking back. Her husband assisted her gallantly into the buggy amid a clamour of waving hands and ancient jests and the wailing of children and showers of well-wishes. Julia did not look toward Pedro, but in that frenzied din, she sensed a crackling maleficent tension as Pedro silently cursed the old man who took her from him.

The horse required no guidance. He often traversed this road and sensed that he headed towards his own manger. Manuel had drunk freely of the wedding wine. For a week he had been unable to rouse his member to rigidity no matter what fantasies he burned into his mind. Fear of failure haunted him and wine reassured him. God knew he would be all right once he got his lovely, sixteen-year-old bride into their bed. His ardour knew no restraint and in his heart he believed he had a way with women. His arm was forever about Julia's body, his hands exploring the rises and heat of her flesh, gently kneading her breasts in erotic delight. Julia protested but he barely heard her. For one thing, her sense of the duties of matrimony, drummed into her all week by Clara, caused her to express her dissent as mildly as her revulsion would allow. Her husband believed her protests were

17

motivated by a mixture of modesty and coquetry. It never crossed his mind that his bridegroom's manifestations of love were unwelcome to his bride. . . .

Manuel's hands crawling over her body were hateful to Julia, but his kisses on her mouth were loathsome to the point of nausea. She struggled when the old man tried to take her into his arms and cover her mouth with his, but her strength, at war with her obligations, was unequal to his stringy old sinews.

'No, no,' she pleaded. 'Not here on the road like this.'

'But you are my bride. One expects a lover to embrace his bride, even on a public road.'

'Oh not yet, Senor. Please. Wait a bit.'

He straightened, wounded in his pride. 'Am I not then your husband? Do I ask too much that I should taste a kiss from the wife I have married? Ah, chica, little flower, my young and lovely wife, how I crave one kiss.' His words gushed and quivered with emotion and yet his entreaty was both command and warrant, lustfully kind but permitting no denial.

Julia surrendered. As his face came closer to her own she shrank from him as best she could and closed her eyes to shut out the pock-marked skin, the wizened cheeks, the wild sparks glinting in his ancient eyes. In that long contact of her husband's parted mouth on hers, Julia would have fainted but for the shock of his breath, that combination of unclean gums, decomposing teeth, wine and wedding viands at war in a deranged stomach.

When Manuel released her at last, Julia fell away from him. She prayed that Manuel's amatory spasm had spent itself in that violent assault. But his appetites were merely whetted, he even felt strange stirrings deep in his loins, and frantically hopeful, he clutched at her again.

The sun slumped beyond the hills like something half-melted. Twilight burned only briefly. When the sun set the hills lost their angularity and sharply defined planes. Darkness settled upward through the ravines, leaving the gaps sombre with chill. Forbidding tall crests loomed in the distance, slashed with bottomless gorges and twisting black canyons, lonely, empty, forlorn places ringing the barren valley.

The heavy odour of orange bloom overflowed from distant

orchards as if nature had prepared a far-flung bower for the bride. A low-flying bat frightened Sal, who lunged sideways on the road. Mockingbirds called, as oblivious of Manuel and Julia as the bride was of the mockingbirds and orange blossoms and crescent moon and evening star. Julia huddled against the iron seat-brace, wrapped in painful memories of the life now lost behind her: Clara's kindliness and love, romps with Pedro, avid for his arms the moment they were alone, Pedrillo's infectious laughter and Concha's baby body nestling against her, the worthless Jose Gonzales of the bold eyes and ruddy mouth. Against this rose her future like acid gorge in her throat. Life as the wife of Manuel seemed in her thoughts as a flat and barren and infinite desert over which blew hot and stagnant winds.

Beside her, Manuel sang in a happy undertone. He rode in a rapture of that anticipated bliss to which his love-making along the way was but an overture. And he was certain now of success. All his old powers would return when he had Julia naked in his bed and in his arms.

Julia looked forward indifferently to Manuel's house and ranch and groves. She accepted as her due that the fertilty of the land would provide her with a livelihood, and the soundness of the structure would offer shelter. It was not for love but for security that she had permitted herself to be espoused to Manuel O'Brien.

The effects of the wine that Manuel had consumed in Los Angeles faded as the liquid swelled his bladder to bursting. With the dying of the wine Manuel's love-making abated.

Julia waited, taut with inner illness. She was not by nature a squeamish girl. She'd grown up in poverty where youth is not shielded from the intimacies of human contact. From her first night in Pedro's home she'd lain and listened, breath-bated, to his erotic assaults on Clara in their bed. When a mild stupor settled over Manuel and he relaxed his attacks upon her, she was grateful, but remained tense and watchful.

It was early evening when Sal plodded into the rancho O'Brien and ambled exhaustedly toward the humpback barn that was his stable. In the darkness Julia could see little. A gateless picket fence toppled along the side of the road, half the pickets missing or hanging awry. A magnificent spreading live oak overhung the house. Against the barnyard fence she saw what seemed to be a walking-plough, abandoned on its

19

side in the weeds, harrow and teeth gone, a grindstone encrusted in knee-high hollyhocks. A one-horse open wagon stood just within the barnyard, serving as a chicken roost.

Manuel alighted rustily from the buggy and helped Julia to the ground. He stretched and said, 'I must feed and water the horse. Please to wait for me. I shall be but a moment, my bride.'

She nodded and leaned against the side of the buggy. Manuel removed the harness and threw it, tangled, into the sump of the buggy and then led Sal into the barn stall. The horse whinnied in hunger. Manuel fussed about in the dark barn, relieved his aching bladder in thick shadow, found corn and hay which he gave to the horse, then fetched a bucket of stale water from the barnyard for the beast.

Julia meanwhile removed from the rear of the buggy the handbag in which she had transported her belongings. It was a contrivance of two grey cloth-covered boxes, the larger inverted and slipped as a cover over the smaller where the bride's effects were stored, the whole bound with two fragile straps of leather. Manuel, when he had finished his chores in the barn, came to carry her luggage into the house. Julia followed him, moving slowly, her slender shoulders slumped round.

She gazed about, troubled, feeling trapped. She saw white splotches in the dark, row upon row of white bee-hives in the field beyond the barn. Rosa tried to walk between them. Manuel kicked sideways at her and, carrying the cumbersome handbag, almost lost his balance. He looked ridiculous, but Julia was too tired, too nervous even to smile.

The rear door of the house, warped and weatherbeaten, was not locked. Manuel admitted he owned no keys to his doors, front or back, and his windows were thrown open, a few of them flaunting brittle white curtains in the darkness. The house was dark. Julia waited in the musty-smelling kitchen while Manuel sought the one lamp the house possessed. After some further searching he located a block of matches and fired the lampwick. Fumes of sulphur from the splintered match and from the improperly trimmed wick filled the already unpleasant-smelling kitchen. 'You'll soon have this place sparkling and smelling good,' Manuel said when he noticed the way her nostrils flared in distaste.

The glass lamp globe had been hastily cleaned and left

streaked with soot. The light when turned high enough even partially to illuminate the dark walls emitted smoke, but when Manuel turned it low so it did not smoke, it offered hardly sufficient luster to dispel shadows.

The kitchen centred around a large, rusty, wood-burning cooking stove. To one side, a table covered with scabrous red oilcloth, a short bench, and a cupboard holding a few battered pans and coarse dishes. The room was lined with ceiling timber and the walls had long before been painted a vivid blue. Smoke, grime and dust had dulled and adulterated the colour.

Forward from the kitchen and adjoining it was the other main room of the house. A bed of marred white enameled iron trimmed with brass ornaments was freshly, if inexpertly made. The sheets and pillow-slips, even in such wan light as the lamp provided, showed that although newly washed, they were less than clean and the quilts were shabby and threadbare. A strip of dyed carpeting, a runner from the front entrance to the kitchen door, was the only covering for the pinewood floor. A wooden rocking chair with a worn cushion, two small straight chairs with laced seats of sagging rawhide and a dusty clock in a jig-saw case, set perpetually at eight minutes before three, comprised the furnishings. Above the head of the bed a chromo-lithograph of the Virgin holding the infant Jesus amid an adoring brace of saints, glowed faintly in a chipped gilt frame. Beside the lamp on the bedtable a coarse drinking goblet served as vase for a bouquet of pink geraniums, calendulas and a single purple iris which Manuel had plucked and arranged as a tribute to his bride.

Off the main room, behind a sleazy curtain, was a hybrid niche, not a room but larger than a cupboard. On its floor lay a ragged mattress covered with shabby quilts. Here Manuel usually slept, and he came here secretively, even when there was no other person in the house, to smoke his opium, a habit he'd been taught in his boyhood by a Chinese gardener who worked on his ranch when it had belonged to an earlier O'Brien. Julia sniffed, smelling, but failed to recognize the odour of the drug that clung to the walls and furnishings. On the walls of this cupboard-room nails, half-driven, supported clothing.

From the kitchen Manuel brought a wicker-covered demi-john of wine which he poured into large, thick, dingy goblets.

21

He proffered one of these to Julia with some show of ceremony as if the drinking of it were a rite.

'Drink, chica.' He smiled, nodding vigorously. 'Our wedding night. Drink to the joys of our union, little bride, and to the son that you shall bear me.'

Julia winced and shook her head. 'I do not wish for the wine tonight, Senor. I — do not feel quite well.' Julia did not object to drinking the wine, but to the toast her husband proposed. 'Maybe I have drunk already too much today at our wedding. Or maybe I ate something that does not please my stomach.'

'Drink,' Manuel urged her. 'To drink will make you feel better. It will restore you. Drink, my pretty bride.' He forced the goblet into her hand.

Julia sipped the wine. He embraced her in his right arm, raised his glass high in his left hand and then half-drained the acrid potion.

He wiped his hand across his mouth, laughing. 'Come, drink now.' Nor would he relinquish the toast he'd proposed. 'Drink to wedding joys, a happy marriage and a lusty son.' His arm encircled her waist; he grasped her wrist and guided the glass to her mouth. Reluctantly she emptied the goblet. Watching her with bright brown eyes, Manuel drained his glass and refilled it. He would not hear Julia's protest, sloshing red wine to the brim of her goblet. The draught she'd swallowed had, as Manuel predicted, warmed and cheered her.

Manuel tossed off his second tumbler of wine and, in the gloom of meagre light, fondled and caressed his bride. A wine-born fortitude sustained the girl and she made no effort to resist her man's gallantry. Her repugnance for him did not involve hatred, although she was unable to comprehend this randy behaviour from the kind old man she'd known all her life. She was not ignorant of what marriage entailed, but she had failed to associate passion with old Manuel O'Brien. Somehow, in her mind, sex after thirty was obscene. Now, even though she could not reciprocate his passion, she must accept it.

She held her breath and remained close in his fevered embrace. She knew what she had to do. Never mind the conjugal duty Clara had drummed into her, Pedro had made it clear. In their one sad, brief encounter earlier in this eternal

22

week, Pedro had spoken plainly, if anguishedly. She must endure at least one assault from old Manuel or her marriage was useless. Manuel must be allowed to penetrate and possess her. She had to make this happen for her own welfare, no matter what she had to do to bring it about. Nothing else in this life was as urgent to her. She had nodded, her black eyes brimming with tears, knowing Pedro spoke inescapable truth.

Now, she felt her throat tighten with tears, her body withdraw instinctively no matter how acquiescent she tried to be. Why did he have to be so old? So ugly and unappealing? This wedding night was essential to her and her marriage. She would buy security, protection, property. Could these be weighed in the balance against the price she paid for them? And why couldn't she deny the vision in the darkness of Pepe's flashing black eyes?

As for Manuel, no matter what he did, no matter how fiercely he fanned the embers of his desire, he felt himself numb down there, as if his loins were cut off from every access to his nerve centres. He wanted her! God knew he wanted her, and yet he remained as limp as the dough of a tortilla. He kept up his outward show of confidence, his simulation of lust, and he sweated with failure. His bravado and passionate ardour convinced the girl. She lay passively, waiting, but Manuel knew he was playing a part; even the words came haltingly like the remembered idiom of some long-forgotten, alien language.

His ecstasies of love failed to rouse him. He no longer questioned the effects of his charms upon his bride. She lay waiting while he felt the need of calculation, of an herculean effort that love had not in the past required of him. Trembling with the lack of spontaneity in his passion, he concentrated earnestly, drank more wine, spoke aloud words that had never failed to arouse his fervour, but which failed him now. He brought to bear an unyielding determination, a forced vehemence, a false fervency; he overacted his ardour.

Julia, however, took his tenders for true pay. She wanted only to get it over with. Her stomach moiled hotly, but she was resigned. Fatalism blends with stoicism in her race; what could not be escaped must be endured. Though she found the old man hesitant and clumsy and suddenly even reticent, Julia had no intention of shirking her obligation. She would obey Pedro because her own well-being depended upon it. the

23

Church had made her the wife of Manuel O'Brien and she was prepared to endure matrimony with him. But in the name of God couldn't the old man get on with it?

She opened the bodice of her dress for him and his trembling hands covered the bare mounds of her firm young breasts. He gasped as if choking but remained inert, clinging to her. However brave her resolutions, when his talon-like hands clawed underneath her chemise, her muscles stiffened in antagonism and she drew away involuntarily.

When Manuel remained unmoving at her side, the girl unbuttoned her dress and whispered, 'Take it off of me. Don't you want to take it off of me?'

He nodded and began clumsily to remove the garments from her. As her bared charms revealed themselves, his breathless comments flattered Julia. She found his admiration pleasing. When only her chemise remained, she smiled at him and got under the sheet, watching him with black liquid eyes.

Manuel's own disrobing was brief. He removed his outer clothes only, retaining as sleeping garments a knitted shirt and woven drawers. He was thankful for his bride's inexperience and virginity. She would not see that he wasn't tumescent. He peered down at himself outlined limply against his fly, hating himself, his ancestors and all his gods. He felt abandoned at the worst moment of his life, and helpless against this cruelest jest. Though his mind reeled and his legs threatened to buckle under him already, he drained the last of the wine from the demi-john and blew out the low-wicked light.

Darkness settled over the room and Julia waited. She closed her eyes tightly and visualized the flashing eyes of the worthless Jose Gonzales. She prayed silently that Manuel might be in her fantasies transmogrified into the hard, muscular body of Pedro Grandos Luiz. She shivered as if violently chilled.

Manuel staggered and toppled across the bed beside her. His hands clawed at her and he mouthed words from the gutters and the whore-cribs of his youth, pleading, telling her how desperately he wanted her. He stopped talking suddenly. Julia had reached down and closed her hand on him. He winced. He had been using words to trample down her fences and all the time she was holding the gate open for him.

'One drinks too much wine,' he muttered. 'I ache for sleep.

24

You must be very tired. Such a long day. So much excitement. So much wine.'

He gave her her chance to escape the hateful contact of his ancient scrawny body, but it was sanctuary she could not accept. She must submit. She worked her hand furiously, trying to hurry him.

'Don't you want me?' she whispered.

'More than life. . . but you must be patient.'

'But I am not patient. I am ready now.'

He swallowed back a hot gush of bile. He lay sweating in an agony of failure. He was overcome with self-hatred. What a fool he was. A lovely, willing young flower and he was helpless to pluck her. Oh, foul gods.

He raised himself on his elbow and threw back the sheet. He spoke with forced bravado. 'Maybe. Maybe if I looked at you.' He was convinced she would from shame and modesty refuse, but she did not hesitate.

She stared up at Manuel in the grey darkness. For the first time it occurred to her that Manuel was not going to consummate this marriage, that for some reason she did not understand, he was unable to possess her. She realized in terror that he would as long as he lived recall his failure. And if he failed, she was lost.

'Naked?' she whispered. 'One wishes to see me naked?'

With a serpentine, fluid motion she peeled off the chemise and tossed it across the room. Then she fell upon the mattress, her slender legs wide apart.

'Look at me,' she said. 'Look at me. Look at me. Look at me.'

She reached up and drew him down upon her. She enclosed his lean shanks in her legs, locking her ankles at the small of his back. 'Oh God,' he whispered. 'Oh my God.'

'Put it in,' she ordered. She reached down and forced his half-rigid staff between the lips of her vagina. She imprisoned him there and fiercely rocked against him with frenzied undulations. He began to whimper, then to gasp. He clutched her with all his strength. A shudder wracked through his body and sighing loudly he fell away from her.

She sat up, releasing him. 'But. . .' She shook her head. 'Don't you wish to come?'

He spoke almost in arrogance, with pride restored. 'I have come,' he said. 'Did you not feel it?'

She nodded, forced herself to smile. 'Oh? Was that it? I thought it another drop of sweat, but I captured it. You can be certain that I captured your strength and your being inside me.'

Manuel nodded and wept suddenly. Totally exhausted, and somehow reassured, he fell away from her and sank at once into a stunned sleep. At first his snoring frightened Julia, but after a moment she felt reassured by the sound. When Julia was sure that Manuel's sleep was deep, she writhed on the mattress, putting as much of the bed between them as possible. But, fatigued as she was, she lay staring for a long time wide-eyed through the darkness. Somewhere a mocking-bird shrilled, a coyote yelped, and as if from some distant planet, a train whistled mournfully in the night.

5

Julia awoke in the first flaring of dawn. She glanced at Manuel sprawled face down on the rumpled sheet and escaped stealthily from the bed. She dressed and walked through the kitchen and out by the back door. Life stirred only desultorily. Rosa, the black bitch, followed her to the outhouse beyond the barn and returned with swishing tail at the heels of her new mistress. Rosa responded with tremours of delight when the girl stooped to pet her. Together they prowled the rows of hives and wandered through the scale-encrusted and anaemic lemon orchard. Distantly she saw the limitless expanse of ploughed and irrigated land of some gigantic estate. She returned through an uncultivated expanse of rough ground surrounded by a rickety fence. She crossed the barn lot, stopping to peer into the sty where four half-grown hogs rested. The pigs lunged grunting and squealing onto their long legs when she approached. She watched them idly for a moment and then returned to the house.

Julia was not disturbed or disappointed that her new home was paint-peeled and tiny. She had not even anticipated what sort of place Manuel's home would be. She liked the quiet and the rich odours. Early California spring cloaked the ground with verdant tenderness. As sunbeams sucked up the dew from grass and flowers, the smells in the clean air were

26

sweet: the lemon bloom, broken honeycomb, the rich earth itself, the myriad flowers that rioted among the weeds, even the pungent odour of the stables. She paused, gazing at her house a moment. She shrugged, finding it adequate. It was shelter, home.

At a pile of broken and discarded bee-hives, Julia broke kindling with a rusty axe and made a fire in the kitchen stove. From the coffee, rice, thick bacon and dry bread she found in the pantry she concocted breakfast and prepared to serve it on the table covered with the shabby red oilcloth.

Manuel heard her breaking the kindling and got up, drowsy and hung-over. His mouth tasted like discarded cotton. He hesitated to enter the kitchen. The swilling and gourmandizing of yesterday had robbed him of appetite or energy. He remembered that he had drunk far too much wine, and recalled vividly only his self-hatred at the failure of his manhood, that limp tortilla which must hang to mock him as long as he lived. He dreaded to face Julia, who must despise him for his failing her. At last, he could delay it no longer. He faced the sad truth. The wedding was over. For better or worse, Julia was his wife, to cook his food, care for his house, revere his authority. His face burned. He had wanted her most to bear his children, and he had failed. He dreaded the look he must confront in her eyes. But there was nothing to say. Domesticity had begun.

He entered the kitcen without ceremony of salutation and sat down to his breakfast. She stood beside the table as he ate, as she had seen Clara stand beside Pedro, her hands folded under her apron. 'So here is the slugabed,' she said, smiling. 'Do you sleep so late every day?'

'No. I am up at dawn.' Manuel could not bring himself to look at her.

He heard her short musical laugh, a bird sound in this old shanty. 'Was your great conquest last night too much for you then?'

'Conquest?' His hands were poised woodenly before him. He still did not look up from his plate.

Her laughter teased him. 'You don't recall then the way you took me?'

Manuel winced; his heart thudded sickly above his taut, empty belly. At first he thought she was taunting him with the cruelty of youth. But when he looked up, her dark face was passive, smiling. He managed to nod his head. 'Of course, I recall. How could one forget?'

'One must not forget. One took his bride with such force. One planted his seeds deep inside her womb.' She sighed. 'With such vigour.'

Like one reprieved at the very threshold of the gallows, Manuel exhaled heavily and relaxed. He nodded again and spoke almost arrogantly, with pride restored. 'One does not forget. One heads his house. One is master in his own house.'

Julia accepted the obligations of marriage. Her household chores did not consume much of her time. She had leisure to sit on a bench beside the house hour after hour sunk in loneliness while Manuel pottered among his hives. She did not care what he did as long as he left her alone, as long as he did not paw at her. She was not going to endure another situation like her wedding night, except by force, and she was no longer afraid of Manuel.

She watched the occasional wagons passing on the road. Sometimes the fine carriages from the great Stockton Farms raced past in violent swirls of dust. The carts of the poor farmers pulled off into the ditch when the great freighters of the Stockton place swept by. She did not even envy the rich and mighty Stocktons; she remained apathetic and passive.

Some days she drove beside Manuel in their buggy down the winding road and across the senile bridge over an arroyo to the store at the crossroads, a place designated Apia by a scabbed signpost. Here they bought food and supplies and Manuel passed the time of day with his acquaintances. He told her that once there had been maybe fifty families in the valley, but now there were fewer than a dozen. 'One day Stockton Farms will own it all, the whole valley.' Manuel swung his arm. 'Only then will their greed be appeased. They will be satisfied only when every farmer is gone or works for the Stocktons.'

Mostly, they remained at home because early in the year the bees were active. Escaping swarms at that time were valuable and Manuel was too skilled an apiarist to leave his filling hives unattended for very long.

The old man spent eternal hours among the bees. When the sun shone with sufficient heat for him not to fear lifting the hive covers lest he kill the unhatched brood, he checked the workers. There seemed a thousand things to do and Julia

28

watched him idly and without interest. He destroyed new queen-cells in colonies so prosperous that the old queen seemed better than a new one might be. He had to bolster the strength of a weak lot with a leaf of brood or a new queen-cell from a stronger colony. He was always adding new super-boxes in which to store the honey. His vigilance was needed to destroy drone brood, to look for signs of foul-brood or other diseases. He had to capture escaping swarms and brush them into fresh hives he'd prepared to receive them.

When the sun was so pallid that opening the hives might hazard the brood on cool days, there was work to be done in the little shed which Manuel used as his workshop. There were new boxes to assemble, frames to be wired and inlaid with foundation wax. Old boxes fell apart from exposure to sun and rain. Those which could be salvaged had to be nailed and cleated together, strengthened to serve their purpose for one more year. But Manuel could not stay away from Julia for very long. She drew him as the moon draws the tides. Throughout the day he came into the kitchen to refresh himself with a draught of red wine.

As soon as his evening meal was devoured, Manuel retired to his cupboard-room to indulge himself in his whiff of opium. He never mentioned to Julia why he went there or what he did. Manuel did not think of his indulgence as secret, still it was something not to be discussed. Julia knew what he did in the niche; she simply did not care. 'When he's pulling on his pipe,' she told herself, 'he's letting me alone.'

Sundays took the couple away to Mass at the stone mission beyond Apia. On infrequent occasions Manuel displayed his bride proudly in the homes of his friends in the vast neighbourhood. Here they gossiped in Spanish and drank enkindling wines which always excited Manuel's passions, so he was already pawing at her before he got her into their buggy.

Manuel's closest friend, Julia learned, was a field worker named Juan de Zaragosa who lived alone in one of the field shacks for permanent hands at the Stockton estate. Juan and Manuel had long memories, found much to laugh about and tippled much wine. They had also shared the sad ties of tragedy. Juan had owned a farm twice the area of Rancho O'Brien; he had possessed a loud and handsome family. Somehow through some legal manoeuvre which neither man fully understood, he lost his land; his wife died, his family dispersed across the face of California; some of them he had not even seen in twenty years. After the loss of his family place, Juan de Zaragosa wandered the San Gabriels in a wine-sodden haze. He might have died from exposure or broken heart or starvation but for Mr Bragg Stockton, who took him on as a permanent field hand with a shack of his own. 'For as long as you live, boy,' Mr Bragg Stockton told him. 'We're all neighbours here in this valley. A man has to take care of his neighbours.'

Juan de Zaragosa could no longer find even a trace or boundary of his old farm. It had long been ploughed up and planted so it looked like all the rest of Mr Bragg Stockton's property.

Julia was bored and miserable when they visited Juan de Zaragosa. No matter how cheerfully the old friends met across demi-johns of wine, they always ended sodden in tears, clinging to each other, swearing undying fealty. She always raged on the journey home about the way they carried on, weeping.

'But Juan is my oldest friend,' Manuel said.

'That's it. He's old. I hate being around him. I feel I am the last young person on this earth. It's scary he's so old.'

Manuel laughed. 'Why, Juan must be eight — ten years younger than I am.'

'That's what I mean,' Julia said with a bleak feral smile.

They could never visit anywhere very long. The bees would not permit of their master's frequent and prolonged absences and so, to Julia's relief, the O'Briens kept largely at home.

Julia was lonely but she had foreseen loneliness. She had expected only security as Manuel's wife and she had that.

Manuel's tentative amatory demands gave his wife scant concern. She quickly learned to repel or circumvent his desires. She didn't care what he wanted, he got nothing except rebuffs, black looks and brazen refusals. When he accused her of coldness, she reminded him of the way he had assaulted her on their wedding night, the way he had penetrated her, the way he had hurt her. Manuel was torn apart by her indifference.

The very pride he felt in her youth and grace and beauty, the unction of vanity that in his age he should have captured this paragon of virtue, his fear of losing her, the egoism of his possession, the nagging doubts of his own manhood, prompted him to deference in dealing with her. Too, he was afraid that if she submitted, he would fail, and this would unman him forever. He chided Julia for the frigidity she showed toward his advances, his love and passion for her. Still he remained suppliant, and inwardly relieved, rather than imperative. He wanted to enforce his authority as head of his house, but he hesitated. Enforced kisses, repulsed embraces and hurried fondling marked the limits of his achievement with her.

Still, he might have asserted himself. The forcefulness and success she related to him of their wedding night spurred him to thrust again to the limit. But that very muddled, confused and agonizing memory made him pause. Deep inside his consciousness was an awareness of his waning puissance which he was fearfully reluctant and simultaneously hopefully desirous to put once again to its test. The truth about his wedding night remained vague to him. He had only Julia's report and sometimes it seemed to him she protested his vigour too much. Sleep and stumbling drunkenness had overtaken him and he had never been sure of his marriage's consummation. He had Julia's ample assurance but, strangely, no memory. If Julia were to believed — and he was avid of belief — her word was warrant for him again to essay his powers. Yet, no matter how fervently he willed it, he could not recall his forceful assault upon Julia on their wedding night. He even began to be afraid Julia was being kind to him, trying to conceal the truth of his failure, trying to spare him from further disgrace. This thought swirled always around the rim of his conscious mind and he was sickened, for if it were true, Julia's was a deadly sort of kindness.

Working the hives he would covertly study her from under the great brim of his hat as she sagged in the shade of the live oak, staring apathetically into some middle distance. His heart lurched at the sight of her, the determined little chin, the taut line of her mouth, the way her black eyes narrowed thin sometimes, even when she smiled. He sighed in despair. It was not like Julia to be kind. She snarled and spat at him like a cat. He could not believe she would lie unselfishly to make him happy. He had yet to discover any sign that Julia was in any way unselfish. . .

The hives waxed. The bees laboured home with loads of

nectar and with hips heavy, overflowing pockets of yellow pollen. New queens made single nuptial flights and drones fulfilled their destinies with love and death. Young workers sunned themselves before the openings of the hives and essayed short journeys to test their wings, neophytes in preparation for duties and devotion to a bloated queen. New swarms followed their old queens to found new colonies, leaving their former estates to such new queens as should burst the caps of their cells and fight their way to supremacy. Manuel was ineffectual and impotent in his house but he dominated his myriad menage, forcing his insect slaves month after month to do his bidding.

Denied by his wife any of those conjugal rights to which he felt himself entitled, Manuel began talking to his bees, muttering as he worked. He had misgivings about pressing his demands. Was it not better, he argued, to defer to Julia's refusal than possibly to chagrin himself even in his own eyes?

He felt ill most of the time, and went about his work with little enthusiasm. Only with God's intervention would he ever have his way with Julia. Then one day in June, he looked up from his work among his hives to find Juan de Zaragosa staring at him, grinning. A bald, obese man with vulnerable black eyes, Juan wore overalls, denim shirt buttoned at the collar, and dung-smeared boots almost as old as he was.

The old friends embraced, laughing. 'In the middle of the day like this, Juan? How do you escape your work?'

'I came for advice,' Juan said. 'I am at that place where I no longer know what to do. I work as hard as ever at the great estate. Harder. But I get less done, I am forever angering el patron Senor Stockton. I can please him in no way. He says I am old. Worthless. A toothless hound. A lazy greaser. I bite my lip to keep from crying. I can see it. He wants me to give up my house, to leave his land. What would I do? Where would I go?'

'Why would he want you to leave?'

'Because I am old. His arrogant sons say I take up space, but do nothing in return. El patron agrees. I fear they will turn me from the house and the farm.'

'Just because you have the years? My God. We all get old. The Stocktons will get old.' Manuel tried to laugh. 'It is easy. It only takes time.'

Juan nodded. 'We all get old. . . . One dreads to age — to

be turned out from the great estate. It is worse that the young Stocktons curse me as a lazy greaser. I was in this valley before they were born.'

'We all were. But the Stocktons have great wealth and power.'

'I was born in this valley. My father came across the border with my pregnant mother. This is my home. I belong here.'

Manuel sighed and nodded. 'What of your children?'

Juan spread his hands. 'What of them? They are blown away like milkweed on the wind. Many may be dead. One does not hear.'

'Don't you have any other relatives?'

'Who would take me in? Don't you understand? I don't want to be driven out. I have nowhere to go. Of relatives, I have cousins in Sonora. In Hermosillo, I think. I visited them once. They had little. A few chickens. A cow.'

'Why not return to them? You have a little put aside, no? They could help you. You could help them.'

'I come for wisdom. You talk like a fool. We would all starve. I am an old man. This is my native land. In Mexico, my cousins are always hungry.'

'Still, here at the great farm, they treat you like an animal.'

'Lower than an animal. Their horses they pet and pamper and curry and stroke — '

'A man must have pride. Would you stay then and be treated like an animal?'

'An animal, yes. But an animal with food in his belly. No. My pride speaks loud, but my belly growls louder. I stay. I shall never leave this valley.'

Manuel sighed. 'I hurt that you allow yourself so to be treated. But this is a bad time for all of us, Juan.'

'And yet I envy you, amigo mio, above all men.'

'Me?' Manuel straightened, pushing his sombrero back on his head.

'You have so much of good.'

Manuel stared at him. 'Do you believe this? Or do you say it to taunt me?'

'Why would I wish to taunt my old friend? I speak true. You have your land. Your bees. Your young bride.'

Manuel bit back a bitter laugh like wormwood in his mouth. 'My bees rule my life. It is not the other way round. . . . And look yonder at my bride. . . . You believe then that this one offers succour to her husband? When I turn to her in our bed, she gives me only the cold rump.'

Juan nodded, not astonished. Manuel had not meant to expose his torment even to an old and trusted friend, but he was helpless and frustrated. The bees could not counsel him; they seemed not even to listen to his lamentations. His heart hurt and somehow it seemed that to reveal his own inner agony might help relieve Juan's pain in some small way. Anyhow, he had spoken the words, and now he could not stop.

'She refuses me her lips, her body, my rights as her husband.'

Juan nodded again and shrugged his shoulders slightly. 'An old mule and a young filly. The mule can only be a jackass to the filly. Worse. Only an old jackass.'

'Why then would she marry me, if not to live with me as my wife?'

Juan did not bother to answer this. He plucked a weed and chewed on it, looking grave.

'She is quick enough to demand of me,' Manuel said. 'Her right. This is her right. That is her right. What of my rights?'

'The young understand only the young, and then only when they wish. The young are very selfish. It is part of their charm.'

Manuel winced. 'But this one is not charmed.'

'It is not easy to live with. It is a trait best admired from a safe distance. Still, if one is plagued with it, one must face it and accept it.'

'I ask little in return. A kiss. To fondle. To see her in her nakedness. Is this too much?'

Juan smiled faintly. 'Evidently. It must be.'

'Enjoy your laughter at my distress.'

'I am not laughing, amigo mio. I hurt for you, but is that any balm for your wounds? Would you have me cry? At the moment I cry easily.'

'I try to take her in my arms, and she twists away, like a cat. A moment later she is after me to send more money to the family of her sister. We have so much, my bride says, and her sister's family has so little. I work. He does not. But when I say this, she seems not even to hear me.'

'One hears what one wishes to hear,' Juan said.

'You are a man of great wisdom. What can I do about her?'

Juan shook his head. 'I know little of women, amigo. But I know much of dogs. . . . If she were a bitch, she would suck eggs.'

Manuel staggered as if he'd been struck in the chest. 'Is this the way one speaks of a man's wife? Must you speak such evil?'

Juan sighed. 'I am your friend. For a long time. I was with you before she came. I will be here when she is gone.'

'Gone?' Manuel trembled visibly, looking around wildly in the blaze of sun.

'As your friend, I say only what you must know in your heart. Watch that one as you would watch a fox among chickens.'

'Oh, you are wrong about her. She is quiet and good and gentle.'

'The dark rivers run silent, amigo. You have dipped into German silver. You must assert your mastery. You must make her see you are master in your house and she must accept this or depart.'

'Name of Mary, I couldn't live without her.'

Juan's lip twisted. 'Do you believe she would leave a feathered nest?'

'I fear to gamble. And yet I know you are right. I need love. It is as though I look on food and cannot taste it. As if I thirst while water is just beyond the reach of my fingers. How can I make her come to my arms as a dutiful wife must?'

Juan considered for a long moment, chewing on the reed. 'Have you gone to the priest about this?'

Manuel retreated a step. 'Tell my confessor of my wife's coldness?'

'Your priest can advise you. But more than that, he can speak with the authority of God to your woman. If she has shame, he can shame her. If she has fear, he can frighten her into the ways of righteousness.'

Manuel rocked back and forth, disturbed. He saw that Juan was right and wise. The fear of God might well move Julia when fear of her husband did not. For a moment he felt encouraged. Then he shook his head.

'One dislikes to speak of this to the priest. . . . There is the matter of my age. . . . There is too the matter of my own self-doubt.'

'At your age you should doubt.'

'How does one say such things aloud, even to a priest?'

'You may not be the raging stallion of your youth, still you have needs. Needs a wife should satisfy. Your priest will understand this, even if your wife does not.'

'True. This is true. I shall gather my courage. I shall go to the priest.'

Juan smiled. 'Maybe you won't have to go the the priest.'

'What is this? You advise and then retract?'

'No. You would suffer much going to the priest with the entire truth. An old man. A young wife. Maybe just to threaten her that you will seek counsel. Maybe this would be enough to convert her. It is true that women don't mind denying sex to their men, but they hate for this truth to be circulated. If you convince her that you shall confess her shame to the priest, she may well change her ways. To me it seems worth a gamble. . . . At least, amigo, your very existence is not threatened, as mine is.'

6

Manuel walked to Juan's cart with him. When he returned from the road Julia was gone from beneath the live oak. He felt a sudden pang of agony. Bees hummed about his head. The valley sprawled hot and empty and eternal around him. Everywhere there were brilliant shadows sliced by the blaze of the sun. These shadows wrinkled across the low hills, upon the road, on the open fields; shadows of lemon trees, olive bushes and eucalyptus, of distant farm buildings, of broken stones. He felt his pulses throb and he felt as if he were a stranger in an alien place.

He tried to resume his chores among his hives and could not. He could not put aside Juan's sage advice. He was struck with the idea that to threaten Julia with his intention to consult the priest might serve his purpose as well as actually to do it. The idea started his heart pounding, parched his throat and provoked a thirst for wine. At least wine was the excuse to go casually into the house where he would calmly unfold his project to Julia.

Empty-bellied, he entered the kitchen, letting the door whine shut behind him. He brought the demi-john from the pantry and poured a tumbler of the red liquid, aware of the way his hands shook. He gulped down the wine. Where was Julia? The house lay silent. Always she was near when he came for his restoring draught, passive, withdrawn but ready to serve him. An interest in his labours provided a relief to her tedium. He called her name. There was no answer.

Disturbed, he searched for her. He found her on their bed asleep. Rosa, the black bitch, lay curled on the floor beside the bed. He stood staring down at Julia. That she should be asleep in mid-morning was incomprehensible to Manuel. He called her name again and she did not rouse. He stepped toward the bed and Rosa, without raising her head from between her paws, growled. At the same time, as if to apologize for the necessity of warning him, Rosa slapped her tail upon the floor.

Suddenly enraged, Manuel stared at the dog. That low growl was uttered in earnest. Manuel approached another step and the bitch raised her head with an angry snarl that wakened Julia.

Julia sat up, for the moment disoriented, her face flushed, her eyes swollen. Manuel frowned, concerned. 'Why do you sleep in the middle of the morning, chica? Is it that you are ill? Or is it that you seek surcease from unhappiness? Are you then lonesome on this ranchito with your husband?'

Julia shrugged, dampening her lips with her tongue. She slapped at her skirt with the flat of her hand. 'I have only an ache of the head. I did not sleep well in the night.'

Now troubled, Manuel leaned against the bed. Rosa came to her feet, interposed her body between the couple and snarled again.

Manuel swore. 'What is wrong with that bitch? She never acted so before.'

Julia smiled wanly. 'Rosa and I are close friends now. That is all. She does not wish it that you should come close to me. She is jealous.' Leaning forward, Julia placed her arm about the black neck of the dog and fondled her with gentle pulling strokes of the silken ears, and caressed her with that wealth of endearing terms in which the Spanish tongue abounds. Rosa laid her head against the girl's leg.

The deflection of the bitch's allegiance from himself didn't irritate Manuel as did the awareness that this allegiance had gone to the woman. Here was one more barrier between them, a mere dog's veto to his needs. Julia's arm languid about the dog forbade him the violence toward the animal that his frustration urged. Vexation, indignation, resentment and wrath fermented inside Manuel, making his stomach queasy. But his love for Julia, his pride in owning her, his tenderness towards her immaturity, the hope of his new plan, restrained the explosion that flared inside him.

His voice shook. 'How is this? Here you offer to the dog, the dog who comes now to hate me, snarls at me, the affection you deny your husband. Is this right? Is this what the Holy Church means by marriage, that you should withhold from your husband the rights your vows have given him?' His words were aggressive but they came from his mouth as a simple plea. 'I married you because I wanted a wife. My love, I desire you. I must have you.'

His eyes brimming with tears of self-pity, he leaned towards Julia. The dog growled again, but Julia restrained her with a strong grip around Rosa's neck. She threw up her other hand as if to repel the man. 'No, no, no, Manuel. Not today. Not now.' She shuddered visibly. 'I shall be your wife. I swear this. I shall. A good wife to you. But — '

'You will grant to me my wishes, my desires, my rights?'

She hesitated. 'No, not now. Not today. Wait. Please wait.'

'When?'

'Sometime, sometime. I swear it. Not now. Not now.'

Agonized, Manuel shook his head. Nothing changed. She merely delayed; he knew she would go on refusing him forever. His heart broke. He drew a deep breath and played his trump card. 'Then I shall speak to the priest. . . . Father Garcia shall say whether a husband must wait eternally upon his wife's whims. The good father shall declare my rights to you. If you have married an old man because he has a rancho and property, only to moon in regret for the pauper youths in the city, denying me the rights with which marriage in the Holy Church endowed me, you shall see, you shall see. . . . You shall see. The father shall say. He will confront you. He shall command you.'

As Manuel spoke Julia rose from the bed and, standing, thrust Rosa gently behind her. A crimson flush stole through the waxen tan of her cheeks and suffused the taut muscles of her throat. The back of her hand pressed against her forehead as if to steady her from reeling. Words started slowly and then

38

poured from her mouth like an avalanche of pebbles. She nodded her head vehemently. 'So. Go then to the priest. Go to Father Garcia. Go! Go! Have him define your rights. Have the good father come in anger to me. Have him say aloud what I should do. . . . Go. See what he will say. See for yourself. Go to him. Go now. Today. Do not put it off. Go to the priest. Tell him the story of our marriage. Tell him. Tell him everything. Tell him how you were drunk and violated your wife's body the night after we were married in the church. Tell him how you spewed your seed inside her. Uncaring. Cruel. Tell him the disgust she felt for the embraces you forced on her in your drunkenness. Go.' Rumbling growls from Rosa provided an obbligato to Julia's tirade. 'Tell him. Tell him all. Tell him your age. And tell him mine. Tell him that you hound me and pester me and importune me daily. Not to procreate as the Church wills. But to satisfy your dirty passions. Go and tell him. Tell him that even now I carry your child in my belly. Tell — '

'Child? What do you say? Child? What child? You are with child?' The old man wilted and paled, as if he would faint. He gasped and his mouth gaped open. He watched her. She seemed to have turned to ice. He waited. The affirmation, the reassurance would never come. It was as if she had withdrawn into her shell and might never speak again. And yet he did not doubt.

'I am prenada. With child. Of course. Do you deny that you knew it?' Julia spoke with a sudden placid calm, detached and remote again. She had won and she knew it. The rage was burned out of the old man.

He stood there between tears and laughter, staring at her. He too had won. Through this new defeat, through this final and utter rout, stalked victory. Tantalus stooped and quenched his mighty thirst.

His throat choked, he whispered, 'Julia. Little darling. Little wife of me. A child. A child for me. A child from my loins and carried in your sweet womb. A child for Manuel in his age. A child for which he has prayed to the holy Mother of God.'

Despite Rosa's sullen warnings, he grasped Julia in his arms, kissing her between his sobs. Julia made no effort to resist his raptures. Her arms hung at her side and her face was calm and tranquil.

Manuel quivered at the pit of his belly. That need for offspring had often been fulfilled for him, only to have his brood snatched from him. It might seem he would have become inured to disappointment, that he would come to accept his role of masculine Niobe, or at least that he would comprehend the hazards ahead for him. He could think only that he had won. He would be a father. The beginning itself was an end. It was proof that he, Manuel O'Brien, could yet beget his kind. The old wolf was grey but he had not yet lost his teeth. His line would continue, the blood of his people would survive.

<h2 style="text-align:center">7</h2>

Manuel heeled about and ran into the kitchen. He clutched the wicker demi-john in his trembling hands. He was anxious to fortify his ecstasy with wine so it might never wane from this moment's high exultation. He turned the jug up to his lips and the liquid gurgled into his mouth, seeped along his chin and burned his throat. His repeatedly declared anxiety for Julia's health, welfare, comfort and needs grew wearisome to her, but her sudden assurance of her position of security made it all tolerable. Manuel's day evaporated in a sodden haze of self-gratification.

Dusk lowered and the pigs squealed and grunted in hunger. Sal whinnied at his supper hour. Manuel, giggling, promised to feed his stock and then procrastinated over one more drink, one more toast to her beauty and immortality. At last, in the half-dark Julia sneaked away and carried rations to the stock. Sprawled at the kitchen table, Manuel rebuked her on her return. It was unfitting, he sobbed, that the wife of Senor O'Brien should slop pigs, the more improper since she was carrying his child. He would have done the chores if only she had waited. He was sincere enough but by now was hardly able to pour his wine without spilling it all over the oilcloth.

Nor did sobriety abate Manuel's solicitude for Julia's felicity. The days were for him a time of satisfaction in the contemplation of his future and of delight in the service of his senora. No longer did he demand anything of her. His amorous persistence gave place to selfless attendance to

Julia's least whim. What had passed for passion became a vigil of veneration. His devotion was such a touching manifestation of his adoration that Julia in her perverse way might now at last in her gratitude grant him intimacies she had previously denied. He racked his brain to find services he could offer her, whims he might fulfill, presents he could buy. He ploughed and planted two kitchen gardens, one of vegetables with beans and peas and onions and chicory that she might have the freshest food, and one of flowers to surround her in beauty: snapdragons, pansies and the gummy sweetness of petunias. A comfortable new rocking chair, carpeting for her floor, lace curtains with incredible flower patterns, made his lady's bower more tolerable. He bought better quality foods and delicacies to tempt her palate, wines smoother than the mordant liquid of his demi-john, bags of many-coloured candies, stylish tortoiseshell Spanish back combs ornamented with rows of glass gems, all the rage at the moment, loose-fitting maternity frocks, anything that he hoped might delight her.

The tide of summer rose. The hives were full with their sweet harvest; robber bees flitted between the colonies and the vigilance of the entrance guards was intensified. Untended roses burst into brief profusion. Rosa grew rotund and whelped another variegated litter of puppies, showing them all impartial devotion and discipline.

That Clara was to bear another child was known to Manuel and Julia. The importance of its advent was minimized only in the anticipation of their own prospects. Early in July, Manuel returned from Los Angeles through rose-tinted dusk with the information that Clara had brought forth another son and that he had been christened Teodore in honour of the esteemed American President. There had been no question about Clara's strength to go through the labour and delivery, but the tidings that she had borne it all in her uncomplaining, complacent way and that the child thrived, reassured Manuel that Julia too might bear her infant without undue travail or risk.

What with Manuel's patience and solicitude, the progress of Julia's confinement and her growing, rather than decreasing, sense of loneliness on the ranchito, she became exigent of her husband's care, devotion and attention. She came more and more to demand them as her right. Luxuries now

41

seemed true necessities to her. She grew imperious, requiring immediate fulfilment of her flightiest fancy. Manuel shared her conviction that his highest duty was instant gratification of her longings, however irrational. Above all, Julia was no longer to Manuel a young girl married to an old man, immured on an isolated farm, removed from friends and family, but the custodian of that new life which was to be the heart of him, of that new being in whose youth he should renew his own. Whatever made Julia content, added to her health or comfort or promoted the growth and well-being of the fetus which was to be the O'Brien heir, the child of which the mother was not matrix but the custodian, was immediately provided. She could have anything she wanted. Only the poverty of Julia's imagination kept her demands within the realm of reason.

She was too hot or too cold, too sleepy or too wakeful, hungry, surfeited; Manuel was too talkative or too silent; the weather too wet, too dry, too windy or too still. The presents Manuel brought from his trips to Apia or Los Angeles she accepted complacently. At first pleased with their novelty, she soon found interminable fault with them: they were too dark or too light, too thick or too thin, too large or too small, too drab or too gaudy. When Manuel's chores required his attention, she slouched in the doorway and complained that she was neglected and lonely. When he remained with her, she was bored with his talk. He listened patiently to her complaints, silently shouldered the weight of her opprobrium; the end, for him, justified the endurance. In fact, he was as nearly happy as she would permit him to be.

Her censure never took the form of open and forthright accusation or condemnation; it was made up of nagging hints and insinuations and a frequently exasperating and unexplained air of silent forbearance. Manuel accepted the blame for her unspecified unhappiness. Julia wept suddenly and for no discernible cause and her weeping desolated and subdued the old man.

Riding in the dung-yellow buggy fatigued Julia, and she loudly complained of being abandoned when Manuel attended to her errands away from home. On most Sundays, she drove with him to the mission at Apia to hear Mass, but early in the summer she gave up going with him to Los Angeles to visit the family of Pedro Grandos Luiz. Nor did

42

the Luiz family come to the rancho; the distance was too great, Pedro owned no horse and Clara's infant was too young for travel.

For this reason, Manuel was astonished when on this September morning Julia suddenly reversed all her decisions. He'd hardly begun his tasks with his bees which were certain to occupy his entire day when he saw Julia approaching laboriously slowly along the path towards the honey shed.

'Go back.' He waved his arms back and forth, shouting. 'The bees. There is danger.'

Julia paused, impatient, and shaded the sun from her eyes with her arm.

'Manuel, I would go to Los Angeles now. I would visit my sister. It makes a long time since I saw her and I have not seen her new baby.'

Manuel emerged from the shed, shaking his head. 'But, chica. This is without reason. I am at work, taking honey from the comb. I cannot break into my day's work.'

She remained impassive, unyielding. 'I shall go. I must go to the house of my sister. I am ready now to go.'

Manuel's reluctance to abandon his open boxes was soon worn down by Julia's reiteration. She did not lift her voice; she offered no reason, no argument, only her unwavering intention in a flat dead tone.

'I fear for you to make the journey. It is taxing your strength to drive so far in an open buggy — and so far back. . . . We can go early to stay with Clara before your lying-in. You can then visit with your good sister for as many days as you wish. We can start in the cool morning and arrive before the sun's heat is vast enough to weary the soul of you and your burden.'

Even as he protested, Manuel began putting the honey shed to rights. He washed down the extracting device, poured the honey resultant from his morning's labour into large tins in which he would transport it to the Los Angeles market. He carefully stored the full frames of honey from which the caps had not yet been sliced so they should not be disturbed. He straightened and put the workroom in order. Then he went out to the barn lot, hauled the harness from the yellow buggy and untangled it, scratched Sal with curry comb and dandy brush. When he harnessed the horse to the buggy and led him out to the spreading shade of the live oak, he found Julia

43

standing where he had left her. She was not yet reconciled. Even when she saw she was to have her way, she raged at him coldly before she turned and went into the house, making certain he did not dare to change his mind.

'Today, Manuel. Now. It is that I would set out at once. The journey I shall endure, the heat I shall tolerate. To go at once is my will.'

II

Pedro Luiz sprawled on the front porch of his East Los Angeles home. His legs stretched across the floor, his back against the wall of the house, he nodded and napped between the gadfly attacks of four-year-old Concha. At last, despairing of sleep, he caught the child in his arms as she assaulted him. He tickled and spanked her until in her frantic, giggling attempts to escape, she wriggled from his clasp and fell from the porch to the ground, scraping her naked shin against the flooring. She wept in pain. The repentant father slid from the porch, gathered the child in his tenderest embrace, whispered to her, rubbed the injury with his callused hand which increased the pain but abated her tears, kissed her mouth gently and begged her not to weep.

Clara, hearing the ruction, appeared at the opposite corner of the house. She chided her spouse mildly for causing their child pain. At her breast was the naked infant Teodoro, whining in petulance and surfeit, repulsing the full breast in rage each time Clara thrust its nipple into his mouth.

Pedro laughed. 'Wait a few years. He'll be fighting to chew on them.'

Clara smiled, pretending indignation at her husband's brazenness. She was a large woman, full in thighs, buttocks, breast and cheeks. Spots of crimson shone through the translucent beige of her complacent, comfortable and contented countenance. Before maternity padded her figure for the fifth time, she had been beautiful and beautiful she was yet in a buxom, voluptuous way. Her eyes were large and flashing. Her mouth was full-lipped and sensual. She no longer thought of herself as attractive; she was tolerant and passive and thought of herself only as the wife of Pedro Luiz.

If Clara thought about her figure at all, she hated the idea of getting fat and yet she accepted this as the curse of the women of her class. The loose cotton shift she wore exaggerated the amplitude of her body, as the apron wound rebozo-like around her head heightened her bovine expression of amiability and acceptance of the world as she found it.

Pedro could do no wrong in Clara's eyes. She scolded him now as a mere instinctive gesture, aimed at reassuring the child that she was deeply loved by both parents. Looking up, she glimpsed the horse Sal drawing the O'Brien equipage in his halting, stumbling gait to the wooden hitching post in front of the Luiz home. Pedro stopped comforting Concha and set her aside. He stretched his lean body in his feline way which betokened a welcome. Clara hurried forward in surprise and delight, crying out Julia's name.

Manuel descended from the boot of the carriage with an air of serious purpose. With ceremonious gallantry he assisted the ashen and fatigued Julia to the ground. Concha, forgetting her scraped shin, scampered about Julia, pulling at her skirt, and Pedrillo, witnessing the arrival from across vacant lots, loped homeward with yells of greeting.

Pedro stared at Julia but spoke to her husband in a bantering way. 'Hey, Manuel, when do you send that nag to the glue factory and get yourself one of these new Fords?'

Manuel laughed and shook his head. 'I would not be caught dead in one of those new-fangled wagons. The only persons I know who parade about in them are the Stocktons and others of the very rich classes.'

Pedro shrugged, still not taking his gaze from Julia's tired face.

Manuel's black bitch bristled and growled her challenge to the sleek, liver-coloured mongrel that appeared from the rear quarters. At the prospect of combat, Rosa's exhausted son sought safety, tail between legs, under the buggy and almost under Sal's rear hoofs. The liver bitch accepted Rosa's challenge. They circled and sniffed each other until, with simultaneous snarl and slash, the fight was joined. Concha ran screaming to the wall of the porch. Pedrillo danced in glee about the low-snarling, snapping, struggling animals. Teodoro, sensing excitement, squalled lustily.

'Jazmin. Jazmin. Come here, Jazmin.' Clara ordered. When the animals continued to snarl and bite, she screamed at her husband, 'Pedro, get them apart. Jazmin. Poor Jazmin. Don't let Rosa hurt Jazmin.'

Manuel waded into the fracas in an effort to separate the snarling bitches. Pedro stretched himself in a preliminary to action. Neighbours and children gathered from all directions. Julia, gasping, wide-eyed, looked around emptily and collapsed in a faint.

A thousand suggestions reverberated from the mob, torn between the double diversions of fainting woman and fighting dogs. At last, Clara, still holding Teodoro, with the assistance of Manuel, and despite the well-intentioned interference of the crowd, succeeded in half-carrying, half-dragging Julia into the house. They laid her on the bed where, while Clara ran for water and wet towels, requesting charms and priests and doctors, the fatigued girl opened her eyes.

'I am so tired,' she moaned and burst into helpless sobs.

Pedro, with many volunteers aggravating the dog fight by intruding, finally quelled the battle by grabbing and holding the slathering combatants apart. Neither animal was injured and Pedro tied Jazmin to the outhouse lest the dogs join battle again.

Inside the house, Julia wept on the bed and her husband crouched desolated in his impotence to soothe her. Clara hastily concocted a gruel, the efficacy of which she was able to warrant. Pedrillo stood at the rear door, solicitous for the battered Jazmin. Concha whined, neglected in the crowd. Teodoro squalled, kicking his naked little legs on the quilt which had been folded and laid on the floor to serve as a pallet. Three or four neighbour women came and went, clucking their concern, offering their advice, all of them long-faced in compassion and curiosity, all of them crowded into the small room into which Pedro sauntered, the only placid person in the house.

Julia's will was futile against Clara and always had been. Julia unwillingly swallowed a few spoonfuls of the gruel her sister had prepared and shovelled deep into her mouth. Also against her will, Julia sipped at a broth hot with peppers which one of the neighbour women had been fortuitously brewing and which she solicitously fetched, greasy and steaming. With difficulty, Julia acceded to Manuel's demand that she sip glassfuls of wine, red and astringent. 'It will make blood. It will give you strength. It will restore you. It will soothe the little one inside you,' Manuel kept saying. All this time Julia was aware only of the way Pedro's black eyes were fixed on her, the way she longed to gaze up at him.

Whether as result of the various libations, or despite them, Julia soon became calm, her tears vanished and she slept. 'I am home,' she whispered. 'I am home.'

'She looks like a little girl,' Clara said, staring down at her younger sister. 'Like a little girl.'

'Like a fat little girl,' Pedro said and Pedrillo giggled from the doorway.

Gradually, quiet was restored. Neighbours returned to their various homes; Manuel unharnessed Sal from the yellow buggy and tied him at the rear of the house. He fed and watered him, taking a long time.

From within the cottage he could hear Clara preparing the evening meal, garrulous in her indecision as to whether Julia had better be roused and induced to eat, or permitted to sleep. Food or rest. Rest or food.

'At such time as this,' Clara argued, 'a woman must have plenty of food. When I carried my babies I have eaten well. . . . And yet, she is very tired. One looks at her and sees her great weariness; she should sleep.'

After a moment, her voice rose again. 'But food is necessary for the child. If she does not eat the child cannot be fed. I always ate well in my time.'

'The girl is worn out from the long drive. She took gruel and broth and wine. She is not hungry. Let her sleep,' Pedro offered his opinion.

His counsel confused rather than satisfied Clara. She countered, 'But the food which you say she took was no food at all. A few spoonfuls of gruel, a cup of broth, and you know how Yolita waters all her soups. It is nothing. The little sister needs food. . . . If I do not waken her, at least I shall keep supper warm for her so that when she wakes, she may truly eat. She must not go hungry into the night. Eh? Eh?'

This matter, continually broached, was the sole subject of the family's conversation during the meal.

The afternoon heat subsided as the sun dissolved beyond the hills. The brief twilight barely lasted through supper; as it faded, a chill settled over the house. After supper, while Clara put her kitchen in order, Pedro and Manuel wandered together into the back yard, finally seating themselves on the front porch. Here they politely bided the time until it should be fitting to go to bed. Despite their having seen little of each other for long months, and each being truly interested in the affairs of the other, they spoke little. Julia's indisposition was ominously unsettling between them. Manuel had discarded his jacket on arrival and Pedro wore only trousers and a faded denim shirt, hacked away at his muscular shoulders. The coolness of the evening caused them to shiver at intervals.

Pedro stretched himself. 'Could you let me take a peso, Manuel? I have need of money until I am paid.' By peso, Manuel meant the American dollar. 'I have pay coming to me on Saturday for three days' work.' He stretched again languidly, staring across the palely illuminated street. Distantly someone strummed a plaintive mandolin.

'I have but little money without taking from the bank,' Manuel said. 'And tomorrow before I sell my honey, I must go to the Chinaman's.' As he spoke he removed a coin from his pocket and handed it to his brother-in-law. Pedro took it without looking at him or the dollar.

Pedro did not impy any intention of returning the money, nor did Manuel expect that it would be returned. While the dollar was neither given nor received as payment for hospitality, both men felt a debt was satisfied. If Manuel and his wife remained a second day, Pedro would borrow another dollar.

2

The only bed in the house was occupied by Julia and the other half of it was intended for Manuel. Pallets were laid down on the floor of the same room for the Luiz family. Pedrillo and Concha always slept together on the floor, except when Concha ingratiated herself into the bed where her parents slept with Teodoro between them, a place until recently dedicated to Concha herself.

The children removed their clothes early and lay down on their pads, Jazmin curled beside them. Julia continued to sleep, almost as if she had not fully rested since she departed this place in March. Her meal, warming on the back of the stove, waited. The cigarettes of the men, minute quantities of tobacco twisted into brown papers, glowed on the porch.

Barefoot, Clara pattered through the house in preparation for the night, laying down pads, tending her baby, putting out food for the O'Brien dogs, watching over Julia's deep sleep.

Going to the front door, Clara announced, 'I am going to wake her up so that she can have supper before we go to bed.'

'I think that is best,' Manuel said, rising. Pedro stretched his arms but made no comment. Manuel went into the house.

Bending over the slumbering girl, Clara grasped her shoulder and said, 'My little sister must eat her supper before we go to bed. It is not good that she should pass the night without food.'

Julia roused herself slightly, passed her hand over her forehead. 'No. I do not wish it, Clara mia. . . I am so tired. It is good to be home with you.' She added this last in a placating way.

'But you must eat. It is necessary for the child.' Clara voiced her convictions. She herself had no experience of not wanting plenty of food regularly.

Julia would make no effort to eat, even as her duty to her unborn. After suffering difficulty swallowing a few mouthfuls, she could take no more. She shook her head. 'It is that I cannot, sister mia. Take it away. The food. It sickens me. I cannot.'

Clara permitted her to lie down again and Julia turned to the wall, sighing. Pedro and Manuel entered the room and prepared themselves for bed with the mere removal of outer garments, which, for Pedro, involved much stretching of muscles and many yawns.

When Clara returned from the kitchen, Manuel was in bed beside Julia and Pedro sprawled on the double pallet which his wife had improvised for them upon the floor.

Julia lay silent but wakeful. Clara began her preparations for bed. 'The little sister shall feel much better tomorrow,' Clara crooned in a solicitous hum. 'It is that she is very tired tonight.'

After a long time, Julia said, 'I am more than merely tired, sister mia. It is the child. The child seeks to be born.'

Clara leaned over the bed, her long black hair plaited over her shoulder. 'No, no, little one. It is far too soon. It is not yet your season for the child to be born. . . . Two months yet must pass. Born now would be a tragedy. It could not survive. It would not live. You are only tired. You must not think of

50

such things'.

Julia bit her lip and writhed on the bed. 'The pain. . . it is the child.'

Manuel sat upright beside her in the bed, fear rattling his voice. 'No. It is not the child. No. It cannot be. It must not be. No. No. . . I wished not to come today. The journey was too much. Yet my wife wished it. I did not wish it. No. It is not the child, but fatigue. It is not the child so soon. It must wait.'

'Clara. The pain. The terrible pain,' Julia whispered in low tones. Then, 'It is the child. Mary, Mother of Jesus, it is the child. It moves. . . it seeks to be born.'

'No. No. I do not wish that the child be born so soon,' Manuel protested.

'It were best to get the midwife,' Pedro suggested, sitting up and stretching on the quilts.

Clara shook her head. 'Not yet. Women suffer long in pregnancy before the first child is born. I have seen this.' She stared at Pedro. 'I have borne five children now, three who live, and I know what it is to suffer.'

Pedro lapsed into silence and lay down again, stretching his legs. In moving, he roused Teodoro who lay at his side. The child wailed and Clara lifted it up into her arms, jostled it into quietude, and thrust the dark nipple of her breast in to its mouth. Anxiety, indecision, helplessness, fatalism, crackled in the silence which was broken only by aspirate sighs from the woman agonizing on the bed. Julia was silent for a long time and they held their breathing waiting, praying she had fallen asleep again.

When Clara could endure the silence no longer, she went to Julia's side of the bed and, Teodoro still in her arms, stared down at her sister. The yellow incandescent bulb suspended in the centre of the ceiling cast strange and ominous shadows against the walls. Julia was awake, but her eyes were closed. Her breathing was deep and laboured.

'You are better and the pains have departed?' Clara whispered.

Julia raised her arm above her head. 'The child strives to be born. Tonight he comes. He comes or I shall die. The dolour is too much. I do not care. I would rather die.'

Clara straightened, her tone determined. 'Senor O'Brien. Something must be done at once. The child will be born.'

Manuel continued to shake his head, his face anguished. 'It

51

is too early. You have said so yourself. It will die. It cannot live.' His eyes filled with tears, he shook his head and waved his arm in surrender. 'Do what you will for her. Do what is best.'

'We must get Senora Ramirez,' Clara announced her decision. 'She has delivered me of my children. We must send at once for her.'

Clara knelt at the pallet where Pedrillo lay beside his sister. She grasped the sleeping boy by the arm, shook him roughly and dragged him, startled and shivering, from beneath the covers. He rubbed his eyes sleepily and whimpered.

'Haste,' his mother said, smoothing his tousled black hair with her palm. 'Haste and do not cry. Put on your clothes quick. Go at once to the casa of the good Senora Ramirez, her who lives in Castalar street in the house with the painted shutters. Bring the good senora without delay to serve your Tia Julia.'

Half-awake, the child groped for his clothes, a torn shirt and knee-length trousers, much too tight. As he drew the garments over his shivering limbs, his mother continued her instructions, repeating them often and slowly.

'And will the Senora Ramirez bring a baby for Tia Julia?' he asked.

Clara shrugged. 'Who knows? Go. Make haste.'

The child set out into the night on his errand. Dark spaces and limber shadows in the ill-lighted street turned the few men he met into ogres, bushes into black bears in his troubled imagination. He shivered in the night chill. Fear and cold hastened his steps and he finally burst into a run. The distance was something more than four squares. He reached the front door of the Ramirez cottage, breathless and shaken. He hesitated in fear of the very noise he would make in knocking which might well rouse sleeping demons.

He struck the door with his fist and after a moment an incandescent lamp was switched on inside the house. A sleepy voice called, 'Who is there? What do you want?'

'Me, Pedrillo. Pedrillo Luiz. I beg you, Senora Ramirez, my mother says come. At once. Quickly. Come to attend my Tia Julia, the wife of Senor O'Brien, and bring with you her baby.'

The door opened, disclosing the small, dumpy figure of Senora Ramirez in more than even her usual dishabille. She wore a soiled wrapper of red flannel over her night clothes, her greying hair was disheveled, and she had removed her teeth for the night. Her right side was partially paralyzed and, in order to steady herself, she leaned against the door, carrying her right arm in her left hand. 'Is this Tia Julia already in labour, boy?'

Pedrillo nodded. 'Quickly, my mother says. My aunt suffers much dolour. And bring her baby along.'

'It was not due yet for some two months.' The midwife smiled toothlessly to herself and nodded. 'But one never knows. Eh?' She shook her head and turned to dress, still muttering to herself. 'What folks guessed was true then. She and that husband of her sister have played the jest on the old miser. Serves him right, serves him right, an old hound sniffing after a young bitch.' She turned and glanced over her shoulder. 'If it comes, it comes, and I go to bring it, soon or in season.' She dressed, laughing.

Pedrillo stood in the open doorway, dancing impatiently from one foot to the other. In moments she reappeared, wearing a black shawl wound around her head and falling over her shoulders, and a limp but freshly washed frock of what might have been white cotton. She had laced her shoes, and her stockings sagged about her ankles. She brought an old sweater and tossed it to Pedrillo. 'Wear this, boy. It is cold out.'

She made no haste. She carefully locked her front door, removed the key and placed it in a pocket of her dress. She carried in her left hand a burly walking cane. In her right hand she carried a wrinkled paper bag containing herbs and medicaments she might require in her profession.

Slowly, painfully, cautiously she descended the steps and eased her way along the broken plank path to her gate. Deliberately, she closed her gate and dropped a metal loop to lock it.

Senora Ramirez could hobble only painfully and slowly. Wrapped in the oversized woolen sweater she'd provided him with, Pedrillo tried to hurry her. He would stride several steps ahead, return to the old woman and walk a step or two beside her, then scurry ahead again, looking back hopefully.

Once he stopped and stared back at her, studying her frantically. 'Oh, Senora, you forgot to bring the baby for Tia Julia.'

53

The midwife smiled and placed her hand on the child's bare head. 'Si, little Pedrillo. This time I forgot. But perhaps the Tia is not ready yet for the baby. Eh? If need be, I can send you back to fetch it after a while. No?'

'And so you do not always bring babies when you go to relieve the pain of ailing women? Do you not then always bring babies so to make them forget their suffering and be well again?'

She smiled down at him with great tenderness. 'I bring them when I can, jovenito. . . . But, you must understand. There are not always enough babies for all who want them.'

'Mio tio, the Senor O'Brien has much money in the big bank. He can buy a baby for my Tia Julia if he wishes, can he not? There are enough babies if you have the money, eh?'

The old woman shook her head. 'There are not always enough for all who wish them, little one. One sometimes has to wait until new ones can be made. But — if one has money, one can usually get one at last.'

'But you brought my baby brother, Teodoro, to my mother?'

'Si, muchacho, and I brought you to your mother, and it was a good service I did for her that night, I warrant you. A fine good boy like you. And if I live a few years more, I shall be bringing babies to your woman when you are married.'

The boy laughed with her at the old woman's prediction and they walked in silence until they came to the house where they were awaited.

The men, fully dressed now, with blankets like serapes across their shoulders against the night chill, were on the porch. Pedro sat with his head slumped across his arms and Manuel paced nervously with banty steps. Clara, the baby in her arms, stood in the doorway.

'Haste,' Clara called as soon as she sighted them in the shadows. 'The little sister has the great pains'

This information failed to quicken Senora Ramirez' hitching steps. She made a deprecatory noise and said, 'It will keep, It will keep.'

Manuel halted his excited pacing and spoke, voice quivering. 'The child is not due yet. Not by two months. It must not be born. Come. Make haste to my wife. Ease her pain, but do not deliver the child.'

Senora Ramirez hobbled past him into the room where

Julia lay, biting her mouth. Casually removing her shawl and setting her herbs where they would be convenient, Senora Ramirez approached the bedside. Julia opened her eyes and stared up at the woman, seeing her only through a haze of agony.

Deeply troubled, Pedrillo tugged at Clara's skirt. 'My mother. It is that Senora Ramirez forgot to bring the baby along. She goes to send me back for it after a while when Tia Julia tells her that she is ready to receive it.'

Clara nodded negligently. 'Take off your clothes and go back to bed. Go to sleep and stay out of the way.'

The midwife looked up from her examination of Julia. 'You have sent too early for me.'

Manuel exhaled his relief. 'So. Then I was right. It is too soon. The child must not be born.'

Senora Ramirez gazed at him, her whiskered upper lip curling. 'You have sent too early. It will be hours before the child is ready to deliver. We can only wait.'

Manuel shook his head. 'You can do nothing? Nothing will delay the child in premature birth?'

The old woman shrugged. 'It is an act of God. The child will come before dawn,' she said.

Manuel resumed his pacing upon the porch, finding himself unable to breath in the little room. Pedro remained slumped with his head in his hands. He altered his position slightly from time to time and stretched himself. Pedrillo came and went, to the porch, into the house again. Clara brewed coffee in the kitchen. Bursts of staccato conversation, everyone speaking at once, alternated with stretches of dead silence. Sleep, after a supreme struggle against it, overcame the boy. His lids drooped and he sagged back in a chair. His mother lifted him to his pallet beside Concha.

To hasten parturition, Senora Ramirez induced Julia to swallow scalding cups of decoctions of herbs which the old woman steeped on Clara's stove. Dry black pepper fed to her from a teaspoon to promote dilation strangled and gagged the girl. Julia writhed on the rumpled sheets and protested weakly; the medication was worse than the pain of labour. 'I want it over,' she whispered, lips parched and fevered. 'I want it to end.'

Midnight approached. Manuel's despair deepened. His thoughts were only for his child who could not survive or, if it

55

lived, was destined to be crippled, stunted or wizened from premature birth. As for the sufferings of the mother, that was a woman's lot. He had begotten so many children only to have them die. He had despaired of being a father again. The desire for a son had become an obsession all these months. Was he again about to be thwarted? Was the line of the O'Briens to perish with his own passing?

Manuel took up his hat and departed for an unannounced destination. It was no secret. Both Pedro and Clara knew he had gone to the Chinaman's. The distance was not great, a few squares to the south and across the Plaza to Chinatown. Senor O'Brien was well known in the Chinaman's dingy little shop, but the impersonal man who served him seemed not to see him at all. He produced a small tin in a red wrapper marked with Chinese characters, laid it on the counter and silently received the money which Manuel counted into his hand. For all the formality of the transaction, words were no part of it. Manuel took his purchase, nodded a farewell and departed the shop.

He arrived at the home of his brother-in-law to find things as he had left them, the place as silent and still as the eye of a hurricane. He retired to his buggy behind the house, searched under the cushions and retrieved a pipe with a long stem and minute bowl. He partially opened the tin, penetrated the foil with which it was lined and with his knife filled the tiny pipe-bowl with its gummy contents. Heating the pipe required more fire than could be derived from the ill-smelling sulphur match from his pocket. It was necessary to find a sliver of wood, ignite it from a match and fire up his pipe. Then he crawled into the buggy, sprawled across the seat and resigned himself to this Lethe from his troubles. The opium sputtered and burbled and the old man sucked in long draughts of its smoke. The acrid, faintly nauseating sweetness permeated the air around him but in it he found surcease from his anxiety, found that negation of unhappiness which passes for happiness itself. A sort of langour crept over him and he gave himself up to pleasant imaginings.

Within the house the struggle went on. The will of the unborn child did not abate; the pain-weakened mother endured as best she could, growing steadily feebler; the midwife prescribed her herbs; the tedious night dragged itself away. Pedro remained slouched on the porch, drowsily caught between sleep and waking.

Worn out from loss of sleep, Clara nodded in her rocking chair. Senora Ramirez moved unsteadily about the house. She was used to night-long vigils and to the suffering of women. Pedro heard the old woman limping back and forth, knew she was bending over Julia. Once the midwife came out upon the porch to beg from him materials with which to fabricate a cigarette for herself. 'A long night,' she said.

From time to time Pedro heard Julia's stifled moans. Then, after a while, he heard a weak, whining screech — the cry of a very young child. He straightened slightly, stretching. Might Teodoro be awake? He heard Clara's chair squeak as she rose from it and heard her quick footsteps. Then he heard Senora Ramirez say, 'Es un muchacho. A fine boy.'

Pedro pulled himself together and went into the house. Clara had produced clothing for the baby from Teodoro's scant wardrobe and the two women were laughing as they dressed the squalling infant. Pedro merely glanced at them. He stood staring at Julia, ashen and sweating on the bed, her eyes closed. In this hour of his triumph Manuel slept peacefully in the boot of his buggy at the rear of the Luiz house. None thought to summon him to see his new son.

3

The sun appeared blearily in the east, like the blazing eye of some tired god beyond the ragged caps of the shadowed Sierra Madres. The dazzling glare and abrupt heat ot sunrise struck Manuel full in the face and he awoke with a start. He needed the better part of a minute to orient himself. At first, he failed to comprehend his being in his buggy behind Pedro Luiz' house. He smelled burning and heard the noisy sizzling of meat, the fumes wafted upward into the dawn, the strong smell of burnt onions making him ill, and that implacable eye watching him from the vast expanse of hills, unsettling him. Remembering the circumstances of the previous night, he descended from his carriage boot, hurriedly hid the tin of opium and his pipe under the seat of the buggy, and went through the rear door of the house, wild-eyed in expectancy of evil tidings.

57

Clara worked over the glowing stove. Senora Ramirez drank coffee at the table. They seemed unaware of him. He caught Senora Ramirez' arm. 'My child. Is he yet born?'

Senora Ramirez gazed at him as if she had never seen him before. Then, shrugging, she got up and limped into the bedroom. Manuel followed her to the bed where the baby lay beside its mother. 'Here is your son, Senor,' the old woman said in a flat tone.

'It is alive then?' Manuel whispered. Again Senora Ramirez merely gazed at him. 'A son you say? A boy. And will he live?'

The old woman shrugged her shoulders. 'Quien sabe? Who knows? Only our good God Knows.' She crossed herself piously.

Manuel too crossed himself. 'But perhaps he will live?' he urged. 'He is not born too early to survive?'

She shrugged again, her mouth twisting faintly. 'He has every chance. Never before have I delivered a finer boy. His development is complete and his cry is lusty.' The woman reassured him in salesmanlike fashion. A satisfied patron assured payment for her services.

'Let me see him. Let me see for myself.'

Sighing, Senora Ramirez lifted the bundle of garments in which the child was enveloped like a nut in its shell and placed it in the old man's arms. Manuel held his son inexpertly, having never paid more than the scantiest attention to his earlier children in their infancy. He handed the child back to the midwife, shaking his head. 'No, no. You show him to me.'

She pulled the clothing away from the red, puckered, amorphous little face. The eyes, large and liquid and black, dominated the other features. She cupped the oval skull in her palm, raised it up and stroked the black fuzz, raised in turn the minute hands to display their tiny nails.

O'Brien nodded but it was evident he was not satisfied. 'No. I want to see my son. Show me my child. Take off his clothes.'

The midwife did not demur; the fee for her services was as yet unpaid. She laid the baby upon the bed. Though her right hand was almost useless, she worked quickly and expertly. Off came the cumbersome vestments in which mankind restricts the freedom of its young from the instant of birth.

O'Brien gazed down at the bowed legs and squirming feet,

felt appraisingly of the frail biceps. He stuck his forefinger into the tender abdomen as if determining whether a cut from this small carcass might tempt a jaded appetite. Finally he said, 'Remove the diaper.'

Only when the woman had loosened the cloth and the red little organism lay before its sire in nakedness did Manuel smile and nod in satisfaction. 'A boy,' he announced, small eyes aglitter. 'A son.' He reassured himself of his own responsibility for the child's being. He nodded again emphatically, glancing toward the woman. 'He shall be for the Church, you know.' He crossed himself again, and the woman repeated his gesture. 'And he shall say Masses for the soul of me when I am dead.'

He continued to gaze down upon the nude infant in growing approval. Drawing a deep breath, he spoke in a tone that implied epochal import. 'His name shall be Jesus. Jesus Jose. Jesus Jose O'Brien.'

Nodding with self-satisfaction, he stepped back and allowed the woman to dress the baby. Only then did he glance towards Julia who lay, eyes closed and unmoving, her cheeks pallid and rigid, her lips broken with fever. 'And how is it with my wife?'

Senora Ramirez gave him a brief smile, nodding. 'She has a fever, but it will pass. She should take of food, but she will not. It is her first child and she is very weak.'

Julia lay immobile. She was aware of voices over her but she did not recognize them and she could not distinguish the words. It didn't matter, she did not care. She was grateful for the surcease from the pain she'd endured last night. She was content, she felt at home here in the house of her sister, more at home than she had ever been. Here she was snug and cozy among the family with whom she had spent the happiness of her girlhood. Here was tenderness and attention and love and consideration. She was content.

She burned with fever and her mind wandered in strange fantasies. Despite her fever she was no longer uncomfortable; she was too weak for anguish. Toward her infant she felt only a shuddering indifference. She had no concern for its looks, its condition, its welfare. She wondered indifferently at her own indifference. A mother was supposed instinctively to care for her offspring. She felt the burn of tears in her dry eyes. If the child were to be removed from her forever

59

without her seeing it, she would have suffered no qualms. If it were to die, no grief would touch her.

Pedro came back from purchasing materials for the breakfast of his family and its guests. He deposited the parcels in the kitchen and entered to make a casual inspection of the new arrival. Julia sensed his presence in the room. She opened her eyes for the first time, smiling faintly toward him. She tried to lift her hand to him but could not. Her eyelids closed heavily but she went on smiling wanly until she sensed that he had plodded from the room. . . .

Pedrillo slept later than usual, exhausted from his tasks of the night before. His sister too remained asleep on the pad beside him. Pedrillo had not heard the noise and talk and bustle going on in the house. Now, something of its tension must have penetrated his sleeping consciousness. Waking suddenly, he leapt to his feet and lunged, unaware of his nakedness, to the bedside where the new baby lay. His mother, stooping to place an arm about his waist, with her free hand uncovered the face of Julia's baby for his inspection. The two boys peered quizzically into each other's eyes. Finally Pedrillo looked up at Clara and shook his head. 'He doesn't look finished, Mama. Is he done?'

Standing aside, Manuel overheard this and his heart sank. His own doubts, appeased as they had been by the midwife, were raised again. How much did the boy sense? Children had a special instinct for these things, didn't they? Had the midwife lied to him from kindness? Was this son of his, sent before his time into this world, mature and sound enough to survive?

As Manuel stood there, tormented, Pedrillo spoke to the midwife. 'Senora, why did you not let me go back for the baby? I might have chosen one more finished.' He spoke with wounded politeness. 'You promised I might go to fetch it.'

The old woman smiled dotingly upon him and nodded. 'Si. But you went to sleep, and I had to go myself.'

O'Brien spoke abruptly into the silence. 'Without delay,' he said.

Clara, the old woman and even the naked Pedrillo stared at him. Manuel nodded emphatically, his decision made. 'Without delay my son must be baptized. He is a frail child, born two months premature. There is great risk. We must take him this very morning to the church.' He turned to where Pedro leaned in the doorjamb, watching the fevered girl. 'I appeal to you, Pedro, and to your good wife, I appeal. Do my son the honour that you will stand as godparents to him.'

Pedro's mouth twisted faintly. 'Senor O'Brien does my wife and me a great honour, but he can see that for us it is impossible to partake of the ceremony. We are but poor folk and humble. We have no such garments as would befit the godparents of the senor's son at his christening.'

As Pedro had anticipated, Manuel was in a liberal mood this morning. The old man merely laughed. 'Clothes are easily obtained, Pedro. I shall anyway have to take from the bank when it is opened in order that I may buy for my son fitting apparel in which to go to the church. You can go with me and we shall buy a suit of clothes for you and a fine outfit for the good Clara. I owe you no less than that.'

Senora Ramirez stirred impatiently at the bedside. She had felt for some hours that her duties were finished here but she made no move to depart, awaiting that payment which might be tendered for her services without the necessity of her asking. At length, she retrieved from the kitchen her wrinkled paper bag of herbs, adjusted her shawl over her shoulders and grasped her cane. 'I have delivered a fine and vigorous son for the Senor O'Brien and, if he will open his purse,' she brought her thumb and forefinger together in a circle, a symbol of money, 'I must return to the chores of my own house.'

Manuel nodded, smiling and apologetic for his oversight. 'How much are the charges, Senora?'

The woman hesitated, calculating. 'What the senor will,' she said, and then, lest she lose in this bargain, added, 'would five dollars be too much?'

Even she was surprised that the old man did not demur at the temerity of her demand. She dropped her gaze and to occupy herself in the silence, bent over the fever-parched Julia, reassuring her out of her own confidence that the young mother's illness was normal and would abate with the passing hours, words to which Julia, if she heard them at all, paid no heed. Formal and polite farewells were exchanged between the Senora Ramirez and members of the household. She kissed young Pedrillo noisily atop his head and took her leave.

Manuel, despite the midwife's assurances, harboured doubt about the strength of the premature infant Julia had borne

61

him. He followed the midwife out of doors, across the porch to the path. He appealed to her confidentially in a low tone, 'You are sure then my son is strong enough to survive? You have known, you yourself, seven-month babies who have survived?'

The money Manuel had paid her was stowed safely in the pocket of her dress, her payment was no longer contingent upon any satisfaction her reply should inspire in the old man. She squinted one eye against the sun, staring into his face. 'I'll tell you true, Senor.' Her tone was as confidential as his question. 'This is the first-born of Senora O'Brien. One need not worry. The child is complete. A woman's first-born often comes too soon, and no harm. It is after the first-born that they perish who come before their time.'

His mind was at rest again and he bade her, 'Go with God.'

4

Sal was harnessed again to the yellow buggy. Senor O'Brien and Pedro mounted to the boot with good cheer and with Rosa, tagged by her son, following the equipage, they drove away waving to Clara and the children.

They went first to a dealer who bought the honey which Manuel had brought from his ranch. Then, until the doors of the bank should be open to customers, they drank puckerish, acrid wine in a Spring Street bodega. Here, all comers were invited to pledge the health of Manuel's heir at the father's expense.

When the bank opened, Manuel withdrew sufficient funds for his extraordinary needs while Pedro looked on in wonder and congratulated himself upon having a brother-in-law who could obtain such major sums for the mere asking. This going into a bank and getting money without working for it seemed like necromancy to Pedro, and he was awed. Manuel's nonchalance in the transaction led Pedro to assume that the amounts available were unlimited.

The shopping expedition was an orgy of indifference to prices. Habiliments fit for the baptism of Jesus Jose O'Brien obviously were not cheap, and for Manuel the best that was offered him was hardly good enough.

Pedro watched with some sweaty trepidation the rapid disbursements of Manuel's funds. Manuel drew secret glee from his own perversity in refusing even to mention the garments he'd promised Pedro until he had bought everything else he required. So many uncontemplated items were brought to his attention by salespeople and the old man spent so lavishly, Pedro began to panic, fearing that the money might not hold out until the time came at last to supply his own particular requirements.

That turn came finally. All apparel in which to clothe Manuel's son and satellites to the ceremony in a manner worthy of that son had been bought and paid for and stowed carefully behind the seat of the buggy, except clothing for the godparents and their children. Pedro's head ached mildly.

He had long admired and wished for togs in which he might stroll peerless among his peers. While Manuel chose the other finery, Pedro visualized the outfit he anticipated O'Brien would buy for him. He saw himself in fashionable peg-top pantaloons, wide at the thighs and narrow at the cuffs, a jacket which reached only slightly below the waist-line with shoulders padded to their utter squareness, shoes of patent leather with high, rounded box toes, a pink shirt with starched bosom and detached cuffs and gaiters for the biceps, a cravat of watery green already made up into a four-in-hand shape and furnished with a tiny hook whereby it might be attached to the collar button, a round hat of soft felt, crown creased in telescope fashion. Pedro could envisage himself so bedecked in his mind's eye as clearly as if he gazed through a stereopticon.

Manuel objected only to the dimensions of the hat Pedro chose. To Manuel, it was the hat that proclaimed the quality and character of the wearer. A rakish chapeau was not fit gear for his son's godfather. He wished Pedro to wear something less extreme. Pedro was desolated, determined, and Manuel in too buoyant a mood long to oppose him.

Nor was Pedro satisfied with mere outward sartorial elegance. He ordered socks, alternately striped with pink and green, linen underclothes, cuff-buttons of pearl, a blood-red handkerchief for the breast pocket of his jacket, and every other supernumerary incidental to the perfection of his costume. He had never in his life owned such apparel; he meant now to go to the limit. He wouldn't consent to wait until he reached home to don his stylish outfit, but insisted upon attiring himself in his new splendor in the shop where it was purchased. The salesman smoothed any wrinkles, stretched the sleeves precisely, jerked the waistcoat into exactness, and hauled at the jacket until it hung smartly on Pedro's lean body.

Pedro emerged into the sunlight, self-conscious with pride, wearing the latest apparel which fashion dictated for the well-dressed young man in that year of the young century. His garments clung to him so snugly and he was so afraid to disarrange the perfection of fit into which the shopkeeper had manipulated the outfit that he restrained himself from stretching and relaxing his muscles, which might have relieved some of his inner tension. In his new costume, with his chiseled, swarthy features, the excellent proportions of his body, and the latent power which rippled visibly through his raiment, he drew sighs of secret admiration from passers-by in the street. He took great care to show himself at best advantage, aware that lovely women glanced his way who had never bothered to look at him before. The Mexican girls, with hair like flowing ebony manes, dressed only in low-bodiced shifts and short petticoats, stared openly from under the chopped fringes on their foreheads. He strode past them and kept his gaze averted, letting them feast their dark eyes upon him.

When Sal again drew up at the Luiz home, he was left hitched in the street because his services would so soon be required again. Bursting with pride and gratification, Pedro assisted Manuel in carrying the parcels into the house. Clara stared at her husband for a long time in awe as if he were a stranger.

'Hermoso,' she whispered, licking at her lips and devouring him with her adoring eyes. 'Muy hermoso, mi corazon.'

Warning the children away lest they soil something with dirty hands, Clara opened the packages, gasping in delight at their contents.

For him who was soon to be hailed formally as Jesus Jose, there were literal heaps of garments, the finest set of which his sire had decided the infant must wear for his pilgrimage to the church in search of his name before God. Manuel requested that his son should be made ready immediately before anyone else should be clothed for the ceremony.

Clara drew over his fragile body a vest of soft silk and wool, material of such delicate texture as the newborn hides of her own children had never felt. Next were added long white petticoats, heavily starched, each hemmed with a deep ruffle of machine embroidery and each more elaborately ornamented than the one beneath it. Stockings and shoes, those emblems of the patrician, encased his feet. Over all was draped the pièce de résistance of his wardrobe, an outer frock of madder pink China silk, frilled and tucked and ruffled and embroidered, against which the red little face looked as if it had been parboiled. A bonnet of alternate rows of white lace and blue ribbon was tied upon his head, the great bow of lawn streamers all but stifling him.

When the baby was dressed, his sire took from his pocket a necklace of garnet beads. The endeavour to place it around the neck of the squirming child so that it should not be entirely covered by the bow on the bonnet gave Manuel and Clara a good deal of trouble. Next, Manuel produced a gilt brooch for the infant's breast, and last, to Clara's amazed delight, a narrow band of gold, specked with turquoise, for the child's finger. The one forgotten item was a ribbon with which to secure the ring to the hand; a strand of red twine had to suffice.

When the small protagonist had been arrayed in his finery, his aunt carried him to the bed that his mother might admire her offspring. Clara smoothed the dress, raised the skirts to display the petticoats, stockings and miniature shoes; she straightened the bonnet-bow, arranging the necklace; she lifted the hand with its ringed finger. Julia's strength was sufficient only to signify, by a wan smile and an effortful nod, her approval of the garb in which her son was about to go forth to his first sacrament.

Clara Luiz devoted her attention next to her own children. Teodoro, who was to accompany his cousin to the church, was forced into new garments his uncle had brought for him, garments just as uncomfortable, but by no means so rich, as those of the young O'Brien. For him, shoes and stockings were dispensed with; the embroidery on his outer petticoat was no deeper than Jesus' innermost one; the outer dress was of less deep a dye and was not tricked out so much with tucks and pleats and lace.

Nor had Manuel omitted to provide new costumes for

Pedro's elder children. Concha was delighted with the blue taffeta dress which she wore over starched petticoats and lace-edged panties, which she endeavoured, for modesty's sake, not to exhibit. The starchy, embroidered blouse, the butterfly bow of red at his neck, the skin-tight breeches hampered Pedrillo's activities, but they caused him none of the actual pain he had to endure from shiny new ill-fitting shoes over ribbed stockings on feet that had known bare freedom.

Though Pedro had chosen debonair livery for himself, for his spouse he had selected an ankle-length gown of ungarnished black. Clara retired into the kitchen to put it on and there strove and struggled with her corsets, adjusted her bustle, combed her rich hair upward into full pompadour over paddings which she called rats and moored with a Spanish back comb of turquoise, finally slipping the bell-shaped, gored cashmere skirt over her head. She bent and stretched and cramped her arms hooking the fasteners down the back. Her hat, also black, turned up in a Cheyenne roll to flaunt her rolled coiffure.

The neighbours watched with approving eyes as the Luiz family set out in purple and fine linen. Julia's fever continued to mount and for this reason Clara asked her neighbour Yolita to sit with her. Julia lay silent and uncomplaining. Clara kept telling her how dismayed the family was that the little sister could not join them in the holiday of christening her baby. But Clara hoped that upon their return Julia could at least join the feast of celebration for which Manuel had provided generously.

The loading of the buggy involved some ingenuity and weighing of precedent. Pedro, as head of the family, felt his place was on the boot beside Manuel, but because Clara was compelled to hold the babies, one on each arm, it was necessary for him to surrender pride of place. He rode backward on the little platform behind the seat, his legs dangling over its spindled railing. Pedrillo shared this space with his father and Concha crouched on the floor at her mother's feet. Nobody was comfortable, but such were their spirits that they were too excited to complain.

Stoically the candidate underwent the ordeal of baptism, the adventure offering him neither pain nor pleasure. To the priest, that same cleric of the swinish, close-set eyes who had officiated at the wedding of the parents, Jesus Jose was just another infant upon whom the bestowal of a name was but another tiresome chore which he performed hastily, adequately and disinterestedly.

The godfather's assumption of his obligation was pridefully solemn. He was unaccustomed to being petitioned for a favour or honour such as godfatherhood to Senor O'Brien's son, just as he'd never worn apparel of such conspicuous and fashionable elegance. He was not used to priestly attentions such as accrued to him in this ceremony. To Pedro this was a serious transaction and seriously he accepted it. It gave a fillip to his self-esteem, invested him with dignity, imbued him with a sense of responsibility entirely new to him. Previously things happened to him; this was conferred upon him. With high resolve he undertook a covenant with the Church of God to renounce sin in the child's name, to help and protect and guide Jesus Jose in the name of the Father, the Son and the Holy Ghost.

To Clara the ceremony meant one more child for her ministrations. She accepted godmotherhood as complacently as she accepted motherhood itself — not so much something to be undertaken as something never to be shirked. She did not object, she was a natural mother, she loved children.

Manuel sweated in the great cathedral. If perchance the midwife were wrong, if his premature birth indeed threatened the life of Jesus Jose, at least, now, baptized, the child was safe from damnation. His very hopes inspired his fears. If the line of the O'Briens were destined to endure or to perish, he had preserved the family allegiance and devotion to its God.

5

Pedro paused on the wide stone steps outside the cathedral, feeling the soft breeze evaporate from his face the sweat of tension he'd brought from that solemn ceremony inside. He was pleasantly aware too of the admiring gazes of passers-by. Some whom he knew casually, he saw in delight, did not even recognize him in his fashionable toggery. Despite the hunger that growled in his belly, Pedro, in the pride of his new responsibility, his new honour, and his new clothes, declined to dangle his legs from the rear of the yellow buggy on the return journey to the Luiz home. He surrendered his seat beside her brother to Conchita and walked homeward, striding with his head up and his shoulders back in the blaze of sun. The remainder of the family arrived, accordingly, well ahead of him.

He found Clara in the kitchen. She was smiling, already escaped from her formal dress and preparing the celebration feast. She told him that Julia's fever had fallen. Perspiration marbled her face and Clara believed the little sister was stronger though she'd murmured only, 'I'm cold, so cold,' when Clara kissed her and spoke her name. Clara's hand on Julia's forehead reassured her, her temperature had fallen. She still seemed weak, she shivered, and her eyes looked glassy. Clara was hopeful. Still, she sensed a crisis and summoned Manuel into the kitchen.

'We must have a doctor for the little sister,' she said. 'Go, Senor, drive your horse with haste to bring Dr Robles for your wife.'

Manuel obeyed. Sal retraced his steps, the olive branch resting over his quarters and lashing him in dead earnest whenever he sought to lessen a crow-hop sort of trot into his usual casual plodding pace. The day was hot, the horse was tired, Manuel was merciless.

A ramshackle stairwell led to the office of Dr Robles. Manuel was breathless when he reached the top of the steps and boldly entered the doctor's waiting-room and living quarters. The coatless physician sat in a spray of sunlight near a window, smoking a cigarette.

'Come. We go to my wife, the mother of my new-born son. We fear for her life. We go without delay.' Manuel's tone was pleading but determined.

'And where does the senora stay?' the physician inquired, unhurried.

'Come with me. Without delay,' Manuel insisted.

Robles rose from his chair and snuffed out his cigarette in a metal ash-tray. He buttoned his soiled white waistcoat over the stiff bosom of his soiled white shirt, affixed no less soiled cuffs to his sleeves, adjusted the heavy, plated watch-chain across his waistcoat, retrieved the skirted coat that exchanged dignities with his profession, twisted the ends of the moustache which rested above his Vandyke beard. He entered a rear room and returned with his leather medicine bag. He thoughtfully arranged a hand on a printed clock face to indicate the hour of his probable return and bowed his readiness to Senor O'Brien.

Manuel was a small man, but Dr Robles was smaller. His manner was dapper to the point of daintiness. His dignified bearing, his unction and austerity comprised an unconscious effort to attain an impressive air which his stature initially denied. If he'd been larger, he would have been pompous. He proclaimed himself to be 'of the faculty of Mexico' whenever he could find or invent an occasion. He also had this distinction blazoned on the windows and door of his office-residence; indeed it brought him many patients. In Sonoratown of Los Angeles it was an earnest of his professional ability.

Despite his nervous gestures, Robles was incapable of haste, even if he had conceived haste to be comportable with his status in the medical profession. Manuel herded him across the dingy hall, half-dark beneath the dust-crusted sky-light, and down the worn and creaking stairwell. After what seemed a sweated eternity, Manuel boosted the doctor into the hot seat of the yellow buggy and swung up beside him, already clucking to Sal.

On the short ride the doctor fidgeted, crossed and re-crossed his neat hands, adjusted his cuffs, twirled the ends of his moustache. In this state of restlessness he listened to his client's recital of his patient's exigency. Manuel held the reins in one hand, the whip in the other, the while he gestured with both hands as he talked anguishedly. The physician barely paid attention; occasionally he uttered a 'si, Senor' to assure the troubled man that the case history was not being related in vain.

Arrived at the Luiz home, Manuel's hand on the doctor's match-stick arm forced him out of the buggy in the same urgent fashion as it had boosted him into it. He hastened the mincing Robles up the walk and into the house.

Clara was attempting to serve her sister, though she did not know what was best to be done. The babies lay side by side on a quilt spread upon the floor. Teodoro cried unheard and unheeded.

Dr Robles went to the bed and laid his hand on Julia's brow, then grunted in some unctuous, unexplained discernment. He lifted her wrist and checked the pulse, finding it

69

slow, laboured, stringy. He produced his thermometer from his coat pocket, shook down the mercury, placed the instrument in the girl's mouth and stood holding her arm, waiting for a reading.

Manuel breathlessly awaited a verdict which did not come. Dr Robles spoke to none of them.

When the physician had read the thermometer, he glanced over his shoulder and asked Clara to bring boiling water. Then he gave his patient a hypodermic stimulant for her heart. The sight of the syringe and needle and the use to which it was put brought consternation to Clara, despair to Manuel. Clara half-turned, grimacing, unable to watch, unable to turn away.

The doctor continued to ignore them. He wrote two prescriptions and only then gave Clara directions about their administration. He closed his medical kit and prepared to leave. He was not unaware that his opinion was awaited, but dignity prompted him to withhold it until it should be requested.

'Doctor.' Manuel's voice shook. 'Is she bad off?'

'The senora is very ill.' Dr Robles nodded solemnly. 'Had you not come for me when you did. . . .' Robles broke off with a dainty shrug. He hesitated, looking from Clara to Manuel, and resumed. 'You really should have come earlier, Senor. But it is well that you did call me.' He nodded. 'I well understand such cases as this. I have treated many of them, both here and when I was of the faculty of Mexico.'

'But my wife. Is she going to die?'

The doctor smiled mysteriously. 'It is wise you called me. Give her the medicine as I have designated and I shall come again tomorrow.'

Manuel craved more information but knew neither what details he desired nor how to ask for them. He wanted reassurance and he received evasion. Dr Robles appeared more interested in his own craft and the impression he achieved than in the patient's recovery. Feeling helpless, Manuel stood silently, trying to formulate a further question.

'The charge is one dollar for a house call. It would have been less had the senora been able to come to my office, of course,' the physician stated. When Manuel produced the money, Robles said, 'If the senor will have the goodness to drive me again to my office. One has many patients who wait,

70

you know.'

During the drive across the Plaza, Manuel remained silent, baffled. He let the little physician out at his door. Then he drove to a pharmacy where the window signs were repeated in Spanish and waited while the prescriptions were compounded.

The medicines that Manuel brought to Clara's kitchen were both in sixteen-ounce bottles. One was a liquid of thin yellowish green; the other a thick syrupy brown slow-oozing mixture. This latter was to be administered hourly in tablespoonfuls. What with Julia's weakness and the nauseating odour of the concoction, Clara had difficulty in inducing the girl to swallow the first dose of it. Manuel stood watching, urging his wife to drink. Manuel had paid a considerable price for the potion and he admired it because it was costly and because it trickled turgidly from the bottle, looked, smelled and tasted so unpleasant. These signs were ample warrant to him that it would be efficacious in restoring Julia's health. 'It's for your own good,' he kept saying.

After that dose of medicine had been administered, nothing more was to be done for her. She seemed to sink into semi-consciousness from which it was difficult to rouse her. Still, her fever appeared to have ebbed slightly. Manuel found the unoccupied waiting dismal. He paced the house, wishing for someway to hasten the results which he confidently expected from the medicine. To relieve the tension of her own impotent solicitude, Clara took the infant boys, one in each arm, and suckled both at once at her swollen breasts.

The fowl which Manuel had provided as main entree to celebrate the baptism simmered on the stove and permeated the whole house with the goodness of its odour. Pedrillo and Concha, anticipating this unwonted delicacy, appeared at brief intervals to inquire when they were to be fed. When at length Clara went into the kitchen, the mingled odours of spiced food and saffron rice grew stronger, dishes rattled and the meal was served.

It was far from the pleasant feast Manuel had anticipated that morning when he provided the cash with which to buy the roasting hen and all the other staples. Stretches of apprehensive silence marked the repast, and when the diners spoke at all, it was in low and muted tones.

Once Pedrillo, after a prolonged and serious silence, asked, 'Is the Tia Julia sick because she does not like the baby that

71

Senora Ramirez brought for her? The senora should have let me go back to get the baby as she promised. I should have picked out a good one for Tia.'

Manuel straightened in the chair, bristling silently. He did not relish this aspersion upon his son, but he continued to eat his chicken and held his tongue. Clara explained gently to the boy that it was not dissatisfaction with the midwife's selection of a child for her that had intensified his aunt's weakness. 'We all love the baby,' Clara said. 'The sickness is something else.'

After dinner there remained nothing to be done except to administer Julia's medicine at the prescibed intervals. Clara, because she desperately hoped it was true, expressed the opinion that her sister's condition was improved. When Clara pressed the question as to whether her strength was returning, Julia gave her a faint affirmative smile and nod, but relapsed at once into that restless half-sleep. Clara had saved broth from the chicken and urged Julia to swallow some of it. Clara supported Julia's body and the girl made the vain effort only to please her beloved sister.

The afternoon grew hot and quiet. The men went out of doors and Pedro propped himself against the wall of the porch. He would have made conversation if Manuel had chosen, but the old man was too distracted to be polite. Jazmin and Rosa, having made up their differences, appeared from behind the house, followed by Rosa's heir. They approached their respective masters who responded with the affectionate attention for which they appealed. Pedrillo's voice sounded in distant laughter from the vacant lot where he had resumed his play with the other urchins of his street. Concha lay down near her father and sucked her thumb until she fell asleep. Clara appeared at the door and told the men to listen for Julia as she'd been summoned urgently but briefly next door to some kitchen crisis in the home of her neighbour Yolita.

After a brief taut silence, Manuel disappeared around the house. After a while he could be heard talking in a low flat tone to his horse as he fed and watered him. And then later, the sickly sweet smell of opium-smoke faintly suffused the atmosphere.

The elastic shadows lay full length upon the ground. All the sky and the haze that veiled distant hills turned pink and yellow.

Pedro slouched on the porch, troubled about Julia, half-asleep and yet too disturbed to sleep. He sat in silence and buried his head in his hands, feeling the hot sting of tears. It seemed that the whole memory of his life passed before his mind's eye. He tried to shut out the memory of the way Julia had looked when she first came to them, innocent and fresh like new flowers. She had stood looking at him, her small round breasts erect and untouched, her eyes open and admiring and vulnerable, fixed on him. He tried to shut out the unsettling vision of her flower-fresh face and her taut young breasts and her eager eyes and he could not do it.

Pedro pressed his hands against the side of his head to crush out the memory. Then from nowhere came the thought of Julia's soft, slender hand when she'd tried to reach out to him, and the outlined mound of her feminity and the erect breasts against the sweat-damp sheet. Whether he wanted to or not he remembered the lines of her naked body, the way it had opened to him like a fresh flower bud opening in the morning sun, and he felt himself go empty with longing deep in his loins. His throat tightened and his heart drummed arhythmically and he shivered as if cold. He remembered the way he'd held her naked body; the way she'd pulled her skirts upward out of the way, frantically; the vivid greed that had blazed in her black eyes every time Clara left the house. He grew restless with excitement and need. He deliberated the wisdom of going into the house, but went on sitting there in anguished anticipation.

Pedro felt as if none of this were real, as if he were caught in a disturbing dream, aching with desire. In his mind he dreamed that Julia was running, in déshabillé, her long black hair flying at her shoulders, across some sunlit glen. Her head was turned and she laughed, calling to him. And though he wanted her, hurt with pounding and relentless need, his rubbery legs failed him, he staggered helplessly, calling her back, trying to stay her. Then Julia paused and reached out her arm toward him and called, laughing and promising, and he could not overtake her.

He sat up, shaken, his eyes blurred with tears. He knew he had to go into that room where she lay on the bed. As he moved to lever himself to his feet he saw that Concha had wakened and stood, thumb in mouth, staring at him in a strange, bewildering way.

His throat ached so he was afraid he could not speak naturally. He smiled at her and found three coppers in his pocket. 'Would you like a poke of candy, Conchita?' When she nodded, he gave her the pennies. 'Run yonder to the market and buy yourself candy.'

She nodded, kissed him and ran down the steps. He stood for a moment watching her run in the sunlight. Murmurs of mixed sounds floated around him from the town and the street and the houses next door. He heard Clara and Yolita laughing together. He could smell Manuel's opium cooking.

He went through the door and into the room where Julia lay on the bed. It did not deter him that Julia had had a difficult labour and delivery a few hours ago. He wanted her, she had always wanted him as mindlessly and he could not believe she would want him to suffer no matter how badly she ached. She would forget her pain. He would make her forget.

He stood beside the bed in the silent room looking down at Julia.

Something about the Easter-lily pallor of Julia's face made Pedro choke back a cry in his throat. He had never seen her look so pale and still. He had never seen such a bleak look in her face, even in her deepest sleep. It frightened him to see her like that. He wanted to turn and run from the room, but he wanted her too badly to leave her.

He tried to say something, but there were no words. When Julia opened her eyes and saw his face, she would know what he wanted. He was bursting inside and couldn't express what he felt for her.

He bent over the bed and touched her arm, finding it chilled. He shuddered faintly, a sense of horror creeping at the nape of his neck. He drew a deep breath and whispered her name. When she did not answer, did not move at all, he shook her roughly.

Her eyes popped open, staring, glassy and empty. Pedro bit back the bile that welled in his throat, the screams of terror that roiled up from the depths of his loins. He touched her icy cheek gently. And then he crossed himself.

III

Pedro stood unmoving. He felt cold and rigid as if he had turned to stone inside. Julia was dead. Name of God, Julia was dead. Death. How he hated the word and dreaded the thought. Death was here, here in this house, stealing his love from him. Its fleshless forefinger had touched this girl and taken her from him. A sense of horror seized him.

His eyes brimmed with tears. The lifeless form on that bed Pedro had loved and it had responded to him, wild with love. She had romped with him in frenzies of delight, had lain beatified in the fervour of his passion. Those lips had eagerly opened to his kisses and had given them again to him. Those bloodless cheeks had mantled at his words whispered in her ear. Those sightless eyes had kindled at his glance. Aye God. Aye God. There could be no God who cared so little.

He did not know how long he stood there. He was aware that Clara entered the room, stared down at Julia's body and then sank, pressing her head into the mattress. For a long time neither of them spoke. At last, Clara whispered through her choked throat, 'One should tell her husband.'

Pedro nodded. He sought Manuel in the buggy behind the house. The husband of the dead girl slumped asleep in the seat of the carriage. Pedro spoke his name. He growled, 'You old bastard, wake up.' Manuel did not respond. Pedro grasped the seat of the buggy and, trembling with rage against death and loss and life itself, he shook the wagon on its springs. The old man in his lethargy slouched deeper into his stupor. Pedro took hold of his shoulder and shook him.

This only caused Manuel's head to topple off the support and hang loosely over the side of the seat. He did not waken. Pedro shook him more violently. Manuel only grunted. Pedro continued to shake the fragile little man until at last Manuel opened his eyes and stared around, lost.

'Senor. Julia. Your wife, Senor, she is dead,' Pedro said, and crossed himself.

Manuel strove to shake off his stupor. He only half-understood the words which Pedro repeated with cold patience while he tried to shake Manuel into wakefulness. Manuel shook his head. 'But the doctor — '

'She is dead.' Pedro shook his head again. 'Julia is dead.'

Manuel finally roused himself. Blindly, he climbed down from the buggy and accompanied Pedro into the house. Pedro's words at last penetrated his consciousness but their sense still failed to involve him. 'The priest?' he said. 'The priest gave her the last sacrament?'

A muscle worked in Pedro's jaw. He spoke in a low, dead tone. 'There was no priest.'

Manuel shook his head, staring up at him. 'Not the sacrament? Why did you not call the priest?' When Pedro did not bother to answer, Manuel said, 'But the doctor? And the medicine? The doctor said she would not die.'

Clara still kelt beside the bed on which her sister's body lay. Clara's sobs shook her. Manuel, his head reeling, looked down at his dead wife. He placed his palm upon her forehead. He nodded. 'She is dead.' Pausing, he added, 'and without the blessed last sacrament.' He crossed himself. When neither of them spoke, Manuel's voice hardened. 'The doctor said she would not die.'

They did not reply. Manuel stood, slump-shouldered. He had been bereft so many times that he was immune to death's terrors. His drugged senses were not jarred into any strong emotion. That Julia had died without clerical ministration was to him of equal import to the fact that she was dead.

He shivered with the chill touch of loneliness which death reserves for the aged bereft, those who have so little remaining and have that taken away. His marriage had not provided him with the delights he had anticipated but he had become used to her presence on the farm, depended upon it. He would miss having her with him on the rancho. Her death would complicate the problem of rearing Jesus. Manuel felt a wave of outrage that she had died leaving the infant without the sustenance from her breasts. However, he had the boy. His son was his own now. No woman, no other person had any rights or interest in him. He need share the child with nobody.

The light glowed yellowly in the room. After a long time Clara's mournful sobbing waned. Manuel saw his life resuming its pattern ahead in the gloom.

'We must go then to the undertaker that he may send for the body of my wife,' Manuel decided. 'The priest too. The priest must come and light candles for her soul.'

Clara lifted her head. 'No, no, Senor.' She knew little of undertakers. 'Let us keep the little sister here. Let her stay near her son till that time comes she must go to be buried.' She wept again. 'I wish not to give up the body of my sister to strangers.'

Manuel seemed not to hear her; he was unmoved by anything she said. At his behest Pedro accompanied him to obtain the services of the undertaker. The distance was short and it was easier to walk than to harness Sal to the buggy.

Manuel made a choice of a coffin, an ornate box of black brocade, festooned with fringes, and elaborately fitted with silver-plated hardware which included an oversized silver crucifix attached to the lid. The two men walked out of the sombre building and plodded in the growing darkness toward Pedro's home. They did not speak. The undertaker's wagon passed them, lumbering noisily on the brick street.

The undertaker and his helper, with mournful faces as if Julia might be their own little sister, folded a white sheet over her body and lifted her into the wagon. The undertaker assured Manuel the the corpse would be properly cared for, and departed. The procedure was so impersonal, so business-like and lacking in ceremony that Manuel felt somehow defrauded. He went at once and summoned a priest to the undertakers' to set candles to burn and to perform those terminal rites for the salvation of Julia's soul.

2

Manuel slept that night at the Luiz house in the bed where Julia had died. Pedro, Clara and their children occupied pallets upon the floor.

At breakfast, Manuel sat without eating. His brows knotted. He spoke almost musingly as if he expected no answer, as if there were no answer. 'What now of Jesusito, now that his mother is gone from him in death, how will he live? How can I care for him? A new-born requires a woman's milk. Or fresh goat's milk. Perhaps that might serve, but not so well as the milk of a woman. I wish my son to have what is best, for it is certain I shall never have another.'

Clara sighed heavily. 'If the senor would leave the child with me. . . . I can divide with him the milk that goes to feed Teodoro. I can eat more and my breasts flow freely.'

Manuel seemed not to hear her. 'A wet-nurse? If I could get for him a wet-nurse, a woman who has lost her own child. One willing to live in the country. My son is frail. A premature child. He needs all the milk one woman can provide.'

Clara spoke with more determination. 'The senor must leave the child here. As his own mother would want it, rest her soul. Jesusito shall be cared for well, and I shall have milk for both.'

Manuel continued to stare into the middle distance as if the grieving woman's voice did not reach him. 'I should seldom see my son if I left him in the care of others.' He looked at Clara now and tried to smile. 'You are a good woman, Clara, and I know you would treat him well, but I want the best for him. He is my only son. He is all my young wife has left me. He is for the Church and I must know he has everything.'

Clara spoke in firm logic. 'I am not only his aunt, Senor. I am his godmother. Pedro is his godfather. Our duty is to look out for my sister's son. Leave the little one with us and fear nothing.'

At last O'Brien nodded. 'The senora is a saint on this earth. . . . I shall leave with her my son until he shall reach the age where he can come with me to the rancho. I vow to you that when he is grown and of the Church, he shall say prayers for the souls of his kind godparents. . . . It is decided that he shall stay.'

It was for this moment that Pedro had waited. He stood up and stretched himself. 'We wish, my wife and I, to serve the senor in his grief, for he is the husband of my wife's sister and one of our family. We desire to be true godparents to the young Jesusito. But my wife forgets that we are poor.' When Clara would have spoken he threw up his arm to silence her. 'Another child means more food for Clara. Already I work too hard, my back is pained and my stomach is delicate. We

78

cannot afford to keep the baby for the senor. It is as plain as that. The Senor O'Brien is rich; he does not understand to be poor.'

'But, my husband,' Clara broke in. 'The young baby will eat nothing except from my breast. Already my milk is too much for our own son and he can share it with his cousin. I wish to have the boy. My heart breaks else I have him near and know he is safe. I shall try to eat no extra.'

Manuel waved his arms and shook his head, trying to smile. 'Yes, yes. You must eat well, Clara. You must make milk for the boys. I shall pay. I shall gladly pay for the keeping of my son. My expenses recently have been great and the funeral of my wife will cost much money, but I shall have enough to pay regularly for my son. . . . Do not vex yourself, good Pedro. If your wife will care for him, my son will cost you nothing.'

Pedro appeared to consider and calculate for a long time. At last he stretched and nodded. 'It is good then. Jesusito shall stay and my wife shall care for him as our humble means will permit. It would be my wish to make no charges, but my back gets weaker and my stomach is delicate. I am not able to work so much as once I did.' He smiled. Then he stretched himself again and said with a rueful frown, 'We need to buy groceries today and there is no money. I can collect money on Saturday, but until then we starve.'

Manuel delved into his pocket, but the amount he handed over to Pedro, ample as it was for a day's rations, was a disappointment. Pedro had indeed overstated the larder's depletion, but he could not forbear from beginning at once to enjoy the profits of this new arrangement, this first day of his improved existence.

Manuel went to the church and arranged with a priest that a requiem Mass should be sung for Julia's funeral. He went again to his bank for more funds with which to meet the expenses of her burial. He drove to the undertakers, gave orders that a grave should be dug in the O'Brien family plot, and made final arrangements for Julia's interment on the following day. Then he returned to Pedro's. Melancholy, he retired again to the seclusion of his buggy and gave himself up to opium and oblivion.

Clara's day was so hectic, filled with household duties, preparation of food, care of two infants, entertaining callers come to commiserate about Julia's death, that she had little time to vent the grief that moiled deep inside her.

Dr Robles returned as he had promised in the afternoon and was embarrassed to find his patient dead. His face flushed and he dry-washed his small hands. 'The case was without hope, of course. You sent for me too late. I declared to the husband yesterday that she would die.' The physician bowed to Clara and took his leave as quickly as he could.

Pedro donned his new clothes immediately after Manuel departed that morning. The coins he'd received from the old miser jangled in his pockets. Clara watched Pedro striding away along the path. She sighed. She could not expect him to return until the money had been spent.

It was well after midnight when he returned. One of the tickets he had bought in the Chinese lottery had returned him more than fifteen dollars, of which he had been unable to spend more than half. He refrained from telling his wife about his good fortune. She might want part of it to spend upon the family. He could not help thinking that since Julia had died, his fortunes had improved dramatically. He almost believed that, across that vale, she was interceding already on his behalf. He crossed himself. Julia was a young innocent. He should fare well with her watching over him.

He staggered into the bedroom. Manuel slept soundly in the bed. Clara lay on a pallet upon the floor. She roused slightly when Pedro came in. He took off his garments and tossed them toward a chair. As he undressed, he gazed at the sleeping Manuel and Manuel's trousers hanging over the bedpost. He wondered how much money the old miser really carried on his person. His heart pounded faster. What would it hurt just to count Manuel's money?

Holding his breath, he felt into the pocket, removed Manuel's money. He cupped the handful of golden eagles and double eagles, awed. He sighed. Would one coin among so many be missed? He chose a ten-dollar piece, replaced it and took a twenty in its stead. The coins jingled as he returned them. Manuel stirred and Pedro backed away against the wall, tense. He clutched the coin in his palm and held his breath until Manuel snored again. Sweating, he almost returned the money he had stolen. He shook his head. If the coin should be missed and even if he were suspected of taking it, he would merely deny everything. If Manuel wanted him to care for Manuel's bastard son, the old fellow had better walk

80

easily around here.

Barefooted and wearing only his underclothes, those rich textured garments old Manuel had bought for him, he went stealthily out of the room and out of the house. He turned over a large rock that lay at the corner of the house. Then he shook his head and replaced the rock as he had found it. He lifted a loose board on the porch, thrust his arm through the opening and placed the coin on the ground, fixing in his mind its exact location. Then he replaced the board as well as he was able and, stretching, crept back into the bedroom and joined Clara on the pallet upon the floor.

3

A closed black carriage called for the O'Brien and Luiz families at ten the next morning. The coach, shining and with a sleek team of horses, was much admired from neighbouring windows. Crowded with three adults and four children, the tonneau of the vehicle was stifling, but was endured without complaint for the sake of its splendor.

Manuel's grief at the loss of his wife was tempered by satisfaction in the pageantry of the obsequies, the arrival of the hearse with plumed black horses, the colourful ceremonies of the Mass, the surpliced and red-stoled priest, the red-clad acolytes, the intoned Latin, incomprehensible and potent, the swinging censer, incense, tall candles, crucifixes, icons, an unusually large crowd of mourners, the tears shed, the elegant bier, flowers, white gloves, the atmosphere of compassion and shared grief, the row of processional carriages, all the pomp of human sorrow.

Manuel did grieve, and aloud. It was expected of him. It was part of the spectacle. But greater than his grief was his pride that he could offer to his beloved wife, dead in the bearing of his son, a funeral commensurate with his bereavement. With these magnificent last rites he made up to Julia for the omission of the sacred last sacrament.

Over the same road the O'Briens had traversed in their final journey from the rancho to Los Angeles, the long line of vehicles in the funeral cortege crawled its way to the graveyard beyond the city limits where an open grave awaited. The return trip from the cemetery was at a faster pace. Life, pausing for a moment, regained its former tempo.

Manuel, emotionally exhausted, was impatient to discharge this reckoning of his unhappiness and to be gone back to his ranch. Solitude was to be his lot again, but solitude was no novelty to Manuel. And he could look forward now to that day when Jesusito should join him in his home. He would make the place ready for the child.

'The consolation left me in the death of my woman is that you are here to give sustenance to my son,' Manuel said to Clara. 'I pray that one more mouth is not too great a burden.'

'So many children are the affliction of poverty,' Pedro said with flat resignation in his tone.

Manuel tried to smile. 'But they will care for you when you are old. Children are a blessing — when they live.'

Pedro stretched, cat-like. 'And your son who nurses at my wife's breast, will he support me when I am old?' Pedro tilted his brow, watching the older man.

'And more.' Manuel nodded. 'Jesusito is for the Church, and he will say prayers for your soul.'

Arrived once more at the Luiz house, Manuel went into the kitchen to refresh himself with wine before he set out for his own home. The older children joined the adults in drinking the acrid beverage and Clara mixed some with water that Pedrillo and Concha might in the restorative juice of the grape forget their sweaty and petulant fatigue.

'I return now to my ranchito.' Manuel drained a full glass of wine and wiped the back of his hand across his mouth. 'I leave my son to you. Do all for him, he must have everything.'

Pedro nodded. 'But the cost is great. To rear a child is expensive and we are poor.' Pedro once more reminded his brother-in-law of his promise to pay for the keep of the child.

Manuel smiled and nodded his head. 'Yes. He is my son and I shall pay willingly.' Removing coins from his pocket, he selected a ten-dollar gold-piece. 'This will serve until I come again.' He extended the money towards Clara.

Pedro's mouth watered at the sight of the coin. He regretted he had not availed himself of the chance to steal more last night. The old bastard had so much and he had so little. He bewailed his modesty and the lost opportunity.

His face flushed and rage boiled up inside him when he saw that Manuel was about to give the coin to Clara. He clutched at the money before his wife could accept it.

Manuel protested. 'But the money must be for the sister of Julia, that she may rear my child.'

Pedro glared down at him, face flushed and taut. 'I am the husband. I keep the money. Money is not for women. Money is then for the head of the house.'

'When he earns it, yes,' Manuel agreed. 'Then money is the man's. But this money is for the good Clara who will use it for Jesusito.' He straightened and his voice hardened. 'Give the money then to Clara.'

Scowling, enraged, Pedro with open bad grace surrendered the coin to his wife's keeping. Once rid of this old bastard, he would commandeer the money. Although Clara's had been a totally impassive acquiescence in Manuel's proposal of a separate budget at the woman's disposal for the maintenance of the O'Brien baby, Pedro was outraged that she should permit her husband to be so humiliated before an outsider. The anger Pedro felt toward O'Brien, as murderous as it was, could not vent itself upon the guest in his house, but must contain itself until Manuel should be gone and he could avenge the smear on his honour upon his wife: for O'Brien's affront to his dignity and for her permitting it. Only so could he re-establish over his own household that authority which accrues to husband and father.

Manuel noted the younger man's livid displeasure and so hastened his preparations for an early departure. He bowed to them and went at once to the rear yard to harness Sal to the yellow buggy and to summon his dogs.

Pedro, shaking with rage, sought a shady spot upon the front porch where he sprawled to nurse the injury which had been offered to him, and to bide his time until Manuel should be gone. Pedrillo and Conchita led a group of urchins in a pantomimic re-enactment of Julia's funeral, with much sobbing and wailing lamentation in the procession.

Manuel brought Sal around to the street and left him standing at the hitching post. Then he returned to the edge of the porch to say his farewells. The need for a show of politeness to his guest brought Pedro to his feet. The two men embraced and patted backs.

Clara brought Jesus, and Manuel bent over the child and gazed into his face for a long time with yearning eyes. He straightened the baby's dress, brushed a fly from its forehead, lifted one tiny hand in his fingers, almost as if he expected the child to kiss his hand in earnest of filial obedience. He pressed the back of his hand against the baby's mouth. Clara called to Concha and Pedrillo to kiss the avuncular hand in farewell.

'Take good care of Jesusito,' Manuel said. The family group followed him to his buggy. Again the men embraced and bade each other, 'Go with God.' The old man climbed up into the seat. His dogs moved round the vehicle, waiting for it to move. Clara called Jazmin, afraid the dog might follow her companions. Manuel jerked on the reins and Sal lurched into his awkward amble amid a chorus of 'Adios. Adios, Senor. Vaya con Dios.'

The family stood watching the retreating buggy. Before Manuel was out of hearing, Pedrillo called. 'Adios, Tio. I'll take care of Jesusito.'

Despite the injury that Pedro considered O'Brien had callously inflicted upon him when he gave money to the wife instead of to the husband, he behaved well enough toward his departing guest. His cordiality had its reservations and that anger which custom and hospitality forbade him to vent upon his guest, continued to simmer and stew within him. The children rounded up their playmates and resumed their funeral services. Clara, the two infants in her arms, went into the house. Her agony at her sister's death was all the more poignant now that the ceremonies were done, now that her brother-in-law had departed, now that she was alone in the silent house. Jesusito would be a constant reminder of her bereavement. Her vow given to the father that she would care for the baby Clara considered a promise to the dead Julia also. She knelt upon the floor to lay the babies awkwardly upon the pallet. Jesus lay staring up at her and, her eyes wet with tears, she pressed her mouth against the lips of her motherless nephew.

Pedro had difficulty in freeing the end of the loose board on the front porch. Without taking the board entirely away it was impossible for him to see the ground. He had to grope with his hand in the earth. His belly went empty when he did not locate the money at once. He thought he had marked the exact spot in his mind, but the coin eluded his grasping fingers. When at length, sweating, he touched the coin, his spirits soared. He slapped the board in place and put the twenty-dollar piece in his pocket.

He stretched in a delicious ecstacy of pleasure. With what remained of the money he'd won in the Chinese lottery, and knowing he could bully Clara out of the coin Manuel had given her, he enjoyed a sense of prosperity he had seldom known. Pedro shrugged. It would not be necessary so much as to ask Clara for the money. If she did not surrender it to him as her husband, head of the house, she would give it to him and ask him to make a purchase out of it. In any event it would be his. He sat smiling in contemplation of his incredible good fortune. Then he sat abruptly upright, amazed to see Sal sidling down the street ahead of the yellow buggy in which sat Manuel O'Brien.

Sal halted at the hitching post and Manuel crawled down from the buggy, gesticulating and stumbling.

'It is that I have lost money,' Manuel called to Pedro, running toward the porch. 'Twenty dollars. One coin of gold. Twenty pesos. Have you found my money?'

Pedro rose languidly from the porch, stretching self-consciously. He shook his head. 'No, Senor. Where did you lose it?'

'I don't know. Somewhere here. I got money yesterday from the bank to pay the burial of my wife. I go to pay and twenty dollars is gone. It was here, safe in my pocket, but it is gone.'

Clara came to the door. She shook her head, troubled. The amount was a fortune in her mind. 'Twenty pesos? Such a terrible loss.'

'Maybe the bank was wrong. Maybe they did not give you enough,' Pedro suggested.

Manuel looked around, distracted. 'No, I counted. I had it and it is gone. I lost it.' Manuel hesitated, his face bleak. 'Or somebody stole it.'

Pedro winced and straightened against the wall. 'No.' He shook his head. 'Nobody stole. Nobody took your money. Maybe you lost it at the graveyard, or where you knelt in church.' He shrugged. 'But why worry? A rich man like you. You have more in the big bank, haven't you?'

Manuel nodded, voice quavering. 'A little more. But I need much. For my son. And twenty pesos is much money. In honey it is many cans, the work of many bees.' Manuel spoke as much to himself as to the Luiz couple. 'No. My money was stolen.'

Pedro felt himself accused. He was conscious of the gold among the lesser coins in his pocket. He defended himself from the charge. 'I stole not your money. Do you charge me with theft? I am not a thief. You come here and use my house and eat my food and then you spend your money and say that I stole it. You bring your wife here to me to whelp her bastard of which it prides you to think you are the father, you who are too old, too much used up to make a baby. And then you say I stole your money. I don't want your money. I am lucky just yesterday in the lottery. I have money of my own. I do not have to steal. And you with so much money in the big bank, you say I stole your twenty pesos. Miser. Gringo. Sinvuerguenza. Chingado. Capron!' Shaken, Pedro paused for breath. That the inapt epithets he used against Manuel were ugly was all he asked of them.

Manuel waved his arms, gesturing for Pedro to desist, but he was so shocked, so sadly injured by what the younger man had said that he was unable to speak.

Clara was able to murmur only, 'Pedro. My husband. Pedro. Shame. Shame.'

Pedro would not be censured or consoled into silence. 'You do me injury when you accuse me of robbing you, Senor. . . . Only last night I came home and found you sleeping in the same room where slept my wife. What was I to think? Do you suppose I am a fool or innocent, not to know what went on? Do you think I should trust you? A rich old man who goes about seducing the wives of honest men. And today you gave her money. In my own presence you gave her gold. Do you think I don't know what that means? And you foist your wife's bastard baby — no, not yours. You are not able to produce a child — foist it on my wife for me to rear for you. And then you say I stole your money. You can go, and you can take the bastard brat with you. You cannot leave it here.'

Manuel staggered, stunned and irreparably hurt. He might have wept but he was to shocked for tears. And, at Pedro's mention of his late homecoming last night, Manuel knew where his money had gone. Before that instant he had not questioned Pedro's honesty. The money now was gone. This was settled and must be forgotten, because he could not take Jesus away from Clara if his son were to live. He looked around emptily. It would have been best had he not returned. Now he must find some means to placate this savage fellow.

'No, Pedro. Mi amigo. I did not say you stole. I know you did not steal. I did not believe that. Have I said you stole? No. No. You would not steal, amigo. You are right, I lost the money. And of last night, the gracious Clara is pure and innocent. I did no wrong to you. The money I gave today was for my son. Do not mistake, amigo. I make no charges against your good name. I wish to leave the child with his good aunt, his kind uncle, with his godparents. I shall pay. I shall pay you well for the rearing of him. See. Ten pesos more. I shall leave it with you. Let me leave the boy.'

The sight of Manuel's gold coin placated Pedro. He was unable to refrain from reaching for the money. He would have liked to spurn the offer for long enough to permit the acid of his invective to grave upon the old man's consciousness the depth of the wrong Pedro Grandos Luiz had suffered.

Pedro took the coin and bowed, thanking Manuel. Both knew that the passage of the yellow disk implied a truce, in which, as in all truces, both sides admitted defeat. His son's welfare, dependent as it was upon Clara's tending the baby, justified O'Brien in his own mind for swallowing the unforgiveable insults Pedro had hurled at him.

Manuel forced a grey smile. 'My twenty pesos is gone. It is best forgotten. We will not speak of it again. Do not believe, mi amigo, that I think for one moment that you took it. I know you do not steal. Use this new money, good Pedro, for the care of my son. Farewell.'

O'Brien was as eager to be gone as Luiz was to have him go. Despite the polite amenities that marked their parting, the hatred each had for the other, engendered by the quarrel, had not evaporated, but festered deeply behind their smiles.

When Don Manuel had driven away, Pedro exhaled in relief. He felt as if he had been holding his breath for ten minutes. His emotions had been so mangled this day: grief for the dead Julia, awe of the terrible majesty of death itself, this stain upon his honour. It was a relief to sprawl on the porch in the hot afternoon and to contemplate the use he should make of the considerable fortune that jangled in his pocket. It was his; he had earned it all.

He lay back and closed his eyes. He did not forget the money Manuel had given to Clara. He calculated the magnitude of the sum he already possessed, more avid than ever to add Clara's ten dollars to it. He had not forgiven Manuel for forcing him to surrender that money to Clara. He would never forgive him, and he included Clara as an object of his rage that she should have stood against him and taken the money. The anger built and roiled inside him until veins stood along his throat and marked his temples like taut cords.

He entered the kitchen with the prowling gait of a stalking puma. He found his wife washing infant clothes in a large suds-swollen pan. Pedro walked up behind her and grasped her by the wrist with one hand while with the other he slapped her across her back.

'Where is that money?' he said. 'Give it to me.'

'But the money is for Jesusito. Don Manuel said — ' Pedro backhanded her with his fist across her face. She sagged but he would not let her fall or retreat.

'Give me the money.' A resounding slap of his open palm against each temple rocked her head. A blow from his doubled fist cut her mouth so blood spurted. Clara reeled in momentary darkness.

'My husband. Spare me,' She begged. 'I get you the money. Do not beat me.'

He stood staring at her, faintly mollified because her flesh was broken and blood spilled untended over her mouth and across her chin. 'Get it then.' He did not relinquish his hold upon her wrist. When she did not move quickly enough to please him he doubled his fist and beat her shoulders and arms.

Pedrillo entered the rear door of the kitchen and stopped, his face grey. He shook his head, crying out because his mother was hurt. He had learned long ago to keep out of the way when his father became violent. But the sight of his mother helpless and bleeding terrifed and deranged him.

Screaming, he ran at his father with his fists doubled. Still holding Clara pinned by the wrist, Pedro staggered the boy with a powerful slap across the face. When the boy fell, Pedro kicked him and Pedrillo, stunned, lay on the floor trying to crawl away.

'My mother,' he wept. 'Please, sir, don't hurt my mother.'

Pedro did not even hear the boy. He forgot him in his savage attack on Clara. 'Puta,' he snarled at her. 'Whore. Selling yourself to the old gringo. Where is the money?' He struck her in the mouth again with his fist. His fingers and hand were covered with her blood. 'You think to put the horns of the goat on me? You think I'll endure it? You and your old miser gringo.'

Clara's head rolled back and forth. Her blood spattered her dress and streaked her throat. She offered no resistance to the beating. She did not fight back. Her resentment at the vilification of her husband's baseless accusation did not hurt her because she knew it to be his rage speaking and not his convictions. She suffered more from the single blow that Pedro had lashed out at Pedrillo than from all the savage pounding he was giving her. The pain and soreness would last for days. Her face would be broken and discoloured to spur the gossips but she did not care.

'Pedro, please. It is enough. I will get the money for you if you permit it.'

He half-threw her from him. She struck the wall and sank along it. She pushed herself up awkwardly, her hair wild about her bloodied face. 'Then get it,' he told her. 'And remember well. It is mine. The money belongs to the husband. You know this. I am the head of this house. The money is mine. Get it for me.'

Clara staggered to the small cupboard where she'd stored the gold piece, tied in an old handkerchief, in a broken coffee cup behind some pans. She untied the knot and handed the coin meekly to her spouse who accepted it coldly and silently.

Clara sagged at the kitchen table, trying to pin up her hair. She did not touch her bleeding face.

Swaggering about the room, Pedro brought from his pocket his entire store of cash. Almost fifty dollars, more than he'd ever had in his hand at one time in all his life before. He spread the coins on his palm admiringly and added this new piece to them. His anger had spent itself and he was at peace with the world. He smiled faintly in satisfaction at his cunning. Clara, slouched in the chair, saw the double eagle in his hand. Her heart sank. She knew where it came from, but she said nothing. He held the coins so she had to see them. He wished she should see the coins, that she might admire his affluence.

When Clara did not speak, Pedro said in a flat savage tone, 'Let us have supper. I go out.'

Clara got up and washed her face at the kitchen sink. She placed food on the littered table: cold beans, pieces of uncooked cabbage, rudely sliced brown bread, a jug of wine, black olives. Before she'd finished the formalities of preparation, Pedro sat down at the table. Pedrillo and Concha crept silently into the room, wide-eyed and afraid to speak.

Clara surveyed her man as she prepared the meal. She was satisfied and even filled with pride at what she saw. She took no cognizance of any signs of grossness. She admired the symetry of his features, the unwrinkled texture of his swarthy skin, glowing with health, his shining, thick black hair, untrimmed, disheveled, giving him the look of some ancient god, the staunch column of his neck, the long muscles of his arms and the powerful shoulders visible where his shirt clung to his flesh, the lean hardness of his thighs. She loved this strong, predatory animal, hungered for his love. The pummeling he'd given her she accepted as the husband's prerogative, evidence of his devotion.

She paused beside his chair and pressed her thigh against him.

'Do not go out tonight, querido,' she whispered, pleading. 'Stay with me now that we are again alone.'

He shoved her away with his shoulder. 'Get the supper. I have said. I go out.' He shrugged slightly, his mouth twisting in an arrogant smile of victory. 'Maybe I shall come home early. Quien sabe? Who knows?'

She gazed down at him, trying to smile with her broken lips. 'Do not spend your money on other women, querido mio. Your woman is here for you. Come back to her early. I have desire for you tonight.'

Pedro glanced up at her with that twisted smile but gave her no promise. He bolted his food and washed it down with red wine. Draining his glass, he rose from the table. For a moment he stood grinning down at his children. He grasped Pedrillo's neck roughly and good-naturedly, if too violently, slapped his face. Pedrillo looked up and smiled wanly in gratitude for the attention. To Conchita her sire's notice was less of a novelty and rib-tickling, which ended with a fierce kiss, was received with a coquette's casualness. Then Pedro was gone with his good humour, out of the door. Clara watched him as he sauntered away from the house, humming the strains of 'La Golandrina'.

IV

The return of Manuel O'Brien to his San Gabriel Valley ranch was a forlorn journey. A few days earlier, he'd traversed this road beside his woman. Today he rode alone toward empty solitude. He reached the cemetery where the fresh earth was a heaped red scab over Julia's grave. He drew reins with intention to alight. The prospect of having his emotions stirred with another leave-taking hurt too much and so he urged Sal forward and did not look back.

The horse's hoofs stirred dust into clouds and the slanting rays of the sun turned it into powdered gold. Cobalt, warm and purpled, smeared the sky and the landscape glowed with ochres, sienna raw and burnt, umbers and Indian reds. Sharp lines demarcated the shadows from the sun. Distant hills lay lost in curtains of autumnal haze. A breeze fresh from the sea tempered the heat. Sal's was a sluggard pace, but Manuel, sick at heart, did not urge the horse to mend it.

Live things along the roadside failed to attract Manuel's attention. All his thoughts were on death. A gopher snake writhed in shoulder-high weeds and the dogs skirted its threatening hiss. Linnets clung swinging to tall grasses, nibbling the summer harvest of seeds. A road-runner scampered ahead of the cart. Rabbits showed white tails to Rosa and her son but ground squirrels remained defiantly upon rocks or fences. An earth-dwelling owl squatted on a boulder. A less heavy heart might have leapt at the golden flight of an apprehensive oriole. A mare trotted to her pasture fence and whickered a welcome to Sal. Of all that lived and hummed or buzzed or sang or vanished in fear, Manuel saw only a vulture where it wheeled and circled against the florid sky, and in the flight of the buzzard he saw not the confident poise of vast wings but the gluttony of death.

His unhappiness at Julia's death was partly compounded of

vexation with Providence that she had not been destined to rear the son she'd borne him. He feared even that both might be snatched from him, because the survival of the premature infant was not assured. He wished for Julia and for his son. His sociable nature craved companionship, not only mere meetings and partings with acquaintances but the steadfast mutuality of interest, support, loyalty and affection, the apotheosis of friendship; such a relationship has ever been a universal human quest.

Pedro and Clara flashed into his mind and he winced. Pedro and the money Pedro had stolen from him, the old man chose to disremember. To recover the money was impossible and he was in no retributive mood; he wanted only what was best for his son, no matter what it cost. To the difficulties and expense of his traffic with Pedro Luiz, O'Brien was reconciled.

Daylight was failing when Sal plodded into the barnyard of the little ranch. Nothing had changed during Manuel's absence. Various-coloured chickens roosted on the wagon, the flat plain lay empty and sere as far as he could see. Manuel unhitched his horse from the buggy and led him into his stall. By the time he'd fed and watered Sal, darkness enveloped the valley.

Manuel went into the house. Heat of the day was imprisoned in the closed structure and the place was rancid with odours of spoiled food. Manuel scraped it up and emptied it in the back yard so that his dogs could eat it. Although hungry, he was too forlorn and dejected to prepare a meal. He trimmed away green spots of mildew from a loaf of dry bread and, with a demi-john of wine, stayed his hunger.

Everywhere he turned in the house he was reminded of his dead wife. Many of the furnishings had been purchased only to please Julia. Her carpeted floors and curtained windows heightened his loneliness. Julia had not made their bed on the day of their departure and it lay as they had risen from it. Ants paraded across a half-eaten apple in which Julia's toothmarks were embedded. On the table a red geranium grew in a tin lard-pail where Julia had planted it. One of her stockings hung on the arm of the rocking chair where she had tossed it in her haste, its mate having missed its mark and fallen to the floor. The wine deepened his despair rather than easing it. Tears might have calmed his anguish, but he could not weep.

He went to bed. Though he'd lain the previous night in the bed in which his wife had died, he could not force himself to lie down on the mattress where they had passed their nights together. He spread quilts on the floor of the little room and lay down there, apart from the memories of his marriage. He decided he would save the bed in the bigger room for Jesusito when the boy was old enough to join him here. The boy should have everything that made for his comfort or happiness, Manuel vowed, because Jesus Jose was the last of the proud clan of the O'Briens, Irish to be sure but the equal of that landed aristocracy of Spanish origin with which the family mingled. Not only was the boy the last O'Brien but he was destined for the Church. Meanwhile he must have that environment worthy of the gentleman he was born to be and of the priest he was fated to become.

Manuel lay down on his pallet, resolved the next morning to undertake that extraction of his honey-crop interrupted by Julia's insistence that he take her to Los Angeles. This work would help divert him from his lonely despair. However, when morning came he could not drive himself to the honey shed.

He invented excuses from hour to hour to postpone that task. He consumed a slender breakfast of undercooked beans, wine and coffee. He fed his horse and stalked the rows of hives. He wandered into the dying lemon grove and traversed the fallow lot which he called his pasture. In the barnlot he found his tangled harness where he'd dropped it last night, untangled it and hung it in the barn on seldom-used hooks. He gave Sal an unwonted currying, but the horse failed to enjoy it, fearing it to be the prelude to another trip.

Manuel did not go near the honey shed. At mid-morning he returned to his kitchen, drank a tumblerful of wine, and another, a third, a fourth. He asked of the acrid fluid only surcease from his debilitating melancholy, but it brought him fresh dejection, from which he took refuge in opium.

The little room was hot and stifling under its low roof, but Manuel was inured to its sultriness. He lay down on the rumpled quilts. He propped himself on one elbow and inhaled smoke from the drug which bubbled in the tiny bowl of his pipe. Stupor overtook him, making him oblivious to sorrow, regret and finally pleasant images too.

Three days he remained so. Mornings, he fed his horse, ate

a few morsels of stale food, drank deeply of the red wine, and returned to his pipe and his dreams. In his visions he beheld himself young and puissant and comely, attired in silken robes of gorgeous hues, reclining on a cushioned couch, attended by a woman of superlative beauty who was his wife and constant companion. Sometimes the woman was Julia, sometimes Anna whom he'd married in his youth, sometimes it was some other woman he had known and loved. Sometimes the woman was a lovely stranger; once it was Anna Smith. Always, whoever she was, she was beautiful beyond human beauty. She poured thick, syrupy wine from great flagons into a golden cup and held it to his lips as he drank, then kissed his lips still wet with wine.

He saw youths and maidens in abandoned dances on lawns strewn with flowers. Rose-coloured and golden clouds floated in a sky of such purple as never was. Low music from myriad strings rose and fell and sometimes faded, and a sweet contralto sang of unrequited love. Gigantic butterflies wafted now and then across his vision, blurring out the world, or alighted in grass beyond his couch to wave silken wings. Perfumes of honeysuckle and orange blossom and heliotrope and jasmine succeeded each other, each blending with the one that preceded it, the one growing stronger while the other weakened and languished. A boy, half-grown, laughed and romped naked with a young girl and made precocious love. He warmed, recognizing Jesus, the son of Manuel and already sought by the women. Other women appeared to Manuel, women different from any of those who had been espoused to him, and they freely bestowed and avidly sought his caress.

The Elysian vision altered in timelessness, sometimes vivid with reality, again hazy and indistinct, but always pleasurable. Even while he experienced its delights, Manuel knew it was a fiction, a mirage, a figment, but he chose to dwell upon it. He didn't desire the dream as much as he sought the refuge from reality, escape from his kinless, solitarity senility upon this senile farm.

The fourth morning when Manuel arose to feed his horse, he staggered, weak and exhausted. He'd eaten almost no food during his debauch, but he was not hungry. He wanted only to return to his floor-bed and his pipe.

He shuddered. From previous experiences, he knew the appetite for opium grew by what it fed on and that incredible strength of will would be required to return him to the work he'd neglected. He temporized that if he could spend one more day with his dreams of splendor, then he would be reconciled to return to reality and labour. He recognized this as a lie. Another day with the drug would demand another and another, as his will weakened. He calculated the costs of the birth of his son and the burial of his wife. He considered the rearing of the boy and estimated its expense. He shook his head, leaning for support against the stall. He must return at once to his chores with the bee-hives because he had to replace those funds he had used and to provide for the upbringing of Jesus Jose.

Reluctantly, Manuel forced himself toward the honey shed. His extraction had been interrupted just as it was begun by Julia's insistence that he leave off his work to drive her into Los Angeles. He'd hung several frames of plump honeycomb from the apiary in empty hive-boxes within the shed. Now he lifted the coverboard of a hive-box and staggered back, crying out and shaking his head. Like some terrible image from his drugged sleep, he saw the combs overspread with feasting ants. A brown thread of the vermin, coming and going, streamed across the floor to a crack through which it disappeared. Another train traced a line down the wall and across the flooring to the empty combs from which extraction had been made. In the haste of departure, Manuel had overlooked the possibility that the hateful cousins of his bees might make such inroads.

Disdaining to employ a bellows hive-smoker, Manuel packed and tamped tobacco into a pipe which he smoked only when he worked with his bees. Taking up the combs, both full and extracted, he returned them into the apiary. The season was a time when honey-bearing blossoms were rare and bees particularly militant, but Manuel, bare of hand and face, chose a hive which he knew to house a robust and active colony. He stooped over and blew long whiffs of tobacco smoke into the hive entrance and waited for the drowsy hum which betokened stupor. Then he removed the coverboard and exchanged the ant-infested frames of honey for others which were free of the pests. He went to a second hive where he withdrew full combs and replaced them with the frames of empty combs. He nodded with a savage satisfaction. His bees would destroy the ants on both the full and empty combs and they would glean the last iota of honey from those combs which had already been through the extracting machine. The old man cursed his own negligence. He should never have left those frames of honey to the pests' mercy, knowing their ubiquitous scouts must find it.

Weak and malnourished, the old man went about his labour in a sort of daze. His long experience as an apiarist guided his actions almost automatically. For this he thanked his God. He returned to the honey shed with full combs, uncapped them and put them singly into his extracting device, and doggedly turned its handle.

When he had thrown the honey from all the combs, he returned the empty frames to the hives to be cleaned by the bees and withdrew another lot of full combs. For hours he worked, stopping only to go into the kitchen for draughts of wine. He sweated, fighting the frantic urge to return to the Lethe of his pipe. He could not indulge that obsession for the drug until his whole crop of honey should be harvested and strained into those new tin receptacles stacked neatly against the walls of the shed.

The work required little conscious thought. As he spun the handle of the extractor, he relived the pleasures of his youth, built new castles in the air for occupancy of Jesus and himself. Dreaming, he refused to permit any unpleasurable experiences he had suffered to filter into his consciousness. When agreeable episodes became tinctured with anguish, he distorted his recollections to eliminate all that failed of felicity and indeed, much of the youthful rapture which bubbled up in his memory was caused by what might have been rather than by what actually had occured.

The beatitude which he projected forward for Jesus ran often into blind alleys and had to be rearranged, and he was never quite able to reconcile the course of sensuous luxury which he mapped for the boy with the priestly calling at which he aimed him. In Manuel's dreams, Jesus was able to enjoy all the revelries of youth and yet enter holy orders in ample time to redeem his own soul and his father's from purgatory or worse. Too, Manuel did not consider the priesthood to be a state of abnegation. He was aware of the vows his son would be obliged to take, but he did not regard them with great seriousness. Their violation amounted to no more than a venial offense. A priest was a go-between in his commerce with God, a being so sanctified as to be incapable of sin.

The whir of the extractor was the only noise. At long intervals a horseman or wagon might pass along the road and exchange salutations with the lonely man. Manuel sometimes spoke aloud his retrospections and his hopes, but his half-audible comments were brief. Frequently his lips moved in soliloquy without producing sound.

. . . If Julia could see my son whom all women long for! . . . Anna was more beautiful than any woman of these times. . . Jesusito will come to the rancho and we shall have everything to make him happy. . . . I must work harder and save more money that we may own all that befits my heir. . . . She begged me to come back, that one, but I never went back. . . I could have had her. She would have left him to go with me. . . . That fortune-teller said that I should live long and have a son. . . . That fortune-teller, she knew. . . .

He cut short his work early on those first days, his appetite for food reasserting itself. He built a fire in the kitchen stove, went into the barnyard and, after much difficulty chasing and heading-off a squawking hen, cornered her in Sal's stall. When he tried to wring the fowl's neck, it resisted the efforts of his wrist which already was exhausted from turning the handle of the extractor. He had to resort to a rusty hatchet. When he scalded the roaster, removed the grey-tinged white feathers and drew the viscera, the scrawny carcass was little more than a skeleton. He severed the tough joints and put the pieces upon the fire to stew. He added pods of dried red peppers, cloves of garlic, olive oil and at the right time polished rice and saffron.

By the time the dish was adequately cooked, Manuel trembled with hunger and his mouth watered in anticipation. The chicken was tough and Manuel's teeth were unsound, but he managed to tear the stringy flesh from the bones and washed it down with relish and much wine.

Stomach full, muscles exhausted, mind weary, Manuel retired to his cupboard and lay down to sound sleep. His pipe tempted him but he resisted. The drug would hinder him from the work which he had begun and was resolved to finish.

The days that followed were all alike. Honey flowed from the machine and filled the square tins. Manuel dreamed of the past and of the future. Only the page of the present was blank, a whir of a centrifugal honey-extractor. As he removed

97

the honey from the hives, he also took away the super-boxes and stacked them, each filled with frames of empty honeycomb, in the shed. The colonies, each reduced to a single box, were better fitted to endure the chill of winter.

One day Manuel discovered his larder nearly empty. He harnessed Sal to the yellow buggy and drove to the country store. Errand accomplished, he did not loiter for conversation, but returned without delay to the rancho. That night he heard rain upon his roof, the first showers of the rainy season. In the morning the glint of the sun's rays was brighter than midsummer. Summer-long incrustations of dust were washed from roof and window panes and trees and hives. Manuel imagined hints of green in the plains that lay brown and barren to the horizon.

Three more days of Manuel's labour and the honey crop was ready for market. The task completed, he felt at liberty to return to the pipe for which he had ached with longing. After supper, he cooked his opium and lay back with his ecstatic visions. The stock of the drug was low, insufficient for prolonged indulgence. Troubled, Manuel conserved it, meted it charily into his pipe-bowl, husbanding the contents of the tin like a miser as it diminished.

V

Pedro walked restlessly in the early evening darkness. Somewhere someone pounded a wailing ragtime from an ill-tuned piano. Melancholy, though he still hummed 'La Golandrina' to an accompiment of the jingling of unaccustomed gold in his pocket, he checked the sad path of the moon across a wan-lit sky. His destination was unknown even to himself, an aimless quest. He wanted to visit his family in his new-found good fortune but many months ago his kin had grown very weary of his insatiable demands for money, which he solicited as loans but forgot to repay. Ill-will crackled, a static charge in the Luiz family.

Pedro was the first-born son; Pablo, the next in line, had at last brought himself to the point of a blank refusal of a loan. Pedro thereupon threatened to reveal to Juan Sanchez what he knew of Pablo's relations with Juan's wife. Pablo laughed at him. Pablo's guilt was no greater than Pedro's own in *that* sullied nest and he persisted in his refusal, confident that his brother dared not betray him. Pedro, drinking heavily one night, did reveal to Sanchez all that he knew of the philandering of Pablo and Maria. Sanchez, after administering a sound beating to Maria, awaited that moment when he should find Pablo drunker than himself and attacked him with a four-inch knife, slashed his face clear through the cheek from ear to chin, and cut his arm so deeply that it hung useless for weeks. If the police had not interfered, Sanchez might have killed Pablo. Juan Sanchez was sentenced to jail for a long term and Pablo Luiz, after the ministrations of his wife and Dr Robles, resumed his gallantry with Maria. But Pablo could not easily forgive his brother's perfidy.

Their father, Andres Luiz, joined with Pablo in his resentment of his first-born's disservice to the family. The paternal posture determined that of his other sons. Carlos and

Cipriano and daughter Felicia, Pedro's twin, married to Luis Villareal, who disliked Pedro instinctively, sided with Pablo and stood with Andres against him. Pedro's mother withheld her opinion. The frail blind Maria Luiz' loyalty to her husband came first, but her love for her eldest son out-weighed every other consideration, even of fraternal treachery. Execrating Juan Sanchez for wreaking savage vegeance upon Pablo, she forgave Pedro the betrayal that incited the assault.

Pedro had been inspired to reveal to Sanchez the truth about Maria's philandering with Pablo not entirely because of Pablo's refusal to lend him money. Pedro raged inwardly in jealousy over the Sanchez woman's preference for Pablo's embraces over his own. He felt justified in what he had done and now he felt unfairly exiled from his family.

Recently, however, he had met and talked with the youngest brother, Cipriano, who had appeared not unfriend-ly, and he had come upon Pablo himself in a saloon and had been subjected only to a hostile stare.

Pedro stretched and flexed his muscles as he walked. He was anxious to return to the family fold. Now, with gold in his pocket and new clothes on his back, seemed an auspicious time to do this. He had no regrets for the injury he had inflicted upon his brother, but deplored the retribution the tribal animosity had brought upon himself. Without real affection for any sibling, unless perhaps some slight measure of regard for Cipriano, Pedro's gregarious urge inspired in him a desire to return home.

Pedro walked faster, still humming 'La Golandrina', going toward Aliso Street and through Aliso to the short lane in which the Luiz family lived. He heard an accordion playing 'Bedelia' and saw in the dusk that the song came from Cipriano's instrument and lips. The younger man recognized Pedro and, knowing Pedro's favourite composition, left off 'Bedelia' in mid-measure and pressed the plaintive strains of 'La Golandrina' from his accordion. The voices of the brothers mingled in the music and Pedro's heart lifted. Forgiveness was inevitable.

Cipriano sat on the steps, the blind mother sagged in an aged, carpet-covered rocking chair upon the porch. The burly Andres tipped a wicker chair against the wall. The song finished, Pedro approached his sire, lifted the labour-scarred hand to his lips. 'Buenas noches, padre mio,' Pedro said as if he had seen his father as recently as this afternoon.

Andres did not reply at once and smiling, Pedro turned to his mother, kissed her hand and then kissed her mouth. 'It is Pedro, mama mia,' he said. 'Your son Pedro.'

'Pedro! Son of my heart.' Her blind eyes filled with tears. 'I feared you would not come again.' Her faltering hands travelled up his arms to his shoulders and to his face. Her fingers explored his features and pictured on the retina of her imagination what he must look like. She smiled and nodded, pleased. Then she sighed and shook her head. 'But you come at a bad time, Pedro. There is no money in this house. Your father has none for you, nor your bothers. All have no work.'

'I need not money. I have money.' Pedro drew the coins from his pocket and let them stare at the heap upon his palm. 'I have plenty of money. Silver and gold.' He jingled the coins back into his pocket. 'Mr rich brother-in-law, he pays me for keeping his baby after his wife, the sister of my Clara, died.'

Cipriano put aside his accordion and arose. He went to his brother and embraced him, patting him on the back. 'Since you have money, brother mine, can you lend a peso then to your little brother until next week?'

Pedro nodded, smiling. 'Yes, Cipriano. Money for all. Take this peso, but don't run away to spend it with a puta so quickly. Women are free to such likely boys as you, Cipriano. A few sweet words and you can have anything you want, for nothing. . . . Stay awhile and play us music.'

Cipriano resumed his seat upon the step. He played 'Bedelia' and 'The Banks of the Wabash' and 'Creole Sue', and old Mexican airs including an interminable bawdy ballad of which he and Pedro sang alternate stanzas while the parents chuckled at the ribald words and neighbouring children gathered to listen.

Felicia came from the house next door, trailed by a girl of three and a boy of four. Pedro exchanged recent histories with the others. Pablo had abandoned his interest in Senora Sanchez. Pablo now had a new mistress. Felicia was going to have another child. Andres had suffered for weeks with rheumatism but, except for occasional shoulder-twinges in chilly weather, had almost recovered. Felicia's daughter, trailing at her skirts, suffered epilepsy. The men had but little work, Carlos an occasional job, but he spent whatever he

101

earned entirely upon wine and prostitutes. Pedro did not relish being told of Pablo's slow and difficult recovery from his injury at the hands of Sanchez, but there was no way to avoid the subject. His mother seemed determined to dwell upon it, blaming Juan Sanchez for it all.

Pedro told of the birth of Teodoro, of Manuel O'Brien and his limitless riches in the big bank on Spring Street, of Julia's death, of his arrangement with Manuel that Clara should suckle Jesus. He laughed in a cold harsh tone of irony. 'The old one believes he is the father of his Jesus.' He shook his head. 'But he is not. He has only whey in his loins. He pays me gold that my wife shall suckle my own baby.' He nodded, laughing. 'I fixed up that marriage. The old one, he cannot get a baby.'

The elder Luizes found much in this story to amuse them. Especially did it seem commendable and cunning that Pedro should have found a husband for the girl who was going to bear his child and the denouement, his receiving money for the rearing of his own child, was high comedy and doubly gratifying, first in the deception of any husband and secondly in any arrangement through which he should come cleverly by money.

Only Felicia did not join the others in laughter. Delicately-made like her mother, slender, small of hand and foot, her skin less dark and bloodlessly pallid, Felicia met so few strangers that she was shy in their presence and Pedro had been so long absent from the barrio that he was like a stranger to her. She was unheard in this barter of news except for her tubercular cough. Cipriano, full of admiration for his eldest brother, played a low accompaniment upon his accordion to the narration of events, the music muted during the preliminary recital of details and rising in crescendo to its climax, like any troubabour. The boy was eighteen and bore a strong resemblance to Pedro. The fine chiselling of his features and his lithe graze made Cipriano look as men hope angels will look. 'And you will have money all the time and no work?' Cipriano laughed. Pedro nodded. 'For a long time. Yes. Until the baby goes to the father.' Pedro sneered at that word father. 'Plenty of money,' He added. 'The Senor O'Brien is rich.'

'Why live so far from us? Why do you not stay here with your own people?' Cipriano asked.

'If I stay not with my wife while she tends O'Brien's bastard,' Pedro said, 'I get no money from the rich old miser.'

'Bring them then,' the father said. 'There is a house here vacant next to us. Seven dollars a month, but we do not always pay.'

Pedro hitched his jacket up on his shoulders. 'But Pablo. Pablo will not like it that I should come.'

'Pablo is well again and he has another woman,' Andres assured his son. 'You have the money now and Pablo will welcome you.'

Pedro nodded. He had suffered in his exile. He delighted in the companionship of his kindred, loved the scandal that he heard from them, enjoyed fraternal quarrels, reciprocated Cipriano's admiration with the nearest emotion to affection of which he was capable. 'I like not to live in a house where one has died,' he said. He nodded again and stretched. 'We come tomorrow to occupy the house.'

He walked with Cipriano to inspect the quarters. It was part of the house in which his parents lived. A long, flimsy shed of old boards, it was divided into three parts, consisting of three small rooms each. An undivided galley extended the length of the whole front. Three pairs of wobbly steps led from the street, from which the structure was removed only sufficiently to permit positioning of the steps between porch and pavement. The Villareals with their children and a boarder occupied one end apartment, Andres Luiz the other end. It was into the middle apartment that Pedro proposed to move. Carlos lived in the same part of the lane and Pablo just beyond the corner in Aliso Street.

2

The October night was languorous and warm. A wind from the south-east, together with a mackerel sky, like mother-of-pearl where the moon shot through a buttonhook cloud, threatened rain. Pedro breathed in deeply of the freshening night breeze. He now had everything which could contribute to his contentment. He was reluctant to depart from this group. He belonged among them and Pablo's anger had kept him too long away. He disliked leaving the music which

Cipriano pressed from the bellows, and yet the hour grew late and his father yawned and broke wind loudly.

At length, unwillingly, Pedro bade farewell to his parents, kissed their hands and invited Cipriano to accompany him to the nearest saloon.

Pedro exhaled heavily. The visit had been the triumph for which he had hoped. He had found his father and brothers to be unemployed and bankrupt while he had money and new clothes. He understood that mead of envy they offered up to him.

In the saloon he found nobody he knew. He and Cipriano drank their beer. Pedro sensed the boy's anxiety to be gone where the peso would buy the love of his most recent fancy. Pedro envied Cipriano the youthful zest with which he went to his amour. The quest of women palled upon Pedro. Lately he had found them all alike and he sometimes experienced difficulty in responding to their ministrations. When he had no money he went home to Clara and when he was in funds he sought variety elsewhere because it was the manly thing to do, but he was unable to summon up the avidity for that kind of adventure which he saw in Cipriano.

It had been his intention to find his pleasure outside his own house this night, and after his brother left him he strolled to the barberia where he could usually find boon companions, only to see that the place was dark. He enumerated to himself those women who would surely make him welcome, especially Mme. Rosa now that he was wealthy, but it was difficult for him to go to any of those to whom he felt himself attracted. A few years before, husbands, rivals, distance, discretion, nothing would have deterred him, as such considerations would not deter Cipriano now. Despite his pocket full of money, Pedro returned to his own home.

Clara sat up in bed when he entered the room. Although she had solicited his early return, she had not anticipated that he would come. Happy as she was at his attention, she feared he had lost his money at fan-tan or dice or some of the other games of chance he liked. She sighed heavily. 'You come so soon. Is it that you have lost again.?'

He shrugged. 'I did not play. I went to the house of my father and then I came back again.' The beating he'd administered to Clara had cleared the atmosphere of any nagging animosity they might have harboured one for the other. Clara's face was battered, swollen and discoloured, but she seemed to have forgotten his brutality. She delighted in her man's mastery over her and Pedro felt elation in his dominance as head of his house.

'But Pablo,' Clara said. 'Was Pablo there?'

'He was not there, but it is well. His wound is healed and he has a new woman. He is no longer angry. So says my father.'

She smiled and nodded, relieved. 'Then you no longer fear. You can then go often to the house of your father?'

He nodded. 'We move in the morning to the house between Felicia's and my father's. I like not to live in this house where one has died.'

'But Don Manuel. How will he know?' Clara protested. The proposal to move met with her approval. She too feared to live in a house where death had recently intruded and even more then Pedro, she relished the gregarious tribalism of the Luiz family.

Pedro shrugged. 'He will find us. He can inquire.'

3

The south-east wind failed to bring the rain it forecast. The following morning Pedro went to the Plaza where he employed the services of a decrepit wagon drawn by a grey mule, fat and weary of standing on corners awaiting employment. Pedro did not wait to consult the owner of the house before taking possession. The landlord would learn soon enough of the Luiz occupancy and come demanding the rent.

The various Luiz families in the Aliso Street barrio had been on slender rations. The feast Pedro provided to celebrate his return from exile restored him to his niche in the affection of his kin. Greasy pork in thick gravy and highly flavoured with pepper and garlic, fresh astringent wine, chicken in a sauce of chocolate, bitter coffee made from beans burned in roasting, satisfied to repletion all who partook. The only reminder of the family schism was the livid scar on Pablo's face which neither he nor Pedro chose to mention. Cipriano pressed from his accordion his entire repertoire, and whoever knew the words, English or Spanish, sang lustily. Esteban Garcia, the boarder in the Villareal household, strummed a battered guitar. The insecure flooring vibrated to the dancing, the walls rang with laughter. Julia's death was forgotten in the merriment. Even her son drank weakened wine from a soaked cloth.

Pedro Luiz was not stingy when he had money. Bankruptcy, categorical and absolute, was for Pedro the only and sufficient reason to refuse what he called a loan to anybody who asked him. He failed to comprehend any motive of hoarding for the future and when he was broke he resented the refusal of others to share their money with him in the same measure.

He found satisfaction in sharing with others on the rare occasions when his pockets were not empty. To be the liberal banker, to succumb to solicitation and dole out money to his acquaintants, gave Pedro a feeling of affluence, a sense of importance, an unction of condescension that, however hollow it might leave the bellies of his wife and children, was worth to him the amount of the outlay. His kinsmen were without work that might provide them with a livelihood, but so long as Pedro's funds lasted none needed to seek employment. And none did. The board money that Esteban Garcia paid to Felicia made work for Villareal dispensable, but when he saw with what free hand Pedro satisfied the importunings of his brothers, Felicia's husband, though he despised Pedro and always had, set Felicia to the task of obtaining a fair portion of Pedro's largesse.

To Don Andres Pedro gave from filial duty, to Pablo and Carlos to display his prosperity and the magnanimity of forgiveness for past injuries. He gave to Felicia because he didn't know how to refuse what was asked of him, but only to Cipriano, who, more than any of the others except their mother, held the eldest brother in approbation and esteem, did he offer anything resembling affection along with the handout. That the boy was so successful with women pleased Pedro; at the same time it excited within him a degree of stinging envy. Pedro stretched uncomfortably, considering. He knew in what kind of debauchery Cipriano spent his money, but too he wondered 'what the vintners buy.'

As days passed the jingle of coins in Pedro's pocket became muffled, and at length the music ceased altogether. Esteban Garcia continued to pay Felicia Villareal his board, and the whole Luiz family now crowded to her table. Felicia, however, was not cabable of miracles and there was in-sufficent food for such a multitude. Credit for any of the Luiz family had by now become difficult to obtain and Pedro's family survived on meagre rations. Esteban doled out as so-called loans the little money left of his wages after he paid Felicia. There was not by any means enough to satisfy so many borrowers.

The flow of milk from Clara's breasts dwindled with reduction of food but, true to her promise to O'Brien, she suckled Jesus before she permitted Teodoro to indulge at that fountain. Her buxom figure remained full but a languor, different from the calm habitual to Clara, evidenced the depletion of her systemic calcium. Teodoro had never been a fat baby; he had large, knobby joints and a protuberant abdomen. He grew petulant, but this failed to impress his harried mother. Teodoro had always whined and cried more than her other children. But she watched him, troubled. Already it was to be seen that Teodoro's mouth and nose were somewhat asymmetrical, the nose tilted left and this side seemed more developed than the right side of his face. His lower lip was thick and straight but the upper part of his mouth, higher on the right, was devoid of bow.

Jesus remained plump and firm. A beautiful infant, he rarely emitted a squall of anger, usually kept an even tenor of placidity, quiet as his mother had been. He was never peevish. Sometimes his face twisted in the flash of a smile which delighted Clara. How she loved this child of her sister's. Pedrillo harboured that sense of his importance in having been sent to bring the midwife for his aunt. He felt a paternal attitude towards the baby though he might have chosen a stronger one if he'd been permitted. He hovered over Jesus' pallet, lifted him up and laid him down with solicitude, renewed nappies and made himself useful. If he felt any jealousy, he was unaware of it.

After his money was exhausted Pedro stalked to the galley and watched the street daily, impatient for the return of O'Brien from whom he expected to obtain further instalments for the rearing of the child. He stretched angrily. 'I'd send the little bastard to the old miser if I had my way. Does he expect me to bring up his brat when I have not the money to feed myself and my own children? It would well serve the rich old gringo if his child should starve.'

107

'No, no, my husband.' Clara touched his arm placatingly, smiling to show him she was not opposing his will. 'Jesusito is the son of my dead sister. And Don Manuel gave much money for his rearing. We shall care for him as if he were our own.'

Pedro stared along the empty street. 'But the money is gone and yet the old miser does not return. It is to feed the bastard of the old caprino that I work and slave to earn money, while I and my own children have not enough to eat.' Though he'd neither worked a single day nor earned a peso since before Jesus was born, Pedro quarrelled daily with Clara, his animosity towards her building together with his hatred for his delinquent brother-in-law.

Clara tried to be compliant. Pedro had no intention or wish to be relieved of the O'Brien child. His protests would be as earnest as her own if Manuel should offer to take the infant away. But O'Brien's failure to fork over funds for Jesus' rearing at least as fast as the Luiz family could squander them, stirred in Pedro bitter indignation which he vented upon his wife in these petulant threats to deprive her of her dead sister's baby.

VI

When Manuel decided to return to Los Angeles, he was actuated by an urgent need to replenish the depleted fuel for his pipe. He had 'to go to the Chinaman'.

Because he was hauling a load of honey to market he would have to harness Sal to the long unused wagon in his barnyard. All summer the flatbed had furnished roosting for his chickens. He found that the incrustations of their droppings covered the bed of the cart to a depth of several inches in the middle and a foot in heaped ridges along the sideboards, as well as the hubs, shafts and seat. The summer sun and autumn rains, followed by heat in October as violent as August's, combined to agglutinate this mass solidly to the vehicle. Swearing, the old man searched through the weeds which tumbled along his barnyard fence and finally retrieved a rusty shovel, edge serrated and dull. With this implement he undertook to scrape the incrustations from the dray. Damp wedges broke away in congealed layers, but the dried offal crumbled and a powdery dust arose from it and settled on Manuel's clothes and face and in his hair and beard. His efforts to dislodge the dung disturbed families of vermin which fed upon the chickens and lived in the cracks of the van. These mites crawled infuriatingly over Manuel as he worked and sweated.

He sagged, trembling with fatigue, against the rear wheel. Cleaning the wagon had seemed to be a twenty-minute chore, but it required unrelenting hours and used up all his strength. When he could scrape no more with the shovel he got an ancient broom from the kitchen. The worn straw was bent sideways into a sort of fat crescent. He brushed and scrubbed, with little result. Weariness argued to him that he could do no more. He was dissatisfied with the state of the wagon but resigned himself to its irremediable condition.

Manuel had planned to set out for Los Angeles that morning, but by the time he had cleaned the wagon, or at least by the time he gave up trying to clean it, he was too tired to make the journey. The trip must wait for manana.

He shuffled into the house and drank tumblers of wine to relieve his bone weariness. He longed for a pipe of opium and resolved never again to permit his store of the drug to become exhausted. His need for the pipe tempted him to make the trip at once, despite his debilitating fatigue. The honey had to be loaded, however, and, somewhat rested and fortified by a demi-john of wine, he carried heavy cans of honey from shed to wagon. The path was crooked and he covered a full hundred yards with each can. Already exhausted from his labours on his wagon, Manuel found the cans of honey heavier than he remembered. After carrying four cans, one at a time, he sat down, drank off another glass of wine and tried to devise some easier method of loading the cargo. He bethought himself of the wheel barrow, but when he got it, he found its wheel was stiff and would only turn freely part of the way round. Manuel did not consider oiling it but tried to use it as it was.

He might have carried a single can at a time on the barrow and saved himself effort, but he tried to carry five cans each trip. He got the first load halfway to the wagon and concluded it was easier to carry the cans one at a time than to trundle the wretched barrow. He removed the cans and left the cart in the middle of the path where he had to walk around it on each subsequent trip. At no time did he consider moving the wagon to the shed where he might have loaded it with only a few steps for each can. He persisted doggedly at his labour, stopping frequently to sit down and drink wine. He had to climb frequently up into the wagon and arrange the cans in rows and his joints ached.

He'd run his apiary most of his life, made his harvest, transported honey to market and obtained money for it. Now, with his son to be provided for, he did not spare himself. Trip after trip he made, can after can he carried. Each can meant money in the bank, money for the rearing of his son. At length he found to his dismay that the wagon would not safely hold more cans. He stowed them in tiers as well as he could, firmly so they would not fall. One load failed to carry the entire crop. His next load would not be a full one, but it would be necessary.

Although the afternoon was not far spent, the sunshine of late autumn paled. The sky was cold green. Manuel sagged against his wagon, pleased with his day's work, but convinced now the trip must wait for tomorrow. He went into the kitchen and prepared a meal: bacon, rice with pimentoes and peppers, red wine. He ate heartily, exhausted. He felt restless. There was no opium to soothe him. Need for it oppressed him. He paced the house and brooded over the past, the present and the future. Despondent doubt, born of fatigue, assailed him and red wine failed to dispel his gloom. At last, deeply depressed, he sank upon the worn mattress on the floor of the cubicle and succumbed to troubled sleep.

2

In the chilly dawn, Manuel harnessed his horse to the wagon laden with honey and set out at a plodding pace for Los Angeles. The day promised to to one of those hazy dreamy times that for weeks on end tread constant in the California autumn. Rosa and her whelp trotted ahead. Sal had not been called upon to pull so great a load since the honey-crop of the previous year. It taxed the strength and will of the animal to drag the heavy wagon.

The night's sleep had relieved Manuel's despondency. His muscles were sore and stiff from loading the wagon, but he was no longer tired. Opium awaited his journey's end and opium, in its very truce to living, was purpose enough for life.

He went first to the commission merchant in San Pedro Street. The price was not at all to his liking, although it was greater than he had ever before been offered. He haggled and waited and threatened to go elsewhere. The merchant merely shrugged, patient. He had dealt with Senor O'Brien for many years. He smiled faintly to himself. Don Manuel would be dissatisfied with any offered price, whatever it might be; too, Manuel would haggle and threaten but he would finally accept the bid. He explained to Manuel that eastern demand for honey was down, Cuban sugar was cheap and why this affected the price of California honey, even explained that the merchant might well lose money on the transaction, that while he was desolate he was unable to offer more. The

111

merchant's explanation, Manuel's reluctance, the haggling were formulae for annual negotiations. However, Manuel was under such stress to go to the Chinaman's that he cut the transaction far shorter then usual. The honey was unloaded and weighed and the merchant's cheque passed to O'Brien, who mounted his wagon and drove to his Spring Street bank. Here, he deposited his buyer's cheque to his account and withdrew funds for his current needs.

His next stop was in the narrow alley where the Chinese opium-dealer kept shop. Here occurred the usual silent and impersonal exchange of commodity for cash. Upon a few occasions, the shop-keeper had spoken, to mention a revision of price, always upward, and, with no other protest than a shrug of his shoulders, Manuel had paid. Now when he left the shop and mounted again to his wagon, he shivered with a sense of relief. Desire for the fumes of the drug increased with his possession of the means to satisfy it.

When he arrived at the house where the Luiz family had lived he was desolated to find it occupied by strangers. Fear the Pedro had removed with Jesus somewhere Manuel would never find him seized the old man. Pain twisted his solar plexus. Sweat broke out on his forehead and his hands trembled.

The yellow woman who stood in the doorway began to shake her head as he inquired. 'Senor Luiz?' She shrugged. 'He move.' She spread her hands. 'Where, I do not know.'

Yolita, who occupied the adjacent house, she who had provided hot soup for Julia the night she'd fainted at the dog fight, came out on her porch. She recognized Manuel and was willing to supply him with information she had, but this proved scant.

Yolita waved her arm in a direction generally eastward. 'They go to live in the house beside the father of Pedro.' Again she waved her hand vaguely.

Manuel sat in his wagon, dejected. He did not trust Pedro. 'What if my son,' he thought in agony, 'prematurely born, has died?'

Yolita seemed to sense his distress. Winding her black apron about her head, she approached his wagon and smiled. 'The muchacho is well.' She nodded her head. 'Clara herself has told me this.'

'Gracias, Senora. Muchas gracias.' He bowed to Yolita and

drove to the barber's shop where Pedro had frequently hung around. He found none who knew where Pedro now lived. Directions, indefinite and conflicting, confused more than they helped him. He inquired at a saloon where Pedro sometimes drank, but with no results. Leaving Sal and his wagon at a livery stable, he walked to the Plaza in the hope of encountering his brother-in-law lounging there. He wandered among the loiterers, inquired from such men as appeared to be about Pedro's age and type. Some knew him. None knew where he lived. One gave directions to the former Luiz residence from which Manuel had just come.

Although in despair, Manuel had no intention of relinquishing his search. He was unsure, though, how to continue it. Tired and wilted by the futility of his efforts, he went into the nearest cantina and, standing at the bar, drank a glass of wine.

Glancing through the batwing doors as a stranger entered, he recognized the cat-like swing of Pedro's shoulders, his idly gliding gait passing on the path. He tossed coins on the bar and rushed through the doorway just in time to see those feline shoulders disappear around the corner. He ran, calling aloud. His breath burned in his throat, more from fear of losing Pedro than from exhaustion. He rounded the corner and overtook his man. It was not Pedro.

'Si, Senor,' the youth said. 'I am Cipriano, brother of Pedro Luiz. My brother lives by our father.' He gazed a moment at Manuel and added, 'Pedro is out of work and there is no money. The family of my brother, they starve.'

'But Jesusito? He is well?' Manuel ignored the news of Pedro's crisis.

'The infant, he is well, yes.' Cipriano nodded. As a sort of inspired afterthought, he added, 'But even the Jesusito is scrawny, like a banty chicken, Senor. He has not enough food in these times.'

Manuel's face hardened. 'But the money I left for Jesuito. Where is it?'

Cipriano shrugged. 'All is gone. My poor brother has nothing. There is no work for any of us.'

'Let us go quickly to my son. Come, take me to Pedro's house.'

Cipriano hesitated. 'It is that I cannot go now,' he said with cryptic inflection.

'Why? I must go to my son who starves.'

Cipriano sighed. 'One owes me money. He promised to meet me today to pay. I cannot go until I meet with him.'

'Then tell me where Don Pedro lives that I may go alone to my son.'

Cipriano frowned. 'It is far and I cannot explain the directions. If you will wait until I collect the money that is owed to me, then I will go to show you the right way.'

'How much are you owed?' Manuel said. To be fair to him, he doubted the youth's tale.

Cipriano scrutinized the old man, remembering all Pedro said of him with such scorn, estimating the limits of his credibility. At last he said, 'Two pesos.'

Manuel nodded. 'I give you the two pesos. Here.' He thrust coins into the youth's hand. 'Come now. Take me to the house where your brother keeps my son. We go in my wagon which is near.'

The boy pocketed the silver dollars with a moue of satisfaction. They hurried to the livery stable, where the patient Sal stood in the shafts of the wagon and mounted to the seat. Manuel drove in accord with Cipriano's guidance. This route was as devious as Cipriano could devise because he sought to justify his refusal to provide Manuel with simple directions.

In the mid-afternoon they arrived at the house of Pedro Luiz. Jazmin ambled out from beneath the stoop to sniff at the O'Brien dogs. Pedrillo recognized the wagon and ran to meet it, calling Manuel's name joyously.

Pedro reclined upon his bed, fully clothed, and twisted Duke's Mixture into a sheet of ricepaper to roll a cigarette. He rose, stretching, to his feet and embraced Manuel courteously. 'One is welcome in my home, Don Manuel,' he said.

The babies lay upon their pad. Clara was visible through a rear window where she hung nappies upon a line to dry, Conchita at her heels. Clara heard Manuel and Pedro talking and came into the house, drying her hands on her apron.

She greeted Manuel warmly. He touched her shoulder in affection and said, 'Good Clara, how is my son? He is well?'

'He is very well.' Clara nodded though Pedro scowled at her from behind Manuel's back. 'The son of my sister has good health. He gives no trouble,' Clara elaborated, to the savage dismay of her husband who stretched and frowned behind their guest. Clara stooped and took Jesus up in her arms.

Awakened abruptly from sleep and seeing the bearded face of the elderly stranger peering into his own, Jesus wrinkled his face and wailed. Clara joggled and soothed until he was still.

Manuel gazed in pride at his son. The new-born redness had disappeared and the baby's skin was translucent, mellowed ivory. Hints of carmine glowed in the cheeks, the full mouth was ruddy. Dark brown eyes, placid and sombre, glinted with tears. Pedro and Cipriano had such large eyes, so coloured, so shaped, as placid. Clara beamed proudly upon the plump baby.

'The child is thin,' Manuel said, not because it was true but because he remembered what Cipriano had told him. 'Has he had enough to eat? The milk of the good Clara flows sufficient?'

She laughed. 'It is plentiful. I have enough for yet another.' She was disappointed that Manuel should withhold his full approval of the gentle care she gave Jesus.

Pedro spoke quickly to forestall any further revelations from his wife. 'Clara could have plenty of milk if she had enough to eat. . . . She has not enough of late. . . a few beans. And the baby hungers. My wife wishes not to tell you the truth because she wishes not to give up the child and so she says that she flows enough milk. Ah, there would be enough, but there is no money and no work and she eats little. A few beans. They do not make enough milk for two babies.' He stretched his muscles fiercely.

Manuel exhaled. 'But my son must eat well. I shall pay. My son must not grow gaunt for want of food. The good Clara must eat. We all must eat. All.' He swung his arms. He drew silver from his pocket and handed it to Pedro. 'Go, amigo. Buy the food for Clara and for us all. We shall have a rich supper to sustain us. All shall come who wish.'

'Must I spend all? What must I buy?' Pedro asked.

'To the good appetite there is no stale bread.' Manuel quoted a Spanish adage.

'Meat. Let us have meat,' Pedrillo said.

'Meat,' Concha echoed her brother.

'Yes, meat,' Clara agreed. 'Or fowls.'

115

Pedro departed. Cipriano disappeared down the galley and returned with his accordion. Clara moved in and out of her kitchen in preparation for the arrival of the food. Manuel found a seat upon something which once might have been a rocking chair and from which the rockers had been removed. He sagged back, tired and hungry, but even more avid for a whiff of his pipe. He shifted his makeshift chair so that he might better gaze upon Jesus, again sleeping beside Teodoro. He felt no urge to take the baby into his arms, no wish to fondle or caress him, only to contemplate him, to satisfy himself of Jesus' wellbeing. He called questions to Clara as she came and went, all pertaining to Jesus. 'Does the little gentleman cry often?' and 'Is the little friend as large as a child of his age ought to be?' When he used terms like 'caballerito' and 'amigito', the diminutives under his inflection denoted endearment. Idle questions enough, but they served to centre his attention upon his heir.

Cipriano's accordion whined softly, an accompaniment to, but not an intrusion upon Manuel's thoughts. It was a long time since the old fellow had listened to music and Cipriano's playing buoyed and rested him. Pedrillo and Concha ran to apprise their grandparents, uncles, aunts and cousins of the feast and to summon them to be guests. They capered to the music happily.

Hours passed, light failed, yet Pedro did not return. Clara kept the kindled fire alive in the stove; all was in readiness except the viands.

Manuel bit back questions, controlling his impatience and resentment. Clara detected his displeasure, not in his words, but in his tones. She grew uneasy, not at Pedro's prolonged absence which was not new to her, but at the rising fretfulness of her guest. If Manuel saw how Pedro neglected them when there was money, would he leave his son in her care? Troubled, she urged Cipriano, 'Go to seek your brother who comes not with the victuals. Some mishap may have come upon him. Bring him with the food for our supper. Say to him that his entire family awaits, as well as his guest.'

The youth finished the refrain of 'The Message of the Violet' which he had been repeating in an effort to avoid the errors of each previous rendition. He placed his instrument in the very middle of the bed upon which he had reclined, warned Pedrillo against molesting his beloved concertina, and

116

set out in quest of his brother.

He sauntered along Aliso Street and had only turned the first corner when he encountered Pedro, empty-handed and grave. Cipriano shook his head, exhaling in wonder. 'Where has one been? Clara throws spasms. The old one is chafed. The family gathers. All are hungry. Where then is the food?'

Pedro shrugged. 'I lost,' was all he said. 'I wish not to return to the house, but at last I must face them.'

'No. No. One must not go back there without food. The old goat would be angry. He might take his child and leave no money. You must not.'

'But I have no money. No credit.'

Sighing, Cipriano produced the two pesos which Manuel had given him.

'Why did you not tell me you had money?' Pedro upbraided his brother. 'Here I starve while you jingle money. When I have money, it is yours also. But you have money while I hunger.'

Cipriano shook his head. 'I got it today from the old cuckold. Come, we must buy food. Say not that you played. You can repay tomorrow, after you have money for the bastard.'

3

Dim lights burned in an odorous little market on the opposite side of Aliso Street. The brothers entered, bought mutton shanks, cabbages, onions, wilted turnips, cornmeal, cheese enough for the entire family. Of the two dollars, ten cents remained and was used to purchase a stale candy that once had masqueraded as chocolate creams. These they divided evenly, piece by piece between them, and consumed them hurriedly before they came in sight of their home.

By the time the brothers returned the whole Luiz clan was assembled in the small apartment. The parcels they carried calmed doubts and relieved suspicions and that Pedro might have used for some other purpose the money Manuel had given him to buy food. To inquiries about his belatedness, Pedro merely stretched and shrugged and made no reply.

Excepting blind Maria, the women joined with Clara to

117

prepare the meal. Rapid-fire conversation, in which all talked and none listened, rattled from the kitchen. Maria sat in the parlour which was crowded with Luiz men, standing, sitting, crouching. Children scurried and scrambled and edged in their play among their elders.

Pedrillo remained close to his blind grandmother. He had in these weeks grown accustomed to caring for Maria and he was her favourite, partly because he was the first son of her favourite eldest and partly because of his vanity which prompted him to exchange solicitude and service for approval and praise. He stood beside Maria's chair and complacently submitted to the affectionate exploration of her blind hands over his face and person.

Pedro brought out the flagon of red wine which his house always sheltered, no matter what might be curtailed otherwise in its poverty. The pungency sharpened appetites already keen. Children begged for a gulp or two from the glasses of their elders. Maria shared her beverage generously with Pedrillo. He became exuberantly tipsy and accidentally stumbled against his sire, giggling. Pedro dealt the boy a blow which was loud in the noisy room and sent him toppling against a wall in surprise and pain.

Conversation ceased abruptly for a few seconds, but quickly resumed. The food, finally served, was plentiful. The family crowded in, tearing meat from bones and gorging stomachs that had almost disremembered repletion. Pedrillo, on the pretext of serving his grandmother, obtained more food then would otherwise have been meted out to him. The frail old woman had only a small capacity for food and the surplus of her plate fell to the lot of her favourite grandchild.

When at last the Luiz kin departed, Manuel retired to his wagon behind the house and there satisfied his passionate need for opium. The chilly night made him shiver but did not deter him or interfere with the pleasure he derived from his bubbling pipe. He sank down on the boot of the cart. The stupor of the drug and the solitary depths of sleep itself overcame him.

VII

Manuel awoke in the first light of false dawn, hours before anyone in this town family stirred from sleep. He sat up, yawning. He'd accomplished all that had brought him to Los Angeles. He had sold his honey, obtained his opium, seen his son. There was nothing to prevent his returning at once to his ranch. But the sights and sounds and smells of the city fascinated the lonely man. Being among people with whom one might converse even though one had nothing to say, the mere passing of people in a street, strangers and unknown though they might be, pleased him.

He dressed, left the silent, sleep-stunned house and strolled about the town. In cantinas near the Plaza he met old acquaintances. He wandered into an exhibition in a North Main Street store-room, where five blonde beauties disported themselves, dancing, buxom, clad only in sheer tights. He whiled away the day and as soon as dark fell, went to his wagon and smoked his opium before he went in to bed. In the following days, Cipriano found in Manuel an avid audience for his accordion. Manuel doled out money to pay for food for Clara's household and some of it trickled, either directly as coins or indirectly as food, to the various Luiz families up and down Aliso Street. Pedro considered Manuel's contributions a niggardly bounty, but withheld his comments from Manuel's hearing.

Pedrillo's honest interest in Sal, his ministrations to his blind grandmother, his solicitude for the babies, his shy friendliness towards Manuel, all combined to draw pennies, nickles and once, a quarter, from the pockets of the old man, who saw in the boy something of what he hoped Jesus should become; though, of course, Jesus was an O'Brien and in him, the last of his race, should flower all the virtues of that blood.

Clara was suckling Teodoro one morning. Manuel sat

119

gazing down at Jesus who had indulged his prior right at the flowing breast. Cipriano pressed his accordion. Pedro ambled restlessly, self-consciously about the house.

Stretching himself, he remarked 'Mme Rosa says that if I should play today at La Madreselva I should win. This is my day.'

'Mme Rosa?' O'Brien looked up, eyes glittering.

'Yes. She. The seeress. But I have no money with which to begin my fortune.' He spoke in an aggrieved tone.

'Mme Rosa?' Manuel repeated. 'Who is she?'

'She who tells the future, on Aliso Street. She knows all. She tells the gone, the now and the to-come. She tells one when to risk and win,' Pedro said.

'And she entertains men.' Clara's mouth twisted in contempt. 'She steals away the husbands of good women.'

'She has great gifts, Mme Rosa,' Pedro continued. 'Her mother was a gypsy who taught her to know all from the cards and from the hand.'

'And her father, she knows not who he may have been,' Clara said. 'And she knows not who is the father of her child. A common puta.'

'But I have not the money to follow her counsel,' Pedro said in that same aggrieved tone, ignoring his wife. 'I have not the means to risk at La Madreselva, though I am certain from Mme Rosa herself this day is mine to risk'.

The hint was ignored, but curiosity about the fortune-teller seethed in Manuel's mind. It was long since he'd had his fortune foretold. He determined he would go secretly to her. He permitted the subject to drop and then, with an assumed casualness, revived it.

'This Madam — how does one say her name?' he asked.

'Rosa,' Clara answered in contempt.

'Do you think she can foretell truly — that she really knows the to-come?' Manuel looked at his sister-in-law rather than at her husband.

'Without doubt she tells the fortune rightly. I have heard many who say this. She has special gifts,' Clara acknowledged. 'But she lures men. A special gift she has for that too. Talismans of love, she sells, but keeps the best one for herself. A puta.'

Manuel was more interested in the woman's clairvoyance than in her morals. 'Where is her house? Where does she

120

foretell?' Then he added, 'It is not that I go to her. I do not believe in such powers.'

No one, least of all Pedro, was deceived by the old fellow's apparent unconcern or by his disavowal of credence. Pedro did not reply to the questions, waiting for Clara to answer their guest. Pedro assumed no further part in the conservation but as soon as his wife had given Manuel explicit directions as to where the fortune-teller resided, Pedro roused himself, stretched vigorously, and took his hat from where it lay upon the bed.

'I have no money to hazard, but I go to watch others play, to see how much I fail to win for want of a few coins.' Pedro spoke accusingly, and departed. He turned towards Aliso Street and walked away rapidly.

Cipriano's accordion wailed a version of 'Hiawatha'. After a cogitative silence, Manuel said, 'I would not give him money with which to play just on the say of a teller of fortunes.'

'Hiawatha' came to an abrupt halt in mid-measure and Cipriano spoke solemnly. 'He would win if so the seeress says. Mme Rosa tells the fortune true. Everbody knows this. She has the gift to fore-know.'

Cipriano's profound faith in the fortune-teller's ability deepened Manuel's interest.

'She knows, but she knows too much,' Clara said, faint spots of red showing in her dark cheeks. 'She uses her philtres to lure men. She steals the husbands of virtuous women.'

Manuel sighed and seemed not to hear. Cipriano sprawled with languid grace across the bed, his arms above his head. Manuel twice cleared his throat as if to speak and then remained silent. At last, he rose and donned his hat. 'I go to meet one with whom I have business to transact.' He was aware his words failed to carry conviction. Leaving the house, he too turned toward Aliso Street.

Cipriano rose to his elbow and glanced through the window. Sinking back upon the bed, he said to Clara, 'The old one. He goes to the Mme Rosa.'

'Yes.' Clara nodded. 'But he has no wife from whom the puta may steal him. . . . For men who have no wives there must be whores.'

When Manuel reached Aliso Street he slowed his pace, looked carefully at each building, read every sign. He walked three blocks, scrutinizing each facade before he reached the saloon known as La Madreselva in a two-storey, clapboard building somewhat crooked and painted a faded blue. The corner of the lower storey was cut away to provide an entrance equally convenient to Aliso and to the side street upon which it abutted. An iron post supported the overhanging corner of the upper floor. A narrow balcony, railed with wrought-iron lace, bedaubed with vestiges of blue paint, jutted out over the path. The single window of the lower floor was quartered with sash-bars which interfered with the normal spacing of the letters, 'La Madreselva, Saloon, Cantina', painted in a flourishing script of blue with yellow shading. Through this hazy, fly-specked glass, against a background of dusty green drapery suspended from a tarnished brass pipe, could be seen time-worn chromolithographs in chipped frames, advertisements supplied by various brewers and distillers — a huntsman in red coat and top hat jumping his mount over a zigzag fence, a semi-nude woman sitting upon a globe which was circled by blue ribbon, a vivid green landscape of a crystal-clear river beside which darker green trees sheltered a vast distillery of glaringly red brick. Accumulations of dust, dotted with dead flies, covered the windowsill.

On the flank of the building opposite the side street was an uncovered stair, with unsteady railing, and weather-worn treads sadly cracked and turned up at their edges. At the foot of this stairwell was the sign he sought: 'Mme Rosa'. Beneath the script letters were pictured a rose, an open palm heavily lined and a pack of playing cards. The red rose and the red pips of the cards had faded to a frosty pink, the black outlines of the palm and the black pips had turned a rusty grey. Mme Rosa had envisaged fortunes of clients in this location for many years.

Manuel gazed for a long time at the sign and at the stairs. Then he glanced to the right and to the left, up and down Aliso Street, guiltily. He grasped the stair rail and mounted hesitantly. He paused before he knocked at the four-panelled door. He heard voices within, a man's and a woman's, but could not understand the words. His heart pounded with temerity as he knocked. The voices suddenly lowered, words rushed more rapidly, but he could not make out what was said. There was a scurry, a scuffle, the closing of a door, tones that implied anger. Manuel felt his advent inopportune and decided to go away. The door opened and it was too late to retreat.

'Good day, Senor,' the woman greeted him. 'One desires something?' Before he could reply, she answered her own question. 'Is it your fortune you seek? All of your life, past, present and future you would have me read for you from the hand and from the cards? Come in, Senor.'

Manuel went in. The room was high-ceilinged, its walls covered with faded paper depicting purple and magenta and orange morning glories climbing over a grey trellis. In one rectangular spot, probably where a picture had been removed, the colours were most vivid. A bed, spots of stain on its thin white outer cover, stood dishevelled in the corner directly across from the door. A dresser with a large mirror occupied another corner. A folding table with a crystal ball and a pack of cards upon it, and a low willow rocking chair behind it, stood near a window. A brass chandelier for gas hung from the centre of the ceiling, one of its arms surmounted by a Welsbach burner, the other two supporting shades of ground glass, one of them cracked. A bleached blonde lady of well-nourished proportions but anaemic flesh tones stared out from a hangar of an advertising calendar of the year before last, askew between the windows. A bird-cage suspended upon a spring from a hook in the ceiling confined a yellow-green and black canary, which filled the room with raucous trill.

The woman who admitted Senor O'Brien was Mme Rosa herself, amiable, gracious, serene. Her skirt of brown woollen material was fitted to the contours of her hips, augmented with a bustle. The hem reached the floor in front and lay in a train behind. Slightly rusty at the seams, a trifle threadbare on one elbow of its long tight sleeves, a blouse of black taffeta silk closely enwrapped her tightly corseted body. The tight, stiff collar carried points that rested behind the base of her ears. Around her neck hung a double strand of amber-coloured glass beads. At the base of her collar glittered a sunburst brooch of glass brilliants. Over her left breast dangled from a pin fleur-de-lis of gold a thick watch with a plethora of birds and flowers in the design of its gold-plated case. Her fingers gleamed with rings of garnet and of turquoise. Back combs with rows of red jewels held her black hair which rose in a great roll from her forehead to a complicatedly woven knob held in place on her crown with many large tortoiseshell hairpins. Mme Rosa was maybe twenty-five, certainly less than thirty. Tiny pits from smallpox marred the otherwise smooth skin of her face. Her cheeks bore heavy spots of rouge, sharply defined, unblended at their edges. Her mouth was large, her teeth sound, her black eyes quick, searching, animated, but benignant and deep with native kindliness. A heavy lily-like perfume exuded from her.

She drew a chair in front of the folding table, asked Manuel to seat himself, and retired to the low willow rocking chair where the light glowed behind her. 'You desire a full reading, Senor?'

He nodded. 'I wish to know all. Past. Present. The to-come. You charge how much?'

'For full reading, one peso, Senor.'

Manuel produced the silver coin. She took the money absently and secreted it upon her person, but appeared to be absorbed in study of her client. 'It is not that you are Spanish,' she murmured at last. 'You are something else; maybe Irish?'

'Yes. I am Irish.' Manuel was pleased and gratified at her discernment and more than a little flattered. 'But I speak the Spanish a little. My grandfather, he was Irish.'

Mme Rosa took up the cards. Thick, worn edges made them difficult to shuffle. She laid them before Manuel, asked him to cut them into three talons. Taking up one of the talons, she looked at it, smiled wisely, placed it back whence she had taken it, examined it, examined the second, nodded her head in approval and changed it for the third.

'You have luck, Senor. You are blessed with good luck.' She went back to the first talon. She spoke rapidly, animatedly, giving Manuel no opportunity to comment upon what she told him. 'You are fortunate, Senor. Many women seek your love. You have always been pleasing to women. A woman, a blonde woman, secretly loves you, but she is not to be trusted. The cards do not say why, just that she is not to be trusted. You are married, no. You are a single man. A

124

bachelor — no, not a bachelor, a widower. Your wife is dead, a dark woman, a good woman who loved you. And you are very lonely. You need one to love.'

Mme Rosa raised her eyes from the cards and looked coyly into the old man's eyes where she saw, not the glitter of adventure that had marked his expression upon his arrival, not a disposition for amour, but a rapt fixity upon the cards and the fortune unfolding from them. The woman saw how credulity gripped him and resumed, 'Your children, they also are dead, all dead. . . .'

She watched his expression, but before he could speak, she resumed, 'All dead, but one.' His face subsided into a satisfied conviction and he nodded, a scarcely perceptible movement of assent. She went on, 'But your son — your baby son from the dark woman who loved you — your son is delicate, too early born.'

'The cards say that?' Manuel stared at her in amazement.

She nodded with a sad smile. 'Yes, Senor. Too early born. You do not keep the boy with you. He stays with his kin, with his kind uncle. Leave the boy with his uncle and he will live and thrive. The uncle is poor, but he takes care of the baby. The aunt is a wet-nurse for your son, but the poor uncle has not money that his wife may eat enough. You must give money to the uncle that the child may thrive.

'It is that you are not poor and that you get more money, much more money. I see money coming to you by water. It seems that it is not from over water but it comes to you in great waves. And it is not water, but something that flows thick and turgid.'

'Honey,' the old man murmured as one talking in a dream.

She nodded. 'Yes. Honey perhaps. You will make much money from thick honey. You must give to your son's uncle. The uncle is lucky at play. This is his lucky time. You must give him money to gamble so that he can feed his wife who suckles your son. Leave the son with the uncle long time and give freely that your son may have luck.'

The fortune-teller dismissed the subject of the child and began to tell Manuel of his own affairs. 'Many women love, but —'

'But my son. Tell me about my son. Will he live and be for the Church?'

'That I cannot tell. It is not for your fortune. It would be in the fortune of the child, not of the father.'

'But can you tell his fortune, the fortune of one so young?'

'But yes. To be sure, Senor. He will have to come.'

Manuel nodded, face glowing. 'I shall bring him when you have finished my fortune.'

'You command the love of women, but the joys of love have gone from you. The wolf loses his teeth but not the inclination to feed. You require an amulet.' Raising her voice, she called, 'Paca. Paquita, bring to your mama the box with the amulets.'

'Yes, my mama,' a child's voice replied from another room. The door opened and a four-year-old girl entered, bearing a pasteboard box which she placed upon the table before the woman.

The child's skin was lighter than the mother's but her hair and eyes were equally black. The unmistakable resemblance was heightened by daubs of rouge upon the small cheeks. The repectful dignity of the child's pace seemed to hold in rein an impulse to break into extravagantly graceful dance. As decorous as her manner was, it seemed to conceal puckish gaiety.

'My daughter,' Mme Rosa said. 'Kiss the hand of the senor, Francisca.' When the child bashfully obeyed and when Manuel had stroked her hair with a phrase of admiration, the mother said, 'Now go to the other room that I may finish with the fortune of the senor.'

The child obeyed but when she went through the doorway, she turned. 'Mama, Don Pedro desires that you should hasten. He needs to go away soon.'

Mme Rosa stiffened, her face growing pallid. She observed the interest her child's remark aroused in her client, but such embarrassment as she may have felt did not betray itself in her manner. 'Go,' she said, 'and tell that great tomcat of yours, Don Pedro, that he is not to leave until I have given him his saucer of milk. Go quickly. Go.'

When Francisca had vanished, her mother hastened to explain. 'The little daughter of mine talks to her great tomcat as if he were a person and believes in her imagination that Don Pedro talks with her.' Then, lest Manuel seek to unravel the fabrication, she resumed the subject of the amulet. 'Now here is a luck piece such as my kindred in Spain, the gypsies there, employ to make one puissant in love. To the ageing it

126

restores the vitality of youth with all its amorous delights. It is magical, it is warranted to bring passion surging like the tides within him who wears it on a ribbon near the heart. It is warranted.' The woman forced the tiny silver disk with cryptic designs upon it into the man's unresisting hand. Manuel continued to glance warily from time to time toward the closed door through which the child had gone. Mme Rosa sought to focus his desire upon the amulet. 'It is warranted,' she continued, 'it is used by the gypsies. It cannot fail. Two dollars for the joventud. It is cheap, very cheap for the old man beloved of many women.'

Sighing, Manuel produced the coins to repurchase his spent youth. Mme Rosa inserted a cord into a hole that pierced the amulet and strung the bauble around Manuel's scrawny neck. In the process of loosening the yellow kerchief which Manuel wore around his neck that the amulet might hang beneath his clothes it was necessary to remove the ten-dollar gold-piece pin which held it. Mme Rosa fumbled, dropped the pin to the floor, and awkwardly attempted to kick it under the dresser. Manuel glimpsed the manoeuvre, rose from his chair and recovered his pin. He placed it in his pocket instead of in the cravat.

'How careless I am,' she said. 'My interest was in the amulet and in the youthful vigour which it will restore to the senor.'

He shrugged, ignoring her attempt to sequester his pin.

'And the palm.' Mme Rosa changed the subject, turning his hand palm up on the table before her, holding it lightly and stroking it gently. 'We now read the fortune from the hand.'

This she proceeded to do, flattering him. The hand confirmed the message of the cards. Long life ahead, unexpected wealth, a serious illness in the past, perhaps something like smallpox; a son who, if he lived, should be a holy priest and whose survival depended upon the father's generosity toward the child's uncle who sacrificed so much for the beloved child and who was lucky at dice. All this she read in his hand.

Setting forth this halcyon future, Mme Rosa stroked and patted the weatherbeaten little hand; she crowded Manuel in his chair that she might share it. At length she slipped her arm around his waist and brought her head, heavy with the scent of lilies, provocatively close to his.

127

Manuel warily felt in the pocket where he had secreted the pin and, finding it safe, disengaged himself from her cloying embrace. 'Wait, Senora. Wait until I have for a while worn the amulet.' He rose to depart.

'The fortune of the Senor is rose-coloured, truly. He must come again to obtain his fortune and to see the fortune-teller who knows many ways to please him. He must bring his son, destined for holy orders, that he may know what the future holds, that he may know how to avoid misfortune.'

O'Brien promised to fetch his son immediately and as he went out of the door, called back, 'Forget not the saucer of milk for Don Pedro.'

3

Rosa stiffened, taken aback for the instant. Had her client credited her story of the tomcat? She stood unmoving, listening to O'Brien's footsteps on the rickety stair, and then she threw open the door to where Pedro Luiz sat, tired with waiting and consumed with jealousy. His voice raged at her. 'Is it that you chose to make love with the old miser that you force me to wait kicking my heels?'

'It is nothing,' she replied. 'The old one left money, and comes again for the fortune of his son. One needs money for herself and her child, one must do what one must.'

'Money.' He wiped the back of his hand across his mouth. 'A woman loves any old cadaver who shows money. I'll cut the throat of the old bastard that comes up here with his money to buy my whore away from me. Me, I love you, and I do not endure — '

'So, so, my Pedro, my beloved Pedrito.' She smiled and stroked his face with her lily-scented fingers. 'It was not I, but you yourself who prompted him to come and it was you yourself who decreed that I should take his money and that I should say in his fortune that you are lucky at play and that he should give you wherewith to throw.' She fondled and touched him. 'But you should not make the child here interrupt me with your messages when I tell the fortune of the aged stranger. The tomcat almost caused me to fail to sell the amulet, and I fear yet the old one did not believe.'

Pedro stretched and gestured savagely. 'But his fortune took long, and the love you wasted upon such an old one because he is rich. If, as the cards declare, this is my lucky day to play, it is needful that I begin. Give me the money you took from the old miser and I go to play downstairs at La Madreselva.'

She stood straight, her face cold. 'Ah no, my Pedro. You must get the money to play from the senor. I need my money to feed myself and my Paca.'

He stared at her, impatient. 'But it is just for the hour. No more. I return quickly and I bring your money, doubled, trebled, many times increased. You have said. It is my lucky day, I need money now.'

'One dollar then,' she offered. 'The others I keep for food.'

'No.' Pedro's cheeks were pallid. 'Two dollars.'

She shook her head. 'But one, take it and be pleased, my Pedro.'

'Give me two dollars.' His voice rasped and he bent over her, his fists clenched.

'But, Pedro. My baby must eat.'

'Then give it all to me. You will not be fair and give half. I take it all. I win with it at La Madreselva and give it back to you again. Eh?' He walked toward the dresser where he knew she kept her money when she had any. She ran and placed herself between him and the dresser. Her eyes glittered with anger. Her child clung to her skirt, screaming. Pedro grasped Rosa's arm and flung her away, half across the room. He opened the drawer and took the money. Pocketing the coins, he grinned wolfishly and stretched his muscles. 'You will have more. The old goat will come again for the fortune of his bastard. Take from him what you will. Read in the cards that the uncle must rear up the child and that the old one must give much money to the uncle.'

Rosa ran to him and grasped his arm. 'Have the kindness. Return me my money. Give back my money. Some of my money. Please.'

'Nothing.' Pedro shook his head. 'I win with it.' He embraced and kissed her roughly, then flung her off and departed.

4

Mme Rosa stood unmoving in the shadowed room. She heard Pedro's steps as he descended the stairs. She walked tiredly out upon her balcony, leaned over its railing and watched coldly as he entered the saloon. Then she sighed and went back into her reception room and seated herself in the low willow rocking chair, dejected. Little Francisca amused herself with a one-legged doll upon the floor where a rectangle of sunshine fell through the window and lengthened as the afternoon waned. At length the dispirited woman reassembled the worn cards that were scattered upon the table. She shuffled and cut them and read her own fortune.

She told her fortune once, but it fell not to her liking, depressing her more. She was in the act of shuffling the cards to read her fate again when she heard footsteps upon the stairs. She set the cards aside, rose and looked at herself in the dresser mirror, adjusted a hairpin, pinched a bit of lint from her skirt.

'Go quickly into the other room,' Rosa told Francisca. 'Wait and be very quiet. It is the old senor of our Pedro who desires the fortune of his son.'

The child took up her doll and reluctantly retreated. She held the door slightly ajar in order to obtain a glimpse of the caller. She was as amazed as her mother to see there were four guests rather than the two anticipated. Clara had refused to permit Manuel to take Jesus away from her to learn his destiny from Mme Rosa. After a long argument, which involved impugnment of the seeress' chastity and disbelief of her auguries, Senora Luiz at length consented to accompany Senor O'Brien in taking the child to the sybil. Clara was hotly curious to see Mme Rosa and her exotic quarters. All during her argument there was hidden in a cranny of her mind the need to see the famous puta in her lair.

Pedrillo was the fourth member of the expedition, as chaperone for his mother and as bearer of the child Jesus in his arms.

Manuel had requested that Jesus be decked in the starched habiliments of his christening, including ring and necklace and brooch. Clara, as a protest against making the trip at all and as display of her contempt for the woman she visited, did

130

not change by so much as the readjustment of a button the solid loose wrapper of calico she had worn all day, through the folds of which it was apparent she was once more with child.

Mme Rosa smiled graciously. 'Ah, Senor, you have returned. And with you the good aunt of your son, eh?' She welcomed them into the room. Clara entered, looking around, scarcely breathing. 'And the strong lad who carries the son. How beautiful a baby. How like his father! How beautiful the clothes he wears.'

As the party entered the reception room, Francisca quietly closed the inner door, but not until Pedrillo's eyes had met hers.

Mme Rosa extended her arms to Jesusito. 'Come, chicito, come that I may find a fine destiny for you in the cards.'

Clara took the child and held it close, refusing to relinquish it. The situation was not without embarrassment for Mme Rosa and Senor O'Brien, but Senora Luiz was tranquil, simply refusing to surrender the baby. 'You need not touch the child to read its fortune.'

While Mme Rosa shuffled the cards, Pedrillo stood, wide-eyed, beside his mother's chair. 'It is needful that the little one touch the cards which his father cuts for him,' the seeress said. Clara hesitated and Mme Rosa shoved the three talons towards the side of the table. 'It is needful, else his fortune will not be his own.'

Clara took Jesus' small right hand in her own and touched each pile of cards with it. Mme Rosa nodded and O'Brien exhaled loudly.

The fortune of the child as revealed by the cards was a hopeful one, full of messages and riches and the passionate devotion of hosts of women. It assured the child to be fated for a profession in some unnamed holy cause. The ointment was not without its fly. The child was delicate, too early born, subject to many ills. If he was to live to enjoy the rosy future the cards promised, he must be given care and sustenance beyond the usual. Such care should be supplied only by his good uncle, his godfather and by his good aunt, his godmother. These two were now very poor and to them funds for the care of Jesus must be generously provided. Mme Rosa smiled in congratulation at the child's rich destiny. She moved around the table and fell upon her knees in order to examine the little palm, which, in the main, confirmed the promise of the cards. It was most difficult to read the lines in so undeveloped a hand; the child should be returned to her a few months later when the hand was more completely outlined but, even so, wealth and women were seen to be in his future, as were the poor, generous uncle's requirements of a liberal allowance with which to rear the babe.

Mme Rosa then sat for a long time and would not speak until her clients insisted. The palm revealed one devastating circumstance which the cards had not: Jesus was associated with somebody who had an evil eye, somebody very close to him, somebody in the very family where he lived.

This information left O'Brien shaken with consternation. He threw at his sister-in-law a look of accusation. The child should be removed immediately from such baleful inflence, he declared. Clara sat stunned at this ugly development.

Mme Rosa took the complacent baby into her own arms and Clara was too shocked to protest. The blame she took for the evil eye in her family and the blame Manuel attached to her, forestalled any objection she might have made.

'The bad eye, it is a terrible thing to have upon one,' Mme Rosa said. 'But to run from the situation is not the answer. There are charms against the evil eye. I have charms, such as the gypsies use in Spain, which if one wear, the bad eye cannot touch one.' As when she'd told Manuel's fortune, she raised her voice: 'Paca, oh, Pacquita. Bring the box with the amulets.'

Francisca came, bearing the same pasteboard box from which her mother a short two hours earlier had sold to Manuel the amulet of love. The little girl stared in fascination at the baby in her mother's arms. She held out the box toward her mother at the same time as she squatted down, better to see the infant. She released her hold on the box before her mother grasped it. The box overturned and amulets scattered over the floor.

'Descuidada.' Mme Rosa's scolding voice lashed out and she slapped the small painted face. 'Spilling many charms over the floor. Pick them up, every one.'

Francisca crawled on the floor to retrieve the tiny silver disks, tears welling from her eyes. Pedrillo joined in the search, bashful, inarticulate. Two amulets had rolled under the bed and the boy wriggled on his belly to retrieve them. One, however, he put in his pocket instead of returning it to the box.

Mme Rosa did not know how many amulets she had, but she counted in a pretence of making sure all had been recovered. 'They are valuable,' she said, 'and it is that I cannot afford to lose any. . . . Now, this charm is against the evil eye.' She seemed to choose it at random from the box. 'My own nation, the gypsies of Spain, they warrant this charm. Who wears it the evil eye cannot touch. You must buy it for the very little one here, for he is in much danger from one near him.'

'How much?' Manuel bent forward, anxious.

'The same price as the other,' Mme Rosa answered.

Clara scowled, uncomprehendingly. 'The other?'

Manuel glared at the fortune-teller, whose smile held the hint of a giggle. 'Yes,' the seeress said. 'The other. The one I sold to the senor this afternoon, the one that serves to — what is it to do, Senor? Oh, yes, it is to make his bee-hives yield much honey. Eh, Senor? Two dollars, very cheap for a charm so potent.'

'Is much,' Clara said.

Manuel paid for the charm and for the fortune. Mme Rosa turned away and tucked the coins deep inside her bodice.

Francisca remained in the room, her interest divided between the baby in her mother's arms and the bashful boy beside Clara's chair. The little girl would have liked to converse with him if only she'd known what to say or how to say it. Instead of speaking, she pretended to confine her attention to the infant, but when she was sure adult eyes were looking elsewhere, she made a face at Pedrillo. Shocked, he turned away from her grimaces but rolled his eyes back so as to miss none of them.

Mme Rosa noted only the gaze her daughter fixed upon the baby and failed to see her wry glances at the boy, at once insult and invitation. 'Is he not sweet, Pacquita?' She placed her arm about her daughter. 'And has he not fine clothes? See his fine jewels, his breast-pin, and the tiny ring for his small finger. And now he has the amulet which will protect him from the evil eye.' She raised Jesus' hand and extended it towards Francisca, adding, 'Observe the tiny hand that holds so grand a fortune which I today have read for him. As the palm grows, the fortune grows, and the good cavalier, the father of the tiny one, will have his fortune read often. Do

133

you wish, my little daughter, to kiss the small mouth of the sweet baby?'

Francisca glanced into Clara's eyes and into Manuel's and then bent over the baby and kissed him. 'Is he not sweet?' her mother said.

'Yes, little mama,' the child answered and made another secret grimace at Pedrillo. 'What is his name?'

Mme Rosa raised her eyes to Manuel in pantomimic repetition of the child's query. Manuel answered proudly. 'Jesus Jose O'Brien.'

'Is it not a sweet name?' Mme Rosa smiled all round. 'He is to be for the Church and will sing the holy Mass. Little Jesus, Paquita, has no mama. His mama is dead and he lives in the house of his generous uncle, to whom the father gives freely of much money that Jesus may be fed.'

'You mean Don Pedro? Our Don Pedro?' Francisca asked innocently. She had heard enough of her mother's conversations with Pedro Luiz to understand these circumstances.

'No. No.' Her mother spoke almost gutturally, shaking her head. 'Have you no sense? The great cat, our Don Pedro, has nothing to do with the matter. Why do you always talk of the great cat? Go now. Go quickly into the other room.'

Paca realized from the agitation in her mother's voice that she had made a serious error. She was reluctant to leave the room, fascinated as she was by the baby in her mother's arms and by the sad eyes of the boy who stood behind his mother's chair and whose mouth twisted into embarrassed smiles when their eyes met. 'May I not kiss the tiny one before I must go?' she asked.

'Yes.' Her mother nodded. 'Kiss the tiny one, but then go, and speak no more of the great cat.'

The girl embraced the baby, hugged him fiercely and planted her kiss upon his mouth with such ardour that the complacent Jesus wailed in protest.

'Go now,' Mme Rosa ordered. 'Go into the room and wait, and think no more of the great cat.'

'But, Mama, it is that our cat has gone,' Francisca said.

Mme Rosa waved her arm. 'Our cat has run away, but he will return. Go now. No more words.'

The child lagged towards the door to the other room where she turned and smiled bashfully at Pedrillo. At that instant the outer door was thrown open and Pedro burst in, almost sobbing. 'Rosita. I lose. I lose all.'

'Senor!' Mme Rosa cried, shaking her head at him helplessly.

'My husband.' Clara leapt to her feet, trembling.

Manuel peered at his distracted brother-in-law but remained silent.

'Our Don Pedro. Our Don Pedro has returned!' Paca exulted, rushing to him and embracing his legs.

Pedro staggered as if struck abruptly. He appraised the situation, shook off the child and summoned his anger before Clara could attack him. 'What is this?' he said. 'What do you go to do that you go ambling about with this man, this miser, this goat, whose bastard you suckle? What do you make that you go to fortune-tellers to waste my good money that you could use to buy food for us who starve?'

Clara straightened, hands on hips. 'And you, my husband, why do you come to this place?'

Pedro made a sharp downward cutting gesture. 'I come to tell the whore of a fortune-teller that I lose. She tell me it is my lucky day to play at La Madreselva, and I lose. I lose all.'

Clara's voice lashed at him bitterly. 'Always it is that you go to many women and never that you stay with the wife whom you marry. Always that you seek whores and waste your money.' Her eyes filled with tears but she held her head high and would not cry. 'Don Pedro, a tomcat. Don Pedro is my husband, whom you seduce away from me, whom you would have for yourself to love and work for you with his weak back and to lay out the money he earns upon you and your bastard girl-child whose father none knows.' Pedro tried to speak, but Clara heeled around, facing him in her heartbreak and rage. 'Play. Play. Always you play. Always you lose. Always La Madreselva gets all your money. And then you come to this place of this whore intead of coming home to your family. Where do you get money today to play at La Madreselva? Eh? In the morning you have nothing. In the afternoon, you lose what you have. And then you come here to —'

'It is enough, Clara.' Pedro's voice hardened. 'The senora here who expounds the fortune tells me that my lucky day has arrived and that I must play to win much. I borrow the money and I play, but I lose all. I come back to tell the senora that her fortune is wrong, that her cards lie. I come only to speak about the cards, and I find you here with the old man, you who should remain at home to care for my house, to rear my children. I find you traipsing around with the old miser of a gringo who seeks the fortune of the little abortion of which he imagines himself the father.' Pedro laughed savagely. 'The old son of a sow, I'll kill the old goat of a gringo who goes to steal my woman from me.'

Pedro rushed toward Manuel, but Mme Rosa tossed, rather than laid, Jesus upon the bed and threw herself between the men, shaking her head, her voice rising. 'No. No. No. Do not harm the old man, Don Pedro. The old senor gives you money to play. This is your lucky day. You are lucky yet though you lose a little. Take the senor's money that he gives you willingly and play. Hurt not the old senor. Take his money. The cards say it is your lucky day.'

Pedro yielded to the woman's pleading and her logic. He had no real intention of harming Manuel; he was raging against the luck that destroyed him in the gambling room and this display of indignation not only checkmated Clara's reproaches but restored to him some of the self-pride that his bad luck had cost him. Mme Rosa made sense talking of more coins with which to further test at La Madreselva the winning streak she had foretold for him.

Manuel crouched in his chair. There was always in Manuel's face the look of one about to be struck with a stick. He was genuinely frightened now. His face twisted, gnome-like, and his eyes glittered with apprehension for himself and for his son who wept upon the bed.

Pedro stood over him. 'Give me money to play then. Give me money to play and I overlook the ill that you have done to me. Give me money.'

Manuel pushed his hand into his pocket. He produced two silver dollars and a five-dollar gold-piece. He studied the coins, undecided as to whether the silver would satisfy his brother-in-law. At last, he chose the gold-piece and extended it. Pedro took it and threw it indignantly onto the floor.

He shook his head, sweating with rage. 'No. I want money to play. Five pesos is nothing. Caramba. I want real money to play. This is my lucky day. The senora's cards foretell good fortune for me if I have money to play. Five pesos. I spit on five pesos.'

Before Manuel undertook to revise his offer, he stooped to recover the coin Pedro had thrown away. Pedrillo, diving at

136

the same time, butted the old man's head and they staggered but kept grasping for the money. The boy's hand closed first upon the gold-piece. He rose, rubbing his head and stifling his impluse to weep. He extended the money courteously toward Manuel. But Pedro was more agile than O'Brien and before the old man could take the coin, Pedro grabbed the boy by the shoulder, turned him and jerked the gold-piece from his palm.

'Give it to me,' he said. 'Is it that you did not see the senor give it to me before? Did you not see me drop it?'

Pedrillo nodded and retreated to the other side of Clara who had gone to the bed to succor the crying Jesus.

With the money in hand, Pedro heeled back to face Manuel. 'Give more, old goat. Give me enough that I may cast the dice boldly on this, my day of fortunate chance.' When Manuel did not comply swiftly enough to please him, Pedro doubled his fist threateningly. 'Else, you can take your brat to some other man's wife to nurse for you. It is my lucky day, and if I have not the money to cast the dice, you can let the milk of another feed your bastard, not the milk of my woman. And it will go hard with him. The cards of Mme Rosa have spoken. Take your bastard away. Take him elsewhere. I care not where.'

Though he believed the threats baseless, Manuel shivered, empty-bellied. Except for the two silver dollars, useless for this purpose, Manuel's smallest coin was a ten-dollar piece. God knew he was reluctant to add it to the five Pedro already had. He gazed at Pedro's face and finally shrugged. 'Here, then. Take this ten dollars to play and give back to me the five dollars which you already have.'

Pedro took the ten but refused to return the five. 'Give back? Give back nothing. As it is, it is hardly enough to test my fortune on my day of luck. If I should fail to win, it will be because I have not enough to cast with assurance. If I had much money — a rancho and many hives of bees to make great cans of honey, if I had much money in the great bank on Spring Street and could have any amount only for the asking, I should give freely, to my kin, to the husband of the wife who suckles my child on his day of good fortune according to the cards of Mme Rosa. A mere fifteen pesos — it is not enough, but it must serve.'

He thrust the coins into the pocket of the suit Manuel had

137

given him the day he stood godfather to Jesus. He jingled the money, ill-concealing his satisfaction. He made an immediate exit. They heard the clatter of his boots on the steps as he hurried. He was unaccustomed to going downstairs in such haste. They heard a crash, a yell of anguish, loud and raucous curses. Pedro's heel had caught in one of the warped treads and he had plunged headlong to the ground.

'It is Pedro, my husband Pedro,' Clara cried. 'He has fallen. He is hurt. It comes of visiting the whore. Do something. Help my husband.' Unable to move, she remained beside the bed on which Jesus lay.

Mme Rosa rushed to the door and down the steps. By the time Clara reached the landing, she saw the woman on the path below with Pedro in her arms. Manuel ran out onto the balcony. Clara hastened as best she could down the stairwell.

'Let go, let go,' Clara raged. 'Do not embrace my husband, puta. He is mine. He is not yours.' When she neared the foot of the stair and saw blood streaked on Pedro's face, she screamed. 'He is hurt, he is killed. Oh, Pedro. My Pedrito, my husband, my man, my beloved.' She flung herself to the path and her arms encircled the injured man, wrenching him from the seeress. With her elbow she struck Mme Rosa. 'Go, puta,' she wept. 'He is mine, my husband. Go, you who would steal men from honest women. Go. Leave me with the man who is my own. But for you, but for coming to your dirty place, this had not occured. Pedro, beloved, are you dead?' With her sleeve, she wiped blood from his face.

Manuel leaned over the railing of the balcony, calling down to her. 'Is it that he has lost the money from his pocket? Look for the money.'

Men came out from La Madreselva and stood in a circle. They chuckled and made remarks about Pedro's wife having caught him with Mme Rosa.

Unmoving, Pedro continued to curse. He cursed Manuel for a miser. He cursed Mme Rosa, cursed her stair. He cursed Pedrillo whose tears of fright annoyed him, cursed Clara for having accompanied Manuel, cursed Jesus, the cause of the entire catastrophe. It was a sustained and able effort. He remained prostrate, Clara kneeling to embrace him.

He rose to his knee, extracted a sliver of wood partially buried in his palm, rubbed his hands together, finding them bruised and burned. He brushed at his clothes briefly, felt his knees, from one of which dangled a V-shaped tear in his trousers. Standing, he realized that his ankle was sprained. He pushed Clara away and took a few tentative limping steps. Then he remembered his coins. He thrust his hand into his pocket. They were safe. Jingling them, he hobbled away towards the door of La Madreselva.

Pausing at the doorway, he turned and shouted over his shoulder to Clara. 'Go home, go home and remain. You are my wife, and you are not to serve the wishes of the old gringo goat, the old miser. Go home, I say.'

Clara glanced up the steps to the landing where little Francisca stood holding Jesus in her arms. Clara threw up her arms, crying out. 'Oh! Care. Care. Do not drop the baby. Senor, Senor, bring down your child. Can you not see him in the arms of one too young? Use care. Use care.' She stood helplessly at the foot of the steps.

Mme Rosa took the baby from the arms of her small daughter and brought him down the steps. Pedrillo met her halfway and accompanied her the remainder of the way down to the path. Last came Manuel.

Clara took Jesus in her arms and walked away without any formality of parting. Pedrillo, at her heels, turned to wave an adieu to the little girl on the landing at the top of the stair. Francisca stuck out her tongue. Mme Rosa murmured to Manuel, 'Come again. Come often for the fortune of the young caballerito. As he grows, so grows his fortune. Come often and see to it that he wears the charm against the bad eye.'

VIII

Manuel returned with Clara to her home, his brain awhirl in total credence of Mme Rosa's decrees anent the future of Jesus. Arriving at the house, he began immediately to search for the owner of the evil eye.

With an elaborate casualness and much smiling, he peered with surreptitious suspicion at Cipriano. The youth had remained with Concha and Teodoro during their mother's absence. When the party returned, Cipriano roused himself from half-sleep on the bed. After determined but stealthy examination, Manuel sighed. If the evil eye was Cipriano's it manifested itself only in a brilliant dark beauty and the shade of lazy lashes.

Manuel examined the children more openly. Seating himself in the low chair bereft of its rockers, he called them separately to him. He grasped them by the shoulders, turned them precisely so the light shone directly into their eyes, and inspected them minutely. Failing to find the evidence he sought, he manipulated their lids with his fingers, searching for something sinister that might be hidden. Concha was delighted with the importance of being suspected. She squirmed and giggled in embarrassed satisfaction during the ordeal. Pedrillo had heard enough of the evil eye to comprehend how serious was the accusation against him. He stood in rigid, silent protest while the old man fingered his lids.

'Have I the evil, Don Manuel?' he said. 'Am I the one then who casts the bad eye on little Jesus?' When acquitted, he ran to Clara. 'It is not I, Mamacita, who looks with the bad eye on the son of the senor.'

Pedrillo wandered about the apartment, preoccupied, searching. At length in the rear of the house he found a soiled snarl of used string which he untangled and threaded through

140

the eyelet in the amulet he had stolen from Mme Rosa. He suspended the charm around his neck and poked it down under his clothes: Pedrillo, too, was safe from the gaze of the ogre.

Jesus lay beside Teodoro on the common pad upon the floor. It was with the ostensible purpose of fondling his son the Manuel knelt beside them. He straightened the rumpled dress; he lifted the tiny hand, turning the ring so that the turquoise should be best displayed; he felt through the clothes to be sure the amulet was in its place, he brushed the fine black hair back from the baby's brow. But it was not at Jesus that he looked. He gazed all this time at Teodoro and it was in his eye that he found the threat he dreaded. Teodoro's pupils were not concentric with their irises, but were placed somewhat lower than normal.

Scarcely breathing, Manuel remained crouched, cold to the marrow of his bones. He had never been sufficiently interested in Clara's younger son to note this malformation. Now when he saw it, it appeared to him as weird, haunted. It fascinated him, drew him, hypnotized him. He was unable to remove his eyes from the baby's. At first he believed the pupils to be narrow, cat-like. He could not formulate in his mind exactly what was wrong. The expression was strange and Manuel could see after all that his diagnosis was wrong. He looked into the normal eyes of Jesus for comparison. Finally, he detected wherein lay the aberration. That he could not keep his own gaze long from the disquieting eyes of the child frightened him. He took refuge in the sign of the cross.

Struggling upright from the kneeling position and rubbing his thighs to erase the twinges from his muscles, he announced, 'That which I sought is here! It is the Teodoro who possesses the evil eye! It is he who looks upon my son with the vile glance! Look and you shall see for yourself. It is he!'

Clara, angered and frightened, came from the kitchen and gathered her baby into her arms. 'No.' She shook her head. 'No, Senor, you err. You lie. It is not my son who has the bad eye.'

'Look,' was Manuel's terse answer. Again he crossed himself.

Pedrillo came across the room to inspect his brother. He felt beneath his shirt to be sure his charm was in place.

Clara gazed into Teodoro's beloved little face. 'I see nothing. Nada.'

'Look close,' Manuel ordered her. 'See you not that the black of his eye is not in its centre? Look.'

Clara kissed her baby, shaking her head. 'It is nothing. It cannot be. He has not the bad eyes.'

Manuel turned to Cipriano and urged him to look. Cipriano shook his head. 'I covet not to see.' The tone of his voice was like muted strings. He crossed himself, gathered his hat and accordion and departed.

Manuel's voice quavered. 'It is as Mme Rosa declared: my son is exposed to the noxious glance. How propitious is it that I brought him to the wizardess and that I bought for him the charm against the banal gaze of one who sleeps beside him, shares his bed, and might, but for the little disk, conjure his life from him, conjure his spotless soul to very hell.'

Clara's confidence weakened. She crossed herself, the while protesting the child's innocence. 'It is nothing. It is only that he looks so. I myself have seen the evil eye, and it is not like this, Senor. Teodoro has it not. It is only that the black spot is low.'

'It is the bad eyes. That is all.' There was finality to Manuel's pronouncement. He resumed his low chair to await dinner. 'Take care that my Jesus wears always the charm — always.'

The meal, which was soon ready, was consumed in silence. Cipriano did not return for his portion. Pedro, in funds, was not expected. After dinner, Manuel fed his horse and stood while Jazmin disputed for meagre viands with Rosa and her unnamed son.

They retired early. Clara and her children lay down upon the floor. Manuel smoked his pipe in the kitchen and at length went to bed. Still, Pedro did not return.

Manuel stared into the darkness. He had, despite the threat of Teodoro's evil eye, enjoyed his stay in the city. It had been a pleasant relief from the monotony of the ranch.

They slept late, waking to find that Pedro had not come home during the night. His absence caused Clara no real distress. She was so inured to the vagaries of his habits that his night-long absence stirred little anxiety for his safety, no doubts of his constant inconstancy.

Cipriano, cautious of Teodoro's evil eye, did not come to

the house of his brother. At midday, Clara went next door to take broth to the blind Maria. There she encountered Cipriano and from him heard tidings of her husband. Pedro had played again at La Madreselva, Cipriano reported, had lost, was penniless. The stake with which Manuel had supplied him had gone the invariable way of all Pedro's moneys.

Clara sighed. She had no true conception of the magnitude of the sum Pedro had gambled away. She thought of the things fifteen dollars would buy for her and her children. It seemed a vast fortune — food, clothes for the young, a carpet for her parlour, a new stove. None of Clara's wants amounted to a cost as great as the amount Pedro had lost; the dissipated funds were sufficient to have satisfied all her longings.

Clara laid the blame for the squandering of the money not upon Pedro, but upon Mme Rosa. Repressed wrath seethed within Clara's breast. This gaudy fortune-teller, this whore, so ran Clara's animosity, induced Pedro to play. The woman's auguries had failed; her magic was but fraud. But for her, Pedro would have brought his money home to spend upon the needs of his children. Clara did not bother considering that, but for Mme Rosa's professional advice, Manuel would not have given Pedro the money at all.

Clara was too shaken with rage to waste time on logic. She blamed this whore for seducing Pedro away from her, a part of her gypsy magic. That the other woman achieved Pedro's affections without any suspicion of magic was beside the point. And Teododo's eyes. More work of the foul slut. That the child's pupils were set low in their irises signified nothing, nothing at all. It was not the evil eye.

Clara shuddered and crossed herself in suspicious fear that the woman might be right after all. But for Mme Rosa this distress and breach in her family would never have arisen. She was to blame for all of Clara's woes, she, Mme Rosa, the puta who crouched like a painted spider upstairs over the cantina, La Madreselva, lying in wait for innocent men. As Clara recounted her sorrows to her mother-in-law and to Cipriano, and especially as those two sought to disparage her charges and minimize her adversities, her indignation mounted.

Maria drank her broth from the bowl in which Clara had taken it to her, but she received it with no particular evidence of gratitude. Clara smelled meat and heard the kettle gurgling

143

in the kitchen. She went out and lifted the pot cover. She had not been mistaken; the kitchen of Andres Luiz was well-stocked with food. Returning to the parlour she saw that Cipriano wore new yellow shoes but she made no mention of them.

At length Clara broached the subject. 'Is it that you have money?'

Maria shook her head. 'No, no. One gives credit to my husband that we may eat. One has compassion.' She crossed herself.

'And el joven, is it that he owns shoes of new, bright leather?'

'No? I do not know.' Maria shrugged. 'I cannot see them.'

'My novia, she gives them to me.' Cipriano offered a specious explanation. He rose to leave to avoid further discussion. As he crossed the floor the squeak of the new shoes did not drown what Clara was sure was the jingle of coins in his pocket. Clara drew a deep breath and held it. She did not believe their tales. She felt her mind whirling with the deceptions and evil charging the atmosphere around her. Sickness churned in her stomach.

Clara returned to her own home along the porch that spread across the front of the three domiciles. She pondered this prosperity she observed at her in-laws' house. It accentuated her own sense of poverty and loss, for which she reproached Mme Rosa. Her ire spread like fire inside her.

2

When she related to Manuel the news she'd received of Pedro, the old man determined to return at once to his ranch. If Pedro came back broke, he would demand more money. That Manuel was to return in a few days to bring to market the remainer of his honey-crop dulled his ache of reluctance to depart. He did not fancy the loneliness that faced him. The opium he was taking with him provided the only solace in the dismal prospect.

He ate his dinner, harnessed Sal to his wagon, called his dogs, was ready to set out. He gave funds to Clara for her sustenance, admonishing her to spend the money upon food for herself to the end that Jesus should be nourished. He cautioned her about the charm, warning her that the child should never be without it, that he be shielded always, always from the malignance of his cousin's glance. His words stirred the embers of Clara's outrage at the fortune-teller's evil, but she remained coldly silent, trembling inwardly.

Manuel climbed up to the driver's place on the weather-worn wagon. Pedrillo and Concha came racing along the street where they'd been playing with Carlos' children, anxious to witness the departure. Sal between shafts gave a fillip to their imaginations, brought dreams of voyages, far into strange territory, to the elegant rancho of their Tio Manuel, or to Mexico whence Maria Luiz had come in her girlhood; such dreams as others conjure of coral isles and palm-fringed reefs when they watched tramp steamers putting out to sea.

'Adios. Adios, Tio mio! Come soon to see thy son Jesus,' they called to the old man. Food was always sufficient when Manuel was a guest in the Luiz house. Manuel took up the reins, then put them down again.

'Good Clara, sister of my Julia, permit it that your son accompany me. Let me take Pedrillo. I shall return him safe to you in a few days,' Manuel begged, dread of the threatened solitude overwhelming him.

As soon as his astonishment at his uncle's suggestion subsided, the boy nodded and his eyes shone with joy. He tugged at his mother's skirt. 'Permit it, permit it, Mamacita, good mamacita, permit. Permit that I go with my good uncle who requests it. I go to be very good. Mamacita, permit it.'

Senora Luiz, after some argument, gave niggardly consent. Preparations for the boy's visit were unnecessary. He scrambled up the wheels and onto the seat beside his uncle, impatient to be gone lest his mother withdraw her permission. When Sal rallied his energy and the vehicle moved away, Clara and Concha and Jazmin stood and watched it until it had turned the corner of Aliso Street.

Concha returned to play with her cousins and Clara went into her house. Her resentment toward Mme Rosa did not subside. She cleared away the soiled dishes, she suckled the babies with anger-tainted milk. She resolved upon action.

She walked into the kitchen and took up the large stiff-bladed knife which she used in the preparation of food.

145

Though dulled and nicked from years of use, it was a formidable weapon in the hand of one with strength enough to wield it. Clara's mouth twisted. She was no weakling.

She took the knife to the rear of the house and whetted it for a long time upon a flat rock under a stunted tree. Whether the knife-edge was sharpened or blunted by the stone, Clara's resolve became keener with every stroke. She knew what she would do. She knew what she had to do. She concealed the great knife beneath the folds of her skirt and set out to search for her antagonist.

Hers was the air of a crusader. Righteous fury became her and she strode with the grace of justice.

She climbed the dilapidated stair that led to Mme Rosa's quarters with hasteless aplomb. Her knock upon the door was forthright, no tapping, no doubts, no indecision. No one answered.

Shocked, Clara knocked again, then pounded. She grasped the knob and shook it until the frame itself trembled. Still no one came. She turned the knob. The door toppled open. An instant of doubt assailed Clara, but only an instant. She entered the hateful apartment. Nobody was in the room.

She spoke in a dead flat tone of challenge. 'You. Puta. Where do you hide, whore? You who steal men from honest wives, I go to kill you, kill you that you die. You who rob decent women of men, come forth. Come forth, dirty whore. Come forth that I may kill you with the great knife.' She held the weapon aloft in her fist. 'No more shall you tempt men to throw the dice and lose their hard-earned money. No more shall you say it is their day of luck when it is their day of adversity. I go to kill you that you shall die. You who tell lies and sell your useless charms against the evil eye, you shall not live. To say that my son, who lies innocent in his bed, possesses the evil glances, it suffices only that you die.'

Clara paced agitated through Mme Rosa's quarters and ranted her paean of retributive justice. Long after she had searched the place and finally convinced herself that the woman was not at home, she continued her malediction, spicing it with every vituperative term in her idiom.

At last, she sagged wearily. Her invective spent itself but she remained standing in the middle of the room holding the knife. The outer door stood open. She heard steps upon the stair. Her victim was returning. Resolved upon murder, she felt no murderous rage. Her fevered words had cooled her wrath. She had come to kill and kill she would, but now no mad fury ordered death. Calm justice guided her knife.

The footsteps on the stair drew nearer. Pedro Luiz stood in the doorway. Clara stared at him. Her upraised hand relaxed its grasp. the knife clattered to the floor.

'What is it that you go to do now?' her husband demanded. 'Why do you not stay at home which is the place for the woman? It is the old one. He teaches you to abandon your place, to go to meddle where it does not concern you.'

Clara stared at him, defiant. 'I go to kill her, the whore who steals my man, who tempts him to play that he may lose, who maligns my son and says his glance is cursed.'

'Kill?' He stared at her. 'Nada. Nada. Go home. Go home to your duty.'

Pedro's hand lashed out and burned her cheek with a slap. He grasped her arm and held her while he dealt violent blows upon her buttocks. His doubled fist bruised the flesh beneath her eye. That this woman was with child did not restrain him. A sense of power, a feeling of mastery, a realization of dominance surged through the man and prompted the beating. His anger was spurious, it did not gush from his heart. He was in a mood too gay for anger, a mood even of generosity, because coins weighted his pockets. He had not lost at La Madreselva; he had won, won handsomely.

He escorted Clara roughly down the steps. 'Go to my house. Stay there.'

Mme Rosa, followed by Paca, approached in the street, but Clara feigned not to see her and walked meekly, battered and bleeding, in the direction of home. Pedro entered the saloon. Mme Rosa mounted her stair.

The beatings Pedro Luiz gave his wife always revived such affection as he had for her and, after a short interval, he emerged from La Madreselva and turned homeward. The Luiz families of the neighbourhood gathered that night at his table and ate to repletion, drank deep of new wine, and danced to the music of Cipriano's accordion and Esteban Garcia's guitar. Pedro scattered lavish largesse among his kin and his ego fattened.

IX

Within a week O'Brien returned to Los Angeles with the remainder of his honey-crop, bringing Pedrillo with him. The boy proudly held the reins over the great horse and clutched the unused olive branch in his fist. He had scampered unrestrained on the ranchito, had been stung by bees and nursed the injury with prideful care, had helped in loading of the honey, but for all the novel experiences he had enjoyed, he had suffered from loneliness. The old man's taciturnity chastened him. He had roamed joyously with Rosa and her son. He had eaten with relish and slept with a kind of ardour. But he longed for home, for street noises in the strange quiet nights, for the shoutings of kindred souls, for his mother, for the babies. He was ebullient in the joy of his return.

Manuel transacted his business in the city and with little delay returned to his home, taking with him an ample supply of his drug. In the weeks that followed he put his apiary in order. In due time the air was redolent of citrus bloom and bees, dusty with yellow pollen, returned to their hives with nectar.

The rains ceased. Green hillsides burned brown. At intervals Manuel jogged in the carriage behind Sal to Los Angeles to see his son and to go to the Chinaman.

Clara's child, a girl, was born, only to die the same day. Teodoro walked precocoiously and later began to use words, chattering. Jesus, however, was supine and languid at an age when he might have been expected to walk and talk. As Teodoro grew older the strange placement of his pupils was more noticeable, and Cipriano crossed himself whenever he looked at his nephew.

Felicia's cough worsened and she was frequently forced to keep to her bed. Pedro's stomach gave him concern, burning with acids, and he consumed various different brands of patent medicines. He also complained of his back and Clara

148

was effusive in sympathy and massaged his muscles often and uncomplainingly.

The honey ripened in the comb. Once more Manuel garnered his harvest and sold it. He continued to supply money to Pedro Luiz who squandered more of it upon gambling and women than he used on the child for whose sustenance it was intended. As often as Manuel came to town he repaired without delay to Mme Rosa, often taking his son with him, to ascertain what the future held in store for them. Upon each visit, that lady embellished her tale with such garnish as might induce the old fellow to continue his patronage. Particularly, she urged him to leave his son with Pedro's wife and to subsidize generously the boy's maintenance, knowing that at least a part of the money Pedro received would find its way into her dresser drawer.

Manuel continued to wear the amulet warranted to restore his youth and enable him to enjoy those numerous loves which, according to the madame, stayed upon his requital. That its potency did not manifest itself failed to prompt the old fellow to put it aside: he had ceased to expect results from it, but wearing it had become a habit. Jesus' charm against the evil eye of his cousin, however, proved entirely efficacious. Clara saw to it that the talisman was at all times about the small neck and Pedrillo was sedulous in his wearing of the charm he had filched from Mme Rosa, which also evinced its powers.

No longer did any doubts persist of the evil influence of Teodoro's misshapen eyes. While his mother remained steadfast in her hatred for the woman who had revealed her son so terribly afflicted, her silence on the subject only confirmed her credence. The adversities, evils, afflictions, ills, and troubles which beset all who came near Teodoro, excepting the protected Jesus and Pedrillo, confirmed the hardening suspicion. The family fortunes had not worsened since Teodoro had arrived to share them, but his evil eye provided convenient excuse for whatever mischances — and they were numerous — lighted on the Luiz house.

This visual deviation from the norm did not make the little boy's visage more unpleasant. It added a piquancy, an interest to a face that, even with normal eyes, would not have been pretty. The abnormal eyes arrested attention, held it until one analyzed the defect and determined what produced the peculiar aspect in the sunny, smiling face. It was elusive. On seeing him one was aware something was wrong with the eyes; it was a short step then to realizing how brilliant the seeress was who first revealed the distortion.

His nonconcentric pupils and irises inspired in the neighbourhood a sullen fear of Teodoro, and fear grew into hatred. Parents warned their children of his malevolence. Adults themselves avoided his presence. As the child grew old enough to play on the porches and paths, passers-by got into the nervous habit of watching for him and walking on the opposite side of the street so as to evade his glances. To spit or to make the sign of the cross was the accepted method of counteracting the effects of the evil eye, but one could never be certain when one might have wandered unwittingly within its range and it was easy to omit the protective rites.

Clara did her maternal duty by her afflicted son, but even she kept as much away from him as possible. This was difficult because Teodoro was a loving and outgoing child who adored people, and worshipped his mother. Clara's affection for him was perhaps even greater than it might have been if fear of him had not caused others to shun him. Her own misgivings were such that she chose not to have him about her more than was necessary. Pedrillo vaunted his immunity to his brother's evil eye. The elder Pedro refused to sleep in the room with his son. Teodoro was relegated to a bed upon the floor in the kitchen. The father cuffed and scolded and threatened the child as often as it came in his presence. The boy learned to stay clear of his sire. Cipriano's music penetrated the walls of the triple house, but its maker came no more to his brother's quarters to play upon his accordion.

Mme Rosa had for sale plenty of her charms to avert the ills, but their cost was prohibitive. Pedro bought one for himself on credit but when he lost the tiny disk, Mme Rosa refused to let him have another without cash in hand.

Jesus in those first two years was not an exceptional child but for the symmetry of his face and body, and this beauty attracted scant notice. Nor did his tardiness to walk and to speak excite comment, although it was foiled by the amazing precocity of his slightly older cousin. Teodoro strung his Spanish words into sentences before Jesus could utter more than a single, uncertain syllables to designate the members of the household. To him, Pedrillo, his favourite, was Driyo.

Teodoro walked and ran and stopped and rose with fine agility while Jesus was able only to hitch himself across the floor to where Jazmin slept in a spot of sunlight, there to snooze beside her and wallow in the warm rays. The bitch resented with snarls the not always painless attentions from the older children but to Jesus' approach she never failed to bang a welcome with her tail upon the floor. Her grimed hide served as pillow for the child and for hours these two would sleep together, changing positions only to follow the patch of sunlight.

As Jesus grew older he developed the dreamy air of his mother, an appearance of gravity, of benevolent disdain for others. As Julia had before him, he seemed content to dwell in a serene, placid and languid world of his own. In the caresses of Pedrillo and of Jazmin he took undisguised delight, and of attention from one or the other he was never long in want. There were no strangers in his existence. To anybody at all his lustrous black eyes would vouchsafe a momentary smile but immediately he would drift away to that tranquil dignity that was not to be disturbed. He ate what was given to him — all of it — but demanded no more. He slept so much that his aunt suspected him of ill-health. He played and wrestled with the dogs. At the sound of Cipriano's accordion, whatever the tune, through the thin partition, Jesus' face would flare with pleasure and his arm would move as if in an effort to beat the time. At Pedrillo's approach he reached out in an appeal to be taken into the older boy's arms, there to snuggle in a sort of beatification. For the rest he seemed to spend his days musing upon remote wonders of remote worlds. At the cutting of his teeth he clung to Pedrillo who was devoted to him and patient with him. He whimpered when his friend abandoned him, but it was a whimper of pain and not of petulance. Otherwise he seldom cried at all. He accepted what was given him, asked for nothing more, seemed to comprehend the position of sufferance he occupied in the household and to emit unspoken gratitude for the tolerance accorded him. Never was a toddler less trouble. He grew steadily, his muscles were firm and strong, quite firm and strong enough to protect him from the active, petulant, vindictive and mischievous cousin of the evil eye.

2

The winter when Jesus was two years old was an ill-fated time for Pedro Luiz. The dice proved fickle; a rival supplanted him in the quarters and favours of his mistress; Clara announced herself again with child; he was worsted in another bloody fight with Pablo and spent a night in jail. His stomach tormented him, rejected food and burned and gnawed until he prowled the floor in pain. Shortly after Christmas a feverish cold confined him to his home and for two days to his bed. His temper seethed with his misfortunes. Peevish and irritable, he reproached the world for his adversity, but particularly faulted the members of his own household, above all Teodoro of the evil eye.

Clara submitted to such chastisement as he saw fit to inflict upon her and made only feeble protest when he abused her children, but she defended Jesus with a loud and bitter virulence, threatened to have Manuel take the child away which would abolish Pedro's chief source of revenue, and herself accepted the beating the baby might have received. Concha escaped with comparative immunity. Pedrillo suffered slaps and whippings and revilings and curses. But upon Teodoro his father's spleen found daily vent, and the small posterior stung and glowed with the unbridled spankings which the man laid upon it. The child could not learn to keep out of Pedro's way. Pedro watched warily for the child's eyes to rest upon him for even an instant, wereupon he would seize the little fellow, throw him over his knee and paddle his bottom until the child's hysterical screams ebbed into muffled sobs. Teodoro failed to understand that his glance was a menace.

But if Teodoro smarted most frequently, Pedrillo suffered most severely. While Pedro was ill one night, he exhausted his wine. Racked with fever, his stomach afire with explosions of pain, he could not sleep without wine, and there was no money. Accordingly, he selected Carlos as the brother most likely to succumb to solicitation and sent his eldest son for what he chose to call a loan of the wine jug. The boy went sleepily into the night. The father waited hopefully and, when the messenger did not return, cursed and whined in complaint. At length he dispatched Clara to seek the boy and as she opened the front door, Pedrillo was coming up the steps. The abrupt opening of the door, the sudden blinding light in his eyes, disconcerted the lad and he dropped the wine jug. Marked with an old crack, the jug struck the wooden porch and fell into halves, the wine spilling in great pools which trickled away.

Pedrillo wept and his mother tried to comfort him. 'It imports nothing, Pedrillo. You could not help it. Do not weep. Do not bother,' she said.

Pedro sensed the catastrophe. He sprang from his bed, furious, his illness forgotten. 'Imports nothing? Not bother? My wine — spilt, ruined, lost! The little son of a bitch wished it. He planned it. He shall suffer. Come in here, come in.' The invitation was unnecessary, inasmuch as he already had the boy by the shoulder and was dragging him through the door. Pedrillo was yelling and Jazmin snarled and barked loudly. This incensed Pedro more. 'I'll teach you. Spill my wine. Deprive me when I am sick of that which would cure my pain. I'll teach you. Denude yourself. Strip off your clothes. Now. At once.' Nor were these admonitions necessary either, since Pedro was jerking at buttons and ripping away the boy's clothing.

The boy wailed in terror and trembled so badly that he was small assistance in his undressing. The few garments tore and ripped as Pedro roughly snatched them from his son's body.

Pedro saw the charm which hung on a string around the naked boy's neck. He had never before known Pedrillo had such an amulet. 'Ho!' he cried. 'You. A charm. A charm against the eye. You? I, head of the house, I who need it, have not the charm against my ill luck. You will suffer, with or without a charm. The charm is mine. Give it to me.' He grabbed the disk, the string broke, the charm bounced across the room, never to be found. Pedro was mindless in wrath.

Pedrillo stood before his sire, naked, trembling — not from cold because the winter night was warm with a gentle rain, but trembling from fear of what was about to befall him. Clara wept in impotent sympathy for her son.

Pedro looked about wildly but could find nothing with which to belabour the boy who stood with arms extended to ward off the blows he knew were to light upon him. The thin covering of his chest revealed his ribs. 'No. Don't. Don't whip me. Father mine, don't. I didn't mean to spill it. I won't spill it

153

next time. Don't, padre mio.'

Pedro, unconciliated, sat on the bed and pulled the child to him. He threw the boy face down and slapped and pummeled him. Patches of fiery red glowed on the olive skin of Pedrillo's back and buttocks and thighs. A punch in the ribs sent the boy spinning and his arm, unprotected, struck the father in the face. Pedro saw this as resistance which he would not tolerate. He leapt to his feet, seized a chair on which a rung hung loose. He wrenched the bar free and belaboured Pedrillo with it. He pulled the boy upright. The blows from the inflexible chair-rung fell upon the child's back and arms with dull thuds, upon his thighs and calves, upon his ribs and buttocks. Pedro clasped him by the arm or by the neck while he rained this torture upon him.

Pedrillo's wild screams rent the house, wails of terror, howls, outcries, groans, sighs, whimpers, sobs. As the beating continued, the cries subsided. They became mere voiceless heavings. The child could make no more noise. He was stupefied with pain. His tears would no longer flow. He sank, a dead weight in his sire's hand.

Pedro released his grasp and the child crumpled to the floor. Pedro was tired from his exertion. He cast aside the chair-rung. 'Now go,' his voice was hoarse from weariness. 'Get out. Go.' The boy peered up at him questioningly. 'Go,' Pedro said again, his voice hardening. 'Bastard. Son of a bitch. Go. Get out.' When Pedrillo remained unmoving, he grasped the boy again and Pedrillo, in fear of further beating, wailed. Pedro dragged him across the floor, shoved him outside, and closed the door. There was no key; he braced the door with a chair so the boy could not return.

'He is not mine. Not mine, the bastard, the small son of a bitch. He is not mine. He shall not return. And now I have no wine and none to lend me wine. I who am sick, I must sleep without wine. And my stomach, aye God, how it burns.'

On the porch, the naked boy knocked and pounded and begged and called, pleading for permission to return into the house. The night was not cold but, after the heat of his terror and pummeling, Pedrillo shivered. He felt no shame in his nakedness, but it was night and he didn't know where to go. He heard Clara begging Pedro to permit their son to return. His heart leaped and then sank at Pedro's adamant refusal. His muscles ached and burned. He was sore all over and cold.

He crept along the veranda to the door of his grandfather's house. He turned the knob, opened the door, and entered. The place was dark, everyone asleep, accustomed to riotous noises from Pedro's domicile.

'Grandmother mine,' Pedrillo called in a muffled tone. 'Cannot I come to bed with you? My father has put me out and will not permit me to return. Take me to sleep here, Grandmother mine.'

Neither Maria nor Andres heard him. His plaintive supplications were muffled by fear and even by a suppressed hope they might not be heard so that he might remain overnight in his grandparents' house without having his presence recognized. The fury of the beating he'd absorbed convinced him that his transgression justified the punishment he'd received, and he was by no means certain his grandparents would see fit to condone its enormity by receiving him in their house and bed. He was tired, totally exhausted, defeated and without will. His bones and joints ached. His bruised muscles throbbed, and he was cold. Cipriano's bed was empty and the boy crawled against it. He saw it not so much as a place of rest as of refuge. To rise was painful, to push his naked, chilled body between the soiled warm blankets cost aching effort. It was not a soft bed, but to Pedrillo it was soft, so downy that it gave him a sinking sensation as he relaxed in it. His head ached with a renewed fury in contrast with the comfort of the pillow upon which it rested. Pedrillo felt himself tentatively, the muscles of his thighs, calves, belly, to ascertain how sore they were.

The beating taught Pedrillo nothing, not even to hate the man from whom he derived life and name. His offense was not premeditated; he didn't even charge it to carelessness. It was a crime which must be paid for and he had paid, was paying. He grew warmer. Stretching his limbs sent a twinge all through his flesh. He released the tensions and slept.

Pedrillo out of his way, Pedro confronted Clara. 'Find the charm.' When she stared uncomprehendingly, he cursed her. 'Yes. The charm from the neck of the rascal boy, the charm that protects from the bad eye of the one who sleeps in the kitchen. I, I go to wear it on my own neck.'

Pedro returned to his bed while his wife got on her hands and knees to search for the amulet. The direction it had bounded, the corner of the room toward which it rolled was known only to Pedro. Clara searched diligently, afraid to admit she could not find it. Her thoughts were less upon the amulet than upon her son, sore, naked and cold, she knew not where. But Pedro swore and threatened and commanded from the bed. Clara continued to search.

At last, Pedro said, 'But the son of the old gringo goat, he has a charm against the eye?'

'Yes, my husband. But the father has ordered —'

'The father be damned. Get the charm for me. You will find the other tomorrow and can place it on the neck of the O'Brien bastard. Get it. I go to protect myself. Get it.'

Clara obeyed. She knelt beside Jesus' pad and with a dull knife sawed the cord that secured his amulet. She brought the disk to Pedro. With a new cord the man suspended it over his own breast.

The scowl lightened on his face. 'Now, I shall not fear the eye of the brat. Now will my fortunes change.' Appeased, tired, satisfied, he slept.

Clara put out the light. Cautiously, lest she waken Pedro, she moved the chair which braced the door and went out. Her son was not on the porch. No hat upon her head, nor shawl about her shoulders, she descended the steps to the street. She was unaware that the rain wet her, only that somewhere it was wetting Pedrillo. She felt no chill herself, but shivered that her naked boy was abroad in this night. She walked the streets, distracted, searching, hoping. Behind buildings, in doorways, empty packing-boxes, under porches, in vacant rooms, she searched. That the child might have sought shelter in the home of his kin did not occur to her. She hurried, searching, retraced her steps, rechecking the same buildings, rooms, boxes, porches and doorways, again and yet again. Her desperation became an agony, her quest became a mania. She could think of nothing except that Pedrillo was naked, wet and cold. She sensed the soreness of his bruises: she had been beaten by those same merciless fists, and Pedrillo was only a child. She pictured broken limbs and torn ligaments. She thought of seeking aid and abandoned the idea in the same instant. Resolute, distracted, feverish, mad, she walked the night streets.

Somewhat after midnight Cipriano returned home. It was still raining and his clothes were damp. He doffed them in the dark, used the thunder chamber, and got into bed. He all but lay down on Pedrillo, but the boy did not waken. Cipriano sat up, shaken, certain there was a corpse in his bed. He grasped the child's arm and shook him, then recognized him in the hazy dark. Pedrillo only groaned from bottomless sleep. The uncle did not comprehend the reason for the boy's being in his bed, pondered a moment, shrugged and settled himself comfortably beside the lad. He draped an arm around the warm inert body, drew it to him and dropped into sleep.

3

Clara searched until dawn. She returned home bedraggled, her clothing soaked, disheartened.

Pedro arose in an amiable mood. His fever had broken and his cold was improved. He dressed, fingering his amulet with satisfaction. He caught Teodoro in his arms and dandled him. The child, who had learned to fear his sire's hands, screamed in terror. Pedro only laughed. Protected by the amulet he did not fear.

Pedrillo returned furtively. He kissed his father's hand as always. His joints were stiff, his muscles twinged, his battered skin was discoloured. He harboured no resentment. He put on his clothes and Clara gave him breakfast. Pedro departed for those haunts from which his illness had exiled him. Clara, in reaction to her anxiety, first clutched Pedrillo against her full breast and then reproved him for his absense. They sought vainly for the lost amulet and, without its protection, Pedrillo avoided his brother.

Pedro approached La Cantina La Madreselva but stopped outside its door, suffused with a sudden murderous jealousy. He watched Jose Gonzales emerge from Mme Rosa's door and descend her stair, the same Jose Gonzales whose burnished eyes had quickened Julia O'Brien's pulses in her girlhood. Pedro held no delusions that Mme Rosa's favours were solely his own; they were purchasable by any and all who had funds and passions. Pedro remembered Julia's fondness for Jose; he had sensed it sometimes at the very height of his own dalliance with her. He had only to mention Jose's name at moments of passion to rouse Julia to even greater heights of response. Damn her, how jealous he had

157

been. Now, seeing Jose come from the quarters of another of his women, the old jealousy flared, renewed and mindless. He was furious that Mme Rosa had been entertaining, not moneyed strangers, but this particular hombre during the absence that illness had forced upon him. Gonzales strode into La Madreselva, a cock of the walk swagger in his fluid movements. Pedro followed him.

Jose ordered a glass of wine at the bar. He greeted Luiz affably but casually. 'Good days, cavalier.'

Pedro was obsessed with the need for vengence, but he hesitated. He needed greater strength than the fever had left him if he were going to fight this man. He thought better of revenge, grunted, 'Buenas dias, caballero,' and passed to the rear of the saloon.

He did not loiter there. As soon as he could leave without his purpose to escape becoming evident, he returned to the front of the cantina, leaned for a moment upon the bar, gazing out of the window, then departed.

He crossed the front of the building and climbed the stairs to Mme Rosa's quarters. The woman heard him coming and emerged from the rear room as he threw open the door.

'Goddamn puta,' he greeted her, showing his white teeth in a snarl. 'You go to hold the night with Jose Gonzales. You know I hate this goat. I'll find him and I'll kill him. What do you mean that you sleep the night with him?'

'Jose Gonzales?' She shrugged, her face bland in its innocence. 'Jose Gonzales does not come here. I have not seen Jose Gonzales. You do me wrong, beloved one.'

'You son of a bitch of a bastard whore, you lie to me, you lie to me. I see Jose Gonzales go down those stairs and enter La Madreselva. I go to kill him. I kill him. You lie.'

He had reconsidered attacking Gonzales in his present state of weakness, but he could handle Rosa despite his debilitating illness. He grabbed her and slapped her back and forth across her face and pummelled her breasts with his fist and struck her low in the abdomen as it was his habit to slap and beat Clara. He cursed and vilified her to the limits of his vocabulary.

The noise of Pedro's tantrum wakened Francisca in the other room. She leaped from her bed and ran to her mother. 'Run,' the battered Rosa sobbed to the child. 'Run, daughter mine, to La Madreselva. Fetch our Jose. Fetch Senor

Gonzales. Bring him quickly in God's name.'

The child obeyed. Her small feet scrambling fleetly down the steps, her nightgown flying, she screamed as she ran, 'Jose. Jose. Senor Gonzales, my mama is murdered. My mama is murdered. Run to help my mama.'

With the departure of the child, Pedro abandoned his attack upon the woman. He sought to escape down the steps but the arrival of Gonzales cut off his retreat and he backed into Mme Rosa's reception room.

Jose swaggered in authoritatively. 'What do you make?' he said to Pedro. 'Why do you beat the woman?' As he spoke, he swung at Pedro's jaw. The sound of the fist against bone, gristle and flesh was sickening. It sickened Pedro. He felt the room skid about his head and his legs went weak at his knees. He could not stand against such brutal force. He shook his head and could not stop shaking it, trying to smile through the blood spurting from his broken lip.

Mme Rosa screamed in her hysteria and agony. 'He is jealous, Jose. Save me, beloved one. He is raging because you were here. He claims me for his own. He who has no money. I must live, Jose. Do not let him beat me. I love you, Jose. Save me.'

Pedro was nodding now and smiling fatuously. 'I go. I go. Let me go,' he urged. 'I wish not to fight. Let me go, eh, caballero? Eh?' Cold sweat beaded upon his face and burned in his eyes. Jose merely watched him, composed and virile and quietly deadly.

Pedro's desire to retreat amused Jose and prompted him to take advantage of a frightened adversary. The woman's laughing, crying, sobbing, encouraged him. He caught Pedro's shirt, grappled with him, tipped him off his toes and threw him to the floor. When Pedro would not get up, but lay there grinning vacantly, Jose leaped upon him, pounded and battered him. Pedro was in no condition to fight and the power in Jose's fists weakened his will even to defend himself. The man could maim him with one blow. He sought only to protect himself but even in this was less than successful.

Jose stood up, caught Pedro by the collar and dragged him through the door. When Pedro grabbed at the newel post, Jose kicked his fingers. Pedro screamed, certain his hand was broken. Jose shoved him down the stair and stood with hands on his hips watching Pedro topple helplessly. Pedro caught at the railing with his smashed hand to keep himself from tumbling and breaking his neck. His nose bled, the fluid spewing over his cheeks and eyes. He was vaguely aware of laughing men watching from the doorway of the cantina.

'This is my whore. Come not here again,' Jose told him, loud against the chorus of laughter from the bystanders.

'No. Come not again,' Mme Rosa said from the security of Jose's shoulder. 'Come not again. No. Never. Never.'

Pedro pulled himself as best he could and staggered away down the street toward his home.

X

The valley around him flowering, his mind and hands occupied with the bees and his chores, Manuel was content. He worked hard and went days at a time when he did not listen for Julia's call from the house. Sometimes his muscles tightened and his bones ached, but the sunshine blazed down upon him, comforting and warming him.

Manuel's existence upon his ranch followed old patterns. Most of the time he was too busy, or too charmed with poppy-scented dreams, to be lonely. Always, pottering in his apiary, hoeing in the small garden he'd made for Julia, gathering fruit in his neglected orchard, cooking his meals, lolling in the sun upon the bench beside his house, reclining on the floor of the cubicle inhaling vivid visions from his pipe, he was aware of the nearness of his son. Jesus was not there in person, but the aspect of him was in some respects even more satisfying to the old man than his child's presence. He sated himself upon dreams, plans, hopes, schemes, designs, projects, picturing of his son's life ahead, his achievements, his happiness, prosperity, piety, puissance and, above all, his love and gratitude towards his father. Manuel was no longer alone, kinless. There existed one to cling to him, one to whom he might cling.

He saw few people on the dusty road that scarred the rich red soil beyond his sagging fence. The Stocktons seemed to own more and louder models of the new-fangled automobiles. The younger Stocktons made the track out there a race-course, clouding the world with dust and frightening the chickens with thunderous roaring of asthmatic engines.

He spoke with few people, the shop-keeper at the crossroads store, the priest at the mission, his old friend Juan de Zaragosa. Juan came less and less frequently, complaining that the Stocktons now refused to allow him to drive the mule

161

cart any more, saying he was too old, no longer trustworthy. Juan clung to his job at the huge estate by his black-rimmed fingernails. Sometimes for weeks the Stockton people forgot to pay him and he was afraid to complain for fear they would drive him away. Infrequently, they tossed him a few pesos and warned him they had young families coming from Mexico and they'd be needing his shack as soon as he could find somewhere to stay. Disheartened, Juan tried to speak of other things when he visited, but there was nothing else in his mind, nothing else in his broken heart. It was for sure the Stocktons wanted to be rid of him. It was equally sure he had no place to go. He came, walking with his plodding, painful steps along the road, calling out to Manuel from a quarter of a mile away, less and less often. Manuel sometimes stood and listened for his old friend along the track, but for a long time Juan de Zaragosa did not come at all. Troubled, Manuel determined to drive out to the vast Stockton estate and inquire about his ancient crony, but he delayed. There was much to do about the ranchito.

He told himself he prepared the place for that wonderful day when his son would come to live with him here in the valley. His heart pounded and his arms and chest ached as if the blood stopped in his aged arteries when he thought about the time when Jesus would come to stay. He worried about him; he was always nagged by the fear Jesus might be mistreated, might not have enough food to eat to grow strong bones and clear eyes and taut muscles.

Still, it was not anxiety for Jesus' welfare which prompted O'Brien's visit to Los Angeles just at that season when the nectar of orange blossoms was filling his hives and when failure to capture emerging swarms meant a deficit in the honey-crop. 'A swarm of bees in May is worth a load of hay', the old rhyme begins, but it treats of apiculture in a clime where springtimes are less precocious than in the San Gabriel Valley. The opium powder had sunk low in Manuel's last tin and nothing less than the urgent necessity to go to the Chinaman inspired him to abandon his watchful surveillance of his bees. Trusting to fortune that emigrated swarms would cling overnight to bush or tree, he promised himself a hasty journey and quick return.

As he entered the town, twilight clouds rose vertically in somber tans and fiery golds against an aqua and cerise sky.

He drove through crosshatchings of shadow to the alley where the Chinese sold him his drug. Darkness boiled from the gutter by the time Sal delivered him to the home of Pedro Luiz.

Concha was first to spy him. Clapping her hands and dancing upon the veranda, she screamed in her delight. 'Mi tio comes. The father of Jesus arrives. Ola! He is here. Now do we eat much food. Now do we eat until the belly swells.'

Pedrillo ran out of the house and across the path to help Senor O'Brien alight from the buggy. 'The son is well. Jesusito is healthy. The arrival of his father will please the small one.' Pedrillo anticipated every enquiry. He grasped his uncle's hand and kissed it warmly. 'It is that the large horse is well? And the many bees? And the very large ranch where one eats much?'

Manuel nodded, smiling, and encircling the boy in his arm, entered the house where Clara was putting the babies to bed. Jesus, entirely nude, wrestled with Jazmin who playfully licked at the dried exudations of his skin. Teodoro wailed on Clara's lap as she struggled to remove his clothes.

'Don Manuel. Welcome.' Clara managed a smile. 'Don Manuel's son — '

'Ah! No!' Manuel took a single look at his son and his face twisted in horror. 'His neck! Without the charm! He is here in peril — with your son! Where is the charm?'

'Is lost.' Clara sighed, blood suffusing her face. She kept her eyes lowered.

'Lost? How?.'

'My father — ' Pedrillo tried to explain but his mother turned on him, her voice rasping. 'Enough. Silence. Enough.' The surprised boy expelled his breath and fell silent.

Manuel shook his head in frustration and dismay. His voice quavered with a deadly patience. 'He must never be without the charm. The danger, it is terrible. And to be with the evil eye, every day with the evil eye, and without the charm.' Manuel trembled, outraged. 'How long has it been so? How long has he endured — without protection — the glances of your son? How long has the charm been — lost?'

Clara looked up, her face dark with embarrassment. 'Many days, Senor. It disappears. None knows whither. There is no money to buy a new one.'

Manuel stared about helplessly. He waved his arms towards

163

Pedrillo. 'Boy, take your brother out. Take him away.' He turned back to Clara. 'Let not my Jesus stay within the range of the bad eye.' When Pedrillo did not move swiftly enough to please him, O'Brien lashed out. 'Take him.'

Nodding, Pedrillo gathered up the struggling Teodoro from their mother's arms and removed him into the kitchen. Manuel spoke in flat cold tones to Clara. 'Put on his clothes. Put on at once. I go to take him to Mme Rosa to purchase for him another charm against the evil eye. Lost? Carelessness. Charms cost much money. Put on his clothes at once.'

As soon as Jesus was dressed, his father took him up into his arms. The child stared at him, dismayed. The tot's fear of this strange, bearded person brought a whimpering cry. Manuel waved Clara away, confident the boy would instinctively recognize his kinship. Anyhow, he was in a hurry to be gone. He ignored the baby's writhing protests. With Jesus struggling vainly in his arms, Manuel put his hand upon the knob to go.

Pedrillo abandoned the weeping Teodoro in the dark kitchen and came running into the parlour. 'Permit it that I go with you, Uncle mine,' he said. 'I help care for the small Jesus.'

Manuel might have assented readily but for Clara's seconding her son's request. 'Permit that Pedrillo go along. Jesus knows you not and fears.'

Manuel was already aggravated with Clara. Her suggestion that his son might fail to know his own father angered him and determined him to refuse Pedrillo's assistance though Jesus was crying and kicking against him by now. 'Knows me not?' Manuel staightened indignantly. 'I am his father. We go and return later.'

However when he undertook the double task of driving and holding in the buggy the squirming, struggling two-year-old who sought fiercely to escape from his father's care and to return to the arms of his foster mother, Manuel was abrubtly anxious to have the aid of Pedrillo who stood disappointedly upon the porch.

'Is it that you would like to drive the horse, muchacho?' the old man called, as if the subject had not been previously discussed. 'Then come with us. Me, I hold to my son that he shall not fall.'

A bright light glowed in the windows of the quarters of

Mme Rosa. Leaving Pedrillo to tend the horse at the kerb, Manuel climbed the steps with the somewhat mollified Jesus in his arms. The night was brassily loud, with laughter spewing from the saloon doors of La Madreselva.

Manuel pounded pre-emptorily upon the door. When it was opened, he blurted breathlessly and without amenities, 'A charm. A charm against the bad eye. My son has lost his charm and would have another.'

'Enter, so welcome Senor, enter with your so beautiful son.' Mme Rosa smiled serenely. She called across her shoulder. 'Paquita. At once. The box with the charms.' She stroked Manuel's arm and laid the backs of her fingers against Jesus's cheek. The child gave her a devastating smile which instantly evaporated. 'The misfortune is great, to lose the charm, the more terrible when one is in the very house with the eye that curses.'

The little girl brought the box as directed. The mother fingered the amulets, all exactly alike, in search of that one which should be of special efficacy against the evil eye. She strung a disk upon a cord, seated herself in a low rocking chair and reached up to take the child from Manuel. The boy smiled again, not at all reluctant to leave his father's arms for those of the lily-scented woman. He smiled again and she laughed. 'A charmer. Such a charmer.'

She placed the cord and charm around the child's neck and arranged the blouse to cover it, crooning words of soothing endearment. 'Querdito, pobrecito, one who has no mother. How small are his hands, how beautiful the visage of the child. How beautiful when he smiles. So, so, little love, recline on the breast of her who loves small ones so deeply.'

Francisca hovered wanly beside her mother's chair, her eyes fixed as brightly upon the child as if with fever.

'Is it not, Paca, that you wish for a brother, small and beautiful, like this one?' Rosa whispered to Francisca. 'See the strong sinews of the small leg.' She grasped the child's thigh. 'See the beauty of the tiny face. Is it not, Francisca, that the lovely mouth is a delight to kiss?' She suited the action to the word. Francisca also kissed the child repeatedly and embraced him as he lay contentedly in Rosa's lap. 'And see the small hand,' the woman continued in that crooning tone, 'the small hand which holds so large a fortune. It is that he should have his fortune read again.'

'No.' Manuel shook his head. 'He goes not to have his fortune read so soon again. No. The cost of the charm is sufficient. And it is that I must give the Senora Luiz money for the feeding of him. No. I cannot afford another fortune for the boy tonight.'

'It is without cost that I shall study his small palm. You shall pay for the charm that will protect him from the eye. I shall read his hand because I love the beautiful one.'

The woman peered at Jesus' right palm, thought for a moment, then looked into the left hand. 'Yes. Yes,' she murmured. 'The same. Many women who love him when he is a smiling man of comely face and virile body. Many adoring women. And money, much money. And many offspring, boys and girls to seek his paternal blessing.'

Manuel waved his arm, objecting. 'But my son is for the Church. A priest.'

'But yes.' Mme Rosa gazed at the palms again and nodded. 'For the Church. The lines declare no wife. True. But — there are many children. Ah, he will be a sly one, this charmer.' Her voice lowered and she shook her head. 'One would it were not so. But the fortune is in the hand. It cannot be altered.'

What she foretold gave Mme Rosa amusement and her tone rose, bantering. Manuel was only mildly interested in the repetition of what Jesus' small palm had revealed on previous readings. He reached out to take the child. Mme Rosa seemed unaware of him. Suddenly, the madame's face clouded. She ceased to speak, sank into a mysterious sort of trance. She examined the baby's hand again, one and then the other. Her manner annoyed Manuel, he was in haste to depart, but the baby grinned, enjoying the fondling and attention.

'Danger,' the madame whispered. 'The child is in danger. In danger. Grave danger.' Her voice came from her throat, husky, troubled. She seemed not so much to speak as to breathe the words. If the fear she expressed were simulated, the histrionics were superb. 'There is danger where this one stays. It is in the evil house where he lives. It is that he must not return there. One there hates him and will serve him ill. The charm protects from the eye, but there is another, a large one, un hombrenazo, who seeks to harm thy son. It is foretold, the boy remains in that place where he stays but to

166

suffer. He must be taken elsewhere for his safety, for many months. Perhaps after a long time he may be safe that he return to the old place. But now, no, not now. He must go away. There is grave danger.'

Manuel demanded details. He sweated, offered to pay for a reading that would explain the peril, but Mme Rosa shook her head and declared that she could say no more.

'But where can I take the boy?' Manuel asked her, desperate.

She shrugged those powdered shoulders. 'But to your own home. To your rancho. Take him where you will, so that he stay not in that place where he has been. There, there is much danger that he must not face. And give not the money which is demanded there. Your money has not been spent upon your son. Give no more.'

Manuel sagged in upon himself. He was convinced, and Mme Rosa had with these few well-chosen words canceled the debt of the beating she had received from Pedro Grandos Luiz.

Manuel paid for the amulet and, with Jesus in his arms, descended the steps. Francisca, coughing faintly, pressed against her mother's skirts and they watched their guests safely to the ground.

Pedrillo lay asleep in the buggy, the reins in his hands. Manuel shook the boy to waken him and tugged at him to hasten his descent from the carriage.

'Get down. Get down,' he said. 'Quickly. I return not to your house. Go. Run to the house of your father. Say to your mother that I return to my ranchito.'

Pedrillo nodded, reaching out his arms. 'And I shall carry Jesus to my mother?'

'No. No. Jesusito goes to drive with me to my house. Say to your mother that I take my son with me to stay.'

Pedrillo stood on the path unable to comprehend what had happened. He refused to believe. He opened his mouth to question but only shook his head, too stunned to think clearly, or to speak at ali.

Manuel struggled into the seat of the buggy, his son half-asleep upon his arm. He was awkward handling the burden, twice almost dropped him. He laid the child down on the seat and, alighting, took a hitch-strap from the harness at the horse's head. Then he remounted to the boot and bound the

167

child's body to his own. Without any more ado, he waved farewells to the boy at the kerb and drove away.

Pedrillo watched the buggy disappear around the corner. Sorrow too deep for words overwhelmed him. His heart seemed to sink in his breast. His throat tightened. His eyes grew moist, burning. Tears leaked down his cheeks and he gulped at the wad of his bereavement which choked him. He turned and walked slowly toward home. He felt such pity for Jesus, because his own mother was the centre of his little universe and Jesus had no mother at all. Pedrillo knew most other children had mothers to care for them, but for the motherless Jesus, Pedrillo felt a deep affection and compassion. He had watched over him, rocked and quieted him, put him to bed and taken him up, had loved the little one as it was impossible to love Teodoro. Now one had gone suddenly with the baby and left Pedrillo alone and bereft in the street, uncomprehending. His steps were leaden, wretched, his tears blinding.

Part Two

THE SON

'But all was false and hollow;
    though his tongue
Dropped manna, and could make
    the worse appear
The better reason, to perplex
    and dash
Maturest counsels.'

John Milton: *Paradise Lost*

XI

Manuel headed his tired horse out of town toward the valley. The heavily travelled road twisted through the countryside, narrow, potted, eroded by gullies, but quiet in the late night. They passed the cemetery where he had buried Julia, but no memories of his bride obtruded into his troubled thoughts. The harried man barely glanced toward that dark rill where faint moonlight revealed gravestones rearing like graven flowers in some sad and silent garden. Julia belonged to his past and he held only thoughts of his future with his son beside him. A light rain fell but he was barely aware of its chilled sting.

He had been content to permit Jesus to remain in the custody and care of Pedro Luiz's wife. Alone, he had woven fanciful dreams of the time when his son should come with him to the rancho, of that time when their camaraderie, affection and tenderness, one for the other, should make existence there a sort of Arcadian idyll. The idea of actually taking Jesus with him had not truly occurred to him. Yet, with the child strapped to his side and Sal jogging through the night, they headed home together. It was a flight into Egypt, an escape from malevolence, as envisioned by the seeress of Aliso Street.

The child, in the confines of the leather strap, squirmed and struggled. Manuel devoted one arm to encircling the small form, holding it in the seat. Jesus alternately whimpered and sobbed and slept. The night chill sent a shiver through Manuel who buttoned his coat. Aware that the boy must be cold with only a tiny thin blouse around his shoulders, he stopped the horse, removed his coarse jacket, wrapped and buttoned it about his son, and Jesus slept.

In his shirtsleeves, Manuel shuddered with chill; cold penetrated to his marrow. He gazed down at the child resting against him and smiled. Any sacrifices he made for his son gave him peace of mind. He exaggerated his own discomfort and thrilled with satisfaction that he endured it that the boy might not suffer. It was the first deprivation he had assumed for his heir.

He shivered partly from cold, partly from the ecstasy of fulfillment. Not even the felicity he had achieved upon that other long-ago night when he brought Julia home as his bride was vaguely comparable to the beatitude that now closed over him, enveloped him like a fog out of Elysium. He shared this treasure of his loins with none. Jesus was his now, his own, only his.

When they turned off the road into the yard of the ranchito, Jesus stirred, half-awake. 'Tia mia,' he called, troubled, not knowing where he was. 'Tia mia, Tia Clara, a te quiero.'

Manuel felt something twist in his sloar plexus. He resented the child's calling for another. 'Quiet,' he whispered. His arm tightened about the boy. 'Your father has you. We reach our own home.'

'A mi tia quiero,' the child insisted.

Manuel lifted Jesus tenderly from the buggy. He threw a cushion from the seat upon the ground and placed the boy on it, pulling the coat tighter around the small body. He removed the harness from Sal, gave the animal his night's rations of hay and corn and hastened back to where Jesus lay on the leather mat. He urged Jesus to rise and walk with him into the house, but the boy was too fatigued, too nearly asleep to obey. Awkwardly, the old man took his son into the room where stood Julia's bed and laid the child down on it. He lighted the lamp with its dingy chimney, the room yellow, shadowy.

Shivering with chill, he found his wine jug and swallowed a tumblerful of the red liquid. It restored and warmed him. The two-year-old stirred on the bed. Manuel poured another glass of wine, half-raised the tot to sitting. Jesus drank avidly. Manuel drank from the glass, gave it to the child again and then drained it.

Manuel had no idea how to go about putting a child to bed. He hesitated over the task, drank another tumbler of wine, pondering it. He removed the rough jacket in which the boy was wrapped and donned it. He was uncertain about the rest. He removed the shoes, Jesus unresisting. He unbuttoned the

171

small trousers, seeking to disturb the child no more than necessary, but the garment clung. Manuel had to peel it off, wrong-side out. Jesus whined and flinched at the touch of the man's cold hands upon his thighs. Sighing, Manuel unbuttoned the blouse but did not remove it. He wrapped the child in quilts and placed him in the middle of the mattress, shoving a pillow beneath the small cheek. Once more he poured wine and raised the boy to sitting that he might drink. When Jesus had gulped down as much as he wished, Manuel finished the glass. Jesus' mouth was moist and stained; the father stooped and pressed his own lips against it. Jesus slumped, asleep.

Manuel shook dust from a rosary which hung on a nail at the bedside and knelt where the gaudy Virgin looked upon his son and told its beads. He knelt so long, prayed so fervently that he staggered, in some pain, when he rose to his feet. He drank another glass of wine, retired to his cubicle, consumed a pipe of his drug and drifted into gratified sleep.

Rising with the dawn was Manuel's life long custom. The next morning he got up from his hard pad and gazed in delight and disbelief at the sleeping boy, arms free from the covers, widespread, hair moist with perspiration. The steady rise and fall of the chest, the utter relaxation of the whole being, evidenced deep repose. The long drive and the wine combined to prolong sleep.

For a long time Manuel looked down at the sleeping boy, tempted to rouse him. He was impatient to begin that idyll of existence of which last night's experience was a foretaste. He went into the back yard and watched the sun as it broke across the vast acreage of the Stockton farms. When he returned to the bedroom, the boy still slept. Manuel chopped kindling, made a fire in the kitchen stove, prepared an elaborate breakfast for two. Jesus did not waken. Manuel was hungry but would not eat until his son should join him. He did swallow a tumblerful of wine, however. He walked out through the orchard, surveyed the entire ranch, seeking any swarms of bees which might have emerged in his absence and gathered to hang on his trees. Finding none, he returned to the house. Again and again, he tiptoed into the bedroom where the child continued to slumber soundly, at once impatient that Jesus should wake and careful not to waken him.

It was midmorning when he finally found the large black eyes open but lethargically unfocused. 'Good day, caballerito,' the father addressed the boy. 'The day goes. Rise now that we may eat the breakfast. For you, I have baked a fresh loaf of bread.'

He slipped his hand under the child's body to take him from the bed. Jesus shrank from him, ready to wail in protest. 'I want my aunt. Where is Drillo? Jazmin? I want Tia Clara.'

Manuel smiled and nodded. 'But you are now with your father. Your own dear father. This is your own home. The place where you live. Now shall we hold the life of happiness together.'

'No. I do not like you. I want my aunt.'

Manuel was hurt by his son's dislike. 'But no,' he said in a calm tone. 'Your aunt is behind us in the great town. You are here on the rancho with your father in the country. Here you will live in health and grow tall and strong. Here we shall be happy. Come. Arise. The good breakfast awaits.'

He dragged the boy out of the bed, buttoned the blouse, somehow manipulated the small legs into the tight trousers, forced the shoes upon the little feet. Jesus, uncertain and shy, stood rigid and gazed vacantly, disinterestedly, about him. Manuel brought a tumbler of wine from the kitchen. The sight of the wine aroused the child's desire; he stretched his arms towards it. He drank greedily; the wine trickled down his chin and stained his blouse. Manuel finished the small amount in the glass when Jesus had drunk.

'Now,' Manuel said, 'the dutiful son goes to kiss the hand of his father.'

This strange rite was incomprehensible to the boy. Previously, he had kissed whom and what he had chosen to kiss, spurred by desire, instinct, affection. To kiss a gnarled and liver-spotted hand for duty's sake, he could not understand. Duty was some new abstract. Manuel persisted, insisted, urged, reasoned, commanded. His kindliness and gentle patience did not forsake him.

Rosa entered the room and Manuel called to her. He caressed her and and extended the back of his hand toward her mouth. The black dog smelled the hand and then licked it.

'You see,' Manuel said. 'The good dog goes to kiss thy father's hand. The dutiful Jesusito must kiss the hand also. Else there will be no breakfast.'

173

The example of the bitch was sufficient. Thereafter the ceremony of fidelity and affection was brought to pass without conflict.

Manuel had no theories on the rearing of children. He took for granted patriarchal authority, believed the father's wish was a son's duty, but he did not feel any necessity to inculcate such self-evident ideals into the consciousness of a normal son. Duty and love were instinctive. Immediate, unquestioning, cheerful obedience was anticipated of a son as matter of course. He did not see that children had to be reared in obedience; they were obedient instinctively out of filial love which was born in them. Still, he did not lose patience with Jesus when the child failed to do what he was told. He had been long in an unpleasant atmosphere; there was much to unlearn. There was none about to note any disobedience, none to witness subversion of paternal infallibility. Further, this two-year-old was the single object in the whole world of Manuel O'Brien's interest, affection or devotion; the only fillip his existence had, wanted or was likely to have; the only reason he wished to continue his life. To force the little one to do what he wished not to do, to constrain, limit or deny him, however much Manuel's principles counselled otherwise, was beyond the father's will.

With all that, Manuel was no slave to Jesus. What the child required, what the child wished, so far as Manuel was able to guess or ascertain, the father sought to supply but he made no show of anxiety for the boy's happiness. In fact, he felt a kind of shame for the depth of his affection for his son. Dignity required solicitude should be of the son for the sire rather than sire for son, and Manuel concealed as well as he could, even from himself, his zeal to satisfy his offspring's every caprice, to please his every impulse, secure his unbroken happiness. The boy was his all. He dedicated what remained of his life to this toddler. His passion was more than paternal; the child was more than a son; he was Manuel himself reincarnated. In the body and mind of this one, Manuel sought to live another, nobler and better, life.

Jesus felt as if he had fallen into a void, strange and yet somewhat pleasant, where he was centre of a lonely universe. No clatter of hoofs on pavements, no quarrelling, laughing voices, no shouts through thin walls, no neighbourhood habitations, none of Cipriano's music, none of the smells of people crowded together, but above all no Tia Clara to take care of him, no Pedrillo to spoil and amuse him. Still Manuel's ministrations were adequate, if awkward. Jesus was aware of no physical need unsupplied. Rosa assumed the role that Jazmin had played. Occasionally, the baby called out uncomprehendingly for Clara, Concha, Pedrillo, Teodoro. No matter what others felt, he loved the mischievous Teodoro deeply and forgivingly. When he called, there was no response. At most, the old man explained that the summoned person was a long way off and could not come to him. The boy lapsed into a languid apathy which Manuel recalled in Julia. Jesus had no comprehension of the meaning of 'a long way off', but he accepted Manuel's loving tone more than his words.

The black bitch caressed the baby's skin with her rough tongue, inspiring in Jesus a reciprocal affection. Rosa offered her body as a pillow in the sun; she licked and indulged him; she walked beside him, steadying his steps, about the sunlit yard. Her intimacy with the toddler fulfilled a need in her nature as in his.

Although Jesus lisped to the dog all the words of affection in his vocabulary, Manuel was not jealous of Rosa. No child would prefer a dog to its own father. Rosa's language of love was more intelligible to Jesus than were Manuel's attentions to his needs. But he lacked for no tenderness. If Manuel was unable to express his love for his son plainly, it was not that he did not feel it profoundly.

They somehow co-existed for a full week at the rancho. This day supper had been eaten and father and son were warm with the fumes of wine. The dusk deepened into sombre dark while Manuel stripped the baby of his clothes in preparation for bed. It seemed to him they'd shared a good week, a time filled with promise. Jesus had toddled about the yard in his shadow. As Manuel worked he talked to his heir of his magnificent plans for the boy's future. 'You go to the service of God,' he said, nodding as he worked. Jesus leaned against Rosa and stared up at the old man. 'Yes. You will be a priest and say prayers for my immortal soul. It is my wish for you. It is my only wish.'

Now, as the litle man leaned over the unclothed child, Jesus encircled the leathery corrugations of Manuel's neck and murmured sleepily, 'Mi padre. A te quiero.'

It was his adjustment to and acceptance of this new life into which he had been thrust, mere complacency, but it was the first evidence of recognition of their relationship. To Manuel it was much more, a declaration of filial passion, a fulfillment of all his fantasies.

He drew his son to him in devotion, lowered his head to kiss the frail neck, the tender shoulder. 'Pobrecita, pobrecita,' he murmured with deep emotion, 'pobrecito sin madre; hiho mio, querido mio, avanzarimos juntemente, juntemente siempre.'

His spiny beard irritated the child's skin and Jesus squirmed free of the elder's embrace with a faint cry of displeasure. The wine he'd drunk with his supper made him drowsy. He crawled upon the bed and fell asleep at once.

Manuel remained for a long time at the bedside in adoration of him he had begotten. At last he retired to his own cubicle and to the fantasies of his pipe wherein he gamboled with a puissant youth who requited a father's love.

Since Clara Luiz had mentioned to Manuel that Jesus was teething and as a consequence irritable and feverish, the father did not trouble himself about the condition. Jesus sucked and gnawed at the round knob on the arm of the rocking chair, but Manuel knew the sore gums of erupting teeth moved the child to gnaw anything convenient and the little fellow had not been petulant.

However, when Jesus awoke the next morning, he whimpered, rubbing his face and temples and kicking in restless antagonism at the covers of his disheveled bed. At first, Manuel assumed Jesus had simply awakened in a bad temper. Lifting the child from the bed he admired the brightness of his eyes which his unwonted spirit gave him. The boy's disposition did not improve in his parent's arms, and, dressing the youngster, Manuel became aware the child had a slight fever. Since this was a usual attribute of teething, he ignored it.

176

Jesus refused food and demanded water. Manuel denied him this, urging wine instead. Jesus drank greedily.

'Where have you pain?' the father said.

'I know not,' the child whined. 'I have pain. I have pain.'

Manuel scowled. He had no idea that a young child was unable to determine the seat of discomfort. He supposed the tenderness of the gums caused all the baby's woe.

Holding the child, cajoling him with Spanish words of sympathy, he explored, with a none too clean forefinger, inside the baby's mouth. He pressed and rubbed the swollen gums, reassuring the boy and himself that all would be well.

He went out into the apiary to work but his thoughts were upon Jesus and he neglected his chores. Glancing frequently towards the house, he hoped to find the boy playing in the back yard with the dogs. He heard faintly the petulant cry of the little fellow. He hurried across the yard and into the house, pausing in the doorway, wincing at the sobs of distress.

'One is not better?' He bent over the bed.

The boy shook his head, 'I hold pain.'

Manuel's concern grew to anxiety. Feeling impotent, he went into the orchard and gathered citrus leaves. In the kitchen he steeped them in water and made tea, to which he added spoonfuls of sugar. With some difficulty, he persuaded Jesus to drink this boiling-hot tonic.

The fever did not abate. The boy ceased to whimper or complain. He lay in his bed, in silence, staring from fever-bright eyes.

Manuel gazed down at his son. His anxiety gave way to fear. He could not leave the child to summon a doctor. Anyway, he associated his worst misfortunes with the medical profession. He was not sure he desired or trusted a doctor for his son. The need of a priest occured to him, but he could not go to summon the padre from Apia. He himself could pray. He sank to his knees beside the bed, gaze fixed in rapturous petition upon the holy picture hung above his head. He told his rosary in trembling fingers and implored the intercesssion of the Holy Mother for the life and well-being of his son. Otherwise he slumped, helpless, impotent.

Jesus struggled in a fitful, tossing, restless sleep. The old man remained beside his bed. To the child's pleas for water, he offered wine in its stead, or that bitter tea of citrus leaves. Through the eternal night, the old man kept vigil.

The following morning the fever had risen. Jesus lay in a stupor, eyes glassy bright, cheeks burning carmine. Through that day, that night, the father maintained his impotent watch, alternately hopeful and hopeless.

On the third day, the child's smooth skin was reddened with a rash. Manuel exhaled, feeling terror and relief. At least he knew what the malady was. Before night the disease's progressed confirmed his diagnosis. Smallpox!

Manuel himself had endured the itching fire of the infection, the oozy purulence of his flesh, the long delirious fever, the drying of the surface of his entire body into thick, prickling black scabs which finally dropped off to leave the skin a vast, pink, slick and tender cicatrix. That contagion had left him ugly and unloved and forever pockmarked. More than that, he had watched his first wife and all her children suffer its torments, seen them rot and die of the pestilence, had been left alone and solitary, wifeless, childless, because of its evil. Then he had been in a stupor of pain, too ill with the disease himself to realize the horror of his bereavement.

Now he remembered. Fear enveloped him. With Jesus dead, all his dreams would be destroyed. And Jesus would die. Death stalked with the plague. Manuel had no hope. His cruel experience inspired no hope. Jesus would die.

Manuel crouched over the bed where the child, burning with fever, suffering with thirst his father feared to humour, speckled with pustules, lay mindless with pain.

The idea of driving to find a doctor occurred to Manuel, but he dismissed it. The boy could not be abandoned while he made the search. Anyway, doctors had always failed him; they'd never been of use to him. Their patients all died. Had he not brought doctors to Anna? And to their children? Had not teenaged Julia died under the care of the learned Dr Robles, he from the famous faculty of Mexico?

He swallowed at the lump choking his throat. No, no doctor. Then in his despair, he saw a faint glimmer of hope. Perhaps if he could reach Mme Rosa in time. Would she not have a charm to turn away even this hideous visitation? A charm. Aye, God, there he had it: this illness was the effect of the evil eye in the house of Pedro Luiz. There he had discovered his son unprotected against the malignant glances of Teodoro. Between the loss of the charm and the father's finding him without it, the cousin had cursed him with a baleful glance, had wished this pestilence upon him. Only necromancy would combat it, only magic could cure. Prayers had proved fruitless. She who had carried her own Son in Her arms had not intereded with the Son in his behalf. He accepted the blame. He had neglected Her in good times; in his woe She retaliated for that neglect. He was guilty. God the Father was a vengeful God. She came from a vengeful family. Only a charm from Mme Rosa might now save his son.

'Agua, agua. Quiero agua. Tengo sed,' the child wailed.

Manuel was unable any longer to refuse the child water, yet water would aggravate the fever. Still, if the charm he was to fetch should be potent to cure, it would cure despite water, despite anything, would it not? He brought water in a cracked cup and the boy, weakened with fever, rose up to clasp it. He gulped down the tepid liquid. There was barely enough to tantalize his rabid thirst.

'Mas. Mas,' he pleaded. 'Mas agua,'

'No more.' With tears in his eyes, Manuel shook his head. 'Water will make you worse. My son wishes to recover. No more water.'

In apathy, the boy accepted the denial. He sank back in his bed. Manuel covered him with a quilt, then sank again on his knees at the bedside, and once more implored the Holy Virgin's good offices with Her own Son. He slumped down, despairing. His prayers were wasted.

XII

Manuel went to the barnyard and harnessed Sal to the yellow buggy. He came back into the house for one last look at Jesus before he set out.

Trepidation, anxiety, bewilderment and despair rode with him. A kind of faint hope flickered in the old man's breast. At least he was doing something. To remain impotently at the bedside was intolerable. On this mission, no olive branch quickened Sal's laggard pace. A flexible eucalyptus sapling stung the horse's scrawny haunches. Sal did not comprehend this new mood of his master, but the pain of the whip sent him trotting. Manuel sat upright and forward on the boot. He wished he could push on the reins; he would willingly have added his own wiry strength to Sal's.

Spring sunshine danced like golden wine full of bubbles. Outlines of distant hills against the blue sky reared hard, distinct and bald with crags. Mustard, lupins, Indian paint-brush, eschscholzia blazed in open fields. Roadways were edged with mallow, green to black. Winter rains had brought the landscape to its vernal effusion. But Manuel saw no landscape, he saw only his horse, thought only of his son burning with fever. He wielded the eucalyptus over the animal's rump. Seconds were like minutes, minutes hours. To reach Mme Rosa's, obtain the charm and return to Jesus was the sole purpose and desire left in his life. Reason advised that the seeress' charm was useless, but he wanted to believe it would save Jesus' life. His heart gave the lie to his brain.

The sun set and darkness clouded in as he pulled up beside La Madreselva. He got down from his buggy and leaned against a wheel, a sense of weakness flooding over him. Tension and the exertion of driving had fatigued him. Before he climbed upstairs to the madame's quarters, he drank brandy, two hasty glasses. He felt better.

He ascended to Mme Rosa's apartment and knocked on the door.

'Do not come in,' Rosa called. 'Go away. It is that I am busy. Come another time. Not tonight.'

Manuel only knocked louder. 'It is that I must come in. I must have a charm. It is I. Manuel O'Brien. I must have a charm for my son lest he die. Let me in now. My son, he goes to die without a charm.'

'Go now and come in the morning, then I can give you the charm. I am busy. I am engaged,' the madame called.

'No, no, Senora. I go not away. I come for the charm. Give me the charm.'

'Get out of here. It is that you cannot. Madame Rosa is busy. Get out.' This was a male voice, angry and challenging.

'I must have the charm,' Manuel repeated. 'My son, he dies. He dies of the smallpox for want of a charm.' Bafflement and despair shook his voice. He tried the knob. The door opened. Mme Rosa lay on the bed with Joze Gonzales.

'Get out,' the madame screamed at him. 'Do not come in. You cannot come in.'

Manuel was in no way deterred. He seemed not even to hear her or to be aware of her voluptuously naked body. 'The charm,' he said, pleading. 'It is that I must have the charm.'

Swearing, Gonzales levered himself from the bed, clad in underpants. He strode menacingly towards Manuel, but Manuel barely saw him. Mme Rosa, reluctant to be disturbed in amour, felt business was business; the old man looked distracted, and he was in the room now. 'Do not harm him, Jose mine,' she said in a cool and serene tone. 'Let him have the charm and depart. Bring the box to me from the other room.'

Jose brought the same box which Fracisca usually delivered to her mother. Mme Rosa extended a naked arm from beneath a hastily donned sheet and took the carton from him. Bracing herself on her elbow, her rich black hair tumbling over her smooth, powder-dusted shoulders, she glanced toward Manuel. 'What then is this charm for?' She sorted casually among the charms, as if seeking a particular one for a particular purpose. Even in his anxiety, Manuel was deeply impressed; his heart lifted a little with hope.

'The smallpox,' he said. 'My small son, the beautiful one, he has the pox. I require a charm which shall cure him.'

Mme Rosa nodded her lovely head and continued to sort among the identical disks, picking them up one by one, scrutinizing and relinquishing them. Finally, her lips widened in a smile. She nodded, extending a disk in her hand. 'This now is for the cure of the smallpox. Let the little one, el pobrecito, wear it around his neck. If it is that he does not then recover, there is at work a bad influence of which we know nothing. . . . This one is for the smallpox. It is such as my people, the gypsies, employ in Spain.'

Manuel reached for the disk, trembling, anxious to be gone. 'How much?'

'For the smallpox, charms are expensive.' Mme Rosa calculated how much Manuel could be brought to pay. He owed her something for this inconvenience. Still, she let the sheet slip away from her taut, full, high-standing breasts to soften the impact. 'This charm now is five pesos, Senor.'

Not even glancing at her exposed breasts, Manuel nodded and paid, unhesitatingly, without question. Taking the money, Mme Rosa redraped the sheet and inquired, 'Is he bad then, the litle one?'

'Muy malo, Senora,' Manuel said. 'I go to take him the charm. Good nights, Senora.'

He heeled about and ran toward the doorway. Jose stood grinning, pleased and freshly aroused by the way she had exposed her bosom to the old man. Excited, he got back into bed, reaching for her, calling her those forbidden names which spoken aloud roused him even more. 'You puta,' he said, trembling with desire. 'You whore. You are a whore, aren't you?'

'For you I am,' she whispered with a smile, but she ceded him only half her mind and none of her heart. She was troubled. She had failed to tell O'Brien that her own Francisca lay in the rear room, ill with smallpox. Paca's had been only a light attack, however. The child had been vaccinated during an epidemic two years previously. Consequently, she'd weathered this with no serious aftermath, and minor discomfort. It was the day following Manuel's last visit here that the little girl had broken out with a few vesicular eruptions which soon formed tiny scabs. Even now these were falling off; the child had hardly been ill at all, but Mme Rosa had kept her isolated lest knowledge of her contagion be noised about, bringing down upon her the health authorities, quarantines, ruin of her trade. She felt a twinge of guilt. The kisses the small girl had planted upon Jesus' lips that night might have — who could say? — brought about the little boy's plight. It did not even occur to her that Jose Gonzales, face now unpitted, would in ten days find himself lying in fever and agony.

2

Manuel paused at La Madreselva for another hurried brandy, after which he set out for home. The way seemed eternally long through the moonless night. The bony old horse was exhausted. He hadn't the energy to return at the pace he had come. Manuel, however, was relentless with his whip. The tired horse stumbled and shuffled along. In Manuel's mind burned a vision of a baby prostrate on a dingy bed guarded only by a picture of the Holy Mother of God. This fearful vision did not for an instant leave the old man. His eyes focused upon the haunches of his horse. He brought down the eucalyptus whip on one side and then upon the other. He was merciless, on himself and on his beast.

It was after midnight when Sal turned off the dark road into the rancho. Manuel climbed from the buggy. Without bothering to unharness the horse, he hurried into the house. As he opened the door, the stench of fever struck him. He groped for matches, broke one from its block and lighted the lamp. He hefted the light above the bed. The child slept. The small chest heaved in slow, laboured respiration. He was alive. Perhaps, after all, the Mother of God had found in Her heart forgiveness enough to listen.

He placed his hand on the hot forehead. He took the charm from his pocket and laid it carefully on the child's chest while he searched for string with which it could be fastened around his neck. Minutes were precious, the presence of the charm might well determine the difference between life and death. He found no cord, was finally reduced to unravelling a burlap bag. He roused the sleepy child who whimpered at being disturbed and at the relentless itch of his eruptions. Manuel handled the boy as gently as he could in his weariness, awkwardness and haste. He lifted the night garment to permit

183

the new disk to fall against the child's chest. He saw the red pustules and a vast tender pity welled in him. Tears stung his eyes. 'This charm will cure my son,' he whispered. 'The charm of the gypsy woman goes to make well my little one. Poor little one. Go now, to sleep.'

The baby was awake, fevered. 'Water, water,' he begged.

Manuel winced. 'Water is not good for one when the fever burns, caballerito. But, yes, a little, you go to have a cupful, for the charm goes to cure, water or not.'

Jesus twisted and squirmed restlessly. He had slept all day and most of the night. Tears seeped along his red-hot cheeks, but he did not cry aloud. His was steady, hot, itching discomfort. From time to time, he pleaded for water which his father postponed giving him. At length Manuel gave him wine which he considered less dangerous than water for one with fever. The little fellow drank all of it his father would permit. Dazed by the alcohol, he toppled back upon his mattress.

Manuel knelt beside the bed, agonizing with every breath of his son, every twist of the discoloured body, every fling of the small arms. Again and again he replaced the covers. Having himself once endured the sufferings of smallpox, he understood, even exaggerated in his imagination, the agony of his son. He prayed to be allowed to take the child's place in this fevered purgatory. He had never felt such tenderness and compassion for any person before.

Jesus thrashed and turned and shrugged, then, worn out with his own restlessness, consumed with fever, sodden with wine, he sank into stunned sleep. Manuel continued to watch. As tired as he was from his drive to Los Angeles, he felt no hunger. Since his body required food, he left his vigil long enough to prepare a meagre supper. Though he had no desire to eat, he craved opium and the surcease it promised. After supper, he got his pipe, but instead of smoking it in the cubicle, he brought it to the bedside of his ill son. The opium afforded him brief respite from anxiety. He lay down on the floor beside the dogs and slept.

Jesus worsened during the night. By morning eruptions broke out. In despair, Manuel even doubted the value and strength and power of the charm.

He sought to induce the boy to eat but Jesus refused food. Manuel then weakened evaporated tinned milk with water and gave it to the patient. Jesus drank it for the water in it which he would have preferred without the milk. Fever dried him out, cracked his lips, burning him at the armpits and the anus, and yet the father feared the effects of as much water as the child craved. He felt to give it was to aggravate the illness; to withhold it was cruelty.

Manuel had bought Jesus only a few garments from the crossroads store at Apia. He found it necessary to wash these frequently. This at least gave him something to do.

After he had washed the clothes and hung them on the barnyard fence to dry, he returned to the house. He decided to anoint the eruptions with a small amount of kerosene mixed into a greater quantity of lard. He had no other ointment. He scooped the lard from a kitchen pail into a coffee cup and added kerosene from the lamp. He mixed these ingredients together by puddling them with his fingers.

He took Jesus in his arms and carried him outdoors into the sunshine. He sat on the bench against the house where Julia once spent so many hours. He removed Jesusito's coarse nightgown. The charm was not about his neck. The flimsy thread had broken. He felt weak and outraged. Fate frustrated all his efforts to cure his son. Then his hopes rose. If the charm were dislodged, Jesus' worsened condition could not be charged against the talisman's potency. Perhaps it was that the charm had not yet failed. Found and restored to the child's neck more securely, it might yet work its miricle. He spread the gown on the ground and seated the boy on it, with the dogs beside him. He returned to the house and ransacked the bed looking for the lost amulet.

The covers were tumbled and disheveled, sheets awry. He yanked at them. Failing to find the disk, he finally took the bedclothes one by one from the bed and shook them over the floor. At last, in the fold of a quilt, string dangling from it, he found the charm.

He hurried outdoors to where Jesus lay on the nightgown. The black bitch was licking his body. The contact of the rough tongue allayed somewhat the burning itch of the boy's flesh. Rosa wagged her tail in satisfaction and pleasure.

'Vete, get out, bitch without shame,' Manuel shouted at Rosa. The dog slunk away, crestfallen.

Taking his son in his arms, O'Brien restored the charm against the reddened chest. Then he filled his fingers from the cup of ointment and smeared it over the mottled body. The kerosene stung the broken skin. At first, Jesus simply winced, then he cried and then screamed in anguish, as if army ants covered his body. He tried to fight the old man, seeking to defend himself, but the strength had gone out of him, he was too weak even to protest. Manuel's pity urged him to abandon his task, but desire to heal his son would not let him relent.

He spread the ointment thickly over the boy's trunk, legs, arms, face and scalp. He massaged it in, using more vigour than he was aware. The boy struggled vainly, his screams ineffective. Exhausted, he surrendered and submitted to the treatment.

Manuel carried the boy to the fence where he tested the clothes for dryness, chose a fresh gown and slipped it over Jesus' head, then returned him to his freshly made bed. Jesus begged for water and, begging, fell asleep, worn out by his struggles.

Manuel watched all day beside the boy. There was little he could do for him. The fever mounted. Late in the afternoon, Jesus uttered gibberish which his father recognized as delirium. Stray words were unintelligible, among them 'priano', and 'musica'. The old man sat frantic with anxiety and despair, waiting for his son to die. Black eyes peered glassily from the pustuled redness of the child's face. In delirium the boy begged for water. Manuel sagged, hopeless. Death was inevitable and at hand. To withhold water from the dying child, however harmful it might be, by however many minutes it might hasten the end of the agony, seemed pointless and cruel. He brought a bucket of water, fresh from the well. As often as Jesus asked, Manuel gave it to him. The boy's thirst was implacable. He drank more than his stomach could retain and regurgitated it upon himself and the bed. Yet, he desired more water and Manuel gave it to him. At length the child slept.

Manuel knelt by the bedside, telling his rosary, waiting for death.

Night came and the minutes crawled into the darkness on maggot's feet. Jesus lived. By morning the fever had receded somewhat, but the child's body was a mass of oozing suppuration. He lay weak, apathetic and exhausted.

Hoping again, Manuel anointed the boy once more with kerosene and lard. Jesus was too weak to resist, too tired to care, existing in a kind of euphoria of agony. The small arms and legs were thin, the belly had lost its roundness, but the boy had survived the water. If the charm were potent, it would prove it had potency against any aggravation of the illness, and Manuel gave Jesus fresh cold water whenever he asked for it.

As the sun declined, the fever rose again, but it was not accompanied by the delirium of the previous day. The eruptions enlarged, more and more inflamed, and spread and flowed together. Pus and serum glued the nightgown to the flesh and Manuel was able to remove it only by soaking spots in warm lard.

Days piled one upon another. Manuel remained steadfast beside the bed. He slept a few minutes at a time, upon his knees, head against the mattress.

He lost track of time. Jesus' festerings dried into scabs which itched constantly. Despite Manuel's pleading and reproofs, Jesus scratched them off as fast as they formed. Finally, the father had to bind the boy's hands to enable the surfaces to heal. Jesus was emaciated, his skin a crust of hard black scabs, oozing pus at their rims. Only while he slept did his whimpering complaints cease. Manuel did for him what he could. This little skeleton on the bed, clad only in putridity, was all that remained to Manuel O'Brien of his high hopes for an heir: a poor object around which to group dreams of happiness. Manuel was no longer interested in future felicity; pride dropped away from him. Nursing the child, Manuel had served, striven, hoped, prayed only that Jesus might recover. This was all he asked. The boy had become the vital part of the old man's being. Earlier, he had drawn satisfaction for having begotten this child, now he had come to love him. Cankered and atrophied as he was, Jesus was to Manuel something to love devotedly, tenderly and unselfishly.

Manuel felt better. The charm had proved its potency. The plague ran its course. Scabs dried, dropping off. He crossed himself, fearing wrath of that jealous family which controlled the destinies of men on earth. Perhaps the charm alone had not saved the little one's life; perhaps the good Virgin above the bed had been moved to pity by Manuel's prayers.

The last of the black scabs peeled from the boy's body, leaving patches of slick tenderness to serve for skin. Jesus was as something scalded, like photographic film addled in the drying. His fingers seemed to have run together at their bases where eruptions conflowed. Both ears were misshapen with scars. The lids of his left eye were grown together at their outer junction. Brows and lashes had disappeared, the hair on his scalp stood in scanty, irregular patches. Even his nose appeared drawn to one side, and a scar on his lip looked like a hairlip repaired with inexpert surgery. Fever had rendered the baby-fat from his flesh. Pock scars scrawled over his shrunken belly until his navel appeared one of them. The gauntness of his ribs striped the molten flesh of his upper torso. His arms and legs were mere bones wrapped in scar tissue. Naked he appeared like some huge, loathsome insect. The left eye squinted, but the right eye shone larger, complacent, Cyclops-like in the shrivelled face.

Manuel was aware of no ugliness in his son. The slick cicatrices were evidence that smallpox was conquered forever. Mme Rosa's charm, with such assistance as the Virgin may have mustered, had driven the enemy of his race from its tiny victim. His admiration for Jesus lost none of its fervour; his tenderness multiplied itself myriad-fold. Jesus was convalescing. Manual was content.

The emaciation of the child distressed Manuel, but food and time would surely clothe the gauntness with round flesh. Manuel's culinary efforts produced strange, nameless, but tasty dishes designed to tempt the boy's appetite, recipes hot with pepper, odourous of garlic. The flock of mongrel chickens ranging the barnyard was halved, its members served up to Jesus in stews with rich sauces and gravies. Along with the food, Manuel urged the boy to drink glassfuls of red wine and after such meals Jesus would lie on the bed or the floor in a blissful langour and, contented, doze into lethargic sleep, waking to eat again. He grew daily stronger. The wine, Manuel believed, served to make blood.

Half a mile up the road, the slattern wife of Manuel's neighbour Milhaus owned a bony cow which grazed a precarious diet from roadside weeds. Leaving Jesus asleep, Manuel harnessed Sal to the buggy, drove to the Milhaus farm and arranged with the woman to sell him a quart of milk daily. A blond, twelve-year-old boy came each morning with milk in a battered lard-bucket which he hung by its handle on a picket of the O'Brien fence. Often the amount was lessened by the hunger or thirst of the messenger, but Manuel made no complaint.

Jesus' skin gradually toughened and lost its tenderness and redness. The scars faded, looking less vicious. But for weeks, despite the chicken dumplings, the milk, wine, honey and fresh-baked bread, the ribs showed plainly, the limbs were cadaverous. The small belly was puffed with food, but its sides sank in. The child was like some victim of horrible famine, crammed abruptly with all the rich foods he could consume.

Manuel ate what he couldn't induce Jesus to devour and his face warmed and filled out, his clothes grew tight. He had for years concerned himself little with food, eating only staples easiest to prepare. Improved nutrition gave him a sense of wellbeing, a satisfaction with life he had long forgotten.

At length, Jesus too filled out his contours and as he thrived, flesh gathered rapidly around his bones. As Jesus recovered Manuel returned to essential tasks among his bees. When the boy's recovery was assured, the old man spent more time at his chores, leaving Jesus in the care of Rosa and her son, with Jesus usually sleeping off the effects of the wine.

By mid-July Jesus showed no lingering ill-effects of the malady, save fading pockmarks that dotted his skin, and these were daily less evident. Brows and lashes renewed themselves, his scalp was covered with its quondam shock of lustrous black. His left eyelid yielded to use, the nose regained its symmetry, and the scar on the lip disappeared completely.

XIII

Jesus finished his breakfast that late spring morning and, sated, slept nude on the floor, black Rosa stretched at his side. One of his thin arms rested across her flank. The sun splashed through a window over the legs of the naked child. Boy and dog rested, content in the silent morning. Manuel had gone out to work in his apiary; the only sounds were the clucking of chickens, the muted hum of bees and distant lowing of a cow.

The knob of the outer door turned. Rosa raised her head and gave a low, sharp warning growl. She remained tense, watching the door. It slowly and noiselessly opened and Rosa got to her feet, bristling. Shyly, furtively, the face of Pedrillo Luiz, eyes astare, presented itself through the opening.

Rosa whined faintly, recognizing the boy. She relaxed her stance and sidled toward him, tail wagging. Pedrillo hesitated and looked about the room before he decided to enter. The past couple of years had taught him to trust no one, nothing. He was almost ten years old now, wiry and handsome, like a miniature of his father, with more of the goodness of his uncle Cipriano in his classical sculptured face framed in rich black hair chopped in ragged locks about his skull. He was barefoot, his ankles and calves scabbed with grey dust.

At last, holding his breath, he came into the room and closed the door. Seeing Jesus, Pedrillo wanted to go at once to him, but the black bitch stood between them, unmoving. The child did not waken; his mouth and chin were stained red with wine.

Pedrillo exhaled and took a step forward. Rosa growled again but wagged her tail amicably. Pedrillo laid the back of his hand in gentle caress upon Rosa's head. He approached the sleeping Jesusito, but Rosa insinuated herself between them. Pedrillo sank to his knees and Rosa showed white teeth

190

in a snarl, so he made no effort to touch the sleeping tot. And so he remained, kneeling beside Jesus, the dog between them, friendly but immoveable, and so Manuel found them when he came into the house for a glass of wine half an hour later.

'What has befallen Jesusito, Tio mio?' Pedrillo greeted his uncle.

Manuel's reply was laconic. 'But you? How do you come?'

'My father, he sends me.' The boy hesitated, his face flushed red in embarrassment. 'He sends me to stay awhile with you and Jesus. Do you permit it, Uncle?'

Manuel went on staring at him. 'And how do you come so far?'

Pedrillo shrugged. 'I walk. I remember the way since the time you brought me here with the great horse.' Pedrillo smiled. 'And the great horse, is he well?'

Manuel ignored the question. 'When did you set out?'

'Yesterday.'

'And sleep? Where slept you?'

Pedrillo smiled deprecatingly. 'By the roadside — for a little while. Something wakened me suddenly and I feared much. I was no longer sleepy. I walked, I was anxious then to be with you and Jesusito whom I have missed with my heart.'

'And you ate?'

'No, Senor. I did not eat.'

'Then you must have the great hunger?'

'Yes, Uncle, I have much hunger. It is that I shall eat with you and Jesus, if you will permit it.'

O'Brien did not believe the tale about his father's having sent the boy upon this visit, but he knew well the violence of Pedro Luiz' temper and he made no further inquiry. One asks many questions, sometimes one collects answers with which one cannot deal. He suspected Pedrillo had run away from home, but to extract the truth would obligate the uncle to return the boy to his parents without a period for cooling tempers. He did not wish this. Jesus needed a playmate and Manuel had always found Pedrillo a favourite, as smiling and as easy-going as his blessed mother. Pedrillo had come at an opportune time. He was a welcome arrival. Pedrillo shared Manuel's love for Jesusito and this mutual interest made host and guest almost closer kindred than ties of blood.

Pedrillo arose from his knees and approached Manuel

where he stood in the doorway. He kissed the old man's hand in belated obeisance. Manuel smiled, pleased with the child's manners.

'Is it that the little one has been very sick?' Pedrillo inquired. 'And that the pox has left him much scarred and marked?'

'No. No. Scarred but little. Jesusito is well. Such marks will vanish quickly.' Manuel made the sign of the cross. The old man's perturbation at his question warned Pedrillo off the subject.

'And is it that he will wake and play with me?'

Manuel nodded, smiling again. 'He will wake soon and play. Meanwhile, you must eat something before dinner shall be ready.'

Manuel placed on a tin plate some pieces of cold fried chicken, saffron rice seasoned with peppers and garnished with bits of pimento, slices of his freshly baked bread with honey over it. He saw Pedrillo wipe at his watering mouth. He poured a glass of wine from his jug, drank it himself and then, smiling and with much ceremony for the guest, poured another and handed it to the boy. 'Drink, drink your wine,' the uncle urged. 'It will fortify anew the strength of one who has not eaten since yesterday.'

Pedrillo nodded and drank. The wine coloured his lips and he wiped them with the back of his hand. He smiled at his uncle in admiration. 'The rich eat much, eh? Always the rich have plenty to eat. I have seen this. Is it not that you have much to eat because you are rich, my uncle?' He shook his head, his black eyes shadowy. 'At home, we do not eat a great deal, for my father is a poor man who has not the work by which to earn. And so we do not eat well. It is pleasant to be rich and to eat well, eh?' The daintiness with which he ate bread and honey and chicken belied his voracious appetite. Manuel said nothing but filled the plate a second time and the boy, grinning shyly, cleaned it, wiping it up with bread.

When he had finished his meal, he smiled and spoke timidly. 'Now it is that I have the sleepiness also. Do you permit, Uncle, that I lay me down to sleep on the floor by the side of the small cousin Jesusito?' He did not wait for the old man's reply but lay upon the floor. He put his arm gently around the child who squirmed but did not waken. O'Brien swallowed another glass of wine and returned to his bees, leaving the boys asleep.

Jesus woke first. Startled at finding a stranger asleep at his side, he cried out and tried to retreat. Pedrillo awoke. 'Jesus. Jesusito. Is it that you remember me not? Do you not remember Drillo? I come to visit and you go to forget me. Jesusito, cry not, but come to thy Pedrillo.'

The baby had half-forgotten Pedrillo but there was a gentle kind of seduction in the plaintive voice which was somehow familiar and welcome to his ears. He smiled, his face and eyes glowing briefly. Pedrillo laughed and grasped him like a great doll, caressing him with gentle spanks as he had caressed him so many times before. Jesus' eyes shone brightly, his small hands buffeted the cheeks of his cousin in satisfaction and delight at finding him again after so long. 'Drillo will take care of Jesus,' the older boy said.

After his nap, Pedrillo found himself sore, not only from the long walk from Los Angeles but even more from the bruises caused by the flogging Pedro had given him, which had determined him to leave his father's house. His heart broke with longing for his mother but bitter resentment toward his sire hardened his will and set his resolve. His was a precocious race and he was old enough now not only to resent but to refuse to endure such brutality. He did not consider that his uncle suspected the lie he had told about his advent into the valley. He kept his own counsel about his pain and was able to eat all of the generous portions of food Manuel heaped upon his plate at the midday meal.

Both children were tipsy with wine by the time they had finished eating and they tussled happily. Manuel sat in a rocker, delighted at their frolicking play. He watched them romp, chase and hide from each other. A twinkle of satisfaction glittered in his eyes. Only when they'd finished playing and succumbed again to sleep did he return to the apiary. That Pedrillo might supplant him in the affections of his son did not occur to the father. He was happy to have this boy around the place to amuse Jesus and keep him company in the lonely countryside.

When night came, Jesus insisted that Pedrillo sleep in the bed with him. Manuel consented because there was nowhere else to accommodate a visitor. He took no thought of the variola which still lurked in the soiled bedclothes, none of which had been washed since Jesus' recovery.

The following morning Pedrillo espied the lad who delivered the milk and, despite an habitual politeness, made hostile overtures as strange children sometimes make toward each other. The Milhaus boy, older and conscious of his greater strength which did not have to be proved, ignored the insults. Pedrillo mistook the other's contempt for fear and ran out of the yard to chase the cotton-haired Anglo-Saxon down the road. It was in fact the colour of the boy's hair which first roused the hostility in the black-haired Pedrillo.

The Milhaus boy refused to run. He stood, legs apart, waiting in the middle of the road. When Pedrillo, slowing, threw clods at him, he coolly returned and gave the young Mexican a mild pummeling. This was easily accomplished. Pedrillo immediately realized himself outclassed but because of pride would not retreat. The blond stranger was older and a good deal larger, if slightly big-jointed, awkward and deliberate. As mild as the chastisement was, it was painful to Pedrillo, who felt his pride crumpled and who had not recovered from his father's beating three days before.

The victor was not implacable. Once supremacy had been established, amity was easy. Young Milhaus remained to play and each morning when he brought the milk he stayed for a game or a tussle with Pedrillo. His name was Hubert. Pedrillo's English was stronger than Hubert's Spanish and it became their means of communication, though both continually were asking, 'What? What does that mean?' When they became better acquainted, Pedrillo was anglicized to Pete. This new name amused and delighted him and he ran to share it with Manuel. 'I am happy to be here, Uncle, with you and with Jesusito, as I am happy to be called Pete. Is that not an elegant name?'

Pedrillo awoke one morning fevered and shaky. Manuel touched his forehead and sighed. It was no surprise to him that Pedrillo should contract smallpox and in this case, Manuel did not consider it a momentous calamity. The life of a Luiz was to him of no such consequence as the life of an O'Brien. Since smallpox was well-nigh unavoidable at some time during the boy's life, it seemed to Manuel that now was as good a time for Pedrillo to have the malady as later. This is not to suggest that Manuel was casual or unconcerned. It was just that the very source of Pedrillo's infection dulled for Manuel the edge of its curse. It was not in him to attribute ill-fortune to anything that derived from Jesus.

Just the same, now that it was too late, he stripped the bed and washed the sheet and quilts in a black pot over the fire in the yard. He allowed the mattress to sun all day.

Pedrillo's head ached and he was feverish and his joints hurt worse than when his father kicked him. It deterred his play but did not stop it. He tried to ignore his malaise and to romp with Jesusito. He had learned at home to conceal his griefs and pains. The following day, though, he was forced to declare himself ill and Manuel hung about Pedrillo's neck the talisman which had served so well during Jesus' illness. As an additional but ancillary remedy he addressed potent, whispered words to the lithograph which hung above the sickbed. He felt no undue uneasiness; what had brought an O'Brien through this pestilence would adequately serve for a Luiz.

The next day a roughness rose over Pedrillo's skin, as if particles were embedded under it, forming tiny lumps. Fever rose, the lumps grew and spread. Finally they burst into hot, putrid sores. These in turn dried into scabs. The boy was weak with fever, pain and unbearable itching. He complained only little. Manuel applied lard and kerosene. The eruptions were neither so large nor so numerous as those of Jesus had been, not did they conflow. This case was one which, for unknown reasons, is described as discrete by physicians. It ran its course. The scabs dropped off the tender skin beneath them. Once more, Mme Rosa's charm had conquered an enemy.

Long before Pedrillo recovered, Hubert ceased to deliver the milk. Manuel drove to the Milhaus farm to ascertain the reason and learned that Hubert was also ill. Thereafter, he went daily to fetch the milk. He did not choose that Jesus should do without. He found that Hubert was bright with smallpox, his mother panicky with anxiety. She had no money to employ medical aid. Manuel offered the woman such reassurance as his experience would permit. He prescribed for Hubert lard and kerosene ointment and even mixed and puddled the dosage. He drove home to get for Hubert the charm which the convalescent Pedrillo no longer required.

When he saw the disk safely suspended around Hubert's neck, he said to the mother, 'Now you have need to fear not.

195

The powerful charm will cure the miserable boy. Trust the charm, and say your prayers to the blessed Mother of God.'

Such faith as Mrs Milhaus had left, however, was of protestant persuasion and her acid reply was an affront to the ears of so ardent a Romanist: 'And if ever it needs prayers to that there dirty Catholic whore to cure him, my boy will die. When I pray, I pray to God Himself, and not to no woman who trifled with Roman soldiers to fix nothing up for me. This charm may cure and it may not. We'll try it. But the Mother of God, as you call her, and all your popes and priests and their hocus-pocus and candles and such, let 'em keep out of this and allow Hubert to get well.'

Manuel, stunned and grey-faced, only shrugged and re-treated. However, he would nourish his son on no milk from a protestant cow and thereafter did not return to the Milhaus farm. It was necessary for him to drive past Apia for milk, but he made the trip daily and increased the quantity so that Pedrillo too might enjoy its benefits and speed his recovery.

Hubert's disease ran its course and he recovered without permanent ill effects save a few pale scars pitting his pale skin. He came daily to play with Pedrillo and Jesus and though Manuel disapproved of his religion, he accepted the boy. The summer passed pleasantly for all of them. The boys prowled in the sunlit valley. One day they dragged home a six-foot snake which Pedrillo and Hubert had killed with stones, thanks to Rosa's diversive actions. Manuel stared at his son and at the fangs and rattles and buttons of the snake and felt ill, but he concealed his terror and congratulated the boys, calling them brave young men.

He watched the children at play, made gardens for fresh vegetables, pruned and fertilized his orchard, and saw his honey hives thrive as never before. He credited it all to Jesus' arrival. His life was renewed since the birth of his son. He prayed to live only long enough to watch the boy grow and develop for a little while. He was already sixty-five and knew he couldn't live forever. He was reconciled to death until he thought of his son and his needs and his beauty which daily intensified and deepened.

Working, Manuel said his little prayers. This was the pleasantest time of his life. He had everything he wanted. He could recall no moment, with his first wife, with the Smith woman, with lovely Julia, or with those half-forgotten belles of his free-booting youth, to compare with the pleasure and delight of this summer.

Jesus grew, rounding out, and babyhood fell from him. Firm, supple muscles rounded his vigorous frame with symmetrical proportions. The cicatrices faded on his face, most disappeared entirely. The disease had weakened a muscle in his left upper eyelid, causing it to droop almost imperceptibly, but giving his languid countenance in repose a hint of stupidity, and when he smiled that rare, brief and enchanting smile, he seemed to be controlling, with conscious effort, an impulse to wink. This fillip added a new fascination to his face when he smiled, giving him a go-to-hell look suddenly there, instantly gone. One felt uncertain about what the beautifully smiling child really thought. It made that lovely, fugitive smile unforgettable.

The child's face was oval, the chin cleft, the nose slightly aquiline, the black eyes, like Julia's, large and liquid. Carmine patches played through the olive smoothness of his cheeks and colour lay vivid upon his full lips. His hair was almost ebony, slightly coarse and chopped awry about his head. The same impassive tranquility which had individualized Julia's face lay upon his. He seemed to possess her placidity, a remote indifference to life that bordered on dullness. Even as a three-year-old his reticence and placidity seemed a kind of dignified quietude. One almost wished to shake him, to wake him up, to demand what he was thinking that was unknown and unknowable to others, but if one did, he only smiled, briefly and devastatingly, and drifted immediately into that unapproachable indifference.

Sometimes Manuel worried about the way Jesus stood slightly apart, even at play with Hubert and Pedrillo. He watched their play eagerly and avidly but somehow seemed aloof, even in the midst of it. Manuel considered discussing it with the wise Dr Robles of the faculty of Mexico, but brushed the idea aside. Jesus was normal. There was nothing wrong with him.

The first rain of the season did not come until mid-October. The downpour freshened the landscape and fringed the valley in green. Manuel pottered all day in the honey-house, preparing for the autumn harvest. He was exhausted when he went in to supper and anxiously awaited the time when the children would go to bed and he could retire with his pipe.

197

He entered his cubicle with the lamp and sought his tins of opium. Sickness flooded through him. His whole body yearned and ached for the surcease of the drug, and the last tin was empty. He stared down at his trembling hands and told himself he'd just have to wait until morning when he and the boys would take a journey into the town. The longer he sat there, his teeth chattering with inner chill, the more he realized that to wait was impossible, foolhardy, without reason.

He went into the room where the boys slept. He placed the lamp on a table and shook Pedrillo awake. 'Arouse the little one,' he said. 'Dress him and dress oneself. I hitch Sal to the buggy. We go at once into Los Angeles.'

Pedrillo slumped, vague with sleep. At the mention of the town, he came instantly awake, his eyes wide and stark. 'Must we go into town, Senor?'

''Yes. We must go. At once. Get dressed and get Jesus dressed. You can sleep on the way.'

'Please, Senor, forgive, but one wishes not to go to Los Angeles. Please, I beg you. Do not command that I go. It is that I am happy here and I want not to go to the town. Not now, Senor. Not tonight.'

Already shaken and impatient, it was on Manuel's tongue to curse the boy and cuff him to speed him. But, looking into that stricken face, he hesitated. All summer, Pedrillo had not spoken of home, as though the place did not exist for him. Manuel had waited but the child had betrayed no trace of loneliness or homesickness. Pedrillo was in terror of returning to his father's house.

Manuel stood a long time, his aching arms at his sides. He looked at Pedrillo, hunched on the bed like a condemned prisoner awaiting his last cigarette, at Jesus sprawled asleep across the mattress, one leg flung over Pedrillo's. At last he said, 'But I must go. I must go now. It is that I must go to the Chinaman. If I return by morning, perhaps you and the child will pass the night safely. I will lock Rosa and the puppy in here with you.'

'Please, Senor. Dear Senor, please.' Pedrillo hoped without daring to hope.

'I had planned to visit in Aliso Street as well. Do you not wish to kiss thy mother?'

Pedrillo winced. 'If thou see my beloved mother, say to her

198

one misses her with all his heart, and say the same to Concha.'

Manuel sighed. 'It is all right then to say you are with me here at the ranchito?'

Pedrillo sagged as if struck and chewed at his upper lip. He shook his head, his eyes welled with tears. 'If you see my parents, say nothing of me, Uncle,' Pedrillo begged. 'If they ask, please say one has not seen me.'

Plodding through the dark valley toward town, Manuel felt overwhelmed with a deep melancholy. He looked forward feverishly to going to the Chinaman. Yet he knew if he told the parents he had Pedrillo at the farm with him, there would be trouble, maybe violence even, and in the end Pedrillo would be returned against his will. Still, if he said nothing, the good Clara whom he admired and respected above all women, to whom he felt deep and abiding gratitude, must suffer the hell of not knowing the whereabouts of her firstborn. This was not fair to her, even if it meant losing Pedrillo.

He sagged on the seat, wishing with all his heart for one soothing pipe of the powder of the poppy, for surcease and escape. If he betrayed Pedrillo's trust and spoke of him to Clara, it would all end. Pedrillo would be threatened and Jesus lonely and heartbroken without his beloved Drillo. Well, the child would forget in time, as Pedrillo might someday find it in his heart to forgive him this betrayal. But there was more. He himself had come to love Pedrillo, next only to Jesus, as much as any man might love a child not of his own loins. He ached thinking of condemning Pedrillo again to Pedro Luiz' cruel fists and thick boots and drunken rages.

He shook his head. If he went to Aliso Street he must visit Clara, and if he met her, he must be truthful with her at all costs. Only if he did not go at all to Aliso Street could he serve each of them according to the dictates of his heart and his conscience. . . .

XIV

By midnight, Manuel was entering the eastern limits of the town. He found the streets unusually busy, with signs of much construction, as if the city had suddenly mushroomed, no longer a sleepy village. Carts, carriages and many automobiles lined the streets, even at this hour. Street lamps cast blurred halos in the mist, drifting like pale balloons in the darkness. The lights and automobiles and strange buildings were changes that distressed him. He was already troubled and these gaudy alterations addled him even more, depressing him. He slapped at Sal's rump with the olive branch, hastening directly to the alley emporium of the Chinaman. The old man greeted him silently and politely. By signalling with his fingers, Manuel doubled his purchases of the small, precious tins. The aged merchant bowed politely and Manuel bent awkwardly in return, backing from the shop with his ricepaper-wrapped package clutched in trembling hands.

Wisdom probably dictated waiting for an appropriate time and place to fire his pipe, but Manuel admitted he was beyond the grasp of reason. He felt sick with need. He drove deeper into the alley and in a niche between darkened laundry plant and restaurant kitchen, he filled his bowl, lit the powder and sucked guiltily and almost frantically upon the syrup gum bubbling in his pipe. He felt no guilt for his habit, its legality or morality; he never had. But guilt had ridden his shoulders like some ugly albatross on the way from the farm, and it increased rather than abated as he smoked. It came from his growing anxiety about Pedrillo and his family, especially about the good Clara who had never dealt him anything but fairness and justice. He owed Clara so much. Could he then continue to harbour her son and not even let her know? But if he told her, would Pedro, learning the whereabouts of his son, leave the matter between him and Clara? No matter how concerned he was for the boy's welfare, no matter his deep affection for him, and Jesus' need, had he the right to keep him without the parents' knowledge or consent? He did not deceive himself as to why Pedrillo stayed hidden on the farm. Pedro had beaten and flogged his ten-year-old son without mercy, and Pedrillo had fled to the one haven he knew. Could he deny him that safety and return the child to torment and torture? And if he himself went to Aliso Street this morning with the daylight, would his efforts buy him more than a running fire of obscenities, taunts, threats and vilification? In growing agony the old man sucked deeply at his pipe, unable to find the surcease he'd come so urgently to seek, managing nothing more than a faint dizziness behind his eyes and a queasy stomach. Despairing, he sat up and doused his pipe, clutching the warm bowl in his palm. He could not face the dilemma and he was exhausting his strength by fighting it and finding no relief in the poppy.

He told himself he had reached no decision, but he held the reins slack and offered no protest when Sal turned the buggy ploddingly toward the valley. By dawn the clouds gathered and thundered across the ranges to the west, threatening a storm. He rode in a daze, barely aware of the warm drizzle which fell soon after daybreak and continued through the morning. He remained slightly sick at the stomach and was nervously anxious to return to the farm. He would have a letter written to Clara who in turn would have the missive read to her. He would explain that Pedrillo had shown up on the doorstep one morning, was well, healthy and sent his deep love to his mother and as her faithful servant awaited her reply. This decision accomplished several things; it delayed a confrontation which might become ugly or costly, or both; it allowed Pedrillo a little more time on the farm with Jesus; it salved his own conscience without placing him in actual involvement; it allowed him to put the matter from his mind for the moment at least.

He massaged his temples and watched the earth lighten and sparkle around him. There was urgency in sending Pedrillo back to his own family, or at least apprising the good Clara of the boy's whereabouts, but this necessity was qualified by his own reluctance, by Jesus' grief and loss and by Pedrillo's disappointment and terror. These were matters better faced after the tempering of time, putting aside the fact that

Pedrillo had been on the ranchito for many months now. Time was the only response Manuel could dredge up. Time might not be the answer, but it was the only one he could find suitable at the moment.

A rising of tension and unease disturbed him before he came in sight of the ranchito. Something was wrong. He did not know what, but the premonition was too fearful to be denied. He laid the whip to Sal and entered the ranch yard in a cloud of pink dust.

He drew up hard on the reins, the buggy surrounded by screaming, laughing children, their faces turned up like imps from purgatory. He sat for a long moment unmoving on the boot. He recognized Jesusito, face illuminated with smiles of pleasure, Pedrillo, strutting and proud and important with news to impart, and Hubert was there, and little Concha and, with despair and a wince of dread, he saw the strange eyes of Teodoro. He resisted the fierce urge to turn away and cross himself. But there was bedlam to deal with, shouting children, barking, lunging dogs, dust, and the terrible sense of irreparable wrong and the threat of doom.

Pedrillo scrambled like a monkey up into the carriage with his uncle. Both Jesus and Teodoro tried to emulate their idol. Only the stolid Hubert and the shy Concha remained on the ground, gazing up at him as if they had never seen him before.

Pedrillo caught the old man's fist and kissed it with some passion. 'My mama,' he said, face twisted with delight, 'my mama has brought the little ones to visit us, Uncle. Is this not a gift of the Blessed Virgin Herself, Senor? Is this not a beautiful gift from heaven?'

Manuel pulled his hand away, confused and sicker than ever. He managed to take up his ricepaper-wrapped package and thrust squirming arms and legs aside so he could dismount to the ground, that insubstantial gauze wavering under him.

'A visit. A visit, Tio mio,' Concha cried.

Even Hubert Milhaus nodded and smiled in approbation. 'Your folks, Senor. They come to visit a spell.'

Pedrillo leaped to the ground in Manuel's wake and the younger boys jumped into his shadow, raging with laughter. Little Teodoro clutched Manuel about the leg, embracing him. 'Candy,' Teodoro shouted. 'Did you bring us candy?'

Manuel managed to disengage himself from the clasp of the

boy only to have Concha embrace him. 'Your rancho es grando muy,' she declared. 'So rich. So beautiful. I greet you with love and pleasure, Tio mio.'

Manuel waved his arms. 'All right. All right.'

Pedrillo spoke, his voice more sedate and uncertain. 'Mi mama,' he said. 'She has come to stay with the good senor for a while if one permits.'

Teodoro, Concha and Jesus greeted this news with screams of delight. Manuel waved his arms again. 'We see. We see what we see.'

Manuel walked slowly across the yard, admonishing the children to stay as they were in the faint mist of rain, to remain at play, promising later to drive them to the crossroads store at Apia for candy if they behaved well while he talked with their sainted mother.

'We shall do as you wish, Uncle,' Pedrillo said. 'If one permits, I let the little ones sit in the carriage while I lead the great horse to food and water.'

Manuel looked back from the front door. He nodded and smiled. 'That would be very good, Pedrillo mio. Perhaps too, you might rub Sal down. It has been a long night.'

He opened the door and stepped into the front room. The first thing he saw was a large wicker basket in which were neatly folded clothes piled high. And then he saw Clara, crouched in the rocking chair.

For an instant the old man's heart seemed to stop, a heavy useless weight in his chest. Clara lifted her head only briefly in greeting but it was enough. Aye God, more than enough. He saw the way she was battered, her cheeks torn, her lip split, one eye swollen and blackened. A sense of sickness washed down through him.

He stood gazing at her and Clara began to talk. It was as if she delivered a poorly prepared speech, like something badly learned, ill prepared, and yet words from deep inside, words which must be spoken. 'The children and I,' she said. 'We have come. We were brought by Senor Esteban Garcia, whom one hopes you recall. Esteban Garcia for some years was Felicia's boarder in the house on Aliso Street.'

'I remember,' whispered a voice Manuel hardly recognized as his own. 'I remember the good senor well.'

'It is that Senor Esteban Garcia is no longer Felicia's boarder,' Clara said as if this were the most important information she had to impart. 'No. Senor Esteban does well and has moved to better quarters, a place of his own. He has plans to marry, and he has bought one of the new Ford cars. It is the first one I or my children have ever ridden in. It is very good, though Senor Garcia was forced three times to change and patch his tyres on the drive out here. But it was his goodness of heart that makes it possible that we have come, the children and I, to the rancho of my dead sister's husband.'

Manuel's heart sank faintly. He understood the import of Clara's reminding him that he was Julia's husband. 'Are you all right?' he said. He felt inane because he could see she was not alright, she was battered and ill, but he had no words. He did not know what to say.

'I am very well, gracias. It is that I have brought the children.' Her voice broke. She continued to stare at the floor, her shoulders sagged. She did not look up at him. 'No. No es verdad, Senor. The truth is that I had nowhere else I might go with my children. You. My dead sister's husband. You are my only family — except for cousins in Hermosillo. Across the border.' She spread her hands. 'They have even less than I, and many mouths to feed.'

'You are welcome here, my wife's sister. You are ever welcome in my house. You have a place always in my heart.'

She caught her breath, her voice choked. 'I had nowhere else.' She twisted her hands. 'You have been so kind to my little Pedrillo. He has eaten well and grown much. And in his face shines happiness one has not seen there for a long time. I have missed him in my heart, but I am pleased he has done well in your house.'

'He too is welcome,' Manuel said, helpless for words.

'We shall try not to be a nuisance,' Clara said. 'And we go as soon as possible. You understand? It is that I had nowhere else.'

'I understand, Clara. You are welcome to stay here. As long as you like.' He spoke in sincerity, yet at the same time he felt a contrary anxiety about the evil eye of Teodoro. This matter would have to be dealt with, but this was not the moment, in Clara's agony and grief and embarrassment. 'You must not feel embarrassment. You must say this is your home. You must stay as long as you like.'

She nodded, pressing a sodden kerchief to her nose. 'It is that I knew you would say this. I knew you would speak from the goodness of a kind and gentle heart. I said to the Senor Esteban Garcia that you were a good man, my sister's husband, my family, and you would welcome us.'

'I welcome you,' he assured her.

'It is with gratitude that I accept,' Clara said. 'In humble thanks because I am without funds or friends or place to keep my children. It is my children I worry about. You understand?'

'I understand, dear Clara.'

'For myself, I might go anywhere. There is many things a woman can do if she must, but you understand, it is not the same for one with children.'

'I understand. You are welcome. I shall fix breakfast for you and the children and you shall stay as long as you wish.'

'Only until I have some place to go.'

'If that is what you wish. As long as pleases you. This is your home.'

Clara drew a deep breath and held it. Her head sank even lower and she spoke in a faint whisper. 'There is one matter more, Senor. Believe me, it is not easy and I speak from the heart what must be said.'

'One may say to me what one wishes.'

'It is a matter of my staying here. I and my children. It is that I want to understand all between us. All, you understand? Whatever you require of me, whatever you want —'

'What?'

'I am a chaste woman. But for my own husband I am pure.'

'I am sure of this, Clara.' He spread his hands. 'You need not speak of such things.'

'I must. I am in your debt. I owe — whatever you wish from me. You must say and I shall try to do for you.'

Manuel was not even sure he understood her, even while at the same time he was afraid that he did understand. He shook his head. 'No. No. What you suggest has no place here. You are my family. You are Julia's sister. I owe you much more than I can ever repay. You have suckled the son of my loins. You have cared for him and succoured him and kept him well. I owe you. Let's talk no more of this.'

'We must talk of it, or I cannot stay under thy roof.'

'I ask nothing like that of you.' He shook his head, the room spinning about him.

Her voice remained low, soft, but implacable. 'I want that

205

you know. I do not protest if you require of me that which pleases you in bed.'

'My God, Clara.'

'I want no strain or discord between us. No agitation of spirit because one desires what one fears will be denied one. I want not you to wish and to fear to speak. I wish no coldness because words cannot be spoken, or because one feels tied up inside.'

'Only the words you speak now tie me up inside,' he said.

'Do not misunderstand. It is not that I think you find allurement in me. I know better. I know I am fat and no longer pretty. But a man has needs. If one has needs, one must satisfy them or go to vinegar inside. . . . I and my children shall burden you enough, I will not add that burden to you.'

He looked around helplessly. 'Say no more of this, Clara. I understand that one is hurt and sad and without much hope. But there is hope here in my poor house. You will see. You will stay. And your children, and we shall eat well, and live good and. . . and say no more of this.'

XV

The first week of Clara's visit at Manuel's ranchito sped past. Manuel could not remember when time had raced along as these days appeared and melted. There was always noise, excitement, the wild and savagely innocent laughter of children. There was no time for melancholy, or for remorse or regret for all that was lost, all that must now never be. The children cavorted as if life were a continual party, as if they inhabited a carefree world of their own in which adults intruded only to feed and tend them. Pedrillo was Manuel's constant companion working among the bees. Patiently, Manuel tried to teach the boy the art of bee-keeping. Pedrillo did not mind being stung. He accepted these shattering attacks with some pride. He was proving himself manly. He shook his head, unable to believe that Manuel was never bitten, that bees crawled on him, his face, nape of neck, and he never batted at them and was never stung. When asked to explain it, Manuel could only shrug. 'One comes to know,' was all he said.

Instead of dragging himself out to his chores, Manuel found himself striding about his farm with new vigour, new purpose, new drive and new interest in life. Despite the fears and misgivings that had caused cold sweats and palpitations when he arrived home to find Clara and her brood descended upon him, life was not hectic and unmanageable. The routine of the crowded little house settled into a pleasant and even leisurely pace.

The bad eye of the child Teodoro had disturbed him most. He feared for Jesus in Teodoro's maleficent company. He feared for himself. He feared for his ranch and for his harvest. One glance from those baleful eyes and the honey-crop would sour or go to the ants, or fall to disease and rot. He owed Clara much, he revered her as the best of women, but he felt he had to tell her that he was not prepared to live under the threat of the evil eye.

Manuel made certain that Jesusito was never without the talisman warranted by Mme Rosa against the influence of the dreadful gaze. He told Clara that while they were welcome, Teodoro must never sleep in the same room with Jesusito.

Clara nodded. 'Yes. One has understanding, Senor. I shall fix a pallet for Teodoro in the kitchen. He shall not vex you.'

Jesus took care of these well-laid plans. Though Teodoro was mischievous, even innocently cruel at times, punching the dogs with sticks when no one was looking, pinching Concha until she struck at him and then beating her and defending himself as having struck only when provoked, Jesus was fascinated by his cousin. From the moment Teodoro arrived, Jesus attached himself to him fiercely, stoically accepting the tricks and deceits and pain such friendship entailed. He went into the kitchen when Teodoro was exiled there the first night, and when he was forcibly removed, he wept until he was permitted to share Teodoro's pad. Finally, making certain that Jesus wore his charm, Manuel surrendered and allowed the boys to sleep together.

On the morning of the third day, Manuel was stunned to find Teodoro wearing Jesusito's charm upon his own bare and nut-brown little chest. 'Jesusito gave it to me,' Teodoro said when Manuel threatened him with a hoe handle. And Jesus supported his adored cousin. He had indeed made a gift of the charm to Teodoro. Teodoro admired the talisman, had never owned one, and wished to possess so fine an ornament. Jesus was only too pleased to part with the trinket if he assured Teodoro's fickle devotion even for a little while.

Almost as disquieting as his fear of Teodoro's bad eye was Manuel's sense that Pedro would appear at any moment, drunk, demanding, violent, deadly. He tried to think what he would do if Pedro showed up suddenly — it had to happen sooner or later. He could not plan a defence, because he could imagine none. He placed bars and old utensil handles and broken spades strategically about the house and yard. He could not really even see himself using one of these weapons against Pedro Luiz because he was practical enough to realize that if he raised a bat against Pedro, Pedro would wrench it from him and use it mercilessly. He did not know what he would do. He delayed making plans until that bridge had to be crossed. In the meantime, he did not even like to think about it. In moments of silence or repose, his mind would swarm abruptly with cold terror.

'One sees the good senor is much troubled,' Clara said to him one day when he paused near where she washed the children's clothes over an open wood fire in the yard.

'No. No.' Manuel shook his head. 'Things go well.'

'Yes. For me and my children, very well indeed. We owe you much for your great kindness. It is not my wish to repay you in bad ways for all your good.'

'I don't know what you mean,' Manuel lied.

'One sees you watching the road out there, Senor. At times when the good senor does not realize it, one sees. You look for Pedro, my husband Pedro. One looks in dread for his coming.'

Manuel tried to smile. 'One does not look for it with watering mouth.'

'One must not fret. If Pedro comes, he will rage at me.'

'This troubles me deeply.'

Clara nodded, wiping a strand of black hair from her face with the back of her soapy hand. 'Yes. And for this one thanks you. But you must not worry about me. Pedro is my man. He has been with me twelve years and I know him well. Sometimes he is cruel, but with it all, there is feeling for me. Or there was. He has now a new woman — no longer the puta seeress of Aliso Street, but now one of the women Pablo Luiz has abandoned. She cried her tears of loss on Pedro's shoulder, and soon he was in her bed to make her forget Pablo's cruelty. This woman had no place to stay when her husband learned of her betrayal of his hearth with Pablo Luiz. This is why Pedro drove me away. I did not wish to leave my house, and so he beat me until I had to run for my life. That is when Esteban Garcia drove me and my children here. One does not think Pedro will seek me. One does not believe he wants one any more. I am fat now and no longer young. Pedro would as soon sweep the front porch as to bed with me — the thrill for him is the same.'

'Then he is a fool.'

Clara shrugged and returned to her washboard. 'I tell you this not to trouble you, but to reassure you, Senor. Pedro will not come. Sometimes, I too watch the road out there, but I know in my heart. He will come no more.'

2

Despite the presence of Teodoro of the baleful glance on the ranchito, Manuel took the greatest harvest of his life from his hives and combs. Pedrillo turned the crank of the extracting machine. Smiling, Manuel decided perhaps Pedrillo's persistent young strength forced out an extra measure from every rack. Anyhow, the harvest of honey was rich.

Pedrillo harnessed Sal to the old wagon. He also swept it clean of chicken droppings, for which Manuel was grateful. But when the boy drove Sal across the yard, backing the old cart to the very door of the honey shed, Manuel stood stunned with awe at such a time and labour-saving idea. When the boy saw that there was too much honey to be secured within the sideboards of the wagon bed, he drove ancient posts and staves along the sides and slipped planks inside the posts, planks supported by and supporting the extra, high-piled cans of honey.

Manuel stood in the shade and watched as Pedrillo loaded the wagon. 'I look with great pride on thee, Pedrillo,' he said. 'You are a smart nino. Like a whip, a great bull-whip, eh? All loaded, and all to be transported in one load. You have earned the right to drive the great horse all the way into the market on San Diego Street. I have great pride in you.'

Pedrillo looked as if he would burst with the pleasure he sucked from the praise of the old man. 'One is happy to work with thee, Tio mio,' Pedrillo said. 'My uncle is kind to my mother and my sister and brother. One does what one can to repay the kind uncle.'

With Pedrillo handling the reins, they drove together into the market where Pedrillo was allowed to stand near as Manuel haggled with the merchant for a better price for his goods, finally accepted payment and came away smiling at his reward. Never before had he taken a cheque of such magnitude to the big bank on Spring Street. Pedrillo was allowed to enter with Manuel and to stand as he deposited the cheque and withdrew cash for expenses. As they walked out of the bank where Pedrillo had glowed with pleasure at the warmth accorded his uncle and himself, Manuel paused on the path and pressed a peso into the boy's hand.

Pedrillo grinned, delighted. 'One does not need to do this,

Uncle.'

Manuel smiled and smoothed his hair. 'One has the wish to do it, Pedrillo. What will you do with so much money?'

Pedrillo walked in silence to the wagon. He climbed up onto the boot and took up the reins, considering his fortune. When Manuel had painfully sagged into the seat beside him, Pedrillo said, 'My mother has the love for the candy which covers the cherries. Does one know this candy? Perhaps I could buy a poke of it for the mother and the little ones.'

Manuel nodded. When Pedrillo asked where they should drive next, Manuel directed him to the Chinatown alley where he bought his tins of opium. This time he refused to allow Pedrillo to accompany him. 'These people hold the young much in contempt,' he said. 'They might be upset with me if I permit you to come with me. If thou wait patiently, we drive next to the store where we buy candy and sweets for the family.'

Pedrillo bought a poke of chocolate-covered cherries and had the bag secured with twine. He set it in the cool beneath the front seat. He and Manuel gorged themselves on the striped canes, nut clusters, jelly beans and orange jellied slices which Manuel bought for the long ride home.

They ate dinner in a Mexican restaurant. Pedrillo was allowed to choose his own menu and he ate ravenously. Manuel too was hungry, but he kept watching the people passing on the street, his heart a heavy lump in his chest. He felt almost compelled to inquire if one knew Pedro Grandos Luiz and what might be the latest information on that caballero. He did not ask; he managed to clean the tortillos and refried beans from his plate. He even tried to joke with Pedrillo. 'Eating all these beans, you and I, we'll play a merry tune all the way home, eh?'

Pedrillo blushed to the roots of his chopped black hair. He giggled and covered his mouth with embarrassment, looking about grinning to see if they were overheard in this forbidden exchange. 'Perhaps if things get too bad,' he whispered, 'I can get out and walk along the side of the wagon, eh?'

'Thou wouldn't want to walk behind it,' Manuel told him. He tried to smile, tried to think about the boy, but he was relieved when they got into the wagon again and headed Sal back toward the San Gabriel Valley.

3

The times flowered, the days passed bright and loud on Manuel's ranch. This was the end of his time of solitude. Except for dreading, when he paused to think about it, that time when the children and Clara would be gone, he was happy and content, with the thought of Pedro Luiz tamped down deep in the pits of his mind. He found the house swept and scoured as it had never been. They slept upon sheets and quilts washed once every week in boiling water and lye soap. Clara named lists of provisions and he and Pedrillo drove the children to the crossroads store at Apia to supply them. They ate as they never had in memory.

It seemed to Manuel that there was more vehicular traffic on the road out in front of his house. Either there were more wagons and more cars from the vast Stockton estate, or with Pedrillo and Clara to help him, he had more time to look up and to look outside himself. Sometimes in a great bulky Oldsmobile, Bragg Stockton, the patriarch of the estate, drove by sedately, at a speed which barely stirred the dust. The farm now boasted dozens of Ford trucks and they passed almost like a far-spaced parade. The open Stutz-Bearcat roadster was the car the children watched for and stood, wide-eyed, to see it race past in gales of dust and tiny stinging pebbles. Bragg Stockton's oldest son drove this fantastic machine, heading toward Los Angeles or careering from one ditch to the other on his way home. Bonnett Stockton spent as little time as possible at the farm; he would have stayed away altogether, Juan de Zaragosa had whispered, but Bragg Stockton had threatened to disinherit him if he did. Occasionally, a blonde vision of such unearthly loveliness sat in the roadster beside Bonnett that the children in Manuel's yard were convinced they were seeing a pale and fragile angel. Bonnett drove more sedately when the celestial lady accompanied him; she was seen not too often in the car.

These passing cars, trucks and wagons provided continual excitement for the children when games palled or they ran themselves into exhaustion and flung their bodies beneath the cottonwood to watch the sky and the road and the misty hills. Sometimes Manuel would hear Pedrillo regaling the little ones with the mystery and glamour and thrill of his journey into Los Angeles where he had been allowed to order his own meal in a real cafe.

Manuel worked in the orchard, trying to repair some of the ravages of years of neglect. Clara told him that when she was a girl she had learned to milk a cow and if they owned one, they could have fresh milk for the children and save a great deal of money. 'You have wide acres for the animal to graze,' she said. 'I am sure Pedrillo should wish to water the cow and stake her to graze. And I should teach him to milk too.'

Manuel bought the cow from the farm beyond the Milhaus place and Pedrillo walked it home, leading it with a short rope, Hubert striding along beside him, explaining how one cared for animals, how they must be milked. 'Only this one don't have to be milked for a long time. She's got to get crawled by a big-staffed bull and ridden good and hard around the field a time or two before she will come in with calf.'

'You're lying,' Pedrillo raged. 'You're making fun.'

'Are you crazy?' The stolid Hubert stared at him. 'Don't you know anything?'

'I know it ain't done that way,' Pedrillo said. 'If it was my Uncle Manuel would tell me.'

Hubert laughed at him. 'Your uncle is so old, he probably don't know how bulls and cows make little calves and milk to drink.'

'You make me sick,' Pedrillo said. 'And if that's the way it happens, I'll never drink another glass of milk as long as I live.'

'You are a dumb greaser,' Hubert said. 'How do you think your old lady got the milk in her tits to feed you?'

'Not from any bull,' Pedrillo said. 'I don't know if I'm big enough yet to beat the shit out of you, but I think I'll try.'

'Don't be dumb, Pete,' Hubert said. 'I'm telling you true. Your old man climbs on top of your mother and puts his jigger up in her and shoots off and then a baby starts to grow in her belly, and her tits swell up with milk. Just like a cow.'

Pedrillo began to cry. 'Shut up, damn you. Shut up to hell. If you ever say that again, I'll fight you. You talk about my mother like that again, you gringo son of a bitch, and I'll fight you.'

'Aw, Pete. I don't want to fight you. Stop crying. I'm just trying to tell you about life. That's all. Hell, ain't you ever jerked off?'

Pedrillo tried to run, but the lumbering bovine slowed him. Hubert kept pace, but he shrugged and said no more. The next time Pedrillo was alone with Manuel, he said, 'Will thou tell me true how cows make milk, Uncle?'

Manuel nodded and smiled. He sat on a stump and picked up a stick to whittle. Pedrillo stared at him, hopeful and yet anxious. 'The cows have in their bellies great vats which fill with milk that is made when they chew their cud. From the grass they eat. When a cow eats strong grass, her milk flows well and rich with much cream on top.'

Pedrillo winced; he wanted to believe, but he was past that stage of innocence. 'And calves, how are they made?'

Manuel drew a deep breath. 'It is like with children,' he said.

Pedrillo smiled, believing that at last they were getting somewhere. 'And what is that?' he asked, holding his breath.

'Your mama goes out in the great cabbage patch, and finds her child there on a cabbage leaf,' Manuel said. 'And the cow does much the same. She goes alone off into a gully or arroyo somewhere, and finds the calf she seeks, bringing it home with her.'

Pedrillo stared at him, his eyes blurred with tears. 'Aw, hell,' he said. 'Hubert told me you were too old to know anything.' He turned and walked away.

Manuel did not call him back. He was relieved and pleased to see Pedrillo go. He had known well enough what Pedrillo wanted to hear but he did not feel he was the one to spell out these complex facts of life for the boy, he had no idea how to go about it. Nobody had enlightened him, he had learned the hard way, and anyhow, as much as he would like to help Pedrillo, he didn't know how to say the words to a child. No, it was better to let him go his way in peace. There was time for Pedrillo to learn the truth.

Manuel had so much leisure these days with help and energetic helpers, he had time to think of things he'd been unable to consider before.

For no good reason that Manuel could formulate in his own mind, he began to worry about the health and wellbeing and even the whereabouts of his old friend Juan de Zaragosa. It was that Juan had not stopped by to share the demi-john of wine for many weeks — perhaps, in this sudden accelerated passage of time Manuel's preoccupation with Clara and her children, it was many months since he had seen the unhappy old man. Again, Manuel grinned, reminding himself that Juan was his junior by several years. But like most aging people, Manuel saw in himself a preserved youth he failed to detect in others around him. 'I have taken care of myself,' he would assure himself. 'I have not aged as most people do who have my years.' But Juan nagged at the rim of his consciousness almost like a robber bee at the hives.

As for Pedrillo, he told himself he was through forever with childish ignorance, foolish innocence and most especially was he quits with the lies and pretenses and hypocrisies of his elders. He still loved his Uncle Manuel, the kindest, gentlest and most patient man he had encoutered in his brief and hectic existence. Still, love was not the same as trust. He did not know if he could ever trust Tio Manuel again.

He prowled the farm for a while, speaking to nobody, and then, as soon as he could get away unnoticed, he left the ranchito and loped along the road in the saffron sunlight to the Milhaus farm. He stood in the yard before the front porch of the unkempt farmhouse and shouted until Hubert came out and stood staring stolidly down at him.

'What's the matter with you, Pete?' Hubert said. 'You look like you got a hate on for everbody in the world.'

Pedrillo merely shrugged his shoulders and motioned for Hubert to follow him. Puzzled, the tow-headed boy straggled in his wake. Pedrillo stalked silently across the bare red yard, chickens squawking from his path. He entered the old Milhaus barn and climbed the ladder to the hayloft. He stood tautly watching until Hubert joined him in this shadowed, hay-smelling upper cavern. Pedrillo flopped down into the straw, legs crossed and face pallid, but rigid and determined. 'All right,' he said. 'Show me how to jerk off. . . .'

4

Dressed in his Sunday best, Manuel drove in his carriage into the Stockton estate. He still had a long drive ahead of him, because the joke of the region was that a man could die of thirst between the time he entered the area marked with stones establishing the perimeters of the Stockton farms, and

215

that time when he finally came to the villa and well-water.

It was a hot and arid day with a faint breeze like the tatters of winds battered to pieces against the hills to the west. The sun lay vague shadows across the ploughed lands which stretched in precise rows as far as the eye could see. Manuel did not follow the main road which rose to knolls and eucalyptus groves and the red-tiled roof of the chateau Stockton, dimly discernible in the distance, almost like the hope of heaven. The clustered shacks of the permanent farm labourers lined both sides of a side artery out of sight of the great house. A mile or two removed, but still set apart and concealed, was the aged barracks where the migrants were accommodated.

Manuel had been often to the shack where Juan de Zaragosa had lived for almost twenty years. He guided Sal directly to it, shading his eyes in the hope of glimpsing his friend on the porch.

The shacks opened directly onto the single-laned road, steps rising from the sun-shattered shoulders to the porches which, like each shanty, were set on wooded pillars. All the houses looked exactly alike and most of them were empty during the ten-hour working day. A sombre silence hung suspended like a kind of miasma in the heat. Manuel halted Sal at the foot of the slab steps leading up to the shack where Juan had lived for so long. Mongrels lunged from the shadows of the porch, savagely snarling at Sal's legs. The barking set off other dogs and distantly, children, startled into troubled tears.

With a sinking sensation in his stomach, the finally accepted sense of something wrong, Manuel called, cupping his small hands about his mouth. 'Juan. Juan de Zaragosa. Are thou home, Juan?'

A dark-skinned young Mexican woman came shyly to the front door, peering from the depths of shadows at Manuel in the sunlight. 'Who does one seek?' she asked.

'Is not this the domicile of Juan de Zaragosa?'

The young woman stepped through the doorway to the porch. When she came out of the house, the mongrels ceased their vicious snapping at Sal's legs and retreated, hair bristling at their necks, beneath the open steps. The girl, who was not yet twenty, had a baby in her arms, a child clinging to her sack dress and her stomach bulging in pregnancy. She shook her

216

head. 'This is the house of Ramon Cortez,' she said. 'I do not know the name of Juan de Zaragosa. Perhaps another house?'

That feeling of illness congealing in his stomach, Manuel looked around and shook his head. At the end of the porch sagged a Mexican-built two-wheeled cart, one wheel missing; wherever Ramon and his family had come from, this was their transportation, disabled until it was needed again.

'How long hast thou lived in this place?' Manuel asked.

The girl shrugged. 'Many months, Senor.'

'And you did not know the man who lived here before?'

Again the girl shrugged. 'I don't know him. I don't know the name. This house was vacant when Ramon and I came here.'

Manuel was too troubled to abandon his quest. He tipped his hat and slapped the reins over Sal's rump. He drove, his belly increasingly empty, to the barracks where the migrants were housed and where a foreman was usually present to receive new workers and to keep labourers from loitering. The shadowed structure resembled a great barn lined with windows along both sides.

Manuel pulled his carriage into the worn area before the double doors of the silent barracks. He called, 'Hello. Is someone here?'

A stout man in a battered sun hat, its brim curled into a point over his ruddy face, stepped out into the sunlight. His denim shirt was stained with sweat at the armpits; he wore khaki trousers and calf-high boots. He squinted against the sun and peered at Manuel from the doorway. Plainly, he was ready to demand what the visitor wanted, what he was doing on Stockton property. Then he recognized the old fellow. 'You Manuel O'Brien, ain't you?'

'Yes, caballero. I am. And I recall you. Mr Church Foley. It is a pleasure to see you again.'

Church Foley shrugged, not caring to exchange further pleasantries. O'Brien was a Mexican, and Foley held for him the same casual contempt he held for all the greasers who showed up here, hat in hand, looking for work. The difference was, and it was slight at best, O'Brien wasn't a migrant or a worker. He was a landowner, and this set him apart from his compatriots, but not by very much; he was still a greaser. 'What you doin' around here, Manuel?

Manuel smiled and nodded. 'One seeks his old friend, Mr Foley. I went to the shack of Juan de Zaragosa. It is occupied by strangers who do not know Juan's name.'

Foley shrugged and shook his head. 'Naw. That's right, Manuel. Your old pal Juan ain't on the place any more.'

His worst fears realized, Manuel felt a tightening in his chest. He drew a deep breath and forced himself to go on smiling; with a fatuous smile a Mexican could always ingratiate himself with the Americano. 'That is too bad. But I do seek Juan. Is it that you might tell me where he went?'

Foley laughed. 'Hell no, Manuel. You know better than that. Greasers come in here from nowhere, and that's where they go when they leave, far as I am concerned.'

'But Juan is a little different, Senor Foley. No? For twenty years he was on this place.'

'Well, that was twenty years too long, far as I was concerned, Manuel. I know old Juan was a friend of yours, but he wasn't worth a shit. He got so he couldn't do more than an hour's work in ten. You know we can't put up with that.'

Manuel nodded, smiling, agreeing, hoping to delay long enough to find some clue. 'And he did not say where he was going?'

Church Foley stuck his tongue in his cheek and grinned in a flat and cold way. 'Matter of fact, now you mention it, I think he did. I got the idea that ole Juan is over at the Valdez farm.' He laughed, shaking his head. 'That's where a lot of the no-accounts go when they leave here. They can't hack a full day's work, they go begging at compadre Valdez' place.'

Manuel nodded, removing his hat and bobbing his head several times in gratitude. 'I thank you. It is a long drive to the farm of Murado Valdez.'

'Anywhere's a long drive from this place, Manuel,' Foley said in a boastful tone. 'Too far for an old fellow like you in this heat. Why don't you give it up? Likely Juan ain't still at the Valdez farm. He was worn out. Not even another Mexican could put up with a no-good whining greaser like Juan.'

Manuel nodded once more. He replaced his hat, continuing to smile. 'Perhaps you are right, Senor Foley. It is a long way. It is hot. Perhaps I go another day. Thank you, Senor Foley. You have been most kind.'

'Sure, Manuel.' Foley lifted his heavy arm in a brief slaute.

218

'You come back any time you want to.'

Manuel retraced his way to the western brink of the unfenced Stockton estate, but he did not turn toward his own ranchito. He pulled left on the reins and Sal moved unwillingly in response. Manuel did not hurry his horse. A drive beyond the limits of the Stockton fields and the Stockton groves and back was a day's travel in his carriage. He would rather sacrifice the day, however, than return to the ranchito still uncertain about the wellbeing of Juan de Zaragosa.

The horse plodded, the sun crested, a few birds tailed away on wind currents and Manuel drove through the planted silence. Often in the distance he could see gangs of labourers at work in the tomatoes, lettuce, olive groves, and vineyards. The lands of Murado Valdez abutted the rich acreage of the Stockton estate. Here sprawled thousands more productive acres, but the entire Valdez ranch, which had been in one family for five generations, would be swallowed in a remote corner of the outreaching Stockton enterprise. Still, it was the second largest farm of the area, Stockton's only true competitor.

Murado Valdez' home was enclosed in a low-fieldstone fence, almost certainly a hundred years old. Outside the wall, which scrambled about ponds, hammocks, lawns and buildings, every inch of arable land was in use. Men worked, stooped over furrows, in every direction. Near the house, but outside the ancient wall, spread grape vineyards and citrus groves. There was no smell of oil and defaced earth here, but a gentle fragrance of blossom and flower and bud.

Manuel entered the open gateway and drove through a shaded lane to the old house on a knoll. The red-tiled structure was built, Monterey style, low to the ground, sprawling about a large patio, with enclosed walkways, decorated with hanging plants, surrounding the living areas.

By the time Manuel reached the front driveway, his presence had been preceived, dogs barked and servants stood in shadows watching him. He was prepared to inquire for Senor Murado Valdez, but this gentleman strode across the patio from the large inner sunroom, crossed the shadowed walkway and stood awaiting Manuel on the wide stone steps, inset with bright tiles, and guarded by marble statues of lovers, hunters and loiterers, all nude.

Manuel nodded graciously and swung down from his carriage, exchanging greetings with the master of the farm. Though his family had lived in California for many generations, ancestors following the priests and fanatics north along the Camino Real, building missions and subduing Indians, Murado's forebears had married only Spanish blood. The family was as pure-blooded Spanish as when they were granted this land by the king of Spain.

Murado Valdez was a rotund man, slightly under medium height, with round shoulders. His keg-like chest was encased in a silk shirt open at the collar, decorated with a lavender kerchief about his throat. His trousers were ornamented with silver and turquoise, as were his boots.

One saw a pride in his moustached face, black hair deeply indented at the temples and brushed back, collar length. He held his head slightly tilted which might have appeared aggressive and even offensive in a lesser man, but seemed appropriate in this one. When Manuel explained why he had driven so far, Murado Valdez scowled at him, shaking his head. 'I do not hire all the workers who come on my place, Manuel. But I would be apprised of any workers from the farms of Senor Stockton. There is a good reason for this. Often Senor Stockton's foremen and occasionally one of his lawyers arrive here, with charges that I have spirited away the better of the Stockton migrants.'

'Forgive me, Senor. I regret having troubled you. But Juan is a very old friend and I have not seen him for many months. I was worried.'

Valdez shook his head again. 'Who told you that one Juan de Zaragosa had come here?'

'I was told by the Senor Foley, he who is a foreman of the Stocktons.'

Valdez nodded. 'I know Foley. I wonder that he would tell you such a tale and send you so far in this heat.'

Manuel's shoulders sagged. His distress and disappointment were evident to the landowner. 'I am sorry, Manuel. Sorry you made such a fruitless trip. Would thou have a glass of our own wine, and rest a little before you start home?'

Manuel thanked Valdez effusively, but he shook his head. He could not bring himself to intrude upon the grandeur of the Valdez home, nor to waste the time of Senor Murado Valdez himself. But most of all, he was too confused and troubled about Juan to be polite in such a stressful atmosphere. He wished only to escape. 'I hope you can forgive my intrusion, my inconvenience.'

'It is nothing, Manuel. I regret I can be of no help to you. If I hear any news of your old friend Juan, I shall send word to your farm at once.'

Manuel turned the carriage in the pebbled drive and started his exit along the shadowed lane. Over and over he told himself to go home and forget the matter, and over and over he told himself he could not do this. Still, if Juan wished to see him, he would come sooner or later to Manuel's ranchito, would he not? With this, Manuel had to be content. The midafternoon heat was stifling now, Sal was fatigued. There was nothing more he could do.

He reached the stone pillars of the gateway, slowing Sal and sitting for the moment in the last shade of tall trees that he would see for many miles.

He heard a hissed whisper from the outer shadow of the thick gatepost. 'Hist, Senor. Senor, Over here.'

Startled, Manuel looked around and saw a man pressed hard against the rough stone pillar as if trying to conceal himself in its shadow. He urged Sal forward and stopped the wagon beside the gate. 'Who are you?' he said to the hidden man. 'What do you want of me?'

'My name is Enrique, Senor O'Brien. I lived for a time in a house near your friend Juan de Zaragosa on the great farm of the Senor Stockton. I saw you visit often with Juan. I worked then in the kitchen at the Stockton house.' With some pride, he added, 'I cooked for the family. For the very family themselves.'

'And you knew Juan?'

'Very well, Senor. Back there, at the casa del Valdez, I heard you inquiring for Juan. The Senor Valdez tells you true. Juan de Zaragosa never came to this place to work. I got into some trouble with the head chef at casa del Stockton. When I was fired, I came here to work for Senor Valdez. They have started me washing dishes, but in time. . . .' He shrugged.

Eagerly, Manuel prompted the slender man. 'What do you know of Juan?'

Enrique spread his hands. 'Not very much. Perhaps a great deal.'

221

Manuel nodded. 'It is kind of you to take this trouble for me. I do appreciate it. Have you then seen Juan since he left the farm of Senor Stockton?'

Enrique shook his head. 'No. No. This I have not. There is not too much that I can tell you, except that Juan, in the courtyard of the great house at Stockton's, came and pleaded with El Patrone Stockton to overrule a foreman who had ordered Juan out of his house and off the Stockton estate. Senor Stockton shrugged and said there was nothing he could do. Juan was old and no longer able to work, and could not expect to live in charity on the great ranch. Juan began to cry and rage, reminding Senor Stockton of the many years he had worked without complaint. There were angry words. This I know. Juan angered Senor Stockton as I have never seen him upset. It was loud and ugly in the courtyard. I thought many times that Senor Stockton might destroy the old man with his bare fists. I do not know what happened to Juan after this. His belongings were taken from his house and burned. I never saw Juan on the place again. But this I know. Juan de Zaragosa never came to the casa del Valdez to work. He was never here. Senor Valdez speaks true.'

Manuel sagged upon the seat of the carriage. He felt very old and useless and impotent. He thanked Enrique and asked if perhaps he might show his gratitude with a peso or so. Enrique shook his head. 'One does me a favour, Senor, never to mention my name. Say not to anyone on the Stockton farm that you talked with me, or saw me at all. I spoke only because I too have been concerned about Juan. I hope you can find him.'

Manuel sighed. 'One would not know where to look.'

The man nodded. 'Why do you not approach Senor Bragg Stockton himself on the matter of Juan de Zaragosa? He alone might help you.'

5

Manuel drove tiredly in the late afternoon. He was ready to surrender, and yet somehow he could not abandon his search for some trace of his dear old compatriot. He had small hope of learning anything new and it frightened him a little to press against the wills of the patronos grandes of the region. He had long ago learned, with some physical pain and mental torment, that this was not the way to live in truce alongside the Americanos. He had with tact and some courage inquired and had been informed: Juan had simply disappeared, an old and unwanted man. This might well be more or less the truth. And yet he had spent the day all over the great provinces in search of the aged labourer. Two or three hours of sunlight remained. He had wasted the day; he may as well make the one last effort, though he no longer expected results.

He slumped in his travel-worn carriage, the vehicle, horse and man powdered with dust. He reached the intersection where the wide road passed between two stone markers on each shoulder, engraved with a flourished S. Drawing a deep breath and holding it for a long time, almost as if he'd forgotten how to breathe, Manuel turned the buggy to the right, entering the far-flung Stockton estate. Shadows lay long from any vertical thing; rocks, markers, posts shone, silvered on one side and ebony on the other. The work day for the labourers was over and the ploughed fields and manicured vineyards and geometrically designed groves glittered in slience. He gazed with some awe across those empty, eternal fields, rich with growth and promise, without movement or sound. Far in the distance, two foremen, picturesque in great sombreros, with spurred boots and drill breeches and white embroidered shirts, rounded up plodding braceros slumping toward the barracks and shacks like defeated armies. Long before Manuel was ready he climbed toward the smooth-walled hacienda crowning the knolls above the belly of the San Gabriel Valley. It unfolded itself in wavering sunlight, with verdant young crops, groves, vineyards, pastures and pools of water, emerald-like, from the blue mists of the remote sierras to a rugged immensity of shoulders reared against the sky, where vast clouds formed and rolled and seemed to curl into themselves.

Manuel's dread mounted as he approached the villa. He had been to this place a few times in the past, but never in comfort or ease, and his own mission added to his fear now. Like inevitability itself the carriage rolled in the unwavering lane toward the casa grande. He felt sharp shooting pains in his chest and across his shoulders at his temerity in questioning the lord of this manor.

There seemed to Manuel some irony in the Spanish architecture and atmosphere of the Stockton villa, because the Stocktons held anything Latin in such low regard. The labourers were less than human beings to the Anglos, despised and mistrusted. Though this was the third generation of Stocktons to dominate the valley, and though they dealt daily with Californos and Mexicanos, they had never bothered to learn more than a word or two of Spanish.

Still, the house itself was a mansion to inspire pride in the soul of any Latin, built around a cool and shadowed patio where a Madonna sat in marble silence, holding a crowned child upon her lap. Servants passed shadow-like through the arched passages or along the broad flights of stone steps leading to the upper floors. All the great windowed rooms on three sides of the semi-circle opened upon balconies and thus into each other and into the corridors. The patio was brilliant with colours, Indian hangings, flower clusters, green and gold tropical birds, parrots and parakeets. The chateau was the heart of this compound of villas and ten-room cottages in groups, with golf courses and pools and tennis courts and lawns tended emerald-green to serve as croquet pads.

The very sight of this vast, imposing, intimidating estate up close was enough to unman Manuel and to weaken his will. Even when he had driven along the long winding approach through the park-like land to the house, he might yet have turned back, lacking the courage to inquire at the front entrance for the caballero grande.

Voices and movement attracted Manuel's glance toward the six-car garage where men worked and chatted in the late afternoon. He gazed in awe at the expensive models of the latest designs. The clumsy, awkward mechanical beasts decorated the drive, all designed after the shape and form of his own carriage with engines appended.

Some of the men noticed the approaching carriage and stopped work. They straightened, staring at the old man and the plodding horse. Manuel's hands shook, his heart battered crazily and he might have turned Sal about and sped away, using his olive-branch whip, but he recognized Senor Bragg Stockton standing beside one of the cars where two mechanics tinkered tentatively with the exposed engine.

'Manuel drove to within a few feet of where Bragg Stockton stood, hands on hips, watching him. Manuel was aware of other members of the family, at ease on a veranda in lounge chairs or drinking at glass-topped tables. He felt ill at intruding upon this scene of luxurious relaxation. He kept his gaze on Mr Bragg Stockton and ignored everything else. A tall, greying man with grey moustache and unwavering grey eyes, he was known behind his back as 'King of San Gabriel'. He was the son of the man who had founded this farm, of reputed capabilities and excellent character, fair and just but unyielding, a member of the distinguished Stockton family, devouring and planting more and more of the valley. He was known to have easy access to the Governor and, some said, even the President and he was always host to important guests, publishers, bankers, importers, exporters, politicians of every ilk from county sheriff to ambassador. Deeply tanned, heavy-shouldered and barrel-chested, he tilted his head in an unconsciously arrogant way. He did not believe himself to be an arrogant man, but he admitted he was serenely conscious of who he was.

By now almost violently ill at his own temerity, Manuel scrambled down from the boot of his carriage and, bobbing his head, approached Bragg Stockton with hat in hand and pressed against the emptiness of his solar plexus.

'Well, Senor O'Brien,' Bragg Stockton said, nodding. He was bluffly hearty, with that exaggerated politeness one shows inferiors. 'What are you doing way out here?'

Bragg's eldest swung up from a chair under a eucalyptus and strode across the drive, carrying a highball glass in his hand. Taller than his father, he wore a pencil-thin moustache. His features were clear-cut and he was almost classically beautiful in the manner of ancient statuary. He was also deeply aware of his appearance. He held himself even more arrogantly than his father and without any apology. He swaggered in his own self-delight.

Behind Bonnett Stockton, Manuel glimpsed the blonde vision who sometimes accompanied Bonnett in his Stutz-Bearcat and inspired the Luiz children to awe and pleasure. She was gently and palely lovely but, Manuel noted, she was as productive as everything else on this rich estate. She was pregnant, as bulky and ungainly and uncomfortable as any peon woman in the pueblo below. Before either Manuel or Bragg Stockton could speak again, Bonnett strode in between them, staring along his nose at the little bee-keeper. 'What the hell you want around here, greaser?'

Manuel shifted uncomfortably, for a moment disconcerted by the savagery of the soft-spoken attack. Bonnett said, 'You're the little Mexican with all the bees, aren't you?' Manuel sighed and nodded. Like many arrogant men, Bonnett built his own self-esteem by categorizing all lesser beings.

Bragg said, 'That's all right, Bonnett. Senor O'Brien is always welcome here. He is a repected gentleman, a landowner, a neighbour.'

Bonnett laughed in a cold way that was like spittle in Manuel's face. 'Hell, Father, they're all neighbours. You know that. Neighbours who steal chickens, vegetables, calves. Anything that's not nailed down. What you want here, greaser? Make it quick and we'll send a mozo to accompany you to the highway to be certain nothing sticks to your hands.'

Bragg laughed indulgently. 'Why don't you see to your guests, Bonnett? Senor O'Brien and I are old friends. Eh, Manuel? We go back a long way. I'll handle this, Bonnett, thank you.'

Bonnett's ethereally beautiful and awkwardly pregnant wife closed her hands unobtrusively about Bonnett's elbow and walked back with him to the people lounging in the growing shadows near the house.

Manuel bobbed his head. 'It is not that I wish to trouble el patrone. No. No. It is that my good friend Juan de Zaragosa has not visited with me as was his practice over many years. And I have the deep worry about him.'

'Well, of course, Manuel. You and Juan are old friends. I'm truly sorry. He left here suddenly and it looks like he didn't even bother to say adios to his old friend, eh?'

'One is deeply worried,' Manuel said. 'It is not like him to depart with no farewell.'

'Well, Manuel, maybe nothing Juan did around here lately is really like him. He's gotten old and all kind of scrambled upstairs, you know? His mind wasn't clear as a crystal pool, I can tell you. Old. Senile. Doing things nobody could account for, not even Juan himself. Why, he even turned on me shortly before he disappeared. Me. And I've always believed if Juan had two friends, I was one of them and you were the other. Eh? I thought the old fellow was devoted to me, body and soul. I'm sorry about this, Manuel, but I'm afraid Juan and I parted rather abruptly. I was upset and even angry with him. I'm afraid I don't know where he's gone.'

'I hoped maybe for some word. I hate to think of him, wandering around.'

'Yeah, that would be a cruel fate, all right. I always say the cruelest. I think maybe when a man gets old and ill and empty upstairs maybe death is the kindest way out. Eh?'

'You don't think perhaps Juan is dead?'

'I don't know where Juan is. I was talking abstractly, Manuel. All I was saying was there's no place in this world for the terminally old. And that's what Juan was.'

'One hopes he might have said where he was going.'

'Well, he didn't. Not to me. And none of the bosses of the campos have said where he might be. Sometimes Mexicans when they get peeved here go over to Murado Valdez, crying their woes.'

'Juan is not there. Senor Valdez has not seen him.'

'Well, there you are. Juan just likely took off. Without a word to you or to me. It's too bad, but I'm afraid that's the answer.'

Manuel nodded, his heart sinking. 'I wish to thank el patrone for his kindness. It was not my wish to trouble the good senor.'

'Of course you didn't, Manuel. I understand that. You're a respected neighbour. Some of the Mexicans who squat on or buy up little parcels of this rich land are worse than a plague. Some of these people get to thinking they're white Americans. They get too damn big for their serapes.' Bragg smiled. 'But you are quiet and keep to yourself, and I respect that, Manuel.'

'I am of Irish descent,' Manuel said.

'Of course you are.' Bragg's mouth twisted down and he winked at his mechanic at his side. 'Of course you are. And a good neighbour. On your own little place. You make no trouble, you don't try to expand. Don't try to buy up every inch of open land. You been a good neighbour for a long time, O'Brien. I don't mind having greasers like you around. It's them sons of bitches like Murado Valdez that turns my ass to clabber. Him and his land grant. Him and his fine airs. He's still a bastard greaser. I don't give a damn how many generations Latins live in California, that still don't make 'em white Americans.'

227

'I thank you, Senor Stockton, and I'll continue to seek for word of Juan.'

'Yes. You do that, Manuel. For your own peace of mind. You let me know if you hear anything, and I'll do the same for you.' He straightened. 'I'd ask you to stay, Manuel, but Birt here is trying to ease up the carburetor on this here new Oldsmobile of mine and I was hoping to run it out for a test spin before dark.'

Manuel nodded. 'I go. Thank you again, Senor.' He climbed back up into his carriage, aware of the silent gazes fixed on him from the lounge chairs.

Bragg Stockton walked over and placed his hand on the rim of the carriage wheel. 'I know you are worried, Manuel. I know you and Juan are old friends. Good friends. Drinking friends.' He winked. 'Friends of the pipe, eh? And I realize how worried you are about the old fellow. I respect that. I admit to a peeve with Juan there at the last, but that's all forgiven and forgotten by now, as far as I am concerned. I tell you what. You keep looking for Juan, and I'll keep my weather eye out. Eh? For old times sake. We all three been here in this valley a long time, eh? You. You come back. Give me time to ask around. Eh? We'll find some word on Juan. You got my vow on that, Manuel.'

XVI

The world was crimson, the early dusk sky streaked with striae of livid red, empurpled. Time seemed to have changed speeds, hurrying all day and now slowing in a strange and unsettling way. Manuel had not hoped to make it back to the ranchito until well after dark, but the valley, although hazed, was burning feverishly red, everything sharply defined in the blaze of sunset when he turned off the washed and travel-rutted road into his yard.

He pulled sharply on the reins, jerking Sal to a heads-jolting stop when he saw children huddled together, mute, just inside the gate.

'What is it? What is the matter?' he asked. 'Que pasa, Pedrillo?'

'It is my father, Uncle,' Pedrillo said. His face was pallid, cheek muscles rigid. 'My father who says he has come for his family. He says he has come to take us home.'

A scream tore across the yard from the house. For an eternal moment Manuel sat transfixed, gripping the reins, unable to move or to speak, unable at last to cope with the time he had expected all these months. He did not know what to do. He was even unsure that he could get down from the carriage seat and, if he did, if his spindly legs would support him. His bowels seemed to have clabbered.

Clara's screams ripped at him. It was a wail of agony and yet something about it throbbed with forbidden pleasure, as if she were being assaulted and yet found in the beating some perverse delight, painful enjoyment. He winced. In Clara's mind a husband had the right to brutalize his woman. If he battered her, she somehow deserved the punishment, she must submit to the pummelling. It was her lot.

Somehow, Manuel managed to leap down to the ground. He steadied himself, his trembling hand against the steel rim of the cart wheel. Clara screamed again and nearer, the children moaned and hugged each other. Only Pedrillo stood aside, angry and rigid and defiant, and helpless. The dogs whined and circled in the yard, behaving in a way Manuel had never seen before, like coyotes about to bay at the moon.

'You stay here. With the little ones,' Manuel said to Pedrillo.

Drawing a deep breath and holding it in his burning lungs, Manuel ran across the yard and grasped the knob of the front door. Pedrillo ran to him, shaking his head. 'My father has barred the door with a chair to keep us out, Senor.'

Manuel nodded, looking around impotently. Clara's scream was muffled, as if she swallowed the agony and pain and pleasure but could not keep it inside herself.

'Stay here,' Manuel said to Pedrillo. It was not that it mattered what the boy did, Manuel was reassured in his terror by the sound of his own voice. Clara cried out again and he shuddered visibly.

Manuel ran around the house to the kitchen. It didn't make sense that Pedro would bar the front door and leave the rear open. Manuel did not even approach the entrance. He saw a broken axe handle where he had tossed it under the edge of the rear porch. He bent down and took it up, hefting it in his hand, but drawing no sense of security from its weight and texture.

The kitchen window was open, a curtain unfurling at one side in a lazy, shiftless way. He levered himself up over the sill and for a moment, clinging to the axe handle, hung half in and half out.

Writhing there, he heard Pedro's voice, a savage, guttural sound that shook the house and rattled in the crannies of Manuel's belly. Manuel went weak as whey, his will deserting him. He might have toppled back to the yard but Clara cried out again in that strange and unsettling wailing.

Manuel pulled himself over the sill. He landed hard upon his shoulder on the kitchen floor. The noise continued unabated from the bedroom. If they heard him, they ignored his presence, coiled in their own violence.

He stood up and, gripping the axe handle, sidled across the room to the bedroom door. In the doorway, he paused, staring at the bed where Pedro held his wife down, assaulting her. Clara's long black hair was loose about her battered face

230

and traced sweaty tendrils across the rumpled sheets. She bit at her broken mouth, holding back sobs and then wailing aloud. Though she was bare above her hips, her long sack dress rolled up over her rotund belly, and although her naked legs and bare feet were widespread, knees locked at Pedro's buffeting waist, Manuel's mind could not accept what he saw. Half his mind told him that Pedro was on his wife, a rutting boar, and that she could not take him deeply enough to satisfy the cravings inside her. He had never, even in a stud pasture, seen such mindless coupling. . . if that was what it was. Manuel's mind rejected this. He could see that Clara was badly beaten, her face torn and bleeding, her arms discloured with contusions. He had come to believe all these months that her fear of Pedro Luiz was as real as his own terror of the brutal man. And it did not seem to an ageing, gentle mind that any woman could willingly submit to such a hombrenazo as was this arrogant bully holding her down and pounding himself upon her. His fist tightened on the axe handle, his muscles tensed, and then slowly he opened his fingers and allowed the handle to slip to the floor.

'No. No.' Manuel heard his croaking voice protesting in the sweating and charged tension of the room. 'No. No, Senor. You must not harm her. You must stop before you hurt her.'

There was a tense delay before Manuel's voice and presence registered on Pedro's mind and he was able to jerk his head around and focus his gaze on the little man in the door. 'Goddamn you,' Pedro growled. 'What you want in here, old goat?'

'Stop, Senor. I beg you. Do not harm her more. You hurt her.'

Pedro had reared up, bracing himself on the heels of his hands on each side of Clara's sweating, writhing body, but while he slowed his tempo, he did not stop thrusting with his hips. He laughed savagely. 'You crazy old asshole. Do you know nothing in your old age? Singame. Singame. I fuck my wife, you stupid old cuckoo.'

The very presence of the wide-eyed old man added spice to Pedro's savage flagellation of his wife. Watching Manuel with a sweetly agonized smile of contempt twisting his face, Pedro caught her full breasts in both hands, twisting as he drove his hips in mounting frenzy. His whole body shook and trembled. He groaned in pained release and clung to her, rearing rigid above her. Clara too moaned, shivered and slumped beneath him on the rumpled sheet. For uncounted moments Pedro remained suspended there, weak and vulnerable. His mouth hung open, his wide shoulders sagged round and he breathed in a rapid, hurting way.

Manuel stood watching them, convinced at last, wanting to retreat but unable to move at all. He saw the colour return to Pedro's pallid cheeks, the old rage kindled again deep in the wild black eyes. Gaze fixed on Manuel, Pedro levered himself up from between Clara's widespread thighs.

Standing, legs braced apart, Pedro shoved his member back inside his clothing but did not bother to button his fly. When Clara would have moved on the bed, he snarled over his shoulder without even looking at her. 'Stay where you are, whore. Stay as you are, shameful puta. Do you think I believe this old goat has not seen you in your nakedness?'

Clara lowered her legs, but otherwise remained unmoving. She was afraid to move against Pedro's command, afraid to speak, for fear he would batter her again with his fists.

'Look at her, old man,' Pedro growled. 'Look your last. I have come to take your fat whore away. Her and her bastard brats. Did you think I would let you injure me in this way? Rob me of my wife. Rob me of my son. Rob me of my children. Rob me even of the son of my own loins. Rob me of the girl that comforted me. Claim the son of her womb as your own. You who are old and limp and shoot only whey and piss. Do you believe that you could make child? That bastard in the yard there is mine, old goat. As this woman is mine. As her sister was mine. You stole from me. You stole all. You are a thieving son of a bitch who deserves not to live.'

Manuel shook his head. He had never seen such madness as moiled in Pedro's wild eyes. Manuel might have cried out, but he saw in Pedro's face that there were no words to reach him, there was no way to placate him in the madness he had seen in this man before. He retreated a step.

Pedro cried out as if Manuel's very movement were insult unbearable. 'Stand still old man. I am not done with the rich old man who seduces away the sons and women of honest men. I come here and find my woman living with you, baring her nakedness to you, living and sleeping in this house with you. Am I asked to endure this? Before God, I shall not endure this evil.'

'No, no, Senor,' Manuel managed to whisper through his taut throat. 'It is not as you say.'

'Do you call me liar? Is that what is to be now? You rob me and now say I lie. Did I ask you to speak? Do I need to hear lies from your ugly old mouth? Why do you come sneaking in here, to watch me upon my own wife? Is it you have never seen a real man singamas before? What do you want in here? Do you think to keep my own woman from me, even now? You think maybe because you are rich with much money in the big bank that she is yours? You can take my woman and my children from me because you are rich? Do you think I'll permit you to take my wife and her sister and my son and my children? No. You son of a bitch. You'll not get away with it. They will not laugh at Pedro Luiz that a juiceless old goat stole his wife from him. I have come to take her home, but first I give you a lesson you never forget.'

Manuel wanted to turn and run, he wanted to protest, but he could do nothing but sag against the door-jamb. He saw Pedro only through an occluding red mist. Pedro moved in a terrible slow motion, taking up the axe handle from the floor, hefting it in his fist and then backhanding Manuel with it across the side of his head. A rasping sound like the breaking of fragile adobe crackled in the silence. Manuel staggered but did not speak. Pedro brought the axe handle back again, this time across Manuel's throat, smashing his larynx. Manuel gasped, but did not breathe. His knees buckled and he crumpled to the floor. He was already dead, his skull and his throat crushed under the furious blows, but Pedro went on hitting him. He stood over him, beating him from his skull to the back of his legs, raging when Manuel remained inert. Pedro panted through his open mouth, venting all his fury and outrage and injury with the flailing bar. He stopped only when Clara's voice intruded into his madness.

'Stop. Please. My husband. Cease. Cease. You have killed him. Hit him no more. He is dead.'

2

'Open this door!'

The voice was loud, commanding, Anglo-Saxon, perhaps an articulation of gringo authority. Pedro went weak, seeing that he had been trapped once more in an unfair machination of fate, ever known to bedevil the underlings of this world. A man was injured, outraged, bereft, and when he struck back, it was again the poor devil who was further violated and mistreated. None of this was his fault, the old goat was to blame, and yet who was to believe him in his adversity?

Fists pounded on the door now. The gringo voice threatened to break it in unless it was opened at once. Biting back the bile that boiled up into his throat, Pedro looked around wildly, cunning replacing the immobilizing terror glittering in his black eyes. He hastily buttoned his fly, straightened his clothing. He gazed at Clara across his shoulder. 'Do as I say,' he told her. 'You will support your husband in whatever I say. Or God help you.'

Clara merely nodded. Her face was ashen, her black hair loose and wet about her face and shoulders. She stared as if transfixed in pity and agony at the small, scrawny little body twisted out of shape and unmoving on the floor. Poor old man. He had been kind to her and her children and she had brought him death. This guilt she must live with the rest of her life and yet it did not matter because she could see no future ahead for herself anyway. Whatever miserable existence she'd had ended with Manuel's savage murder.

Pedro stared down at the bloody axe handle in his fist. Though the weapon was badly smeared with blood, thank God there was none on his own hands or his clothing. He threw the shaft across the room. It struck at the base of the wall and fell in the shadows at the edge of the bed.

'Cover your face with your hands,' Pedro ordered Clara in a hoarse whisper. 'Weep — as if you weep in distress. You will agree with all I say.'

Clara nodded again. She pressed her splayed hands over her battered face and wept. Her body shook with her sobbing. Her teeth chattered. She was afraid that now she had started to cry she might never stop crying on this earth.

Pedro stood one more moment as the pounding on the door

increased, rattling the house. His mind spun. He looked about, like a trapped animal. Though unknown gringos beat at the door there was still one chance to run, to go out at the rear of the house as old Manuel had come in. He wiped the back of his hand across his mouth. He could run, but he could not keep running. And he had no money. He had come out here to reclaim his family and to get money out of the old miser, even if he used force. God knew, he hadn't meant to kill the old goat; he had wished only to teach him a lesson and to get money from him. It had even been in his mind to leave Clara and her bastard brats here as long as he got enough dinero from the old man. God knew, he should be paid for the injury done him by the evil old bastard. But he had no money. That was all that mattered now. He had nowhere to go without funds.

A shoulder struck against the door facing, but Pedro did not yet move, trying to find some answers inside his own reeling brain. Perhaps there was a solution even the coldest-hearted gringo would believe. He could swear before the Mother of God that he had arrived here, without rancour, only to find the rutting old goat in bed with his wife, and in that sudden temporary madness which is known to over-whelm an outraged husband, he had killed him — the right of common law. But even as he thought this he could hear deep inside his mind the laughter of the hombres along the bar at La Madreselva — laughing at him because a scrawny old goat took his woman. He would be alive if he invoked the right of the common law that a betrayed man may protect his home and hearth, but he would not want to live with that savage laughter of his friends at La Madreselva like cold spittle in his face from now on. No. He wanted to live. But he wanted the world to know he was a man. A man who acted in fury but in righteousness.

There seemed only one choice left to him. He must act in truth and humility. He must open this door and throw himself on the mercy of the gringo. He saw this was indeed the precise answer he had sought, this gave him the one chance to resume his life as it had been before Manuel O'Brien injured, outraged and betrayed him. This one chance had nothing to do with common law or with any claim of justice. The simple fact was, what Americano gave a damn in hell for the life of one more shrivelled old greaser?

'You watch yourself, woman,' he said from the side of his mouth and crossed the room to the front door. 'One moment, Senor,' He called in a warm and gracious tone. 'I shall open the door at once.'

He shook his shirt up on his wide shoulders, took up the chair and set it aside against the wall. He opened the door and stepped back, bowing slightly, inviting the gringo in, the rich-looking gringo, aye God, dressed to the nines. Distinguished. The real upper crust.

Bragg Stockton stepped through the doorway and paused just inside the darkening room.

Bragg looked around with the instant comprehension of the speed reader, the man who had tasted at all springs in life and was astonished at no evil, no greed, no savagery of the human animal. The room reeked of death. He saw the rumpled bed, the helplessly sobbing woman, the twisted body crumpled out of shape as if the corpse had tried to dig his way to freedom.

Stockton drew a breath. He didn't have to touch O'Brien to know the old man was dead. No mortal could lie contorted as he was, head hanging back over his own shoulder, and live. O'Brien looked like nothing more than a crushed spider on that floor.

'What happened here?' he said to the smiling Mexican who watched him meekly and respectfully.

'We have a tragedy, Patrono,' Pedro said in an agonized voice.

'I can see that. What happened? That's what I want to know. A boy ran out into the middle of the road to flag me down. I almost ran over him. He was sobbing and hardly able to talk.'

'A child, Senor. A young boy. All a mistake, Patrono.'

Bragg Stockton's voice hardened. He despised Mexicans who tried to play games with him. He'd known them all; he knew all their tricks. He said, 'The child didn't think it was a mistake. He was hysterical. Screaming for help. He would not move. If I had not stopped, he would have been killed.

'I understand, Patrono. One holds you in no way to blame.'

'I'm not talking blame, hombre. I want to know what happened. Who killed old man O'Brien?'

Pedro smiled, nodded and washed his hands. 'It is all an error. A terrible error, Patrono. . . . The boy, he misunderstood. He was in the yard. He heard words. We talked loud,

Manuel and I, but we did not speak in anger.'

Bragg Stockton bit back an ironic smile. 'No anger. Old Manuel just had a fit, twisted himself out of shape and fell dead on the floor, while you did all you could to succour him. Is that true, hombre?'

Pedro winced. 'It is not precisely thus, Patrono.'

'I figured not. How was it precisely?'

'We argued because Manuel had come home, sat for a while with his pipe, and then in a kind of madness, set upon Clara, accusing her of much evil. I am Clara's husband, Patrono, and I reasoned with Manuel, begged that he not treat poor Clara in such an evil way. But he was much driven by the fumes of the pipe. He would not listen to my pleas.'

Bragg Stockton was silent for a moment; in that flash of time his entire attitude altered. A look of sorrow, almost as false as Pedro's humble smile, crept across the arrogantly distinguished features of el patrono. Stockton nodded and spoke in a tone of grieving understanding and compassion. 'It has long been known that O'Brien was on opium. We had never heard stories of his violence. Usually these people become tranquil, almost comatose. . . . Well, we never know, do we?'

'He had never been so wild before, Patrono. Never. But he attacked Clara. Then he went wild, falling on chairs and hurting himself. Clara and I tried to do what we could for the old man, but he died. He died in my arms, Patrono.'

'I see. Very sad.' Stockton shrugged. 'He was a good man, but there is nothing we can do for him now.'

'We want to do all we can, Patrono.'

'Who are you? What is your relationship to the old man?'

'He was my dearest friend, Patrono. Despite the years between us.'

'But not related to you?'

Pedro looked as if he might weep. 'Not by blood, Patrono. No. But the Senor O'Brien married Julia, sister of my woman, Clara here.'

'And this Julia? where is she?'

'It is sad, Patrono. Julia died in birth of the son she bore to the old senor.'

Stockton almost smiled. 'Well, I'm damned, the old greaser was still begetting. At his age. I'm damned. And the child? Is he alive?'

'He lives, Senor.'

'And the child is the sole heir of Senor O'Brien?'

'Es verdad, Patrono. True. The poor old man. He was alone in the world with no family, except Julia and his child.'

'And his pipe,' Stockton said, nodding to himself. 'I think I see how it must have been here. You people have my deepest condolences, of course. But now, there may be a few things to be done. I shall contact Morris Redding for you.'

'Perdone, Patrono. Who is one Senor Morris Redding?'

'You don't live around here, then?'

'No, Senor. We have been visiting Clara's brother-in-law, the Senor O'Brien.' Pedro nodded, smiling. 'We live in east Los Angeles. On Aliso Street.'

'Well, that's why you don't know Morris Redding. Morris is the deputy sheriff out this way. Morris and his under deputies are the law in the valley. He is a good friend of mine. A reasonable man. I shall explain in detail precisely what happened in this regrettable tragedy here. I believe he will understand. I believe you may rest assured that he will see that the death certificate is marked accidental death.'

'Gracias, Patrono. Mucho gracias.' Pedro's eyes now filled with tears.

Stockton gestured with his hand. 'Yes. Well, these things happen. No cause to disrupt the lives of everyone, even the old man's child, when an elderly man, drugged with opium, kills himself. I believe Morris Redding will concur in that thought. As for you and your wife, I suggest that you straighten up here. If I were you, Senor — what is your name?' And when Pedro told him, Stockton shrugged. 'All right, Pedro. I think you should go at once to the mission church at Apia and notify Father Garcia. He will know how to handle all arrangements for the Mass and the funeral.'

Pedro was weeping now and nodding with every word Bragg Stockton spoke. He shuddered inwardly, his stomach moiling. He had witnessed a miracle here. He was seeing goodness and decency in action and he had expected abuse and accusation. It was all going to be handled for him. The old man was dead and el patrono would notify the law and handle the matter of the death certificate, and the priest at Apia would see to the funeral and church ceremonies. He had been vindicated; he had been spared.

Stockton was looking around the room. 'Morris may come

over to talk to you folks. But there is nothing to worry about. Just tell him as you told me. You'll find him extremely cooperative and compassionate. A good man. I've known Morris for a long time. But if you are going to have the priest here — and it's important that you do — I think you ought to clean this place up. I don't believe that Morris would object if you put the old man's body on his bed — after you've made it up, of course.'

'We will do all as you say, Patrono.'

Stockton nodded. He stepped around Clara and took up the bloody axe handle. 'I'll just take this along. Get it out of the way. Looks as if the old man must have fallen on it a dozen or so times before he died.'

3

A dreadful silence settled over the ranchito and the valley with the lowering darkness. Clara twisted and plaited her hair in braids on each side of her face. She changed the sheets and quilts on the bed. When she told Pedro it was time to place the corpse on the bed, he looked up from where he knelt beside Manuel's body. He had removed Manuel's battered pocketbook from the old man's trousers and was transferring the money, paper and coins, to his own pocket. He replaced the wallet gingerly, his face twisting. 'I cannot touch a dead body,' he said. He shuddered, his shoulders rising and falling. 'You will have to do it. Besides, my back is in great pain.'

Clara only nodded. Without speaking, she caught Manuel's body by the boots and dragged him across the bare floor to the bed. Squatting, she lifted his shoulders and torso, letting him topple onto the mattress. Then she straightened before the corpse could fall back to the floor, caught his legs and heaved them onto the covers. She rolled the thin little body until it lay on its back in the middle of the bed. She folded his arms across his chest as she had seen cadavers in funeral parlors. She sighed. The old man looked peaceful in death. She turned and looked at Manuel who was counting the money. 'Well, it is done. Perhaps, as the senor said, you should go now for the priest at Apia.'

Pedro shrugged. 'That can wait until morning.'

'Are we to spend the night, then, in this place?' Clara asked.

'What else? You heard el patrono, he is sending someone from the sheriff's office to talk to us. How would it look if we ran away in the night?'

'I hate to stay here,' Clara said. 'In this place of death.'

Pedro stared at her, his face rigid. 'You have stayed here all these months. You can stay one more night. El patrono goes to help me in this matter. I go to do as he instructs. And you will do as I say.'

The lamplight merely intensified the shadows in the room. Clara called the children from the front door. She bade them to go around to the kitchen where she would let them in and feed them their supper. The children nodded silently and plodded around the dark house. They entered the lighted kitchen and sat down without speaking.

Clara cooked eggs and ham. She worked silently, moving about the room on bare feet. Pedro brought a demi-john of wine, got a tumbler and sat at the table, drinking. The children did not speak to him and he said nothing to them. When the eggs and ham were prepared, Clara placed the plate upon the table and told the children to eat. She did not sit down. She prowled the room, restive and silent. She heard Pedro emit a slight chuckle and she turned from the window and looked at him. He had finished off his meal, wiping up his plate with a slab of bread. He poured another tumbler of wine and sat turning something in his fingers. 'What have you there?' Clara said.

'The tie-pin the old man always wore. He'll need it no more.'

'Perhaps one might wish to give it to Jesusito. A gift from Manuel. He would want Jesus to have it, one feels.'

Pedro hesitated a moment and then shook his head. 'Well, that's too bad. This thing is real gold. A gold ten-dollar piece. Why should one give it to the child? The little bastard would only lose it.'

Clara shrugged and did not reply. Pedro laughed and said, 'If one wishes the child to have something, maybe we can give him the long-stemmed pipe the old cabron loved so much. Eh?'

The whole family slept that night on pallets on the kitchen floor. None entered the bedroom where the corpse lay, none

240

mentioned the old man. Clara did not sleep. She crouched against the wall, a quilt, serape-like, about her shoulders. Sometimes her eyes filled with tears. Sometimes she merely stared unblinking into the darkness. Sometimes she dozed and wakened, biting her mouth to keep from crying out. In the false dawn, she finally fell asleep, fatigued.

Pedro shook her awake. Sunshine splashed into the room through the open door and opened window. 'Get up. Get up,' Pedro said. 'It is time one prepared breakfast. The jerif may arrive at any hour. We must be ready for him. There is much to do, and I wish to get back to town before dark. I have no wish to spend another night in this house.'

Clara got painfully to her feet. The muscles of her body ached and her face was bruised and tender, as sore as a festering boil. She made breakfast and the odours of cooking food wakened the children. They played, subdued and sombre, on the floor until she told them to eat. She tried to talk to Pedrillo but he merely stared at her emptily and said nothing.

After breakfast, Pedro said, 'Pedrillo. Hast not the old man taught you to harness and drive the horse and carriage?'

Pedrillo nodded. 'Then I would have you drive to the Catholic church along the road at Apia. One will say to the priest at the manse that there has been a death here at the ranchito. One will say an old man has died. An old man who has many years has died. One will say no more than this. One will ask the priest to come that he might say Mass and arrange for the funeral.'

Pedrillo nodded and left the house, as if relieved to escape. They heard him in the yard and then saw him drive past the window, sitting alone on the boot of the carriage, slapping the reins and speaking quietly to the horse.

Pedrillo had been gone along the road to Apia less than thirty minutes when two uniformed horsemen rode into the yard of the ranchito and dismounted. One of the officers stayed with the tied-up animals, the other looked around the yard a moment and then approached the house.

Watching the stout, heavy-hipped, thick-legged man come toward the door, Pedro slumped, sick at heart. He felt his throat choke and a sense of dread moil in his stomach. This deputy was an Anglo-Saxon, the kind of gringo Pedro had learned to fear. There was no look of compassion or weakness

241

about the tanned, leather-hard face or the sun-faded blue eyes. Even the mouth, beneath a stylish trimmed moustache was cold and unsmiling. Pedro's heart battered in his ribcage; his breathing shortened and his breath burned in his throat; he was afraid to speak for fear his voice would crack. It was not a sense of guilt that immobilized him; he felt no guilt. By now he had accepted El Patrono Stockton's version of Manuel's death: the old man had died from opium madness. Pedro's dread came from his fear of the gringo deputy. Here was the kind of officer who would beat a suspect to get from him the answers he wanted. Pedro had lived through the night with hope; suddenly he was sick with anxiety.

He went on quivering legs to the front door and held it open, even before the deputy came up the steps. Pedro nodded, trying to show grief and to smile obsequiously at the same time.

Morris Redding introduced himself and said, 'I hear you folks had some trouble here last night?'

Pedro nodded, swallowing at bile. 'An accident, officer. A sad accident. The old man was on opium. He fell and was killed. We tried to do all we could for him. There is no guilt. No crime, Senor. No. It is the sad death of an old man, a very old man.'

Redding made a sharp cutting gesture with his muscled arm. 'All right. All right. Let's get on with it.'

'Does the noble sir wish to come inside to view the body?'

Redding squinted and shook his head. 'Ain't no sense in that, Mex. Why don't you come out here?'

Overcome with sudden fear, Pedro nodded and stepped through the doorway to the porch. He was unable to go on standing on legs that had turned to whey and refused to support him. Pedro slumped against the wall. 'Let me tell you my side of it,' he said in a whining tone. 'Please, noble, let me explain to you the accident.'

Redding shook his head. 'I got no time for that, boy. I don't want to hear about it. I already heard what happened, from Mister Bragg Stockton hisself. I don't give a shit what you say, but whatever Mister Bragg Stockton says is pure gospel to me and Mister Stockton has spoken for you. You got good sense, you'll let it go at that.'

Pedro nodded. 'Whatever you say, jerif. It is as you wish.'

Redding grinned coldly, a smile never meant to be shared.

'Yer damned right it is, Mex. Now, let's get on with it and stop wasting my time. What I want to know is, who owns this property?'

'The deceased, noble one. He owned it.'

'And what kind of family does this deceased leave? I mean, who will inherit this place, this house and land, now that the old man has passed on?'

'The old man had no blood kin, sir. His only kin is his son. Jesusito is his only blood relative. The child makes two years old.'

'Two years old, huh? The only relative, eh?'

Pedro drew a deep, painful breath. 'And the child alone will inherit?'

'That's none of my business, hombre. And none of yours. I reckon I can tell you this much. Looks like the child will inherit. It'll have to go through the probate courts, and it'll take a while. But, yes, I'd say the two-year-old will inherit everything.'

Pedro felt a new sickness bubble and boil in his belly. He shook his head. 'The child? The little one? Who makes only two years? He will get all this — and too the great amounts in the big bank on Spring Street?'

'Why not? It's all his. Like I say, it'll take a while. Courts are slow.'

'But Jesusito is a child, Senor. A helpless child, to be left so much money.'

Redding stared at Pedro, unsmiling. 'If I was you, hombre, I wouldn't worry about that. You don't need to worry about things that don't concern you none.'

'But everything, Senor? To the child?' Pedro shook his head, his fear and dread now less acute than this new sickness, eating at the lining of his stomach like hot acid.

'Like I say, don't fret it, Mex. The court will appoint a caretaker for the child and his estate. That's the way it is done. I can tell you, with Mister Bragg Stockton interested in this, it may be speeded up some. Yes. It will move pretty fast.'

Pedro shook his head, seeing himself injured and defrauded one more time by the old cabron. All this money and land to a child barely able to say his own name. It didn't make sense. It wasn't right. 'A caretaker?' he murmured. 'What does the honourable senor mean, a caretaker?'

'An executor of the old man's estate, hombre. I can't explain it to you. Maybe in a few days Mister Bragg Stockton will send a lawyer to talk to you. He'll be able to tell you about an executor.'

'An executor? And who will this be?'

Morris Redding shrugged and grinned coldly. 'I told you, don't fret it. Right now what ought to concern you is that I am having the coroner sign a certificate for accidental death. As for the executor, Mister Stockton's lawyer can tell you about that. Hell, you say you are the kid's uncle, maybe they'll name you executor. Who knows?'

The funeral of Manuel O'Brien was held with graveside ceremonies the following day. Father Garcia had arrived at the ranchito with Pedrillo in the carriage. He was angered when he found the deceased stiff with rigor mortis. He wanted Pedro to notify an undertaker at once. He said a few hasty prayers over the cadaver and departed.

The day of the funeral was overcast, with the threat of rain, and a blowing mist in the atmosphere. A raw mound of earth was dug in the O'Brien cemetery plot beside the grave of Julia, with that of Anna on the other side and surrounded by long-dead children of Manuel's first marriage.

Father Garcia conducted the funeral service. He spoke swiftly and without emotion, reading much in Latin. It was as if he had never known the deceased and was in haste to be out of this place.

One could scarcely blame the padre. The service was meagre and poorly attended. Chairs had been placed near the open pit, but most were empty. Mme Rosa and her daughter Francisca were there, the madame in black and the daughter dressed soberly, but with many bows and ornaments. Mrs Milhaus and her son Hubert had driven in from their farm to pay their respects. They sat together on the back row, the first to arrive, the first to leave. Clara and Concha sat with Pedro who wept loudly and sank from the chair to his knees sobbing in the midst of the rites. Cipriano too was there, along with the sad, pale and coughing Felicia and her former boarder Esteban Garcia. Esteban showed neither sympathy nor concern nor even very much interest. The truth was that he was present solely because he owned an automobile, transportation for Felicia who had been kind to him and for her family in a time of grief. The only other person to attend was

244

an aged Chinese gentleman, wearing a pigtail, a black armband and ceremonial robes. He did not sit down, but stood to one side, his head bowed. As a matter of fact, the only tears shed during the hurried ceremony were in the eyes of the ancient Chinese and the sobbing Pedro Luiz.

The ceremony was abruptly ended by Father Garcia who muttered something in Latin, crossed himself and waved incense over the open pit before he turned and strode away, followed by his acolytes, without speaking to any of the bereaved. Pedro gathered his family in Manuel's carriage. In the intervening time between Manuel's regrettable death and the funeral, Pedro had been advised by an attorney, sent to represent him by Mr Bragg Stockton himself, that in all likelihood Pedro would be named as executor of the late Manuel O'Brien's estate by the courts. At least, the attorney would request this, and he foresaw no problem. In the meantime, as executor, Pedro would be allowed to draw cash from the estate to cover expenses of burial and livelihood for the two-year-old heir. The attorney had advised Pedro that unless he planned to live at the ranchito, he might wish to remove anything of value so that it would not be lost to vandals.

Pedro drove in silence into the valley. Clara and the children said little on the long ride. At the ranchito, the children leaped from the carriage and played under the eucalyptus tree. Pedrillo fed the horse, the cow and the chickens.

Pedro went into the silent house. For a long time he ransacked the rooms but found nothing of value. He allowed Clara to fill a small poke with old Manuel's belongings to be held as mementoes of the senor for his son. Pedro checked through the bag but finding nothing of use, shrugged and returned it to the silent woman.

When he had searched the house, Pedro went into the yard. He gathered kindling, pieces of wood and paper and set fire to the honey shed. He stood watching with silent satisfaction as this last symbol of the evil old man's livelihood went up in smoke. With a long rake, Pedro then went among the hives. He shoved them over, leaving them in broken rows along the ground. When this was done, he whistled for the dogs. When Rosa and her son approached him, Pedro killed them and left them lying in the field for the vultures.

He returned to the yard, tied the cow to the rear of the carriage and set the children to catching the chickens which he piled into a wire box. He yelled for Pedrillo to come help the little ones run down the chickens, but Pedrillo did not answer. When at last the carriage was loaded with everything of value and the family was ready to return to Los Angeles, Pedro shouted again for Pedrillo, growing angrier by the moment. They could not find the boy; he was gone and finally they were forced to leave without him.

XVII

By the time Jesus was nine years old all memory of the ranchito, the bees, the black bitch and her mongrel son had dimmed and faded from his mind. He had forgotten the farm and he would have misplaced Manuel O'Brien deep in his recesses of abstraction but for Clara. Clara would not let him forget. She saw this obligation as her debt to the old man who had been kind to her and paid for his kindness with his life.

While she was careful never to mention the old senor in the presence of her husband, she found many opportunities to remind Jesus, to talk to him of who he was, who his sire had been, and what his father expected of him. 'He wanted you for the Church,' she would say often. 'Your loving father wished you should be a priest and say prayers for his soul, and for the soul of your poor mother and, if it occurs to you, you might say one for your Aunt Clara who loves you.'

Clara took Jesusito, Teodoro and Concha to Mass every Sunday. Her own children found nothing in the huge cathedral to stir them, but she had not hoped for this. She watched Jesus avidly, if secretly. She waited for that moment when his eyes would glow with a healing light, when he would see truths denied ordinary men and women, when he would find a dedication to God within himself. No matter how diligently she studied, she found nothing to reassure her. She saw plainly enough that Jesus sat still only when she ordered him to, his mind wandered, he yawned often, bored and restless and apathetic. She could rouse in him no sense of awe or inspiration or devotion.

Clara took hope in the mind-bending effects of the Catholic school where Teodoro and Jesus were under the tutelage of devout, pious and reverent nuns. The cost of the church school for her children was excessive in the mind of her husband, but Clara was quietly adamant. She prevailed.

247

Concha, Teodoro and Jesus attended the school of the sisters. Concha became a little prude, simpering and beatific, often sitting with her hands pressed together as if in prayer, and her head tilted to available light. This would have troubled Clara but she remembered what a little actress she herself had been as a child, always pretending, forever enmeshed in some secret fantasy. This pose of Concha would fall away, Clara told herself with a faint smile, on that hot day when Concha discovered boys.

Clara sighed. In the meantime, it was fun to watch Concha in her solemn little games where she was purer than the Virgin Mother Herself. Teodoro said sometimes it was hard to believe that Concha went to the outhouse like ordinary people.

Teodoro was, to Clara's shock, the best student of the three. He was a quiet and placid child with his elders, though there was about him as he grew that old streak of meanness. Teodoro got good marks at school, the sisters liked him and often let him stay after lessons to clean blackboards and pound erasers. Clara felt sickness when she realized why the nuns kept Teodoro in the classroom until the schoolyard should be almost empty. The children, reminded and reinforced by their elders, never let Teodoro forget that he was the one with the evil eye. Sometimes girls would approach him in coveys and then race away screaming that they had been damaged by the bad gaze.

Standing looking at Teodoro at night when he lay on his pallet asleep beside Jesus, Clara would bite back tears. Teodoro was damned by that evil puta of Aliso Street, that lewd and wanton fortune-teller who had lied about her child to sell her rotten talismans. Clara's shoulders sagged. She was helpless to aid Teodoro. As he became aware of the way people turned their faces from him, and cursed him, and even threw rocks and sticks at him, and crossed themselves when they met him by accident, he maybe even in his own mind accepted the guilt of the evil look. If everyone said he was bad, then he might be bad. She could only love him and reassure him and hold him in her arms when he wakened screaming from nightmares.

Though she had Teodoro and Concha, and was responsible for the welfare of Jesusito, Clara lived with a constant sense of loss. She was bereft. Her eldest son was gone. No

248

one had had word of him since, as an eleven-year-old boy, he had run away alone from the ranchito. She had not seen Pedrillo for seven eternal years, but he had never been out of her mind for more than moments at a time. Waking, sleepless at night, Clara would walk out onto the porch of her house and stand with a shawl about her shoulders, watching the night street, waiting for Pedrillo to come home to her. If he lived, he would be a young man now, eighteen years old, with that classic profile and those beautiful black eyes, and she would not even know him if she met him. She might pass him on the street and not recognize him. She prayed, standing alone in the misty night, that wherever he was, Pedrillo was warm and healthy and with food to eat. In all the cruelty she had endured in God's name, this was the most devastating. Sometimes her throat closed and ached so badly she could hardly breathe, and sometimes she didn't even want to breathe any more at all.

And as if to torment her she saw Jesus growing to look like Pedrillo, to remind her, to keep in her mind him she would not see again on this earth. And although Pedro did not say so aloud, he too recognized Pedrillo in the young cousin and he treated the boy with the same casual cruelty that had made Pedrillo's life an unending hell. Pedro would playfully cuff Jesus when the boy came near him, sometimes striking him with his fist or sharply with the flat of his hand, but laughing as if it were a game and he was teaching the boy to be a man and to weather the hard knocks ahead of him. 'You got to be a man, Jesusito,' Pedro would say. 'You got to stand up for yourself. You got to be fast on your feet,' and he would hit him again before the boy could evade him.

If Jesusito protested at this treatment, Clara never heard him. There was a serenity and apathy about the child that brought Julia back as if the younger sister still lived. It was as if Jesus expected nothing of life, was inured to cruelty, and no longer cared. He seemed remote, removed. He loved Cipriano's music and tried to get his uncle to teach him the accordion, but Cipriano was too busy with his senoritas, and he warned Teodoro and Jesusito to keep their hands off his instrument.

Jesus went quietly and phlegmatically to school, but as surely as he took nothing with him to the convent, he brought nothing from it. He loitered with Teodoro on the way and entered the classrooms silently and indifferently. The nuns complained to Clara about that faint smiling way that Jesus had, looking as if he were about to wink. 'It is almost,' one furious nun said, 'as if he is saying to you that the two of you share some shameful and obscene secret. And the rest of the time there is about him the look of stupidity.' Clara tried fruitlessly to explain about the smallpox, the weakened left upper eyelid, but the sisters did not listen; they did not want excuses. They wanted Jesus warned of the dire consequences if he continued to appear, every time he smiled, about to wink at the holy sisters. In God's name, it was intolerable.

And too, Jesus entered into the games of the children at school only if he were forced to do so. He was reticent and withdrawn, his placidity a kind of dignified wall between himself and his playmates. If they approached, he gave them rare shy smiles which seemed to involve a disposition to wink about something. He watched with eager, avid interest the play and games of the other children, but he was unable to emerge from his bashful shell and abandon himself to pranks and screams. He gazed longingly at their roughhouse playing but stayed aloof from it.

It was as bad in the classroom. He appeared to comprehend English with difficulty. One could almost see him translating to Spanish and struggling to answer in English. The nuns refused to allow him to speak in Spanish; if he did, he was punished.

Jesus was satisfied to listen and observe; he was fascinated by the bright, loud and irreverent children around him. His closest acquaintances remained in many ways strangers to him. He would have been content in his self-imposed solitude, but the good sisters refused to permit him to stand aside. He tried to please the nuns, but seldom did. He never defied instruction, but what was offered to him never impressed itself upon him, and he had no will to study or to learn. He never shirked obedience or questioned the authority of the teachers. Clara sent him to school and he went unquestioningly. He sat there in lethargy, waiting only for the three o'clock bell.

His serenity aroused displeasure in every authority. He was compliant to the wishes of all in charge, but his was a passive compliance which outraged his elders more then his defiance might have. They wanted active reaction and he had none for

250

them. He was willing to submit, but he had no idea of what they wanted from him. He failed to learn; he remained isloated in crowds.

Only in his consuming devotion to Teodoro did he break free of his torpor. He and his cousin were inseparable, and because they were, they arrived at the Luiz home off Aliso Street every night battered and bloody. When Teodoro was attacked or tormented or teased about his evil gaze, Jesus joined Teodoro in battle and, when Teodoro refrained from the conflict, fought alone until he was too weak and too sore to stand. 'You're so stupid, Jesusito,' Teodoro told him. 'You don't know how to quit. You don't know how to lie down and play dead. They will kill you. As long as you fight them, they will kill you.'

Jesus spat blood and shrugged. He had nothing to say, and even if he had, there were no words. Cruelty to Teodoro was an assault on his own person and he would not endure it. If they hated Teodoro, they hated him. If they fought Teodoro, they must fight him. He knew no other way.

In many ways, these years had passed in a kind of bland serenity for Jesus. There was money always for food at the Luiz house, though sometimes Pedro handed it over grudgingly. There were moments when Clara was forced to remind her husband that if it were not for the boy, Pedro would not be the executor, able to withdraw money at will from the big bank on Spring Street. Pedro cursed, but he provided food and clothing for Jesus and for Teodoro and Concha. Nine years earlier, the probate judge had warned Senor Luiz that what he was doing, taking the orphan into his home and providing for him, was a selfless and admirable thing, but nevertheless would require an accounting of the funds expended. Sometimes, needing money to gamble at La Madreselva, he would resent being forced to lay out cash on Clara and the bastard brats, but he wanted no inquiry into his administration of Manuel O'Brian's estate. He fed and clothed Jesusito adequately.

A whole new lifestyle prevailed at the Luiz triplex off Aliso Street. Pedro would have moved into better accommodation as befitted his new station, but he lived in an inescapable dread of the watchful eye of the probate court. The Los Angeles County Courthouse intimidated him; he feared the law itself; he despised the police; he was unmanned by the dignity and solemnity of the judicial chambers. Though he was treated with repect and courtesy down there, he knew from bitter experience how quickly the winds of gringo friendship could alter, darken and devastate the unfortunate of his class. Still, he had moved up in the world. He was providing home and sustenance to a ward of the court; he himself represented that awesome court as executor of old O'Brien's estate. One thing appeared certain in his own mind. He could no longer slouch about La Madreselva and Aliso Street and the neighbourhood in the shabby suit Manuel O'Brien had purchased three years earlier for the man-child's christening. He had torn the knee of those trousers; a tailor had botched the repair. Those trousers would always look to be what they were, patched and dowdy.

Pedro entered his new existence with the cautious purchase of a single new suit from the haberdashery on Main Street which he had first entered with old Manuel. Planning for this event, he carefully hoarded money, from the food budget, a few extra dollars charged against the rent. He relinquished everything except whores and gambling. No man should be required to forsake the essentials of existence, else life itself became an eternal season of Lent. He was not a man to live like that.

He decided to gamble. Heart in his throat, he bought a new teal-green suit with feathered felt hat to match. He ordered the outfit in trepidation. It was not that he suffered any sense of guilt; he did not. Where was guilt in a successful man's looking at least marginally prosperous? Could any reasonable person ask less? What he feared was the cold, heavy hand of the probate court closing on his shoulder. For Pedro there was no sin in supplying one's needs at any cost to family, neighbour or society; a man and his own necessities had to come first; the crime was in being apprehended and punished by the impersonal and dehumanized system of the law.

He stood before the triple mirrors admiring the extraordinary dark Latin male beauty God had lavished upon him but at the same time keeping a sick, weather-eye on the street entrance. He bought a pongee shirt with high detachable celluloid collar such as he saw in photographs and lithographs of the best dressed college men. He set off the shirtsleeves with red arm garters and gold-plated cufflinks. Upon the watered-silk blue tie he secured the ten-dollar gold-piece pin he'd inherited from Manuel O'Brien.

He was not courageous or foolhardy enough to wear the new outfit from the shop. He had the goods packaged and carried them home under his arm. It was almost three days before he summoned the audacity to venture out upon Aliso Street so bedecked. He had made a date with a woman he hoped to impress and thus to join her in her husband's bed, the fellow being absent for a period of six months to a year.

He took a long time dressing, splashing cologne about his crotch and in his armpits, shaking hair tonic into his thick chopped curls and massaging his face with shaving lotions. Not even a bath would have made him smell better. He strode from the house in the early evening darkness, faintly secure in the shadowed night. Clara watched him silently. He was one of the most handsome men she had ever known, and the least moral. He made no secret of the fact that he was on his way to his latest assignation. Clara would see him next when he tired, exhausted his funds, or was caught by some jealous lover. She made no protest. She was resigned.

Pedro promenaded proudly with his new paramour along Aliso Street. They drank tequila together at a discreet booth under a Tiffany-style lamp in La Madreselva. They danced the tarantella in the ballroom. Pedro spent freely but not all his sweat was excreted in passion and pleasure. He did not look over his shoulder all evening, but he sure as hell wanted to.

Nothing untoward occurred to mar the delight of the evening. The lady was indeed impressed with his largesse and his charisma. She'd known few men who spent as freely. Whatever she wanted, he bought for her at once. The senora was in her early twenties, beginning to be heavy in the calves, matronly about the hips, robust at the half-exposed and thickly powdered bosom. Younger and prettier damas circulated in the plaza, the bars and dancehalls, but lately Pedro found the younger sluts demanding and insulting and sometimes contemptuous of his prowess. To hell with them; a woman got a few years on her, she knew what was expected of her, she knew what a man wanted, she knew how to please an hombre and performed willingly; she was grateful for a handsome man's attentions; she reciprocated his interest. And this young senora on his arm was still young and flashy enough to get him noticed, admired and envied by his peers. She smelled good and she felt good and she laughed at everything he said.

He spent the evening abroad with the lady and encountered no representative of any court. No one appeared to be watching him. Encouraged, he bought a new suit the next week, and another the week following. His shirts rose in a tall stack in his bedroom cupboard. He did not permit Clara to wash these precious items, they were hand-laundered and folded by the Chinese laundry in Aliso Street.

Reassured by his purchases, he no longer approached the big bank in Spring Street in trepidation and tension. If he needed fifty or even a hundred dollars, he boldly scrawled his withdrawal slips and received the funds as easily and with as much gracious attention as old O'Brien ever had. The bank employees came to know him. The guard smiled and called him by name. The tellers asked if it was hot enough for him, and did he think America might enter the war raging in Europe? To such inquiry, he only shrugged. He paid no attention to the weather and he had no idea where Europe was or why anyone would would fight over it.

Striding through the barrio with money in his pockets, Pedro came to consider himself one of the elite; if not on a social par yet with say, El Patrono Stockton, at least recognized and, in many ways, sponsored by that supreme gentleman.

When Pedro looked back infrequently to the onset of his good fortune, he never reached that tragic moment when poor Manuel O'Brien had died in his arms on the ranchito. It seemed to Pedro that Mr Bragg Stockton had set in motion all those wheels which had improved the lot of Pedro Grandos Luiz. The great landowner had erased the moment of tragedy for him when Manuel died. Stockton had sent an attorney to represent Pedro before the probate court. Through the good offices of these gentlemen, Pedro had been named executor of the O'Brien estate; he had been elevated in the condition of life and the bottomless vaults of the great bank in Spring Street had been opened to him.

There had been uneasy moments at first which Pedro now recognized as grounded only in his own mistaken doubts. He had nothing to fear from Mr Bragg Stockton, and Mr Bragg Stockton with one word could protect him from minions of the law, even the deputy sheriff and the sheriff and the judges themselves. Pedro had never imagined any gringo could be so friendly, considerate and helpful as Senor Stockton had been to him. He even told himself that whatever he wanted, he had only to request it of El Patrono Stockton. Senor Stockton was a good man. For a gringo, he continually proved himself incredibly warm and generous and understanding.

Pedro's first touchy moment had come soon after he had been appointed executor by the probate court and he hesitantly and sweatily cashed his first draft for twenty-five dollars at the Spring Street bank.

He was at home one morning when an automobile, an official new Ford of the Los Angeles Sheriff's Department, parked at his curb. The entire neighbourhood spilled out into the street to stare and whisper and point.

Deputy Morris Redding was alone in the car. He got out and came up to the door and knocked, his huge fist rattling echoes from the frame building. At first, sick in his belly, Pedro had ordered Clara in hoarse whispers to say he was not at home. He considered putting on his shirt and shoes and sidling out of the kitchen door. He could run along the alley and hide until Deputy Redding tired and departed. But at the commanding tone of Redding's hard voice, Pedro quaked, too weak-legged to run. 'Come out here, Pedro. I want to talk to you.'

Pedro's mind swarmed with a hundred ills, dreads and guilts. Buttoning his shirt across his bared chest, he plodded to the door, feeling as if he waded in a calf-deep surf. He tried to smile, washing his hands together and bowing. 'I've done no wrong, sir,' he whimpered. 'I swear it.'

'To hell with that.' Morris Redding waved his arm. 'Get your clothes on. You're coming with me.'

'But I've spent only twenty-five dollars, sir. Food. Clothes. Spent most frugally.'

'Mr Bragg Stockton wants to see you. Out to his place. I'll drive you.'

Shaken, unsure that he would ever return to Aliso Street alive, unsteady on his feet, his eyes burning with unshed tears, ready to sob out his innocence of any and all crimes and to plead no guilt and to beg for mercy, Pedro got into the Ford. He felt the eyes of his neighbours on him. None seemed astonished to see him in the clutches of the law.

It was a long, silent and rough drive into the country. It was also by far the longest journey Pedro had ever made by car. He was too sick inside to enjoy it.

Morris Redding did not bother talking to him on the trip into the San Gabriel Valley. Driving consumed Redding's entire attention. He did not drive well. He gripped the wheel with both hands and kept turning it back and forth in short, quick jerks, as most drivers of his day did, as if piloting a boat in choppy seas. Pedro was quite seasick by the time they reached the Stockton mansion.

Pedro was rendered speechless at the splendour of the vast estate, the elegance of the Spanish-style villa, the cars in the drives and garages, the tennis courts, the swimming-pool, the telephones set conveniently and profligately on tables or walls, the electric chandeliers which glowed in the entrance, day and night. Pedro had never encountered such magnificence. He had never beheld such marvels before. He had never even in his most heated fantasy supposed people actually lived in such luxury, casually and indifferently, taking all this fashionable beauty for granted.

Pedro and Morris Redding waited in the flowering patio, standing, ill at ease, though wicker chairs were placed about the stone-paved court. Bragg Stockton and his eldest son came out of a sun parlour at last and greeted the deputy and Pedro coolly. Stockton wasted no words. He said, 'I brought you out here, Pedro, because I want to buy that O'Brien land.'

Pedro stared at him, unsure what this desire had to do with him. 'Sir?'

'Don't play games, Luiz.'

'Games? Me? Oh, no, sir. I am most serious. Most anxious to please el patrono, if the good gentleman will be kind enough to tell me what it is he wishes.'

'My God,' Bonnett Stockton said, shaking his head.

Bragg Stockton gestured toward his son and said, 'I told you what I want. I want to buy the O'Brien place. I don't know what offers you've had. Nothing there of any great value. Vandals have destroyed thousands of dollars worth of bee-hives and equipment. I want to buy, and I don't anticipate that you will raise any obstacle in my way.'

'Oh no, sir. I wouldn't do that.'

'You don't understand me yet, do you?' Stockton scowled at him.

Seeing the great man displeased unmanned Pedro. He felt he might wet his pants, but he was at a loss. 'Understand, Patrono? Understand?'

Stockton shook his head, spoke with terrible patience. 'Your nephew — the three-year-old child — Jesus O'Brien — owns that section of land. I want to buy the parcel. Since you represent your ward, I've brought you out here to offer you a fair price. Whether it's market price or not, I don't know, I haven't inquired, but it is what I am willing to pay.'

'Of course, Senor. I have no wish to hold the land from you.'

'That's very wise of you, Pedro. I am willing to pay you five hundred an acre — quite a generous offer for unimproved land. And anyway, quite generous under the circumstances.'

Pedro gave him a false and ingratiating smile. 'I am more than anxious to trust el patrono in this matter.'

'I hope so.'

'The good gentleman has been most kind to me.'

'You better remember that.'

'Oh, I'll never forget it, El Patrono.'

'You'd do well not to.' He shrugged. 'It's settled then. I'll have a check placed in the account of the heir. Bonnett has a couple of papers for you to sign. You may make an X if you like — '

'I write fluently, El Parono.'

'Well. How nice. Just your signature.' The landowner smiled faintly. 'You seem to be living high on the hog, Pedro.'

Pedro nodded. 'One gets along, Patrono.'

'One will get along best if one never forgets who his friends are, Luiz.'

Pedro went cold with fright, without knowing why. The three men smiled at him, nothing had changed, the atmosphere was redolent of jasmine and yet Pedro leaked chilled sweat. He tried to smile. 'I don't understand, Patrono.'

Bragg Stockton shrugged. 'As long as you understand one thing, Pedro, you and I will get along and you won't have to fret the details. Just remember this, amigo: There is no statute of limitations on murder.'

XVIII

Changes ripped at Jesus' familiar world of Main Street and
Aliso and Sixth. The old safe boundaries disappeared and
there followed an unsettling invasion of the strange and
unaccountable. Everything seemed to move faster. Aged
buildings were wrecked, torn down and replaced with
structures soon as dusty and battered and scarred and pigeon-
streaked as the old. The unquiet streets were far more
crowded and faceless people hurried, shoppers swarming the
paths, strangers blowing the horns of their new cars.

Teodoro was fascinated by these new machines. He could
stand for long minutes on a kerb just staring at a parked car.
He boasted that he would be an auto mechanic when he
escaped the convent; one day he'd own his own garage where
people would bring their vehicles because no one could fix
them as well as he. Jesus had little interest in the smoky,
balky, bouncing ogres. When Teodoro challenged him, he
declared he preferred horses though they left the streets
stinking and messy. He didn't care; he would as soon walk, he
wasn't in any hurry and wasn't planning to go anywhere.

Like Teodoro, Pedro was hypnotized by the wonder of the
automobile. To own a car seemed to him the ultimate symbol
of status, the final proof of manhood unquestioned, unques-
tionable. He talked constantly of buying himself a touring
sedan, the open four-door with jump-seats so the entire Luiz
clan could drive out to Griffith Park or to the Zoo on Sunday,
Pedro at the wheel, of course. The only reason he delayed
was the initial high cost of the vehicle. A new family car, Ford
or Chevrolet, cost over three hundred dollars.

He was certain there were amounts waiting in the big bank
in Spring Street where he had only to sign a draft and make
the withdrawal. But he was afraid that such a large sum
withdrawn would certainly and finally bring the probate court

259

investigators down on him like crows on a June bug. As badly as he wanted to own a car, he didn't want to spoil the easy existence he had enjoyed for more than nine years now. There had to be a better way. He invented a scheme which took longer but which protected him as he withdrew money from the account. He wrote many smaller chits, slips marked for doctors, medicines, hospital, food, clothing, school fees. He set these funds aside until he should have hoarded the cash to pay for that beautiful new car he coveted, a model he revisited two or three times a week in its Main Street showroom.

Some of the changes in the street and in the neighbourhood aroused Jesus' interest, in varying degrees. Apart from one instance, he didn't care very much. Uniforms, khaki, with leggings and flat-brimmed hats, appeared everywhere: men home on leave from the training camps. The nuns told the students how war against the heathen raged in Europe. The cinemas showed pictorial evidence of the inhuman blood-thirst and brutality of the godless hun, and the patrons in these crowded amphitheatres booed, hissed and stamped their feet. Teodoro was vastly moved; the game he wanted to play all the time was soldiering. They marched and did battle in all the alleys and open lots and gulleys of the barrio. Jesus joined in only because he wanted to please his beloved Teodoro.

The one occurrence which stirred Jesus totally from his lethargy and made him willing, anxious, to expend energy was his ability to read the coming attraction posters outside the cinema. He could tell if a film starred Bronco Billy, Tom Mix or William S. Hart only if the bright lithograph face was recognizable. The words, English or Spanish, were jumbled, incomprehensible.

This need and inability to read brought him out of his shell long enough to learn to string letters into words and words into phrases with meaning. It enraged him that Teodoro could read all the words on those one-sheets glittering outside the Granada Theatre and that he could read none. Within a week of diligently applying himself, of listening and responding and questioning, he could read as well as Teodoro. The nuns watched his progress excitedly. The child showed promise after all. But as soon as Jesus had accomplished his goal, he slipped back into his old passive lethargy, from which nothing, threat, promise or reward, could rouse him.

He and Teodoro went directly to the Granada Theatre every afternoon from school, doing anything to come by the five cents fee for the matinee. They sat rapt, enthralled. They heard that these films were made a few miles up the road in the beanfields of Hollywood, but they were unimpressed. This magic had to come from another world. It never even occurred to them to want to visit this wonderland. Deep in their minds they doubted that such fantasy came from their mundane region.

One evening they emerged from the darkened auditorium enthralled, in an almost trancelike state, the reality of the film far more compelling than the irrelevant ugliness surrounding them.

They sauntered, wordless, through the dusk crowds to Aliso Street. They turned the corner, entering their own barrio, barely aware of the sounds of movement around them. Somewhere a band played martial music, people sang and uniformed men milled about among the bright dresses of the girls. The entire street was like a fiesta, with people dashing in and out of traffic, strolling the paths, singing and laughing.

Evidently this informal celebration had sprouted soon after noon and by now, at the supper hour, was palling, fading and fragmented. Crowds of children, unwilling to relinquish the festivity, roamed in packs, looting, pilfering, snatching wallets or jostling their elders off the kerb. Horns blared and brakes squealed and strong men cursed helplessly.

A bevy of little girls between six and twelve, still wearing their blue and white blouses and skirts, their convent uniforms, giggled along the shop fronts, unwilling to surrender the excitement of the heated afternoon. One of them spotted Teodoro. She wailed in frantic ecstacy, punching and shoving the girls nearest her. 'Mother of God,' she screamed, laughing in her panic, 'it's him of the evil eye. Oh, don't let him look at me. The bad eye. The bad eye.'

Not only her companions reacted. Old people retreated, crossing themselves, pressing against walls to escape the evil glance. Even some of the soldiers neglected their senoritas for the moment, staring at this dangerous freak of nature.

The covey of convent girls crowded forward, giggling, wailing and covering their eyes. 'Bad eye. Bad eye. It is

261

Teodoro of the evil eye. Run. Run. Run for your lives.'

An old man cried out in horror and staggered from the path of the boy.

'Leave us alone, bitches,' Jesus said.

The girls chanted. 'Jesus cursed. Jesus cursed. We're going to tell Mother Superior. Jesus cursed.'

Jesus swung at them. Teodoro caught his arm. 'Leave them alone, Jesus,' he said. 'They're idiots. Must you be an idiot because they are idiots?'

'Idiot?' The girls took up the cry. 'Who's the idiot? You of the evil eye. You would drive us mad with the evil eye.'

Angered, Teodoro opened his eyes as wide as he could. He raised his arms as if he were a demon from one of the films and ran at the girls. They stopped laughing. They screamed in terror and flushed out like quail in every direction. Grown people raged at Teodoro. Jesus caught his arm, trying to pull him away to the corner where they could cross the street past La Madreselva and escape into their own lane.

Horns pealed, yapping like mad dogs. Brakes grated and men shouted. Cries of terror and sorrow rent the sudden silence. The band broke off and women screamed. As the newspapers would report the next day, they were all present at an historic event: the girl in the blue and white uniform was the first child run down and killed by a car in East Los Angeles.

Part of the crowd ran out into the street and surrounded the car. Its driver stood up behind the steering wheel, staring down at the lifeless child tossed from under his front tyre. He shook his head, sobbing. A new litany was created as he wailed, 'I didn't see her, I didn't see her. I tried to stop and I could not. She ran out from nowhere. God help me, I didn't see her.'

People knelt over the dead girl, others crowded forward, staring at the driver. But on the path, the largest mob surrounded Jesus and Teodoro. A man in his fifties growled his rage. 'It is he. He who caused it all. I saw it. He looked at her with the evil eye. The evil eye. He looked at her. He looked at the car.' He raised his cane like a club and began to strike Teodoro with it across the head and shoulders.

No one in the mob attempted to stop the man or to reason with him. There were those who took up the chant, 'Evil eye. Evil eye.' Someone threw a paving brick and struck Teodoro above the eye. His forehead broke open and blood spurted. The sight and smell of blood maddened the mob.

Incensed, the crowd crushed in around Teodoro. Jesus ran at the cane-wielding old man, screaming at him. The old man shoved Jesus. The boy lost his balance and fell. People walked over him, trying to get at the bleeding Teodoro.

Jesus could hear only the insensate scream, 'Evil eye. Evil eye. The evil eye has killed.'

Jesus tried to fight his way into the core of the mob where Teodoro was being beaten with fists, canes, rocks and cans. He was shoved aside. It was impossible to get to where Teodoro was being beaten. Sobbing helplessly, Jesus looked around him, trying to think from where help might be brought. His terrorized gaze struck the window of La Madreselva.

He thrust through the crowd, ran out into the street where traffic had clotted and congealed. Crying, he pushed people aside, his gaze fixed on the swinging doors of the saloon. When he reached the pavement, he saw thirteen-year-old Conchita, surrounded by two neighbourhood boys and two uniformed soldiers. Concha was gradually being weaned from the unctuous chasteness of her convent. She no longer sat with her hands folded prayer-like. She smiled and simpered when boys came near. But while her eyes and smiles promised much, she remained prudish and untouchable. Still, she was incredibly pretty, with classic nose, full lips and dark-lashed black eyes under wing-like brows.

Seeing her, Jesus cried out, 'Concha. Run. Tia Clara. Bring Tia Clara. They kill Teodoro up the street there. Go to Tia Clara.'

He did not wait to see if Concha tore herself from her devastated swains. He thrust open the doors and stepped inside the forbidden cantina. Panting, his legs apart, he searched the bar and all the tables. Already the bartenders were shouting at him. 'Get out of here, muchacho. Get out before I throw you out.'

Men looked up from their games and drinking and women to laugh at the child who stood unmoved by the threats of the bartenders.

Jesus saw Pedro, hat back on his rich hair, face pallid and sweating, at a poker table. Pedro, engrossed in his cards, was one of the few men in La Madreselva as yet unaware of Jesus in the doorway.

Jesus ran between the tables. Men grabbed at him, laughing, but he broke free, shouting. 'Tio Pedro. Tio Pedro. Come. I pray you, Tio Pedro. Come at once. It is that they go to kill Teodoro.'

Jesus shoved his way to Pedro's table before Pedro set aside his cards and stared at him, face twisted. 'What does one do in this place? he demanded. 'What do you want, muchacho?'

'Teodoro. They kill him. Please, Tio Pedro, come help Teodoro before they kill him.'

'Get out of here,' Pedro said. He drew his arm across his chest to backhand the child when his gaze struck the sour glance of his old enemy at the table. Jose Gonzales, his face deeply pocked and pitted with smallpox scars, no longer found himself pursued by avid females and so spent more time gambling than in courting.

'Your child is in peril, Luiz,' Gonzales said.

'Stay out of this, Gonzales,' Pedro said. 'What do you know of it?'

'Only what the child says. It must be true to bring the child in here. If the crowd is punishing your brat for the evil eye, they may kill him. There are such fools as one knows.'

Pedro winced and lowered his arm. He stared at Jesus. 'Do you lie to me?'

'I speak true, Tio Pedro. Come. Please. Before it is too late.'

Jose Gonzales laughed. 'Perhaps it is that your uncle Pedro is scared. Your uncle is great with the threats, but weak with the fists. He who cannot satisfy a woman can beat on her, but must take to his heels when a real man comes. I am afraid, kid, your uncle Pedro would rather sit here where one is safe.'

Pedro shoved his chair back so abruptly that it fell over behind him. He did not look at Jose or the other grinning men at the poker table. He caught Jesus savagely by the arm. 'Come, boy, show me where is Teodoro.'

Jesus nodded and ran, breaking free of Pedro's grasp. Pedro pushed between the tables. As if moving in unison, men rose and followed him in a growing tide that spewed through the saloon doors to the dusk-beiged street.

From the street rose screams of women, snarls of men against the wail of police whistles. Jesus raced across with Pedro in his wake. He went between parked cars to where the mob had knotted over Teodoro on the pavement. 'They go to kill him, Tio Pedro,' Jesus wept. 'Stop them. Make them stop.'

Pedro followed Jesus to the kerb, but moved no further forward. He watched in dazed horror as canes and sticks and stones were raised and driven down savagely into the centre of the mob. He shook his head, biting back the sickness that rose into his throat.

Believing his uncle was at his heels, Jesus tore at the rim of the crowd, breaking his way into the storm centre. In the crush of people he heard someone scream that Teodoro's eyes were gone. People yelled that Teodoro was dead as if it were some noble achievement.

Pedro stood unmoving. Jesus clawed his way forward. By the time he reached the place where Teodoro was twisted, bloody on the ground, the blows ceased. Those nearest the child's shattered body retreated as much as they could, still nodding in satisfaction, but no longer rabid to kill. At the edge of the mob, it began to fragment. People broke away, some walking slowly, other moving without looking back.

Jesus fell to his knees beside Teodoro. He wept, calling Teodoro's name, begging the boy to speak to him. Holding Teodoro's bloody head against his chest, Jesus began to understand the truth. The mob had gouged Teodoro's eyes out. They had crushed his cheekbones with paving bricks and cracked his skull with canes and clubs.

Jesus stayed there for a long time. The crowd receded, dispersed and disappeared. A horse-drawn ambulance from the hospital rounded the corner into Aliso Street, bells clanging and people shouting as they leaped out of the way. Doctors sprang from the carriage. Some ran to where the girl had been covered with somebody's jacket, others came and stood looking down at Teodoro clutched in Jesus' arms. 'This one is dead,' a young doctor said over his shoulder. 'Nothing we can do for him.'

'The girl is dead too,' another doctor said. 'We can take them in to emergency. Get death certificates, let the undertakers pick them up.'

'That's about all we can do.'

Sobbing, holding her arms across her breasts, Clara pushed the doctors aside. She knelt beside Jesus. Gently, she reached out for the child and Jesus let her take Teodoro's body to her bosom.

Jesus stayed there on his knees for a few moments. He said nothing. His grief was too deep for words, too numbing for tears. Agony knotted and twisted inside him. He could not cry, he couldn't speak even to his beloved Tia Clara. He was helpless. There were no words, no tears.

At last, he stood up and walked towards the kerb. He saw that Tio Pedro had turned and walked, shoulders slumped round, back towards the silent doors of La Madreselva. He followed him with his eyes but he no longer cared what Tio Pedro did, or where he went. He hated him, but not even this set his uncle apart. He hated God and God's world.

As the boy straggled towards the lane off Aliso Street, going to the Luiz house because he had nowhere else to go, someone spoke to him. 'I am sorry, caballerito. For the little Teodoro, my heart aches.'

Jesus glanced up at Mme Rosa, his face blank. The seeress stood at the base of her stairwell, immobile. Her face was bright with rouge and powder, her eyes heavily made up to hide the ravages of crow's-feet and wrinkles. The child did not speak, but continued to plod towards the alleyway.

Mme Rosa went on standing there, her beringed hands pressed tightly against her stomach. After a long time, she turned and slowly climbed the steps to her apartment where she had left the door standing open.

XIX

Jesus began to think of the runaway Pedrillo with sympathy and understanding and even with some envy. He might have forgotten the beloved older Luiz boy in the intervening eight years since Pedrillo disappeared from the ranchito but Clara could not forget, and she did not let Jesus forget. The death of Teodoro intensified her sadness. After the Luiz clan returned in Pedro's rented sedan from the graveside ceremonies for Teodoro, there was little laughter in the old house off Aliso Street.

Clara seemed to withdraw into herself. She sat for hours during the day in an unmoving rocking chair, lost in deep depression, staring into a distance she could not share. She seldom combed or brushed her long black hair, wearing it snarled in a bun at the nape of the neck. She had no interest in herself, in hygiene, in the house or her children. As for Pedro, she seemed barely aware of him unless he struck her across her face trying to rouse her from her lethargy.

Conchita was yanked from the selfish core of awakening girlhood. She had little time for dreaming, for posing or simpering. There would be no food on the table at night unless Concha prepared and placed it there. The table would sit, the left-over food spoiling and smelly and turning green unless Concha dragged herself in to clean it up. Sometimes these tasks were too burdensome, too degrading for Concha, they made her smell and they spoiled her hands. 'My lovely hands,' she wept, standing in front of her immobile mother. 'Look at my lovely hands.'

Clara seemed not even to hear her. Frustrated and despairing, Concha, who had basked in the brilliance of family attentiveness all her life, wailed in tears and outrage. 'I will not stay here and be a kitchen-slavey. I am no slave to work in the kitchen, without help, without anyone to care. I will leave before I endure this. Do you hear, mama? I will run away. I shall. As Pedrillo ran to escape this ugly place, I shall run.'

Clara appeared to hear this in that distracted void where she passed her empty hours. She shook her head. Her eyes welled with tears. She clutched Concha's soap-reddened hands in hers, kissing them, pressing them against her mouth.

Sometimes Cipriano brought his accordion and played lively music, trying to cheer Clara. She seemed barely aware of him or his compositions. Jesus was fascinated, but Cipriano remained distant toward him. And too, Jesus found himself little welcomed in the apartment of Andre and Maria Luiz. Andre was polite, but Jesus had the feeling that the greying man didn't even know his name. With blind Maria it was different. She knew his name, all right, but she kept him at arm's length. She never smiled at him, never asked him to stand while she studied his features with her fingers. Though he lived in the house, he was not of Luiz blood; he was not one of the family. Maria treated him like an uninvited stranger. He stayed away from them as much as possible. Maria called him 'the O'Brien bastardo.' She did not care whether he was within hearing or not; she believed in speaking the cold truth. One who was not of Luiz blood had no place in her life.

Even when Clara slowly climbed from the depths of depression to a kind of lethargic adjustment to what went on around her, the quality of life was little improved. She wandered the house at night, unable to sleep, unable to lie in the bed with Pedro. Lying awake, Jesus would hear her whisper at shadows. 'Teodoro. Is that you, Teodoro?'

Sometimes, waking, Pedro would hear her whispers. 'Is that you, crazy woman?' he would say. 'Are you talking now to the dead?'

'I thought it was Teodoro, there at the door,' Clara said in a flat empty voice.

'The child is dead, damn you. Why do you pretend you do not know this?'

'I know Teodoro is dead. I know. You killed him.'

'Aw shit, Clara. Don't start that at this hour of the night. If one does not shut up, I go to break your nose.'

'Si. You would hit me. You are a woman-hitter. You hit women, but you have no courage to stand and fight for the life of your son. You let strangers kill my son because your guts had turned to whey. You killed Teodoro. You.'

Pedro's voice shook, savage with rage and self-pity at war inside him. 'They killed him, Clara. He had the evil eye. They killed him because they feared him. There was nothing I could do.'

'You could have stopped them.'

'No. No. They meant to kill him. Nothing could stop them. The child, Clara. He did possess the evil eye.'

She moaned aloud in the darkness. 'You lie. Your whore lied. She lied to say my Teodoro was a demon. He was a good and loving child.'

'Everybody saw the evil eye in Teodoro, Clara. Everyone. Could they all be wrong?'

'They were wrong.'

'No. Console yourself. Face the truth, Clara. Teodoro was possessed. He had the evil eye. I myself felt it. If I — his father who lived in the house with him — feared him, God knows that outsiders would hate him. Those people hated him, Clara. They feared him. They never meant to let him live.'

'You could have spoken. You could have torn them apart. You could have hit them with your fists as you hit women. You could have saved my baby.'

'It was already too late.'

'You did nothing.'

'I wept, Clara. I wept as you did.'

'You lie. Bastardo. You lie. I wept for my child. You wept for yourself.'

'For myself, crazy woman? Where is the sense in that?'

'You wept because you feared. You feared to stand up to that mob for the life of your own child. Yet, unless you wept for Teodoro, your macho friends would revile you. You wept so your friends would believe you would have acted but there was nothing you could do.'

'That is the truth, Clara.'

'You stood there and watched as that mob slew your son.'

'They would have killed me if I had tried to stop them.'

'But you could have saved your son.'

'No, woman. Listen to me. I will hear no more of this. By the time I got there, Teodoro was dead — '

'How then do you know this?'

' — they would have turned on me, and Teodoro was already dead. Would it have brought Teodoro back to life if I were killed? Who is to protect and feed this family if I am killed? Say no more, woman. I warn you. I shall not tolerate that you should speak against me. I am the head of this house. You will not speak against me.'

Pedro went to the automobile sales agency in Main Street and paid cash for the touring car he had coveted for so long. He felt exalted and generous in this act. He was not doing it for himself, but for Clara.

'It is that I need only to be understood,' he said aloud, driving the new car home. 'I do not act for myself. I act to make those around me happy and pleased. When I have money I share. With my family. With my brothers. Even with the rotten Pablo, I share. With my friends. What I have is to share. To make others happy makes Pedro Grandos Luiz happy. Why do not people see this in me?'

He drove swiftly up to the kerb before the Luiz triplex, stepped hard on the brake and skidded to a stop. With his head back, laughing, he sounded the horn furiously, slapping the button with his fist until the family and the neighbours spilled out into the street to stare in awe. At once, Felicia and Cipriano, Felicia's children, Andre and blind Maria, clambered into the car, making room, or sitting on laps.

Pedro strode around, polishing the car with the sleeve of his coat, answering questions about make, model, price and speed. With one eye he kept watching the door of his own house. Clara, alone of all the neighbourhood, had not come into the street.

At last, enraged, he shoved children aside, strode up the steps and across the porch, yelling Clara's name. He found her sitting alone at the kitchen table staring at the cold stove.

'Damn you,' he said. 'I do for you. I do all I can for you. I spend a fortune to buy a car to cheer you. I bring this fine car home to please you. And what do you? You hide here in the kitchen. You insult me before my family and all the neighbours by refusing even to look at it.'

'I do not care, Pedro.' Clara shook her head. 'I do not want a car.'

'Well, goddamn it, you got one. You will not sit here and make the neighbours laugh at me. You will come for a drive.'

He caught the loose bun of her hair in his fist and twisted

until she came to her feet, grimacing in pain. 'You will come outside. You will smile around at the neighbours. You will smile at your new car. You will get into the front seat and we will take a drive. You will be happy or by God I break your nose.'

Her hair twisted in his fist, he piloted her through the house to the front door. There, he released her. Her hair toppled loosely about her shoulders, but he ignored this. He grasped her elbow, squeezing with all his strength. Clara walked out across the porch, a sick smirk contorting her mouth, her eyes wild with terror. When Pedro pinched her arm she nodded her head at her neighbours and gazed at them with that wan smile.

Cipriano held the front door of the car open for Clara. When she got in, he sat beside her and slammed the door. Pedro went around the machine, swung in under the wheel. He turned on the switch, set the petrol lever and retarded the spark, then he got out, warning Cipriano not to touch the levers. He strode to the front of the car, engaged the crank and spun it until the engine caught. 'Now the spark,' Pedro yelled at Cipriano. 'Pull down the spark and let up on the gas.'

Cipriano stared at him helplessly. The car engine raced until Pedro ran around, got under the wheel and tamed the monster with dexterous manipulation of petrol and spark lever. The neighbours laughed and cheered.

'Where would you like to go, Clara?' Pedro asked with a bright smile. 'You tell me where you would like to drive, and we shall go there.'

After a long moment, Clara said, 'I would wish to to go to the cemetery. I would visit the grave of Teodoro.'

Sickness rose up from the pit of Pedro's stomach. The burn of acid choked in his throat. 'No,' he said. 'No, damn you. No.'

She stared straight ahead. Her voice was low. 'There is nowhere else I wish to go.'

Pedro peered at her helplessly, then engaged the clutch. The car leapt and bucked forward. The children and some of their elders ran alongside it to the corner. Pedro Grandos Luiz owned the first car in the barrio. There was none now who dared doubt his splendor of status. He was a man set apart.

Once they were out of the neighbourhood, the family shouting and yelling at each other, and waving back at the bystanders along the street, Pedro tried again. He asked Clara where she would like to drive. When she said she wished to visit the cemetery, Pedro's mouth whitened into a thin line. His eyes narrowed and he drove as one possessed. They drove for hours until the petrol ran out. Cipriano walked a mile and brought back enough to start the car and get it to the nearest petroleum pumps.

Everybody was tired and sore from bouncing over the rough roads, from being crowded, from the tensions that steamed from Pedro. They were relieved to return to the Luiz house. They shouted their appreciation, congratulating Pedro on his latest acquisition, but went quickly into their own houses. When they were all gone, Clara remained where she was, staring ahead silently.

'Get out of the car, loco en cabeza. We are home. Get out of the car.'

Silently, Clara obeyed. She stepped down to the street, crossed the pavement and went into the house without looking at the new car.

From that day, Pedro spent less and less time at the house. During the day he could be found at the gambling tables of La Madreselva. He made friends by lending money; he kept their friendship by not demanding repayment, even when a recipient struck it lucky at the numbers.

He financed his own gambling by writing cheques on the Spring Street bank. He had long ago stopped fretting about the probate court's inquiry into his stewardship of Jesus' inheritance. Over the years he had forgotten where the money came from; it belonged to him now; it was his. He was the executor, only his decision about the funds mattered at all. He lived well because a man in his position was obligated to live well.

When he was introduced to new women during the day at La Madreselva, he hastened to the bank to cash withdrawal slips for fifty dollars for his dinner and hotel dates. He had come to be known in the barrio as an easy spender, as a ladies' man. He had many assignations, seldom going out with the same woman more than twice. They simpered and smiled and writhed against him like cats in their pleasure, but they did not accept his invitations for more than a couple of trysts.

272

This troubled him only because when his brother Pablo made a conquest, the woman trailed after Pablo, enslaved, for months, leaving him only when Pablo abandoned her.

In other ways he was able to lord it over Pablo, especially since he had bought the new sedan. A car made a difference with the women. Women were easier to meet when a man arrived in a fashionable, shining new touring car. Women were attracted to automobiles; they were entranced by the men strong and powerful and wealthy enough to possess them. Never in the history of man had there been such a symbol of manhood as a sleek and speeding car. He saw his magnificence in the awed eyes of females. When he wore a new suit and a new hat with boots and pongee shirt and tooled along the avenues in his polished car, he was incredibly handsome, desirable and attractive. Women were weak vessels. He had only to nod toward them and, without formal introduction, was able to arrange an assignation.

Recently, however, a run of bad luck at the gambling tables of La Madreselva had undermined Pedro's rugged self-confidence. He remained a man set apart, a person of consequence, but fortune was fickle. No matter what five cards he held in stud, another held better and raked in the pot. No matter the power of dreams, of intuition, even of prayer, his numbers always missed and he tore up stacks of useless tickets. And the women he met and bedded were less attractive than formerly by far, some unacceptable even by his lax standards. Usually, he could find some redeeming beauty in any woman willing to go to bed with him, but lately this was not true. They were older than he liked his damas. Some were even older then he and this, in its way, was enough to turn a man's stomach. Spanish women broke early, and God knew most of them had moustaches by the time they were thirty. Still, a man had to have something. Sometimes he could get no female at all except through the offices of some simpering cabronazo. Without the recompensed services of a husband willing to prostitute his own wife, he would be reduced to picking up one of the peso-per-trick whores loitering on the corners of Sixth Street.

He had cashed his second cheque for fifty dollars that Monday morning and lost it all before noon at the cards. He told himself he could afford no more and yet when he walked out of La Madreselva, he admitted he was on his way to

Spring Street for additional funds. He needed to spend freely to reverse his failing fortunes; a man who dared was destiny's darling.

Pedro was so deeply involved with his inner thoughts and woes that the girl spoke to him twice before he was aware of her at all. She said, 'Senor.' He heard the female voice and realized that he was being addressed in the busy street in the middle of the hot morning. Music wailed from within the cantina. Horns sounded and he brought his gaze to the girl who had stopped him.

Mouth agape, Pedro stared at her. His mouth watered and his eyes stung with tears because she was so young and fresh and desirable and he was aging and bulky and even gross, though he sucked his belly in as well as he could. This girl was no more than fourteen, but there was a reticent sensuality about her: the rouge massaged and blended into her cheeks and the mascara about her eyes made her as ageless as the first whore. She looked sleekly made, avidly voluptuous, delicate and flowerlike, and yet indestructible. Hot damn. This was Pedro's immediate reaction. She had been born to flit uncaring across the hearts and minds of enchanted men, born to captivate, entice and finally desolate the ensnared. She looked as if she had been slowly poured into a tight-fitting, calf-length dress, which itself was a badge of shame, the ankles exposed. Her frock was cut low at the bodice, swollen but taut at the high-standing young bust, designed with flowered flair and seeping, like liquid linen, down the wealth of her shapely hips and thighs.

God knew, a female like this would cost a pretty penny. This one looked worth every exorbitant cent. She walked as if that lovely, auburn-tinted head had been set upon the exquisitely fragile perfection of her lithe young form after every precise consideration of effect, shock-value and symmetry. Her large, thick-lashed, olive-black eyes glinted with promise of inward fire. Her brows were plucked wings in flight. Her nose was delicately shaped, her face made more tempting in its breathtaking beauty by the molten gold of her smile. Hot damn, he thought, looking at her. He had never seen anything more alluring before. He stood there, feeling impotent in his insolvency, yet caught in that richly rewarding, lingering moment of adoration and appreciation of the beautifully packaged little wench.

He found it hard to believe she had accosted him, spoken to him, but her gravely smiling eyes were fixed on him in unsettling intensity.

'You don't know me, do you?' Her throaty voice teased and yet soothed.

He stared at her, trying to find in her exotic beauty the sudden flowering of one of Concha's schoolmates. But he had never seen her before. She was a stranger to the barrio. He shrugged: she was merely pretending to know him as an easy introduction. Would God he had that hundred dollars he had thrown away at numbers and poker in the cantina.

'I don't know you,' he said. 'If ever I had seen you, I would not have forgotten.' He sighed and smiled. 'I could not have forgotten.'

'Why, how gallant you are. No wonder I was always so enslaved by you, even as a little girl.'

He grinned. He believed he had heard every come-on known to woman, but this was different. 'Where did I know you?' he asked. He would do anything, say anything, to keep her from disappearing like the mirage he feared her to be.

She smiled up at him and licked the tip of her tongue across her lips. 'One used to be called Our Pedro in my house. Our great tomcat Pedro.'

Stunned, Pedro stared at the lovely teenager. He would have taken oath he had never seen her before. There was no trace of the child he scarcely recalled up those steps at Mme Rosa's. He had never looked at little Paca, as Rosa called her daughter, unless the girl was in the way when he was rampant. He shook his head, trying to smile. 'You are — the little one — Mme Rosa's daughter. Why, I have not seen you since you were — were — '

'Four years old,' she said. She made a faint moue. 'I should be insulted. I remember you. I could never forget you. And yet you don't remember Francisca at all.'

'But you are all grown up.'

Francisca laughed at him, a lilting sound. 'It happens to children,' she said. 'They are underfoot, and suddenly they are all grown up.'

'None ever grew up more expertly than you, Francisca. My God, my God. The baby Paca. Francisca. How it all comes back. Forgive me for not knowing you, beautiful and grown up like this.'

275

She gazed up into his eyes, without smiling now. 'You'll never know how grown up I am, talking with me on the street like this.'

'Of course. We have so much to say to each other. I must inquire about your mother. About you. We have so much to say.' He looked around. 'Where shall we go?'

Her voice dropped, more throaty than ever. 'We can go where you like, great Pedro. Yet shouldn't we talk money first?'

'What?' Not even a Sixth Street whore had ever been so blatant as this.

She smiled, totally at ease. 'Singame,' she said. 'Singame. I have dreamed of being mounted as I used to watch you mount my mother.'

'Oh my God.'

'I watched them all. But I watched Pedro the great tomcat the most. It was his claws I longed for.'

'My God.'

'Still, if a man of your age molests a fourteen-year-old girl, that is rape, even in this god-forsaken barrio.'

'I would never rape you.'

'If you touched me, I would scream rape.'

'What? Are you crazy?'

'Not at all. To be taken unwillingly by a man is something I would not endure.'

'But you — you are the one suggested — '

'Singame? Of course. But if you pay me, it is not rape because I would not call it rape if you paid me well enough. You paid my mother, but you will never get me for two pesos. Enough money silences my mouth.' She writhed slightly and dampened her lips again with her tongue. 'Enough extra money makes me use my mouth to do tricks to please one even as sated as you.'

He was trembling with desire, sweating. Francisca stuck her extended third finger between her lips and delicately nursed it, watching his face. Francisca was not subtle, but she was effective. He was ready to grovel.

'Eh?' he said. 'How much do you wish, Francisca? How much singame? And — for the extra — for the other — how much?'

'How much for one to go down on you? For the great tomcat? Perhaps fifty dollars for the singame, naked you and

276

I together on a bed. . . . For the tongue, for going on my knees to you — another fifty.'

'A hundred dollars.' He sweated, nodding. 'Yes. I'll pay that. Gladly. Willingly. It is that I have lost that amount in La Madreselva this morning. Could I pay you after I go to the bank where I have plenty of money?'

She laughed at him and shook her head. 'I am Francisca. I am Mme Rosa's daughter. One pays in advance, or one walks away from me before I scream rape.'

'Yes. I pay. Of course I pay. But you have stirred in me the great ache. I have lost all at cards. I need only time. I have the money.'

Francisca shrugged. 'Yes. One hears the great tomcat Pedro has mucho dinero in the big bank. But is one to believe he cannot get one hundred dollars in advance — money to get me naked in his bed — and naked on my knees to him?'

Sweating, Pedro clutched Francisca by the elbow and propelled her along Aliso Street to his parked car. He trembled with fear and apprehension that something, some cruel, sick prank of God, might interfere before he could undress, gaze upon, kiss and possess this lovely, golden young body, restore his shaken faith in himself and perhaps return the old rigidity and vigour and passion he had recently found lacking in ordinary intercourse. Of all the women he'd ever possessed, he had never wanted anyone as he desired this enchanting creature.

He held the door open and Francisca got into the front seat. She did not remark on his car. Obviously, she was accustomed to limousines, to swank cabriolets and to the superior men who drove them. 'We must hurry,' he said. 'We would get to the bank before it closes.'

Francisca shrugged. She said merely, 'You will need money for a nice hotel room, too, tomcat. I will not enter a dump. And you cannot expect me to pay for the bed.'

'Do not worry. You are worth whatever you will cost me, Francisca. We will enjoy a day and night you will never forget.'

She shrugged. 'We will. If you pay me first.'

Pedro parked his car directly in front of the aged stone and marble building of the Pan-American bank. The sun slithered across its facade, heightening the spray of light and shadow. The institution was old and respected, quiet and forbidding.

277

Through Pedro's mind flashed the memory of the first time he had entered this high-ceilinged foyer with old Manuel. A long time ago. Another lifetime. He closed his fingers on Francisca's elbow and steered her through the heavy doors and past the armed guard who bowed politely and called him by name. Pedro flushed with pride.

He glanced from the corner of his eye, but Francisca seemed not unduly impressed by the deference shown him. He winced, wondering what it would take to impress this girl. She was only fourteen and yet entirely blasé and sophisticated.

Francisca stood quietly to one side while Pedro used a bank pen, dipped into the secured inkwell, to scrawl out a withdrawal slip for two hundred dollars. He signed the chit with a flourish, and gave Francisca a brief, faint smile and approached one of the tellers with whom he had dealt for many years.

He nodded towards the bank clerk and pushed the withdrawal slip under the grille. The teller did not smile as usual or call him by name. Instead, he sat unmoving for what seemed a sweating eternity to Pedro, staring at the slip of paper. 'What is it?' Pedro said. 'What is the matter?'

The clerk only smiled and shook his head. 'Sorry, Mr Luiz. One moment, sir.' He walked back to a row of ledgers, thumbed through one of them, checked and double-checked it, and studied the withdrawal slip again.

Pedro spoke louder now. 'What's the matter?'

The teller only shook his head and gave him that imitation smile again. 'If you'll wait one more moment, sir.' The man went between desks and spoke to one of the bank officials. The official nodded, listening, then got up and accompanied the teller to the ledger. Both studied it now as if neither trusted the other, or the ledgend entered on the books before them.

The teller turned and walked back to the counter. The official took a few steps in his wake and then stopped, studying his nails. The teller pushed the withdrawal slip back beneath the grille. 'Sorry, sir. You have no funds in this bank.'

Pedro was torn between outrage and savage laughter at these bankers' stupid idea of a joke. What a hellish time to play games with him, as Francisca stood watching. He glanced

278

towards her, found her faintly pale and annoyed. Hell, why shouldn't she be annoyed, he was raging. 'What do you say? I always get funds here. You know me.' He glared toward the official who stood uncomfortably watching in neutral territory. 'You both know me. For ten years you honour my signature.'

'I'm sorry, sir,' the teller said. 'I hope you will understand.'

'I don't understand,' Pedro raged. He shoved the slip under the grille again. 'Give me money.'

'Sir. It is quite simple. Quite easy to understand. Your account has no money in it. You are overdrawn.'

'Overdrawn? Overdrawn?' Pedro was shouting because he had no idea what the teller was talking about and so all he could do was bluster. 'What do you say — overdrawn?'

'Please don't shout, sir. It is quite simple. There are no funds left in your account.'

'Jesus Christ, I don't care about that,' Pedro shouted. He caught the grille in his fists, shaking it. 'Put some more in my account. You have money here in this bank. Why do you do this to me?'

The official came to the teller's shoulder. His face was pale and he looked ill. 'Please, keep your voice down, sir.'

'I shall not. You shall not rob me like this and get away with it.'

'Sir, you have withdrawn money for ten years from this account without ever depositing one dime into it.'

'Don't talk to me about deposit. I know nothing of deposit. The old man got money here. I get money here. Give me money.'

'Sir, we will have to ask you to lower your voice or to leave at once.'

'I won't lower my voice. I shall yell for the police. You rob me. You give me my money. I want my money now.'

Other officials ran across the bank floor with the armed guard in the lead. This gentleman did not draw his gun, but he pressed himself close beside Pedro and spoke from the corner of his mouth. 'I would advise you to leave before you are in trouble.'

Pedro swung around. He shoved the guard away. He peered at the officials and advanced upon them. These gentlemen retreated. One of them called over his shoulder, 'Fetch the police. At once. Call the police.'

Pedro heeled around. Francisca remained where she had waited, but she was poised for flight. Her face was pale with contempt and her eyes glittered. He said, 'Francisca. Paca. Wait. We settle this.'

'Call me when it is settled, you rapist.' Francisca laughed at him. She turned on her heels and walked towards the front entrance. Pedro sobbed, calling her name, but she did not look back. She set her shoulders and pushed through the heavy doors. Once she was in the street, she turned along the pavement, lost to him.

He wept, crying for her. The guard closed in on him and Pedro grabbed a chair, holding the security man at bay. He was swinging the chair when the police ran through the front doors, guns drawn. They closed in on him. He threw the chair at them. They rushed him — using gun-butts as clubs they overwhelmed him and beat him to his knees. When he stopped fighting, they put handcuffs on his wrists and dragged him out to the police wagon.

XX

Pedro had been five days away from the house in Aliso Street. Driving his car, which was dusty and pigeon-streaked from sitting in a police lot, he detoured around his familiar haunts, approaching his home from the alley. It was the middle of the morning. He parked his car at the kerb and got out, looking around guiltily before he crossed the pavement and climbed the steps to the porch.

His face was dark and patchy with scruffy beard, his clothes were soiled and torn; he had been wearing them since he was arrested in the Spring Street bank for creating a public disturbance, threatening bodily harm and resisting arrest. He felt as sweaty, miserable and unclean inside as his skin and clothing was outside, caked with filth. His heart pulsed, tight in his chest. His stomach was sour and his mind spun, wheeled and revolved with the hatred that had been born in the Pan-American Bank and festered over five long, evil days in the city jail.

The front door stood open and he strode through it. The house was silent and shadowed. He saw Clara crouched in a rocking chair and at the sight of her, withdrawn and staring, he flushed red with rage. Nothing had changed in this goddamned place, she was as he had left her. She tilted her head and looked up at Pedro but did not speak.

His rasping voice clawed at her. 'Well, bitch, don't you wish to know where your husband has been? It's been five days, Clara. I've been in jail.'

She gazed at him but shrugged and said nothing.

He stood over her, trembling with surpressed rage moiling deep in his belly. 'Don't you wish to know why your husband was in jail?' He waited but when she merely stared up at him bleakly, he said, 'One was in jail because of old goat O'Brien's fine bank on Spring Street. It is there I have gotten funds for ten years — and old O'Brien for God only knows how long before this. It was the place where we got our funds and none ever refused until five days ago. Suddenly, no more. They refuse me my money. They say I have no funds in that bank. Singame. I've always had funds in that bank. When I protest that they rob me, they club me to my knees and jail me. Five days I rotted in that jail.'

He prowled the room, stretching and flexing his muscles, moving with the lithe supple step of the puma. He walked to the door, stood staring into the sun-struck street. 'They impound my car. The police. They had it hauled from in front of the bank where I parked it to the police impounding lot.'

When Clara did not speak, he turned, working his shoulders inside his shirt. 'Don't you hear me, loco bitch? My car. They took my car from me. Do you know how I was able to reclaim it, to get back my own car? I had to pay them money. I was able to borrow a few dollars from those acquaintances who do not yet know that I have been cut off from my funds at the bank on Spring Street. Well, if this is the way the fine gringos treat Pedro Luiz, I know how to get even with them. I'll have my revenge on them. I've made up my mind. I'll do it through the bastardo O'Brien.'

At this reference to Jesus, Clara sat up slightly. Pedro saw that the woman had responded and this pleased him. He was suffering, in hell on earth; there was no reason why he should suffer alone. He drew in a deep breath, clenching and unclenching his fists.

He walked past her and went into the kitchen. He unbuttoned his pongee shirt and threw it on the floor. There were great stains around the armpits. He sloshed water into a metalware basin on the draining-board and set a small mirror in a patch of sunlight on the windowsill. He used a bar of lye soap and washed at the evil and grime on his face, the dirt he had brought home from that jail. He slapped water into the black hair at his armpits and shuddering, dried himself with a towel. His face soaked and caked with lye soap, he shaved with a straight razor. 'Is there food to eat?' he said when Clara trailed him into the room. 'It is that I am hungry and have much to do.'

Clara spread her hands and shrugged. She pulled out a cane-bottomed chair and sat at the table, slouched against it, resting on her arm. She sat there silently, watching him.

When he had shaved, he tested his face with his fingers and, pleased, splashed cologne on his cheeks and hair and dried his fragrant-smelling hands on the tufts of his armpits. Then he ran his hands through his thick shorn locks. He began to feel better, at least a little clean.

He smiled faintly when Clara spoke, in a halting, uncertain voice. 'What is it you say of Jesus?'

As he dressed in fresh underclothing, new trousers and fresh pongee shirt from the laundry stack in the cupboard, he talked coldly to her, his voice loud and accusing. Nothing of what had happened, nothing that was to happen was any fault of his; he did not want to be blamed, he would endure no censure.

'It's very simple, Clara. It is over. The gringos refuse to pay me any longer for the great sacrifice I made to take the bastardo O'Brien into my home, giving him as much and even more than I gave my own children. Well, it's over. No longer can I feed and clothe and house the O'Brien bastard.'

Clara straightened at the table. 'What madness do you talk now?' she said, trembling.

'I speak no madness. It is you who is loco in cabeza. It is simple. I am not paid, I can no longer keep the bastard orphan.'

'For ten years it is his money we have lived on.'

He heeled around, his voice savage. 'It was my money. It was money paid to me by gringo courts to care for the bastard. This I have done. But now the funds are gone. There are no more funds in the big bank on Spring Street. Well, there are no more funds in the casa Luiz for the tending of the bastard. And so it is over. I can no longer afford to work and support him with no help from the gringo bank.'

Dressed, he nodded in satisfaction. In talking it out with Clara, he had straightened it out in his own mind. He had placed all guilt where it truly belonged, in the uncaring hands of the bastard gringos. He shifted his jacket up on his wide shoulders and looked around, preparing to leave.

Clara stood up. 'What do you do? Where do you go?'

'I go to do what I must. I go to get rid of the O'Brien orphan. They stop paying me to care for him, I stop feeding him and clothing and housing him. It is that simple. I go to get rid of him.'

She shook her head. 'You must not do this terrible thing,

Pedro. We have had hurt enough in this house. Do not do this evil thing to me.'

He flexed his muscles and shrugged. 'It is that your words prove how loco you are. I do no evil thing. I do only what must be done. It is the gringo who has done the evil hurt to me. I will say no more. I want no words from you. I warn you that I will tolerate not one more word against me. No. Not one. Get together his things. At once.'

2

Pedro, his hat in his hand, walked along the silent, shadowed corridor of the convent. He knocked at the door of the fourth grade classroom. A young monitor from the first seat, first row, leaped up and, face shining, answered the summons. Pedro stared down at the simpering child. 'I wish to speak with Sister Angelina.'

'It is a gentleman, Sister,' the monitor said. 'He wishes to talk to you.'

The nun nodded and set her pointer across her desk. This staff was used as much for discipline as for designating. She gazed coldly out over the pupils and warned them to be silent on pain of fearful retribution. She went to the door, her shoe-length skirts rustling.

Pedro nodded and gave the nun a smile of great and practised charm. He had learned to use smiles to disarm the sisters in the first grade. He saw that it still worked here too. 'I am the father of one Jesus O'Brien, Sister,' he said.

'Oh yes, Senor O'Brien. It is good to meet you.'

'No. My name is Luiz. Pedro Grandos Luiz. It is that Jesus is adopted.'

'A foster child?' She said this as if many things were suddenly revealed to her.

Pedro shrugged, stretching and flexing his muscles. 'It is that I regret to have to disturb you and your classroom, Sister, but I have come to take Jesus from the class.'

'Is it that there is some emergency?' the sister asked. 'Some family problem? Nothing of great seriousness, I hope.'

Pedro only smiled and shrugged. 'I have come to take him,' he repeated.

The nun nodded. She turned and spoke in a voice to strike at the rear of the room since the children were seated according to their marks achieved in class. Jesus sat in one of the rear seats in the row of desks beside the windows. 'Jesus. Jesus O'Brien. Do you hear me, Jesus? Come. Stop your woolgathering. It is that your father has come to take you from the class.'

Yawning, Jesus got up from his desk where he had sprawled, twisted, on his spine, only half awake, watching two pigeons on a wall of the playground. The other children stirred and stared at him, envious that he should escape this prison of learning before noon.

His face flushed at the flurry of unaccustomed attention, Jesus came slowly from the rear of the room, smiling in a shy and uncomfortable way.

The sister gave him a vinegary smile and touched his shoulder briefly. 'We will see you in the morning, Jesus.'

Pedro shook his head. 'No. He comes no more.'

Jesus loitered in the wake of Pedro, who strode along the corridor without looking over his shoulder. Jesus had learned many years ago to keep as much distance as possible between himself and his Tio Pedro, even when that caballero was in a playful mood. One could be hurt badly by those fists, and be punished if one cried from the pain. He had never liked his uncle and since the death of Teodoro, he had despised him.

He felt a band of tension loosening across his chest the farther he got from that classroom where he was called upon by Sister Angelina only to be made the goat of her attention. She asked him only questions that not even the brightest child in the class could answer, and she asked him only to show that the dolt was uninformed, and others should listen lest they be likened to him.

The brilliant sunshine warmed Jesus when he followed Pedro from the building and across the pavement. Pedro nodded towards the car and said, 'Get in.' His uncle had indicated the front seat but Jesus climbed over the rear door and toppled in the right-hand corner of the back. He was astonished to see his belongings tied in a colourful, but badly faded tablecloth. He was intrigued, but he said nothing.

Pedro cranked the car and got in under the wheel. 'We go for a long drive, you and I,' he said.

Jesus sighed. 'Where is Tia Clara?'

Pedro glanced over his shoulder, but did not bother to answer. Jesus shrugged and laid his head back into a patch of sunlight on the oilcloth cushion. He yawned and blinked sleepily. Pedro engaged the clutch and the car bucked into motion, moving swiftly east through the streets and out into the country.

Jesus watched the town dissolve and slip away behind them. He recognized the cemetery where they had buried Teodoro in the O'Brien plot and where Tia Clara told him his mother and father were buried. He shivered and looked away, watching the sun on distant hazy hills.

They drove swiftly into the lightly travelled San Gabriel Valley highway. Jesus did not even feel any distinctive familiarity with this place. It seemed a vast ploughed land as far as one could see in any direction, beanfields and groves and an occasional shack in the distance.

There was nothing to mark where the ranchito once had stood, the honey shed and barn and rows of hives. He remembered none of it, and the last sign was gone, even the trees had been removed. The section where Manuel O'Brien had lived was now cultivated and absorbed into the abutting acreage of the vast Stockton farms.

'You used to live out here once,' Pedro said loudly over his shoulder against engine noises and the scream of wind in the open sedan. 'A long time ago. Do you remember?'

Jesus only shook his head. Pedro laughed and nodded. 'You will like it out here.'

They turned from the highway into the wide, hardpacked orange road through vineyards, groves and fields to a mansion on a shaded knoll. Pedro slowed but did not hesitate. He drove between the gates and along the lane to the Spanish-style chateau.

Jesus sat forward on the edge of the seat, awed and fascinated. He had never seen such an elegant estate, never dreamed of such a place. Why, there were more cars parked casually about the driveways and garage aprons than one saw in a car display lot. Looking at those splendid machines, Jesus saw how cheap and insubstantial his uncle's car was.

Jesus saw more than his eyes could register, or his mind assimilate. Young people shouted and dived into a lime-green swimming-pool. Others raced about a tennis court, screaming with laughter at triumph or defeat.

Pedro pulled his car up near the side terrace of the house and turned off the engine. 'You will sit here,' he said. 'You will wait. One will not be long.'

Jesus did not answer. He sat, staring at the beauties wrought by man and money, speechless with excitement. After some moments Tio Pedro returned, walking between Senor Bragg Stockton and one of his foremen, Church Foley.

Pedro said, 'Get out of the car, boy.'

Self-conscious, Jesus got out of the car and stood squinting in the sun. He was aware he was hungry; it was past the lunch hour at the convent and his stomach growled.

'This the young fellow you been telling me about?' Bragg Stockton said, peering at Jesus as he might inspect a young hog or a lamb.

'Si, Patrono.' Pedro nodded, smiling widely. He did not grovel, but one almost expected him to sink to his knees at any moment. 'Si. He is ten. Eleven now. Big for his age. I have heard el patrono much approves hiring young boys to work the fields.'

Bragg Stockton smiled and nodded, but Church Foley spoke. 'Greasers get lazy, older they get. They get so you can't prod 'em. If any of them brecheros got any energy it's the young ones.'

'It is that he will work well for you, Patrono,' Pedro said. 'He will make you no trouble.'

'Shit. All greasers make trouble,' Church Foley replied. 'One way or another.'

'Not this boy,' Pedro said, his voice quavering. 'He is a very good boy. Strong. Quiet. He makes no trouble.'

Bragg Stockton was frowning. 'Is he one of your sons, Pedro? He kind of favours you.'

Pedro shook his head, smiling falsely. 'It is only the resemblance of the family, Patrono. He is the son of my wife's sister.'

Stockton frowned again. 'This ain't Manuel O'Brien's kid, is it?'

Pedro nodded, smiling but his cheeks rigid and pallid. 'Si, Patrono. One has the excellent memory. One remembers the old senor. One recalls his son. One knew me when I walked toward you.'

'I remember all my friends, Pedro,' Bragg Stockton said. 'Folks I can do favours for — and sometimes folks who might do me favours. Eh?'

'I am eternally in your debt, el Patrono.'

'I know,' Bragg Stockton said in a flat tone.

Church Foley laughed. 'So you want Mr Stockton to take O'Brien's kid off your hands, eh?'

'He works well. This I promise. He makes no trouble.' Then suddenly Pedro's shoulders sagged, his face contorted and the words spewed from his mouth. 'It is that I have the great need, Patrono. The money left to care for the boy is now exhausted. There are no more funds for me in the great bank in Spring Street. My own family starves. I cannot feed another mouth when my own children go hungry, Patrono. I can work only infrequently, Senor. It is that my back is bad and my stomach gives me great trouble. There are only jobs of labour, and heavy lifting causes me pain of my back. I can make only a little money. Almost none. And my own family starves. I would keep the boy gladly, but I am helpless, Patrono. My own children go hungry.'

As Pedro talked, Jesus' attention wandered. A youthful man, elegantly attired in riding breeches, boots, silk shirt and kerchief at his throat, walked from the shadowed terrace toward them. He held by the hand a little girl who looked to be eight or nine. Jesus looked at the golden vision and could not pull his gaze away. No radiant cherub in the Sunday church bulletins was as heavenly. He had never seen anyone so fragile and delicate, so breathtakingly lovely, and it was as if even her beauty was merely promissory, it whispered of the loveliness ahead for her. She wore a white dress, anklets and pumps and Jesus was entranced.

'What's going on, Father?' the young man said. The little girl clung to his hand, but her gaze was fixed on Jesus. None of the adults noticed the children.

'My old friend Pedro Luiz here has brought a boy to work on the place. Says he's a good worker, Bonnett. What do you think?'

Bonnett Stockton glanced down at Jesus, raking his gaze across him in a casual way. He shrugged. 'He looks healthy enough. If he can be made to work, we can use him.'

'He works well. He will do as you tell him.' Pedro nodded, looking frightened. 'I would never leave him but my own family — '

'You told us that, Pedro,' Bragg said, laughing. 'The

problem with you is that you don't look in the right places for employment.'

'Eh, Senor?' Pedro winced and shifted inside his shirt.

'Hell, boy, if your back hurts and your stomach gives you trouble, you don't want a day-labour job. Hell, that kind of work will kill a strong man.'

Pedro's eyes brimmed with tears of self-pity. 'Si, Senor. Es verdad. But what other work is open for a man such as I?'

Bragg Stockton shrugged. 'Who knows? You won't know until you ask around. You got friends. I'm your friend. Hell, I'll make you a wager. If you go from here to the office of Deputy Morris Redding, he'll hire you. No hard work. Been telling Morris, we need a deputy who can deal with Mexicans. I figure a Mexican deputy would be great boon to old Morris Redding.'

Pedro almost laughed, nodding, filled with sudden hope. 'Do you believe he would hire me? I would be a deputy?'

'You might have to take some kind of civil service exam. But don't worry about that. You don't pass, Morris will fix it so you do.' He laughed. 'Old Morris himself had to take that exam three times before he could pass it. And look at Morris. One of the best deputy sheriffs this county ever had.'

'Is it that he might hire me then?' Pedro begged.

Bragg Stockton grinned. 'If you go right on down there to his area office. I'll be pleased to call ahead and tell him you're coming.'

Now Pedro did burst into tears. He wept openly. 'I can never repay you, Patrono.'

Bragg shrugged. 'Oh, I think you can, Pedro. I think you will. I choose my people carefully. I like my friends to owe me a little something — in advance. Eh, Pedro? I feel more secure that way.'

'Oh, you need never but ask of me, Patrono. I owe you much.'

Bragg laughed. 'And don't you forget it.' He moved to turn away, then stopped and looked at Pedro. 'Things a little tight, Pedro? You need a little something to tide you over?' He reached into his trouser pocket, removed a fat wad of paper money and peeled off a hundred-dollar bill. He extended it between his fingers. 'A kind of down payment, say, on the boy here.'

Pedro took the bill, nodding. 'You are the most kind and

generous of men, Patrono. I am ever in your debt.'

The little blonde girl gazed at Jesus without blinking. He gave her a brief, shy smile, his weakened left eyelid fluttering slightly, almost in a wink, as if the two of them, strangers, shared a wild and wonderous secret beyond the ken of the adults around them.

The blonde vision did not smile in return, but she did not lower her gaze. She closed her own eye in a secret wink of understanding and accord and of unsettling promise.

Part Three:

THE UNLAID GHOST

'Some say no evil thing that walks by night,
In fog or fire, by lake or moorish fen,
Blue meagre hag, or stubborn unlaid ghost
That wreaks his magic charms at curfew time,
No goblin, or swart faery of the mine,
Hath power o'er true virginity.'

John Milton: *Paradise Lost*

XXI

There were no good hours of the working day on the Stockton farms, and Jesus was neither happy nor miserable. As his mother before him had been to those around her, he was to acquaintances and superiors, almost inscrutable. No matter what happened to him, good or ill, he remained remote, withdrawn, with that outward calm and inner resignation in which Julia had passed the heated days of her own brief life.

He ate with the single labourers in the dormitory mess-hall, usually meals of beans, rice and minced beef cooked in onions, peppers and water. The labourers were charged ten cents a meal. He slept on a barracks cot, again at a cost of ten cents a night. During the harvest season, the place was bedlam: loud, overcrowded, never really clean, stinking of sweat and unwashed bodies. Jesus did not complain. He silently accepted these conditions just as he passed through those comparatively rare times when there were no more than a dozen men and boys in the spotless, sanitized and fumigated dormitory.

He worked without protest and sans enthusiasm at any tasks the foremen found for him. He was by no means a diligent, strenuous or even an energetic labourer. He finished off his chores without interest, working steadily but with no haste and yet without dawdling quite enough to earn the curses of the overseers. In time, working in the vast fields, he became like a sunspot, almost like the growing plants; he blended in with the groves or the ploughed earth, practically disappearing against the sun-bleached sky. He was so quiet and unremarkable that one almost forgot him and he seemed very carefully never to do anything, good or bad, that might draw attention to himself.

The sun burned him almost black. The pain in the small of his back from endless stooping never really released him. He didn't speak of the ache because no one else did. The Mexican workers knew they were hired because few Anglos would perform this type of labour; stoop labour, as it was known.

Jesus, as always, watched everything and everybody with silent, unyielding attention, forever slightly apart, never really belonging anywhere. He was a Latin, but he was not one of the braceros because he was not from Mexico and because he was not an illegal, they did not trust him, or accept him. These, wetbacks, lived in constant fear of immigration officers, though they had been transported from the border without incident in farm or army trucks.

Jesus soon was aware of the pragmatism of the American agricultural establishment. There were state and federal laws against wetbacks, illegal Mexican emigrants or alien workers. None spoke more vehemently than the wealthy landowners against the flood of Mexicans across the border, the migrants who came to work the lettuce fields, to harvest tomatoes, grapes, olives, citrus, all the bounty of the rich California valleys. Yet, even to one as uninterested and uninvolved as Jesus, it was obvious that the huge farms, ranches and groves could not exist without stoop labourers. Not only that, but officers of the law rode convoy on the very trucks which rolled up the highways from the border towns, delivering the illegals to the immense estates. These men, women and children were paid ten cents an hour, one dollar for a ten-hour day in the fields. They were charged half a day's wages in rent for scantily furnished shacks or barracks beds and for food purchased in dormitory commissary or mess-hall. They were also dunned ten cents a day for transportation to and from the harvest regions, though they walked in crowds, morning and night. Not one Mexican national family ever left the farms without being in debt to the growers, for food and rent and for passage to and from the border at the onset and end of the harvest seasons.

Jesus watched indifferently as the wetbacks came and departed. They arrived, anxious, but their faces warm with hope, with their beautiful young girls, slovenly older women, ambitious children. The men prowled, watchful, with their darkly handsome, bronzed, high-boned faces, shiny black hair, glistening olive eyes, broad-chested, sometimes sporting an earring or silver belt-buckle, their single worldly possession. During the lunch breaks, they sprawled sleeping in the sun or played cards or dominoes in stolid silence.

It was at night that they came alive. After ten hours of stooping in the blazing sun of the fields, they gathered between the barracks and the shanties, with mandolin, accordion, guitar, fiddle and mouth harp. They sang and danced the passionate, up-tempo music they'd brought across the border with them. The women were beautiful by firelight, the men gallant and rugged and laughing, their bodies glistening with sweat, their eyes illumined by wine. The foremen on night duty sat apart, waiting, talking quietly or simply smoking their pipes and cigars, their heads drifting in lamplit clouds of smoke, the sensuous beat of music throbbing and pulsing in the fire-splattered night.

For Jesus this was the good time, the nights of laughter and music and excitement. He watched fascinated, standing with warm, shy smile, but without a word to anyone. He longed to plunge into the middle of the hilarity, to dance and sing and hold the young girls close — those sloe-eyed little ninas who eyed him expectantly and confidently — but he could not. To the emigrant girls under twelve who found him comely, he soon was rated apathetic and dull, unfriendly and withdrawn. It was as if he were helplessly slumbering through his childhood, needing to wake or to be wakened.

Only the infrequent sight, from afar, of the golden little princess from the castle beyond the walls could rouse him from his lethargy. All others who thought about him at all, saw him as they might see a silent, deep-bellied volcano, with violence tamped down, leashed and hidden. Most, giving him any casual scrutiny, found him a serene, removed, dull-minded and unfeeling boy. He had no parents; he never spoke of them, or seemed to need them. Late at night he lay sleepless and his eyes brimmed with tears, longing for Tia Clara and for Teodoro, but no one saw him weep. Because he was timid, he gained among the other labourers the reputation of false pride, of snobbery, of feeling he was better than the rest of them, somehow set apart, heartless and uncaring.

Sometimes, for no good reason that he could discern, he would be called out of the ranks of the stoop labourers and sent up to the big house to work in the kitchen, or to trim the hedges, edge the lush grass, or clean the swimming-pool. These tasks were like excursions into heaven for him. He saw the smiling, golden little girl a dozen times a day. He would look up from his work and find her watching him, smiling faintly.

He never spoke to her. He never dared, and yet the dullest moron could see his face come alive, flushed with colour, alert and exuberant, his full lips parted in that faint smile, his breath quickened to flare his nostrils, his eyes fiery with exultation, adoring, entranced, enchanted. She saw it. She returned his smile secretly and winked at him, bringing back that wondrous, life-altering moment when he'd first beheld her.

He learned that her name was Leonora. He had never heard a name with such beauty and poetry and delight in it. He was not content merely to be in her orbit, but he knew his place. It was better to be near her, where he could see her beauty and inhale the faint unsettling musk of her gleaming golden hair, even denied the right to speak to her or to say her musical name aloud, than to be banished to the fields from where she'd be as remote as the farthest star. He was resigned to working silently if only he could be in sight of her fragile loveliness. To look at her was like the jolt of strong wine, as heady as the faintly remembered whiff of opium from an almost disremembered pipe in the mists of the past. To see her walk near was a prayer answered. The hope that he might encounter her about the house, the terrace or the formal gardens, even for a moment, gave meaning and high expectation to his life.

The moments up at the chateau were few and far between. He was afraid to ask to be sent to work at the mansion for fear this would motivate the foremen to deny him that privilege. He didn't ask but he prayed a lot. Only Leonora could stir him from his lethargy, but she boiled his blood and sauteed his brain, she made him look for something in life other than stoop labour in the fields. She haunted his dreams, fired his waking fantasies. He could work all day in the fields, almost unaware of the agony in his back, the burn of the sun, the sweat in his eyes, the thirst in his throat, because inside his mind he was with Leonora in some rich, lush and breeze-cooled bower. She was his and somehow, he was worthy of her.

Despite himself, he was caught up in the life of the migrants. They swarmed around him, day and night, with their woes, their triumphs, their disasters, their fears. They laughed or wept, loved, hated and fought, and he was swept along at the brink of their onrushing tide. They bore children, and lost them at birth, and he saw the priest come from Apia, saw the child blessed and buried, the mother stolid and returning to work, the father as cold as ice, immobile as any Indian, staring, hating, but not daring to question. Some of these people possessed such strong personalities, such magnetism or physical strength or unusual beauty that they stood out from the mob, admired, envied and sometimes even hated by the peons around them, but always prominent.

Such a man was Alzado Salazar. That late afternoon the border truck arrived with the migrants, Jesus watched Alzado leap down from the tailgate and hold out his arms to his lovely young wife who dived from the crowd into his embrace. Everyone laughed and applauded and from this moment the young Salazars stood apart. Jesus watched them, fascinated, admiring. Loud, boisterous and macho, young Salazar might have recalled Tio Pedro unpleasantly in Jesus' mind, except that the twenty-five-year-old Salazar treated his seventeen-year-old wife as if Dolores Maria Constancia were fragile china. He saw other women but he looked with desire only at his own esposa.

Salazar was muscular, dark, of medium height, with bole-like thighs and sculpted calves. He was forgivably vain of his masculine beauty. His thick dark hair shone and his black eyes gleamed with his inner strengths and pride and delight in himself and his wife. She was all he had; he had not a peso in his pocket and yet watching him prowl in that easy, graceful way, one might have thought him a millionaire. He had worked in Mexico but times had been disastrous at home this year, worse than ever. His family urged him to seek work north of the border but to leave Dolores in the safety of his father's house in Guaymas. Alzado knew he must find work in order to feed, clothe and pamper his exquisite wife, but he could not endure the prospect of life separated from her. California, despite the danger of illegal entry, seemed an exciting adventure to Dolores. She accompanied him, crossing a hole in a border wall late one night. They were quickly rounded up by national guardsmen but instead of being returned to Mexico, they were crowded into trucks and sent north to work the harvests.

Jesus was not the only one who gazed in delight upon the symmetry and bright elegance of Dolores Salazar. Dolores was of such beauty as one seldom encounters outside some idealized painting of the Latin senorita. Her face was dark cream, smoother than any damask, unblemished, with vast, expressive, seeking eyes. Salazar had wed and bedded her, but he had not tamed her. He had whetted in her appetites she had not even suspected in herself before her wedding night in Alzado's passionate embrace. After months of marriage, she still carried herself in that tantalizing way of the maidens promenading the sunset plazas. She writhed her hips in an almost serpentine twist when she walked. She gazed boldly back into the eyes of men who, seeing her for the first time, doubted their own senses, and looked again. Her wide-lipped mouth, glittering with white teeth and sensuous tongue, spread in a smile for everybody — man, woman, child, old and young alike. Unfortunately for her reputation in that strict society where appearances are everything, there glowed in her smile that quality which permitted, and even encouraged, one to feel he alone was the sudden and adored centre of her fantastic universe. Unfortunately again, for all outsiders, this simply was not true. Her smile lied. Alzado Salazar was the core of her life, but strangers and gossips could hardly know this. Sometimes, Dolores herself appeared not to know it.

When she plunged from that canvas-topped truck which had transported her and Alzado and forty other wetbacks north from San Diego, every eye, Anglo-Saxon and Latin, struck as one upon her, stayed and grazed there, over high-standing full firm breasts, unfettered by any chemise, the rounded hips and thighs that broke a man's heart or rekindled in him old dreams and fantasies. They were as entranced as misled by that vivacious smile which seemed to whisper, 'I've been looking for you, all my life, I've been looking for you alone.'

Bonnett Stockton was endowed with that instinctive genius for appreciation of feminine pulchritude, plus the God-granted power of being instinctively and advantageously in the right place at the right time. In his Stutz-Bearcat he had careened along the highway into the barracks area of the farm just ahead of the national guard truck which had been commandeered for this transport of labour. He stood, sweating, senses reeling, with two of his foremen when the emigrants were discharged from its tonneau. Hector Swain and Church Foley, sober, but enthralled, whistled at the sight of the exuberant and incredible Dolores.

'Got us a load of trouble this trip, boss.' Hector spoke from experience. He had seen a decade of wetbacks come and go; he had learned to spot problems at first glance. This black-eyed senorita was too beautiful to be true and too much beauty meant trouble in any work crew.

Bonnett laughed at him. 'I see big tits, but I don't see any trouble.'

'That's because you don't have to live down here with them, boss. Look at that Mexican girl, bouncing her boobs and swinging her hips and eyeing all the men. A female like that can cause more trouble in the fields than a plague of locusts and a hell of a lot quicker.'

Bonnett only laughed again. 'Well, maybe we can keep her out of the fields, Hector. Maybe I can find things for her to do up at the house.' He wiped sweat from his mouth with the back of his hand. 'Ought to be able to find something for her to do up there.'

Hector shook his head. 'Before you do that, boss, you better look at those muscles on her man. See that arm around her waist? That hombre has got muscles growing out of his muscles.'

'So has his wife,' Church Foley said.

'Yeah, but his muscles will kill you quicker. Look at him, the way he is holding on to her, he's just about daring any other cock to come near her.'

'How can I look at him when I've got a hard-on looking at her?' Bonnett slapped Hector's shoulder, laughing.

'Not me. My pecker crawled back up inside when I looked at that hombre with her,' Church said. 'That female is good to look at, but I wouldn't want to die for it.'

'Nor me,' Hector said, shaking his head.

Bonnett laughed at them. 'You fellows have got to stop being afraid of greasers.'

Hector shrugged. 'No greaser alive that I'm scared of. But I've seen a lot of greaser machetes that scare me shitless.'

'Amen,' Church Foley said. 'You get a jealous wetback with a machete in his hand and you got blood. Every time.'

Bonnett peered at them, amused. 'If you think I'm going to

298

let that luscious little puta get away from here without getting myself a sample or two of those sweet juices, you're loco.'

'Jesus, boss,' Hector said. 'We got troubles enough worrying about the illegals without you stirring up that hornet's nest.'

Bonnett swung his arm. 'Look at her, for God's sake. She's made for bedding down. It's God's intention for her to pleasure men, and I never question God's will.' He exhaled heavily, steadying himself against Church Foley. 'Will you look at the way she smiles at me?'

'She smiles at everybody like that, boss,' Hector Swain said.

'Maybe. But I'm the one who takes it personally. At least, I'm the one who takes it personally that's in a position to do something about it.'

2

The next morning, when the newly arrived labourers were gathered outside the barracks to be assigned to work crews, Dolores Salazar was told to wait behind the others. She was summoned into Hector Swain's office inside the barracks building, along with Jesus. Jesus felt exultant; he was certain this meant he was to be sent up to the great house for the day. Though he had been assigned to a section and told to march with it to the lettuce fields, Alzado Salazar stood outside the barracks in the sun, cracking his knuckles, pacing in small circles, awaiting his wife, his face pallid.

Hector Swain sat at a pine desk. Jesus and Dolores stood before him. It was almost as if Hector had Jesus there as chaperone; he had the will perhaps, but not the audacity, to bring the Mexican beauty into his room alone. He smiled at the girl and asked if she'd ever worked as a domestic. She said that she had done housework. 'I don't mean that,' Hector said. 'Have you ever worked for nobles, in a rich house where everything must be polished and dust-free?'

Dolores only shrugged.

'Well, we'll try you out up there,' Hector Swain said, because he had no choice. He had his orders from a sniggering Bonnett Stockton himself.

'You wish me to work as a maid?'

'As a maid. Yes. It will be far easier.'

'If I may, Senor. I'd wish to be with my husband — '

'In the fields?' Hector stared at her as if she were insane. The girl sighed. 'I came north to work beside my husband.'

'You'll see him at night.'

'But that is not as I wish it, Senor, if you please. Forgive me. I do understand that one does me honour to offer me a job that is not in the fields. But I wish to refuse it.'

Hector shook his head. 'Listen. You better ask your husband what he'd rather have you do, if he'd want you burning up out in those fields — or working in a cool and beautiful house.'

'It is very pleasant up at the great house, Senora,' Jesus ventured to say.

Hector jerked his head around. 'Stay out of this, boy,' Hector warned him, but Dolores' smile made it worthwhile. Hector waved his arm. 'Now, listen Senora. You do as I say and you'll stay out of trouble. You try it a few days up at the big house. You don't like it — well, we'll talk about it then. Now, you just go on up there. Jesus here will walk up there with you. And when you get there, you do as you're told.'

Dolores sighed, but did not protest any more. She and Jesus walked outside the barracks. They found Alzado standing alone, looking grey and troubled, frightened for both of them in this alien place.

'What is the matter?' Alzado greeted them.

'It is that I have been sent up to the house of el patrono — as a maid,' Dolores told him.

Colour returned to Alzado's dark cheeks and he nodded, exhaling as if he had not breathed since Dolores had entered the barracks. 'Bueno, Dolores. Muy bueno. It gets hotter than hell in the fields.'

She shook her head. 'I told the senor it is my wish to be with you.'

Alzado looked pleased, but he shook his head. 'No. Go up there. If one works well, perhaps they will like you and keep you. Perhaps it will lead to good, a place to live, work for both of us.'

Dolores kissed Alzado, her eyes brimming with tears. Salazar clutched her close in his arms and then hurried away, running towards his work crew along the dusty road.

300

Dolores and Jesus walked together toward the mansion. She asked his name and if he came from Mexico.

'I was born here,' Jesus told her.

She gave him a warm smile. 'You are a pretty boy.' She nodded as if foretelling his fate. 'You will break many hearts in a few years.'

Jesus smiled at her in his shy way, that left eyelid wavering as if about to wink. 'One believes that such a beautiful senora as you would indeed know all there is to know of breaking hearts.'

Dolores laughed. 'Why, what a charming little heartbreaker you are. But it is not nice to wink at an old married lady. You charming little devil, you will give her ideas.'

Jesus walked with Dolores to a rear door where he knocked hesitantly. When a servant appeared in the doorway, Jesus introduced Dolores Salazar and said she had been bade to work as a maid. When Bonnett Stockton appeared suddenly behind the servant, his face flushed with whiskey at eight o'clock in the morning, Jesus heeled about directly and ran around the house to the old gardener, feeling frightened without being able to say why. He feared both the patron of the estate and the eldest son equally, but for different reasons. He feared Bragg Stockton because here was a man whose very word on this rancho meant life or death to its hirelings. But he feared the violence and drunken temper of Bonnett Stockton as he was afraid of the devil himself. When he worked at the mansion he spent most of his time seeking glimpses of Leonora and trying to stay out of her father's way.

The next time Jesus saw Dolores, the young woman wore a maid's black dress, trimmed with white lace. She was sweeping floor rugs on the terrace. Jesus raked eucalyptus leaves, gathering them down to the last stem in a peach basket. She seemed adjusted to her position, resigned to her tasks and awed by her surroundings.

Working silently, almost invisible against the hedges, Jesus saw Bonnett Stockton sidle out on the terrace before Dolores was aware of the landowner's son. Holding his breath, Jesus watched them. Bonnett Stockton's first precaution was to glance hastily across the windows of the house. Jesus drew out of sight against the bole of a tree. Bonnett stepped across the terrace stones behind Dolores. Hearing him, she cried out and turned quickly, facing him. He said something to her, but

301

her English was imperfect and she only shook her head. She flushed, embarrassed, and looked around, anxious to get away. Bonnett caught her arm in his hand and spoke again to her, under his breath and close against her black hair. She averted her face and spoke in frantic Spanish. Stockton glanced around again and slipped his hands under her biceps, closing his palms on her full breasts. Dolores understood this all right. She broke free and shoved him away. Laughing, he reached for her again, but she ran into the house.

Bonnett remained standing there a few moments, then he shrugged, laughed and disappeared into the shadowed sun-room.

Jesus was immobilized by a fear he didn't even comprehend. His stomach felt empty, tied in knots. The backs of his legs seemed suddenly incapable of supporting him. He leaned against the tree, gripping the rake handle as if it were the straw which would save him.

'Why are you standing idle like that, you worthless boy?' Stunned at the sound of Leonora's voice, Jesus heeled around.

He felt something tear free in his chest, the pain sharp and unrelenting. The first time Leonora Stockton had spoken to him, and in her face there was nothing but hatred and rage. He shook his head helplessly, unable to speak. He could only stare at her, shaking his head from side to side.

Her voice quavered with anger. 'Why are you standing there like that? Why do you sneak around, spying on people?'

He swallowed at the knot choking his throat. 'I'm sorry,' he managed to whisper. 'I beg you. Forgive me.'

'Don't lie to me,' she said. 'Don't you dare make up lies to tell me. I warn you, unless you are tired of this farm, that you tell me why you spy. Why?'

She looked as if she might weep, except that weeping was an admission of weakness, and she would die before she would let him see her cry. Jesus shook his head, feeling angered at the falseness of her accusation, but aching in deepest compassion for the pain he saw swirling in the little girl's face. 'I spy on no one,' he said in a flat and anguished tone.

'I warn you, boy. Don't lie to me. I see you — spying. Watching all the time.'

'No. No. If I look — it is to find only a glimpse of you. That is all. I meant no harm.'

'Well, I won't have it. Do you understand? Do you hear? I shall tell Grandfather not to let you near this house again.'

He shook his head, pleading. 'Please forgive me.'

'No. I cannot forgive you. You have no right to spy on my father like this. What my father chooses to do is no concern of yours. Do you hear me? What evil is it that you do? Do you spy on us here at this house — and run back with your lies to amuse your dirty wetback friends? Is that what you do?'

He straightened. 'I speak to no one. Of anything. You accuse me falsely. Wrongly. I would do nothing to hurt you. Ever. I speak to no one.'

'See that you don't. What happens in this house is private. Of no concern to you or any of your people. If you wish to work at this house, see that you say nothing of anything you hear, anything you see. . . . If you think I won't tell my grandfather that you spread lies, you are wrong. If you lie about my father, you do hurt me, you understand? You break my heart and I hate you.'

Suddenly crying, tears running down her golden cheeks, Leonora turned and fled across the terrace from him. She entered the sunroom through the tall open French windows and she did not look back. Jesus stood, empty-bellied, feeling a constricting sadness for the little girl, knowing she vowed her hatred for him only because her heart would not permit her to hate her own father who had distressed and offended her. Her anguish and heartbreak had to find some outlet and she could castigate him and pretend in her mind that it was he who had roused her outrage in the first place.

Somehow, moody and unhappy, he got through the rest of the day. He stayed as far from the terrace as his chores would permit. He glimpsed Leonora sitting on her father's lap on the terrace, laughing and chatting with him. Emptily, he retreated, praying she had not seen him. Late in the afternoon he heard Leonora's mother raging, her voice drunken, the same liquored passionate words he'd heard in Aliso Street. He was disenchanted. The home was larger, the land vast, the fortune huge, but the people after all were not so unlike the ones he had known in the barrio. They laughed and drank and fought and either faced their problems or ran from them, in one way or another.

When he started back toward the barracks in the dusk,

Dolores called out his name and walked along with him. They tried to talk, but found little to say; both were dejected and gloomy, their thoughts turned inward.

Jesus walked to the door of her shanty with her. She gave him a faint and twisted smile, thanking him. She went into the house and he returned to the barracks. He sighed, miserable. One thing was certain. He would not be sent again to work at the mansion. He would see the golden Leonora no more. From a driving inner enthusiasm, he sank again into the old apathy. He fell across his cot and was asleep before dark.

When Alzado Salazar returned, back aching and legs trembling from the eternal ordeal in the sun, he had one hope. He prayed that Dolores would scrub him down with soap and hot water and that she would massage the burning tendons of his back and legs. He asked little else of God that night. He was too exhausted to wish for more.

He entered the shanty and called her name. She did not reply at once and he found her slumped in a chair at the bare pinewood kitchen table. The lamp was unlit, the wood-burning stove was cold. Dolores had been crouched with her head on her folded arms, but she straightened and tried to smile when he came into the room.

'What is it, Dolores?' Alzado sank to the floor on one knee beside her, his fatigue forgotten.

Haltingly, reluctantly, she told him of her day, of Bonnett Stockton, the son of the patron of the estate. 'He treated me like a puta. He said to me things in English. I do not know the words, but the tone I know well. I know what he said to me. I know what he tried to do to me. He found me in a bedroom and locked the door. He let me go only when I screamed.'

His eyes blurry with tears, Alzado closed his arms about her. 'I go to kill him,' he said. 'I will not endure the infernal evil of him. Because he is rich and he owns much land, we are nothing to him. He believes he can take what he wants. Well, I show him the truth. I swear I'll kill him.'

Dolores threw her arms about him, holding him with all her strength. 'Do not go to seek revenge,' she begged. 'Only you and I can be hurt. If you go to kill the evil man, you in turn must die, and I must live — a living death without you.'

'My God. What can we do?' His voice shook. 'We cannot let them do this evil to you.'

'I will not go back there to the great house,' she said. 'I will

304

stay with you.'

'I do not think it is that easy,' he said. 'If we stay here, they will make us do as they wish. We must leave.'

'Where would we go?'

'I would go back home. This is a strange and heartless place. We will find a little land. We will grow enough to eat. We will not dream of California. We shall be content.'

'Yes.' For the first time she smiled and nodded. 'Yes. I too wish to go home. When can we leave?'

He stood up. 'I will talk to the straw boss, the one called Swain. I will ask for the two pesos they owe us and we will leave.'

She sighed out the agony that had constricted her insides. She stood up, smiling, looking forward to escaping this place, to returning to her homeland and her family and her friends, of going home again with Alzado. 'Yes. Talk to him. I will prepare our dinner while you are gone.'

Salazar strode from the shanty, his weariness shoved aside in his mind. He felt a ray of hope, a sense of triumph that he would take Dolores and go back home. He wanted to laugh. What renewed life had flowed into Dolores at the wondrous thought of returning across the border!

Hector Swain ate his supper alone. Salazar knocked on the door and entered when Swain called out to him. Swain sat at his desk, his meal before him. When he recognized Salazar, he scowled. He had heard nothing of what had transpired at the mansion, but looking at Salazar's face he did not need to be told. It was all there to be seen. God knew, he had seen it often enough.

'Well, Salazar, what's the matter? They work you too hard out there?'

Alzado shrugged. 'I come not to talk of the work. I knew it would not be easy before I got here. It is not the work. It is my wife. Dolores is unhappy here. She is very unhappy here. She wants to return to Mexico. And I came to tell you, I go to take her home,'

Swain stared up at him. 'Just like that, eh?'

'My wife is unhappy. I wish to say no more. It is that we wish to leave.'

Swain shook his head. 'And it is equally that we can't spare you to go right now, Salazar. We are in the midst of a harvest. You might have noticed the smell of rotting lettuce out in those fields. We need every hand we can get.'

'Still, it is that you do not need me. Nor my wife. It is great trouble if we stay on this place. I ask only that you pay me two pesos — the money my wife and I earned today. We will leave. We will make no trouble.'

'Two pesos, eh? I'm afraid you can't add and subtract very good, Salazar. You are right. You and your wife each make one dollar a day. Money paid when the harvest is in. But already — for two days, you owe the grower one dollar for rent of your shanty, and twenty cents for food.'

Salazar winced as if Swain had struck him across the eyes. 'With no money we cannot eat. It is many miles from here to the border.'

'Don't worry about it, Salazar. You and your woman wouldn't never get back to the border, even if you had money for food. Don't you know what will happen to you the minute you step off this farm? The US Immigration officers will get you. They'll put you in one camp, your woman in another. You may get out in a week, a month, a year. You'll surely be deported back to Mexico, which is what you want. But it is not likely you will be sent back together. Or even to the same place. You may have one hell of a time finding your pretty little Dolores once the Immigration people separate you. I'm telling you this for your own good. I'm trying to be friendly. Trying to give you good advice.'

Salazar drew a deep breath. 'If you will not pay us the eighty cents that you owe us — '

'Oh, we'll pay you every cent we owe you people, Salazar, just as we are supposed to do — when the harvest is in and the trucks are here to return you people to the border. But right now, we owe you nothing. You try to leave, and I warn you, we'll have to call the Immigration people.'

'Why would you have to do this evil thing?'

'Well, it's only evil, Salazar, depending on your view. It seems evil to you, because the Immigration people will arrest you and keep you from going where you want to go. But from our view, it is the legal and patriotic thing to do. It is what we are sworn to do. The Stocktons get a special state and federal dispensation to bring in migrant workers. In return, if any workers decamp, run away or try to leave the farm, we are bound by law to notify Immigration, and I promise you, that's what we'll have to do.'

'You are holding us — in slavery.'

Swain shook his head. 'Well, there you go again, Salazar. It is slavery only if you take that view. I can see it might look like slavery to you. But you and your woman crossed the border illegally. Nobody asked you to come up here. But you came. You take your chances. I can tell you this. Your chances are not too bad if you stay here, keep your nose clean, and do what you're told. If you try to leave, you got no chance at all — and this slavery, as you call it, will look like the good old days.'

'We wish only to go home. We ask nothing else.'

'Well, I'm sorry about that. I might even wish I could help you. But I can't. You stay here until the lettuce is harvested, you'll get paid what is coming to you and a ride back to the border.'

'My wife wishes to return home and I must take her.'

Swain shook his head again. 'I don't think you are that big a fool, Salazar. You know I'm telling you straight. You and your woman got one chance of getting back home together. Stay here and do what you're told.'

Salazar sighed deeply. 'We cannot do this. Already, my wife refuses to go again to work in the casa grande. She will not go. You must not try to make her go. She must stay at my side.'

Swain laughed at him. 'You're in no position to bargain with me, Salazar. You people will do what you are told. Or we'll turn you over to Immigration. Go on home. Talk it over with your woman. I think you're both smart enough to make the right decision.'

XXII

Jesus awoke reluctantly, a splinter of daylight scratching at his eyelids. He felt tired for no good reason, overcome with the old lethargy and a new gloomy sense of despair. He lay for a long time, unwilling to open his eyes to the daybreak and the fevered noises and activities around him. During the past months, he'd begun each day with vigour and enthusiasm, driven by the hope, however baseless, that he would be assigned to the ranch-house work-crew, that he would pass the hours in the cosmos of the golden Leonora. He was fascinated, awed and inspired by her. He sought her all day long, gratified by the briefest glimpse, and she trailed after him into his dreams at night like a tantilizing wisp of remembered perfume; he could not grasp it, but he could not escape it, either.

His head rolled restlessly on the straw pillow. He remembered the bitter scene with Lenora yesterday, the hatred glittering in her violet eyes. She despised him. Aye God, as much as he loved her, she hated him. She would speak against him to her grandfather. He would be exiled to the fields or the groves. He would go up to the casa grande no more.

He ate his breakfast of beans and ham without relish and stood listlessly, shoulders slumped, in the crowd outside the barracks as work was assigned. When he heard his own name called among the select few to report to the mansion he was at first disbelieving. It could not be true. Leonora was giving him a second chance. God knew he would stay out of her way; he would avert his face when her family neared; he'd do nothing to displease her.

He was sent into the kitchen to wash dishes and cooking utensils from the family breakfast. He placed the china in suds, washed it and set it to rinse in scalding water. He scrubbed the pans. It was hard to believe so many utensils could be required for the preparation of one meal. As he worked, he listed in his mind the entrees prepared since six a.m., when Bragg Stockton stalked downstairs and ate alone, to ten when finally Bonnett and his wife appeared. These two were the last to eat. They allowed the cooks to prepare eggs Benedict, poached eggs, pancakes, hot cereal, coffee and juice, before declining anything except black coffee. The meal was scraped into metal drums to be fed to the hogs.

The cooks escaped the kitchen while Jesus still worked at the huge tubs and drains, the steam misting up around him, turning his face and hands a bright crimson.

He heard the low murmur of taut voices. He winced, looking around, wanting to escape. Bonnett Stockton and his beautiful young wife were arguing at the breakfast table over their coffee. They did not know whether workers remained in the kitchen, but obviously they did not care.

Bonnett's voice rose first. 'Goddamn it, Tory. What kind of crap is this, drinking straight whiskey at six o'clock in the morning.'

Her laugh raked at him like hawk talons. 'I have to get up pretty early in the morning, Bonny, to get ahead of you. Well, I decided to get ahead of you today. And I may be ahead of you tomorrow. If I must stay prisoner in this damned horrible and ugly old barn and watch you sniff after the Mexican maids, I've got to be fortified — I've got to have my own friends with me — good old Jim Beam and Jack Daniels.'

'You want to know what you are, Tory? A bitch, that's what you are.'

Tory laughed, her voice quavering unsteadily. 'Certainly I'm a bitch. I have to be a bitch to live with a son of a bitch like you. . . . But I wasn't a bitch when you married me. There were people, good people, who thought I was something special. I was pretty and I was smart and I cared. Well, thirteen years later, I'm not pretty any more. If I were smart I'd walk to hell away from you, and I don't care. I don't care. Do you hear me? I don't care. I don't give a goddamn any more. You can run after the Mexican women like a mongrel in the streets, and I don't give a damn. But I won't have you trying to tell me how to live.'

'You are my wife. By God, you are a Stockton now, and you'll behave like one.'

She laughed at him, her voice rising and echoing. 'Oh, you

want me to rut around like a boar in the mud, like you do?'

'Keep your goddamn voice down. You know what I want you to do. I want you to stop thinking about yourself all the time. I'm sick of your moping around here, full of self-pity, accusing me of all sorts of crimes I don't commit.'

'Do you mean that we didn't catch you in that bedroom, behind locked doors with that fat-titted Mexican whore who was screaming for her life?'

'I mean it wasn't what it looked like. I was in that room. She came in. She locked the door. She didn't understand English. When I tried to get her to leave, when I put my hands on her — on her shoulders — to escort her out, she started to scream.'

'Oh Jesus, Bonny, you're not even a good liar. No good in bed. A faithless husband. A lecherous drunk, and you can't even tell a convincing lie.'

'That's because I tell the truth and you don't recognize it.'

'No, dear bastard. It is because you have the upper-class mentality. You can do no wrong. You are not subject to the same laws which govern the common herd. You truly believe that because you are a Stockton, you are above decent morality.'

'I believe I'm sick to death of your nagging, your drinking, your neglecting our daughter — '

'Jesus, Bonny. How dare you bring that up? It is you who turns Leonora against me with your lies. I have only one hope as far as poor little Leonora is concerned. One day she'll know the truth. She'll know you for what you are.'

'Sit down. Damn you, where do you think you're going?'

'I can't stay in the same room with you any more. The rarified Bonnett Stockton atmosphere is too rancid, too rotten for me. I've got to have fresh air.'

'Sit down. I'm not through talking to you.'

'Well, I'm through listening to you. I don't want any more coffee, and I don't want any more of your lies. I want you to leave me alone, do you understand? Leave me alone. . . .'

In the kitchen, Jesus stood with his arms immersed to the elbows in the scalding suds. He was unaware of the hot water. He was afraid to move for fear he would be overheard, be accused of eavesdropping. His stomach was tied in knots. He could not tell whether Bonnett Stockton had followed his wife from the breakfast nook or not. After a long time he dared to exhale and inhale a deep breath. He panted, grinning wanly. He had forgotten to breathe. When at last he dared lift a frying-pan from the steaming suds, he heard voices again from the breakfast nook and he stopped; as if caught in commission of some unforgivable crime.

He recognized Bragg Stockton's voice, the deep-chested tones accustomed to being heard and obeyed in high winds. 'Good morning, Bonny. I couldn't help overhearing you chatting with your wife. I doubt if they could help overhearing you at Apia.'

'I don't give a damn about anybody at Apia, Father.'

'Neither do I. But I do care about your screaming at your wife so the whole house echoes with it.'

'Would you like coffee, Father.'

'I'd like you to listen to me, Bonny. This internecine warfare between you and Tory must cease. Stop trying to destroy each other. Stop trying to hold Leonora as hostage between you. I won't tolerate it. It has got to stop.'

'I can call a servant for a fresh cup if you'd like coffee.'

A taut moment of prolonged silence. When Bragg Stockton spoke again, his voice was low and controlled. 'If I want coffee, I'll drink from Tory's cup, Bonny. I hope for your own good you will listen to me.'

'I've heard all this before, Father. I've told you how Tory and I can get along, how we can stop raging at each other like animals in a cage. Do you somehow think I enjoy this daily ranting between us?'

'One would think so, the way you indulge yourself.'

'We behave like caged animals because we *are* caged animals, Father. We can all profit if you will only agree to a divorce. Let me divorce her. Let us try to find some kind of life apart.'

'I won't do that. You'll never divorce Tory as long as I live. I shall make it part of my will that all my property, all my money will go to your younger brothers if you divorce Tory after my death. I want you to be a man. This farm, this name is a great responsibility. Your responsibility.'

'You ask too much,' Bonnett said. 'Goddamn it, you ask too much.'

'You chose Tory. You wed her. In the church. Before the priest. Before the world. Before God.'

'Before I knew what was happening to me.'

'I don't appreciate your smart-ass answers, either.'

'Then you'll forgive me.'

'Where are you going?'

'To get a drink, Father. To get several drinks. To escape you. To escape Tory. To escape myself. We all need something, Father, and it seems the only thing I'm permitted around here is the key to your liquor cabinet.'

Jesus waited a silent eternity in the kitchen before he dared continue working with the pans. One of the underling cooks came in and cursed at him. 'My God, boy, we'll need those things for lunch before you're through with them.'

Jesus worked furiously, a sense of dizziness reeling behind his eyes. When he could escape the kitchen at last, he went to the housekeeper for his new assignment, praying it was removed from the mansion itself. He was sent to scrub the black ring from around the swimming-pool with bucket, rags and ill-smelling acid.

He crawled on his knees at the rim of the lime-green pool. The chilled water was inviting against his fevered flesh. He did not lift his head or glance toward the house, afraid his action might be noted and misinterpreted. He had heard and seen too much at this house today. He wanted only to escape. He had not glimpsed his little golden goddess, but he was afraid to encounter her now. He wished to God he didn't know so much about her parents. His entire vision of this place was tilted, slightly out of focus, disturbing. Only his passion for Leonora remained unaltered.

He heard a faint splash in the pool, the whispered sound the striking of a trout might rouse. His head jerked up. Stunned, he watched Leonora, in a blue, knee-length swimsuit, slither otter-like beneath the wavy, translucent green surface.

Treading water easily, working her legs and waving her arms as effortlessly as reeds might in a stream, Leonora surfaced. Her golden hair slicked back from her forehead, her pale cheeks marbled with drops, like the smooth soft face of a lily. Jesus bit back the agonized delight her beauty roused in him, always fomented in him, and would forever, he was feveredly certain. If the romantics were right and true lovers were fated, meant one for the other, he knew whom God had made for him and him alone, even as he knew it could never be and was, likely, another of God's little jests. Still, he wanted only her, despite God, despite her family, despite all the odds against them, despite everything.

Leonora gazed up at him, unblinking, like a water nymph. 'Do you want to kiss me, Heysus?'

She heard him catch his breath in sudden anguish. He shook his head, cheeks pallid. 'Oh no. I would never — '

'Never think about it? Never think about kissing me? Heysus, anybody can look at you and know you want to kiss me. From twenty paces you can see how much you want to kiss me. Why, Heysus, you're lying to me. Yes, you are. I can look at you up close like this and see what you want.'

He looked around, frightened. 'No. Please.'

'Why do you look so miserable? Are you afraid of me?'

Jesus sighed. She was teasing him but he had no weapons, no armour against her. She had learned to flirt in kindergarten. He said nothing.

She peered at him. 'Do you want me to go away?'

He exhaled heavily, tried to smile and tried to keep his voice as light as hers. 'It's your pool.'

She nodded contentedly. 'Yes. You're right, Heysus. So it is. My pool. My home. My lands. My world. . . . So what are you doing in it if you don't want to be near me?' She laughed, shaking her head, water spraying as if from a spaniel. 'Do you know how to swim, Heysus?'

He shook his head. 'I never learned. This is the first pool I ever saw.'

'Really. It's just too sad, the first pool you ever saw and you have to sit wiping at it with a dirty rag. . . . I'll just have to teach you to swim. Would you like that?'

Again he tried to match her airy tone. 'I don't think your father would.'

She laughed. 'My father doesn't like you, Heysus. You know why? Because you're too pretty. Because he can see in your face that you like me. And he's not sure yet how I feel about you. . . . But Grandfather likes you. He told me so. He spoke with the priest about sending you in to the convent school at Apia afternoons. He must like you. I'm thinking about asking Grandfather to have you brought up to the house full time — to live with the servants up here. I've got to be careful, got to work it so he thinks it's his own idea, but I could do that if I wanted to. Then you'd be around all the time — whenever I need you. Wouldn't you?'

313

She laughed again and, unsure whether this was simply more taunting to amuse herself, he remained silent, scrubbing at the rim of the pool.

'Stop that, Heysus,' she ordered, her voice sharp. 'I'm talking to you.'

'It's my job. Somebody's got to do it, Miss Leonora.'

'Maybe they do,' she shrugged. 'But not right now.'

She levered herself up from the water, sitting on the beveled rim, dangling her feet in the pool. 'And don't call me Miss Leonora. I hate it. I can't stand it. Call me Leonora, or don't speak to me at all.'

'All right.'

'Well. Do it. Say my name.'

'Leonora.'

She laughed. 'You sound like you've had a lot of practice saying my name, Heysus. You think about me a lot — when you're by yourself? When you shouldn't be thinking about me at all?'

His face reddened to the roots of his chopped black curls, but he did not speak.

Leonora gazed at him intently. 'Do you think I like you, Heysus?'

'I don't know.'

'I don't mean just like you, do you think I like you better than anybody else, better than any other boy?'

He sighed heavily. 'I wish you liked me.'

'As much as you like me?'

He was forced to smile at that. 'I don't expect miracles.' His left eyelid flickered and his face was illumined, abruptly darkly beautiful. She caught her breath, staring at him, her own face suddenly vulnerable.

'Why not expect miracles, Heysus? Miracles are the only things left that are fun any more. Few people can work miracles. Wouldn't it be nice if you and I could?'

2

When Bonnett walked out of the breakfast nook to escape his father, he strode directly to the bar in the sunroom and poured straight whiskey.

He drank it down and blowing loudly, his mouth parted wide, he strode about the room. He wandered through the downstairs. He asked a maid if she had seen Mrs Stockton. 'I haven't seen Miss Tory,' the girl said.

He shrugged and got another drink before he checked the rest of the downstairs. He saw maids and men-servants, but he did not see the maid he sought, nor did he find any trace of his wife.

Angered, he finished off a third straight whiskey in the sunroom, prowling from wall to wall, trying to walk off the effects of the uncut booze. He paused in a splash of sunlight through the French windows. Something in the garden snagged his attenion and he growled aloud. Leonora was swimming in the pool. He smiled at first and then discovered the Mexican boy cleaning the far side of the pool. Leonora was like her mother. He had to watch her like a hawk. He sure as hell had to watch a horny twelve-year-old Mexican kid. He started through the door and then hesitated, something else on his mind.

He strode across the sunroom into the foyer and mounted the stairs, two at a time. He went along the silent cavernous first floor to his wife's bedroom. He opened the door. A maid was making the bed. He said, 'I'm looking for Mrs Stockton.'

'She is not here, sir. She left the house. More than an hour ago. She said if you asked me I was to tell you she had packed a small bag and gone into Los Angeles for the night. She said she might be gone for a couple of days.'

He nodded and retreated from the room. He went along the corridor, checking through the open doors, but finding no trace of the Mexican maid. As empty-bellied with yearning as he was, he could not bring himself to ask the servants where she was because of the scene she had created yesterday. Damn her, she'd pay for that impudence, and pay, his way. He grinned coldly.

In his own bedroom he found a bottle of bourbon and drank from it, wiping the back of his hand across his mouth. Setting the bottle back in its portable bar, he went downstairs, his face glowing, with a sense of wellbeing, of urbanity. He checked beyond the sunroom windows and found Leonora in rapt conversation with the Mexican kid. Now what in hell would she have in common with that greaser?

Irate, he sought the housekeeper. The fifty-year-old

woman had the look of a society dowager and she appeared to gaze along her prominent nose even at the Stocktons themselves.

Bonnett gave her his most amiable and casual smile. He said, 'That new maid, Mrs Hollister. . . I'm not sure I remember her name. Mrs Stockton was asking about her. Dolores? Oh yes. That's right. Dolores. Where is she working at the moment?'

He held himself aloof and disinterested, a poise spoiled mildly when he braced himself against a table and staggered slightly. Mrs Hollister gazed at him, unsmiling. 'I'm sorry, sir. The Mexican girl, Mrs Dolores Salazar, did not show up this morning.'

Feeling anger and frustration rising up on the hot acid from his stomach, Bonnett forced himself to go on smiling genteelly. He wanted to rage aloud but heard himself saying good-humouredly, 'Well, it doesn't matter. These people. They don't seem to realize when they've been shown preferential treatment. Do they?'

'No, Mr Stockton. Some of them don't.'

If there was a trace of irony in her tone, he ignored it. He didn't give a fart in a whirlwind what this old woman thought of him. He turned away and then paused, glancing at her as if in an afterthought.

'By the way, Mrs Hollister. There's a young Mexican boy working around the house. His name is Jesus O'Brien. I don't want him around up here any more. Leonora is young and impressionable, and she won't stay away from him. He's not the kind of influence I want for my daughter.'

'I understand, Mr Stockton.'

'As soon as possible, I want you to write a note to Foley or Swain down at the barracks. Tell them to keep the little bastard greaser away from this house. Call the boy in, give him the note and send him with it down to the barracks. I want him out of here.'

Feeling faintly pleased with himself, satisfied that he'd accomplished something, at least, he put on a hat and went out to his Stutz-Bearcat. He started it up and raced out of the drive.

He slammed on the brakes, skidding to a long stop directly in front of the barracks. He looked back in pleasure at the long arc of rubber he had laid down in the hard-packed clay roadway. He yelled, 'Swain? Swain, you round here?'

Hector Swain came out of the barracks. He winced when he saw Stockton's flushed face and liquid, reddened eyes. He had been here a long time. He recognized trouble by the first scent now. He didn't have to ask Bonnett what he wanted; he had been expecting the Stockton eldest son ever since the Salazar bitch had simply followed her husband into the lettuce fields despite his direct order to her to report to the mansion.

He managed a smile that any man not three sheets to the wind would have recognized as phony and empty and forced. He spoke in a loud, hearty tone, full of false warmth. 'Well, Bonny. What the hell you doing down here in the heat of the day?'

'You know fucking well what I'm doing down here, you betraying rat. Where's that Salazar bitch with the big tits?'

'You mean Alzado Salazar's wife, boss?'

'I don't give a damn whose wife she is. I want to know where is she? I told you to send her up to the house to work as a maid. Every day. That's every day, damn it. Not just when it pleases you.'

Swain tried to laugh. 'She wouldn't go, boss. Said she had to stay with her man. Tell you the truth, you came on like a freight train yesterday. You scared hell out of her.'

'Hell. She's a Mexican whore. She knows what I want. She's playing hard to get thinking she can get extra money out of me. I know whores like her. Meet 'em all the time. You tell her I want her back up at the mansion tomorrow or we'll fire her and her husband.'

Swain shook his head. 'Don't think that'll hack it, boss. Firin' em is just what they want. Salazar tried to quit. When I told him he'd get no pay for either one of them until harvest was over, he wanted to quit anyway. Why don't you pick out something else? They ain't all as hard to get as that Salazar dame.'

'Because, damn you, it's the Salazar dame I want. I'm not like you, Swain. I never settle for second best. I never make optional choices. I see what I want, I go after that. Now tomorrow, you tell her and you tell her tough-assed husband that she can't go into the fields. Tell her we need her to do maid's work at the house. If she don't want that, she can stay in her own house until I get down here. Tell her I want to talk to her. Tell her and Salazar that if they got sense enough to

317

pour piss out of a bucket, they'll start taking orders from the man that owns this place, and do it now.'

3

Leonora followed Jesus around the pool until he had finished scrubbing it down with acid. As he straightened, Mrs Hollister called him from the sunroom doorway. Leonora smiled at him and disappeared into the house. He walked over to where the housekeeper stood with a folded sheet of paper in her hand. 'I've a message here that must be delivered to Mr Hector Swain down at the barracks, Jesus. You'll deliver this note to Mr Swain and stay there until he gives you an answer.'

Jesus nodded. Mrs Hollister gave him a terse, faint smile and re-entered the house. He glanced across the windows, seeking one last glimpse of Leonora. There was no trace of her.

He sighed. He supposed that as long as he lived he would look back on this morning beside the pool as one of the supreme moments of pleasure in his life. Leonora was hard to understand. She had vilified him one day, her face showing her hatred. Today she had gazed at him raptly, chatted with him intimately, as if the things she had to say to him she could say to no one else. He grinned wryly. He supposed he should feel something like a fish snagged on her line. She threw him out and she reeled him in. Hell, he didn't care. He had been sure she would never speak to him again and she had been kind and pleasant and warm. Whatever happened to him, it was worth it to be near her when she wanted him.

He walked around the rear of the house, passing the garages, the servants' quarters, the stables, the dog runs. The Doberman pinschers ran against the wire fences, snarling and yowling, trained to kill intruders.

He loitered, empty-bellied in the midmorning sun. He lazed through the shade of the eucalyptus, smelling the citrus groves, the formal gardens. This setting was perfect for Leonora. It did not matter how she treated him, even if tomorrow she destroyed him with a frown, today he had basked in the brilliance of her golden smile. No one had to tell

318

him what a difference Leonora made in his existence. Without her, he was empty, lethargic and withdrawn. When she came near she wakened him to dreams, to ambitions, to magical hopes, no matter how foolish. She brought him alive. For the first time, he was stimulated, enthusiastic, excited by everything around him and impassioned with the possibilities of the future. The high road ahead was rosy and open and bright with promise, and all because Leonora had smiled at him.

'Heysus.'

At the sound of her voice, Jesus stopped as if someone had struck him with a stone in the small of his back. Incredulous, he turned and saw her hurrying after him in the blaze of sun. He stared at her, entranced. She wore a towel wrapped turban-like about her damp hair, white square-collared blouse and skirt. She looked like a little girl and she didn't look artless or young or innocent at all. She had stoped by the kennels and brought out one of the Doberman pinschers on a leash, the strap looped about her wrist. 'Where you going?' she called.

She came near him, staying across the road because the Doberman snarled if Jesus approached. 'I had to bring Master along,' she said. 'Father says I can never go near the fields — or the workers — without a guard dog. I'll walk with you if you like — even if we must stay across the road from each other.'

'I don't know what I've done to deserve this, but I'll burn candles if it will help.'

She sighed, her voice tinged with sadness. 'I don't think it will help, Heysus. I think Father has forbidden them to send you up to the house any more. I'm sure of it. I asked Mrs Hollister. He was angry because I spent the morning with you. I'll talk to Grandfather, but I don't think it will help. Grandfather does like you, but I know he won't go against Father's orders. I'm sorry, Heysus. I'm really sorry. We could have had such a nice time.'

He nodded. 'I'll miss you,' he said.

'And I you. I planned how we might sneak into the gardens and have picnics, just the two of us. I was going to ask Grandfather if I could teach you to swim in the pool. I had such lovely plans. But I know better. If I went against Father, he would send me off to school. He's threatened to do that anyway. He torments Mother with the threat of sending me away to school.'

He tried to smile. 'He torments me with it.'

'He might just do it. But he's gone a lot. There may be something I can work out. I'm at least as smart as he is.'

'I don't want to get you in trouble.'

She laughed. 'Worry about yourself. That's what I'm thinking about. Nobody can get me in trouble. I'm Bragg Stockton's granddaughter. But I could get you in bad trouble. . . . I've just got to be careful, that's all. . . . I'll tell you one thing, Heysus. I've known a lot of boys in my life. I've thought I cared about a lot of them. One especially at dancing school. Dorrance Perry. But I truly care for you. Better than anyone else. Anyone. That won't buy you a ticket to Paris, but it's true anyway.'

'I don't want to go to Paris.'

'You're such a sweet boy, Heysus. Such a sweet innocent.' She stopped and looked back over her shoulder toward the big house on the knoll, rising from a green beard of trees. 'Can you see the house from down at the barracks, Heysus?'

He nodded. She walked again, the dog pulling at her arm. 'I'll tell you something, Heysus, if you want me to. Something that can be ours alone, and a secret between us. Something nobody can ever take away from us.'

'Please,' he said.

She nodded, pleased, conspiratorial. 'When I was a little girl, when I was four years old, I had a nightmare. It was so terrible that the whole house was in an uproar. They sent for doctors. They sent me to doctors. After that nightmare I wouldn't sleep in a dark room. They had to leave a nightlamp for me. I kept a nightlight until about three years ago. I was nine when I let them turn off the nightlight. For a long time I would lie sweating. In terror, afraid I would have that dream again. It finally went away. It hasn't bothered me any more for the last three years.'

'What was your nightmare?'

She glanced at him, brow tilted. 'Do you want to know? Really? That's not important — it's the nightlight I want to tell you about.' She shrugged. 'Well, since I'm going to have that nightmare again, I might as well run through it now. I dreamed that my grandfather and some of his foremen came and took away my favourite doll. I got up and followed them

320

— in my dream — and they buried my doll, by lantern-light, in a dark grove. I screamed and pleaded, but they wouldn't listen, they just stared at me as if they were strangers and as if they were afraid — of me. I used to get cold all over, with goosebumps just thinking about it, and I'd wake up in the dark, screaming.'

Jesus shivered in the brilliant sunlight, the sweat turning cold on his shirt. 'I get goosebumps now,' he said.

'Do you?' She smiled and nodded. 'So do I. For a long time I was hysterical. If I have that nightmare now, I can start screaming and they'll give me the nightlamp again. . . . Don't you see, Heysus? It can be our signal. Our very own signal. You can see it. All night. Any night. Every night. And you can know I am thinking about you. Would you like that?'

The big Stutz-Bearcat skidded to a stop in a crimson cloud of dust that enveloped them. Bonnett Stockton reached across and slapped open the door on the passenger side. 'What in hell are you doing out here, Leonora?' he said. 'I left word you were to stay away from this — Mexican.'

Leonora gave him a calm, unruffled smile, letting the dog lunge into the car ahead of her. 'I know you did, Papa. But Heysus came right in the house after me. He had this great huge machete. And he said unless I walked out here with him he would chop off my —'

'Never mind. I don't think you're amusing, young lady. And when you have to stay year round at some finishing school in Los Angeles, you won't be very amused, either.'

'Quick, Papa,' Leonora cried, slamming the door after her. 'Drive away before he takes out his machete and chops off my —'

'That's enough, damn it.' Bonnett's voice was furious. He did not engage the gears. He stared over the side of the car at Jesus. 'I warn you, boy. You come within a mile of this house again — ever again and I'll turn these dogs on you. And you think I'm joking, you bastard greaser, you try me.'

XXIII

A heavy rain blew in across the valley from the west that night, but by ten o'clock the next morning it had cleared away. When Bonnett Stockton got out of bed, nagged by a teasing sense of wrong that he couldn't pin down, he walked to his window and gazed across the planted fields. The foremen had the migrants out there. Lazy bastards. Always griping about being overworked, but they wouldn't do anything at all unless they were harried and driven all day long.

He stood in a wan patch of sunlight, yawning and scratching himself; then he remembered what toubled him. Tory had not returned when he went to bed around midnight. No sound of cars had disturbed his restless sleep. He tied a robe about his waist and went through the connecting bathroom to Tory's suite. It was silent and unoccupied. Damn her. She had not come home. God knew what she was doing in Los Angeles. She was fascinated by the motion picture people there and had many friends among them. He had heard that one of the directors at Mack Sennett Comedies was a leading supplier of cocaine to the industry. Tory had acted as if she were on something more stimulating than liquor recently.

Anger boiling in him, he returned to his room. He got out a bottle of bourbon and drank from it. He washed his mouth out with the liquid, spat it into the bathroom lavatory and then took a long swig, shuddering.

He went downstairs, refusing breakfast, brushing aside his brothers and his father when they attempted to converse with him.

He found the housekeeper at work in one of the linen cupboards. He said, 'Did that new maid show up this morning, Mrs Hollister?'

She glanced over her shoulder at him, pausing in her towel-counting. She shook her head. 'No, Mr Stockton, she did not come up today.'

Rage out of all proportion to the situation rose up in Bonnett, but he smiled faintly and raised an eyebrow, debonair and casual, he was certain. 'I left word she was to be sent up here.'

Mrs Hollister shrugged and said nothing. After a brief pause, she returned to her counting of linens. He winced and strode away. He crossed the kitchen, went out of a rear door and to the garage.

He got into the Stutz-Bearcat, filled its tank with petrol at the farm supply pumps and raced away from the mansion. He told himself he had no firm destination, but he did not slow down below fifty until he entered the city limits of Los Angeles. The post-war metropolis was a boom town. People from all over the country were flooding into the glamourous environs of Southern California. The Chamber of Commerce was placing advertising in eastern newspapers trying to discourage the young people from coming west seeking work in the films. Of the hundred thousand who had come in 1915, the ad said, no more than five had found enough work to support themselves. But the town burgeoned anyway, bright with sunshine, its streets lined with palms which were no more native than most of the people who worshipped them. The gaudy, dirty streets, pocked with single-storied or double-storied buildings, were being torn out and replaced with paving and Spanish architecture. Bonnett drove through dry and dusty avenues, crowded with people awed to find themselves in a different world from anything they'd ever known before. He shrugged. The place was becoming alien even to him after thirty-five years.

He drove to the Biltmore, downtown at Pershing Square, where he and Tory usually stayed. He left his car in the loading area at the hotel entrance and crossed the lobby. The clerks knew him, but they shook their heads, they had not seen Mrs Stockton recently. She was not registered, nor was she at the Ambassador up at Wilshire and Normandy.

He wandered the town aimlessly, calling at homes of friends where he received no news of Tory, but was plied with a drink or two and one for the road. By noon, he was at Hollywood and Highland outside the Hollywood Hotel, and wearing a rosy glow. Tory was not registered at the popular motion picture inn and he returned to his car. He sat for a long time, slumped behind the wheel. He had searched the city. Not only had he found no trace of Tory, he'd not even found anyone who would admit to having encountered her in recent weeks.

Rage boiled inside him. He bought a bottle of bourbon and set it on the seat beside him for the long drive home. He yelled back at the conductor of the trackless streetcar that almost ploughed headlong into him. He sweated, the top down, the car seats blisteringly hot, the wind dry and cutting against his face.

As soon as he reached the San Gabriel Valley highway, he floored the accelerator, blaring his horn at anyone who got in his way. He was shaking by the time he reached the migrant workers' barracks at the farm. He parked, got out and went inside. Church Foley and Hector Swain looked up from cane-bottomed rocking chairs. He stared at them, bracing his legs apart and biting down hard on his teeth to steady himself and to bring them into focus. He said, 'That Salazar bitch didn't show up at the house again today.'

Hector Swain glanced at Church Foley and shrugged. 'She would not do it, boss. Said she is not a maid, she says she's a fieldhand.'

'Goddamn it, did you tell her she's what we tell her she is, and I say she's a hardheaded whore?'

'Not in those exact words, boss.'

'So, you let her go on out in the fields with her husband, eh?'

Again, Hector glanced toward Foley. 'No. We wouldn't let her do that. We told her — and her husband — that unless she worked where we needed her and assigned her, she couldn't work at all.'

'So. What happened?'

'We told her to go back to her shack and stay there until we decided what to do about her.'

'Okay. So I've decided what to do about her. Let's go talk to her.'

Swain stood up, shaking his head. 'You think that's wise, boss? Just now?'

'What's wrong with now, Swain? You not happy here? You start giving me orders now?'

'You know better than that, boss. I do whatever you tell

324

me. I always have. Just thought you might want to think it over.'

Bonnett sniggered. 'I haven't thought about anything else, Hector old son, since the little whore showed up here.'

'Your old man ain't going to like it,' Church Foley said.

Bonnett laughed. 'So we won't let him in on it. This little party will be just between us boys — and the little greaser puta.' He stopped laughing abruptly, his face going cold. 'I've had a bad day. I'm in no mood to take any crap from either one of you. You fellows going along with me? If not, tell me what shack she's in and I'll go alone.'

Foley stood up and got his hat. 'We better go along, boss.'

Bonnett nodded. 'Well, that's better. There's plenty for all of us.'

2

Dolores heard the big car stop outside her shack, its engines like the guttural snarling of an ogre. She braced herself against the wall and peered through the window at Bonnett Stockton and his two foremen. She watched them get out of the open touring car. Holding her breath so it burned in her throat, she ran across the room and slammed the front door. Looking around wildly, she caught up a straight chair and braced it against the knob.

Poised, tilted forward on the balls of her bare feet, her arms taut out at her sides, she listened to their boots on the plank steps. She heard them cross the pinewood porch. The knocking started, at first muted and polite. She did not move, only went on standing there, shaking her head, her black hair rich and thick about her shoulders.

Abruptly, Bonnett Stockton's voice, irate and intemperate, blared through the door facing. 'We know you're in there, bitch. Open up.'

Dolores didn't understand the words, but she comprehended their meaning. She looked around, feeling trapped. When Stockton's voice raged again, it acted as a spur upon her. She heeled around and ran through the rear room toward the back door.

The threat in Stockton's tone made her ill. She glanced

over her shoulder as he battered at the front door, shouting, 'Open up, or we break it down.'

Hands trembling, she turned the knob, opened the kitchen door, and glancing back one last time, started through. She stopped, gasping, shaken, her legs turning to whey. She was afraid she was going to fall. She was too weak and terrified even to cry out. Through her mind kept running one word, one name, 'Alzado. Alzado.' It spun in her brain, round and round, when she was too mindless with terror to think anything else.

She stared up into Church Foley's smiling face.

Foley shook his head, his voice soft but threatening in its implacability. 'That's far enough, missy,' he said. 'Why don't we just go back inside?'

'Let me go,' she pleaded. 'Please let me go.'

Foley caught her elbow and turned her. Despairing, she did not try to fight him. She could not pretend she had not anticipated some confrontation today. It was just that when it came it was so much more unsettling, frightening and deadly than she had been able to imagine, that she was incapable of coping with its threat.

The other two men hammered on the front door until Foley called out to them, 'Take it easy. We're coming.'

He prodded Dolores ahead of him across the kitchen and the front room which served as parlor and sleeping quarters. He did not release his grip on her arm as he kicked the chair aside and opened the door.

Bonnett Stockton walked in, Hector Swain at his heels. Stockton stepped up close to where Foley held the girl. He stared down into her eyes, his face rigid. His voice shook. 'You bitch,' he said. 'Don't you ever try to lock me out of my own property.'

Uncomprehendingly, agonized with fear, she stared up at Bonnett Stockton. She saw that he was drunk, but she had never seen him in any other condition since her arrival at this terrifying place.

Hector Swain, his voice low, translated for her. She shook her head and broke into voluble protest. She had barred the door because she was afraid. She wanted only to work in the fields. She wished only to return to Guaymas with her husband. She and Alzado would gladly leave, today, if the patron would release them and permit it. She meant no disrespect in barring the door. It was that she was alone and frightened.

Bonnett spoke across his shoulder to Hector. 'Tell the bitch to shut up and listen to me.'

Dolores didn't need these words translated. She understood the commanding tone. Panting, poised as if to run even yet, she stood with her bare feet apart and stared up at Stockton, her black eyes both defiant and terrified.

'The kid's scared half to death, boss,' Swain said.

Bonnett was peering at Dolores, but he jerked his head around. He snarled at his foreman. 'You don't want any of this spicy litle tamale, Swain, you go outside and stand watch.'

'Stand watch?' Swain said. 'Who could stop you now?'

Bonnett laughed. 'That's right, old son. Nobody. So you just relax. You tell the bitch to relax and enjoy it.'

Swain exhaled and leaned against the wall. He spoke quietly in Spanish to the trembling girl. 'Do what the boss tells you, Dolores. It'll be a hell of a lot easier.'

She glanced towards Swain and nodded, but remained taut and rigid. Her liquid eyes brimmed with helpless tears. She heard Stockton speaking, his hot soured breath searing her face. She had no idea what he was saying.

'I told you to come up to the house to work, whore.' He waited until Swain translated. The girl stared up at him and shook her head.

Her opposition enraged Stockton. 'Goddamn it, you're going to learn to do what I say.'

Swain translated in a flat dead tone, but the girl only shook her head again. 'I cannot,' she managed to say. 'Please to tell the patron it is that I cannot.'

Stockton waited until Swain translated, but he seemed not even to hear what his foreman said; he waited only for him to stop talking.

'Tell the puta I'm going to teach her a lesson.' Stockton spoke to Swain but stared down into Dolores' grey face. 'One hell of a good lesson — one she'll love once we get started. You tell her she's going to get seven the hard way.'

Swain said nothing. He pressed his shoulders against the wall, feeling the bite of the unsealed wood against his flesh. He stared at the boss and the Mexican girl, his belly going empty.

Stockton reached for her but Dolores retreated a step. Cursing, Stockton snagged the front of her peasant blouse and yanked downwards. The fabric ripped like brittle paper in his fists. Her breasts spilled free, golden, swollen and full, tiped with crimson, the nipples rigid.

Dolores tried to cover her bosom with her arms but Bonnett caught the dollar-sized button at the waist of her ankle-length skirt and broke it free. The garment toppled loosely about her ankles.

Standing naked, the girl wept. She stared up at Stockton, her eyes pleading even when she saw he was without compassion, that she, Alzado and all the other migrants were less than human beings to this man. They were part of his property. It was his undisputed right to use them as he willed. They had no rights in this place except the tenuous rights he granted them and recalled at any whim.

She looked at Swain, but his face, though grey, held no hope for her. His eyes were riveted upon the soft brown puff at her thighs. She heard Foley whistle faintly between his teeth and she did not even bother glancing toward him.

For an eternal moment, Stockton did not move. He only shook his head, his eyes glistening. What he had anticipated paled at the reality. He had never seen a lovelier, riper female in all his prowling.

His heart slugged against his ribcage. God help us all. When God had started making pussy, this ideal must have been what he had in mind all the time. 'Come here, bitch,' he said.

She shook her head and retreated a step. Her resistance angered and roused him at the same time. Having a woman was no good anyhow unless you could dominate her and beat her down and humiliate her. You had to have her on her kness begging or you had nothing.

He reached down and ripped at the buttons securing his fly. When his staff appeared, rigid, in her view, Dolores screamed, turned and tried to run.

'Grab that bitch,' Stockton ordered Foley.

'It's my pleasure, boss.' Foley caught the girl in his arms, his hands closing instinctively over her full breasts. He held her nakedness against him as she writhed.

Stockton caught her arm in his left hand and yanked her forward away from Foley. As she toppled forward, Stockton's fist struck her in the face, stunning her. She sagged, and holding her, he shoved her back across her bed. Before she could turn her body, he fell upon her, forcing her legs apart. When she fought him, he struck her with his fists, hitting her in the face and breasts until she lay quiet. . . .

In less than two minutes, Stockton gasped aloud and fell away from her. The other two men remained, half-crouched, staring at the naked girl sprawled, legs wide, across the bed.

Stockton said, 'Help yourself, boys. Gives you an extra charge knowing you're being watched while you're hosing it to her.'

But at the sound of his voice, Dolores doubled forward, vomiting. She came up off the bed and staggered into the kitchen.

Stockton sat up. 'Stop her.'

'She ain't going nowhere, boss,' Swain said. 'She's just trying to throw it all up.'

Stockton laughed. 'Hell, she ain't had it all yet.'

Dolores' scream was high-pitched, a keening wail of agony which sounded half-choked as though she'd tried to bite it back.

'Jesus Christ,' Swain said. He ran across the room, thrusting Foley aside. He stepped through the kitchen door. He stopped, swallowing back the bile that flushed up through his throat. He was aware of Stockton and Foley at his shoulders but he did not move. He felt as if he might never move from this spot, as if he'd turned to stone.

Dolores hadn't fallen yet, but she was leaning far forward, blood spewing from her stomach. She had gutted herself with a long-handled butcher's knife. Her hands, legs, body and face were covered with blood. Her head sagged forward. She did not look up. She fell slowly and when she struck the floor she did not move.

Neither Swain nor Foley spoke. Swain stood, his head moving slowly from side to side. Foley sagged against the door-jamb. Only Bonnett kept his poise. The death of another Mexican was no more to him than the killing of fowl or pigs on the farm. He was outraged that she had caused inconvenience, that she had denied him the rest of his pleasure. Otherwise he felt nothing, neither guilt nor remorse. What was there to feel guilty about? He'd tried to show her a good time, he hadn't told her to kill herself. And remorse? What was there to regret? The Mexicans would keep flowing across that border. Tomorrow another beauty would take her place. Maybe the next one would know the score; she might even have a little commonsense.

Bonnett was instantly cold sober and totally in command. He scarcely glanced at the dead girl in the pool of blood on the pinewood floor. He said, 'You fellows clean this up. Wash up the blood, wrap her body in quilts so we can get rid of it. I'll call Redding and Luiz from the house. They'll take care of it.'

Swain spoke in a dead tone. 'Who's going to take care of Salazar?'

Bonnett laughed sharply. 'We will, Hector. Just as we've taken care of every other chicano who ever got in our way.' He stopped laughing abruptly. 'What makes this greaser any different from all the others?'

'God knows, boss,' Swain said.

3

Like a ripple across the green face of a pond, the migrants stopped chopping lettuce and straightened in the sun. Alert to problems, the assistant foreman tensed, looking for the trouble. A man, a stick figure in the distance, ran across the eternal green furrows. By the time he reached the brink of the crew he was staggering with fatigue and work had ceased completely. The foreman yelled at those nearest him, but when he got no response, he gave it up for the moment, watching the runner.

At the edge of the party of workers, the man hesitated, asking a question. Workers pointed and he ran again. The foreman saw Alzado Salazar wave and then run towards the messenger. The supervisor yelled and hurried along the rows toward where Alzado and the runner met. Before he got there, the two men raced away across the fields to the barracks. The overseer shouted, but when neither man even slowed, he desisted and stood watching them.

For a brief distance the messenger kept pace with Salazar, but his steps lagged and he fell behind, finally slowing to a walk in the sun. He watched Salazar race away from him, never slowing, never appearing to tire.

Alzado came out of the ploughed fields and ran along the dusty road. He passed the silent barracks without slowing his pace. He saw two sheriff's Ford cars outside his shack, but he still did not slacken his speed.

Breathing through his mouth, he ran between the cars and up the steps. He paused on the porch, calling, 'Dolores?'

Receiving no answer he ran through the door. It was as if the solid earth fell away from him as he crossed into the shadowed room. Someone backhanded him across the belly with a blackjack. He gasped and doubled over, clutching his arms across his agonized stomach. When he bent forward, the man in the shadows expertly struck him at the back of his skull. His straw hat flew across the room and Alzado plunged into a pool of fiery pain. He was unconscious when he hit the floor.

XXIV

Alzado swam up slowly from the green, suffocating depths of a drowning darkness. Slanting blades of light pierced his eyeballs and set off new alarms of agony in his brain. He massaged the swollen soreness at the base of his skull with one hand and with the other pressed his fist into the queasy sickness in his belly. For a long time he had no idea of where he was, or why he was there, or what had happened to him. He wavered in a sodden sea of anguish, sickened on the taste of his own blood. He kept waiting for his mind to clear and for the pain to ebb, at least enough so that his mind could grasp at another thought.

But the pain did not pass. Any idea that flared in his mind fragmented at once, and he was able only to mewl in agony like some animal on the floor. After a long time he heard voices distantly above him and much later he could even disentangle words.

'He's coming out of it.' Alzado recognized Church Foley leaning over him. 'Better put cuffs on him, Redding. He'll be crazier than ever when he does revive.'

Alzado was vaguely aware that his arms were grasped roughly and twisted at his belt. The metal cuffs were tight; they cut off the blood to his hands and fingers. But he could not care. It did not seem to matter very much what they did to him now. The fevered warmth of agony subsided and a momentary chill ran through his body.

Alzado felt himself fainting, but he did not faint. By some incredible and reluctant exercise of will, he retained his consciousness. His swollen hands ached and shook and he tried to control their tremor. It seemed somehow important that the men standing over him should not be allowed to see him tremble, even when he could not say why it mattered. He wanted to vomit up the pain that seared his insides but he knew that he could not.

Foley was speaking again and by holding his breath and tensing his body to keep from flying apart, Alzado was able to understand the foreman. 'You taking this greaser in to jail, Redding?'

From some remote place of darkness another man answered, his voice strangely high-pitched and amplified in Alzado's eardrums. 'Yeah. Help me get him out there.'

'Hell, drag him,' Foley said. 'You and Luiz ought to be able to drag him. He ain't going to hurt you now, he's cuffed up tight.'

'I ain't scared of him, Foley,' Redding said from that unknown place. 'I just want a little help from you bastards, that's all.'

'You're going to have him in the car by yourself. Luiz has got to stay here and help us with the woman.'

The woman. Alzado's brain cleared, abruptly lucid, and then spinning out of control, like a rollercoaster on an eternal downrun. He moaned and cried out, 'Dolores.'

'You better get moving, Redding,' Foley said.

'I'll handle it, Foley.'

'Sure you will. But when you get him in the car, he'll be all yours. . . . You might have to kill him because it's dead sure he'll try to escape.'

Redding cursed. 'Just lay off me, Foley. You bastards make the messes. I clean 'em up. Just don't try to tell me how to run my business.'

Alzado was aware that two men had grabbed his shoulders, hefting him just off the floor. A third man lifted him by the boots. He was transported out of the door into the blaze of the sun. They lifted him and threw him into the front seat of the Ford. They straightened him so that he sprawled against the passenger side, his head back, his arms handcuffed between his legs.

He heard them talking in low, desperate tones, but he could not understand any words. Slowly, memory returned to him. Elia Perez running across the field calling for him. Something wrong at the shack. His running across the miles of ploughed and greened lands, the bludgeon in his belly and across his skull. Dolores. Dolores.

He stirred on the seat. He opened his eyes, aware that Redding had got in under the steering wheel. The car had been cranked, the motor raced. He heard Redding yell something at the men in the roadway and then the Ford was moving, going swiftly through the ploughed lands. The wind burned Alzado's face, reviving him.

'Coming out of it, are you, Mex?'

Alzado rolled his head on the seat rest, peering at the deputy through a red and occluding haze. 'Where is my wife?' he said.

Redding hesitated but when he answered he did not speak of Dolores at all. 'You've really fucked it up now, haven't you?'

'My wife,' Alzado said. 'Where is Dolores?'

'Hell, you bastard wetbacks. You come up here like you own the world, like you think you got some rights. Well, you ain't. You're illegals and lower than rat piss as far as I'm concerned.'

'I worry about my wife, Senor. Please. Where is she?'

'That's the trouble with you people,' Redding went on, his face straight ahead, both hands gripping the steering wheel. 'You won't do what you're told. If you and your woman had done what Senor Stockton told you, you'd of been fine, both of you would have been fine.'

'Please, sir, where is my wife?'

Redding seemed not to hear Alzado. 'But you're sure as hell not fine right now, are you? You got to prove you're a big man. What's the word? Macho. Ah? You can't do what you're told, you got to prove you're a better man than anybody else. . . . Well, amigo, I can tell you, you ain't a better man. You're not even a man at all.'

Enraged, Alzado said, 'Are you such a fine one, Senor? You're not a man. You. You're a gringo nanny goat, bleating when the great one pokes you.'

'Maybe, but I'm the nanny goat driving a nice car, living good on a good salary with retirement. You got nothing but handcuffs. You don't even have your woman no more.' Briefly, his voice cold and flat and without emotion, Redding told Alzado a censored version of what had happened to Dolores. 'One thing led to another. They tried to talk some sense into her, but she wouldn't listen.'

'She told me that Senor Stockton tried to rape her when he got her alone up at the casa grande. This is why she would go there no more.'

'Well, that may be. I don't know nothing about that. All I know is they tried to talk to your woman, but she was hot-headed and wouldn't listen to reason. She ran into the kitchen, and before they could stop her, she had slashed her belly open with a butcher knife.'

Agonized, Alzado rolled his head back and forth on the seat rest. He moaned deep inside but he did not speak at all.

'Now, you got to look ahead. I'm trying to tell you true, the way it is. You got a right to grieve for your wife. I understand that. But you got one chance to come out of this on both feet. You can go back to Mexico. I'll see that you get there. All you got to do is stay there. Forget what happened up here. Forget Senor Stockton. And forget your wife. She'd dead, and no matter what you do to try to avenge her, you ain't going to bring her back, you're just going to get your own tail in a sling. Do you understand what I'm saying?'

Alzado did not speak. He sat tense, his eyes blurred with tears.

'You try to strike back at Senor Stockton, you'll end up on a slab. He's too big for you. You got no chance against him. If you got any sense at all, you'll listen to me. You'll go on back to Mexico and forget all about all of this. That ain't just *one* of the things you can do, amigo. It's the only thing you can do and go on breathing.'

Alzado sobbed, deep inside, his stomach shaking with his sobbing.

'Grief. That's one thing, boy. But revenge, that's something else. That's something you can't afford. No way. Now, hell, it don't matter to me. I don't give a damn in hell what happens to you. I'm just trying to help you. You had a bad time, and I'm sorry about that. But I'm trying to keep you from making it worse on yourself.'

'Or are you trying to keep me from repaying Senor Stockton for killing my wife?'

'No. I ain't trying to do that, amigo. Not at all. You got no chance of getting back at Senor Bonnett Stockton, because you'd be dead three times before you got near enough for him to spit on you. Ain't you got sense enough to see that, boy? Are you as dumb as all the rest of them chicanos? Revenge. You can't live without revenge, can you?'

Alzado did not speak. He sat, tense, staring straight ahead. After a while, Redding stopped talking and lapsed into silence. Occasionally, he glanced toward the man handcuffed on the seat beside him, but by the time they reached the crossroad settlement of Apia, he had given up on the Mexican. The hell with him. He was too stupid to listen. That meant he was too stupid to live.

As they drove past the last house west of Apia, a mongrel dog ran out, barking savagely at the tyres of the Ford. Redding laughed and said, 'Watch this, amigo. We'll have some fun with the dog.'

Alzado said nothing. He glanced toward Redding, his eyes cold. Redding inched the car to the right on the narrow road, edging the dog toward the shoulder and the abrupt ditch between the roadway and the ploughed fields. Suddenly, Redding yanked the wheel hard right, trying to run down the dog.

Alzado threw himself across the seat and grabbed the steering wheel with his cufflinked hands, pulling it around with all his strength.

Redding cursed, grabbing for the gun in his holster. The car swerved off the pavement, bounced across the shoulder. Its front wheels plunged into the ditch, throwing Redding forward.

As Redding toppled over the wheel, still grabbing for his gun, Salazar brought his cuffed arms upward, using his doubled fists and the metal as a weapon. He caught Redding in the throat and then struck him again on the side of the chin, driving his head back.

The car tilted at a precarious angle, its front tyres at the bottom of the ditch, one of its rear wheels off the ground and spinning wildly.

Alzado acted coldly and deliberately, without haste. Redding was sprawled back against the seat rest, wedged under the steering wheel, unconscious. Salazar took the keys from the deputy's belt and holding the handcuff key between his teeth unlocked the cuffs securing his wrists. He placed one cuff on Redding's left arm and then linked it through the steering wheel and locked it. He reached around the stout-bellied deputy and took his gun, which he shoved under his own belt. Still holding the keys, he started to get out of the car, then hesitated. He needed money. Whatever Redding had would have to suffice.

He searched the officer's pockets, found a handful of

change and a few paper bills in a wallet. He thrust it all into his own pocket and got out of the car.

He paused, wincing. The mongrel dog lay dead beside the road, tyre marks showing on its fur.

Exhaling heavily, Alzado threw both the car keys and handcuff keys as far as he could into the ploughed field.

2

Alzado loped west for a long time along the roadway. It seemed to him he was exposed, helpless in this flat, planted valley. The sun was like a huge, unblinking spotlight fixed on him.

Distantly to the west, he saw a cloud of dust and then an open touring car, a late model Oldsmobile, racing toward him. He touched the gun tucked under his belt, stood in the left lane of the road, waving his arms before his face.

The car approached, speeding, and not slowing down at all. When he saw that the woman, driving alone, had no intention of stopping, he drew the gun and stepped out into the middle of the road, holding it fixed upon her.

Alzado pointed the gun directly at the lovely head of the blonde woman. At the very last instant she stepped hard on the brakes and the open Oldsmobile skidded to a stop beside him, so that he stood at the door of her car in the billowing dust.

She seemed untroubled by the gun which he held, hammer back, inches from her head. She appeared only vaguely aware of him, and not at all afraid. Her throaty voice was almost casual in admonition. 'Pointing guns at people can get you in trouble.'

'It e-stopped you, Senora,' Alzado said. 'That's all I want.'

She gave him a faint, go-to-hell smile. 'Well, now that you've stopped me, what do you want?'

'I want you to do what I tell you. That way maybe you won't have to get hurt. I got no wish to hurt you, you do what I tell you.'

'You're digging a grave for yourself a mile deep,' she said, watching him without even really seeing him as a person. 'You can still put up that gun and walk away and I won't say anything.'

337

'Sorry, Senora. It is that I cannot do that.' Holding the gun on her, he stepped on the running board and swung his leg over the rear door, getting into the tonneau of the boat-like vehicle. He inched across and then slid into the front seat beside her. 'It is that I tell you to do me the favour. Turn this car around. Real slow and easy.'

'Shouldn't we talk about this?'

'I'll talk to you while you drive, Senora.' He thrust the gun snout into her ribcage. 'Now, you want to be a healthy gringo lady, you do what I tell you. Turn this car around.'

She shrugged and obeyed him. 'Where are we going?'

Alzado was silent for a long taut moment. There was time for his life to have flashed across the mental screen of his brain. There was time to consider this woman, to think of home and family, of freedom. Nothing occupied his mind except Dolores and his loss. Dolores. Dolores. 'I am going home to Mexico,' he said. He hesitated again for a long time. The car rolled slowly west. 'It is very hard for one like me to get back home when the gringo cavalier decides I must stay. But I can stay here no more. I go home. You are going to drive me.'

She shrugged again. 'It's a long way to Mexico.'

He shook his head. 'We will do it. You will drive as I say. On the roads I say. You do what I say, you'll be all right.'

She glanced at him and saw that he was deadly serious and drawn taut, ready to erupt. But even as he threatened her, held the gun low in his lap but trained on her abdomen, she reacted mildly. She was barely aware of him, except that he was sweating, dusty, dirtied and trembling. She was not concerned for her own safety, or afraid of him. He was another Mexican gone berserk, an agonized national trying to get back home. Not even his goal or anguish was new to her. In her thirteen years as Mrs Bonnett Stockton, Tory had seen too many migrant workers to fear even this wild, driven man beside her.

She sighed, gripping the steering wheel with both hands and watching the road ahead through the dust-crusted windscreen. She had seen these poor devils try to run before; she'd seen them brought back in leg irons, weeping and sullen, but she had not heard of one wetback who made it back to the border safely. They were captured by Immigration, shot by some farmer for trespassing, or found wandering

338

in the hills, lost. She might even have felt some pity for them, but her mind was on something else.

Her pale eyes blurred with tears. She could not fully concentrate on the Mexican at her side or upon the danger he threatened. Her mind was on Leonora and Bonnett's newest threats to take the child from her, to separate them. He was having her shadowed; she knew that. He wanted evidence against her, of her drinking, her use of drugs, her illicit friendships, anything that would prove her an unfit mother. Unfit mother. Name of God, a good mother was all she was, all she wanted to be, all she had left of her life. Leonora was her life, the life she had been denied by her painful marriage to Bonnett. From that union had come one beautiful thing, Leonora. Through Leonora, Tory wanted to live the life she had missed. Leonora would have everything Tory had lost. From the first she had dreamed of the beautiful existence she would provide for Leonora. But when her marriage soured, Bonnett looked for ways to control and harass and humble her. He soon realized that all she cared about any more was her baby daughter. Since that moment a tug of war had existed between them; a war that Bonnett was winning.

That which she had always feared was about to befall her. How many nights had she awakened from the nightmare of having Leonora taken from her and found only little comfort in reaching across her bed to touch her baby sleeping beside her. Later, when Bonnett insisted that Leonora would be happier and healthier in the nursery and her daughter was taken from her, she could still reassure herself, knowing that the child was near, a few steps down the corridor, in the big old house with her, safe and secure. But from the bitter day that Bonnett learned he could hurt Tory through Leonora, the threats started, the new rules were instigated, new governesses hired with orders to keep the mother from the child in the event that Tory might have been drinking and might unknowingly harm the baby.

Tory, hating Bonnett, had done everything possible to ingratiate herself with him, to make him think she was his willing slave, dutiful and uncomplaining as long as he let Leonora stay near her. But all her carefully laid plans had failed, falling apart as she conceived them. The heart-clutching anguish of her nightmares had become a reality. As Leonora grew older, Bonnett did all he could, in covert and subtle ways, to discredit Tory in her daughter's eyes, to turn Leonora from her. Her daughter was leaving her though she remained at her side; it was as if she were gone down that eternal road through the ploughed valley and Tory would never see or hear from her again. The worst part of it was, there was nothing she could do about it. Bonnett laid his own plans carefully, impersonally, implacably. He made plans to send Leonora to a finishing school, a boarding institution for young women. He was forever investigating such schools; they might be in Los Angeles, in Boston, or London, Paris or Switzerland. She could not convince Leonora that she had lived two years in such a school; it had been a prison; she had escaped, heartbroken; she had even married Bonnett Stockton to ensure she'd never have to return to those forbidding walls. Bonnett talked of the glamour, the fun, the rich and exciting people she would meet, the elegant young friends she would make. Listening to him, Leonora's eyes would glow, starry.

Until recently, with Bragg Stockton reinforcing her, and the weight of opinion from the others of the family, she had been able to keep Leonora near, even though the girl was taught, almost daily, to treat her mother with contempt. They grew farther and farther apart, though Tory did all she knew to win the girl's love. Now, Bonnett was using Leonora as a new bargaining chip. Unless Tory agreed to a separation, he would send Leonora to France to school until she was eighteen, and there would be nothing for Tory at Stockton Farms.

In vain, Tory pleaded with Bonnett. She could not leave this house, her daughter. She had invested thirteen years of her life. She was past thirty, and while she was still beautiful, she wanted no other man, and her religion forbade divorce. Here she was reinforced by Bonnett's father who was adamant against a break-up of the marriage. In all these confrontations, with Bragg's support, she was victorious, but the cost of victory was unendurable. Bonnett revenged himself in a hundred cruel and spiteful ways. He made plans for the immediate departure of their daughter for France.

All Tory's pleadings and promises could not deter him. After the row at breakfast with her husband, she had run away to Los Angeles, registered at a small hotel uptown where nobody knew her and tried to plan some strategy that would stop Bonnett. She had been reduced to drinking, to finding cocaine. She had lain, sweating and miserable and alone on the hotel bed, knowing she was defeated. Leonora was all she had, all she wanted, and yet she had to let her go. But without her daughter, life would have no purpose for her. Without Leonora to plan with and dream for, there could be no life for her at Stockton Farms or any other place. If Bonnett took Leonora from her, she would die. She would surely die.

She glanced at the countryside drifting past unseen, the sun sparkling in the dust, the flat rich fields, the infrequent trees, a lonely house lost in the brown foothills. She turned her head and really looked at the young Mexican at her side. Stunned, she saw that his eyes were blurred with tears. But she also recognized there was no weakness in his crying. His squared jaw was set, a tiny muscle working in it. His full-lipped mouth was taut. He was watching her, the road ahead and behind them and he was watching for dust clouds in the distance that would mean they were being pursued. The poor young bastard. He had no chance at all, any more than she had with Bonnett.

For a long time they drove in silence, each lost in his own despair. She had reached a conclusion secluded in that hotel. Damn Bonnett Stockton. Leonora would not be sacrificed on the altar of his hatred for her. She would go directly to Bragg Stockton. She would lay her case entirely before her father-in-law. Blood might well prove thicker than water. But Bragg Stockton loved his granddaughter almost as devotedly as Tory did; he would want what was best for the girl. She would make him see that Leonora's place was with her, and freed of Bonnett's irresponsible threats.

She sighed heavily. She truly believed this plan might succeed. But if it did not, she had made up her mind. She would lull Bonnett into a false sense of security and she would take Leonora and run away east. She would give up everything else. At least she would have Leonora; she would give the girl a good and rewarding existence, among civilized and cultured people. She would do everything she could for Leonora except abandon her to Bonnett. She could go where Bonnett and all his money and influence could not dislodge her. Where the opinion of decent people, and the edicts of the courts, would weigh against him. With this in mind she had started back home. She saw this detour as only a brief delay; the sheriff's office would soon stop them and drag the Mexican away to wherever they incarcerated illegals.

She put on her brakes at the junction with the macadam-paved two-lane highway north and south. She glanced at her passenger. 'Which way, amigo?'

'Go south,' he said. He jerked the gun slightly to the right and then fixed it on her again. He did not speak until they entered the village of Glendora. Among other Anglos like herself, people walking, driving, parked along the sun-braised street, Tory considered slamming on the brakes, stopping the Oldsmobile in the middle of the street and screaming for help.

She breathed out, unaware she had been holding her breath. She discarded the idea instantly because she glimpsed the madness swirling in the Mexican's anguished black eyes. Any attempt at heroism by her would only get somebody killed. This was evident in the sad, terror-ridden face. When they were out of town, heading south again, he said, as if he had read her thoughts, 'You were smart to keep your mouth shut.'

'Oh, I'm a very smart girl, Senor. What is your name?'

He gazed at her, but did not reply. Tory shrugged. 'I'm afraid it is you who is not very smart, my friend.'

'Don't worry about me, Senora. Just drive.'

In Covina she found a petrol station and filled the tank of the Oldsmobile. Salazar sat silently beside her, the gun concealed beneath his denim shirt. She could have spoken a dozen times to the curious, watchful attendant, intrigued to find a lovely and obviously wealthy Anglo woman driving with a shabby and sweaty-looking chicano. But she merely smiled blandly. She refrained from speaking only partly in fear. She felt a deep sympathy for the youthful Mexican because of the agony she saw moiling in his eyes. She was aware of him now as a human being, one with whom she had something in common — pain.

She told him she had to go to the rest-room at the rear of the station. He shrugged, allowing her to go. He reached over, took the keys, and let her see in his face that at her first outcry, he would leap from the car with the gun firing, with her in his line of fire. He said none of this, but she understood him clearly. The attendant stood braced against the front wall of the building watching until she returned, got into the car, started it and moved out into the street. 'He's not going to forget us,' she told Salazar. 'When the police ask him, he will remember us well.'

She did not know what she expected the youth to say, but he answered only, 'Nothing is ever easy, Senora.'

She gave him a faint, sad smile. 'I'm not talking easy or hard, Juan. I am talking impossible. The police are already looking for you by now. Soon they will be looking for both of us. They will wire and telephone ahead. We will not get too much farther. Maybe if we turned around, it would be easier for you.'

'My name is not Juan. My name is Alzado,' was his only answer.

'I think you made a bad choice in selecting my car for your little jaunt,' Tory said in a teasing way.

'Senora, this may be a little joke to you. A little joy-ride. For me it is more. My wife has been slain. It is as if I myself were already dead. You do not frighten me by saying of the police. I wish to return to Mexico. I wish to go home to my people in my grief. I am prepared to kill to get there. I hope I do not have to kill you.'

'Well, I certainly hope so too, Alzado. It's just that I was telling you that my family is very wealthy. A very prominent family. If you had abducted some ordinary person, you might have had a better chance. You could not have made it, but you would not be pursued as you will because you have kidnapped Mrs Bonnett Stockton.'

She heard him gasp in a sharp agonized breath. She was aware that his body trembled on the seat beside her. 'What's the matter with you?' she said.

'You are the Senora Stockton? The wife of the patron Bonnett Stockton?'

She sighed. 'I'm afraid so. Why? Does that make a difference to you?'

He turned on the seat, his eyes filled with tears. 'I am afraid, Senora, it makes a great difference. To both of us.'

They drove on through the waning afternoon, passing through the sleepy hamlets with Spanish names and Spanish missions, houses set back from the street, behind long avenues of eucalyptus and palms. She drove south through Whittier, Anaheim, Santa Ana, and as darkness lowered, she entered the town of Costa Mesa. They passed through

343

valleys, foothills, and in sight of the ocean at San Juan Capistrano. Just before dark they approached a bridge over a dry riverbed.

Tory exhaled a long sigh of relief. She saw the police cars and the blockade of armed men ahead. Every passing moment brought her nearer to the end of this ordeal. She would be free to return to Stockton Farms and to Leonora and whatever life lay ahead for them. She glanced at the dark face beside hers. This boy's life — at least his freedom — was almost over. She felt compassion for him but she was glad the end was in sight.

'Slow down,' he ordered. 'Turn around.'

'In the middle of the road?'

'In the middle of the road, now. I was worried that I might have to hurt you if you refused to obey me. Now — because I know who you are — I hurt you with a free heart unless you do as I say. At once.'

His voice rattled, hard and resonant and resolute, even in the high wind. She sighed and stepped on the brakes. She turned the car in the road and headed north. 'You think they don't see us? You think they won't follow?'

'I think only they have not caught us yet, Senora Stockton. That is all I think.'

'Well, you ought to look ahead. It will go easier on you if you surrender. Maybe I can even speak for you.'

'I want no word from the Senora Stockton in my behalf.'

She caught her breath, realizing for the first time the depth of his hatred for her, for anything named Stockton. When he had not known who she was, he had been polite, almost apologetic. Now he was savage. His voice quivered with rage when he was forced to speak to her at all. 'My God, you do hate me, don't you? Even though I've done nothing but try to help you, you hate me.'

'That road, to the east. Turn. Now.'

'It's not much of a road, Alzado. It may not go very far, at best into the desert.'

'I do not ask you where it goes. I tell you to go.'

She slowed and turned off the paved road into a hard-packed lane that seemed to lead only into chaparral and saguaro cactus land. The hills rose distantly in the darkness.

She turned on the car lights. He cursed her. 'Turn off those lights.'

'I need to see.'

'You need not signal to the police. We will drive as best we can in the dark. We will hide where we can. We will head south again tomorrow.'

The lane wound down through the sparsely grown country and crossed a dry creekbed. 'Stop,' he told her. 'We turn south here and follow the creek.'

'We'll break a spring or an axle in that creekbed.'

'You will do as I say, Senora. I spend most of my life in Mexico following creekbeds to the place I wish to go.'

'But not in an Oldsmobile. How long do you think the tyres will last?'

'When I wish a word from the rich Anglo dama, I shall ask her.' He waited until she manoeuvred the big car into the creekbed and rolled along it slowly. 'You are right. You drive slow. I watch for obstacles. You need not ask me. I shall tell you what to do.'

Tory had no idea how long they rolled along the incline of the pebbled creek. Darkness closed in around them and the dry stream wound into low hills which closed tighter and tighter upon the sides of the bed. Finally, they were stopped in an arroyo, unable to go forward. Tory said, 'You want me to back out of here?'

'I want you to turn off the engine, Mrs Stockton.'

'By morning they will have possees all over this country. If you are going to get free, you better keep moving now.'

'Stop the car.' She obeyed, turning off the engine. The night silences of the open wasteland settled upon them. For the first time Tory realized how tired she really was. She was exhausted from tension, from unhappiness and from the long drive south. She sighed and leaned back against the seat rest.

His voice was low beside her. 'Since you were not home, it is that you do not know that your husband raped my wife. Your husband killed my wife.'

'Oh my God, Alzado. I'm sorry.'

'I am sorry too. But this will not bring Dolores back to me, will it? Nothing will bring her back to me. She is dead and your husband killed her, and yet he thinks to go on with his fine, rich life as he has before.'

'I am sorry, Alzado.'

'Do not say of sorrow to me. You Anglo. You white Americano. You blonde woman. You know nothing of sorrow. Nothing of pity. We are not people to you. We are animals. Less than your animals. We die, it does not matter to you. Your husband rapes and kills my wife, and you are sorry.'

'With all my heart I pity you.'

'Save your pity, Anglo. Pity your husband. Maybe you live to return to him, I don't know. But I know you will not return untouched.'

'Don't be a damned fool,' she said. 'If you want to be free, you better think about that.'

'Yes. You and your husband. You have left me so much to be free for. Eh? What does it matter? Freedom to me? Dolores is dead.'

'They will kill you, Alzado. Maybe if you ran. If you kept heading south.'

'I go south, Senora. But first, I take myself the blonde woman, the wife of the great patrono. He will know that a wetback has fucked his wife. A Mexican peon has shared his woman. Sometimes, when the chicanos talk of heading north, they talk of having themselves an Americano blonde woman. I never talk like this. I have what I want. I have Dolores. But now, I don't have Dolores. Do you think it is right, rich woman, that your great patron should have his wife — while I have none?'

She drew a deep breath. She shook her head. Oh God, the terrible irony. This poor half-mad creature, broken-hearted, living only for revenge. Revenge against Bonnett Stockton. He wanted to take her body to revenge himself upon the evil patrono of Stockton Farms. If the Mexican youth raped her, the joke would still be on him, because of all the people in the entire civilized world, Bonnett would be the only one who would not care. . . .

'I know you are hurt,' she said. 'Don't throw your life away trying to avenge yourself on my husband. Or on me. Run. Get away.'

He laughed, a half-sobbing sound. 'Si. Run. No singame. Run. Leave the white bitch untouched for the murdering patrono. No, Senora, it will not be.'

His voice shook. He caught her and drew her over on the seat against him. Tory felt the raging pressure of his mouth upon hers but she did not turn her head away. His lips were hard, brutal, smashing her lips against her teeth. She felt his tongue shoved into her mouth. She tried to keep her jaws closed tightly, but he struck her and she opened to him. His tongue thrust deep, searching. She fought him, but he was enraged and she was helpless against him.

He pulled her body closer against him, kissing her with savagery. She tried to turn her face away. His hand closed on her throat and she gasped, nodding and opening her mouth to him. His face pressed close to hers, demanding, and yet she felt the burn of his tears on her cheeks. He was in agony, but this did not stop him, nothing would stop him. His arms tightened around her, his fingers caressed her neck and shoulders, tearing at the bodice of her dress. His hands slipped under the torn fabric. The calluses of his palm were like abrasives against the soft rise of her breast and when his fingers closed painfully, she cried out. He did not release her. He kissed her harder, forcing her mouth wider. He pulled away the front of her clothes. She struggled but did not try to speak. He could have forced her to remove her clothing, but this was not what he wanted. He wanted her found naked, her clothing yanked away, her body violated, nothing else would satisfy him.

His mouth, hot and gasping, moved along her throat and nuzzled her breast, closing, nursing upon her nipple. Now, her own neglected body betrayed her. His mouth sent a stream of desire flooding downward through her. Her hips undulated involuntarily, she had to fight the complusion to abandon herself to him, overcome with a passion she could not resist. God only knew how long it was since she had had a man. It had been an eternity since Bonnett had come near her, except in anger. She had no other man. The wild blandishment of his hands and mouth almost conquered her until she realized that not even this man truly wanted her body. He wanted only revenge.

She tried to push him away, but succeeded only in slipping under him on the wide front seat, her head under the streering wheel. His hands ripped away her skirt and underclothing. She lay naked. For some moments he touched her down there, rousing her feverely whether she wanted it or not. His hands fumbled with his own clothing. He pushed between her knees and with his rough hands, caught her hips and lifted her to him. She cried out, half in agony and half in ecstasy as he thrust himself into her.

'They'll kill you,' she sobbed against his face. 'If you do this, they will kill you.'

There was no reason left in him. He said nothing, clasping her to him and driving himself deeper and deeper up into her. She lay back, her blonde hair loose against the leather seat and in the faint night light she saw his mouth slack and his eyes glazed with agonized desire.

'You're hurting me,' she gasped. 'My God, you're hurting me.'

Vainly, she struggled against him, hitting at his face and ripping his worn shirt. He was unaware that she fought him. She cried out and to stop her screaming, his hand closed on her throat. His passions mounted, and as he raged toward a climax, his fingers tightened. She shuddered and sagged beneath him, but he did not stop battering at her until at last he cried out and fell prostrate across her.

He did not know how long he lay there. He pushed himself up to his knees over her. She did not move or speak. Her bare arm flopped limply off the side of the seat. He lifted it in his hand, but when he released it, it fell lifelessly. Slowly, he realized what he had done. He had killed her. He had choked her to death and had not even known he was closing his hand upon her throat.

His eyes filled with tears and his throat choked painfully. He stood up feeling as if he might howl out his agony to the desert moon. When the headlights of half a dozen cars suddenly illuminated the night, fixed upon him, standing up in the car over Tory's dead body, his mind could not credit what was happening. As if upon a signal, the officers around and above him opened fire with rifles. They kept shooting him until their guns were empty.

XXV

Bonnett Stockton wore a black armband for a year after his wife's death. He was a changed man. Everybody said this. In the recent past there had been those who had considered him self-centred, prone to unreasonable and unreasoning violence, unjust, inflexible; one of the most class-conscious men in the caste-aware California society with its Orange County core. These people had found him often ill-tempered, vengeful, a swaggering braggart, insolent, haughty and domineering. They rated him vain, demanding and imperious — and these were estimations of his closest friends, acquaintances and associates, those likely to be most charitable.

The brutal rape and slaying of his wife changed all this. Tory's death seemed to rip away the old framework of his arrogance and rebuild him in a new image: more malleable, and if not gentle, at least temperate. He broke into tears when questioned or consoled. That black band and his new quiet demeanour won him sympathetic entry into many salons and even some bedrooms where he'd been suspect and unwelcome before. Everyone who encountered that drawn, pallid face and those sad eyes tried to ease upon him that intolerable burden of loss which he wore with such fortitude. For example, when a group of Mexican nationals arrived from Guaymas with questions about the fate of the spouse of the young Mexican who'd been caught with Stockton's wife and slain on the spot, those in authority refused to permit the delegation even to confront Bonnett Stockton. The consensus was, the poor man had suffered enough, too much. The ordeal was too painful. There was no way that he could be allowed to be interrogated. In his tragic loss and heartbreak, he must never be subjected to a cruel reminder of that old tragedy.

Even those who had formerly believed that Bonnett

Stockton was arrogant, uncaring, almost inhumane in his treatment of the migrant workers, now professed a new understanding of his attitude. They no longer censured him. They understood that cold, implacable hatred which now possessed him. The scum had attacked and killed Bonnett's beloved wife, violating her as wild, rabid animals might. One could see why Bonnett Stockton would treat such beings as animals, because this was what they had proved themselves to be, animals.

The difference was there for all to see. Once, Bonnett had strode among the migrants, pitiless and uncaring. Now when he was driven to action against them, the world could see the justification in his merciless retribution. He had tried to be fair and just with them, but they had repaid him with murder and rape. He had tried to treat them as if they were his children; they had seen his kindness as weakness. He was no longer weak, but the world saw him in a different light.

They called him a gallant gentleman.

Like all the big farms, groves and vineyards in the vast valleys of California, Stockton Farms continued to have its problems with migrants. The tide of inflowing humanity increased. Every year they came in ever-swelling numbers. There were those who believed that because the illegals were not shot at the Mexican border, they assumed rights and privileges to which they were not in the least entitled. They became more demanding. Some of the great farms were forced to make concessions, but there were no concessions made or contemplated at the Stockton estate. These people could work or they could starve; unless they worked Stockton Farms had no use for them.

Nobody had even heard of farm labour union problems then. Communist-inspired radicals had whipped workers in western wheat fields into a frenzy against the owners. Crops had gone up in flames. The militia had been brought in, rebellious workers had been killed. There were those who foresaw such disaster ahead for the California growers. But the landowners did not believe that day would come in the Golden State for one very good reason. They would not tolerate it; they would nip any insurrection in the bud. Besides, they weren't dealing with citizens here. In the wheat fields the scum had been the dregs of humanity, but most were natives. It was an entirely different situation in

California; the workers were wetbacks mostly and consequently, much easier to deal with legally. The joke was that there was nothing illegal one could do to illegals. These greasers had no rights in California and the sooner they were made to realize this, the better for all concerned.

In the five years following Tory Stockton's death in a desert arroyo, Jesus remained in exile at the barracks and in the fields. He was never again assigned to the ranch-house work-crews. At first, he lived in an agony of loneliness. Leonora was the first person he had loved since Tia Clara, Teodoro and the dimly recalled Pedrillo. His love for Leonora was quite different from any devotion he had felt towards the only family he had ever known. He loved Leonora in a way that shook him and stirred him to the depths of his soul. For a little while she roused him from lethargy, she enkindled dreams and ambitions and fantasies within him. She made him see that there was a life outside the barracks and the tomato fields, a world he could aspire to only through total sacrifice and dedication. For her, he was willing — anxious! — to sacrifice, to dedicate himself. But when she was taken from his orbit, he gradually sank back into that old apathy.

In five years, Jesus saw Leonora fewer than a dozen times, and then always at a distance. He knew when she was at the mansion because he might see her race past in her father's car. And always, when she was at home, the nightlamp burned in her window. But its poignant meaning lost its reality for him. That light was like a star, fading in some remote, lost and irrecoverable galaxy.

He worked silently, uncomplainingly, and without interest, in the crops or in the people around him. As he grew taller, willowy thin, sun-blackened, hard-muscled, the young senoritas among the migrants eyed him hungrily. He came alive at those night fiestas which gathered and flourished in the migrant camps. The music inspired and excited him. He felt a stimulation that made him want to burst from his own skin, as if somehow he were imprisoned, fettered inside his body. The music lifted him up, brought him fighting for deep breaths of air, wanting something he had never had, something he didn't even understand, or have any name for.

The senoritas taught him to dance, and they pressed their heated, musky bodies to him. They closed his palm over their nascent breasts. They drew him into the shadows and plied

351

upon him the wonder and splendor of maidenhairs, of virginity and of promiscuity. They roused him for that brief encounter, but only for that instant. He found he could never get enough of the hot and sweating crotches they opened to him. But sadly, by morning he had forgotten their faces, their names, their thighs, and he had slipped back into that indifference which fell like a veil upon him.

When he saw cruelty dealt out to the helpless braceros by foremen and by the deputy sheriffs called in at the least disturbance, he felt a sudden rush of outrage at the injustice. The injustices went on, but his outrages faded quickly, and he retreated, pretending not even to see or care.

With Leonora gone from his life — if she'd ever truly been any part of it — he was left uncaring. When his blood boiled at the wrongs perpetrated upon the seasonal workers, he dismissed his indignation as unreasonable, the residue of wrath at his loss of Leonora. He had suffered heartbreak and pain at the hands of opponents against whom he'd been helpless. It distressed him to see injustice to people unable to defend themselves. But, there was nothing he could do. Nothing he wanted to do. It would not profit the migrants for him to get his own skull cracked with a club. And anyway, he told himself, his was not anger at the wrongs to other vulnerable men and women, but only memory savagely reawakened of his own impotence against implacable authority and casual cruelty.

Ever since his arrival at Stockton Farms, he had heard of the rich foods and viands removed untouched from the mansion dining-tables and carelessly heaped in galvanized drums to be fed to the farm swine. But with new regulations enunciated by Bonnett Stockton and enforced by his foremen, the galvanized garbage cans of wasted food assumed new importance in the hearts and minds of the migrants. The workers now were fed in direct proportion to the quality of labour expended by the least of the braceros. The purpose of the edict was to speed up the slower stoop-labourers through the enforced pressure of the other peons; if the sluggards loitered, every worker was penalized at the dinner-table or at the commissary. Some nights, after ten hours stooping and crawling in the rows, the fieldhands returned to a dinner of weak broth and bread. The foreman, quieting the uproar with clubs beaten on table tops, explained it quite simply. There was not a being in the huge dormitory too dull to understand. If they wanted to eat well — by Stockton Farms standards — they had to work well, and they had to police their own ranks; they had to push their freeloading laggards to produce well too. There was no sense in blaming the landowners for their plight. They brought it on themselves and they could alter it themselves. They could earn a full meal pail with a full day's work. It was that simple. There was no other way.

Those rebellious workers, with stomachs growling emptily, and their children crying for food which had not been delivered after a day's backbreaking toil in the farm fields, attempting to take matters in their own hands, soon learned how futile — and even fatal — it could be to strike back at the estate authority.

The talk began about the fires after another supperless night. The angered workers recalled what they had heard of the waste of food up at the mansion. It seemed cruel and inhuman that people who sat in luxury and wasted in one day food enough to feed a Mexican family for a month, should impose restrictive and vicious punishment upon their labourers who fed them.

Secretly, three men stole away into the darkness soon after the first accordions were tuned up around the campfire. They crept in the shadows to the low wall enclosing the mansion. Here they delayed for a long time, finally driven to action by their hunger and the hunger of their children.

They approached the house through the gardens. They pressed close to the deepest shadows, unaware of the smell of gardenias, the night-blooming jasmine, the rich budding roses.

From the shadows, they gazed in awe through the lighted windows of the ground floor. They inched around the building in the blackest dark seeking the kitchen and the refuse area. They were almost at the huge garbage vats when half a dozen Doberman pinschers attacked, snarling and slashing, from the garage. Nightlights flared on, turning the yard brighter than noon.

Security guards, armed with shotguns, ran out of the servants' quarters. The peons, blinded by the light, fled, the dogs snapping at their heels. The guards opened fire. The dogs were ordered back and the thieves were cut down by gunfire before they escaped the rim of the light.

For the next week, this was the talk of the migrants. Three men were dead, riddled with 12-gauge pellets. The bodies were buried in a common grave and the three dependent families were turned over to Deputy Sheriff Pedro Luiz and U.S. Immigration officers from Los Angeles. None of the workers ever learned what happened to the families removed by legal authorities. The more courageous enquired of the foremen but were cursed and warned to put the entire matter from their minds. 'Those men trespassed on private proper-ty,' Church Foley told them. 'They were thieves and they were treated like thieves, and that's all there is to it. Forget it.'

Most of the workers tried to forget, because it was easier to live in this place without that tragedy on their minds. Jesus was, briefly, the most aroused of all, but his indignation died quickly. He was outraged because he knew what it must be like to be attacked in the dark up at the mansion by guard dogs trained to kill. He had himself been driven from that rich Eden, but the hungry peons had been slain. Still, there was nothing he could do about it. He felt compassion for those wounded and bereaved, but he did not see how it could be otherwise.

He shook his head, trying to drive the thought away. If the braceros learned only how impossible it was to storm that citadel, the lesson might be worthwhile. They could not hope for justice up at the mansion. If they found they could not take anything from up there, no matter how justified it might seem in their own minds, they might live better for this season until they departed.

2

Soon after her mother's death, Leonora was enrolled in a girl's school in Los Angeles. She was seldom home, except for holidays and the summer, spring and Easter vacations. Old Bragg Stockton made no protest when Bonnett decreed that young Jesus O'Brien be kept away from the mansion. He did not care; he was busy and only barely aware of the boy anyhow. But when Father Garcia from the mission at Apia came on one of his frequent fund drives, the two men strolled in the formal garden and the priest recalled the boy to the farmer's mind. 'The youth O'Brien,' Father Garcia said. 'I have not seen the boy for a long time. Has he left the farm?'

'Oh, no,' Bragg said. 'I don't think so. He's around somewhere.' He was about to laugh and say that 'all those greasers look alike to me', when he realized that Father Garcia for all his education and gentility was a Latin. He only shook his head again. 'He's around.'

'We talked about enrolling the boy in the convent school at Apia.'

'That's right. We did. Something about the O'Brien boy attending afternoon classes?'

'Yes. We need more students to keep the school open. Those who come usually are taken out by their families during harvest season.'

'Well, I can't see that a little book-learning will ruin the O'Brien boy. Never hurt us all that much, eh? Eh, Father?'

'May we count on your sending him into Apia to classes?'

'I'll take care of it when we go back into my study,' Bragg said. 'I'll make a note, that way I won't forget and have to do penance, eh, Father?'

A tiled-roof adobe barn had been remodelled into a large single classroom with tall, deeply inset windows and large double barn doors which were folded open on hot days. Two rows of low, wide desks, procured second-hand, lined each side of a corridor which divided like some invisible wall the girls from the boys. Boys were caught in the left aisles on pain of punishment by unsmiling sisters, or banishment by the good priest himself. Even to smile in the direction of that open barrier was cause for instant retribution. The desks faced a blackboard across the entire width of the forward wall, and it was toward this bleak area that students were expected to focus their eyes and their attention.

All grades, from the first to the twelfth, were taught in this room. The lower grades occupied the first seats in each row and the higher classes were assigned to the rear. There were fewer of the upperclassmen. There might be ten or twelve first graders, but there were seldom more than two or three studying above the tenth year.

On this first afternoon at the convent school, Jesus was subjected to a probing examination by Sister Ilona and though he was twelve years old at the time, he was assigned to

355

the third grade. This caused a great deal of giggling among the girls across the wide aisle, and even the unhappy males around him looked at him with some contempt.

Jesus was thankful for a seat beside one of the tall windows which opened on the alluring world beyond, a eucalyptus tree, a slide, swings, fields and sky. He arrived just after noon every day, exhausted. The enforced quiet of the schoolroom, the muzzing of flies, the warm breezes all combined to seduce and overwhelm him and he learned to sit straight in his seat, asleep with his eyes open.

He sat quietly, never bothered anyone, seemed never even to glance toward the girls' side of the classroom. The sisters seldom called on him and sometimes seemed to forget his presence completely.

He was far less than unhappy at the convent school. The dear God who loved the place knew it was cooler than the lettuce fields, less taxing than the stockyards.

Everyone who noticed him at all remarked upon how handsome he was growing up, dark-skinned, black-haired, olive-eyed, with features such as one saw engraved upon ancient coins. He was quiet, obedient and undemanding. The sisters were impressed by him because he was so little trouble to them in a school where they sometimes believed the little imps were gathered as God's own test of their patience and strength and religion.

Jesus came and went quietly, and during the short afternoon break, he sprawled alone under a eucalyptus tree and because he was a threat to nobody, no one bothered him. No one seemed to like Jesus very much, but none disliked him, either. He might have been the stuff of fantasy in the secret hearts of the girls across the forbidden aisle, but they never spoke to him and certainly never dared smile in his direction. He seemed to ask nothing of any of them, nuns or students alike, except that they let him alone. He loved to watch them at play, smiling and pleased. He responded to music, seeming only then to come truly alive, but he attended classes because he had been ordered to do so. He seemed to expect no reward or profit. It was simply a matter of obeying orders and keeping out of trouble. Without Leonora in his life any more, he was like a sleepwalker, and it did not matter what he did or left undone. By the time he was seventeen, he had been promoted to the eighth grade.

XXVI

Three weeks before her sixteenth birthday, Leonora was at the farm for a weekend. On Saturday afternoon, after she'd swum alone in the pool and laid herself out to dry on a huge printed terrycloth towel, her father came out and sat at a glass table under a striped parasol. When a Mexican woman brought drinks and petit fours, Bonnett called to Leonora and invited her to join him.

She levered herself up, yawning, and flopped into a chair across the table from her father, not bothering to smile because she read the disapproval in his face. 'A one-piece bathing suit, Leonora,' she said, imitating his sternest tone. 'What in God's name is this generation coming to?'

Bonnett did not smile, but he did not bother to answer her, either. After a moment he said, 'Let's try to be better friends, Leonora.'

'Why?' she inquired in an idle tone as if it did not matter to her, one way or the other, as if, in fact, this conversation did not concern her. They might as well be discussing two other people.

'Because I think we ought to. Because I'd like to be your friend.'

'Who are you?'

'I'm sick of this smart talk, Leonora. This jazz age disrespect for one's elders. I am your father, damn it.'

She nodded, grinning at him. 'That's right, you are. I apologize, Papa. It's just that I see you so infrequently, I forget. I do have a great deal on my mind, you know.'

'Yes.' His voice was drier than his martini. 'I get regular reports on you and your conduct from Miss Hamilton's School for Young Ladies. I must say, the reports on your conduct are always most voluminous.'

Leonora shrugged her golden shoulders and shifted her

willowy body in her chair. 'You know what they say, Papa. One day at Miss Hamilton's School for Young Ladies is equal to one year in the seventh ring of hell.'

'You seem to have a pretty exciting time.'

'I'd have a good time in hell itself, Papa, if I had to. I take after Mama. I adjust well.'

'I don't call your latest activities adjustment. Who gave you the idea that I would tolerate your becoming a stunt pilot?'

She laughed. 'You've never seen those barnstorming pilots, Papa. Most are aviators from the war. They were trained to fly, but never got into any real combat. They are a class apart. They live free, going from fair to circus and flying to thrill people. It sounds like the freest, most exciting existence possible.'

He took a deep drink and shrugged his shoulders. 'I suppose it is. For tramps.'

'Oh God, Papa, you'll never understand.'

'I understand only one thing. You're totally rebellious. Against the rules of your school, against my authority, against anything that seeks to discipline and mature you. You've bobbed your beautiful hair. I'm heartbroken, but I've learned to accept it. You have been demerited at school for — let me count the ways — smoking in the bathrooms, drinking, curfew violations, insubordination and trying to sneak boys into your dormitory bedroom.'

She smiled faintly. 'And just think, that's only the list compiled by Miss Hamilton's trained finks.'

'Do you truly think, Leonora, that a school like Miss Hamilton's could exist without laws?'

'I think just as you do, Papa. Laws are made to govern other people.'

He spread his hands. 'My God. Sometimes I feel helpless. I'm only trying to save you, Leonora.'

'From what?'

'From yourself, it looks like. I know it's all the rage to rebel against old standards, old rules, but I can tell you we have laws so we can govern.'

'Laws are made for one reason, Papa, and you know that better than I do. You have laws so families like ours can prosper and protect our wealth from the unwashed rabble.'

'My God, what kind of talk is this?'

She shrugged. 'I get around, Papa. All over Los Angeles.

Despite the rules at Miss Hamilton's, I see the real world. I see what is going on. I'm neither blind nor deaf nor even dumb as good little girls are supposed to be.'

'The school and I are only trying to protect you against the ugliness of the world, Leonora. You don't have to live in that sweaty, nasty environment. You can remain above it. You were born above it. You can stay above it.'

She shrugged her shoulders and said nothing. When a servant poured lemonade for her, she refused to drink it until gin was added to it. At last, Bonnett merely threw up his arms and surrendered. 'Add gin,' he told the servant. He stared at Leonora. 'There seems only one way to get along with you, tö do everything your way.'

'Isn't that funny, Papa? That's what I think about you.'

Bonnett exhaled heavily. 'Well, we seem to be at cross purposes, don't we? I want only the best for you — and I'm unreasonable.'

She gave him a taut smile. 'You don't have to be,' she said. 'You can just face facts, Papa. Since the war, the whole world is changing. I'm changing with it. You're just fighting change. You want things to stay as they always have, and they're not going to do that.'

'I'd feel much more secure, if men could still be men and women would be content still to be women. What do you want, Leonora? What are you looking for? What do you really want?'

She gazed at him, her tongue in her cheek. 'I want to invite Jesus O'Brien to this sixteenth birthday bash you're insisting upon throwing for me.'

'Jesus O'Brien? The Mexican labourer? The greaser boy that works around here? You're joking.'

'No, I'm not. I never joke with you, Papa. You have absolutely no sense of humour.'

He nodded. 'I certainly have none where you and wetbacks are concerned. You should know better.'

'The Jesus O'Brien I'm talking about is no wetback, Papa. And you know that as well as I do. He was born right down the road.'

He scowled, staring at her. 'How do you know that?'

'Grandfather told me.'

'Why would you discuss the labourer with your grandfather? Why would you ask him that?'

'I didn't. Grandfather just told me. Just as he told me that Jesus has been going to school for the past five years.'

'Yes. Jesus O'Brien. Your grandfather thinks maybe he can be groomed to become a foreman for us someday down at the barracks. Isn't that elegant? Uplifting? Just the career you'd want for a man in your life.'

'I don't give a damn about his career, Papa. I just want him at my sixteenth birthday party.'

'Why would you want him?'

'Because he's beautiful. I got a glimpse of him the other day as I was driving in. He's even prettier than he was five years ago.'

'Pretty. For God's sake. Men aren't pretty.'

'He is. And he's very polite and well-behaved, even housebroke, Grandfather says —'

'Well, you just stay away from him.'

'From Grandfather? Why?'

'You damn well know who I mean, young lady. The boy is a Mexican. A goddamn greasy, stupid, dirty, unwashed Mexican.'

'I'll send word for him to take a bath before he shows up for the party. You might have to buy him a new suit and suitable shoes.'

'I'm damned if I will.'

'Well, it doesn't matter. Grandfather will do it.'

'Will you just tell me one thing? Why should you want a fieldhand among your friends — young people from the very best families?'

'Why not? When you brought up the idea of this party, I opposed it with all my heart and all the fervour at my command. You said this would be my party — my very own party — and that I could have anything I wanted —'

'Anything within reason. A society band from the Ambassador Hotel. Any entertainment you wanted. Anything within reason.'

'What that really means is that I can have anything you want for me.'

Bonnett sighed heavily and sank back in his chair. 'Must we fight every time we're together?'

'Looks like it,' she said in a bland voice, as if this were one more fact of life which she accepted and to which she adjusted. 'So. . . may I invite Jesus to my party?'

'You know damned well you cannot.'

'It's what I want.'

'Maybe. But you'll get over it.'

'How do you know?'

'You said so yourself. You adjust well. And this is one situation to which you're damned well going to have to adjust.'

'And if I don't?'

He smiled at her, a chilly light glinting in his eyes. 'But you will. I know these things. You'll mature and you'll thank me. In the meantime, if I'm pushed, I still know ways to cure you, young lady.'

'Oh? Do you?' Her gaze struck against his defiantly.

He sighed, realizing he had said too much. To dare Leonora, to challenge her was the wrong approach. He retreated slightly. 'Let's say, if you push me too far, I know ways to cure the greaser.'

'And if they fail?' she inquired, her gaze unyielding against his.

He shrugged. 'I'll get rid of him if I have to in order to protect you, Leonora. I know this is a silly young girl's infatuation, and nothing more. But I'll get rid of him if you force me. And you know goddamn well I will.'

Her expression did not alter. Her voice remained calm and unruffled. She said, 'Suppose I tell you, Papa, in graphic Anglo-Saxon Terms, exactly where to stick that sixteenth birthday party?'

'You don't mean that, Leonora.'

'Give it. And see. I sure as hell won't be here.'

He sat forward, staring at her. 'And all because I am trying to do what is best for you? Trying to shield you from a Mexican stoop labourer? You know I can't let him near this place. I warned him away from this house — away from you.'

She appeared to have lost interest. 'That was five years ago.'

'It still goes.'

She shook her head. 'I thought you might have come to your senses in five years, Papa. I'm sorry. I see that you haven't learned a thing about me. You still won't let me have anything I want unless it has been purified and sanitized and blessed by you.'

'I'm thinking only of your welfare.' He laughed. 'It might

trouble me that I am refusing you something, Leonora, that I might seem harsh and unfeeling, and even unreasonable. Except that I know you pretty well. You are headstrong, wilful, rebellious — what's the word? One of the flaming youth of these godless twenties. But I have faith in your intelligence. I know you are far too intelligent to want that bracero among your school and social friends. It would be humiliating for me, cheapening for you, and miserable for him. You pretend to want him only to upset me.'

'Oh? Is that I want?'

'It seems to be.'

She stood up. 'Well, Papa, I'm going back into Los Angeles. Back to the seventh ring of hell, better known as Miss Hamilton's School for Young Ladies. I'll come home for summer recess — on my way to Europe. I won't be home before then. I hope you have fun at my party. I hope you get a lot of favours, pin tails on dozens of donkeys, and meet scores of delightful socialites. I'm sure you won't miss me, you'll be far too busy being the ideal parent.'

Bonnett stood up too, and caught her arm. He gazed down into her pale eyes. 'What do you want, Leonora? What do you want from me?'

'I don't want anything, Papa. Honest to God, I don't want anything.'

'Jesus Christ, Leonora. Sometimes you sound exactly like your mother. God rest her soul. Sometimes you even look like her.'

'Insults will get you nowhere, Papa.' She gave him a faint smile, full of guile and treachery. 'I have the same memories of my mother that you do, Papa, only I begin to look at them in new ways, in different lights.'

'I'm sure you do.' She tried to pull free of his grasp but he would not release her. He sighed heavily. 'All right. Let's compromise.'

She laughed at him. 'Compromise? You mean talk around this and end up doing it your way?'

'No. I see how stubborn you are. I'll give a little. If you will.'

'Tell me about it, Papa.'

'All right.' He exhaled heavily again. 'It goes against everything in me. It violates every precept I live by. But I'll tell you what I am willing to do. The compromise I will make with you. If you insist upon having Jesus O'Brien in this house for your sixteenth birthday party, I will arrange it in the only way suitable or acceptable — to either of us, if we're honest about it. I'll have him outfitted in new serving garb. I'll have him sent up here to serve drinks and hors d'oeuvres. That will bring him at least physically to your party, but not as a guest, which I could not tolerate. You will then have the boy at your party — in the only way that makes sense. It may even serve a reasonable purpose. It may serve to show you how inapropri-ate this whole ugly business is.'

Leonora laughed up at him. 'It sounds good to me,' she said.

2

Jesus felt a smouldering exhilaration, a new, galvanizing sense of excitement which he could not decipher, or explain, even to himself. He walked back from the convent school at Apia with his heart beating faster for no good reason, with a growing feeling of pleasant change in the very atmosphere. The valley looked the same, and yet it was not the same at all; the sun was sharper, the lines of distant foothills more distinct with shadow and sunlight, a kind of serene blue haze sifted up from the trackless ploughed ground itself.

He felt the need to do something, to expand the unusual surge of energy rising inside him. He wanted to laugh aloud. He felt as if, like the summer snake, he had shed his old skin, the apathy and lethargy falling away, freeing his body and his mind and his heart, even if this were far too poetic for him even to understand.

He was summoned by the dinner bell into the dormitory mess-hall. He had no desire to eat; he answered from habit. He felt hungry, but the thought of food repelled him. He sat at his place at the long table, bombarded and surrounded in the charge of conversations, a babble of English and Spanish, but the sense of none of it touched him. Incomprehensible, it swirled about his head, a remote and meaningless buzzing, as though he were somehow set apart from these people and could never truly belong among them, though he knew he belonged in no other world, either. He felt as if he belonged nowhere. Yet, for this warm interval, it was not a lonely or disturbing sensation.

He left his food untouched. When darkness fell, he wandered, restless. Campfires glowed in the migrants' quarters, as they did every night. Fiddles, guitars, mandolins and accordions serenaded the night, rising on the smoke, filling the valley but, somehow, not touching him. He heard the songs and the singing but they did not summon him urgently as always before. Though he was nightly drawn irresistibly by the emotion-charged music or the promise he'd detected that morning in some senorita's half-averted face, tonight he did not go near the noisy fiesta.

He strolled the roadway, aimlessly and without direction. When the light appeared in Leonora's window up at the mansion, it was as if something burst inside him. He stopped in the middle of the road, tall, slender, his legs apart and his head back, staring at that light as some mariner lost at sea might gaze at the suddenly appearing north star.

When at last he returned to the dormitory, Hector Swain called him into his office. Jesus entered the small, airless cubicle and stood before the desk. Swain peered up at him. 'You must have got off the shitlist up at the house.'

'What?'

'Tomorrow morning, and every morning until further notice, you are to report to Mrs Hollister up at the house. You ain't on the work-crews. And you are to stay up there every day only as long as Mrs Hollister says, and you're to do whatever she says.'

Jesus felt the old excitement released inside him again. He nodded. As he turned away, Swain's voice stopped him. 'There is one more thing, Jesus.'

'Yes?' He looked back over his shoulder.

'Yes. Word from the boss himself. From Mr Bonnett Stockton. He says you are to do as you're told, keep your nose clean, and stay out of trouble. He says if you fuck up this time, you're in the kind of big trouble that Mr Bonnett Stockton hisself likes to deal with. Understand?'

After an eternal and sleepless night, Jesus drank black coffee for breakfast and went quickly in the saffron morning sunlight up the road to the mansion. He heard songbirds, and the dogs in the kennels, but he was truly attuned only to the rising excitement inside himself.

He presented himself at the kitchen door where none of the chefs or workers remembered him. Five years was several eternities in the kitchen at Stockton Farms. He asked for Mrs Hollister and was shown through rear passages to the housekeeper. She nodded and smiled at him. 'My, how you've grown, Jesus,' she said. 'You must break all the female hearts down at the camps.'

He smiled, but was afraid to speak. Mrs Hollister explained why he had been assigned to her staff. 'We're going to have a huge party, Jesus. It must be the most splendid affair in the history of Stockton Farms, or Mr Bonnett Stockton will be most displeased. They are sparing no expense.' She gave a faint laugh. 'They've even brought you back out of exile.'

He listened as the housekeeper talked. A tailor was brought in and he was measured for serving garb, formal-wear trousers, jacket and detachable shirt-front. He was fitted for a white shirt, collarless, a birdwing collar and bow tie. His feet were measured for black socks and black patent leather shoes. Mrs Hollister laughed. 'You'll look like a dream, Jesus. Except that every butler looks so funny in those formal liveries, you'd be the smash of the evening.'

He was instructed in the art of serving trays of food, drinks and canapes to self-involved, preoccupied and sometimes insolent or inebriated guests. 'Whatever their condition, manner or attitude,' he was warned, 'they are right. They are always right. You have one answer, no matter what is said or done to you. You smile, bow your head and retreat. Or you follow the guest's instruction, no matter what it is, no matter what else you have to do.'

'You will be polite and retiring, obedient,' Mrs Hollister said. 'A good servant isn't one who excels in service, he's one who gets his work done and is not even noticed. No attention is ever called to himself. Ever. That's why I truly think you will get along at Miss Leonora's party. You're a well-behaved boy, Jesus, and I want to be proud of you. I'm sure I will be.'

Jesus was less certain. He went every morning to his instructions and rehearsals and every day he looked for Leonora, but he did not even glimpse her once; there was not even the faint trace of her perfume in any room he entered. She was not there as far as he could tell, and yet the feeling of her nearness stimulated and intoxicated him, and at the same time filled him with dread.

He felt alive, robust, almost reckless, emboldened and even infused with courage. He was driven by needs he'd never known before or always denied and repressed. This magnificent house, this luxury surrounding him, the sense of Leonora's presence, even though he never saw her, aroused in him dreams and desires and ambitions unknown and unsuspected. For Leonora there was nothing on God's earth he couldn't do. Bring on the lion to be bearded, the dragon to be slain, the hill to be climbed.

He shivered. Against that feeling of strength, there rose, like acid gorge from the depths of his belly, the fear of failure, the fear that he would be a clown in the eyes of her friends, callow and clumsy and stupid, all the traits he owned to deep in his mind. He was being carefully tutored, but he did not really know how to act among a crowd of rich young people who had had everything they wanted all their lives. He was afraid of them and of their contempt. He wanted to be near Leonora, but he didn't want to fail in her eyes. In the meantime, he could only fight the sickness and wait, sustained by that light in her window, like some grail in the darkness.

XXVII

The driveway, the facade of the Spanish Monterey mansion and the spring garden, flush with flowers and augmented with incredible floral arrangements, all had been transformed into a gala motion picture theatre premiere. A large band played at one end of the veranda, another group tuned up for dancing in the sunroom and upon the terrace beyond its wide open French windows. The theme of extravagant world debut included great spotlights weaving beams across the night sky, brilliant balloons, streamers and young people arriving in limousines and alighting to fanfares and selected themes from the hidden band. No Graumann's display — on which this extravaganza was patterned — was ever more exotic or glamourous. Theatre personalities were not represented but the young men and women typified the cream of Southern California society, handsome, arrogant and lively.

Even the most sophisticated and blasé among them, including those who went east to school, the Ivy League, were impressed. One could almost see the creativity and imagination at work here and certainly one smelled the money lavished to define every detail. Magic had transformed the night into a bewitching garden of gleaming jewels, sapphires, rubies, emeralds and opals glittering in the soft darkness. For this single night whatever lay beyond the borders of the formal gardens, the kennels of guard dogs, the migrants shacks, any ugliness was removed or concealed. The garden flowered with handsome young people and florists' creations, dance pavilions or serving tables set along every gravel path, scented by gardenias, jasmine, torrents of blossoms.

From the darkness of a recessed balcony on the second floor, old Bragg Stockton gazed upon the lighted garden and the young guests moving about the statuary and flowers and trees, youths in formal black, girls in fashionable knee-length silks and muslins of mauve and lavender and ice-blue. Although Bragg had been invited to join in the festivities, he had chosen to stand removed and aloof. Watching the crowd below, he thanked God he had made that choice. Why would he want to be down there? They were just kids. The oldest was probably just voting for the first time, and not even shaving regularly. For all their finery and cynicism, they were kids at a party and he felt remote and withdrawn from his granddaughter's guests.

His gaze found Leonora and his heart swelled with pride. Among the brightest of the golden girls down there, she stood out. Even admitting part of his delight arose from kinship, he was certain any unbiased onlooker would agree. God Himself, looking down from His own removed eyrie, must be pleased with her, the most brilliant culmination of taming a trackless wilderness and amassing fortunes and polishing away at perfection. She was still a child, though at sixteen, she was to him wilful, spoiled, savagely stubborn, but extraordinarily gifted and delicately lovely. Her dark blonde hair was chopped above her shoulders and loose tendrils fell across her high forehead. Her eyebrows, her nose, lips and faintly squared jaw were chiseled to a jeweller's perfection and her lily-smooth complexion was a soft gold. Her slender throat held her lovely head erect and just arrogant enough to be delightful. Her peach-coloured georgette gown had a curved top, a draped neckline and shirred long sleeves. Her shoulders were padded and her tulip skirt reached just below her shapely knees. He was still too old-fashioned to approve knee-high hems, but young women these days wore their skirts short even to formal affairs.

Fascinated by Leonora, old Bragg watched her move among her guests, like quicksilver through dross. She was not, after all, the granddaughter of Bragg Stockton for nothing. She'd inherited many of the troubling traits of her father, but she'd been endowed with the refined and inexpressible loveliness of her mother.

From his vantage point, he watched Leonora's father being lionized down near the front porch. The children of the best families had all heard of Bonnett's tragic loss in the insane and violent murder of his beloved wife; some of them had not met Bonnett until tonight. They were awed at the sad, gallant face of the father, smiling, but disenchanted and somehow remote and stricken, even after all these years.

For a long time Bragg watched this little drama unfold when guests were introduced to Leonora's father, and his nostrils quivered impatiently. Bonnett belonged down there among those affected and unreal brats. He was in his element being consoled, admired and deferred to. Leonora had moved away from her father with a handsome six-foot blond youth, joining a group gathered about a brilliantly illumined table where green punch, green ice and green slices of cake were being served. A dozen young men crowded about a vast silver punch bowl, drinking, talking, drinking and drinking. Obviously, though they were still children, the punch had been spiked with bootleg hooch. Kids grew up too damned fast for him. He shook his head and leaned back into the shadows, resting against the stuccoed wall. 'Brats,' he said aloud. 'They're all brats. Obnoxious goddamn brats.'

2

Rupert Hayes, handsome, blond, admirable, wanted to dance. He was without any question, and he saw this himself, the handsomest, most striking-looking and charismatic man at this provincial social. He'd just returned this day from back east where a man was truly outstanding or he was absorbed in the mob. He'd stood out. He'd come home from Princeton for the spring break, but really because Leonora Stockton's letters had pleaded with him to make her sixteenth birthday party unforgettable by attending. For weeks he'd been corresponding with Leonora, using barely acceptable euphemisms for what he wanted, as they traded sultry promises for this magic night. Making it across country by Super Chief was going to entail fast movement, juggling of schedules and some inconveniences; she promised that all his sacrifices would be worth it. She could not truly move forward a year in the eyes of the world unless he were her escort. This seemed a fair enough assessment to Rupert.

He recognized the breathtaking impression he made upon the females in his orbit. As he approached or departed their groups they fell to whispering in awe among themselves, which in no way offended, humbled or really surprised him.

369

He saw his idealized male beauty reflected in every feminine eye tonight. There was about him the courtly, debonair and cavalier air which set Princeton men apart. He was, besides taller than the other men, better developed physically, lean and muscular, flat-bellied, long-legged, in excellent shape, from shock of pomaded yellow hair to polished black dancing pumps.

When he stepped from his car in the arc lights at the striped awning before the veranda, Leonora had run forward as the band struck up the Princeton fight song. Every eye turned toward them and Leonora greeted him effusively and thus staked her claim upon him for the evening in all envious eyes. He'd kissed her deferentially and moved with her under the awning, looking about without any expression of awe or pleasure. 'My God, Leonora, how do you stand it, living this far out in the country? One thing I'm convinced of. The sun sets between here and any city.'

She smiled up at him. 'Oh, I have your visits to look forward to, Rupert.'

He nodded, only partly in jest. 'That's true. But I thought we'd never get out here. But I suppose this land is worth its weight in gold. Anything that won't grow out here probably won't grow anywhere else. At least I hope so. There had to be some reasonable explanation for your family's living secluded from civilized society.'

'It just seemed far because you were so anxious to be with me,' she teased.

'That's the God's truth.' He bent over her and whispered. 'If these people only knew my fantasies you've starred in, they'd know what this premiere is really all about.'

'Why, Rubert Hayes, what a bold and ungentlemanly thing to say.' She laughed. 'But don't stop. I like it.'

Rupert took her arm and tried to guide her toward the vaguely illuminated sunroom where a few couples danced to a new love song. When she resisted, he said, 'Come on. I want to dance with you.'

She smiled at him in a preoccupied way and shook her head. 'You'll just have to be patient, Rupert.' She glanced around the crowded party area, looking beyond his splendid shoulder. 'I am hostess, you know.'

'And I am very roused. I've been waiting a long time. I crossed three thousand very dull miles just to get you in my arms.'

'And you will,' she said absently. 'But I must see to my guests.'

'These people can find drinks for themselves. Most of them are just like me, with a flask in their pockets. Come on, Leonora. I can't wait to get you in my arms — as your letters promised.'

'I'd have promised you anything to get you here tonight,' Leonora said absently. 'You know that, Rupert. Why, it would have been no party at all without you.'

'Then prove it,' he whispered against her fragrant hair. 'My God, how I want you in my arms. The dance floor isn't what I want, but in my present condition, just holding you close and hard against me will just have to do.'

'Soon,' she promised without really looking at him. 'You won't be sorry you waited.'

'I am already sorry,' he said. He closed his hand on her elbow again. 'Come on, Leonora. One dance.'

'Soon,' was all she said, moving toward another group of revellers around a serving table.

He spoke in a taut, low voice full of threat and frustration. 'I could have any woman I wanted here tonight, Leonora.'

'I'm sure you could. You're even more fascinating to us poor little country girls than you are to yourself, Rupert.'

'You might keep that in mind,' he said. 'I came all the way west, and all the way out here because you promised me — certain rewards.'

'Why, Rupert Hayes. I thought just being my escort for the evening was all the reward you wanted. That's what you told me last time I saw you.'

'I've aged a lot since then. I've read a lot of letters from you since then. I didn't have to read between the lines.'

'Maybe you should have,' she said, not looking at him.

'What in hell does that mean?'

'It means you're behaving like a boor. All you can think about is getting me in the back seat of a car, and you care for nothing else.'

'I care for everything else,' he whispered, sweating. 'It's just that there are priorities. I thought you meant what you said in your letters.'

'Why, Rupert Hayes. I do believe you Princeton boys are just as gullible as the ones from U.S.C.' She walked away from him and he followed her, angered and growing desperate. He could be as urbane and smooth as any other man, but her missives had not prepared him for the coldness she was showing him beneath the facade of her entranced smile.

She glided from group to group as if being the conscientious hostess. She introduced Rupert warmly, searing him with the splendor of her smiling, letting him bask in her pride. But he was not so easily deceived. She seemed to be looking for someone, distracted and barely aware of him. He'd never been dismissed so casually, and he didn't like it, and he was enraged with himself. He'd lost his poise. He had let her unsettle and discompose him in the first ten minutes. He knew he damned well had to recover his aplomb, take charge of his own emotions and of the deteriorating situation between them or all was lost. The long trek was fruitless and she would be laughing at him from now on. The very thought of this was untenable.

She ceased her odyssey as abruptly as she'd started it. She reached a serving table at a lantern-lit corner on the terrace. A few guests gathered around it, but she took no notice of them. She spoke to the servant. 'May I have a drink, please?'

Jesus went tense. Rupert saw the way the youth's shoulders straightened, the way he remained unmoving for a long breath, the way he smiled, pallid and rigid when he finally turned with the try of punch.

'Good evening, Heysus,' Leonora said. Of only one thing was Rupert Hayes certain in that moment. She'd forgotten all about him.

She took a glass of punch in fingers that trembled, Rupert saw. She went on gazing up into the face of the servant. If Rupert had not witnessed this little scene he would not have believed it. She had eyes only for this slender young Mexican in serving livery. Rupert stared down at him, trying to find the attraction. 'Aren't you going to say hello, Heysus?' she asked.

The servant nodded. 'Good evening, Miss Leonora,' he said. There was nothing irregular in his manner or his words and yet, burning inside, Rupert had the painful sense that he was intruding on something private and personal and insulting.

'You look incredible all dressed up, Hey,' Leonora said.

Rupert spoke in a low, taut tone, crackling with suppressed rage. 'What is this, Leonora? Fraternizing with the servants?

My God, you must be lonely out here.'

Leonora appeared to hear him for the first time. Her head jerked up and she peered up at him. 'Why don't you be a nice little prig, Rupert, and run soak your head?'

'You're insulting, Leonora. You insult me, flirting with a servant when I'm with you.'

'You can always leave, can't you?'

'I'm going to leave,' he said. 'and you're going with me. Now. Come on, Leonora. I want to dance.'

'Well, run do a shimmy solo, sweetheart, because I don't want to dance with you.'

'Do you plan to stay here and make moon eyes at this servant?' Rupert said.

'If I want to. It's none of your affair, Rupert. None.'

He caught her elbow tautly in his fist and spoke between his gritted teeth. 'Well, I make it my affair. I'm leaving, and you're going with me.'

'Let me alone!' Leonora cried out suddenly, her voice breaking across the muted music and the drone of conversations. For a long moment everybody stopped talking, staring at them.

'People are looking at us, Leonora,' Rupert said, his voice hoarse. 'Come on. We'll go dance. You can come back for your assignation with the greaser. But you're leaving with me right now.'

'If you don't take your hand off my arm this instant, Rupert, Heysus will hit you.'

Rupert straightened, quivering with rage. 'I wish to God he would. How I wish that son of a bitch would raise his hand to me.' He jerked his head up. He saw that Jesus' tray was empty. This provided the compromise Rupert sought. 'Get me a drink, boy. Get it at once.'

'If you want a drink, Rupert, you get it yourself,' Leonora said. 'I've never seen anyone as ill-mannered and boorish as you.'

'It's all right, Miss Leonora,' Jesus said in a low voice. 'I'll be pleased to get Mr Rupert's drink.'

'Now you're showing some sense,' Rupert said. He waited until Jesus brought a glass on a tray, then he clutched Leonora's arm again. He spoke in a low tone. 'If you don't walk away with me right now, Leonora, I'm going to poke this son of a bitch right in the face.'

373

She tried to jerk free. Her arm, swinging round, struck the goblet on the tray, flinging the coloured liquid all over Rupert's shirt-front. Rupert didn't even glance towards her. He spoke to Jesus. 'You stupid, clumsy bastard. You get back to the kitchen and you stay there.'

Leonora's voice rose, raging. 'Don't you dare speak to Heysus like that, you stuffed shirt.' If she could have lowered her voice, she would have, but it was already too late for that. She saw her father striding toward them across the bright lawn. Her heart sank. She said, quickly, 'Come on Rupert. You're right. Let's go dance.'

Rupert wasn't even looking at her. Unless he humiliated this servant, he was humbled and he was damned if he would stand for that. He said, 'You stay in the kitchen. I can promise you one thing, greaser boy. You haven't heard the last of this.'

Leonora shook her head defiantly. Her voice was low, now that it was too late. Her eyes filled with tears of rage. There was no sign of weakness in her voice, either. 'And neither have you, Rupert Hayes. If you ever speak to me again on this earth, I'll spit in your eye.'

Bonnett Stockton stepped between them. He did not need to be apprised of the situation. He was not even astonished to see that the chicano boy was at the heart of it. He spoke almost regretfully. 'I'm sorry if you've been inconvenienced, Mr Hayes. I was afraid something like this might happen. If you can forgive us — and go dance with my daughter, I'll handle this. I promise you one thing, sir. You won't be troubled by this particular servant. Not again. Not in my house.'

XXVIII

In the deepest shadows of lawn eucalyptus, Jesus stood in a patch of Stygian darkness, watching across the distant brilliantly illuminated garden where stirred vague forms and sweet sounds and bright colours. He was too empty and forlorn to think, not conscious of any thought at all.

Night winds rose crisp and brisk, shaking the Japanese lanterns on their strings and whipping gay skirts about the trim thighs of the laughing girls. Longing to be in the midst of that music and pleasure, Jesus moved against the tree trunk which hid him from that magic festival. This world was barred to him and the sure, final knowledge gave him a feeling of profound melancholy, left him haunted with desires and staggered by the dreary truth of who he was and what he was, but mostly of who he was not and who he could never be. As if he lacked some golden membership card he was denied entry to that garden where gay colours fluttered in clouds of popular love songs. He did not belong, he could never belong and this desolated him. They laughed and chatted and lured him across an unnavigable chasm where winds blew cold as misery and burned in his eyes tears that would not dry.

The dreams aroused in the past weeks of anticipation and promise and half-formed hope died abruptly. Without that sense of elation which had sustained him and beckoned him and tormented him, the enchantment was gone and he stood cold and bereft in the dismal spring night where he found only sadness in the gorgeous impressions from the bright terrace, and emptiness in the wind-tattered love songs that were never meant for him anyhow.

Reason warned him out of here and back to the barracks, but he had walked this far and he could go no further. Not yet. He watched for the golden girl in the peach-coloured dress and finding her made him clench his fists and shiver and

375

mutter moronic phrases without meaning and feint sharp, menacing gestures at imaginary rivals in formal dress and armed with all the correct credentials. The foe was totally unequal: the right schools, dimensionless bank accounts, family name and family fortune and social acceptability. This was something he could never attain no matter how hard he struck Rupert Hayes in his face. Still this silent confrontation filled him with painful pleasure and gave him a sort of compensatory triumph. He became a planter with thousands of rich California valley acres and in time took over the Stockton farms. He stepped from a smart new Packard car and strode, head tilted in a son-of-a-bitch attitude, into Los Angeles' most exclusive club where people bowed and fawned. He vanquished a tennis opponent with laughable ease on those tennis courts and people applauded because his devastated adversary was the unbeaten — to that moment — marvel from Princeton, Mr Rupert Hayes himself.

He shivered, knowing how totally and finally, and with what casual cruelty, Rupert Hayes had removed him from even a disputed view of that world. He had set down his tray on the Japanese-lantern-lighted serving table and plodded through the house to the kitchen where Mrs Hollister, with her shoes off, directed the servants. 'What's the matter?' she said. 'What have you done?'

He shrugged. 'I've been ordered off the place again.'

'By Mr Bonnett Stockton himself?'

He nodded. She shook her head, staring up at him. 'Why the devil can't you get along with that man? He gave you another chance. You promised me you'd be careful.'

He spread his hands, still too caught in a state of shock to feel anything. 'Where do I put these clothes?'

She gestured meaninglessly. 'Anywhere, Cinderella. Here you are, all finery stripped away and it's nowhere near midnight.'

'I didn't make it.'

'You certainly didn't. I'm sorry, Jesus. You were good. I trained you well and you were willing, intelligent, quiet and honest. I don't know what they want of you.'

'I wasn't lucky.'

She nodded again. 'All right. Just put on your things and leave the suit in the pantry. Take care of yourself, Jesus. You're right. You're not real lucky — and you can be in

376

trouble if you make the wrong enemies around here.'

He undressed, thinking not that he was exiled again, and this time for good, but about the beautiful little goddess who had smiled up at him for a brief moment out on that terrace. God knew she was inexpressibly lovely. She was a heart-breaker at sixteen; there was a great deal of misery ahead for a lot of men. And he would willingly have traded places with any one of them. One thing nobody could deny. There was a spark, a fire between them. He could feel it and even that stranger from Princeton had perceived it. She seemed to pull him deep and drowning into her sultry violet eyes. And her passion for him was there, undeniably there, shining in her perfect face and her slender body in a kind of heated glowing.

He remembered the first time he saw her, a golden vision, like some cherub, fragile and delicate and flirtatious at nine years old. Some women are born full of desires and promise and fires. She had looked at him and smiled and winked and embedded herself in his heart.

Mrs Hollister came to the door of the pantry. He had put on his demin shirt, faded levis and scuffed work shoes. 'How the mighty have fallen,' she said. 'Why don't you keep those new shoes, Jesus? They're no good to anybody else. I don't know what good they'll be to you either, but if you want them, you may as well have them.'

He thanked her and carried them under his arm. They came into the kitchen and Bonnett Stockton stood there, eating canapes at the serving table, a martini in his hand. He smiled at Mrs Hollister and when he spoke his voice was calm and unruffled. 'Well, I see you're sending him back to the barracks. Sorry it didn't work out, Mrs Hollister.'

'He's a good boy,' was all Mrs Hollister said.

Bonnett Stockton glanced at the housekeeper, an eyebrow tilted slightly, but he did not answer. He spoke instead to Jesus, his voice almost benign. 'You will return to the barracks, boy, and we'll say no more about this.'

'All right, sir.'

Stockton sipped at his martini, watching Jesus over the rim of the glass. 'But there is one thing I insist upon. You are to stay away from this house and the grounds around the house. From now on. Do you understand?'

Jesus nodded. He was shocked that Bonnett was letting him go so easily, with no more than this warning repeated from five years ago.

Stockton sighed and took up another canape. He watched the slender young Mexican cross the kitchen and go out of the rear door into the night. He smiled tautly. That young bastard didn't know how lucky he was. From the moment he had witnessed that scene on the terrace, he had made up his mind to rid his farm of the Mexican. He didn't need his kind of trouble. He didn't want him around; he wouldn't have him on the place.

This decision to return Jesus to the barracks and deny him entry to the house and grounds was the result of another compromise between Bonnett and his daughter. Leonora had interceded on the chicano's behalf. It was really more than intercession, it was pitched battle.

She had charged into the den and demanded to know what her father intended to do about Jesus. He didn't bother to tell her it was none of her affair. He was pragmatic enough to know that this was an issue that had to be resolved between them. Rupert Hayes had entered the booklined room behind Leonora and had hesitated just inside the door. He remained in the shadows. Bonnett saw that the youth had already been scourged by Leonora's wrath, and slumped, almost unmanned.

After a few moments old Bragg Stockton came into the den. The landowner smoked an expensive cigar, his face wreathed in smoke. He smiled devilishly. 'Wouldn't miss this for the world,' he said. And so they were all involved while the party eddied, in somewhat abated tempo, outside the room. Faint strains of popular love songs trailed in around them, shattered by the tensions.

Rupert watched helplessly and Bragg in amusement as Leonora and her father engaged in heated dialogue, punctuated by Leonora's taking up thick, leather-bound tomes from the shelves and throwing them on the floor.

'You cannot be so mean,' Leonora said wildly, panting. 'You cannot be my father and be so totally unfair. It was not even Hey's fault. Tell him, Rupert. Tell him I knocked the glass over and you accused Hey even when you knew I was to blame.'

Rupert reluctantly admitted this was true. Leonora even demanded an apology from Rupert for his boorish behaviour, and she got that.

Further argument ensued. Bonnett had one telling point, and this was the unrelenting core of his argument. Where this Jesus went, trouble followed. He would not have him around the house. Not any more. Not ever again. Only Bragg found any comedy in the situation and from time to time he laughed. It was priceless seeing his headstrong granddaughter and unyielding son locked in combat.

The contention was resolved very simply really. Bonnett held to his firm determination to punish the youth, even run him off the farm. Coldly, his daughter stared at him and countered, 'If Heysus is harmed, is reprimanded, I'll leave home. I'll stay at school until college opens and I'm damned if I'll come home even at holidays.'

A desperate silence settled over the den. Not one of the men even suspected that Leonora was joking. Her face was set, her jaw squared, her gaze fixed unblinkingly upon her father's pallid face. The ball was clearly in his court. He backed down and compromised because he knew Leonora was his daughter and what she threatened she would carry out, at whatever cost to any of them. The enormity of her threat intimidated him as nothing else could. He saved face enough to shave by agreeing only to return Jesus to the barracks, with no word of reprimand, but insisting that the boy be exiled from the house and grounds as long as he remained on the farm.

She shrugged. She found that agreeable. She even kissed her grandfather's cheek, smiled in a chilly way at her father and, taking Rupert's arm, returned to her party.

2

Jesus did not know how long he stayed there in the darkness, in desperation clinging to wisps of his reawakened dreams.

He was in a restless way content as long as he could keep Leonora in his vision, that ever-fixed mark. He remained frozen in the shadows, watching her, entranced. Then three things happened which left him forlorn and lost and defeated.

First, he found the golden hair, the peach-coloured dress, the vivacious girl glittering in that setting, perfect for her. She belonged in that world; no one could deny that. It was as if it had been created for her. She was wafted across that bright garden like some volatile vision on winged slippers. Her laughter drifted toward him on the night wind. For no clear reason his eyes brimmed with tears, blinding him for a long moment. And when he blinked away the tears, Leonora was gone and though he searched the lighted terraces and verandas and paths, he could not find her.

He did not know how long he stood there, puzzled and desolated. He knew that if he left here, she was eternally lost to him, like sand trickled through his fingers. All he had left of her were the memories he would take from this place and he could not willingly let her go.

The party rattled on, empty colours, patterns, textures, faces, like something empty, dead and lost and stripped of meaning. He turned slowly, his slender shoulders slumped round, and began to walk away in the darkness, the new shoes under his arm.

'Hey. . . Heysus.'

Jesus stopped.

'Heysus,' the whisper snagged at him. 'It's me.'

He nodded, turned and gazed down into that lovely shadowed face, that smile, grave and unsettling and conspiratorial. 'One of the security guards told me you were out here,' she whispered, taking his hand.

Jesus winced. 'If they know, your father —'

'Don't worry about it,' she whispered, leading him across the dark lawn. 'My father isn't the only Stockton with friends and authority around here. People do things for Papa because they're scared of him. They do things for me because they like me.'

He followed her willingly, as he might through fire or across hot coals. He said, under his breath, 'Where are we going?'

She smiled across her shoulder. 'What do you care, as long as we're together?'

'They'll miss you —'

'Let them —'

'They'll look for you.'

She paused and walked back close to him, the fragrance of her faint perfume and the heated musk of her hair enchanting, baffling and debilitating him. 'Whatever time we have together,' she said, 'they can't take that away from us, can they?'

He grinned down at her, his weak left eyelid trembling. 'What are we standing here for?'

She nodded and turned, hurrying again toward the darkened area beyond the garages where visitors' cars were parked. 'Do you know you have the most beautiful smile I ever saw?'

'I thought you did.'

'We both do.' She led him to an open touring car, its top down. Cautiously, she opened the rear door.

'Whose car is this?'

'What do you care? We're only going to use the back seat.'

Leonora scrambled into the tonneau of the car and toppled giggling upon the seat. Jesus followed, trembling visibly. She caught him in her arms and laughed. 'My darling boy! You've got to relax.'

'How can I relax? I'm with you, and I'll never learn to relax when I'm with you. They'll kill me for this, and I don't care, but I can't help feeling a little squeamish.'

She caught his face in her hands. 'We've a little while, Hey. There's a maid behind the locked door of my bedroom. Anyone who knocks will be told I developed a splitting headache. After my scene with Papa, even he will believe that.'

Her hands caressed his cheeks and his throat and his shoulders and she leaned towards him, her mouth parted. When he remained unmoving, his hands at his sides, she shook her head impatiently. 'Haven't you ever been in the back seat of a car before?'

'No.'

'Then you don't know what to do.'

'I know what I want to do.'

'Then do it, for goodness sakes. If you've never made love in the back seat of a car, you have delights ahead of you. The automobile is the new American bedroom. It takes the place of hotels. Oh, my dearest Heysus. Don't sit there staring at me with that beautiful face. We don't have time for it.'

'What do you want me to do?' he whispered, voice hoarse.

'Oh ye gods. Have you ever made love to a girl — gone all the way making love with a girl — girls?'

'Love?'

'Oh, my poor innocent. I'd think this was a line, but I can look at you and know better. But you must have made love to some girl. You must know what I mean. Haven't you — done it — with a girl?'

He exhaled heavily. 'I've — done it. . . . But I've never made love.'

Leonora laughed helplessly. 'My God. Is there a difference?'

'There is to me. I can do it. . . . But I can't love them, even while I'm doing it.'

She brought her face close to his. 'Why not?'

'Because they are not you. Because I can love only you.'

She whistled softly between her teeth, her eyes liquid and warm. 'You know, I never thought about that in my life, but you're right. . . . Boy. . . . Either you've got the fastest line known to man, or you're devastating. . . . Or both.'

'I do love you,' he said. 'I might be scared to say this to you, but I'm not going to see you again anyway. I want you to know. I've loved you — and only you — since the first time I saw you.'

'I do know, Hey. Truly I do. I'd leave my bedroom light on all night and think maybe you saw it and thought about me.'

'I never thought of anything else.'

'Oh lordy, Hey, you're turning me to jelly. Hot jelly. You're making me ache, even at the base of my throat.' She pressed close to him, her arms going under his biceps and closing on his shoulders, imprisoning him against her. He ached, rigid with desire, and she pressed herself upon him. 'I never forget you either, Hey. . . . Not really. . . . I might have made love with a lot of boys. . . . Only one reason why I didn't. They weren't you.'

She opened her sweet-smelling mouth to him and he kissed her and the night world spun around them, turned upside down, never again the same. She clung to him, panting wildly, her hands exploring him.

She held on to him tightly, talking against his mouth. 'Want to know a true secret, Hey, something I couldn't tell anybody?'

He managed to nod. His hand had closed over her taut high breast, its nipple hard upon his palm and he was truly unable to think of anything except this.

'I lie awake at night at school and think about you — until I can't stand it. . . . I've even told boys about you on dates. I told one boy in Los Angeles about you. We were in the back seat, petting, and I wouldn't let him do anything. He got mad

382

and I told him about you. That I loved you. That even if I couldn't have you, I loved you. You know what he said? He said I was lying. He said he was a U.S.C. psychology student and had read Freud and he knew what was the matter with me. I was afraid of sex. Afraid of men. And I pretended to be in love with you because it was impossible — and non-threatening, and therefore I felt safe. I laughed so hard he took me home and he never spoke to me again.'

For a moment, neither of them spoke. She closed her hand on him, moving it, delighted with him. He held her, kissing her open mouth, nursing her tongue and caressing her breasts. 'Oh God, Hey,' she whispered. 'I don't want to be safe.'

'They'll kill me.'

'I'll die if you don't.' She kissed him savagely, tears seeping along her smooth cheeks. 'Oh, Heysus, why do you have to be so poor?'

'God knows. Why do you have to be so goddamn rich?'

She laughed because she couldn't help it. 'Honest, Hey, rich is better. You've got to leave here. You've got to do something. Anything. You can be anything you want to be.'

His voice sagged in defeat. 'I don't even know *who* I am, much less *what* I might be.' He sighed and held her close, feeling as if they were on different planets about to be torn apart and hurtled separately and eternally through space. 'You're a Stockton. I don't even know who I am.'

'Well, find out.' There was no compassion in her tone. 'You can be who you want to be — you can be whatever you want to be — for me.'

'It's easy for you. . . . You know who you are and that nobody can ever get in your way. But I don't even know who I am — a half-breed father and a Mexican mother. I'm not Anglo. I'm not Mexican. Who am I? What am I? I'm nothing. Nobody. Your father is right about that.'

'Oh, Hey, you're a fool if you believe that. There's so much you can do. You might even make it possible for us — someday — to be together. . . . But even if you didn't, you could get away from here. You could be somebody. Something. I'd be so proud of you.'

He drew away from her, feeling more helpless than ever. 'Without you, I can't even want to do anything. No matter what I did, it would be empty without you — and I know

383

that's what my life is going to be — empty, without you in it. There's no way it could be anything else.'

She drew him close. 'You can have me, Heysus. Right now. You can have me. Everything you want of me. You can know me — like the bible says — you can know whether you want me or not — whether I'm worth fighting and studying and working for.'

She held his face, kissing him. It was as if the world exploded in light at the touch of her lips. It was some seconds before he realized that the light was real and unflinching, from flashlights in the hands of half a dozen men. Bonnett Stockton grabbed open the door, snarling like a rabid animal. Leonora screamed and Jesus held her, trying to protect her, when it was him they wanted.

They stared up at the men ringing the car. Besides Leonora's father, barely able to restrain his rage, there were Rupert Hayes, face twisted with contempt, Church Foley and others assigned as security guards for the party.

Bonnett Stockton crouched over Leonora and Jesus, his face contorted in light and shadow. 'Well, thank God we got here in time.'

Leonora sat forward, her voice and her rage matching her father's. 'In time for what, Papa?'

Her father ignored this, he did not bother answering her. He glanced over his shoulder and spoke in cold formality, his voice under taut control. 'Mr Hayes, would you be kind enough to escort my daughter back to her guests?'

Rupert only nodded. When Leonora did not move quickly enough to please him, Bonnett caught her arm and wrenched her upward from the seat. He half-threw her past him out of the car door. Two of the guards caught her to keep her from falling.

Leonora broke free from them. 'What are you planning to do, Papa?'

Bonnett spoke over his shoulder. 'Get back to your party, Leonora. See to your guests. You needn't burden yourself about what happens out here.'

Rupert Hayes touched her arm, but she shook his hand down. She leaned forward, bracing her splayed hands against the car. 'Listen to me, Papa.'

Bonnett no longer even looked toward her. 'Get her out of here,' he said. His voice lowered. 'If you'll go with her now,

Mr Hayes.'

One of the security guards caught Leonora's arm on one side and Rupert tentatively clutched at her other arm. Leonora allowed them to move her away from the car, but her voice rasped in the faint light. 'If anything happens to Heysus, Papa — anything — it's all over between us. All over. I'll never come back here. Never.'

At this, Bonnett did turn, standing in the tonneau of the car. His voice was modulated, but quivering with suppressed savagery. 'To hell with your threats. You behave like a child, you'll be treated as a child. You say one thing to me, and then sneak around and hide in the dark with this greasy half-breed bastard. I won't have you trying to command me. Not any more, Leonora. I'm master here, and I'll handle this greaser — my way. Now, go back to your party. Please. We'll talk later, you and I. We'll talk later.'

For what seemed a breathless eternity, Leonora stared up at her father, but she did not speak. Rupert said something under his breath to her. She did not glance at him, but heeled around and walked away in the darkness. Rupert took a few hasty steps, overtook her. He touched her arm. She did not try to free herself. They walked away, followed by the young security guard. The guard's convoying them looked like a matter of protection, but everyone who knew the Stocktons, father and daughter, knew better. The guard was there as insurance that the wilful girl obeyed her father's orders.

Bonnett remained unmoving until the three reached the rim of light around the house. Then he jerked his head at Church and two of the three remaining guards. 'Get him out of here.'

When Jesus would have got up to go willingly, Bonnett backhanded him across the face. 'Don't try to get away, bastard,' he said. 'You're not getting out of this.'

Jesus remained prostrate across the seat rest where he'd fallen. Church Foley and one of the other guards caught his arms and helped him from the car. Bonnett Stockton followed and slammed the door behind him.

Bonnett came close to where Jesus was held between the guards. Jesus was slightly taller than Leonora's father. Their eyes met, held.

Though Stockton stared unblinkingly into Jesus's face, he did not speak to him. His cold voice was deadly. 'Take this son of a bitch out of here. Take him out beyond the barns and the kennels. I want you to work him over. With hoe handles. That'll soften him up without too many marks. I want him worked over good. A lesson he don't put out of his mind soon, no matter how stupid he is. We'll make this a night lover-boy here will never forget.'

Two of the guards caught Jesus' arms. 'Tie him up good, Church,' Stockton ordered. 'Stretch him out good.'

Church Foley's voice was low, as if deeply concerned for the sensibilities of his aggrieved employer. 'Don't you worry about it, Mr Stockton, sir. You got enough on your mind. You go back to your party. I know how to handle this. I know what you want done.'

'I want the son of a bitch hurt,' Bonnett said. 'The way I hurt.'

Stockton turned on his heel and strode across the dark lawn toward the light and music. A tenor was singing 'I Love You Truly.'

The guards marched Jesus between them past the garages, the kennels, the feed barns to a corral in the darkness. One of the guards brought hoe handles and ropes. Church cinched the rope knots on Jesus' wrists, making certain they were secure. He felt no particular animosity toward the boy, but he was moved to no leniency toward him, either. He had always liked the kid, quiet, never making trouble around the barracks, but he had his orders. Jesus was no longer one of the workers, no longer one of them. He was an outsider with whom they had been ordered by the boss to deal, and Church Foley followed orders. He could look at the Mexican youth almost as if he had never seen him before. The only thing he said to Jesus was, 'You're lucky the boss didn't order you killed, boy. He could have. He was sure as hell mad enough.'

'Yeah. You're lucky we broke it up before you started humping her. If the boss had caught you screwing her, he would have killed you, hisself. On the spot,' One of the other guards said this, almost off-handedly.

Church Foley grunted in a kind of amused assent, but he said nothing. He tied an end of the rope to the corral fence. Another guard secured the other end of the line to a post so Jesus was spread-eagled, his arms out at his sides, his legs parted.

'You want him nekkid?' one of the guards asked.

Church hesitated. 'No. Boss said don't mark him. His clothes will keep him from being cut as much.' Church wadded up his bandana and stuffed it into Jesus' mouth. Church said, 'Ain't no use you disturbin' the nice folks with your yelling. Huh?'

Jesus sagged against the fence, waiting. He had seen other workers beaten for infractions of Stockton Farms rules. In a strange way he was glad for the gag. He had never been able even to watch a man being beaten.

Armed with the hoe handles, the men stood on both sides of Jesus. They were neither avid nor reluctant. This was simply another chore. Sometimes it was amusing to see the gagged prisoner writhe, trying to scream, but this was the only fringe benefit in this business. It became damned hard work before it was over.

'Don't hit him in the head or face,' Jesus heard Church Foley instruct his men. 'Nothing above the shoulders. Best to aim for his ass, upper legs and the small of his back. That there's where it hurts. And watch it. Don't crack his nuts. The old man wants him hurt, not maimed.' He exhaled heavily and nodded in the darkness. 'All right. Go ahead.'

The first blow caught Jesus in the small of his back. He felt as if his spine shattered. His head jerked up. The next blow caught him at the backs of his knees and though the fire in his middle forced him to stretch tall, his legs would not support him. When he sagged, they rained blows upon his body, methodically, but without mercy. They battered him so fiercely that his body swayed on the ropes, from side to side, under the impact.

Jesus moaned, writhing. The handles caught him again and again, almost in a rhythm of pain. The sound of the poles upon his flesh was dull. The pain was unbearable. He had ground the bandana into a wet wad between his gritted teeth. He almost swallowed it, choking, but this did not matter. He grasped for breathing, mewling. At last his body slumped against the fence and it was as if the men were pounding a sack of grain.

Church held up his hand, calling it off. He told one of the guards to get a truck. Distantly, Jesus heard the Ford engine. He felt the ropes loosen from his bleeding wrists. He sagged to his knees. Two of them lifted him and hefted him into the flatbed of the open truck. He heard the clutch engage and the truck rolled along in the darkness. The wind was cool against Jesus' face.

When the truck stopped, the men carried him between them into the barracks and to his cot. They dropped him heavily upon it. The migrants awoke when they turned on the lights. Church was pleased. It wouldn't hurt the wetbacks to see what they could expect when they stepped out of line.

Jesus lay face down on the cot. He was aware of the light of morning, of the men moving around him. Finally, there was silence when the workers had departed for the fields. No one came near him. He tried to move, but he felt as if his body were covered with fire ants, as if his bones were broken, his tendons whipped to pulp.

Gradually, he became aware of his surroundings, the sounds and the sights of the barracks. He seemed to see everything through an occluding haze, as if blood sprayed across the lenses of his eyes. The third day he got up and ate breakfast with the men. The other braceros would not sit near him. It was almost superstition, as if his ill-fortune might in some way be contagious.

He sprawled on his bed. He looked up and saw Hector Swain coming along the aisle. Swain sat down on a cot bed beside him. 'How you coming on?' Swain said.

'I can't go out to work. Not yet.'

Swain shrugged. 'It don't matter.'

'Why not?'

'Look, kid. I always liked you. You never hurt nobody. Never made me no trouble. But I can tell you, I don't think you ought to go out to work in these fields no more.'

'What?'

'I'm being friendly as I can, kid. It's like all hell is blown loose, up at the Stockton house. Miss Leonora is gone. She swears she'll never come back out here. She refuses to communicate with her old man at all. Not by phone, or letter, or through her grandfather.'

'Oh God,' Jesus whispered.

'Yeah. Well, for you, it's even worse. Mr Bonnett Stockton blames you for everything. All the trouble with his daughter. Her leaving. Everything. I've seen him hate people before. For a hell of a lot less. I'm telling you. Nobody will bother you until you're up and walking again. You can stay here and recuperate. Don't think nobody'll say nothing about that.'

Jesus sagged on the cot. He stared wordlessly at the foreman. He shook his head, defeated.

'It'd be a hell of a lot healthier, kid, if you just sort of walked away from here as soon as you're able. No matter where you go, you'll be a hell of a lot better off.'

Jesus nodded, but did not speak. As if to underline everything Hector Swain had said, he awoke in the late afternoon and saw his uncle Pedro Luiz standing in the barracks doorway. Pedro was staring at him, not as if he really saw him, or recognized him as part of his family, but as if he were watching him, as a scavenger might. The sun flared at Pedro's back, illumining him in the doorway, highlighting his black hair and polished boots. Tio Pedro looked healthy, heavy in the chest, the belly, hips and legs. His deputy sheriff uniform was fresh and pressed and new. Tio Pedro looked as if he were living well, successful in his new career. Jesus wanted to ask about Tia Clara and Concha and if there were any word from Pedrillo, but he did not speak. Pedro Luiz looked more like an apparition, an omen of doom, than a human being. Jesus' gaze fixed on the ten-dollar gold piece that Pedro wore as a tie-pin. It seemed in Jesus' agonized mind that this ornament had once belonged to his own father, and yet standing there, it was as if Pedro Luiz denied him, refusing to acknowledge even that he knew him. Jesus did not speak to his uncle because there was one thing he was certain of: Pedro Luiz would not answer him.

Jesus closed his eyes and remained unmoving on the cot for a long time. When at last he opened his eyes, his uncle was no longer standing in the doorway. The barracks was silent and empty and eerie in the sunlight. Jesus felt his body wracked with an involuntary shudder. Terror washed through him as if he'd not seen his uncle at all, but the angel of death.

Driven by a sense of fear he didn't even really understand, Jesus waited only until the workers were in their cots and the lights extinguished for the night. He got up and dressed as quietly as he could. He catfooted his way along the aisle and to the open front door of the barn-like barracks.

He walked outside, feeling as if he had been holding his breath for a long time. He went down the steps and stood for a moment in the middle of the road which led west away from the Stockton farms. He turned and gazed forlornly at the mansion on the tree-tufted knoll. The house was dark, and there was no sense of yearning toward it now. He knew it was empty for him. He gazed for some moments at that window where Leonora's signal to him had burned so long. The window was dark. Like an inconstant star in a vast and empty night, the light was gone from her window, forever gone.

XXIX

Although it was mid-Autumn of the year of Our Lord 1928, to
the shabby young priest standing outside the aged adobe
mission at Apia, nothing in the entire San Gabriel Valley
seemed to have changed since that first time he'd stood
reluctantly upon this spot in childhood. The world had
marched on, had been at war, in unprecedented prosperity
now sliding into a mild recession, had seen a revolution in
mores, morals and ethics, a change even in religion. But the
village, this church and this valley appeared untouched. He
felt the old sense of despair, insecurity and dread which had
long ago tied his stomach in knots and silenced his tongue,
dulled his mind. Not even the prospect of his new post, the
first true assignment since he'd been ordained, gave him any
counterbalancing lift of excitement or anticipation.

The valley remained unchanged, except for an encroaching
urban sprawl blemishing its far rims. Beyond the brown
foothills the mountains reared, seared by the sun and striped
with shadows like huge scars. Nearer, the eternally ploughed
and growing fields devoured everything except the blue lines
of the highways, the church property and the shrinking
skeleton of the village. Distantly, he glimpsed, like a green
postage stamp of colour, the park-like knoll and the
Monterey-style mansion. He brought his gaze quickly away.
There was nothing up there for him. There never had been,
but by now he was reconciled to his insignificant station in
existence and resigned to whatever role the fates cast him in
life. He even found some irony in his present condition, but
he did not bother to question.

He exhaled heavily, the frightened schoolboy reclaiming
his mind and heart again after all these years. He felt as if he
were that reluctant child trudging unwillingly to class in that
converted barn out beyond the church, the manse, the

outbuildings and the walled gardens. He carried a khaki-coloured canvas tote bag in one hand, a battered guitar case in the other. He walked across the crisp groundcover to the rectory porch, not expecting any overt or even gracious salute of welcome.

He knocked on the heavy front door and stood waiting, slender, black-haired, hatless, dark-skinned, an inch less than six feet tall. He wore a threadbare broadcloth charcoal grey suit. Only his turned-around collar was fresh and white and new. He inhaled several deep breaths and exhaled them as he waited, barely aware of what he did. On his olive-tinged face he'd pasted a faint smile against that moment when the door should be opened.

Finally, an aged Mexican woman he'd never seen before opened the door and peered up at him. She smiled wanly and even gave him a tiny, answering wink and he realized his left upper eyelid had sagged again with his smiling. Damned unseemly in a priest, even a pretty priest, he'd been told more than once.

'I am Father Jesus Jose O'Brien,' he said. 'I am Father Garcia's new assistant.'

'Si. You are expected. The good father awaits you in his study.'

Holding his breath as if he were diving into cold water, deep and over his head, Jesus followed the woman across the silent foyer where a marble Christ gazed coldly at him, into the book-lined study which had changed even less than the valley, less even than the shrivelled old man in the tall-backed throne chair beside an inadequate reading lamp. The old, faintly remembered seminal odour of the place struck Jesus; it was also unaltered, unfreshened.

When Jesus stood before the aging priest's chair, aware of time-crisped curtains rent by seamless sun rays, old, leather-bound books, dust glinting everywhere, a cold grate, a mantel bearing a single icon of Christ slumped upon the cross, Father Garcia muttered something unintelligible and lifted his head slowly. Deliberately, he set aside first the book, with page-marker fringed in place, and then his glasses on the thick cover. He pressed his thumbs against his eyes for a long moment and then peered up at Jesus. One could not say at once whether he did not recognize his former parishioner or simply did not care. His ricepaper-textured face remained

392

expressionless. About the padre was that passive resignation of the man passed over by the church hierarchy, by friends, flock and by time itself. There was not even bitterness any more to foul his digestion and twist down the corners of his mouth. There was simply an overwhelming weariness of soul. Father Garcia no longer believed in anything in heaven or on earth or in the realms below, but even this caused no upheaval inside him; he'd never believed very deeply since his seminary years when his idealism had been mulched to hash in the ecclesiastic grinder of commercialism.

'Put down your bags,' he said. 'Put them down. Yolanda will take them to your room. On the third floor I'm afraid. I've lived in this house a long time. Almost thirty-five years. In all that time I don't think we've ever thrown anything away. They'll have one hell of a time cleaning this place up when I die, eh? But, in the meantime, there's not much room to put anything new, not even a person, not even a new priest.'

'It's all right,' Jesus said. 'I don't need much room. Most of my life I've had a cot in a dormitory. A room to myself will be quite a luxury.'

'Yes. Yes. That's what I told Yolanda and Sister Mari-Jean. One reason I was glad to have you here. You wouldn't expect anything extra.'

'I wondered how you'd feel about my coming back here,' Jesus said. He set down his tote bag and guitar case. Yolanda seized them up and scurried from the room.

'Why would I care, one way or the other?'

'I don't know. I wasn't much of a student or convert.'

'I know. That's why I didn't expect anything. I remember you as a boy. I remember you best as a sun spot in the back of the room near the windows. An empty desk. Passive. A cipher.' He shook his head. 'When you were in a room or out of it, you made the same impression.'

Jesus smiled. The old man's head jerked up. 'Don't wink at me. Priests don't wink.'

'Neither do I, sir. It's something left over from smallpox. A weak left upper eyelid. It flutters every time I smile.'

The old priest shook his head. 'Well, you ought to try to control it. It won't look good to the parishioners. But since there's nothing you can do about it, I suppose it doesn't matter. I think you won't find too much to smile about here at Apia.'

'You didn't want me here?'

'Son. . . . Don't get me wrong. I didn't care. I don't care now. What difference can it make? I just hope you manage to like it here. You'll find you have a hell of a lot to do. In this parish. In the church. In this house. In the school and out in the fields. I'm older than God Himself.' He crossed himself. 'Comparatively. I'm just about two steps and a stumble from being put out to pasture.' He shook his head. 'Oh, Christ. I tell you I don't look forward to spending my golden years rotting in some Catholic retirement home for the indigent.'

'I'll try to be of as much help as I can.'

'You certainly will. What the diocese plans to do with me was my number one fret until now. Now I must chafe about leaving my poor flock in your hands. I never saw you care about anything outside yourself in all the years I knew you.'

'I cared. Sometimes I cared.'

'You concealed it well. Tell me something, why did you — of all people — decide upon the priesthood?'

Jesus sighed and decided to joke about it. 'Well, it was on account of you, sir. When I used to work in the fields at Stockton Farms, only you came and went in an automobile, as you wished, when you wished, staying no longer than you had to. You got in out of the sun with great alacrity it seemed to me. You never stooped, except to pray. It seemed an enviable career.'

The old priest remained impassive. accepting Jesus' words at face value. 'Seems as reasonable a motive as any other I've heard and a hell of a lot less involved. Maybe we'll get along better than I hoped. You work hard and keep your nose clean, even if you have to use your whole surplice to do it, and I'll find no fault.'

Jesus smiled, looking away in case his weakened left eyelid winked and offended the old man again. There was a long moment of silence, as if they had exhausted all they had to say to each other, all they ever would have to say to one another.

Father Garcia nodded and spoke, almost as if to himself. 'So. It's true then. I did save you for God as your poor old father used to tell me he wanted. He used to bore hell out of me telling me how you were for the Church and would pray for his soul. He did bring good buckets of honey, though.'

'I'm glad my decision pleased somebody,' Jesus said with a wry smile.

'Oh, I'm sure you'll be a good priest. If there is such a thing as a good priest. I've never been a good priest, and I've known a lot of them and I've never known a really good one, one who lived Christ-like which seems to me the ideal. Never saw anything like it. Only one thing I pride myself upon. I never went into battle with an army, pretending that my presence signified God's endorsement of their goals and methods. I stayed at home. Shelley said it, war is a statesman's game, a priest's delight. Well, it's not my delight. I don't believe in many things, war least of all. I have not endorsed or encouraged or ennobled war. I imagine that's my single achievement as I look back.'

'It could be a lot worse.'

'I doubt it. The establishment believes in war. It's good for business. It weeds out global competition. It kills off swollen populations. Most people find a great many good things to say for war. And you will too, if you want to succeed.'

'Succeed?'

'Aren't you ambitious? Aren't you looking forward to a church in Los Angeles? To become a bishop, a cardinal?'

Jesus shook his head. 'As you don't believe in war, I don't believe in ambition. They sent me here and I'm satisfied.'

Father Garcia leaned forward, unsmiling. 'That's why they sent you here. Because you were satisfied to come. You would have been sent even if you'd been dissatisfied, but it doesn't matter to you and it doesn't matter to the Council. I have been passed over for thirty-five, forty years. You have been passed over. That's why you have been sent here to assist and then replace me. Make up your mind, you'll die here.'

'Well, I'd better start looking for some way to enjoy it, hadn't I?'

'Enjoy it, or hate it, you'll stay here. This is the backwater of the Church conduit. You will be forgotten here. Hell, you are here and you are already forgotten. The Church promotes its own, and you're not one of them. Just as I am not, just as I never was. They promote from their cliques. The hierarchy supports its closest friends. I don't know whom you offended along the way — '

'Probably everybody.'

'Probably.' With that deliberate lack of haste, Father Garcia took up his rimless glasses and hooked them over his ears and across the bridge of his aquiline nose. He took some folded papers from a small drawer in the table beside his chair. He perused them for some moments. 'Here's a report sent from the Holy See concerning you. You told a congregation that God is like a loving parent, forgiving, understanding, forbearing, that God realizes how weak and unlearned even the most brilliant of us is, and He wants to help us as any kindly father would want to help his beloved child who stumbles and falls. You said they were not to worry because it is not God's wish to punish us. . . . What kind of heresy do you call this?'

Jesus smiled and shrugged. 'I just find it hard to believe — no matter what I've been taught by the Church — that true loving parents, like Joseph and Mary for example, parents who suffered so much at the cruel hands of vengeful and unyielding authority, would rear their sons to be vengeful. It goes against commonsense.'

'Christ almighty. Whether it does or not, you can't be naive if you expect to get along inside this Church. And you did choose it as your vocation willingly and of your own free will.'

'I suppose so. It seemed as good as any opened to me. There wasn't a great deal. I had just about grown up orphaned except for the Church.'

'Well, it looks like you'd have learned the simplest truths. Priests don't create the canons of this Church. But we must live by them. . . . I find it very simple to do, and I hope for your sake that you will. Say what the Church wants you to say and let it go at that.'

'Yes. I'm sure you're right.'

'You're damned right I'm right. Never ask a wise man for advice, ask a fool. A fool makes the mistake the wise man avoids, so he can speak from experience.'

'Were you a rebel when you were young?'

'Me?' Father Garcia shook his head. 'Oh, no. Not me. Never. I did as I was told. As far as I am concerned there is but one canon.'

'And what is that, Father?'

'Never makes waves. Never get the bishop's people mad with you. They are never going to promote you, but they can make your existence hell on earth. And they will. Stay out of their way and out of their thoughts if you can. You cannot count on rising in the Church. You have been stuck away here and forgotten. But you can make it easy or difficult to get along inside the see.'

'I'm not ambitious. I won't make trouble. I'll try not to offend you. I am content here.'

'You may as well be.'

2

Jesus sat alone at the window of his room stroking out wisps of love songs from the strings of his guitar, giving only half of his mind to his music while he went back over all the old priest had said to him.

He gazed unseeingly through the open window and smiled faintly, remembering what Father Garcia had said about saving him for the Church as old Manuel O'Brien had wished. He wondered idly what rearrangement of recall permitted the aging priest to make this claim.

Jesus remembered the night he had walked away from Stockton Farms. While no migrant could possibly stray past the farm boundaries without permission, no one had attempted to stop or even delay him. He'd plodded slowly and had seen no one. When he came into Apia, somebody's mongrel bit his ankle and with the pain in his body and the weariness, fatigue and hopelessness, he felt he had to rest before he resumed the night trek.

He recalled the cardboard box of discarded coats and mufflers collected in the cloakroom of the convent school. The church and its grounds were silent. He wrapped a rag around the lacerated ankle and climbed into the classroom through an unlocked window. In the cloakroom he made a mattress of the cast-offs and curled up on it. Sister Ilona found him there the next morning.

The prune-dried nun treated him with a kindliness he'd never suspected in her. She washed his slashed ankle with stinging disinfectant and bound it neatly in gauze. As she worked, she questioned him. After she'd fed him a breakfast of eggs, pancakes and cornflakes with frosty-cold milk, she took him in to Father Garcia.

Father Garcia had slouched in that same tall-backed chair, listening to the nun and growing more ashen by the minute.

397

Father Garcia had not said so, but he had not needed to put into words his fears, that the Stocktons might well disapprove his taking in an exile from the vast estate. If Bonnett Stockton wanted the boy off the big farm, Stockton likely meant he wanted him out of the valley.

'It is the only Christian thing we can do, Father,' the nun said.

'I suppose so. But it's likely one of the biggest mistakes we'll ever make. We're orphans too you know, Sister. We don't live out of our own poor-box. But we might as well.'

'We have enough to share with a homeless boy.'

'Perhaps. But we stand to lose a great deal if we alienate the wrong people. You don't truly think Los Angeles or San Francisco or Rome are really going to help us, do you?'

'You mean financially?'

'What other way is there, Sister? Look, the boy is seventeen. He's old enough to be on his own. Many boys are on their own at his age. What would we do with him around here?'

'He can help us. He's a strong and willing boy. A good boy. And we cannot go on turning our backs, Father.' There was a kind of unspoken threat in the nun's tone; whatever it was, it was not lost upon the priest.

'This is turning the other cheek, Sister, and I'm running out of cheeks to turn. I'm getting too old for games. We need too much. Too much depends on support and friendships of inflential people.'

'What will such people care about one young boy?'

'I don't know, Sister. They cared enough to want to get shed of him. Think about that, Sister.'

'Why should I, Father? Why should both of us fret about it?'

Jesus realized he had strummed his guitar faster and faster as his thoughts and memories flowed like white water, all stirred up in the rapids of this place. Father Garcia had let him stay a month, then he'd told him he'd found, at great inconvenience and difficulty, a place for him at the mission at Ventura.

Sister Ilona had driven him to the nearest bus-stop where he had boarded a Statewide going north. The sister had permitted him to buss her cheek lightly in farewell. She had sat in the old church truck until the bus pulled away. He had looked back and seen her sitting there. He never saw her again. The last time he'd heard of her, she'd been forcibly removed to a Catholic retreat where she was confined mouthing obscenities, lewdness, ribaldry, vulgarity and blasphemy. He'd wanted to visit her, but had been dissuaded. She was cared for well by doctors and nurses; there were many sisters like her up there and she lived as well as could be hoped for one in her condition and, anyway, she wouldn't know him. She didn't know anybody.

Ventura hovered on the brink of the Pacific. Jesus found it beautiful and exotic and pleasant. He worked hard and as his body repaired itself, he felt no more pain from the brutal beating until at last there was only the memory of pain. Leonora faded too from his mind because he knew if he wanted to remain sane, he had to forget her. He never forgot her but he accepted the truth he'd always known: she was not for him, she never had been. She existed in a world he could never enter.

He traded his labour for board, education and clothing. He worked out in the town when the Church found employment for him. He saved his money because he had nothing to spend it on. He studied hard and in a year had completed the high school course at the convent school. He dreaded working as a stoop labourer, a bell-hop in some resort hotel, a sanitation employee, or any of the opportunities open to him. He went to a Catholic university. He worked and studied because he was driven by the fear of sinking to the bottom of the economic ladder, of becoming a migrant worker, a dishwasher. He drifted into the priesthood, passive and placid and unresisting.

He had his problems in the school and in the friary and in the pulpit. He was a man of deep repressions: innate sensuality, passion, fevered restlessness and frustrated cravings that flared in constant conflict with his vows and his vocation. His dreams were haunted. He worked and he studied constantly and he sweated febrilely. He knew the accepted remedies, but rejected all four of them because the only one that appealed to him, led directly to excommunication. The Church was all he had and there was one way to play, by Church rules. And he had only to plunge once into voluptuous excess and indulgence and he well knew he'd drown there. Even when he saw he was shackling himself with those same unnatural repressions and restraints which had sent Sister Ilona into a padded cell crying out that forbidden word so dear to her in heart-rending anguish, there was no other way for him, as there had been no alternative for the good sister.

He had no idea how fiercely he was battering at the guitar strings until the pounding at his door intruded into his consciousness and brought him to his feet.

The Mexican housekeeper stood there smiling and shaking her head. 'It is the wish of the priest that I deliver a message to you, sir. The father says will you please cut out that goddamn cat yowling or move back to Ventura?'

XXX

Jesus went out to the converted barn classroom, disturbed by a strange sensation, almost as if he were a child again, and nothing had changed here, as if the teacher were Sister Ilona and not the youthful, ardent and eager young Sister Mari-Jean.

The faces of the children were all the same faces and he had the odd feeling that he could give them the old names and he would be right. His gaze sought his desk in the sun near the window. The boy slouched there was larger than his class-mates, remote, withdrawn. Jesus felt the hairs stand in hackles across the nape of his neck.

He stood, silent, beside the teacher's desk, his battered guitar case in his hand. Sister Mari-Jean held up her arm for silence and, truly looking at her for the first time, he saw that she was indeed not like Sister Ilona in the least. Life had turned Sister Ilona to vinegar inside. No repression, restraint or inhibition yet stiffened Mari-Jean's apple cheeks, or calmed the dancing in her blue eyes. When the fabric of her habit tautened across her bosom, Jesus saw she was lavishly endowed and he put himself doubly on guard.

He heard her speaking. 'Children, this is father Jesus O'Brien, who will be assistant pastor to the good father Garcia. Father O'Brien has generously offered to assist me in teaching some of our classes. I hope you will make him welcome.'

The brown faces, turned up like sunflower blooms, smiled. Sister Mari-Jean said, 'I've heard you play your guitar, Father. You're very good.'

Jesus smiled and winked broadly at the class. 'Sister has just revealed that she is totally tone deaf and knows nothing of music.'

The children laughed, as if released suddenly from invisible

401

straitjackets. Sister Mari-Jean was unperturbed by his teasing. She sat down behind her desk and said, 'Maybe Father O'Brien will play for us. We can inaugurate our new class in music appreciation this morning. We'll let the classroom decide how good you are, Father.'

'The walls may fall in on us,' he warned, removing the guitar and pick, setting the case aside. He leaned against the desk, half-sitting upon it, facing the classroom. He began to play, first a sacred song, then one less sacred, another faintly classical and then surged into a medley of popular love songs, ending with the sensational new novelty, 'Yes, We Have No Bananas.'

The children were laughing and wriggling at their desks before he had finished, and when he stopped playing they burst into applause.

'You've made quite an impression,' Sister Mari-Jean said. She had come around the desk and stood beside him. 'I wonder if we can get them quieted down for arithmetic?'

'That's my problem,' Jesus said, smiling at her. 'I never know if God is with me, or the devil is after me.'

'God is with you,' Sister Mari-Jean said. 'Don't worry about that. God is with you.'

2

At Mass four weeks later, Jesus played his guitar at the services, adding it to the wheezing emanations from the asthmatic organ which was far older than even Father Garcia.

The good priest would never have permitted the godless guitar into his church, but the sounds from the organ pipes only vaguely resembled the notes punched into them, and Sister Mari-Jean, when he called her in to protest at the sounds of music and laughter rising from the schoolroom, told him that her classes had grown since Father O'Brien started teaching with her. Part of that growth had to be attributed to the music. The children responded, they came alive at the delight of it; they told their friends and the fame of the school spread.

'Are you saying the children can learn — in all that confusion and chaos and caterwauling?'

'I say they are learning as they never learned before, Father. Willingly. They suffer through maths, agonize through English, speed through history, just to get to music appreciation.'

'Ah, so that's the fancy name you've given this heathen display, is it?'

Sister Mari-Jean nodded, smiling. 'That's what we call it. And that's what it is, Father. It's like we're living in a new world of learning out there — a place where learning suddenly is fun and exciting.'

'Sounds like the teacher herself might be enchanted by this guitar-strumming piper.'

'The children love him, Father Garcia,' was all she would say. 'If Father O'Brien played the church music — '

'He does play. The organ.'

'No one can get music from that organ, Father. You know that. There's nothing sinful, or irreligious about the guitar. Its music can be just as holy. Why don't you try it and see?'

'I'll tell you why I don't. And why I won't. The bishop's spies are just lying in wait for me to do something like that.'

There vibrated a sprightliness, a lightheartedness in the church that first morning Father Garcia reluctantly permitted Jesus to supply guitar music for the hymns. They were the same sombre old spirituals Father Garcia recognized and felt comfortable with. But the atmosphere glowed with something new and discomfiting that the head priest was not sure he approved. And God help him, the bishop's spies would have him on the carpet, in the rack, up before their modern version of the Inquisition. Still, looking down at those beaming faces of his congregation and at the gentle humanity and warmth and goodness of the fine and beautiful young assistant priest, Father Garcia felt a new fire in his own aged heart. 'To hell with the bishop,' he thought. 'I can always claim senility.'

Father Garcia waited for the axe to fall upon his scrawny old neck in the weeks that followed, and when it did not, he attributed his security to the fact that the diocese had forgotten him. They no longer cared what he did.

He did not end the experiment of music during the services, and for a very good reason. The second week the congregation filled the first six rows instead of the first three. The third week, a whole section was filled and in six weeks there was a full congregation, even at early Mass.

Father Garcia was careful. He never spoke a word of praise to the younger priest. He never commented in his company about the growth of the congregation, nor did he mention the increase in the collections. It was not his intention to be cruel or neglectful. He still anticipated trouble from Los Angeles, and when that came he wanted to be separated from the actual culprits. He had long ago learned that the bishop's investigators would believe anything they wanted to believe. They would accept any explanation that they could live with and reconcile with Church policy.

Those were dire months of initiation for Father O'Brien. He officiated at weddings of ordinary communicants. He performed burial ceremonies in the paupers' graveyards. He was sent in the church Model T sedan when a bracero slashed himself or someone else in the fields. Jesus returned with an empty sense of trepidation to the ploughed lands of the Stockton estates. He felt like a trespasser, but no one confronted him. The migrants changed each year; the crops were rotated, but the braceros were ever strangers, coming north in new waves. Even those overseers who had been at the farm when he left five years ago appeared not to recognize him. He didn't believe he had changed that much. On the other hand, as Father Garcia assured him, he made only a slight impression on people, and perhaps all the brown Latin faces came to look alike to impersonal, dehumanized foremen, most of whom these days carried guns, as convict guards might. When he asked about guns, he got only a shrug. 'There's a threat of trouble, Father. We got to be ready for it, that's all.'

One Sunday, a covey of giggling Mexican girls awaited Father O'Brien outside the church. They surrounded him. They had asked permission to invite the young priest to play his guitar at the parties in the migrant camps after dark. 'Why would you want me there?' he said. 'A priest? I'd only cramp your style. I'd put a crimp in all your fun.'

'Not you,' they cried. 'You're not like other priests.'

He sighed and didn't even bother to argue that one.

He finally agreed to come one night, perhaps in the middle of the week, if Father Garcia consented. He would see. Perhaps after he had been once to their firelight fiesta, they would ask him no more. He remembered, with some inner heat, those parties of his boyhood.

He threw himself into his work with all the tamped-down fire and energy in him. He felt a deep compassion for the people he worked among, and when he was able to relieve their grief and burdens even for a little while, he felt a rewarding sense of exaltation. He counted himself lucky to be as free as he was, with an opportunity to expend the dynamic forces boiling within him for which there were no other acceptable outlets. Work of any kind relieved the fearful pressures inside him. The more tired he became, the less thinking he did. He looked forward to nothing; he accepted his position placidly and passively. To the world he seemed the most serene and calm of men. He thanked God he could stay busy.

He answered a midnight call at the Stockton migrant shacks with a sense of release. The Mexican housekeeper climbed to the third floor and wakened him. 'Three men at the door, Father,' Yolanda said. 'There is trouble at the labour camp. I didn't waken Father Garcia. He's so tired. He needs his rest.'

'That was thoughtful of you, Yolanda.' Jesus smiled, knowing he winked involuntarily. 'You go back to bed. I'll let myself out, and I'll let myself back in. You needn't stay up.'

Three Mexicans, awed with the terror of their mission, met him on the front porch. They went silently out to the barn and one of them insisted upon cranking the Model T. They rode in silence with Jesus through the night.

Lights burned in several of the migrant shacks and a silent knot of men and women gathered in the road. Jesus parked the Ford. No foremen were in sight. Jesus remembered this was policy, let the migrants kill each other as long as they showed up at work call. One of the Mexican braceros led him to the front door of a shanty, but would go no further.

Jesus knocked on the door. From within he could hear a baby's sobbing, a woman crying. A man's voice shouted, drunk and raging. 'Who is it? Go away.'

Jesus said, 'It is Father O'Brien. I would like to talk to you.'

'Well, I don't want to talk to you, you pious son bitch. You have one job up here, keep the workers in line, meek and obedient. Well, I ain't meek and I ain't obedient and I got nothing to say to you.'

'Well, I have something to say to you,' Jesus said. He tried the screen door. When he found it locked, he yanked on the handle, jerking it open. The knot of people gathered in the road cheered.

When he entered the house, he wished he had not. He willed himself away, miles away. It was as if he had stepped back in time to those years when he and Teodoro came into the Aliso Street house and found Tio Pedro beating Tia Clara with his fists and kicking her in the breasts and belly with his boots.

At the sight of the battered woman, Jesus shivered and a kind of outrage burned through him. It was mindless anger, not directed at this man at all but at Tio Pedro. It was as if he saw his uncle's face instead of that of the sweating and belligerent bracero.

The woman lay on the floor, whimpering, in her own blood. It looked as if her nose were broken; it bled profusely. Her mouth was torn. Her arms and shoulders were bruised and lacerated.

Jesus had to fight against the fury that swelled up in him, the hatred that moiled and rose up inside his empty belly.

He managed to speak in a cold flat tone. He ignored the man who stood poised, fists clenched at his sides, balanced on dirty bare feet. He said to the woman, 'Do you wish a doctor?'

She managed to shake her head. 'I don't need a medico, Father. I have been beaten before — '

'And she'll be beaten again,' the man said, only in Jesus' ears it was not the Mexican's drunken voice at all, but the bitterly recalled tones of Tio Pedro. 'She is my woman. I beat her if I wish.'

'Don't let him hit me any more. Blood fills my mouth and my nose. It is that I cannot breathe.' The woman lifted her head, whispering, choking.

'Shit,' the man said. 'The bitch is lying.'

Jesus managed to shrug as if he had no interest. 'Perhaps. But she does not want you to beat her any more.'

'Who's to stop me, Padre? You going to stop me?'

'If I have to,' Jesus said.

'Don't try it, Padre,' the man said. 'I've never hit a priest. I don't want to hit a priest.'

'No one has to be hit any more,' Jesus said. 'If you will help her up, tend her bleeding, get her and the baby into bed, we will say no more about it. If I have to come back, I will not be so lenient.'

'Don't come here telling me how to treat my woman,' the man said.

'I'm telling you. Tend her. Don't hit her any more.'

'A dama expects her man to hit her.'

'She says she doesn't. Or she has had too much. No more.'

'She likes it, Padre. All women like it. They know then they got a man.' Listening to the braceros, Jesus felt a sense of dizziness, as if this were the house off Aliso Street and that voice Tio Pedro's voice. 'You know nothing of such things, Priest. How can you know? You who know no women? What can you know?'

'I know this must stop,' Jesus managed to say in a level tone.

'Why? A woman must be beaten if she is to respect her man. She respects only a man's fists and a man's hard cock that gives her the good horsefucking that every woman must get in order to keep her in line, working and behaving herself and obedient to her husband who is her master.'

Jesus spread his hands and shook his head. 'I've heard that all my life, but I don't believe it. If it was ever true, it is the way of the past.'

The man's face twisted in contempt. 'Are you going to change our people and our ways, Padre?'

'If I have to.'

'Eh?' This amused the bracero. 'And how will you do that?'

'We will start here. In this house. You and I. We will learn what it means to be beaten, as our women are beaten. We will be able to go about telling others of the pain where there is no pleasure, of the agony where there is no relief. We will learn much to say.' He smiled as he spoke and the husband was deceived by the faint winking of the priest's left eye. When the bracero feinted in swift reflex and caught at Jesus' doubled left hand, the priest drove his right fist deep under the man's belt.

When the bracero doubled over, retching, Jesus hit him in the face, breaking his nose so blood spurted. As the man weaved, gagging and moaning, Jesus hit him in each temple. The bracero lost control of his bladder and wet his pants helplessly. Jesus kept hitting him relentlessly, but without passion or fury until the husband lay mewling on the floor.

Jesus stood over him, his knuckles raw and his arms aching.

407

He forced himself to smile, kept his voice level. 'If I must come again into your house, I will not be so easy on you.'

The agonized, sobered man stared up from the floor. 'Kill me,' he muttered. 'Or I kill you, Priest. You humiliate me, humble me before my woman. You leave me nothing. I will not forgive. I will kill you.'

3

Jesus' ministry, which had started in a mildly promising way, now began a swift and exciting augmentation, carrying Jesus along with it in all sorts of diverging directions. More and more the communicants brought their problems to the Church, to young Father O'Brien, asking for him at the front door of the manse. His experiences had been limited by poverty, by deprivation, by working from childhood and by his own passive and incurious acceptance of what was going on around him. Suddenly he found that ordinary human beings faced crises and situations in their everyday lives that he had never dreamed of in heaven or on earth or even the outskirts of hell. He sat stunned, slack-jawed at the flat recitation of discord and deviation he'd never suspected in human existence and which he was asked extemporaneously to meditate.

The days of indecision and the nights of self-doubt were finished for Jesus for the simple reason that he had little time for introspection, for looking back, for regretting or even dreaming ahead. Once daydreams had sustained him when the reality of existence threatened to overwhelm him. Now, the casual events of the day resembled the most disturbing of a restless night's inventions.

Shortly after his emergency call to the shack of the migrant worker Ramon Perez and his wife, Jesus got into the old Model T touring car and drove over to the camp at the dinner-hour. He hoped to talk with Ramon; if he had to endure invective, he was prepared; if an apology were demanded, he would offer it. He wanted to know that Ramon's wife was better treated. He wanted to wipe the ugly memory of his fury from his mind, because only part of his rage had been directed towards Ramon.

He was not to be released from guilt or concern so easily. A new family occupied the shack where Ramon had battered his wife. One of the neighbours who had summoned the priest during the violence at the Perez house shook his head when Jesus inquired. 'Ramon took his Lupe back to Mexico. He demanded that the patrono release him. He said the ways of the Americano undermined the stability of the Latin family. He would not live exposed to such vile godlessness. Finally, el patrono called the deputy jefe Pedro Luiz, and Ramon and his wife were driven away in the deputy's car. They have not been seen again, nor has any word been heard of them. One supposes they are back across the border.'

Jesus crossed himself. 'One hopes so,' he said.

More and more, Father Garcia delegated his own duties to the younger priest. The elder padre seemed not to know how many parishioners requested audience with the assistant pastor. He turned over the chore of hearing confessions to Jesus.

Jesus disliked this most of all. He felt imprisoned, confined in the booth which seemed constructed for pigmies. There was never the breath of fresh air, only the stench of soured humanity, the garlic breath, the cheap cologne, the acrid musk. Worse, there was the sense of embarrassment he felt for the poor frightened souls who sought release and absolution without atonement in that cubicle. He thought with some irony that he was pleased to be able to spare God the pettiness of most of the entreaties and revelations. The ones with the most to confess said the least. He was left to infer truths at which they barely hinted. The poor devils certain they'd sinned were only those with the most puritanical consciences. One was shocked at what some human beings considered mortal sin. They were the ones with the searching questions. They all had questions and he was the only one who had no answers.

This late afternoon, months after his return to Apia, he left the church after hearing a dozen confessions and intoning admonitions designed to sting the imagination of the confessor. They wanted to believe they atoned for sin; it was his duty to convince them this was so. And, always in the back of his mind was Father Garcia's counsel to him, 'Say what the Church wants you to say and let it go at that.'

He entered his bedroom, opened the window to the still

dusk, removed his collar and jacket. He was unbuttoning his shirt when Yolanda knocked at the door and presented a fourteen-year-old boy, slender and reluctant, but not prepared to be sent away.

Yolanda closed the door and the boy stood staring at the priest, his black eyes liquid and warm. 'I have just made my confession, Father, but there was something else I could not say,' he began.

'I'm afraid the confessional's the place for those things one cannot say.'

'No. I could not be overheard. Please. Hear what I have to say.'

Jesus shrugged, wondering what choice he had. One truth continued to amaze him, how inflexible were the meek. They bowed and apologized, but they never retreated. He smiled to himself and sat by one of the open windows, watching the boy. 'Sit down,' he said. 'We may as well be comfortable.'

'I can never be comfortable again, Father O'Brien. I have committed a terrible sin. Against purity. Against God. It is so awful that I could not speak of it where I might have been overheard by any but you.'

'What have you done?'

'I have fallen in love. I am obsessed with it.'

'We all fall in love, sooner or later.'

'This is a forbidden love, Father.'

'You have fallen in love with an older woman? She is married?'

'It is nothing like that, Father. Nothing. Bless me, Father, for I have sinned. Help me, Father, for I am damned. In God's name, help me. For only you can help me.'

Jesus caught his breath and stared at the boy in the shadowed room. The youth's eyes were filled with tears; he clenched and released his fists, his body quivered. The atmosphere of this place suddenly sickened Jesus. He knew what he was about to hear. He had heard professions of passion before, in the friary at Ventura, in dormitory rooms at the university, on campus knolls, in cars.

He began to shake his head. 'I don't want to hear this, Alfonso,' he said. 'If you wish to confess, you must ask to see Father Garcia. This is nothing for you to say to me.'

The boy trembled and sank to his knees, weeping. He began to crawl across the floor on his knees. Jesus watched him in pity, in distaste, in a kind of sick horror.

'I can think of nothing else, Father. I am in love with a man. The most beautiful of men. The most wonderful man. I beg you, let me work here at the church. I will do the most menial of jobs. I ask nothing but to be near you. Please. My life will end. I will live only in agony. Forgive me, Father, but it is you I love.'

'Listen to me,' the priest said. 'This is a phase you are going through. You are confused.'

'No. I know what I want. I know what I am inside. God help me. Father, help me. Forgive me, Father. Love me, Father. Bless me, Father, let me live in the pleasure and safety of your shadow. It is only there, on my knees in adoration before your shadow that I can find the ecstasy of existence. You must help me. I have dreamed of you. I am haunted by you. Possessed by you. It is what I want of life. It is all I want of life.'

Jesus went on watching him, sickened. He thought of other youths like him, the hot fevered afternoons, all of them wanting something from him, something he would not and could not give. The boy went on talking, pleading, babbling, until suddenly he cried out and slumped, face down, gasping, his head on his arms.

Jesus stood up and walked to the door. 'I have chores,' he said. 'I am going out. You need not confess. You may leave when you wish. We will say no more about this. It may be of some small comfort to you that we all love, rightly or wrongly, and not all of us are loved in return. But this is not to say we are wrong to love. Sometimes it is the object of our love that is wrong for us, not our love. I know that is no help to you, but it is the best answer I have.'

XXXI

About fifteen months later, Father O'Brien sat in an old leather chair in the vestry or sacristy which had come to be used at Apia as the chapel when services separate from ordinary ceremonies were required. The young man sitting in a small pew with a Mexican girl was not a Catholic, and this was why they were gathered here.

They had been verbally sparring for some moments without ever reaching any point that Jesus could settle on. At last he said, 'Vera, why don't you walk into the church? You might wish to burn a candle. Maybe Homer would then find it easier to tell me what it is he wants.'

When they were alone, the blond young man found it no easier to talk to the priest. There was more than distrust, there was discomfort and dismay. Looking at Homer Bates, Jesus found his mind slipping back across the years to that time when he and Pedrillo had played pirates and Indians with Hubert Milhaus at the now-vanished ranchito of Manuel O'Brien. In many ways young Homer reminded him of the long-lost Hubert. Homer was stolid and blond-headed, not slow-witted, but no genius either.

He explained once more that he had fallen in love with Vera when she came to work as a maid in the home his parents had recently built in the valley. At first there had been great disapproval from his family, but when he finally convinced them that he loved Vera, and would never love anyone else, Anglo or Latin, and they gave their reluctant blessing, he then found the Church standing like a vast immovable barrier between him and happiness.

'My folks want me to go back to Iowa and forget Vera. I can't do that. But it looks like I can't marry Vera, either, because she won't — she says God will not permit her to marry outside what she calls The Church.'

412

'And what do you wish me to do, Hubert? Do you wish me to speak for God and to give you His blessing?'

'I want you to give me instructions.'

'What?'

'That's what Vera says it will take. Instructions. Teach me how to be a Catholic.'

'You wish to convert to Catholicism?'

'It ain't what I wish, Reverend Father. That has nothing to do with it, it seems. What I want is to marry Vera as quickly and totally as I can. That's why I want you to instruct me in being a Catholic and then I can join her church and we can get married and get on with our lives.'

'But you have no great wish to be a Catholic?'

'I got nothing against it, Father. I've heard a lot about what it means to be a Roman Catholic, but I never paid any attention. And anyway, I don't care. I just want to be allowed to marry Vera.'

'I don't think you ought to.'

'My God! You too? What have you got against me? Why shouldn't I marry Vera just because I happen to be Lutheran and not Catholic?'

'I believe if you truly love Vera, and at this moment you certainly seem sincere enough, you should marry her.'

'Why did you say you didn't think I ought to?'

'I don't think you ought to convert to Catholicism, Homer. Listening to you, I find you as sincere in opposing it, even while you plead.'

'Oh my God. Excuse me, Father. But for God's sake, don't put new rocks in the way. I'm willing to be a Catholic. I'm willing to be anything just so Vera and I can get married. Look, let me say it as plain as I can. I love Vera. I want to marry Vera. So I want to be a Catholic, and I want you to help me do it.'

'I don't think we need you as a Catholic, Homer. That's what I'm trying to tell you. We've got enough half-assed Catholics. Forget being Catholic. Be whatever you are, whatever you want to be, to the best you can.'

'I want to marry Vera.'

'You can marry Vera. Here. In this chapel. Not in the church, but here. The ceremony will be binding, it will join you. You might agree to let Vera raise your children as Catholics. This ought to please her and satisfy the Church.'

413

'You mean if Vera agrees, it's that easy?'

'If Vera agrees.'

Before Homer could grasp Jesus' hands in his own and gasp out his appreciation, Yolanda appeared at the vestry door. 'It's Father Garcia, sir. He says he wishes you as soon as convenient. But I can tell you, sir, he means at once.'

Jesus smiled and thanked the housekeeper. They called Vera in. She listened solemnly, but was less than sure that her marriage could be blessed if her husband remained outside the Church. Only Father O'Brien's assurances convinced her. They wanted to thank him effusively and lingeringly. They wanted to discuss plans for a wedding ceremony as quickly as such rites could be arranged, but he had to excuse himself. He left them standing together, holding hands and beaming at each other. As he hurried away, he said a little prayer that in ten years they would still regard each other as warmly. Maybe remembering how hard it had been to get together might bind them tighter.

As he entered the musty, book-lined study of the manse, Jesus saw that the old priest was not alone. With an electric shock that almost stunned him for an instant, he recognized Bonnett Stockton. The elderly priest sat in his tall-backed chair, stained and indented with the imprint of his body, the reading lamp beside him. The landowner slouched in a club chair placed by a window in a shard of sunlight. Jesus walked slowly into the room.

He felt young, helpless, impotent and doomed again, all those sensibilities of his boyhood, revived by the presense of the patrono. The sight of Leonora's father fermented everything, stirring it through Jesus' mind, the good, the thrilling, the evil, the hurting. In the space of a breath it was if his life flashed before his mind's eye, as if he were drowning in old agonies and unforgotten losses.

He exhaled. Bonnett Stockton had not changed much in six years. He looked lean and hard and suntanned, his well-fed cheeks and jaws leathered by sun and wind and rain. If anything, he appeared more distinguished than ever, in hand-tooled boots, casual Scotch tweed jacket, slacks and silk shirt, open at the collar.

'I'm sorry, Father,' Jesus said. 'I didn't know you had a visitor.'

Both men stirred enough to look up at him. There seemed

414

no recognition or interest in Stockton's chiselled face. All these years Jesus had wondered what the patrono's response would be to his returning to the San Gabriel Valley and there was nothing. Stockton's steel-hard eyes betrayed no emotion, no real awareness. His gaze raked across the dark-suited young priest and discarded him.

Jesus sighed because nothing could have satisfied him more.

With a slow and deliberate movement, Father Garcia sat forward in his chair and waved his arm in a gesture that included his guest. 'That's all right, O'Brien,' Father Garcia said. 'I sent for you.'

Jesus nodded. 'But I thought you were alone. I wouldn't have barged in.' His empty-bellied need to apologize for his very existence was as old and as hateful as his acquaintance-ship with the man in that club chair. He felt ill at ease in Stockton's presence, as if he were alien, an intruder, as if he did not belong and never could. He hated himself for feeling that way, but he could not help it.

'We wanted you here,' Father Garcia said. Jesus cast a puzzled glance toward Bonnett Stockton. He found no trace of interest in that cold face. The landowner nodded but avoided meeting Jesus's gaze.

'We were discussing the impending strike,' Stockton said. 'We are expecting bad trouble at the farm. There have been outbreaks in San Jauquin, Imperial, even up in the grape country. A lot of unrest. I dropped by here to find out what support I could expect from the Church.'

'What would you expect us to do?' Jesus heard his own flat, unnatural voice.

'I think Father Garcia understands my position. Father Garcia and I are old friends. Very old friends. I think we understand each other, eh, Father?'

'Oh, precisely.' Father Garcia nodded his head.

'I will do whatever the Church wants, whatever Father Garcia tells me to do,' Jesus said. 'Naturally.'

'Naturally,' Stockton said, nodding.

'It's just that I'm not sure what role we — the Church — can play — what part we would be expected to play.'

Stockton's voice hardened. 'Well, I'm certain Father Garcia can explain the role of the Church in these matters. But perhaps out here in Apia, where we are so close to the

415

people, and the people are almost entirely Catholic, members of this church, your role can be much greater than in other areas.'

'We've never had any troubles here,' Father Garcia said.

'And we don't want any,' Stockton replied as if they recited some litany.

'If the people are patient,' Father Garcia said, 'troubles resolve themselves. I've always seen that. I'm sure we shall see that now.'

Stockton nodded, but sounded less than convinced. 'I'm sure we shall, Father. But I believe it might be wise to base your sermons on obedience, on the role of the meek on the face of this earth, of the kind of forbearance the Church expects of its children. A great deal of trouble can be avoided in advance if the people are prepared correctly by their church leaders, if the example of the Church is one of patience and obedience to law.'

'What kind of troubles are we talking about?' Jesus said. Neither of the other men had suggested he sit down; he remained standing just inside the doorway, his hands at his sides.

'Haven't you been reading the newspapers?' Stockton said. 'It's in all the newspapers. Labour unions. Pinko communists. They're behind it. Illiterate migrants, a lot of them wetbacks, with nothing to lose, are easy to rouse up. They cause the trouble, the losses. Then the illegals are gone, back across the border, and the farms are left with the losses, the destroyed crops, the spoilage, the lost harvests. These migrants are led to believe that these pinkos are working for them. Hell, anybody with commonsense knows better than that. You could give the illegals what the agitators demand. Or you could have them all deported. It wouldn't matter. There's thousands more next season.'

'What is it you want?' Jesus asked, voice low.

'It's what I don't want,' Stockton answered, as if he were speaking to Father Garcia. 'I don't want trouble. We don't need trouble. We've never had it. We don't need it now. We furnish transportation, housing, food and medical care. We pay the going rate for stoop labourers.'

'What is it the labour unions want?'

'Who the hell knows what those pinko commies want? It's like a contagion. Trouble started back east. Factory workers that had to organize. There were riots and death and fires and damage in the millions. There was real and actual warfare in the wheat fields, whole crops were burned by vandals who came in, owned nothing, had nothing to lose, stirred up trouble, and then walked away, leaving devastation and waste behind them. Crops destroyed. Farms in bankruptcy. A whole economy torn down by people who have nothing, own nothing and want to take everything.'

'Whatever I can do to assist you, Mr Stockton,' Father Garcia said. 'You have only to call on me.'

'I know that, Father Garcia. We've counted on you and your loyal support for a long time out here. But it hasn't been a one-way street for us. We have supported you. We have responded in supporting this church every time we've been approached. We've had a long friendship, a long understanding. We are strong. We shall stand against these vandals and pinkos. But we realize the tremendous power of the Church in the hearts and minds of these Mexicans. We can't make them see that we're doing everything we can for them, as much, more than we can afford. They are illegals, without rights, and yet we treat them fairly. I think if the Church told them this, they would see it best. They might be harder to rouse up against law and order.'

'We shall base all our sermons, all our counsel on patience, on the duty of good people to follow the dictates of their Church and their leaders, to live by the commands of the Bible, to obey their superiors, to be thankful for their daily bread, to accept their fate, to make no trouble against those who would aid and succour them.' Father Garcia stood up, quite emotionally moved by his own mini-sermon. He smiled and nodded towards the landowner. He kept nodding.

Bonnett Stockton stood up. 'I was sure we understood each other, Father. The important thing is that we all understand each other.' Now, for the first time he looked toward Jesus, his gaze striking hard against the young priest's. 'Preach obedience to these people. Preach it for their own good. We can be as rough as any rag-tag army of labour agitators. But we don't want it that way. We don't believe in violence at Stockton Farms. Violence is always a last resort with us. But we can use violence if we are driven to it. We have before, and we will again.'

XXXII

When the telephone rang, Father Garcia was preparing his Sunday sermon based on a verse from the Book of Job. Father Garcia was of the generation which feared and mistrusted the telephone, but since his housekeeper was of his age too, though he waited, Yolanda did not take the receiver from the hook. Finally, she even called out to him, 'Telephone, Father.'

The caller was Bragg Stockton. The ageing landowner's voice was terse and demanding. 'Sons o' bitching agitators comin' onto our land, Father. Got the word just now. Think you and young O'Brien ought to get out among your people. Try to keep them calm. We don't want anybody hurt, Father. But we are not going to lose our crops, either.'

Troubled, Father Garcia mumbled some words of assent and replaced the receiver on its hook. He sent Yolanda hurrying across the churchyard for Father O'Brien and Sister Mari-Jean.

'We want you children to leave school quietly,' Sister Mari-Jean told her classroom. 'Go to your homes. You have the rest of the day off.'

'There may be some trouble in the farm fields,' Father O'Brien cautioned. 'Stay away. If we see any of you there, you will be kept after classes for two weeks, starting tomorrow.'

The children departed noisily, leaving behind a tension that crackled in the silence. When Jesus started from the school and Sister Mari-Jean followed at his heels, he said, 'Do you think you should come along, Sister?'

'Perhaps *you* should not go,' she said.

He glanced over his shoulder and gave her a chilly laugh. 'Don't tempt me. You give me an excuse to stay here and I'll stay.'

418

'Well, I won't.'

'That's because you're naturally a belligerent.'

She smiled. 'If there is violence, they'll need a nurse.'

'If they need someone to stand helplessly, I'll be there.' Jesus tried to smile, but he admitted inside that he was serious. He dreaded violence, he had no sympathy for the planters, he had no wish to see migrant workers get their skulls bashed in.

He went out to the converted lean-to stable and cranked the Model T Ford touring car. By the time he returned in it to the manse, Father Garcia and Sister Mari-Jean, in straw sombreros, stood in the drive awaiting him. Sister Mari-Jean carried a wide-brimmed hat for him. He pushed it down on his head and thanked her.

They did not speak on the drive to the intersection of the Los Angeles highway and the county road which penetrated deep across Stockton property.

Two dozen men — most of them Anglos — and some in cars with out-of-state licences, gathered in preliminary council at the road intersection. Jesus parked near their cars. Sister Mari-Jean and Father Garcia got out at once, but Jesus sat for a long beat gripping the steering wheel.

'Who are you people?' A stout man, in his forties, wearing levis and denim shirt, hobbled toward them in painful, runover boots. He tongued a cigar to the corner of his mouth, surveying them disapprovingly. 'Muh name's Salinksy, Father,' he said. 'Rodney L. Salinsky. What you folks want here?'

'We come in the name of peace,' Father Garcia said.

Rodney Salinsky laughed. 'Then you've come to the wrong place, Padre. You folks ought to go back to your church and wait there. In all sincerity I suggest you do that.'

Father Garcia shook his head. 'I'm sure you are friendly and sincere, Mr Salinsky. But we'll stay. We'll try not to get in your way.'

The labour leader winced. 'Look, Padre. We got troubles enough without you three, like some agents of a disapproving Church, here to weaken the wills of these people. A strike is all in their own interests. What we are doing is for them. But if we can't get them to work with us, whole-hearted, well, you can see we can't do a lot for them.'

'Why do you object to our presence — as the clergy?'

Father Garcia asked.

'Of the Catholic Church?' Salinsky shook his head. 'Come on, Father. I'm a Catholic. I was. Polish Catholic. Let's not try to con each other. You and I are old hands at this. The whole, main and approved goal of the Catholic Church is to keep the poor docile, uncomplaining and full of the fear of God and authority. Why else would governments write off billions of dollars in Catholic Church taxes every year? Because it's cheap at twice the price, that's why. The Catholic Church is one of the best tools known to capitalism to enslave and exploit the poor.'

'Do you have some kind of open line to God denied to me?' Father O'Brien inquired with some irony.

'Look, Padre. I'd like to stand here and engage you in a philosophical discussion. But I got no time. We got twenty trucks coming out here this morning from L.A. We going to block these farm roads. No farm trucks get out until the landowners agree at least to talk with us. Things could get unpleasant. You could get hurt. That's my concern. It's no place for you two men of the cloth and the good sister.'

'Sounds like exactly where we belong,' Sister Mari-Jean said.

Salinsky ignored the nun. 'You get in our way. You try to work against us, or stop us, Father, and there are men among us who have no fear of attacking the turned collar of the Roman Church. None. They'll treat you just like they'd treat any other scabs, strike-breakers or rich farmers. As our enemy.'

Father Garcia nodded, but did not retreat. By now four or five other men had joined in a sombre knot, facing them. Father Garcia studied their sweating faces and cold, deadly eyes. His question was almost casual. 'Do any of you gentlemen speak the language of these migrants and illegals?'

'What do you mean?' one of the men said.

'Well, these nationals call their language Spanish, sir. But it is a polyglot — Indian, Spanish and some Americanisms. If you cannot speak their language, how do you expect to communicate with them?'

Rodney Salinsky exhaled heavily, sweat streaking from his felt hat brim down across his cheeks. 'Look, Father. We appreciate your concern. But we didn't come out here unprepared. We got our own people stoop-labouring among these migrants right now. When our trucks get out here from Los Angeles and when the loaded farm vans try to leave, we'll be able to communicate. Believe me, we'll be able to handle it. For the last time, I'm warning you folks to clear out. You won't do that, stand well back.'

Two late-model black Buick sedans raced along the highway, were braked and were brought to a screeching, rubber-burning halt in the middle of the road a few feet from where Salinsky stood. Two men were in each car and the four emerged as one and strode towards Salinsky.

'Bad news, Rod,' one of them said.

'Where are the trucks you men promised me?' Salinsky asked.

The newcomer spread his hands. 'That's the problem, Rod. The trucks are going to be here. It's that I can't say when. There'll be some delay. The minute one of our trucks turns out onto the San Gabriel Valley highway from Los Angeles, the California highway patrol begins to stop and ticket them. Five miles down the road, and another highway patrol roadblock. And another ticket.'

'The bastards.' Salinsky chewed at his cigar, sweating. 'Well, we knew we were up against rich and powerful planters out here.' He shrugged. 'Nobody said it would be easy.'

'We're just beginning to find out what kind of political influence and establishment power we're fighting,' the newcomer said. 'These people own the legislators, the courts, the police and the governor.'

Salinsky shrugged again. 'Well, Teddy boy. They ain't stopped us yet. So, our strike will be delayed.' He paused, scowling. 'The highway patrol ain't turning your trucks back, are they?'

Ted L. Ross shook his head. 'They weren't as we came out . Not so far. Just delay and harass and intimidate. We've warned our drivers not even to talk back to a highway patrolman. That's what the patrol is looking for — an excuse to use clubs, impound our trucks and indict for resisting arrest.'

The labour men returned slowly to the shade offered by their open cars. At last the Buicks were removed from the right-of-way and parked with the other vehicles along the shoulders of the road. No one seemed very excited, although tensions crackled in the air. The men remained quiet and calm. They were old hands at this. For many of them it was simply another job. Some had never even heard the fancy word crusade.

The first empty trucks began to arrive. Salinsky wasted no time going into action. He lined up the trucks, as they pulled in, to form a barricade across the Stockton property access road.

Two dozen trucks arrived at last, one by one, shadowed by two dozen police vehicles, motorcycles or patrol cars. Defiantly, Salinsky went from truck to truck, collecting the police citations. He had two fistfuls by the time he was through.

Making a ceremony of it, he walked to the middle of the roadway, heaped the papers, now wadded in balls to keep them from blowing away, into a pile and set fire to them with a smelly cigarette lighter.

The senior patrol officer stalked out to the small pyre in the middle of the road. He wrote a citation and thrust it out toward the labour agitator. Salinsky accepted it with a polite bow, wadded it up and threw it into the guttering flames. The two men stood in the middle of the highway then and glared at each other.

Someone called out an alert. The first of the loaded vans from the morning harvest in the Stockton fields approached them on the county road.

Everybody gathered at the side of this hard-packed artery, standing along the egress to the highway where the union-hired trucks were parked, bumper to bumper. The men sweated, waiting, taut, silent. Any who had arrived in jackets discarded them. Their shirts were discoloured, damp.

The high-stacked farm van pulled all the way to the highway entry, inches from the truck which blocked its way. The driver stopped his vehicle, turned off the engine. He swung down from the cab. He spoke toward the knot of labour men on the road shoulder. 'Which one of you owns this here truck? Get it outta here.'

Salinsky said, 'You want it moved, mister, you move it.'

The patrol captain stepped across the road and stood beside the driver. 'Mr Salinsky,' he said in his best formal tone, 'I order you in the name of the State of California to move this vehicle. You are illegally blocking a public thoroughfare.'

When the labour union men simply stared blankly at him,

the police officer, raging, yanked out a pad and wrote a citation. The labour agitators laughed at him; even the other police smiled in a sick kind of frustration. When the officer tried to serve the citation on Salinsky, the big man simply shrugged his corpulent shoulders and motioned toward the black ashes in the middle of the highway. 'Just file it, cop.'

By now, other vans rolled out from the Stockton loading docks toward the highway. They approached the roadblock, blowing their horns, but grinding finally to a halt.

Down that side artery, one of the farm vans pulled off the county road and detoured into the tilled field, bumping and rattling over the high furrows, intending to bypass the blockade. Everybody watched with interest. The farm drivers yelled encouragement until the heavily loaded van mired, sinking to its axles in the red ploughed earth.

Three breakdown vans raced to the roadblock from the direction of Los Angeles, horns blowing and sirens wailing.

The patrol officer in charge walked out to the lead van. He had armed himself with a megaphone and he spoke through it. 'Will you people remove these illegally parked trucks from this public roadway? At once? Peaceably?'

The strike leaders hooted in response. Still speaking through the loudhailer, the patrol officer ordered the two lead vans to remove the truck which blocked the Stockton access road.

This proved to be tedious and time-consuming operation: much backing and manoeuvering to get as close as possible between the forward and aft trucks in order to hitch grappling hooks and winch the vehicle up enough to turn and drag it, brakes set, out onto the highway.

The strikers made no attempt to interfere as the two vans removed the truck, an action which consumed almost an hour. As the truck in the roadway was removed a driver immediately rolled the next truck into its place before one of the waiting farm vans could be driven through.

With terrible doggedness, the breakdown vans rolled in place to repeat the slow operation of removal. Now the men in the Buicks acted. As the breakdown vans were reversed across the highway, suddenly grappling hooks were heaved from the Buicks. Police yelled warnings, but the three heavy chain hooks were in place. The Buicks strained forward at top speed, as one car. In an incredible slow-motion the van tilted upward and slammed over on its side in the middle of the highway in an explosion of metal and glass and revved engine. The driver screamed in pain and terror, trapped in the twisted cab.

The police converged on the Buicks then, guns drawn, but as if on some unseen, unheard signal, hundreds of migrant workers, wetbacks and farm hands appeared in a kind of rushing, hurricane whine, out of the fields, running toward the highway, armed with machetes and knives.

The police slowed, then stopped, and finally holstered their handguns and lowered the riot guns. They stood watching impotently as the mob stalked across the fields. The workers shouted something, but it was unintelligible. They looked like some rag-tag army left over from Villa's days on the border. The injured van driver was forgotten. He went on crying out from his shattered cab.

Jesus and Sister Mari-Jean ran across the highway. They managed to pull the driver from the cab. His face was slashed by glass shards and his leg was broken. Sister Mari-Jean stalked up to the patrol commander and demanded that the police get the injured man to hospital. The officer hesitated, worried. 'Right now I can't spare any of my men, Sister.'

'Then his death will be on your hands,' Sister Mari-Jean said. 'He was working for you. He was following your orders, doing your will.'

'All right. All right.' The captain threw up his hands in surrender. He ordered one of his patrolmen to drive the victim to the nearest hospital. 'While you're in there,' he ordered, 'you call for reinforcements. This damn thing is gettin' to hell out of hand. You tell headquarters we got big trouble out here, and it's gettin' worse by the minute.'

Jesus and two patrolmen helped lift the driver and settle him as comfortably as possible into the rear of a police car. By the time this vehicle was turned around and headed along the highway, the stoop labourers from the Stockton fields were massed, chanting, around the barricades, the overturned breakdown van and the stalled farm vans.

When the patrol captain spoke through his megaphone, ordering the farm labourers to disperse and return to their jobs at once or face arrest for trespassing, the workers hooted, shook their machetes above their heads, daring the police to advance upon them. 'Unless you people are

424

working,' he warned, 'you are trespassing on private Stockton property and subject to arrest.'

Salinsky clambered up on the bonnet of one of the barricade trucks. He waved the crowd off the fields and onto the highway. When they quieted again, he harangued them in street English. Brown faces turned up to him blankly. Until his words were translated, they didn't know if he were friend or foe.

Father Garcia walked along the farm road, holding up his arms and speaking with some passion, pleading with the workers for patience, for respect of authority, for rule by law.

Salinsky waved his arm toward his hirelings. 'Get that old son of a bitch out of here before he gets hurt.'

Jesus winced. Those last words were the key to Salinsky's entire message. They sounded like a well-intentioned warning to the priest, but Jesus knew better. Those words provided a licence for the strike leaders, or any worker with the courage of heresy and sacrilege, to attack the ageing padre.

No one from the mob of shouting workers moved toward Father Garcia, but stones and clods of clay were hurled at him from within the faceless crowd. Jesus ran along the road and stood beside Father Garcia. He hoped to accomplish nothing except by his presence, along with Father Garcia's, to remind the migrants of who they were, what their church was, to calm them. A clod struck Jesus in the temple, making him stagger slightly. He set his legs apart and shook it off, though the world skidded around his head crazily for a few seconds.

He gazed out at that sea of sweating brown faces as if nothing had happened. He whistled between his teeth. Salinsky had not lied or exaggerated. The labour agitators had done their work well. They had quietly but expertly orgainized these workers, one by one, group by group, until they were primed and honed for this action today. He wondered what in God's name the union leaders had been able to promise the labourers to make them enlist so fanatically.

A stalemate settled tenuously over the sun-baked valley. The vans could not move, harvested vegetables rotted in ninety-five degree heat. The police threatened but remained impotent, outnumbered and overwhelmed. The police held every advantage, sidearms, shotguns, riot weaponry, but the workers had machetes and a mindless rage driving them. One wrong overt move and a blood-bath could well ensue. Jesus thanked God that the police were clever enough at least to recognize this.

It looked as if the confrontation might wane into a stand-off. The day's harvest would be lost, the day's work in the fields left unfinished. But there seemed no immediate solution. The police made no futher attempt to breach the barricade with the remaining breakdown vans and even when police reinforcements arrived, sirens wailing, the two sides merely stood, armed, tense and sweating.

'Look at that stuff rot,' Salinsky shouted from the bonnet of a barricade truck. 'That's your power. That's where you can hurt these conscienceless thieves who grow rich on your misery. You hurt them in the pocket. You keep hurting them. You can stop these robber-baron landowners. You can break the backs of these lawless growers. If they can't get the produce to the markets, they are beaten. And if you will follow us, we will beat them. We'll go on beating them until they grant us the right to decent wages for humane working hours and respectable living conditions.'

Jesus stared at the shouting, sweating labour agitator. This was the first of his kind Jesus had ever seen. But at the moment, without translation, Salinsky might as well be talking to himself. Not more than a dozen of the braceros understood a word he was yelling.

A cry rose from the labourers and Jesus jerked his head around. From the farm came Los Angeles County Police cars, farm pick-up trucks and open touring automobiles, racing through the dust. He had the terrible and sick feeling that the balance of power was about to shift again.

He recognized Church Foley in the lead car, driven by Pedro Luiz.

Jesus' heart sank. He stood, legs apart in the blazing sun, watching the approaching cars. Things had been evil enough. Labour troubles and worker unrest had been established here today as part of farm existence. Growers were being given warning. They were going to lose part of every harvest — perhaps every day — until they reached some compact with these new farm-labour representatives. Now, with this retalia-tory move from the Stockton forces, he saw the challenge accepted: the farmers' answer was going to be violence.

Church Foley, with his own megaphone, a loud-hailer

emblazoned with Los Angeles County Sheriff across it, crawled up on the bonnet of the police car. Pedro Luiz got out, handgun at his side, and stood beside the open door. The protests ebbed in waves rolling back across the workers.

Church's voice was dead and flat and it carried in the still heat. 'You people get back to work. You people let our trucks pass. You people obey the law and Mr Bragg Stockton has empowered me to say there will be no retaliation from the growers if you return to work, stay at work, and strike no more.'

This had the air of conciliation. Its tone was congenial, but the words and the implied threat were inflamatory, as Church Foley knew they would be, as the Stocktons might have known they would be. Anyhow, it was like hurling a bucket of kerosene on an open fire.

The explosion followed abruptly. Raging, the workers turned from the barricade of trucks and, screaming, waving their machetes above their heads, they surged towards the county police and the farm foremen.

Jesus shouted, waving his arms, trying to slow them, keep them back from the confrontation Church Foley invited. None of the workers, including the savagely smiling Rod Salinsky, realized that Church Foley's words had been designed to cause them to react exactly in this way: to make them attack farm authority.

Jesus, watching the mob, kept glancing back towards Tio Pedro Luiz because he believed he could read from Pedro's actions what the plans of the farm security people were. Pedro calmly took out his handgun, brought it up and fired it over the heads of the mob. This slowed them for the moment.

In that brief time, the state police captain leaped up onto a barricade truck bonnet. He yelled through his voice trumpet. 'Don't do this. Don't do this. In the name of the law, I order you. Put away those guns.'

Jesus' heart pounded. It was incredible that the state police and the county officers should oppose each other. At least the trooper was reacting sanely, trying to stop the planned slaughter by Stockton's hired gunmen and indebted law forces. Jesus shook his head. Only he seemed to have heard the captain. The crowds regrouped and thrust forward again.

This time, Pedro fired directly into the mob. One of the workers fell. Screaming in outrage and blood lust, the labourers ran forward, waving their machetes, the steel blades gistening in sunlight. Before they could get anywhere near Pedro Luiz and Church Foley, other farm guards suddenly jerked open wire cages on the pick-up trucks and a dozen Doberman pinschers lunged outward, trained to kill on signal, snarling and slashing, prodded and encouraged by their trainers.

For a long moment, Jesus stood immobile beside Sister Mari-Jean who knelt over the worker shot by Pedro Luiz. In that moment Jesus felt as if this were a nightmare. His legs refused to move. His arms felt weak. Hatred for Pedro Luiz surged through him, impotent as always in every other nightmare. There was a confusion of dust, yelling, yowling of animals. As the dogs sprang at the workers, these people cried out, striking at the animals with their machetes, but retreating.

One of the labour agitators had grabbed up an iron jack. But his will failed him at the sight of the wild dogs, slashing and snarling. He stood stunned in the roadway.

Hardly aware of what he did, Jesus snatched the jack from the man's hand. Turning, he ran toward where Foley and Pedro Luiz stood, the jack upraised.

He never made it to the county police car. The first dogs had slashed and bitten the workers, but after the initial shock, the labourers used their machetes and the dogs were helpless against them, falling mutilated. Horrified by what was happening to the expensive, trained guard dogs, the trainers called the animals off and rushed them back into their pens. They had lost more than half of the animals.

The farm foremen and county police stood armed, in a line, guns across their chests.

'Get your people back out of here,' the state patrol captain was yelling through his hailer towards Foley and Swain and the other Stockton hirelings.

Foley pressed his megaphone to his face and yelled back. 'These people are trespassing. We'll protect our own property.'

The raging exchange of threats and accusations flared on both sides, words spewing, but after the blood-letting of the dogs, the vicious lacerations from the animals, the wounding of the labourer, some of the fury had ebbed. Neither guns nor machetes were employed at the moment. Rocks and clods were hurled spasmodically from deep within the mob, but both sides held their ground, unmoving.

Jesus could not see clearly. Sweat leaked from his hat brim and burned his eyes. The whole ploughed region was like one vast crimson sun spot. His heart pounded wildly. He slowed, stopped, stunned at his own behaviour. What he'd always known would happen, had happened. In the crisis, he had thrown in with the workers. God help him now by the time the Church and the establishment were through with him. They would chew him up and spit him out.

Suddenly, in the taut, sun-baked madness, he heard a woman's voice call his name. 'Jesus.'

He went cold. At first, he told himself it was Sister Mari-Jean. But even as he thought this, he knew better. The nun would call him Father O'Brien, even in the privacy of the manse. And that was not Mari-Jean's voice. There was something disturbing, exhilarating in that tone, something half-remembered, half-forgotten, totally tormenting. 'Jesus. Hey-sus. Heysus O'Brien.'

He turned slowly, his throat taut, his legs weak. Even when he saw Leonora approaching, hurrying toward him from the aureola of a sun spot, he could not believe his eyes.

She did not come from the farm trucks, but from the newly arriving union buses which blocked the highway behind them and from which union strikers spilled.

Leonora wore a man's shirt and levis — the first woman he'd ever seen in trousers. Her lovely blonde hair was cropped raggedly about her delicate, fragile face. Her violet eyes glowed, her perfect teeth glistened in her smile. 'Oh, Heysus. It is you.' Then she stopped, staring at his turned collar. She shook her head, whispering. 'My God, Heysus, you. . . a priest.'

He could hardly speak. Tears clotted his eyes, choked his throat. He forced himself to smile, his weakened left eyelid sagging in a wink. 'And you,' he managed to say. 'You. A labour agitator.'

XXXIII

Jesus stood and stared at Leonora on the shoulder of the county road. Name of God, she was fascinating. He was fascinated. He was twelve years old, seeing her for the first time, he was seventeen and wrenched from her embrace and lashed, and she was still more enchanting than any forbidden fantasy. Her own beauty was a warning; she was truly taboo, lovelier and more desirable than in his hungriest dream. She lent elegance even to outsize, wrinkled male clothing and not even the clipped boyish bob could destroy her fragile beauty.

'Heysus. It's really you.'

He smiled, nodded, and gazed at her, incredulous, but he didn't speak. She caught both his hands in hers, clinging to them, gazing all the time up into his eyes, her own eyes drowned in tears. She threw her arms around him and embraced him for a long moment with all her strength. He had the strange, mindless feeling that he should run, but that it was already too late to run.

She stood beside him then, silent in the dust and crackling confusion and tension. He felt a panic that had nothing to do with this violent confrontation, or with the threat of death around them. He could not help looking at her again. He felt he had at least that much due to him after all these empty years. When their eyes met, Leonora smiled, but they did not try to talk. It was if they were caught in a racing current and hurtled along helplessly.

Noises raged around them, shouting and threats and curses. From the cages the dogs yowled.

From that moment the farm-strike confrontation bristled, at an impasse. The farm security men and county police stood waiting with guns and clubs. The strikers faced them with machetes gripped in trembling fists. The sun blazed down, melting away the last shreds of sanity.

Jesus saw Sister Mari-Jean tending the wounded, those slashed by the guard dogs. He knew he should go and help her, but he went on standing there as if he and Leonora were removed, insulated from the heat and dust and hatred enveloping them.

Sister Mari-Jean signalled the highway patrol and the worker shot by Pedro Luiz was removed in a car to hospital.

The tensions stretched thinner in the heat, but for that instant in time nobody moved. And then, almost with some sense of cosmic inevitability, advantage shifted totally over to the growers and the first San Gabriel Valley farm-workers' strike ended abruptly in failure.

A half-dozen large trucks, all carrying migrant workers from outside and brought in as strike-breakers, arrived and pulled alongside the empty barricade vans. More than a hundred strike-breakers swarmed from the truckbeds and, under the leadership of foremen shouting orders through megaphones, began to transfer farm produce from the stalled vans and load them into the newly arrived carriers.

It was all over that quickly. The strikers protested, crying and waving their machetes, but even the most fanatical of them knew they were beaten. They spat and cursed at the strike-breakers. But these newcomers worked silently, implacably and diligently. They seemed neither to see nor hear the striking labourers. Soon a truck was loaded and it rolled away along the highway, with police escort, toward Los Angeles.

That first truck was like a terrible symbol of victory for the farmers and defeat for the workers. When the labour union leaders saw that they were beaten, they signalled their drivers to break the barricade line and remove their trucks from the area. There was a cloud of exhaust fumes and dust, caterwauling of horns and grinding of gears and soon the highway was cleared, the last van departed. The remaining Stockton trucks pulled away, loaded, their cargo saved from spoiling.

Jesus stood slump-shouldered in the blazing sun. He watched the lost cause falter, stagger backwards, retreat and disintegrate. On the county road, the Stockton foremen, county police and security guards joined the newcomers. The strike-breakers were marched along the road toward the fields. The strikers were driven off the Stockton property to

431

the highway. They milled there, shattered, confused and impotent. Not only had they lost the battle, they'd relinquished their jobs and forfeited any pay due to them. They were even refused permission to return to the work camp for their families or possessions.

'Any of you people got families at the labour camp,' Church Foley said through the megaphone, 'you can just wait here on the highway, your people will be coming out to you. Any of you caught — from this moment — on Stockton Farms property will be shot.'

At last the buses were hired by the labour people to remove the fired strikers. These people morosely got into the vans and sat, staring through the windows. The state highway patrol left four patrolmen to ensure order and departed. The breakdown vans were hired by the Stockton management to remove the mired truck from the field. Gradually, the whole area cleared. Nothing remained of the revolt except a few blood spots, almost unseen against the red of the earth.

Rodney Salinsky, Ted Ross and the other union leaders gathered around Leonora. With a shock, Jesus realized she was a recognized principal in this labour movement. He stared at her, unable to reconcile her new role with the girl he remembered from six years ago at Stockton Farms. Her leadership in the union only proved how insane the world was, everything topsy-turvy and unreal.

He saw that Sister Mari-Jean and Father Garcia had retired to the old Model T Ford touring car. They sat, awaiting him silently. He clenched his fists at his sides. Whatever role he had in this affair was ended and he should clear out. Father Garcia was impatient and totally unsympathetic to these strike leaders. Jesus knew he ought to say goodbye to Leonora and get out of here. But he did not move. He seemed to be rooted to the spot until Leonora herself might release him.

Salinsky said, 'Well, we got another hundred migrants to feed and clothe and find work for. That's about all we got.'

'It's worse than that,' Ted Ross replied. 'We took a bad beating here. It won't be easy recruiting strikers or arousing workers to the cause once this word gets out.'

'We've been beaten before,' Leonora said.

'Amen.' Salinsky laughed sourly. 'Word of defeat doesn't travel very far or very fast, thank God. We'd be better off, all

432

of us, if we could get the word out, if we could get the world to watching. They couldn't beat us down like this if they knew the world was watching them.'

'I don't think they care very much,' Ross said.

'Hell, I know they don't care.' Salinsky shook his head. 'We just need the weight of public opinion on our side, and we don't even have that.'

'Well, we're never going to get that,' Ross said. 'I think you're dreaming again, Rod. This is a capitalistic country and the people are on the side of the capitalists because that's the only side of any story they ever hear.'

'One thing we can do,' Leonora said. 'We can keep on fighting.'

'Oh, we'll fight,' Salinsky agreed. 'We fight. And we are defeated. That never changes.'

Jesus saw the way Leonora laughed, and in her laugh he saw something of her father's and her grandfather's obstinate resolve, ironically turned in all its unyielding tenacity against them. 'But we keep on fighting,' Leonora said. 'And that never changes, either.'

2

Jesus held the steering wheel and stared at the sun-hazed road ahead. The midafternoon world was bleached white; heat waves shimmered up from the highway pavement. He was barely aware of the world around him, the cars that passed him, horns sounding. He was conscious only of Leonora on the seat beside him. For the sake of propriety she had left a small five-inch corridor between their thighs. She had laid her hand in that space, palm upward, but when he did not close his own fingers upon it, she withdrew it to her lap with a sigh. 'The whole damned world's crazy, isn't it?' she said.

He glanced at her from the corners of his eyes, wondering if she had any suspicion of just how insane this entire universe really was. He felt as if he existed on an insubstantial ice flow twisting and turning in boiling tropical waters. It had begun when Leonora asked if he could drive her into Los Angeles. 'We've so much to talk about,' she said.

He had agreed this was true and had tried to deny the

savage way his heart pounded in his ribcage. Salinsky and the others departed in their big cars. Jesus walked with Leonora to where Sister Mari-Jean and Father Garcia waited in the Model T. He introduced Leonora. Except that Father Garcia was obviously stunned that she should have appeared at this place under any circumstances, and as a strike leader, the aging pastor revealed nothing except a rigid disapproval for the entire situation. He sat silent all the way back to the church.

Leonora sat in the tonneau of the touring car with Sister Mari-Jean and fared little better. Jesus heard one exchange between them and this was enough, too much.

Leonora's voice had been gentle, friendly, and certainly with no criticism implied. If anything she was trying to pay the young novice a compliment. 'You're such a lovely girl, Sister Mari-Jean.'

'Thank you, Miss Stockton.'

'So lovely to — to hide yourself in the habit of a nun.'

'Am I, Miss Stockton? This is what I want. This is the life I've chosen.'

'I understand that. I'm sure you are most content. Still, you are a lovely girl.'

'Personal vanity has nothing to do with my life, Miss Stockton. What I look like is not important. No more than for you — dressing up as a man and leading farm strikers against the people who pay and feed and house them.'

'Underpay, under-feed and under-house them, Sister.'

The silence from the tonneau of the aged car was brittle. Leonora was still smiling when she and Jesus started alone on the drive into Los Angeles. And even this trek was undertaken in tension and ill-will.

When Jesus announced his intention of driving Leonora to her hotel in the city, Father Garcia was stunned, shaken with disbelief. 'Alone? You are going to drive alone with her into the city?'

'I plan to.'

'Well, I can't permit that.'

'Short of sending me to my room without supper, Father, I am afraid there is no way you can stop me.'

'This is against every rule of the church.'

'I suppose. But I find no evil in two very old friends driving together in a car.'

434

'Alone? There is the appearance of evil, as well as the evil, Jesus. I should not have to remind you that you are expected to avoid even the appearance of evil — especially the appearance of evil.'

'I shall try to do that, Father.'

'I'm afraid that's not good enough. If you must go, Sister Mari-Jean will have to accompany you. I'd go, but I'm too exhausted for such a drive. Sister Mari-Jean will go along.'

Jesus grinned and shook his head. 'We've got the old case of the goose and the fox and the river to cross, Father. Sister Mari-Jean and I would have to return alone — and God knows what might happen — or as you suggest, what the Church will suspect might happen.'

'The Church looks only to your best interests, to the best interests of all of us,' Father Garcia said stiffly. He simply turned and entered the manse without saying goodbye. Sister Mari-Jean followed. She did not look back. The sense of tension was almost tangible within the old Ford and followed them along the highway.

Leonora laughed. 'Poor Father Garcia. He can't wait to tell Father on me. Leonora Stockton, dressed outlandishly, hair cropped, working with strikers and labour unionists — and riding alone with a priest. One thing, I'm damned in hell from this moment. Father Garcia will see to that.'

'He has only our best interests at heart,' Jesus quoted.

'And the nun! Such disapproval. She looked rigid as china, and as ready to break. I don't envy you, going back there, Jesus.' She laughed and stared at him in the car. 'Why do you go back, Heysus? Come with me. Work with me. We don't accomplish much. So far we haven't accomplished anything. But we are fighting for what is right. . . . And, no matter what else, you and I, we'd be together.'

'I'm afraid it's too late for that.'

She exhaled heavily. He expected her to say something more about them, but when she spoke it was about herself. 'When I came home from Switzerland,' she said. 'That's where they sent me after they caught me with you that night in the back seat of that lovely old car — when I came back home, they sent me to the University of California at Oakland.' She laughed wanly. 'They should never have done that. I learned about the oppression and exploitation of the workers, the way they're enslaved.'

'They're not slaves —'

'You better believe they're not. None of the growers are fools enough to own these migrants as slaves. Slaves would cost them ten to a hundred times what it costs to underpay the migrants, to overcharge them for substandard housing, for rotten food, even for transportation. Slaves have to be cared for. The migrant can be used for a season and then thrown out. So, I believe it is time to pay decent wages, provide food, housing, transportation.'

He shook his head, laughing hollowly. 'I can't believe it.'

'What can't you believe? That I've taken up the workers' cause? That I'm out fighting the growers? My own people?'

'No.'

'What then?'

'That we're together. Riding along like this.' He sighed, smiling. 'I've had hundreds of fantasies about you and me over the past six years, Leonora, but never one as wild as this.'

'Come with me. Leave the Church.'

'Just like that?'

'Just like that.'

'I'm afraid it's not done that way. Not these days. Not in the year of Our Lord 1930. When you enter the Church, you start off on a road from which you cannot turn back.'

'Oh, you can turn back. You may be excommunicated. Despised. Bedeviled and reviled. But you can do it.'

He shivered. 'Don't think I haven't gone through this a thousand times in my mind. If Leonora came back. If Leonora comes back. If you find Leonora. Only I never thought it would happen.'

'But it really has, Heysus. I'm here. I've come back.'

'Your parents must be raging that you are a strike leader —'

'You'll just never know the wild rage in that house at the mention of my name.'

'Still, if you wanted to go back, they'd forgive you. They could always fall back on the old saw, she's a woman, a weak vessel and she doesn't know any better. But take up with me, they'll never forgive you.'

She laughed. 'Do you think they can forgive my being a communist?'

'Yes. Easier than they would forgive your entering a liaison

436

with a failed priest, a chicano, a half-breed. I know what they think about that possibility. I still have the weal marks to remind me.'

Now she did close her fingers on his hand on the steering wheel. 'I am sorry, Heysus. I'll never forgive them that. Maybe that's what truly turned me against them. They call me a communist. But they know better. I'm really a registered Democrat. But to arch-conservative, Hoover Republicans like my family, that is synonymous with pinko. But the real reason I truly hate them is the way they treated you.'

'Looks like we're at an impasse,' he said in a hollow tone.

'Why?'

'Because I'm on a road from which I can't turn back. And even if I could, I could never ask you to do that one damning thing that would end everything forever between you and your family.'

'Not even if I wanted to?'

'Not even if you wanted to.'

There was a long silence, quiet intensified by the whine of the wind, the mutter of the engine, the whisper of the tyres on the road. Eventually Leonora sighed, her voice empty. 'Oh God, Heysus. It's such a shit of a world.'

'I couldn't have said it better myself.'

XXXIV

Until the thought of Leonora took charge of him, the idea of being near Leonora obsessed him, the consideration of joining the strike leaders or of leaving the priesthood had never crossed Jesus' mind as more than a faint vagary. There was much about his union with the Church which frustrated him and left him dissatisfied and less than fulfilled, but he had never considered acting upon that discontent. His was the passive nature of Julia. With the resigned serenity and lethargic acceptance of his lot he'd inherited from his mother, he'd found the lack in himself and not in his surroundings. He never complained. He worked dutifully, doing whatever the Church asked of him. Even, he saw with a sense of horror, even to going out to bring the influence of the Church against the pitiful goals of the miserable migrants. God in heaven. God in heaven. The Church demanded this of him and yet he did not see how God Himself could forgive him for it.

In the next weeks, while he struggled and raged inside himself, Leonora dominated his mind to the exclusion of everything else, everyone else. It was as if that nightlight had been turned on again in that distant window, as if really it had never been extinguished. He could not put out of his thoughts the fact that she had come back. Leonora was near. She had begged him to join her in her fight, a battle which had his total loyalty, and which offered him the magic opportunity to be with Leonora again, constantly. This troubled him most, because whatever he did, this would be his driving motivation. He was throwing over everything else. She had asked him to leave the Church. The Church had taught him well for ten years. He'd needed her forever.

It was not as if Leonora had returned to her crusade and that he saw her no more, or did not hear from her again. She was in touch with him constantly. She called him daily, sometimes two or three times a day, often, to Father Garcia's indignation, late at night, the telephone bell clanging through the silent old manse like laughter from hell itself.

Leonora called him with good news; if there were a tiny victory anywhere in the labour movement, she had to share it with him. If there were defeat, she needed the comfort of his voice. If there were no news, she wanted to apprise him of this. If she were thinking of him in the midst of hectic, busy confusion, she had to tell him so. When she called late at night, she spoke in a tired, husky and throaty voice, remembering the way she had always loved him, no matter how forbidden that love had been, how even when she was kissing some handsome and eligible boy at college, it was Jesus' face she saw behind her tightly closed eyes.

One day when she called, her throat was choked with tears of agony and defeat. The labour union had sued Stockton Farms in state courts over the violence during the strike. Stockton attorneys had counter-sued, and other area growers had joined in the action. The growers, led by Stockton lawyers, had worked out an 'agreement' which they presented to the court, and which the court accepted as the only basis on which the suits could be settled. The growers offered a ten cents an hour wage increase to migrant workers, declaring to the court that this was the union's principal demand — one the growers found ruinous, but would meet. This meant that workers, paid one dollar for a ten-hour day, would now receive two dollars a day. The growers would accede to no other demands. Rents, transportation and commissary costs would be raised slightly higher as only fair.

'The bastards,' Leonora wept. 'Oh, the bastards. They're not giving anything. Once the raised costs of rents, commissary and transportation are deducted, the workers will be no better off. Worse. Because the courts have ordered the labour people to accept the settlement under threat of restraining orders permanently in place until that agreement is ratified.'

'I'm sorry,' Jesus managed to say.

'Oh, Jesus. I get so tired. So tired. How can we ever win against such inhumanity, such cold and heartless cruelty? It's almost as if the are all just laughing at us. Just laughing at us.' Her voice caught. 'Oh, Heysus. I can't endure this without you. I can't. I've got to have you with me or I can't stand it at all.'

'I am with you,' He whispered, anguished. 'You know I am.'

'Oh, Christ, Heysus,' she wept. 'That isn't what I meant. You know that isn't what I mean.'

Father Garcia was somehow, perhaps instinctively, aware of the consternation and deranging anguish in which the young assistant rector passed his days. He watched Jesus in a kind of awed horror. There was little doubt in his mind that the young priest would be censured, perhaps severely disciplined. He tried to warn him of what terrors lay ahead for both of them. 'I'm too old to fight Los Angeles,' he complained. 'I don't want to be put in the position of having to oppose the bishop or the Committee of Examination.'

He peered up at the quiet young priestling in the shadowed room. His black alpaca soutane accentuated the slender figure. His cropped black hair topped a lean face, drawn with pallor, lit by the calm yet defiant intensity of the dark eyes. The old priest sighed. He was such a beautiful boy, so deep in error, so cruelly misinformed and misled.

'It's like the devil has him by the hand,' the old man mumbled, half to himself. 'The very devil himself.'

'Sir?'

'What?'

'I didn't hear what you said, sir,' Jesus told him.

Father Garcia shrugged. 'Doesn't matter. Wasn't talking to you. But I am talking to you now. I have a letter from the diocese office. It concerns you. I think we ought to discuss it.'

Jesus waited silently, his hands at his sides.

'For your own good,' Father Garcia said after a moment. 'As I warned you, the matter of your indiscreetly driving with that — young woman — alone into Los Angeles has been brought to the attention of Monsignor Newman.'

'My God. How?'

'How? My dear boy, a hundred ways. We cannot even rule out the angry denunciation by Miss Stockton's heartbroken family itself, can we?'

Jesus replied with some irony, 'I suppose not.'

'There are many ways. Many eyes are on us. It is no longer even important how they learned. What matters now is what they learned.'

'Oh, what did they learn?'

'Enough apparently that they believe you should face a

board of examination. Apart from your indiscretion in being seen alone afternoon and evening with the young woman, there is for the Church, the matter of your intentions.'

Jesus peered at the older man but did not even bother to answer this.

'Did you and Miss Stockton enter a speakeasy — an illegal saloon — while you were in Los Angeles?

'Of course not.'

'Did you drink with her, intoxicating beverages?'

'No.'

'You went into her hotel with her.'

'Yes.'

'Did you not eat dinner with her?'

'In the public dining-room.'

'Did you not engage in tête-à-tête during this meal?'

'What in God's name does that mean?'

'I think you know what I mean. This report says you bent often across the table to your partner, exchanging secret whispered things, and that she leaned often toward you as if afraid she might be overheard.'

'I don't know that we whispered, but I do know that if we'd known we were being so closely audited, we might well have.'

'You feel no regret for what you have done?'

'I've done nothing wrong.'

'You've sinned in the eyes of your Church, your fellows, in my eyes. You may as well answer these questions for me, you'll certainly have to answer them when you are called into Los Angeles.'

Jesus stood silently again, gazing at the older priest with calm, black eyes. 'There's nothing I can say to you that you will understand.'

'You'd better hope I understand. You had better try to make me understand. Because you are going to answer to the committee.' Father Garcia waved his arm. 'What did you do after you left the dining-room?'

There was a protracted silence. At last, Jesus shrugged. 'We went up to her suite.'

'You went to her hotel room?'

'Yes. She has a suite. A parlour, bedroom, bath, balcony. I suppose that does not matter.'

'What happens to your intentions now?' Father Garcia's voice quavered with shock.

'We wanted to be where we would not be disturbed.'

'God help me. I'm sure you did.' Father Garcia spread his hands. He drew a deep breath. 'Did you have sexual intercourse?'

'No.'

'Then what did you do, why were you there? What reason can you give our Church for your actions?'

'None, I suppose. I know what I did. But making you people believe it is something else, isn't it?'

Father Garcia drew the back of his thin hand across his eyes. He shook his head. 'Why do you persist in suggesting that the Church is some entity against you?'

'Isn't it?'

'The Church is your life. The way of your life that you have freely chosen. The Church must protect you as it must protect itself. Your good name is most urgent. You must not only remain pure, you must keep also the appearance of purity. I think you'd better tell me the truth.'

'I haven't lied to you yet. I don't want to lie to you. I don't want to endure this inquisition, either.'

Father Garcia cried out, as if wounded. 'Open your eyes, my dearest boy. See things as they are. Not as you might wish them to be — under some disturbing influences. I have given my life to the Church. I don't boast. I accept, because it is the choice I made long ago. It is the choice you made.'

'At this moment I find that hard to believe.'

'I am trying to help you. I want you to present an adequate defence when you are questioned. But even more, I want you to take a serious look at yourself and the sudden sickness that obsesses you. This Church is my life. I will do anything to help you serve it. I will do anything to keep you from serving it badly. I have given my life to this Church. I ask no more of you, Jesus. No less.'

'Maybe I've reached the place where I cannot give what is demanded of me.'

'It is not a demand, my dear boy. An expectation. You would want no less if you were well, if your mind were clear. That's all I am trying to do, to help you prepare yourself, to make you see — yourself and this predicament — as it really is. To see it clearly.'

Jesus sighed and there was a brittle silence in the shadowed room for some moments. Scowling, Father Garcia sat forward on the edge of the chair, his fingers pressed together in a tent before him, staring upward in the sombre darkness.

'Maybe you *have* helped me to see clearly,' Jesus said at last.

'I hope so.'

'So do I. And if you have, I want to thank you.'

'Thank me?'

'Yes. You've done something for me today, Father, something that I couldn't do for myself.'

'You have my prayers. You have a bad time ahead, but not an impossible time. The Church asks only that you confess and repent and sin no more.'

'I didn't mean that, Father. I meant, you made up my mind for me.'

2

When Jesus walked into the dingy union headquarters in downtown Los Angeles, Leonora looked up from a desk near a window which overlooked a narrow side street. At first, she merely glaced at him indifferently, then her violet eyes widened and she cried out his name and he knew he'd made the right decision, the only one possible to him.

'Heysus. My darling Heysus. You've come.'

He nodded but he didn't speak. He stood inside the doorway, holding his canvas tote bag and his guitar case. The room was crowded with desks and people but he saw none of them. He saw only Leonora and the way she watched him, smiling, her eyes brimming with tears of delight. She seemed to draw all light in the shadowy room. She stood in a lazy halo of cigar smoke. He could hear the filtered sounds of subdued voices in the shadows around them, but the words were unintelligible.

Leonora got up from her desk. She wore a dress, but it looked like some ordinary knee-length frock from the racks of a discount store. She seemed to have run as far as possible from the protected, pampered existence of her father's home. He winced, wondering in a passing question too swift to be a thought, how much was idealistic fervour and how much rebellion against her father?

443

He brushed this aside. The hell with that. He had enough problems with his own indecisions and doubts. He was here for only two reasons: he wanted to be near Leonora, and he knew in his own mind that his desires destroyed whatever usefulness he might have had in the Church.

He drew a deep breath and held it. The sorry plight of the migrant workers occupied only minimal space in his mind and his heart. He would do what he could for them; they had his sympathy; but he did not see how he or anyone else could accomplish very much against such unequal foes as the growers and the supporting establishment. He deserved no accolades for this decision and he gave himself none. He might give his life for the labour cause, but only Leonora would ever have his whole heart. He knew that much for certain by now. She was more than his loved one: most men find a woman or women to claim their minds and hearts, but it had gone far past this with him. She obsessed him.

Leonora came around her desk and ran to him. Vaguely he heard the taunting whistles and sighs as she threw her arms around him, holding him fiercely.

'Put down your bags, fellow,' someone hooted. 'You'll find it easier that way.'

Jesus smiled and released his tote bag and guitar case. Distantly they plopped upon the uncarpeted floor. He held Leonora against him, overwhelmed by the sweet and sensuous musk of her hair, like something remembered in all its inspiring and ravening destructiveness. All problems, all troubles, all doubts were for that moment obliterated from his mind. He was conscious only of her beauty, her softness, and the scent of her hair.

When the hoots at last rose to catcalls, Leonora glanced around laguidly and said, 'People like you cause wars. And pestilence. And homicides.'

She took his hand and led him into a small side office marked private. She closed the door and leaned against it. 'Oh, Heysus. My dearest Heysus. I prayed you'd come. You don't know how I've prayed.'

He laughed emptily. 'I've prayed about it a lot myself.'

'Oh, my dearest Heysus. You're not still afraid, are you? You don't think you're doing the wrong thing?'

'I haven't the least idea of what I'm doing.'

'You're living. Truly living, Heysus, for the first time.

Doing what you want to do. I promise you one thing. You'll never regret it.'

He sighed. 'I already regret it. In some ways. I've been in the Church a long time. I'd even come to believe there was a reason for it, that maybe that's where I belonged.'

'Oh, Heysus. That's such a waste for you. There's so much you can do.'

He smiled down into her face. 'Whether there is or not, I am with you. And, finally, this is what it came down to.'

'Of course it did. That's what I tried to tell you. I've loved you since the first moment I saw you — and I was nine years old. That has to count for something. And I knew you were devastated by me. I could look at you and tell you were devastated.'

'I was devastated.' He nodded. 'But I also knew the distance between my world and yours boggles the mind, it makes a trip to the sun a short spin.'

She laughed. 'Oh, that's all in your mind. You're as good as anybody, Heysus. Better. And I'll prove it to you.'

'Anyhow, I came because you were here, and because you were, there was nothing else I could do.'

She pressed against him, clinging to him. 'Of course there wasn't. And you won't regret it, Heysus. I won't let you.'

She introduced him around the headquarters. None seemed impressed by his enlisting in their ranks. There didn't seem much a priest could do.

'What we really need,' Rodney Salinsky said, 'is a street tough.'

'I was one of those,' Jesus said, smiling.

'A street kid who can crack skulls with a crowbar. Can you crack skulls, Father?'

Jesus shrugged. 'Maybe I can learn.'

3

To Jesus the days were endless, the nights a brief harried time of planning and regrouping on a dozen battered fronts. Life was a hectic battle campaign, a time of travel, of bottomless cups of coffee, cheap, hurried sandwiches and lack of sleep. It seemed to him he crossed the smeary wastes of California's valleys a dozen times. He traversed the farmlands until they became shapeless, seamless depressions, hacked from high-walled mountains reared like parapets on every side. Names of towns and people and roads and places blurred in his exhausted mind. Grass Valley. Marysville. Napa. Fairfield. Barstow. Fresno. Salinas. Squaw Valley.

It didn't matter where he was, the faces were the same, the desperation and hopelessness never altered, never lifted, but hung like a stormy cloud over every union gathering. Sometimes he felt as if he were buried alive in a tomb of despair. There was not enough oxygen for one, and a whole doomed people were trying to share it. He did what he could. But he remained tired and sodden with fatigue. He was most conscious of his own sense of melancholy, of inadequacy, lack of experience, lack of the crusader's fire, his incompetence and ineptitude. Salinsky was right in his original estimation. Street fighters were of more value than he. At least they could crack the skulls of scabs and security with a mindless sort of delight and fervour.

There was much that he could do, and gradually, almost grudgingly, the union people came to depend upon him to do it. His guitar music drew the workers like the strains of the famed piper. People streamed to the open meeting places where the tired young priest played the songs they loved, and sang with them from the flag-draped, raised dais.

And he could speak, with passion and sincerity and without bombast. He was never a major speaker; they let him talk between songs, while the crowds were gathered and whipped into enthusiasm for a cause that was failing on every front.

Leonora watched him, starry-eyed, as he talked to the people. He never promised them victory or a dollar an hour, or recognition of their status as indispensable in the agriculture empires — without them there was no planting, there was no harvest. He told them only that they were right, but that no one was ever going to hand them their due deserts just because they were right. They would have to fight for every gain, no matter how slight. And they would have to go on fighting, no matter how often and how badly they were defeated. Against his quiet appeal, sometimes the bombastic oratory of the imported guest speaker had a hollow ring. Despite the continued list of failures, the movement slowly gathered members and though Salinsky angrily disputed her,

Leonora insisted Jesus' 'ministry of music and love' deserved most of the credit.

'Love,' Salinsky raged. 'There is no place for love in this dog-eating world. You're dreaming if you think there is. This Father Jesus can keep turning his cheek until it's chopped off. That's not going to win anything for these poor bastards.'

Leonora remained quiet, calm. 'They're uniting,' she said.

Others agreed with her. In the months that followed, requests came into headquarters for the young priest to spearhead rallies in all remote parts of the state. Soon, he had the workers dancing and singing, and believing that if they trusted God and worked as if there were no God, they must one day prevail. This was in no wise the union message, and leaders like Salinsky tolerated his approach only because it was effective, it drew the workers, it enlisted them, it kept them united when confrontations were bloody failures. In many areas, Jesus was the only union organizer who could go back after a defeat; the shattered workers welcomed him, and they believed him when he told them that every failure, no matter how awful, was one more slight break in the growers' defences. 'The world knows what these conscienceless men are doing to you,' he told them. 'We will make the world know, and we'll make them care — and someday, someday, they will come in to this on your side.'

He helped care for the wounded, performed ceremonies over the dead, comforted the bereaved, challenged the survivors. The people rallied around him. They waited for him to come with his guitar and his quiet and calming voice, his indomitable spirit. When they stood against the guard dogs and fire hoses and guns of the establishment, he walked with them.

He seldom saw Leonora. He was dispatched on a hundred errands of mercy, of repair, of condolence. But she saw what most of the organizers were slow to recognize: Jesus was the catalyst that held the failing movement together.

There was much to destroy the organization. There were newspaper headlines of graft and pay-offs within the farm union. Leaders accepted payment from growers to refrain from striking their lands; they were paid by growers to strike farm competitors and thus enhance the profits of the growers permitted to market.

Leonora raged against them. 'Sometimes I think nobody

cares. They're all evil, the growers and the union people. They are in it for what they can get out of it. And the government! We appeal to the President, and you know what he does? He appoints another commission to study the labour unrest and to report back within a year. He appoints commissions to study unemployment and commissions to study hunger. There are more unemployed in this country now than ever before in history, and yet this President needs a commission to study it. And it isn't as if he takes no action. He does. He sets the US Army under Eisenhower and MacArthur with guns against US war veterans. He drives them out of Washington. He lowers taxes on growers and canners and distributors so that they can afford to plant more and hire more and let some of the money seep down to the masses. They don't care. They don't give a damn. Their stupidity is like something instilled in them. Nobody cares, Heysus. Nobody but you and I. And I'm afraid we are outnumbered.'

'Still, we are together. For this moment.'

She laughed and came into his arms. 'Oh, Heysus. What would I do without you? What would these poor bastards do without you? Exploited by their organizers and by their employers. Starved and cheated and lied to. And yet, it's so terrible because even now, I am happy. Almost happy. For the first time in my life, in the middle of hell, I am almost truly happy for the very first time.'

'I guess that's all I truly want,' he said. He looked about the empty inner office of the headquarters, shadowy, dusty, arid.

'Is it?' she said. She clung to him. 'Didn't you listen, Heysus? Didn't you hear what I said? I said I was *almost* happy.'

'I heard you.'

Her eyes brimmed with tears. 'Are you as cruel as the rest of them? Don't you care about what I need? I need you, Heysus. I need you to make that final break with the Church. It holds nothing for you, Heysus. Not any more. But I offer you everything — everything I am — everything I want. Only, don't try to make me go on like this, Heysus. I can't. And you must not ask it.'

He nodded, closing his arms tightly about her. He felt an emptiness deep in the pit of his stomach. He clung to the Church only as a solid base, something eternal in this confusion and despair. Yet, he was being true neither to the Church nor to Leonora. Most of all he was being dishonest to himself.

Still, holding her, pulsing with need for her, he could only ask that same old question without answer. 'What have I to offer you?'

'Happiness, Heysus. Happiness for you. Happiness for me. Don't we deserve at least that much? What else do we have to look forward to in this ugly, hopeless business?'

A knock on the door, almost like an instrusion of an unyielding, unforgiving God. Jesus winced. If there were a God, He sure as hell was the God of the Old Testament. A vengeful God.

'Who is it?' Leonora's voice rasped, almost with the imperious insolence of her father.

'May I come in?' It was a woman's voice.

Angrily, Leonora wrenched free of Jesus and crossed the room. She unlocked the door and held it open. Jesus retreated a step involuntarily. He stared at Sister Mari-Jean. The young nun looked grey, her pallid cheeks were rigid, her eyes unsmiling. Jesus spoke his first thought. 'What is it, Sister? Has something happened to Father Garcia?'

Sister Mari-Jean shook her head. 'Something has happened to me, Father. I have tried to believe the good priest. I have tried not to read of all you are trying to do, and are unable to do. And I know what I have known from the first. You are right. You are right to be doing this. It is the only true work of God. I believe that, and I want to help you. I want to work with you, if you'll let me.'

4

In the days that followed, Jesus fought for an opportunity to be alone with Leonora. She certainly put no obtacles in his path. She wanted to be with him as often as possible, under whatever conditions prevailed. But a new crisis arose within the union and time seemed speeded beyond endurance. There was never enough time for anything.

Judge Deyo Methard issued his decision. The union had thirty days in which to show cause why it should not accept the 'formula of agreement' presented in compromise by the growers' association. This was the infamous 'capitulation' of the farmers, composed by Stockton attorneys, allowing the workers a rise of ten cents an hour. According to the judge, this was a fair and reasonable document which reflected the common accord and consensus of the growers. They were willing to give in on union wage demands for an end to the disruptive strikes. Though the accord was just for both sides, the union had delayed and procrastinated and had, in defiance of the judge's decree, continued to bring wildcat strikes against farms and farmers. The date was set for a hearing in his office where the contracts would be signed, or from where the judge would issue total restraining orders against all strikes.

Several growers from around the state, among them Bragg and Bonnett Stockton, along with attorneys for all these men and corporations, as well as union leaders Salinsky, Ross, Leonora Stockton and their lawyers, gathered in what Salinsky vowed would be a stalemate hearing in Judge Methard's chambers.

Leonora sat icily at the foot of the long, polished table. She returned her grandfather's faint smile, but refused to look at her father. She was the only woman in the room. She was dressed fittingly for the occasion in one of the expensive outfits her father had bought for her, sheer stockings and sleek pumps. She held her head tilted slightly, aloof, faintly arrogant, and she would have been enraged if anyone had dared suggest how much she resembled her father in that moment.

Nothing had been accomplished, but this was the implicit goal of the union people. They would stall until hell froze over. The growers, on the other hand, wanted the contracts because this would legalize whatever action they took against organized workers in the future.

'It is a fair contract because it gives the workers their increase, and it is judged by competent and experienced growers to be a fair wage in these increasingly uncertain times,' Judge Methard said a half-dozen times. As often, the growers and their attorneys nodded and spoke in support, while the union people merely growled and delayed.

Growing impatient and frustrated because despite his robes and his position the judge was a human being and was sincerely convinced that he was improving the lot of the workers, Methard prepared to sign his injunction against strike, trespass or solicitation on farm properties.

A knock on the door. The judge called, 'Yes? What is it?'

His secretary, a slender, harassed woman who wore her brown hair in a ball at the nape of her thin neck, opened the door. 'A grower, your honour. A Mr Murado Valdez of San Gabriel Valley. And a union person, a Father O'Brien.'

The judge nodded and the two men entered the room. All the growers were acquainted with Murado Valdez and some moments were spent in greeting him. The judge said, 'Am I to gather that you two gentlemen have something new to present in this matter?'

Murado Valdez bowed with Latin courtesy. 'I think so, your honour. I have not been struck at my farms, but when Father O'Brien came to my home and presented both sides of this dispute between the growers and workers, I became interested enough to accompany him here to lend whatever influence I have toward a fair settlement.'

The judge smiled and nodded and several of the planters — neither Bragg nor Bonnett Stockton counted among them — spoke in agreement and welcome.

'Would you care to make your statement, Mr Valdez?' the Judge asked.

Again that deep, courteous bow. 'I believe that Father O'Brien can express my views best, your honour, because our views coincide.'

There was a gasp, as if each man in that room inhaled at the same instant. The union organizers stared coldly at Father O'Brien; the growers stirred nervously, eyeing the Latin farmer. After a brief delay, the judge nodded towards the young priest. 'Go ahead, Father.'

Jesus exhaled heavily. He glanced toward the growers, feeling that old sense of inferiority at the sight of Bragg and Bonnett Stockton. He saw that Leonora watched him, puzzled, and that the expression on Rod Salinsky's face was that of open contempt. Bonnett Stockton's eyes were deadly.

Jesus said, 'Your honour, I told Senor Murado Valdez that I believed the dispute, as you have worded it, pertains entirely to the matter of a wage increase which you believe the workers should accept because it is a fair settlement, the highest amount farmers can be expected to pay for harvest,

451

seasonal and migrant workers.'

The judge nodded. 'I believe that is a fair assessment, Father.'

Jesus continued. 'And the union leaders oppose it, because they find it too little and unfair because it includes raises in other costs, such as transportation, housing and commissary prices.'

'That's right,' Salinsky growled.

'The growers are being unusually lenient, Father,' the judge said. 'I have interviewed the growers' association exhaustively, and I find that at this time a ten cent an hour raise is adequate, fair to both sides. As to the other matters, they must be dealt with separately.'

'But that's it, sir. They are not separate. Also, this agreement among the growers amounts more to collusion than to any honest consensus meant to aid you in reaching your decision.'

Attorneys for the growers spoke sharply, protesting. The judge help up his hand, demanding silence. He peered at Jesus. 'These are very serious charges against honourable businessmen, the backbone of this state.'

'I know that, sir. That's why I drove out to Senor Murado Valdez' farm and urged him to come in with me. Senor Murado Valdez agreed — months ago — to pay his seasonal workers three dollars a day. He collects no rental for their housing; he stipulates this as part of their wages. He does not charge the workers for transportation, no matter whether they come from nearby farms or from the border.'

The growers shouted, furious. 'This is outrageous,' one of their attorneys protested. 'This would be ruinous for the growers.'

'It has not ruined Senor Valdez,' Father O'Brien said.

'What is the purpose of this, Father?' the judge asked. 'Do you expect me to alter my ruling on this one set of testimony from one farmer?'

'From a goddamn greaser son of a bitch,' Bragg Stockton growled.

'My family was in the San Gabriel Valley, Senor Stockton,' Valdez said in a taut, yet somehow gentle tone, 'when your family cleaned slop jars in Europe for sustenance.'

'You're an insulting bastard who ought to be driven out of our valley,' Bonnett Stockton replied furiously.

'That's enough,' Judge Methard said. 'I sincerely believed, gentlemen, that I was working with a consensus here. I see that I am not. Therefore, I am adjourning this hearing, with cause, until such time as I am presented with a representative consensus from all growers.'

Attorneys for the growers protested, threatened, cajoled, but Judge Methard remained adamant and cold. The meeting was adjourned; he was not prepared to hear further arguments from either side. Gradually, the hearing broke up, the growers departing in cold silence. Bonnett Stockton paused across the table, staring down at Leonora, but she would not look up at him. After a long time he followed his father and their lawyers from the room.

Salinsky stood up, staring at Jesus. Suddenly, he thrust out his hand. 'By God, Father,' he said. 'You are everything Leonora says you are. And more. By God, welcome aboard.'

XXXV

In the six p.m. shadows and silences of the union headquarters office, Jesus sat at his cluttered desk. He supported himself on his elbows and kept his throbbing head from fragmenting by pressing the heels of his hands against his temples.

He didn't want whiskey, but he sure as hell needed it. Leonora didn't stay away from him on purpose, but the demands of their jobs kept them apart, except for brief, unsatisfactory, stolen intervals. His memories of her, even in these past months, were shards and shattered pieces of despair and excitement blown past on a gale. Looking back, he could not even sort out the truly happy moments from the bitter and empty hours of loneliness.

Every moment they managed together was like opening an old wound and finding fragments of glitter that had to pass for happiness. All the old intoxication flooded back through him when she kissed him. She had only to look at him — their eyes brushing across a busy room — and she disturbed the crannies of his soul. 'We must be careful,' she'd whispered to him once. 'My father is paying to have us watched. I don't care, but I am afraid for you.'

Jesus shrugged, but there was no way to erase from his mind that glance of cold hatred raking him as Bonnett Stockton walked by him in Judge Methard's chambers. Hatreds as old as their first encounter still rankled in Leonora's father against the chicano. Hatreds compounded because Bonnett had always known how deeply Leonora cared for Jesus. A devotion Bonnett meant to destroy at all costs, and one flourishing because they were thrown together now.

He sighed. It was clear that Bonnett Stockton's operatives had reported his and Leonora's first meeting and evening together, and that Bonnett had arranged to have that information presented to the bishop in Los Angeles. He didn't care except that there was never any way to anticipate when Bonnett would decide stronger tactics were indicated.

He straightened and glanced through an open window to the silent street, almost deserted at the supper-hour. A single car was parked at the far kerb. A man sat alone in it, staring at nothing. There was no proof that this was a Stockton investigator, but it was enough to give a sane man paranoia, and Jesus was not certain he was all that sane any more.

He could not even recall the name of the town, or even of the hotel where he and Leonora had found themselves alone and desperately, irresistibly drawn together. He remembered it wasn't much of a hotel, the sort travelling salesmen and union organizers frequented. An acrid breeze bit at him through an open window; the town was dark and silent beyond it. The walls were thin; he could hear movement in other rooms, not intelligible sounds, but annoying noise, almost like mice skittering about.

They had parted after a late-night snack, exhausted after another organization meeting in some shop-front office, draped with flags and hand-lettered signs and smelling of overbrewed coffee. Yawning, they had said goodnight. The way Leonora had looked at him snarled his insides and twisted like barbed wire drawn to breaking. He entered his room and prowled it. He strode toward that corridor door a dozen times, wanting to go to her, fatigued, but restless and sleepless and driven.

When Leonora tapped lightly on his door, he was not astonished, only slightly despairing that she had the courage he lacked.

The door was unlocked and she entered his room. She wore a nightdress and dressing-gown, her face scrubbed free of makeup so that, with her tired eyes, she looked like a sleepy little girl. She locked the door and leaned against its facing, smiling wanly at him.

His breathing sharpened, the emptiness spreading in the pit of his stomach. 'Leonora.' It was all he could say. They had reached that moment when he broke finally with his vows, or together they lit the fiery hot fuse that would blow them to the deepest pits of Father Garcia's hell.

She smiled. She did not move from the door. 'I got tired of

waiting,' she said. 'That's all.'

'I wanted to come to you. You know that.'

She laughed faintly, teasing, but breathless. 'All I know is that you didn't come.'

'I was afraid to,' he said honestly.

'You're not afraid of me?'

'No. But you're about the only thing in God's world I'm not afraid of.'

'We can be afraid, but we mustn't waste time. It's wrong to do that. We have so little time.'

'But I'm still a priest. You're still Bonnett Stockton's daughter.'

'We can change that first part. You'll just have to accept that I'm Bonnett's daughter. We can't change that. We can just ignore it.'

'I want to. God knows I want to. But there's more to it. We can't get your father to ignore it. What do you think he will do when he finds out you were here in my room tonight?'

She spread her hands and tried to smile. 'Then we've no reason to wait any more, do we? If we're to be hung, we may as well be guilty.'

He came to her and took her in his arms. 'I wish to hell it was that easy, Leonora, or that simple. I don't care about the Church any more. I suppose I broke with the Church the day I walked out and came to you. It's just the formality of the unfrocking, the excommunication. I can take that, but there is the fear of what your father will do to break us up.'

'What can he do, Heysus? I'm a big girl now. See. Feel what a nice big mature girl I am.'

He laughed in spite of his agony. 'God, how I wish I could laugh like you do.'

'You can. It's easy. You just say to hell with it, to hell with everything outside this room, and then you put your head back and the laughter pours out.' She drew his head down and kissed him with a fierce passion, a long, aching hunger. He felt himself fly to pieces inside. He shook crazily, his whole body trembling with his need for her. 'My poor baby,' she whispered. 'My poor beautiful dearest baby.'

He was caught in the need now, the ageless desire for her, the unending, unceasing, unrelenting need for her. He swung her up easily in his arms. She laughed and locked her slender, fragrant arms about his neck. At last, her laughter, her excitement intoxicated him and drove everything else from his mind. He managed to declaim, in mock anguish, standing beside the bed with her in his arms, 'You will be gentle with me, won't you?'

She put her head back, laughing. 'I never promised you that.'

He placed her on the bed and lay down beside her. She writhed free and shed her nightclothes, wanting him to look at her, to touch her and love her so that every fantasy they'd known apart must now at last be shared in violent ecstacy.

'I love you,' she whispered. 'I truly love you.'

His hands closed on her fevered body. Excitement and thirst inflamed him and it seemed wondrously that all his life, every thought, every word, every road he followed, had brought him here, to this moment. There was no past, no present, no future, only the fires that consumed him and the needs that drove him, as though only when he was finally a part of her could he be complete and fulfilled and entire.

He gazed down into her wide, tear-starred violet eyes, watching him intently, hungrily, heatedly. But even now, he shuddered with dread. No matter how devoutly they willed it, they could not shut out the world, or cancel tomorrow. He could find true happiness, finally, here, but as certainly he could destroy her. 'Oh God, Leonora,' he whispered, anguished. 'Be sure this is what you want of me. Be sure for both of us — because we can't turn back now, we can never turn back.'

She caught his shoulders in her soft hands, pulling him down to her. 'God knows, I hope not,' she said.

2

Now he existed in an ecstasy of recall, an anguish of remembering. It was as if they were caught in some swift torrent that bore them along helplessly. He was accepted as a leader in the union movement, promoted to the inner council where the strategy was created and plotted. He found this another mistake of the organizers, taking people from jobs they did well and putting them in positions where they were out of their depth. And what he truly hated was that it effectively kept him from Leonora.

Since it was Leonora he lived for, he existed in a state of despair and unfulfilled need. And worse than that, as he had learned in the Church to doubt God, he learned in the council to doubt the union. He discovered, as a member of the inner committee, that except for secret contributions from radicals and closet radicals, from senile multi-millionaires trying to buy clear consciences, from almost overt bribes and graft, most of the union income and operating expenses came from Leonora. She not only believed in the cause of the migrant and the farm worker, she used the fortune inherited from her mother to support the local organization. He found that Leonora's mother, slain mysteriously long ago, had possessed a large personal fortune and she had willed every cent to her daughter, stipulating that her husband must never be permitted to touch those assets. Her father was impotent to keep Leonora from spending her inheritance in any way that pleased her, but Bonnett Stockton opposed her in this squandering of her fortune in a fight he deplored. Shadowing her constantly, he obviously sought some means to interdict what he called her 'mindless waste'.

Jesus lived with that pulsing headache, that empty-bellied dissatisfaction. For the first time in his life he found himself in agreement with Bonnett Stockton and this in itself scared hell out of him. With Bonnett, Jesus believed Leonora gave enough to the union when she dedicated her life to it. The union had no right to squander her money because she allowed it. The greed and penury and total absorption of the Church hierarchy with money had been his first disillusion in the ministry. This dishonesty and callous appropriation of Leonora's inheritance disgusted and disenchanted him with any moral aims the union might otherwise possess. He'd had enough and yet he knew he could not leave as long as Leonora remained dedicated to its mission.

He heard an odd, troubling sound from the outer office. The corridor door whined open and then someone crossed the foyer as if striking the floor with a metal cane. Whoever it was made no effort to be quiet, but did not speak, either. Jesus called out, 'Who's out there? What do you want?'

That odd halting walk stopped and a voice answered, 'I'm looking for a priest named O'Brien. Father O'Brien.'

Jesus got up from his desk and went out of the small inner

office to the larger shadowy room where a stranger stood. Jesus walked toward him, waiting for him to speak. The young man — he looked to be a few years older then Jesus — said nothing at first but continued to stare at him in the vague half-light. At last the man said, 'Are you Father O'Brien?'

Jesus nodded. The man was Latin, likely a Mexican, tall, slender, with short-cropped curly black hair like a halo about his lean, olive brown face. There was something faintly familiar about the fellow, and then Jesus realized it was not that he knew the stranger; it was as if he looked into an oddly wavering mirror. This was his own image, faintly distorted. A name flared into Jesus' mind from the deepest crannies of his memories. He said, 'Triyo?'

The man laughed, coming forward with his arms extended, lunging, and then catching his balance. 'Jesus. Is it really you? Jesusito. God in heaven, after all these years.'

'Pedrillo,' Jesus whispered. 'Pedrillo Luiz.'

'Almost.' The man caught Jesus in his arms, embracing him fiercely. 'That was my name. Once.' He grinned sourly. 'But it also belonged to my father. And so, as soon as I could, I changed it. I wanted nothing of him. My name is Pete Lewis. L-e-w-i-s. Pete Lewis. But I am Triyo.'

3

Tia Clara Luiz no longer lived in the triplex off Aliso Street, though she told Jesus and Pete Lewis that all the Luiz family did live there still and that they should visit them. 'The hell with that,' Pete said. 'I came back only to see you, Mama. Not even God in heaven knows how I've missed you.'

'You were never out of my prayers,' Clara told him. She clung to his hand. She smiled up into his face and wiped away the tears of delight.

'You should have used a few prayers asking for a better place to live than this hovel,' Pete said, looking around in despair. The three-room shack faced on a rubbish-littered alley. Other houses like it in similar stages of disrepair lined the ugly street.

Tia Clara looked around, shrugging. 'I see nothing so terrible. It is all I can afford.'

459

'Is not Tio Pedro providing?' Jesus asked. 'He has such a well-paying job as a deputy sheriff.'

Tia Clara shook her head. She reached out her lye-reddened, rough hands and caught his hand in hers, clinging to it. Jesus stared at his beloved aunt, anguished by what time and privation had done to her. He knew she was in her late forties; she must be nearly fifty, he thought, and yet except for being as heavy as ever, heavier, she looked sixty at least, her eyes weak, her grey hair stringy about her face, her slippers overrun. 'It is that I have not seen Pedro. It makes many years. But Conchita. She comes often.'

'Will she be at home tonight?' Pete asked. 'I would love to see her.'

Clara shook her head. 'It is not that Concha lives with me. No. The place is not for her. It is too crowded. And I must take in a boarder to make ends meet. Concha has a very good job. She is a waitress up at the Biltmore Hotel. Sometimes she sees her father. Sometimes when she comes, she brings a few pesos which she says that her father asked her to give to me.'

'The son of a bitch,' Pete said. 'The dirty son of a bitch.'

'No. No.' Clara caught her son in her arms. 'You must not curse your father. It is the commandment. Honour thy father. He is your father, Pedro.'

'The hell he is. If he is, it's an accident. He cared like a mongrel copulating in the street.'

'You must not hate him so. It breaks my heart.'

'I am sorry. But I do hate him. What was I, ten, twelve when I ran away? I went because I could not endure to live in a house where he came and went, like a rutting animal. Like a dirty, selfish rat, chewing up and destroying everything he touched.'

Clara closed her arms about her son. 'You must forgive, Pedrillo. For your sake. For my sake. For the good of your own heart, you must forgive. Tell Him, Jesus. Tell him, Father O'Brien. You are a priest, you belong to the Church as your dear father dreamed for you. Tell him he must forgive.'

Jesus winced. 'I could not tell him to forgive, Tia Clara, when I cannot. I regret not to have seen you since the day Tio Pedro took me to the Stockton farm and got a hundred dollars for me — '

'Name of God,' Pete Lewis said under his breath.

' — but I did not return to Aliso Street, though I longed to see you once more, because I did not wish to meet with Tio Pedro.'

Clara stood with her arms about both of them, trembling. 'It must not be. He is your father, Pedrillo. He is your uncle, Jesus. If you love me, you must forgive my husband.'

'My God,' Pete Lewis said. 'Are you saying you can forgive the bastard?'

She spread her hands. 'I forgive. Long ago. I know him so well, Pedrillo. Better than he will ever know himself. He longed only to be loved. Admired. Envied. Respected.'

Pete laughed. 'He went about it a hell of a way to get respect.'

'He went the only way he knew. He is like you, Pedrillo —'

'Christ almighty, don't say that, Mama. I've spent twenty years denying him, trying to alter every sign of him I saw in myself. I changed my name. I changed my life to escape that son of a bitch.'

'And yet, you look so like him. When he was young as you, and so beautiful. No wonder all the women turned when he strode past, walking like a puma, your beautiful father.'

'Well, I managed to change the way I walk,' Pete said. He slapped the thigh of his amputated leg.

Clara forgot Pedro. Her eyes brimmed with tears. She stared at her eldest son, anguished. 'What happened?'

'It's a long story.' Pete laughed. 'But I don't mind telling it. Then, Jesus and I will take you out to some fine Mexican restaurant for dinner, and you may order all the hot and spicy items on the menu. Eh?' He smiled, remembering. 'When I was a little boy, Jesusito, I went in to Los Angeles from your father's rancho with him in the horse and wagon and we sold his buckets of honey. When it was done, he took me to a fine Mexican restaurant and let me order my own dinner. I loved him from that moment. I have been around the world since then, but I remember that moment as one of the happiest of my life. I have eaten in Shanghai, in Rio, London and Oran, But I've never found a dinner to match that one in my memory.'

'The sainted Manuel O'Brien. He was a good man,' Tia Clara said. She clung to Jesus' hand. 'And he wanted you for the Church. It was the wish of his life. Thank God you have honoured your father. Such a beautiful priest. You and my

461

Pedrillo. Like brothers. And so warm in my memory, because you used to fight to defend our poor little Teodoro. As Pedrillo, his own brother, would have fought for him had he been here. And now, you grow to look so much alike. It a miracle. It is that my prayers are answered.' She crossed herself and tried to smile between her tears.

Jesus said nothing about the priesthood, or his unremembered father. He said, 'You lost your leg, Pete. How did you do it? Where?'

Pete grinned. 'It was in the Atlantic Ocean somewhere. The north Atlantic. In a gale. During the war. I joined the navy when I was twelve. I said I was sixteen, and they needed seamen, and they took me. I was in Mobile, Alabama. Do you know where that is, Mama? Mobile, Alabama?'

Tia Clara shrugged. She had no idea. 'It sounds so far away.'

'Believe me, it is. And it took me a long time to get there. I rode a lot of trains, walked a lot of dusty roads, washed a million greasy dishes, and ended up in Mobile, Alabama. I was hungry. I panhandled. A man gave me a dollar. I spent it all on food at the first greasy spoon.'

'Greasy spoon?' Tia Clara said.

'Cafe, Mama. There I met two boys, a few years older than I was. They were going in the navy. Three meals a day. Clothes furnished. A place to sleep. A war in Europe. What the hell? Soldiers fight, sailors sail.' He laughed. 'You know what is funny. I was on navy transport that carried soldiers to Europe, and brought some of the same ones back. A lot of them didn't come back, but a lot of them came back whole. Me. A caisson broke loose from its lashings and rolled wild on a deck during a storm. It rolled over my leg and then broke through a railing and plunged into the sea. I managed to stay, clinging to a rail, bleeding like a stuck pig. But they sawed my leg off and put me off the ship in New York. One hundred percent disabled. All I wanted to do, Mama, was to come home to California to find you. Me with a hundred percent disability pension, we can live like royalty. Huh? How about that?'

'I wish to be no burden to you.'

'Mama. You are no burden to me. Even with but one leg, I can carry you like a little girl.' He looked around, grimacing savagely. 'We'll find us a nice place, and you'll wash other people's clothes no more.'

'You should see your father's family,' Clara said. 'They would be so proud of you. A hero from the war.'

'Why should I? Did they keep you with them when that bastard abandoned you? You don't even have to tell me. They did not help you when Pedro Luiz was gone, because you were no longer a Luiz — not by blood.'

She shook her head. 'It does not matter. You are one of them.'

He laughed. 'The hell I am. My name is Pete Lewis. You ask the Navy Department. When I needed someone to swear to my name and my age, I found the man who gave me a dollar. He went with me to the recruiting office. He said my name was Pete Lewis and I was sixteen years old, and he had known me all my life. And that's who I am. Pete Lewis. Hell, can I help it that my mother's name is Clara Luiz?'

4

In the next hectic days, Jesus did not see Leonora at all. She was never in Los Angeles, going as far away as San Francisco, Salinas, Merced and Modesto. She called him, at his office and at his hotel room, hurried, harried, full of love and suppressed excitements. 'No other man stirs me at all,' she whispered across those humming lines, 'yet the sound of your voice turns me wild inside.'

She promised she would see him at the Apia union meeting. This rally the union had daringly attempted to hold in the workers' camp on Stockton Farms property, but Stockton attorneys stopped this with a court injunction. It was decided to invite workers from the entire area to the roads and streets outside the general store at the Apia crossroads. 'We'll be together at Apia,' she promised. 'And then, after the rally is over, you and I will go away for a weekend — maybe for ten years — together alone. Would you like that?'

He lived for that moment. There were other rallies, organization meetings and membership drives. Sister Mari-Jean was with him constantly, as were Pete Lewis, Rod Salinsky and sometimes Ted L. Ross. Ross was no real asset to the cause at the moment. A grower-inspired state's attorney's investigation charged Ross with accepting grower bribes, and if convicted he faced up to twenty years in prison. 'And the men who bribed me, who came to me with their offers? They are heroes to the press, and that makes them heroes to the public.' It was certainly a fact that Ted L. Ross was one of the most hated men in California that year.

Pete Lewis attached himself to Jesus as his aide, his bodyguard, his liaison with the rabble, his shield against those who would waste his time or threaten him.

Salinsky entered Jesus' office the morning of the Apia rally. He looked Pete over sourly. 'Do we need this guy, Father? Where'd he come from? What does he know about unions?' He jerked his head around and peered at Pete, eyes narrowed. 'What can you do for us, mister?'

Pete gave him the old smile that Jesus swore to himself he almost remembered from the infancy beyond recall. He spoke softly, casually. 'I can do whatever Father O'Brien asks me to do, mister. Anything that will serve him.'

'Big union man are you?'

Pete shrugged. 'It is Father O'Brien I believe in, mister. If he does union work, then so do I. If he gives to it all his heart, then the union has all my heart.'

Salinsky scowled, chomped on his cigar and turned his head enough to peer toward Jesus. 'How you know he ain't another grower spy?'

'I don't,' Jesus said. 'He may well be.'

Salinsky relaxed slightly, mollified. Pete said, 'You'll just have to trust me. I don't know you, but I have to trust you.'

Salinsky exhaled. 'Don't know if we can pay you anything.'

Pete grinned. 'Didn't ask for pay, mister.' He slapped the thigh of his amputated leg. 'I am a hundred percent disabled. Seven years in V.A. hospitals. I have saved some money. I can live on that if I must, as long as I can serve Father O'Brien —and through him, mister, serve you and your cause.'

'What kind of bodyguard are you, with a gimpy leg?' Salinsky asked.

Pete shrugged. 'I don't know. Try me and see.'

Salinsky spread his hands. 'Okay. You can hang around, I reckon. Just don't expect no salary. I can't afford new expenses.'

Jesus stared at Salinsky, his look of contempt telling the union leader that whatever was spent was mostly Leonora

Stockton's largesse; nothing came out of Salinsky's own pocket. Salinsky got the unspoken message, loud and clear. He shrugged. 'Okay. Maybe we can come up with with a salary. Hell, we'll see how you work out.'

The day wore away. Excitement built in Jesus at the thought of seeing Leonora again at Apia. It had been such a long, lonely and empty time without her. At last it was time to leave the union headquarters to meet Leonora at her hotel for the drive to Apia. Sister Mari-Jean and half a dozen others rode in a union-rented bus. Pete drove a union Buick, with Jesus taut and sweating on the front seat beside him, and Salinsky lounging in the tonneau with his cigar.

Pete parked at the kerb outside the Angelino Hotel. Jesus got out and bounded across the path. Salinsky lumbered out of the car and followed. They entered the hotel. Jesus asked the clerk to call Miss Stockton's room to say they would meet her in the lobby.

The hotel clerk shook his head. Miss Stockton had come into the hotel earlier in the day, but then had gone away with two men. No. He had no idea who they were. Miss Stockton seemed to go willingly enough but, he now remembered, each man held her tightly by an elbow, across the lobby, out of the revolving doors and to an expensive foreign-made car parked at the kerb.

They drove in silence to Apia. Here, when Salinsky got out where the roads were tightly packed with workers, Jesus remained in the car.

'What fool thing are you planning to do?' Salinsky asked, bent forward and peering into the car.

'I'm going up to the Stocktons,' Jesus said. 'You must have known I would.'

'No. I thought you had better sense. You could get killed up there. For trespassing, for spitting on the grass, for the way you move your lips when you talk. You know that. They'd love to get you up there — uninvited.'

'I've got to find Leonora.'

'Do you think they would tell you anything, even if she were up there?'

'I don't know, Rod. I've got to try.'

'You're putting your life in danger, Jesus. And for what, for God's sake? If she's up there, her own father ain't going to harm her. And anyway, you don't know for sure that's where she is.'

'I know I've got to find out if she's allright. I've got to know where she is.'

'Hell, Jesus, the hotel clerk told you. She went willingly.'

'I've got to know that for sure, too.'

Jesus and Pete Lewis drove in silence into the vast Stockton estates. They approached the park-like region surrounding the Monterey-style mansion. Jesus felt his heart slow, seeming to sink in his chest as they drew near to the house. It was as if he were being transported back across time into the savage wilderness of his boyhood in this place. He had lived here in empty-bellied dread, and all those old fears crowded his mind, bits and shreds of memories that left him sweating and shaken.

Pete drove the union car to the front veranda of the chateau. Jesus got out, legs weak, crossed the tiled flooring and rang the doorbell.

A butler opened the door. Jesus didn't know the servant. He gave him his name and asked to see Mr Bonnett Stockton. The butler nodded. 'If you'll just wait here, sir.'

The minutes dragged past. Jesus looked around, remembering everything, refusing to remember, recalling in painful pleasure the night he had held Leonora in his arms for the first time and in retaliation had been beaten senseless. He supposed he should be thankful they let him live. There were many workers who hadn't survived confrontations with the Stocktons.

At last, the door was opened. The butler appeared, ashen and pallid, his eyes stricken and his cheeks rigid. 'I have been asked to deliver a message to you, Father. From Mr Bonnett Stockton. He says to tell you to get off his property while you still can walk: He says to tell you to get out and stay out on the pain of death. He says if you are not gone in three minutes, he will have the guard dogs turned on you. He says you will understand this next part. He says to tell you he knows about that hotel in Barstow. All about it, and that is reason enough to kill you.'

Jesus straightened. His fear mutated, turned back upon itself and converted into rage. He kept his voice modulated. 'Is Miss Stockton here?'

'I can't answer that, sir.'

'Is she here?'

'I've no quarrel with you, sir. I would lose my job. I have

466

been told what to say to you. That and no more.'

'All right. Then you deliver my message to Stockton. Tell him that Leonora is an adult, free to make her own choices, and that to take her against her will is abduction. Tell him that I will be back, with a search warrant.'

The butler nodded, but he looked ready to vomit. It was not only in ancient times that the messenger with ill tidings had been destroyed along with the message.

Jesus turned and started across the veranda to the car where Pete sat, watching him silently, disturbed. A voice behind Jesus stopped him. 'Jesus.'

He turned. Bragg Stockton, still thick-shouldered and heavy-chested, still distinguished, but somehow looking older than God, came through the door. He said, 'Don't get a warrant, Jesus. There is no sense in battling with my son. Only you can get hurt, and it won't gain you anything. Leonora is not here.'

'Where is she?'

Bragg straightened. 'I want you to understand, Jesus, I am not obligated to answer you. I don't owe you anything. I am trying to avoid trouble. We have enough of that. But I am going to tell you more than I should, more than you have any right to know, because if you have the commonsense I know you do have, you will let it go, you will end all this. . . . My son has had his daughter followed. He says he has proof that she is being criminally influenced to waste her inheritance by people who control her mind. . . . He says that she is emotionally irresponsible. . . he has reports of her sexual misbehaviour. . . and of her mental incompetence. He had the leading psychiatrist in Southern California talk to her. The doctor's diagnosis is mental instability. She has been declared legally incompetent. Her father gave her a choice. She could be institutionalized in the doctor's sanatorium for the mentally disturbed, or she could leave immediately for Europe. She has elected to go at once to Europe, with a companion. She will not be back. When you've had time to think, my boy, you will see that it is for the best. It's best for both of you.'

S.

XXXVI

For a long moment Jesus stood unmoving. He was afraid he could not walk to the Buick in the driveway. He felt Bragg Stockton's gaze on him. He managed to straighten his shoulders and plod across the tiles and down the wide steps. On the drive, he staggered and stumbled against the car. He clutched at it and hung on. He buckled over as if he had been savaged in the belly, and threw up. Finally, he sank to the running board and sagged there with his head bowed between his legs.

Pete stumbled around the car. Bragg Stockton crossed the veranda to the top step and stood, silent, legs braced apart, face expressionless, a monolith of shadow in a long shaft of light through the open door.

'Come on, Father,' Pete said in a gentle tone. 'We better go.'

Jesus nodded but he did not move. Pete caught his arm and helped him to his feet. He opened the door and Jesus sagged upon the seat. Pete slammed the door and lumbered awkwardly back around the car, got in under the wheel.

'Take me back to the hotel,' Jesus said, voice raw with pain.

'We better go to the rally.'

Jesus sucked in his breath, raging. He spoke in a taut whisper. 'Rally? What rally for Christ's sake? You heard him. I can't go back there.'

Pete started the car and moved it along the driveway. The night wind was chilly against Jesus' fevered face. 'What's back at the hotel for you?'

'Nothing, goddamn it. Nothing. I can't face people now. I want to be by myself. I hurt, damn it. I hurt.'

'So you want to be alone with your hurt?'

'Yes, damn it, I do. Is that so hard for you to understand?'

'I understand,' Pete's gentle voice reached for him in the darkened car. 'But I just don't think it's very smart, that's all, to sit around doing nothing but feeling sorry for yourself.'

'What the fuck do you know about being hurt, about loss?'

Pete laughed. 'Some. I even qualify as an expert. I spent seven long years in V.A. hospitals, feeling sorry over the loss of a leg, with nothing to do but grieve about it. My life was ruined. My usefulness was over. I was a fucking cripple to lie around government hospitals, feeling sorry for myself, with people taking care of me. . . . I swear to you, Father, it was when I stopped grieving and started thinking about something else that I started to live again.'

'I'm sorry I flared up like that, Pete. Forgive me.'

'Don't worry about it. I just don't want you to give up living.'

'I don't give a shit for living. If this is living you can have it. In my whole life, I had one thing — one person — who made me happy, that I loved. I don't give a goddamn for living without her.'

'I understand that, too.'

'Then take me back to the hotel. Let me rip out my guts for a while, then maybe I'll be all right.'

'Only it doesn't work that way, Jesusito. There is only one time to give up to agony.'

'When is that, expert?'

Pete laughed, his voice low against the hum of the engine. 'I learned the hard way. You should face agony only when you can plan how to defeat it. I know you hurt. I know how bad you hurt. But work will help. Nothing will change the hurt, or even lessen it, or the loss. No matter what you do, she will still be gone, she will be lost to you. You can't change that. All you can do is adjust, give in, surrender, try to live with it.'

'Christ, you sound joyful.'

'No. It's not easy. Only we human beings are lucky in one way. Just one. Our minds are capable of holding only one thought at a time. It can be a good thought, or it can be evil. Our minds don't give a damn which. It's just that there can be only the one.'

Jesus said nothing. Pete did not speak again, either. They drove out of the unfenced Stockton estates and along the road to the brilliantly illumined rally in front of the general store.

Five hundred migrants were gathered there. Pete parked the Buick and sat silently until Jesus got out. Then he painfully writhed out of the door and followed him.

The union organizers sat on the general store porch which tonight served as the speakers' dais. When Jesus and Pete stepped up there, the crowd screamed in approval. Somebody handed Jesus his guitar. Jesus sat on the edge of the porch and played 'Ninety-nine out of a hundred want to be kissed, why don't you?' It was a vibrant song, full of fire and excitement. The crowd responded. They sang. They sang a dozen songs, all upbeat and full of promises of love and goodness and devotion.

He got through that rally, and all the rallies during the next long, eternal months. People cheered when he appeared at the meetings. Children sat in knots before him when he played. They danced and laughed and worst of all, they believed.

He found it harder every day to tell these people that by fighting they could win. This had always been his sole promise; he no longer believed it.

He wanted only one thing: he wanted to escape. He needed to extricate himself from suffering people who believed he could in any way at all alleviate their suffering. He needed respite from that sense that he was worse than Ted L. Ross or Rodney Salinsky, no matter how hard and cynical they had become. They at least had their own motives for working in the union; he had none. He was more dishonest than the slimiest snake-oil dealer. He was selling to vulnerable and gullible and miserable people something he distrusted, disbelieved and would have disavowed if only he could.

He prowled his room at night, sleepless. God knew there was right in the cause. What there was not was hope. There was no hope. The establishment was too strong, too rich, too powerful, too formidable, too preoccupied and uncaring. There was no way to reach it. And every day the unemployment rolls swelled all across the country. Unemployment was now at twenty-five percent. President Hoover had appointed a new commission to study it. He had lowered taxes on investments, on factory improvements, on personal income. What hope was there for migrants — many of them illegals and wetbacks — when they had suffered in times of plenty?'

Escape. This was all he asked. For him this was the only

470

answer. He no longer believed he would see Leonora Stockton on this earth again. He accepted this. It was his compromise with a vengeful God. Anything else was the direct route to insanity. But he had to find refuge from faces that smiled and opened like flowers with radiant hope when he appeared, poor bastards who trusted him and his snake-oil when he no longer trusted his God, his mission or himself.

Every morning, he got out of bed after a sweaty, restless night. He vowed he would leave that day. But the union sank, mired in deep trouble since Leonora and her money were gone. Few union people — only the office staff — were paid salaries any more. He got only expenses, room and board. He wanted to escape this hopeless maze, but he could not bring himself to walk out when these other people were still struggling desperately, still depending on him, still needing him. He didn't leave because he truly had nowhere to go anyhow.

He stayed. He and Sister Mari-Jean and Pete Lewis prowled across the state. They organized, they recruited, they begged for financial support. When they were in direst need, they asked the Church to help them. They were rejected there too.

He did not get Leonora out of his mind or out of his heart. Whatever news he had of her now came from the society columns of the Los Angeles newspapers. Leonora sunned with Americans at Nice; she gambled at Monte Carlo; she attended fashion shows in Paris, she visited the wine country around Reims. Headlines, accompanied by a three-column-wide photo of the couple, told of her engagement to the Baron Anton Ivan Katequezane-Speranski at Lido. A definite date for the marriage was not set. There were rumours that the couple might be married in the United States. For a long time then, there was no news of her. It was almost as if she slipped through the column seams of the social pages. And, when after months of silence, Leonora was next reported at Cannes, there was no mention of the baron, or of the engagement. Reading the news account saved by one of the secretaries in the union headquarters, Jesus wondered emptily what Bonnett Stockton had paid, said or done to be rid of the baron.

Time and money became increasingly critical in the union. Most of the organization's dwindling coffers were used to defend Ted L. Ross against an indictment on fourteen counts of extortion. The union looked as if it were finished. Now was the time to leave: it was stupid to stay on in this hopeless cause.

Ross' trial was sensational and lasted for three weeks, during which the whole labour union cause was aired in headlines. The newspaper consensus was that the labour leaders were racketeers, thieves and criminals, somehow battening on workers who needed federal laws protecting them against such thugs. The Hoover administration was preparing to ask Congress for such legislation. A jury found Ted L. Ross guilty on all counts. He was sentenced to twenty years at Alcatraz. The union suffered so brutal a defeat, it could barely hope to recover. Contributions were at an all-time low. Membership dropped daily.

The union itself altered with Ross' conviction and imprisonment. The faces changed. Rod Salinsky remained as president of the local chapter, but Jesus was moved upward to second in command in Ted Ross' place. Clearly, the union hoped that a turned collar, even of a failed priest, might improve its image and find it new financial support.

That support did not come. Jesus, with Sister Mari-Jean and Pete Lewis, could still unite a crowd of unemployed, migrants and farm labourers. They could even laugh when they sang 'Yes, We Have No Bananas'. But nobody promised them three dollars a day for a nine-hour day. The desperate crowded outside the union hall begging for work, for loans, for food money.

When word came that Murado Valdez, the farmer esteemed as the model employer, had cut back to ten cents an hour and had even been forced to lay off workers, the union leaders knew they were driven to the last ditch. Jesus asked if he could at least drive out and talk to Murado Valdez. Despite his earlier success, Rod Salinsky denied the request. Everything rode on their recruiting Valdez' support and promise of better employment and even a modest pay increase. Without it, they were beaten. Rod would go alone.

Rod was gone from the headquarters office less than an hour when he called in and asked urgently to speak to Father O'Brien. Rod's voice crackled across the telephone wires, apprehensive, shaken, totally out of character. Knowing Rod Salinsky, one had to say the organizer no longer feared the devil himself; but he was scared now. He sounded uncertain, tentative and hesitant. 'I think I'm being tailed, Jesus,' Rod said. 'Four men in an old '23 touring car. They got behind me just after I left town and I haven't been able to shake them. I'll go on out to talk to Murado Valdez, but. . . maybe I'm nuts, but I'd feel better. . . I mean, I thought maybe you and Pete Lewis could drive out and meet me at Apia. . . . Tell Pete I said it might not be a bad idea to be armed.'

Jesus replaced the receiver, troubled. Had it been any man other then Salinsky, he would have chalked up part of his apprehension to nerves. But Rod had no nerves, unless he'd sprouted them this morning. Jesus called Pete, told him what Salinsky had said. They went down to the old union car at the kerb without delay. Pete drove swiftly out of the city and then pressed the accelerator to the floorboard once they had turned out onto the San Gabriel Valley highway.

A mile beyond Apia they found Salinsky's car, tilted oddly off the shoulder into a drainage ditch. They prowled around the vehicle but found nothing, not even shoe prints to show that Salinsky had walked away from the abandoned vehicle.

'I think we ought to drive on to Valdez' farm,' Jesus said. 'It doesn't look like Rod ever got that far, but he may just have had car trouble and hitched a ride from here.'

Pete shrugged. He didn't believe that Salinsky had proceeded to Valdez' farm, but he had no alternative idea to suggest. They got back in the union car and went swiftly along the highway, the wind screaming past the windows, almost like a cry of terror.

They did not talk. There was nothing to say. There had been no key in the ignition of Salinsky's car, no sign of a struggle. Yet, on the other hand, there was no trace left, either, that anyone had walked on the road shoulder around the vehicle.

They left the rim of the Stockton farms, a limit indicated by flat stone markers. As they approached the edge of the nine square miles of orange groves inside the Valdez estate, they saw a cloud of dust smoking up from the hard-packed side road which skirted the trees, an artery used only in season by truckers, pickers or maintenance.

Pete slowed to under fifteen miles an hour, trying to reach the side road as whatever vehicle was causing the dust should emerge from it. They were still half a mile from the intersection when a sedan careened out of the lane and turned onto the highway, coming toward them. They saw that it was a Los Angeles County Sheriff's patrol car. Two uniformed officers were in the front seat. They sped past without glancing toward the union automobile.

'Wasn't that Tio Pedro?' Jesus said.

'I don't know,' Pete replied. 'If it was, the hell with him. I got nothing to say to him. But at least we know it's not the '23 touring car that Salinsky said was tailing him.'

Jesus nodded. He turned, watching the patrol car speed away. Pete said, 'Son of a bitch.' Jesus didn't bother asking whom Pete was talking about; his own hatred for Tio Pedro was exceeded only by Pete's loathing.

Senor Murado Valdez invited Pete and Jesus into his cool, Latin-style living-room, sunken, fitted with Persian Carpets, the walls draped with the subdued reds of Spanish scenes in hand-woven wool. He shook his head at their enquiries. He had not seen Senor Rod Salinsky for some weeks. 'I know why he was coming to see me,' Valdez said. 'I know why you are here, Father O'Brien. It was with deep regret I was forced to retrench, even to release many workers. I may as well tell you, my land and its yields have been under ruinous pressures from the growers' cooperative. I am a member of that cooperative.' He laughed in sad irony. 'A charter member. But I am now a pariah. An outsider. They have as much as advised me, I will break, and follow the will of the majority, or they will use any means at their disposal to ruin me.' His smile was cold and frustrated. 'So far they are doing an excellent job.'

They drove back along the highway only as far as the access lane to the Valdez groves. Neither spoke their thoughts aloud, but they were in agreement. They estimated the distance from the highway at which they'd first glimpsed the dust of the speeding police car. Pete drove a few hundred

474

yards beyond this place and parked.

They got out then and walked along the hard-packed lane. They had gone less than a quarter of a mile when they saw where a car had pulled off the roadway onto the soft red shoulder. Here there were boot prints and a path that led into the wall of citrus trees.

With a mounting sense of sickness, Jesus plodded beside Pete. They did not speak. Even when they found a place where the ground was marked and slashed, as if by men in a struggle, they said nothing. Not even the raw, hastily covered hole brought a word from either of them. They were too sick to speak, too filled with agony and besides, there were no words.

Whoever had dug the hole had attempted to cover it over without leaving too high a mound of fresh red earth. Jesus prowled around this broken spot, fascinated, horrified, going back in his mind over the unsolved disappearances of workers during those years when he had lived at Stockton Farms. All the Stocktons needed was somebody to do their dirty work and a place to conceal the evidence. What better site than the remote and silent citrus groves of their despised neighbour? If skeletal remains ever were uncovered, they would be on Valdez land, with nothing to link them to the Stockton estates.

Sickness churned in Jesus' belly. Somebody to do their dirty work. Once it had been a deputy sheriff named Morris Redding. God only knew what blackmail threat they had used against him. And now one of the deputies who actually worked for the Stocktons, for secret bribes and bonuses — and to keep concealed whatever hidden criminal knowledge they held over his head — was Pedro Luiz.

Jesus trudged, moving slowly, as if calf-deep in a rough surf, with his head down. Anguish chewed at him. He could hardly bring himself to speak aloud his thoughts to Pete, even knowing that Pedrillo had grown up detesting his father.

Something glinted on the rim of the shallow grave. Jesus hesitated, unsure whether it was a reflection refracted by the helpless tears that welled in his eyes. He knelt and stared at the coin. He took it up in his hand, recognizing it. It was the ten-dollar gold-piece tie-pin his father had worn and which Pedro Luiz had appropriated as his own when Manuel died, and had now lost here in the brief, violent struggle with the

475

dead man in that grave.

'We better notify the sheriff's office,' Pete said. 'We better let them dig up the body. We better let them handle it.'

Jesus nodded, but for a long moment he stood, unmoving.

3

Jesus sat at his desk. Two eternal days had passed since he and Pete had located that grave and notified the sheriff's office. The body retrieved by the officials was that of Rodney Salinsky. The union organizer had been brutally beaten to death, a killing the sheriff described to reporters as 'racketeer style'. It was unfortunate, lamentable, and yet, the sheriff pointed out, who lives by the sword dies by it, and who sinks into racketeering takes his chances with racketeers.

Jesus and Pete had called the sheriff's office from the general store at Apia, giving exact directions to the murder spot, but refusing to give their names. Pete had wanted to stay and be of whatever assistance they could when the police arrived, but Jesus had objected. 'One of the deputies sure to investigate, Pete, will be Tio Pedro. You and I know he and at least one other deputy were out there in that grove today. Are you ready to testify against him?'

Pete looked grey about the mouth. He shook his head. 'I'm ready,' he said. 'But I don't know if I could.'

Jesus showed him the gold-coin tie-pin he had found at the graveside. 'You recognize this, Pete?'

Pedrillo winced, nodding. 'We know Papa was in that exact spot, don't we?'

Jesus exhaled. 'We've got to be sure what we do next. Once we turn in this tie-pin, we'll never be able to turn back. Tio Pedro will be destroyed.'

'Like a hundred prayers suddenly answered,' Pete said. He shook his head. 'He's got it coming. We both want him to get it, me even a hell of a lot more than you do. But there is one thing that we have to consider, Jesus.'

Jesus spread his hands. 'If we destroy Pedro Luiz, we also destroy Tia Clara. I know goddamn well I'm not ready to do that.'

They had said no more. Sitting alone in his musty, shadowy

office now, Jesus placed the gold-piece tie-pin directly in the centre of the worn, ink-stained green blotter before him. He gazed at the little round ornament as if in it he might discover the secret to existence. The time-dulled, oil-smeared coin and metal pin, which Manuel had worn proudly with his colourful kerchiefs and which Pedro Luiz had claimed as his own, caught the faint light and glistened dully, almost obscenely, taunting him.

A knock on his door roused him from his anguished reverie. With almost a sense of welcomed physical release, he said, 'Come in.'

One of the office women held the door ajar. 'A Senora Pedro Luiz to see you, Father.'

'Tia Clara!' Jesus sprang up from the old swivel chair, leaving it spinning and whining. He went around the desk and held out his arms to his aunt.

Clara shivered, ill at ease, nervous, ready to retreat at the first rebuff, stunned at her own audacity. She'd donned her single 'Sunday best dress', the taffeta grey frock she wore to Mass, to funerals and weddings. It was much laundered, faded, losing its elasticity. She was so much heavier then she'd been when she'd bought it at the May Company uptown that she'd let it out to its final seams. She bulged in places and the fabric constricted her where it could give no more when she pressured it with rolls and knots of fat.

Clara came into his arms and kissed him fiercely. Then, standing rigid and uncomfortable, she inquired about his office, his work, declaring herself pleased to see this important place where he made his grand achievements.

'You are busy,' Clara said. 'I should never have come. But I knew I must.'

'I'm glad you did, Tia Clara. Did Pete know you were coming in?'

'No. No.' She shook her head. 'I said nothing to Pedrillo. I waited until he told me he was to be out of town. I hoped to see you alone. What I have to say is for you alone.'

His heart sank. He led her to a chair. She sat in it, but could not relax. She fussed with her dress, folded and creased her small white kerchief. She tried to smile, failed. At last she got up and walked to the window, staring unseeingly down at the side street below.

'What's the matter, Tia Clara? What's troubling you?'

Jesus had learned in the ministry to ask questions he didn't want to ask, to elicit the answers he dreaded or didn't want to hear.

She turned and gazed at him. She looked tired, as well as frightened. 'I fear,' she said. 'I feel terror that grips at my heart. It is that Concha came night before last to see me. Pedrillo was not at home, so Concha could talk plainly.'

'Yes. What is it? What's the matter?'

'It is that Concha has visited her father in the past days and finds him ill. Sick with an illness of the soul. It is that he fears you and Pedrillo mean to charge him with a crime.'

Jesus stared at the gold coin. He tilted his head, looking at his beloved aunt. There was no easy way to say what had to be said. 'He has committed a crime, Tia Clara. Probably many crimes. But Pedrillo and I have indisputable evidence that he was at the place where a man named Rodney Salinsky was killed and buried.'

Now his aunt sat in the chair, poised on the edge of it.

Jesus persisted, reluctantly. 'Tio Pedro either killed Salinsky, or was most certainly an accomplice, before the fact or after. It doesn't matter. I know he was there. He struggled with Salinsky. I know he did because he lost this, Tia Clara.' He held up the small coin between thumb and forefinger.

Tia Clara took the pin, staring at it, her eyes brimming with tears and her mind teeming with old and painful memories. She nodded. 'This pin belonged to Manuel O'Brien. I knew poor old Manuel would have wanted you to have it when he died. But it was so beautiful. Poor Pedro. So vain. He could not part with the ornament. . . . Yes. . . . Pedro has worn it since — since that night poor Manuel was — Manuel died.'

'Well, Tio Pedro lost it at the murder site. Beside a new grave. Rod Salinsky's body was found in that pit. Pete and I notified the sheriff, but I don't know how Tio Pedro knew it was us who reported the crime. . . unless he recognized us in the car as he passed us. . . . He must have.'

Tia Clara could hardly speak. 'And you told lo jerif of the gold pin?'

Jesus shook his head. 'No. Not yet. But I must. I am sick, but I know this is not the first murder committed by Tio Pedro and other deputies — there were at least two others — and I know they've disposed of those bodies in the Murado Valdez citrus groves. God help me, Tia Clara, I even know the evil, vengeful reason why the bodies were buried on Valdez land. The murders will implicate Murado Valdez and not the Stocktons or the deputy sheriffs. Murado Valdez is a good and decent man, Tia Clara. Honourable. But most of all he is innocent. I can't let him be charged for murder when I know better. I can't let that happen. You know I can't. Tio Pedro is guilty. I know he is. This pin is the final proof.'

The woman bowed her head and wept for some moments. Jesus wanted to go to her, to comfort her, but there was no balm, no words of solace. At last, she whispered, voice choked, 'And it is that you feel he has this guilt of murder alone?'

'No. I don't, Tia Clara. I know better. But he is the only one I have true evidence against. He knows the guilt of others. Maybe he will not want to take the whole blame to himself. Perhaps he will speak out. I pray to God he will. But whether he does or not, he must be stopped. And he is guilty of murder, we can't escape that.'

She sighed heavily and folded her hands in her lap. She gazed at him, anguished, and nodded her head. 'It is that I too know of Pedro's guilt. But it is that you must not betray him to the sheriff, Jesus. You must not.'

Tia Clara, I must. I must — or I am as guilty as he.'

'It is that it is not that simple, my dearest one.'

'I know. It never is.'

'I know of Pedro's guilt. Of murder. Not of these murders you talk of now. And there is much that you do not know. Of former days.' She held up the gold coin. 'The night that Pedro took that gold pin from poor old Manuel O'Brien — Pedro was guilty of murder that night. A murder of passion, of hatred, of rage. He beat poor Manuel to death with an axe handle and threw the bloody thing to the floor. It is that when El Patrono Stockton came he took the axe handle with him. He has that weapon in his possession now. I know this. Pedro has told Concha it is true and Concha tells me. El Patrono Stockton uses this to force Pedro to continue to do his bidding. Si, Pedro is guilty, Jesus. But the true guilt of these other murders belongs to Patrono Stockton. He orders what is to be done and Pedro cannot refuse.'

Almost under his breath, Jesus said with acrid malice, 'Could not refuse, even if he wanted to.'

Tia Clara's head jerked up. 'Ah, dear Jesuito! Such hatred

479

as poisons your dear heart, as well as that of Pedrillo. If you did not hate Pedro Luiz so bitterly, would you be so anxious to destroy him by letting him pay alone for crimes which belong as well to the fine Patrono Stockton?'

Jesus got up. He leaned against the desk, feeling a terrible fatigue. 'A hundred wrongs don't make one right, Tia Clara. I am sorry. I have hesitated turning in that evidence for one reason, and one alone. I would cut out my guts before I'd willingly hurt you. . . . But this man you try to protect is evil, Tia Clara. Before God I swear it. He was cruel to you, to Teodoro, to me and to Pedrillo — and even to my father. You yourself admit Tio Pedro killed my father.'

Tia Clara sat for a long time staring at her lye-reddened hands. At last she looked up. 'No, Jesusito. Pedro killed Manuel O'Brien.' She drew a deep breath and held it as if almost physically unable to speak the next words. 'But Manuel O'Brien was not your father. Poor, sainted, limp old Manuel deceived himself that he was the father of Julia's child. . . . I deceived myself as well. . . . All these years I refused to admit what I knew to be true. I believed Manuel to be your father because I would not let myself believe that my Pedro had violated my beloved little sister and then arranged her marriage to a foolish old man, vain and stupid. . . and deceived.'

Jesus felt as if he'd been beaten mercilessly in the solar plexus. The breath was knocked out of him and he gasped, struggling for air. The world, so long an ugly and lonely place, became suddenly as rotten and vile as the pit beyond hell.

He sat down heavily and stared at the wall. He was forced at last to see himself in a new and soul-gutting light. He saw new reasons for the conflicts between his vows to the Church and the carnal needs of his flesh. He had been a rotten priest because he was the son of a rotten son of a bitch. There was no good in him, none of the reconciling decency of the old beekeeper. He was the bastard son of a bastard.

Tia Clara said nothing. After a long time, she replaced the gold-piece pin on the blotter. Her eyes brimming with tears, she gazed at Jesus. Then she turned and walked out of the office. He hardly was aware she was gone. He sat, unmoving, and stared at the wall and all the past days of his life as seen in this new and garish and merciless light.

XXXVII

Pete Lewis got out of his car, conscious most of all of the weight of the gun in his jacket pocket. Irrationally, he felt conspicuous, uneasy and ill at ease in the quiet east Los Angeles residential street. It was as if alert watchers crouched behind every window curtain, silently regarding him. He suffered the unreasoning fear that anyone who saw his face understood his intent. He had come here to kill his father. The concealed faces behind those shadowed windows winced in shock. His own father. He had come into this quiet neighbourhood like some violent demon to kill his own father. Despite his doubts and his certainty that he was revealed as a murderer to unseen witnesses, he did not hesitate. Nothing, no one could stop him now. He had lived in his own mind too long with this obsessive desire. He had come, an avenging angel, to this place to kill his father, and he would do it. If ever a man deserved to be eradicated, it was Pedro Grandos Luiz. Somebody had to stop him in his insidious evil. They should have wiped him out a long time ago.

Pete limped around his car and to the path before the four-room Spanish-stucco cottage. This neighbourhood was a patchwork of stucco and frame houses with small lawns, detached garages, flowers banked against the foundations, erected feverishly in the boom times of the twenties. The front garden of Pedro Luiz' habitat looked as if it were arid, as though it had existed a year without water or care. In a kind of sick irony, Pete told himself that though this house was light-years removed from the Aliso Street triplex, he still could have selected Pedro Luiz' abode: the one dwelling wholly neglected along here.

He hesitated, glancing at the Los Angeles County Sheriff Department vehicle parked in the driveway, windows down, wing dented, dust-pocked. This would be Deputy Luiz' official car, probably down to its last two or three gallons of petrol, needing oil, tyres ill-inflated. God almighty, how he hated the slovenly bastard who went on and on doing his evil — and getting paid for it, with annual vacations, retirement pay, and all the graft he could stash away.

Pete walked in his stiff stagger, lunge and halt way to the front door. He stared down at the word 'welcome' on the mat. He drew a deep breath, held it. He pressed the doorbell. The sound from within the house reverberated inside his head. He felt sick. The only thing he didn't feel was the need to turn and walk away while he still could. No. He had run away before. He was not going to default in his duty, he was not running any more.

A young girl — within four or five years of his own age — opened the door. She wore a cheap wrap-around, her dark blonde hair in curlers.

He winced at her youthfulness, though he saw a hardness and sophistication about her. Still, she was just a girl. He'd known his father had a new live-in mistress. He had not expected anyone so young. Remembering the way he'd accidentally — though not infrequently — walked into his house from play to find his father mounting Tia Julia in frantic, sweating passion on his mother's bed, when Julia was thirteen or so, he supposed finding Pedro Luiz still chasing young women should be no surprise.

The girl's face warmed in a lovely smile, recognition lightening her dark olive eyes. 'Why hello,' she said. 'Look who's here.' She called over her shoulder. 'Pedro. Agui. You'll never guess who has come to this house to visit us.'

'If it's any of my goddamn family, tell 'em I got no money for them,' Pedro's well-recalled voice raged from within the house.

Pete felt his hackles crinkle and crawl along the nape of his neck. Ugly, violent, hateful and long-suppressed memories swarmed like robber bees in his head. 'Tell him I don't want any of his goddamn money,' Pete said to the girl.

She laughed and relayed the message. 'He says to tell you, he doesn't want any of your goddamn money.' Still smiling, she looked back up at Pete's face, as if fascinated and stirred by memories of her own. 'You don't remember me, do you?'

Pete shrugged. He could have told her that he didn't even give a damn who she was, that he would not have cared in

482

ordinary circumstances.

'Francisca,' she said, as if astonished that he could have disremembered her. 'My name is Francisca. I am Mme Rosa's daughter. I saw you steal one of her gypsy charms, but I did not tell.'

More memories flooded back into Pete's mind, as if from an unblocked sewer: the exotic fortune-telling parlour upstairs above La Madreselva, the talismans against evil, the tarot cards, the formidable, formally attired woman who smelled of faintly soiled lilies. The little girl who'd made faces and stuck out her tongue. His childish fascination with her.

'What's a girl like you doing in a place like this?' Pete managed to keep his voice light.

'Nicely.' She smiled, gazing up at him. 'Your father and I have been in love for some years. We have been together a long time. . . . I'll bet you never thought I'd grow up to be your stepmother.' She held the door open, still smiling, still pleased with him. 'Come in. Come in.'

Pete limped past her into the parlour. He heard her catch her breath. 'Why, Pedrillo,' she said. 'What's the matter with your leg?'

He shrugged. 'I don't know. I haven't seen it in years.'

He held his breath, aware that his father had entered the small square living-room, filled with a clutter of worn carpeting, wicker sofa, bargain-basement furnishings and cheap, framed copies of Spanish art. Pedro stopped, stunned at the sight of his son. He shook his head in disbelief and then tried to smile. 'Pedrillo,' he said. 'My son. Pedrillo.'

'My name is Pete Lewis.' At this announcement in the flat cold tone of hatred, Pedro stopped, arms upraised. He let them sag to his sides and for a long moment the two men stood in awkward silence. Pete shrugged and said, 'You never wanted me as your son. Now, I don't claim you as my old man. I would die first. I came to see you about something else.'

He saw Pedro's face go pale, as if all the blood rushed down from his head. Pedro retreated half a step and shifted his shoulders in a familiar movement. He stared about warily, without looking at either Pete or Francisca.

Pete turned his head and glanced at Francisca. 'Don't you have somewhere you can go, Mother? Somewhere you can visit? You might run and have Mme Rosa tell your fortune.'

'This is my house,' Francisca said.

'I want to talk privately to your husband,' Pete told her. 'You may not find it pleasant.'

Francisca started to speak, but Pedro cut her off, flexing his arms. 'It's all right, Paca. Don't worry about me. What can this one go to do? Gimpy leg. Christ. Look at that. He can hardly stand up on that gimpy leg.'

Francisca sighed and shrugged. 'I'll go to visit down the street.' She glared at Pete. 'Right down the street.'

'That will be very kind,' Pete said, as if she were already dismissed from his mind.

Pedro prowled the room, almost like a fighting-cock circling an opponent. He clenched and loosened his fists, worked his arms inside his shirt. His voice crackled with bravado learned in years as a sheriff's deputy. 'What you want here, gimp?' he asked. 'You want money? I got no money for you. It is that my expenses are great.'

'I'm sure they are,' Pete said. 'I don't care. I don't want your money.'

'If you think to threaten me unless I go back to live with your mother,' Pedro shook his head, 'you can forget that too.'

'My mother lives good without you. Even when she had to wash clothes to stay alive she was better off without you. She is well rid of you.'

Pedro straightened his shoulders, tilted his head slightly. 'I am a deputy sheriff now.' There was flat warning in his tone.

Pete smiled grimly. 'Can't tell the thugs from the cops without a programme.'

'You watch your tone, gimp.' Pedro stretched and worked his shoulders. 'I have the hope you did not come here to make trouble — you and your gimpy leg.'

Francisca returned to the living-room. She'd removed the curlers from her hair, run a brush through the thick tresses, and slipped into a sheath dress and pumps. She carried a red purse. 'I'll be back soon,' she said. 'Adios, Pedrillo.'

He shrugged and did not bother to glance her way. When the front door closed behind Francisca, Pete said, 'My mother said you came to her the other night.'

'Clara is my wife. In the eyes of the Church. In the eyes of God. I can visit her if I like.'

'Only she is not your wife in my eyes. You abandoned her years ago. You forfeited her when you beat her until she bled

484

from broken nose and blackened eyes, when you cheated her, and starved her, and lied to her and disgraced her in the eyes of her neighbours.'

Pedro Luiz shrugged his shoulders. 'Still, she is my wife.'

'No. You came to her now only because you thought she might save your worthless hide, because you knew Jesus O'Brien was going to bring charges of murder against you. You wept and pleaded with my mother, sobbed about what a good man you were, doing your duty, following orders.'

'I do not lie. That is true.'

'You lied all your life. No matter what evil you did, you excused it inside your own empty head. Evil was right if it got you what you wanted.'

'All of us. All. You as much as I. We all do what we can in this world. What we have to do.'

Pete smiled coldly. 'I know. I still bear the scars of your having to beat me without mercy when I was five years old. I started hating you then when you started beating me because you were drunk and needed to hurt somebody — somebody who couldn't hurt you back. I've lived all my life for this moment, this one moment. I have come to kill you because you are not fit to live.'

'Kill me, gimp?' Pedro's mouth twisted, his brow tilted. 'How will you go to do that?'

Pete removed the gun from his jacket pocket. He held it out where Pedro could see it, a .38-caliber Smith & Wesson.

Pedro stared at the gun. He lifted his eyes to Pete's face, found it implacable, the eyes without mercy. Pedro seemed to go to jelly inside. He looked as if he might have wet his pants. His face twisted. His eyes brimmed with tears of self-pity.

'You — you are my son,' he whispered, shaking his head. 'Why would you want to kill me?'

'Because I am your son. Because I am the one who must do it. Because somebody should have killed you before you battered Teodoro for having inherited the off-centre irises of your mother, and before you battered my mother and me. Somebody should have killed you before you robbed Jesus O'Brien of a considerable fortune and spent it on whores and cards and fine clothes. Because no matter where I went on this earth, I lived only to get back here and kill you. That thought kept me alive when I had nothing else to live for.'

Pedro shook his head, as if he could not believe what he

heard. 'I am your father, Pedrillo. My God. I am your flesh. Blood. How could you hate me? How could you wish to harm me?'

'Easy. I learned to hate, to harm — I learned from you.'

Pedro wept openly. 'No. No. This cannot be. That my own son, my flesh and blood, should turn against me — with murder in his heart.' He shook his head and held up his hand as if he could physically delay his son. 'What of your poor bereaved mother when you harm me? What of her?'

'She's lived all these years without you. She will go on living.'

'If you harm me, Clara will despise you before God.'

'Don't worry about me, Pedro. It's too late for your concern.'

'No. . . you cannot, Pedrillo. My dearest Pedrillo. I beg you. You want money? Si? I give you all the money I have. I get more money for you. You want money for Clara? Si? Take it. Take all I have. I've meant to provide for her all along —'

'Stop whining. Stop lying, you snivelling son of a bitch. I'm sick of your lies. God must be sick of your lies. No. I've got something here for you, Pedro, something from me. For all the times when you beat me bloody when I was a child. For the way you beat my mother in front of me. Something from my mother, too. Something from God Himself. If there is a God, He would want this for you.'

He brought the gun up.

Pedro screamed like a woman and toppled to his knees on the floor. He wept, pleading, promising, sobbing. He would reform. He had been evil in Pedrillo's eyes, he saw now how that could be. In the past there were mistakes, when he was misunderstood. Maybe he had been in error. But in his heart he meant well. Always. Always he'd tried to do what was best. 'All I have wanted,' he sobbed, 'was someone who truly understood me.'

'At last you've got him,' Pete said. 'I understand you totally. I know you exactly for what you are.'

When he brought the snout of the gun up, Pedro screamed again. All the time he'd talked, he'd kept his gaze fixed on that gun. As Pete's finger tightened on the trigger, Pedro lunged forward, prostrate, grovelling, his face pressed into the carpet at Pete's feet, crying, begging for mercy, pleading that his life be spared that he might atone for any wrongs.

Pete stared at Pedro, seeing his father whimpering and writhing on the floor, middle-aged, greying, gross, fat, as useless as a slug. He gazed down at him for a long time. He thought of the years he had waited for the triumph of this moment.

A sense of sickness and loss flooded through him. Now that the final moment had come at last, it was no good. Now that it was here, there was no triumph. There was nothing. There would be no exultation in killing this worthless lout. There was no victory in exterminating vermin.

Pete shook his head. His voice was low, hollow, disbelieving. 'You are not a man at all. You're slime. You're not worth killing. . . . Oh God, to think I wasted my life, poisoned my guts, cheated myself, hating scum like you.'

XXXVIII

From the window of his hotel room Father O'Brien stared down into the shadowed, sun-streaked street. A late afternoon sun probed among ill-lit crannies between gloomy walls, light seeping down over lurid dark like some pallid absolution. In the cafe downstairs a man at the piano extracted the latest downhearted wail from the instrument.

Jesus saw nothing of the shabby street, barely heard the bored pianist squeeze the last drippings of sentiment from those trivial ballads of last week, last year, last love. He no longer waged any mental battle of right against wrong, of whether or not he could present his evidence against Pedro Luiz to the sheriff. He had settled that matter. He no longer possessed any evidence against Pedro Luiz. He had thrown that gold-piece pin down a drain.

He had stood a moment looking down between the metal grates of the sewer drain. He felt no regret, no remorse or guilt. God knew withholding evidence was its own kind of criminality. He was now as guilty as Pedro Luiz. He shrugged. Why not? Wasn't he the criminal's off-spring? He had sprung from the loins of that conscienceless bastard. And what is the old saying? Can the fruit fall far from the tree? He still possessed the residue of a hated conscience. He couldn't help this. He'd grown up developing conscience, responsibility, believing decent men were so equipped, and honing it in repudiation of the reprehensible example of Pedro Luiz. His own dear father.

He had walked away at last, entering the moderately priced hotel where he stacked his few belongings in a single room. He suffered a grief that stunned his mind and stilled his tongue. His agony cried out, but so deeply inside that only God could hear, that uncaring, busy and unheeding Jehovah. He had destroyed the evidence against Pedro Luiz only because he owed Tia Clara his life and he owed the law forces of Los Angeles County nothing. Let them solve their own crimes. They committed them without his help.

He had lost Leonora. Hell, he'd never had Leonora. Not even when he possessed her body and held her in his arms with frantic passion had he ever really had her. They would kill him before they would let him live with her. And now, knowing himself and his antecedents as he did, he could not blame them for opposing him. God, how he missed her. He never knew about loneliness until he loved Leonora.

Still, she was gone, and he adjusted to this or fitted himself for a straitjacket in some concealed Catholic retreat. He had given up the priesthood, and looked back at it without regret. Now, he had lost his final grasp on human decency: he had learned the truth about his own bastardy, his own proud bloodline, straight from the lowest of human animals.

He was stripped down to essentials now. He knew who he was, what he was. There remained only the union. He must now walk away from this organization, because he could not go on leading that cruel hoax against gullible workers. He could not. He would not. He did not know what he would do. It crossed his mind that Manuel O'Brien, who'd given him his name at least, had found solace and release in the opium pipe. This was, anyhow, a viable alternative. When a man surrendered totally, at least he no longer pretended to be what he was not in a world that spun without meaning, without reason, without cause, without purpose.

He was, at last, a man for all those seasons.

A knock on his door shook him from his abstacted reverie. The muscles of his stomach tightened. Whoever it was brought tidings, demands, requests, pleas from the outside world. He wanted none of it, no matter what it was. He stood unmoving against the window, the sheer, lifeless curtain fabric flicking against his leg.

'Father? Father O'Brien? Are you there?'

Jesus winced, recognizing Sister Mari-Jean's voice. As if plodding through thick mud, he crossed and opened the door. Sister Mari-Jean hesitated and then stepped inside. 'Please close the door, Father.'

Jesus closed the door. 'It's not much,' he said. He slung his arm, indicating the sagging iron-posted bed, the dresser, the two chairs, a stack of magazines, his guitar in its case, a small cupboard with his clothing. 'But it's no place like home, and for that I'm thankful.'

The beautiful little nun tried to smile, failed. 'I was alone at the union headquarters, Father. The telephone rang. It was Father Garcia. He sounded most upset. There's been a confrontation between foremen from the Stockton estate and workers. Near the store at Apia. Several of the workers are badly hurt and receiving no attention. . . I must go to them. I hoped you would go with me.'

It was on his tongue to refuse when Sister Mari-Jean said, 'Father Garcia did not ask for me. He asked for you. He insisted. He begged that you come.'

Jesus spread his hands and nodded. He shrugged into his jacket and followed her into the corridor and down the staircase to the musty, ill-lit lobby. They went out to the road and got into his union car.

As he moved the vehicle through the traffic, heading north and east toward the San Gabriel Valley, Jesus glanced at Sister Mari-Jean beside him.

'I'm glad to be alone like this with you, Sister,' he said.

He heard her soft intake of breath, saw her gentle cheeks grow pink. Rage festered inside him. If he were truly his father's son, here was opportunity. He had never realized how deeply Sister Mari-Jean cared for him. Hell, the truth was he'd never given her that much thought in all the years he'd known her. 'I'm always glad to be near you, Father,' she said.

He kept his voice firm and impersonal. 'I've been wanting to talk to you.'

'There is nothing you cannot say to me, Father.'

'What I want to say may sound ungrateful, stupid even, as if I were blind to all you've achieved, all you have given to the union.'

'I know better,' she said. 'I try to give more than I can, because I see you doing that. . . and I must be worthy of working with you.'

'That's what I'm trying to say, Mari-Jean. You are far too worthy for me, far too good and generous and trusting for the union.'

'What are you saying?'

'What I should have said years ago, Mari-Jean. I should never have let you join me in this labour movement — '

'You could not have stopped me —'

'I should have sent you back to the convent school where what you did had meaning and proved something.'

'Father. Jesus. I cannot believe you are saying these things.'

'Sister. In the name of God. Have you not seen the ugliness in the union, the greed, the lack of true caring, most of all the hopelessness of what we are trying to do — you and I?'

'If we help one poor soul, Father, we have not failed.'

'Well, that's it. We haven't helped anybody. We have failed.'

Sister Mari-Jean stared at him, disbelieving, incredulous. He said, 'You must return to the Church, back to the Sisters of Mercy.'

'Where would my mercy be if I abandoned these poor people now?'

'Where it should be. Stop closing your eyes to the truth. The truth is that we mislead the workers, the migrants, the illegals. We lie to them. We promise them results we can never deliver. We can only make their miserable lot worse for them by giving them false hope for something better.'

'Are you saying we should walk away, quit, leave them?'

'That is exactly what I am saying. There is nothing we can do for them. In our own way we hurt them as badly as the growers. Worse. Because we hold out false dreams to them. You must get out of it. You must return to the Church.'

'No.' She stared straight ahead. 'I do more good here.'

'But you have vowed yourself to do God's work, Mari-Jean. And this is not God's work. It may seem to be — if you close your eyes to the evil — but it is not. It is useless, pointless. Worse, it's cruel because it gives that false hope to a hopeless people. We've no right to do that.'

'And we must just abandon them?'

'No. Not entirely. You can teach their children in school. You can tend their needs when they come to you — at the church. That's where you belong.'

'And you?' She gazed at him, her eyes brimming with tears.

'God knows where I belong. But not here. Not in this work. Not any more.'

They sped along the San Gabriel Valley highway. In the distance ahead they saw the tattered forms of the houses and buildings of the village of Apia. The sun was setting, the entire valley was bathed in blue-hazed mists.

Jesus exhaled deeply. He prayed that Sister Mari-Jean would follow his advice and try to save herself from this evil failure. He no longer hoped to salvage anything out of this mess. Someday maybe someone would come along with strength enough, integrity enough, courage enough to help these people. He could not help them. The best service he could do them was to admit his inadequacy, his weakness, his guilt. He shook the thought away.

They crossed the bridge over a dry creekbed, the tyres of the car humming against the road. Glancing at Sister Mari-Jean, he saw that though her eyes still glittered with tears, she appeared composed. She would think about what he had said, and she had to know he was right, that he wanted only what was best for her. He sighed, relaxing slightly.

Then he saw the two cars speeding towards him in his rear-view mirror. Racing cars on this stretch of highway was not all that unusual, and yet he felt a sense of something wrong as the cars bore down on his relentlessly. The village was only a few miles ahead. He would feel better about Mari-Jean's and his own safety among witnesses. He said, 'Hold on, Sister.' He stepped hard on the accelerator.

They gained on him as if he were motionless. There was no doubt they pursued him. The two cars sped abreast on the narrow road. As they closed in, he saw that there were at least half a dozen men in each car and that they wore masks or hoods over their faces.

He stepped harder on the accelerator. Sister Mari-Jean had looked over her shoulder and recognized the peril. She sat stiffly, silently, her hands gripped in her lap. There was a nightmarish quality of frustration and helplessness against the speeding cars. Wind screamed past the open windows, shrieked in his ears, and he could hear the roar of the car engines.

The two cars, still side by side, came up behind him, almost touching his bumpers. They separated, closing him between them.

One of the men nearest him shouted, 'If you care about that woman, you best stop before you're both killed.'

Jesus nodded. The village lay ahead, but he could not make it, and he saw no sanctuary up there. These men need not have worn masks. He knew them, at least he knew whom they represented. He removed his foot from the accelerator and allowed the car to slow down. The car on his left kept nudging him to the right. The other car slackened speed and then he was forced off onto the road shoulder.

He cut the engine and sat there. The hooded men got out and surrounded the union car. 'Get out of there,' one of the men said. 'Both of you.'

Jesus opened his door and stepped out. When Sister Mari-Jean joined him, he caught her arm, holding her close against him. He could feel her shiver.

'What do you want with us?' he asked.

'Never mind askin' goddamn questions,' a man said. 'You'll find out what we want with you soon enough. You ought not to have brought the woman with you.'

'What the hell,' a hooded man laughed. 'we'll take care of her.'

Another protested. 'Christ, man, she's a nun.'

'All right. So she's a Catholic whore. What the hell, he's a priest, ain't he? What's the difference?'

'The difference is, it's him we want.' Jesus listened to the voices, trying to recognize them. This man had the cultured, coldly savage tones of Bonnett Stockton, yet he found it hard to believe that Bonnett would not keep an arm's distance between himself and violence.

'What you want us to do with him?'

Jesus caught his breath sharply because he recognized that voice, all right. Deputy Sheriff Pedro Grandos Luiz. Jesus wanted to laugh in wild savagery. He had spared Pedro, he had destroyed the evidence against him. But his father felt no such loyalty for his blood.

'I want you to hurt him good,' the voice that sounded like Bonnett Stockton said. Jesus wondered what crisis was fearful enough to induce Stockton to take an active part in his destruction. 'I want him out of the way. Is that plain enough?'

'Cut off his balls,' somebody said, laughing. 'Those bastard greasers won't follow him when he sings falsetto.'

Before anyone else could speak, a man dropped a looped rope over Jesus' head. When Jesus struggled, three men caught him, pinning him down until the noose was secured about his chest. He saw the other end tied to a trailer hitch on the rear of the lead car.

'Leave him alone,' Sister Mari-Jean wept. 'We're only out

493

here to tend the hurt at Apia.'

'Christ, woman. How dumb are you? They ain't nobody hurt up at Apia. Not yet.'

Sister Mari-Jean gasped, but said nothing more.

A man Jesus recognized as Church Foley spoke to his face. 'Ain't you been told enough to get out of this part of the country and stay out?'

Another said, 'This here is a warning. Kind of a rough warning. But it is better than you'll git if you don't clear out and stay out.'

The man that Jesus was increasingly certain was Bonnett Stockton said, 'There'll be no more union, no more union workers in this valley. There'll be no need for you here, even if you're able to crawl back.'

The men were still talking at Jesus, like accusing, faceless voices in the dusk when suddenly the car sprang forward, the accelerator floored, the tyres squealing. The men yelled in savage unison. Jesus was jerked off his feet. He struck the ground on his right knee, felt it smash, felt the bone of his leg break through the skin in a compound fracture. Behind him, somewhere in the insubstantial distance, he heard a woman scream.

Jesus was yanked and thrown along the road like the tin cans on the car of a couple just married. His body lunged and bounced and was dragged along the highway.

At last the car was brought to a halt. Church Foley's laughter spewed back from the car like something vile spat at him.

Jesus rolled and skidded to a halt. He lay for a long time, almost overcome by the pain in his leg, by the savagery of the laughter that rattled inside his skull. Slowly, he pushed himself up. It was important to him that he stand, even if his leg were broken.

The car driver let him struggle upright. As Jesus pushed himself up from his knees, putting all his weight on his left leg, Church Foley gunned the engine again. The car lunged ahead and Jesus was jerked off his feet and dragged another hundred yards.

Behind them the hooded men followed, shouting and laughing, urging Foley on. Jesus twisted behind the car, which pulled just fast enough to prevent him from freeing himself from the noose about his chest. When he loosened it just enough that it might pull over his arms, the car was speeded again and he was yanked forward onto his face. He dangled there, rattling along at the end of twenty or twenty-five feet of rope.

Every time the car slowed, he struggled frantically to free himself. He could not do it. There was too much tension on the rope. The car speeded again and he was jerked along helplessly.

Laughing, Foley hung his head out of the car, staring back and yelling his savavage glee.

When he stopped again, Jesus, covered with grime and bleeding profusely from his face and head, struggled up to his knees.

Foley roared with laughter, slapping the side of his car. He thrust it in gear and gunned the engine. Jesus staggered and plunged forward on his face.

The masked mob, with Sister Mari-Jean in their wake, ran along the highway, following the trail of blood on the road. Jesus was weakened now. When Foley stopped the car, it was a long time before Jesus could move at all. He was almost too far gone to know what was happening, but he still clutched at the rope, trying to peel it up from his armpits. This one idea of getting free was all that remained in his mind.

The mob ran up to where he lay and surrounded him. Mari-Jean pushed her way through and stood, her eyes brimming with helpless tears. She shook her head. The flesh was torn from Jesus' face and head, his hands bled, skin ripped away. His right leg was twisted oddly and she knew it was broken. She screamed at them suddenly. 'Stop it! Stop it, damn you. You beasts. Stop it.'

One of the men waved his arm over his head. Still laughing, Church Foley got out of the car. He stared down at Jesus who was no longer trying to get to his knees. The bloodied priest still fought at the rope about his chest.

'Cut him loose,' a man ordered. Shrugging, Foley bent over Jesus, loosened the rope and yanked it over his head. It came away bloodied.

Jesus sprawled on the road and rolled over on his face. Though the rope was gone, he kept struggling, kept trying to free himself from it.

Foley and five others went to his car. They got in. Foley accelerated hard, throwing dirt and pebbles as he burned away.

The other car rolled along the road. The remaining men got in. They drove away silently.

Jesus sprawled there, smeared with grime, blood and dirt. He struggled faintly as if the rope still cut into his chest. Sobbing, Sister Mari-Jean knelt beside him. She whispered, 'Forgive me, Jesus. I didn't know. I believed him when he called. I didn't know. Dear God, forgive me.'

He struggled, grimacing in a spinning cosmos of pain. He tried to speak, to tell her he understood. His senses failed him and he could not form the words. He sagged on his face, barely conscious, weak and dazed. After a moment, he started tugging again at the invisible rope about his chest. . . .

XXXIX

The speeding express train roared and twisted through gorges and tunnels down out of the mountains and charged across the wide valley in the sodden and perilous darkness. Only its brilliant headlamp showed in the depthless night. Whistles blasted the silence and the carriages teetered and wavered dangerously along the footless track. The engine screeched to a stop inside his head, the huge light blinding him, the pain rattling inside his skull.

He opened his eyes slowly, cautiously. The dazzling whiteness of the hospital room fired shafts of agony through his eyeballs to the crown of his head. It was worse than he had believed possible. He hated the sterile stench of the industrial-strength disinfectant: it stank to heaven and was as effective as a soft drink against strep infection. There was no way to escape the blandly cheery compromises with death, the horrible grotesqueness of the smiling nurses bending close above his face and smelling of cloves and mint and Odorono. He lived. He was not dead, after all. Damn it, he was not dead.

He drifted again into the blessed dark of sleep.

The next time he wakened he recognized the whispering voices of Pete Lewis and Sister Mari-Jean across the room, just inside the door. He lay with his eyes closed, letting them believe he still slept.

'Workers. Coming. From all across the state,' Sister Mari-Jean was whispering as if fearful of being overheard. 'From as far away as Arizona.'

'They're planning one hell of a protest.'

'The largest in history. And it's called in Father O'Brien's name. They are protesting the evil done him.'

'They're nuts,' Pete said, and mutely Jesus agreed. 'No protest is going to stop Stockton and men like Stockton.'

'Maybe not. But they will let the growers know they cannot mutilate people as they did Father O'Brien, and then casually announce that union workers will no longer be tolerated in the San Gabriel Valley.'

'All right. It's another damned hopeless cause, but I'll be there. I don't know what I can do, but I'll be there.'

'None of us know what we can do. We have no one to lead us. Maybe we can't do anything,' Sister Mari-Jean whispered. 'But we must make the growers see. If they destroy our people, we will retaliate.'

'Christ. I see nothing but a lot of bloodshed.'

'I've already seen bloodshed,' Sister Mari-Jean said. 'I no longer believe the only blood shed should be ours — and that of people like him.' She nodded towards Jesus' hospital bed.

'You're getting bloodthirsty as hell.'

'I've always been bloodthirsty. I just never knew it until that night out there in the valley.'

They wavered and dissolved and disappeared, and he was not even sure it was anything more than a dream, like the raging train which rushed down at him every time he slept. . . .

The newspaper was real enough. It was God only knew how many days, how many light-years, later. The social pages of the *Los Angeles Times* left on his bed table. Leonora Stockton had returned to America. Her engagement to a meat, hotel chain and packing company heir was announced, along with their photo. She was as lovely as ever, lovelier. Even the tears that welled in Jesus' eyes hurt. Rosson Den Eyck was fourth-generation blue-blood. Jesus smiled wryly. How much more acceptable could one man get in the jaundiced eyes of Leonora's father? Bonnett Stockton was prideful. There were no objections. Plans were being made for the 'marriage of the century' — the newspaper's term — in Los Angeles.

Jesus felt the sickness, the loss, but by now, it was more the memory of despair. She had been gone from him for a long time. She had been lost to him forever, even since before the first time he saw her. The news account was impersonal; it was like reading of a stranger's nuptials, except for the sharp, unrelenting pain, the sense of total emptiness.

There was nothing he could do to stop this inevitable merger of family names and family fortunes. There was nothing he wanted to do. If he had been Manuel O'Brien's son, there might have existed the faintest glimmer of hope for him and Leonora, but there was no shred of hope for the bastard whelp of Pedro Grandos Luiz. And this was who he was, no matter how ill it made him to face that truth. He could not go to Leonora, knowing who he really was. He would have felt less guilty if he were taking her a communicable disease. The blood of Pedro Luiz. What a gift to offer any woman, what a hellish burden even to live with.

His bruised, torn head rolled on the pillow. No. Whatever he did now must have a single purpose. He must atone, not only for his own inner evil, but for the evil of his natural father. He felt a raging desire to laugh. He longed to throw his head back, laughing, letting the sound pour from him, spew from his mouth, vomit from the depths of his belly. He wanted to laugh until he cried, until he wept, until he sobbed with laughter, until he cleansed his soul with the scourge of laughter. But he didn't laugh. He was too weak, too tired, too beaten, and after a long time he sank back into sleep. . . .

The next time he opened his eyes he found Sister Mari-Jean sitting in silence beside his bed. Perhaps she was truly there this time. He managed a hideous caricature of a smile. 'Is that really you, Sister?'

'I come every day, Father. Every day I can.'

'You don't have to.'

'I know.'

He sighed. 'Have you taken my advice?'

'What advice is that, Father?'

'Have you returned to the Church?'

Sister Mari-Jean shook her head. 'I never will, Father. My place is among these people. They have hope. They need me.'

He winced. 'And, as you're leaving unsaid, they need me. Eh?'

'I didn't say that. Or leave it unsaid. Or think it at all. You've been hurt enough. You are right to quit. We both know what they will do. Next time they would kill you.'

'Do you think they won't kill you, if you don't stop?'

She shrugged her shoulders. 'When I watched those men torturing and mutilating you, I knew only one thing. I would never quit. They will have to kill me to stop me. They are evil and I could never stop fighting them.'

'They're something else, Sister. Something you overlook.'

'Vicious?'

'Rich. Powerful. Influential. They believe laws were made for lesser souls. They believe what they do is right, or at least justified. They'll do anything to gain their goals. Your life won't mean much to them.'

She sighed. 'Maybe it doesn't mean much to me. . . .'

Pete Lewis stood beside his bed. His face twisted. 'Forgive me, Jesus. It is my fault. I went to Pedro Luiz' house to kill him. I should have killed him. He would not have attacked you.'

'You must not blame yourself, Pete. He was only one of many. Whether Pedro was there does not matter.'

'It matters to me.' He exhaled heavily. 'Well, at least it's over. When you're out of here, you and my mother and I will go away. We'll get a little farm somewhere. There is much we can do. I'll keep bees, as old Manuel did. We'll live well.'

Jesus managed to smile. 'I keep thinking I've had enough.'

'You have. God knows you have.'

'I keep remembering Teodoro.'

'Teodoro?' Pete scowled. 'What's Teodoro got to do with it?'

Jesus' head rolled back and forth. 'When kids taunted Teodoro about the evil eye, Teodoro and I used to fight them.' He smiled wanly, remembering. 'Teodoro was a hell of a lot smarter than I was. When he got hurt fighting, he'd quit. I never had sense enough to quit. The worse I got hurt, the madder I got, and the harder I fought, until sometimes I was a bloody mess. I remember Teodoro told me to stop fighting. He told me that as long as I fought, they'd keep trying to kill me. Now, after all these years, I know he was right.'

2

He opened his eyes slowly and saw her standing beside his bed. At first he thought it was a vision, an illusion, a trick of light and shadow and insatiable longing. She wore a sable hat, jaunty on her blonde head, a sable coat, open, casual, in that 'doesn't everybody?' way. She was so lovely, far too lovely to be real, and yet God knew, far too real to be a dream even in his confused mind.

'Leonora,' he whispered.

'My dearest Heysus.' She pressed close over him, the scent of her distracting, her warmth overwhelming. She touched his torn hands gently, she covered his lips with her warm, sweet-scented mouth. All the old devastating memories and needs and longings washed through him. He would always want her. As long as there was breath in him, he would want her.

'What are you doing here? he whispered.

She smiled, violet eyes drowned in tears. 'I've come back to you. This is where my heart's been. All these years.' She bit at her underlip. 'Maybe I've come back to pick up my heart, if you're not using it.'

'Oh Christ, I could never spare it.' His own eyes filled with tears. 'I would die without it.'

'Then you'll live forever,' she assured him. She kissed him lightly. 'I've come for you, Heysus. The only way Father would permit me back in America, back in California, was when I was "safely" engaged. Rosson — the boy I met in France — is nice enough. Sweet. Good. I suppose he loves me, but I announced our engagement only so I could come back to you.' She sighed. 'I tried before. I tried being engaged to royalty — thinking a royal ceremony would lull Father so I could get back here. But he wouldn't have the baron. To him, the baron was a fortune-hunter. . . . Well, I learned. Rosson Den Eyck's family could buy Father ten times over.'

'I'm glad for you.'

'What are you saying? I'm not marrying Ross. . . . You and I. We are getting out of here. I have money. Plenty of money. We'll run. We'll take a plane to Mexico and we'll keep running from there until we find our own sanctuary. I don't care where it is, as long as we're together.'

'We can't.'

'We must.' Pain constricted her lovely face. 'It's all I've lived for.'

'And I. Only, as I lived — as time passed — I knew better. There's nowhere to run, no place to hide. Your father would always find us. He hates me far too deeply to let me be with you. He wants better for you. And in that, I finally agree.'

'Oh, Heysus. You're just ill, just weak.'

'I'm beaten. Badly. But I've sense enough left to know that your father would never stop looking for us, never stop hounding us. In his mind, it would be justified. It would be a crusade, the only right course for him, saving you from yourself and from the bastard chicano.'

'Oh, Heysus. We can try.'

'No. We've tried.'

'But I've come so far. I know God meant you for me. I know He did. I've lived only to be with you again.'

'We still have that. We'll always have that.' Jesus laughed wryly. 'In one way, we've beaten your father. He can keep us apart, but we've got something he can never take away. Our love. It will stay strong, unchanged, fixed. Forever. There's nothing he can do about that.'

'That's not enough for me. That's not what I want. I want us. You and I. Together. Away from here. Away from this place. Away from these poor, miserable, dirty people. My father is right about them, too. There is nothing we can do for those poor devils. Nothing. Because Father is right. They'll keep coming, always a new flood of wretches, willing to work for less and less. Win something for one group, new ones will come to take their places and work for less. There is no way to win, no way to help them. They're coming from Oklahoma now and Iowa and Kansas, not only just from the border. They are starving. The President won't help them, the state can't. They're miserable, homeless, wretched. I just don't care any more. I'm sick of it. Tired of it. I've done all I can for them. I want to get away. I want to enjoy my life. I want to be happy.'

'Yes. You should get away from it. You must.'

'And you. I have nothing without you. You must go with me.'

'I can't.'

'Why not? Are you so afraid of my father?'

'No. I know he'd overtake us if we ran. He'd separate us. He'd put you in some plush sanatorium until you agreed to live his way, or I was dead, whichever came first. But that's not the reason why I can't go with you. I can't go because I'm one of those wretches you're so tired of.'

'Heysus. Don't say such things.'

'It's true. We're from different worlds, never meant one for the other. Never. We pretended. Refused to admit the truth. Your father was right about us too. There's a rift between us wider than your father's valley. And I can't cross it. You know it. And I've learned it, the hard way.'

502

'Oh, Heysus. I've loved you so.'

'And I you. I owe everything I am, or can ever be, to you and your love. It was like I slept and you woke me up. You made me dream. You made me fight to make those dreams come true. I couldn't quite do that — we were too far apart — but I came a long way. I'm better than I might have been, without you. Whatever I am, it's only because I tried to be more — for you.'

'Don't, Heysus. Please don't break my heart.'

'I'm trying not to. I'm only saying aloud what I've learned, alone, without you, and lying here. You and I were never meant to be. Not for a minute. You knew it, and wouldn't admit it. I didn't know it — because until I found you, I didn't know or care about anything. I'm not even sorry for what happened, not even for the worst of it. When you started me to dreaming ahead, you brought me alive. You made me care. First about you. Then about learning, about improving, about working, even for others. And now, I've fought against that as long as I can. . . . I know you've brought me to the only place where I can be worthwhile to anybody. . . where I can help those poor bastards who can't help themselves, whether I want to or not. You're rightly sick and tired of them and God knows, so am I. But the difference is, they belong to me, and I belong to them. I am one of them, as you are part of the world you belong in — your father's world.'

She gazed at him, forlorn. 'Oh, Heysus. What will I do without you?'

He sighed. 'All the things you should have done, and would have done, if our eyes hadn't met when you were nine years old.'

She wiped away a tear. 'That's a long time to love someone, Heysus. I deserve better.'

He nodded. 'In your father's eyes, you'll have better. You'll be where you belong. At last. It's just that we don't have what we want, that's all.'

'Because you're tired of fighting my father?'

He shook his head. 'No. I'm going to fight your father. Probably as long as I live. But — for something other than you, other things. Not for you. I won't fight him for you any more because he's right about you, and always has been. You deserve better.'

She caught his hand, holding it tautly, yet gently. 'There is

503

no better, Heysus. Not for me. Not on this earth.'

He smiled faintly. 'Then different. I want you to be happy, Leonora. Truly happy. That's all I want. And I know your true happiness is in no way linked to me. . . . God knows it took me long enough to learn. But now I know. . . . I love you with all my heart, wherever you are, and I always will.'

'Heysus. What will you do?'

He sighed. 'I'll lie here weeping about what a gallant son of a bitch I am, that's what I'll do.'

'Oh God, I love you.' She kissed him fiercely. 'You gallant son of a bitch.'

XL

The valley sprawled prostrate in the heat and blaze of sun, silent and motionless as the eye of a hurricane. Cars, trucks, pickups of every age and make and condition lined both shoulders of the highway. Any traffic in either direction had ground to a halt. A terrible, coldly implacable silence gripped the farm workers who slouched, waiting, unmoving, unspeaking, in any wisp of shade. State police had been brought in by the busload, armed with shields and riot gear. The incredible numbers of the gathered protesters, well over ten thousand, officers estimated, tempered the troopers' plans for quelling the disturbance. And, so far, there was no disturbance. There was only the threat which crackled like electric charges in the tense, breathless atmosphere.

The state police patrolled the roadway, making a symbolic gesture toward keeping a narrow artery open on the road. People silently and sullenly stepped back when ordered and then melted into the street again as the troopers passed.

In the dead centre of the mobilization was the single rasp of sound, the lone sweaty activity. Here, in the bed of an open truck, backed across the intersection with the county road which served the Stockton estate, labour union agitators took turns shouting to the multitude through megaphones. 'We are here. . . crusade. . . right before God. . . there will be no movement of grower vehicles allowed. . . prepare to stay here. . . days. . . weeks. . . months if we must. . . these godless growers. . . show humanity. . . living wage. . . submit to our demands. . . or face ruin. . . .'

Watching silently, detached and remote, almost as impersonal as if viewing some simplistic Punch and Judy show, Bonnett and Bragg Stockton stood just inside their land markers. Around them were gathered their managers, foremen, supervisors and field bosses. Supporting them was the might and armed personnel of the Los Angeles County Sheriff. They stood, also unspeaking, though occasionally someone remarked on the unheard-of size of the rabble mob. 'Every unemployed son of a bitch in California must be here,' Church Foley said.

Hector Swain grinned tautly. 'I know now how General Custer felt.'

'You've only got to stand your ground,' Bonnett Stockton told Hector in a cold, contemptuous tone. 'You do what I tell you, and only what I tell you and you'll be all right. I'm glad it's come to this. We break their backs once and for all, here and now, and this is the end of it.'

Hector Swain nodded and said no more.

In a union car, Pete Lewis tooled at three miles an hour through the clot of human beings along the road. The protesters shouted at him. Some bent and peered into the sedan. When they saw Sister Mari-Jean on the front seat beside Pete and the bandaged Father O'Brien on the back seat, they whispered first, turning to pass along the word. Gradually, a shout went up, a cry that became a sustained wail of exultation, resounding and reverberating across the ploughed lands and rising like smoke toward heaven.

The car ground to a halt a few yards from the flatbed truck being used as a dais by the union people. A highway patrolman bent over the window and said to Pete, 'You can't leave this car here.'

Pete got out of it. He squinted against the sun, peering at the patrolman. 'You move it,' Pete said. 'It ain't my car.'

Pete went around the car. He and Sister Mari-Jean helped Father O'Brien struggle from the sedan tonneau to the ground. A dozen men and women crowded in, trying to help.

Panting, already exhausted, Jesus stood beside the open door of the car, steadying himself against it. He settled his crutches in place at his armpits. The people closest to him gasped and nudged each other at his pallor and unsteadiness. He was pale and he trembled. But when someone spoke to him, he smiled and nodded, his black eyes glittering with a strange and deadly fire.

All who had known him well in the union movement withdrew slightly at this new appearance of him when he approached. They had never seen this unnatural light in his sunken eyes, the ashen, rigid and pallid cheeks, scarred and wealed, not fully healed, the twisted smile that showed his teeth in a kind of canine grin. To the perceptive, he looked like a soul who'd been led by the hand into the hottest hole beyond hell and then abandoned there. At every painful step he took, he shuddered and bit hard on his underlip, the pain transfiguring his face.

'Please wait in the car, Father,' Sister Mari-Jean begged. 'It is enough that they know you are here.'

He shook his head and looked at her coldly. 'It's not enough for me.'

He tottered and toppled toward the open flatbed truck. It took four men to hoist him up onto it. A shout of shocked exultation spewed up from the throats of the assemblage. Waves of fevered gratification rolled across the upturned faces. He stood for a long time, supported on his crutches, his right leg in a cast, his face terribly scarred and torn, his bandaged head tilted in silent, passionate defiance.

The crowd roared his name, but he made no gesture of acknowledgement. He seemed not even to hear their wails of adulation. He was not looking at them. He seemed to gaze at something far beyond their heads. Whatever it was he saw, he suffered alone, he thrilled alone, it was something exquisite that he could not share. There was only the anguished and yet tranquil expression for those close enough to see. Whatever it was he watched, his gaze followed it across the blazing valley from one horizon to another.

When Bonnett Stockton recognized the slender, battered figure on that flatbed truck, he stepped forward, his mouth tightening into a grey line, his fists clenched at his sides. 'The bastard, the greaser bastard. Looks like he didn't believe our warning we'd kill him if he ever came back out here.'

'Maybe he doesn't care any more,' Hector Swain said.

'He cares. Those union bastards. They've got him up there to fire up the mob. Look at the poor battered son of a bitch, they're whining. He fought the cruel growers. He was beaten, but survived and he's come back. Jesus Christ, it's enough to make you puke.'

'He's rousing them up,' Hector Swain said. 'Damned noise. Deafening.'

'We'll stop that soon enough,' Stockton told him. 'We'll quiet the bastards right down. Bring up the first trucks.'

'Boss, we ain't got any trucks loaded,' Hector said.

Stockton stared at his foreman, his mouth twisted in contempt. 'You stupid son of a bitch. It don't matter. It's all symbolic. Symbolically, they're stopping our trucks. When we drive through them — over them if we have to — they've got their fucking symbolic answer from me. Start up the trucks.'

A man in his early thirties, sweating in battered felt hat, rumpled Palm Beach suit and saddle shoes, clambered up on the truckbed beside Jesus. He said, 'You Father O'Brien?'

Jesus pulled his gaze back from the hazed distance and nodded.

'My name is Howard Brannon, Father. I'm a publicist. From Hollywood. Movie premieres. Studio celebrations. Parades. Star arrivals. That's my ordinary game. But I been hired to run this thing for you.'

'Hired? By whom?' Father O'Brien stared at him. 'We had to borrow money to feed this mob.'

'No.' Brannon shook his head. 'It's all taken care of. A Miss Leonora Stockton. Said to tell you, she can't be with you, but her money is. Her money and my public relations expertise. No matter what happens here today, Father, you're going to win it.'

'What are you talking about?'

'About them.' Howard Brannon waved his arms and Jesus stared down at the dozens of newsreel cameramen, sound men, reporters and crews. 'They all belong to unions of some kind, Father. They'll get your story out — all over the country. Hell, all over the world. There's Hearst Metrotone News from M-G-M, Pathe, Fox Movietone News, Paramount News, Universal. Anywhere those newsreels are shown, people will see what's going on here today. We'll show your side of it. There are reporters here from the *New York Times,* from Washington, D.C., from *Time Magazine, Literary Digest.* God knows who all. Whatever happens to your union here, it won't be hidden and lied about. The whole world is watching you, thanks to Miss Stockton. They can't kill you or any of your people now and lie about it. Give 'em hell, Father. The world is watching.'

Jesus stared down at the cameras and reporters and his eyes brimmed with tears. The world *was* watching. Those cameras would change the world. They would show the truth, no matter what lies were broadcast.

Sudden screams, growls and yells of protest raged up from the throats of the farm workers. The first of a long line of trucks, their beds covered with tarpaulins, rolled steadily toward the highway.

Three men from the crowd ran along the county road. The sheriff's officers bawled at them, ordering them out of the way. They refused to move. Watching, Jesus felt immobilized by a sense of horror. He saw that the driver of the first truck was Church Foley.

Jesus jerked his head around. 'Get me down from here,' He yelled, his voice almost lost against the ululation of the mob, the grind of approaching truck engines. Howard Brannon and Pete Lewis grabbed Jesus' arms and hoisted him down to other men who set him on the ground and supported him until he steadied himself on his crutches.

Church Foley pressed on the truck horn. The three men did not move. The truck was driven forward. At the last moment, the man in the middle of the road shoved his partners hard so they toppled aside, tumbling into the ditch. He leaped, but the truck bumper struck him and sent him sprawling forward. The truck ran over the small of his back as the cameras ground.

The men near the victim ran out of the ditch in the stunned silence and clouds of exhaust smoke. The man was dead. The wide treads of the truck tyre marked his back. He lay sprawled across the road, lifeless.

In the truck, Church Foley accelerated and did not look back. At the intersection of the highway, he pulled around the union open-bed vehicle and started west towards Los Angeles.

At the Stockton cars, Bragg Stockton grabbed his son's arm. 'Bonnett. Stop them. Look. The cameras. The radio reporters. The whole fucking world is watching you.'

For a moment, Bonnett Stockton hesitated. In that breath of time, he and his father heard the raging screams from the highway. One second, their truck was inching its way along the clotted artery, the next it was tipped on its side. There was a crash and screech of metal as it was overturned. The driver was yanked from the truck cab. The Stocktons could hear Church Foley's cries of terror change to whimpers of agony and then fade.

Bonnett stared at his father, at the waiting mob, at the grinding cameras. He knew only one way of life, the imperious drive that had motivated and served him since childhood. This was his land, his valley, no one had the right to stop, hinder, interfere or intrude. The fucking world would see that on that film.

He turned and ran to where Hector Swain had slowed and then stopped the second truck in the convoy. Bonnett jerked open the door and leaped into the cab. 'Move this damned thing,' he said. 'What are you waiting for?'

'We're killing people, boss. For nothing. For empty trucks.'

'Then kill the sons of bitches. If they are in our way, kill them. If they try to stop us, kill them.'

Hector Swain stared at his employer. He shook his head. 'I got no stomach for this, Bonnett. I'm sorry.' He opened the truck door and stepped out. The mob, seeing Swain refuse to drive the truck forward, roared approval, but Hector heard none of that. He heard only the curses and threats from Bonnett Stockton behind him in the cab of that truck.

Hector stood a moment on the shoulder, watching Bonnett slide under the wheel and shift into gear. Then Hector walked around the truck and plodded over to where Bragg Stockton stood. The old man did not look at him. He did not take his gaze from his son at the wheel of the empty truck.

With long sprawling movements of his crutches, Jesus went around the overturned truck and into the middle of the county road as Bonnett Stockton moved the farm van toward him. He heard Sister Mari-Jean scream his name and then she was beside him, walking forward with him. A moment later, Pete Lewis fell in step on the other side. They moved forward and the truck rolled toward them. From the crowd, the small surpliced figure of Father Garcia appeared. He ran out onto the road and they walked forward, four abreast. The cameramen ran along the roadway shoulders, recording it all.

The crowd hesitated only the space of a breath. They spilled out and crowded, shouting, behind Jesus and the others.

Jesus kept plodding forward awkwardly on his crutches. He stood in the middle of the road. The farm van's horn wailed at him. He seemed not to hear it. The sun glittered in his eyes. He kept his head up, staring unblinking at the oncoming vehicle. Sister Mari-Jean was crying at Pete to carry the young priest off the road forcibly if he saw that the truck would not stop. 'You touch me,' Jesus said between gritted teeth, 'and I'll kill you. Get away and leave me alone.'

They walked beside him. From the crowds, surging forward, women wept and men shouted curses. The truck rolled forward. At the last instant, its bumpers inches from where Jesus stood, the truck stopped. Bonnett Stockton slumped in the cab, gripping the steering wheel as the cameras focused on him.

Bragg Stockton and Hector Swain pushed their way through the mob. Swain climbed up on the bed of the open truck and took up a megaphone. Bragg Stockton agreed to rehire union workers. He agreed to two dollars a day. Free rent. Free Transportation.

In the raging exultation, Jesus stood unmoving.

He gripped the crutch supports, hearing the triumph of these people. For the moment, they had won. He did not believe the road ahead was anything but rough and slow and in places impassable. It seemed to him that down that road fifty years ahead, the workers would still be fighting unequal foes for decent treatment, but for the moment, there was a break in the darkness. What the hell? Things change. When he'd been born there was a Roosevelt in the White House. Now Teddy's cousin FDR was going to be President. Who knew what hope might survive this moment? FDR might at least care about the hungry and homeless, unlike the bastards in at the moment. The new President might listen, he might even make a difference. But whether he did or not, this day brought them one new chance. They had to celebrate it and cling to it and never let it go.

He felt Father Garcia grip his arm. 'You are a good man, Jesus,' the old priest said. 'Truly a man of God.'

Jesus stared at the wizened little old man, biting back the savage laughter that rose up bitterly into his throat. A man of God. Well, maybe he was. Perhaps we all are. Weak. Empty. Doing the best we can. The best we know. All men of God.

Jesus' eyes filled with tears. A man of God? Well, at least maybe just now his father would be proud of him. . . his father in heaven. . . or in hell. Manuel. . . the wretched Pedro. . . his father. . . whoever he was.

THE END

San Francisco, California, 1960

Indian Rocks Beach, Florida, 1985